THE KING SLAYER

ALSO BY CHRISTY R. HARRILL

The Blood Vier

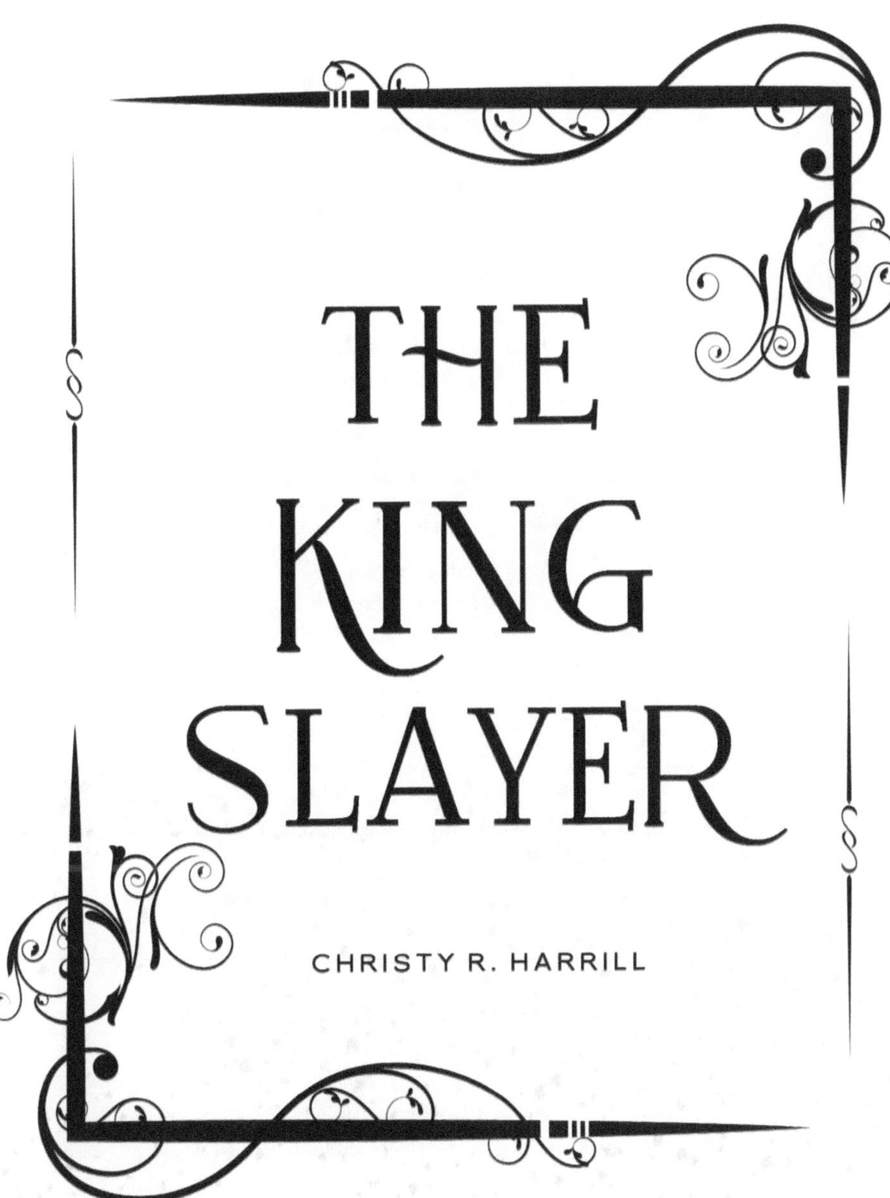

THE KING SLAYER

CHRISTY R. HARRILL

Rose Hollow Press

The King Slayer

Copyright © 2023 by Christy R. Harrill
Cover Art and Design by Franziska Stern
Map by Christy R. Harrill

Published by Rose Hollow Press, LLC
Oklahoma City, Oklahoma
christyrharrill.com

Cataloging Data
Harrill, Christy (Christy R.)
The king slayer/ Christy R. Harrill. –First edition.
p. cm. (The Blood Vier series; bk 2)

Summary: When a foreign mission goes awry, Taryn is caught between the warring sides of the Crown and the Kavari. She must become the master of deception to regain the Crown's trust as Vladimir does everything he can to heal the rift without bloodshed, but far darker forces twist them into doing things they never imagined, including risking the fate of the kingdom—and the lives of the people they love.

Library of Congress Control Number: 2022918801

ISBN 979-8-9859243-3-6 (hardback)
ISBN 979-8-9859243-4-3 (paperback)
ISBN 979-8-9859243-5-0 (e-book)
[1. Fantasy. 2. Action and Adventure—YA Fiction 3. Conspiracies
4. Kings, queens, rulers, etc.—YA Fiction] I. Title

First Edition, March 2023

For Dad,
Who will literally never read this book because he
hates fantasy and runs for the hills at the mention of
watching Lord of the Rings—*but we still love you*
anyways.

CITY OF ISO
DELLWYN
GAPSVAR
BRENDEN
HYTHE
PALAZAAR
ALGARAR

ADELLAIA
CARNA
THE CAPITOL
NAVARRE
GHARRIDAN
VARRA RIVER
JIDERO RIVER
THE COVEL SEA

CHAPTER ONE

TARYN

DEATH STRODE ALONG with me like an old friend, his fingers trembling with anticipation. He'd hung heavy by my side the past few weeks, never more than a handsbreadth away. Waiting. He was always waiting. Waiting to see what I would do. I could have told him to leave, but the truth was, I didn't want him to.

Not yet.

I reached the tent and one of the guards parted the canvas flap for me, granting me entrance. Death did not follow. I looked over my shoulder, saw his smile as he drifted away, shrinking into the shadows.

I stepped inside the immaculate tent, lanterns bathing me in warm light. I was early. No one else occupied the interior, so I moved to one of the outer walls, sinking into the soft cushions of a chair, its shape conforming to my body. This was a rare comfort I had thought I might never experience again. A slow sigh escaped my lips as my gaze wandered over the contents encased between the four canvas walls. A clay water basin sat outside the personal quarters with a tray of food next to it. The center of the room held a simple table surrounded by four chairs. Strewn across its rough wooden surface were crooked stacks of parchment, their pages filled with maps and various official documents; a dull feather quill lay off to the side, a half-empty bottle of black ink resting beside it.

I fiddled with the gold ring on my finger, spinning it round and round, admiring the way the light glinted off its shiny surface. Such a small item that bore the heavy weight of regret. I closed my eyes, picturing my father's face from when I was younger, choosing to dwell only on the fond memories and forsake the sorrows of the past.

I peeked at the door, heartbeat quickening within my chest as my nerves bubbled within me. They should be here by now. I twiddled my fingers, linking and interlacing them out of a desperate need for something to do. Footsteps approached from outside, and I stood. The outside flap and the curtain to the personal quarters opened simultaneously.

Queen Adamara's face lit with surprise when she found me already inside her tent, but her features quickly darkened. She took the seat at the head of the table, chin lifted, eyes darting around with impatience while she waited for everyone else to find their place.

Vladimir's forehead creased with concern as he took the seat to the left of the queen. The circles below his eyes had grown darker since the day before, purpling nearly like a bruise.

Ever since leaving my father's grave, he'd been unusually quiet, but I had hardly spoken since then as well.

William's movements were stiff and rigid, his expression cold as he sat to the right of his mother, ignoring her scrutinizing stare. His arm swung freely, no longer confined by the sling, and the remnants of our captors' abuse had almost completely faded from his face.

Katherine stepped around the chairs with light feet to sit across from the queen, her blood-red hair pulled back in a thick braid that swept over her shoulder. I hesitated for a moment, waiting for an invitation to join them, but it never came and I sank back down into my seat with disappointment. If they wanted me at the table, they would have placed me there. Irritation swelled within my chest, but I pushed it away. I was not an asset of the government, nor was I of any importance. I was only here because Vladimir had insisted on my presence. When he'd sent a letter to the queen by falcon, he hadn't anticipated her traveling out to meet us in the wilderness. None of us had. We'd all been surprised when we came upon her camped in the valley with enough guards to form a small army.

"Your letter implied that time was of the essence, Vladimir," the queen said. "What has transpired since you left the capital in search of Zedekiah?"

I leaned into the chair and crossed my arms, knowing it would be a lengthy explanation. My stomach growled, quiet enough for only me to hear, but dinner would be postponed. I gazed longingly at the tray of food on the other side of the room. The mere sight of the fresh meat made my mouth water.

Vladimir began speaking, starting with Silas's abduction of William and me. I shuddered over the details, rubbing my wrists where the coarse ropes had cut into my flesh, my skin still crawling from the lingering looks of the men. William and I had escaped, but only to end up nearly freezing to death in a blizzard. After finally making it to Gapsvar, William endured a severe beating from the prejudiced guards. We managed to find Marco in the prison—almost getting executed in the process—but we killed Zedekiah.

The queen's expression remained stoic and hard as Vladimir and William each gave their accounts, covering every detail of our extended excursion. Vladimir's calm voice never rose nor fell as he spoke. It stayed grave; his dark brows remained pulled low over piercing blue eyes. When he finished speaking of Zedekiah's demise and the ricochet the traitor had thrown to the ground before his death, Queen Adamara leaned back in her seat like she'd taken a blow to the gut.

"A ricochet?" Her fearful eyes grew earnest as she questioned Vladimir. "Are you certain?"

Vladimir nodded assuredly, slipping a hand in his pocket and returning with a piece of worn cloth that he dropped onto the table. His fingers pulled apart the frayed edges to reveal a tiny silver crescent, thin as parchment but sharper than a sword's edge. Choice weapon of the assassins of Brenden. The small object looked so insignificant, yet it had occupied my thoughts over the endless days in the saddle as I'd debated how we could use it as evidence.

The queen seemed at a loss for words.

"After obtaining the ricochet, I realized another connection to Michael's death." Vladimir's eyes briefly met mine. "Michael's attackers were burned to ash. Originally, I thought it was to conceal their identity, but then I remembered Brenden remains are ceremonially burned, not buried."

A hush fell over the room, Vladimir's words hanging in the air like a haunted whisper.

Seven bodies.

All burned beyond recognition.

The evidence had lingered before us for months, waiting for us to put the pieces together.

"What do we know about the assassins of Brenden?" the queen asked.

Vladimir offered a humorless smile. "Not much. Most people don't even know of their existence, but they are highly trained, ruthless, and wield unique weapons such as the ricochet. Their arrows are spiked, and their precision is deadly."

"And as far as we know, they've never crossed the Gharridan border until Michael's death?"

Vladimir nodded.

I cocked my head. How had Zedekiah made his deal with them? Meeting with Brenden's king would have sent him on a noticeably long hiatus—unless someone had met with the king in his stead.

"Is there any other evidence implying Brenden's involvement?" the queen asked.

Vladimir hesitated. His gaze flicked to mine. "While in Gapsvar, Taryn intercepted a missive received by a Captain Dugal. She only managed to see the first part of the letter, but it did mention that Brenden was ready."

Queen Adamara turned to acknowledge me. "Who sent this missive? What else did it say?"

I squirmed beneath the sudden attention. "It mentioned the terms of a treaty to be met, that Brenden was ready, but that's all I know. I was looking over the captain's shoulder. I never saw the bottom half of the page."

The queen frowned, tapping her fingers methodically on the chair's armrest. "If we accuse Brenden of this crime and they are guilty, they are the only ones to have caused harm. But if we accuse them and we are wrong ..." Her voice trailed off, the question lingering behind unanswered.

I understood the dilemma. Accusing Brenden of a crime they didn't commit would breed unnecessary warfare, but if Brenden was involved in my father's murder, that in itself was an act of hostility. Queen Adamara would have no choice but to declare war on Brenden. No matter which path we chose, war was imminent.

The queen sat up, creating an arch with her fingers as her mind clamored for a solution. "I fear what you suspect may be the truth. Thanks to Michael, Brenden has been our friend for many years. It pains me to believe they are the perpetrators behind this, but I'm afraid I have some grave news of my own to share that I now realize coincides with your findings."

I stiffened, fear clawing at me over the words preparing to leave her mouth.

"In part, it is why I set out to meet you." Her voice faded, eyes glazing over in deep concentration.

"What is it?" Vladimir asked.

A slight tremor affected the queen's hands. "Several weeks ago, a severely wounded messenger rode into the capital from Dellwyn. By his account, Brenden troops marched into Dellwyn and took over, burning half the city to the ground and taking the survivors prisoner."

Vladimir's fists clenched. "Have we retaliated?"

"I sent two battalions to reclaim the city. They should have arrived by now. I've kept the matter quiet as I didn't want to cause a panic, but there have been no signs of aggression from Brenden since then. I communicated with our spies, and there has been no movement along the Brenden border. The attack appears to have been isolated, as if it was carried out without rhyme or reason."

"Dellwyn is north," Vladimir said. "That city holds no military advantage for them whatsoever. If they wanted to wreak havoc or gain ground, they would have overtaken one of the cities along our southwestern border."

The queen shrugged. "It doesn't make sense. I have found no strategy within the attack, which makes me fear they may have set a far more complicated plan in place."

"Brendens are masterminds of wit and cunning," William added. "And wielders of brute force and superiority."

"Perhaps they've changed their tactics," Katherine mused.

Both William and the queen ignored her.

"Either way," Vladimir said. "We can't simply sit and wait for them to conduct their next attack."

"No, we cannot." Queen Adamara spoke with authority. "Some other form of foul play is at work here, and I want us to get to the bottom of it immediately."

The intonation of her voice implied a plan was already brewing behind her sparkling eyes.

"What do you propose?" Vladimir asked.

Queen Adamara gazed absentmindedly at the papers on the table before slowly bringing her hands to rest on each arm of her chair. "We have a spy stationed in the Brenden government right now that we planted years ago. If anyone can figure out exactly what it is that Brenden has planned, it will be him, but digging deep into these matters will compromise his position. Sending correspondences back and forth right now is too risky, especially with this brutality on Dellwyn. I can only hope that doesn't mean that his identity has already been discovered."

She hesitated.

"I propose we send an ambassador to retrieve him, to save whatever intel has been accrued over the past few years before it is lost, and to learn of whatever treachery Brenden has planned for us. A declaration of war must be made against Brenden, but I want absolute certainty about why this atrocity was committed and how involved Brenden was in the sinister matter of Michael's death before it's decreed."

I perked up at her words, my eyes catching Vladimir's. He assessed the desire burning within me, knowing that going to Brenden was precisely what I wanted.

"I can leave with a squadron at first light," Vladimir said. "You've caught us early enough that there won't be too much backtracking. As soon as I uncover anything, I can send a message to the capital by falcon."

Queen Adamara's gaze flicked between Vladimir and William, absorbing his words. "No."

My eyes narrowed at her assertion.

"The unrest in the capital has escalated since the slaughter in the throne room. Our people demand justice, and they want answers. They *deserve* answers. I believe your presence will help calm their fears and smooth things over until we can supply them with a more definitive answer. I need your help ruling our country. I need *you* there, Vladimir."

Her sudden dependency on Vladimir was unexpected considering that only a few months ago they had been at complete odds, but that was back when she had Zedekiah as her adviser. Now she had no one.

Perhaps the queen had always needed someone by her side.

Her cold eyes landed on her son. "William will go. He's visited Brenden before, and he needs more experience with foreign affairs." She turned to Katherine, the first acknowledgment she had shown the healer all night. "Katherine will accompany him."

William bristled, spine straightening, a vein protruding from his neck. The queen was punishing William for leaving the capital when she had strictly forbidden him to go, but why send Katherine? The queen hated her more than anyone else, and it didn't make sense to send her on such a vital mission unless this was also some sort of punishment for Katherine.

"I will accompany them as well," I said.

Queen Adamara didn't even bother to look at me. "That won't be necessary."

Heat flared in my chest. Her displeasure with me had not dissipated. It was alive and burning strong as ever. "With all due respect, Your Majesty, I feel it is my right to see this through."

If there was a chance of finding out who orchestrated my father's murder, I would not be left behind.

Flames lit within the queen's eyes when she finally turned to me. "With all due respect, *Miss Gallows*, you are not a part of this government. You are neither an ambassador nor a Kavari and have no business meddling with our affairs. I fail to see why you are even present for these proceedings."

My breath shuddered out of me as I tried to stay calm. "I may not be a Kavari, but I have the right of a Blood Vier—"

"And look how being a Blood Vier affected our country last time. Dozens of deaths in the throne room."

I stood abruptly at her stinging remark, desperately wanting to hurl something at her. That desire treaded on dangerous ground. I stormed out of the tent, arms shaking at my sides. Those deaths were not my fault. They were Zedekiah's. I'd never wanted to be a Blood Vier in the first place, and the queen was still angry with me for disrupting her plans for the next Kavari. No doubt her pride was wounded from being betrayed by her closest adviser, but she had no right to exclude me from the matter: this was not a frivolous governmental issue, this was my father's murderers we were talking about. I had every right to both see and ensure that the proper justice was carried out, or to even carry out that justice myself.

Anger trembled throughout my body as I marched back to my tent, plopping down on the ground in front of the flap instead of going inside. I'd spent so many nights out in the open that I yearned to see the starry sky spreading out above me.

The anger abated after a few moments, and I hated myself for begrudgingly admitting that the queen had a point. I was not a part of this government. I hadn't taken the oath of the Kavari, nor did I plan to. My fingers dug into the earth, still damp from the last snow. Dirt pressed beneath my fingernails, making them feel clogged and heavy. I'd been making my own decisions ever since my mother's death; now, I found it strange and irritating to have someone instructing me on what I could and could not do.

"She's right, you know."

My fingers dug farther into the ground as I worked my jaw. Vladimir hovered over me, indicating that their deliberations had finished. It hadn't taken long.

I glanced up at him before glaring at the dark sky. "Are you going to let her stop me from going?"

Vladimir shuffled his feet. "You're too close to this, Taryn. Dealing with international relations is precarious at best, and we can't afford for anyone to have clouded judgment."

I scoffed, flinging the dirt from my hands. "Right, because Katherine is definitely able to think straight."

Our eyes met.

Katherine was the one who had released the arrow that resulted in Zedekiah's death. I'd seen the vengeance burning in her eyes, the same vengeance that had once burned so brightly in mine.

"That was the queen's decision," Vladimir said. "Not mine. She wants representation from both the Crown and the Kavari in Brenden."

"Is that what you believe, or are you just willing to go along with her because she now favors your opinion?" I regretted the words as soon as they left my mouth, but it was too late to take them back. "I'm sorry."

Vladimir's jaw ticked. "I am only swayed by what is right, Taryn. Not by who favors my opinion."

I crossed my arms in frustration. I was not a Kavari. I wasn't really anybody. I was nothing more than a girl caught up in circumstances outside of her control. I was nothing before I came to the capital, and I was nothing now. When I had vied for the Kavari, I had almost been something, and I yearned for that brief spark of hope, of purpose, that it had offered me.

"What are you going to do?" Vladimir sounded hesitant.

I looked up at him. "What do you mean?"

He shrugged. "You fulfilled your bargain and are no longer under any obligation. Where are you planning to go? Back to the capital?"

My gaze fell on the road leading back. I'd been so consumed with finding my father's killer that I hadn't even considered it yet. Nothing was waiting for me out in the world. I was alone.

I reached for my mother's clasp at the base of my throat, clutching it to my chest. I had her family name now, but the only thing it told me was that my mother was not from Gharridan. Hardly any coin resided in my purse. My talents were few, and none of them could make a living anyway. In all honesty, I wasn't any closer to finding my mother's family from when I had first set out from Navarre. I wanted to find them, but there was something that I desperately wanted to do more. Something I would have to accomplish on my own and something that I couldn't tell anyone about. Not even Vladimir.

I glanced sidelong at him; my mind made up. "I'm not sure."

But I was.

I sat on the ground for a while after Vladimir left before going in search of William. Most of the camp was already asleep, but his tent stood empty. The crackle and pop of dying embers permeated the quiet along with the low moaning of the brisk wind as I waited outside, pacing back and forth on the soft grass, sure that he had to return soon.

But he didn't.

I frowned, making my way through the sleeping camp and

searching for any sign of him until I found myself near the queen's quarters again. Light still shone from within, and I stepped toward the canvas, hearing hushed voices. I stood quietly outside, unable to discern who was speaking or even what they were speaking about, but the voices abruptly stopped.

The flap of the tent billowed open, and a figure stormed out into the darkness. His heavy footfalls thudded against the ground as he passed me, oblivious to my presence in the shadows. After waiting a moment, I padded softly after him.

"William."

He spun around so quickly that I nearly ran into him. I took a step back as his startled eyes stared back at me in the dim light. They burned with a mixture of hatred and frustration, but the fire evaporated when he recognized me. He turned away and kept walking.

"It's late, Taryn."

I picked up my pace to keep step beside him, unsure of what to say. "I guess your mother had a lot to discuss?"

He looked sharply at me. "Were you listening?"

I quickly shook my head, surprised at his sudden accusation. "I was just looking for you." I stood there helplessly, worried about whatever was bothering him. "What's wrong, William?"

He stopped, raking a hand through his golden hair, jaw clenched.

"Is it because she assigned Katherine to go with you?"

William remained quiet, staring at the ground with a distraught expression. We'd talked so little in the past few weeks that our conversation felt stilted and awkward.

"I'll go with you," I offered. "First thing in the morning, I'll ride ahead and go with you and Katherine to Brenden."

William shook his head. "You can't come with me."

"Your mother doesn't have to know."

"I don't care; you're not coming."

I lifted my chin in defiance. "And if I do?"

William raised an eyebrow. "Then I can arrest you. Going against the Crown's direct orders is a criminal offense."

"Then shouldn't you be in jail?" My eyes bore into him.

I turned to leave, but he sighed and caught my arm. He stepped forward, face sincere. "I need you to trust me, Taryn. Don't go to Brenden."

Suspicions welled within me. He was hiding something. Something that had to do with what he and his mother had just discussed. William could be finicky, and I had no doubt that if he wanted to keep me from coming, he would.

"All right," I finally agreed, but my compliance was only to pacify him.

A twinge of relief touched William's face, and he moved away, turning back once more before he left. "Then I'll see you back in the capital?"

A question hovered in his eyes, a hope that we could eventually talk.

I nodded.

I stood there for a moment, watching as he disappeared into the darkness. I had no intention of returning to the capital. Not yet. Not when I had other business to attend to.

I returned to my tent, scavenging through my saddle bags until I found ink and a small piece of parchment. When morning broke, my tent would be stripped of all belongings except for a small square parchment with a message scrawled on it— and I would be nowhere to be found.

CHAPTER TWO

TARYN

THE DYING SUNLIGHT splayed through the swaying branches above, casting dancing shadows that concealed us from the searching eyes. I stood frozen next to Stryder, holding my breath, and steadied his head in an attempt to discourage a nicker from betraying us. The outlines of two soldiers moved slowly as they scanned the woods, and I hoped the descending night would distort their view of the shadows enveloping us. Stryder's head shifted in my hands, and I squeezed tighter, begging for silence. With one last sweep of the woods, the soldiers turned their horses away, returning to the larger group that awaited them.

I released a shuddering breath and it streamed out before me, visible in the cold air. The hoofbeats faded, and I tilted my head, paying close attention to which direction they headed.

When the chirping of the crickets was the only sound remaining, I mounted Stryder and slowly crept through the forest after them, watching my back. I needed to get as close to them as possible without being detected. Moments ago, I'd gotten too close. Stryder had stumbled over a branch and broken it, which sent the two soldiers out to uncover the disturbance.

A flame materialized ahead, and I pulled Stryder up, sliding from his back.

This would have to be close enough for tonight.

Stryder grazed beside me as I stretched out on my weathered bedroll, gnawing at a piece of stale bread. I wrapped my cloak tighter around me, staring longingly at the flames of the fire in the distance and wishing for its warmth, but if I could see their fire they would definitely see mine. The light would beckon to them like a beacon. My stomach growled, hungry for more, and I closed my eyes, trying to suppress the desire for food and cursing myself for not snatching more when I'd had the chance.

Pale moonlight shone brightly through the trees, the night unusually clear as I gazed up at it through the interweaving branches. I wouldn't be out here by myself for much longer—they had to be getting close. The forest would eventually dwindle away, leaving me vulnerable and exposed to their eyes. It had been a hard journey, and the endless days of creeping behind them blurred together.

I glanced at my diminishing food supply, which hadn't been much to start with. If they went any farther, I would run out of food before we reached our destination. I shivered at the thought. There had been no game out here, none that I could find anyway, and straying too far off their trail would be dangerous. If it had been summer, I might have been able to find some berries, but at least the cold wasn't as bitter as when we'd traveled to Gapsvar. Stryder had managed to find tiny shoots of grass here and there, and most of the water we'd stumbled upon was still flowing. In the mornings, it was sometimes encased in a thin sheet of ice, but it was thankfully easy to break through. Loneliness preyed upon me, my first few days on the road feeling strangely reminiscent of when I'd split from William after learning where Marco was being held prisoner.

I swallowed, worried about what would happen when they found out I'd followed them. I had to join them before we reached Brenden, or I might end up in an even worse situation. If they were involved in my father's murder, they wouldn't look lightly on his daughter sneaking across their borders—even if they didn't know who I was.

I reached down and pulled the dagger from my boot, turning it over in my hands. The sharp metal gleamed in the moonlight; the leather-bound hilt was worn from use but still dependable. Such a small object, but when used with force it transformed into a deadly weapon. My jaw clenched as I stared at it. Death whispered in my ear, told me to wield this dagger for one person and one person alone.

But I knew that wouldn't give me the peace I was looking for.

Vengeance no longer controlled me, but now I was haunted by a need that burrowed deep inside of me. The need to know who ordered the death of my father and why.

I returned the knife to my boot and wrapped my arms around my legs, staring off into the woods.

A figure stared back at me.

I bolted upright, my breath catching. A thick braid hung over her shoulder. Blood dripped from her hands.

"Helvah?" I called.

Her eyes briefly met mine, full of terror, full of hurt, but then there was only the surrounding darkness.

I blinked.

She was gone.

Tears slid down my cheeks as I buried my face, the pain overwhelming me. It was my fault that she was an orphan. I should have never involved her mother or her. I should have gone *back* for her. Helvah's ghost followed me everywhere I went, tormenting me. I'd see her face in the shadows, certain she was there, but it was only my guilty conscience conjuring the image. At night, sleep evaded me. Whenever I closed my eyes, my dreams were plagued with monstrous nightmares bombarding me with grotesque images.

"I'm sorry, Helvah," I cried softly. "I'm so sorry."

I rubbed my hands together furiously, trying to entice warmth into them. It would be colder tonight. Colder than all the other nights before. My chilled limbs ached for a fire, but I dared not risk it. Stryder plodded slowly beneath me, the soft thud of his hooves the only sound around.

But then a branch cracked to my left.

I spun at the noise, gathering the reins and preparing to send Stryder into a run. Another disturbance came from my right, crashing through the underbrush, and my heels dug into Stryder's sides. He took off, hooves now pounding against the forest floor. A horseman appeared through the trees ahead, and the set of hoofbeats behind me multiplied. I swerved to avoid the one in front of me but was immediately faced with another. We bounced back and forth off one another as I sought an escape, but there was none. I pulled Stryder to a stop, my breath coming in ragged gasps as I surveyed the Gharridan soldiers surrounding us.

They didn't raise their weapons or show aggression, but the wall of horses penning me in knit tightly together. Another horse approached from the ridge, cutting down through the forest to meet us. I swallowed, my stomach dropping as William came into view. I knew this encounter was inevitable, but I'd hoped to be closer to Brenden first. Our eyes locked. Fury lined his face, his short, rapid breaths barely controlled. He brought Othello up beside me, expression dangerous.

"What are you doing here?" He kept his voice low but restrained, like a dam cracking, just barely able to hold the mass of water back.

"Going to Brenden," I stated.

"You were told not to."

I cocked my head. "If I recall correctly, I was simply told not to go with *you*."

William's jaw ticked, fists clenched around the reins. I knew he was holding back, knew his temper boiled dangerously close to the surface. He hadn't expected my presence, which was carelessness on his part. Both he and Vladimir were fools for thinking I'd give up that easily. After my perseverance in finding Marco and going after Zedekiah, they should know better.

William's eyes snapped to one of his men. "Escort her back to the capital immediately."

"I am not your prisoner." Defiance lit my eyes like a wild-fire.

One of the soldiers broke formation to approach me, but I backed Stryder up, bumping into another rider whose mount didn't appreciate the close proximity with an unfamiliar horse. He half reared, kicking out at Stryder and nipping at his rump. Stryder retaliated, hooves flying. The other horses shuffled uneasily at the squabble, stomping their hooves and chomping at their bits.

"Enough!" William motioned them to widen the circle. Frustration marred his features. "This is official business, Taryn. Not a wild-goose chase across the countryside."

My gaze flicked to Katherine standing outside the ring of horses, but she only offered me an imperceptible shake of her head. She couldn't help me with this. William didn't need another reason to despise her.

When I said nothing, William asked, "How long have you been following us?"

"Since the day you left."

He cast a disapproving gaze over each of the soldiers. It wouldn't bode well for them. If they had missed me tailing their group, they could have easily missed someone else. Someone more deadly and with the intention of hurting them.

"If you don't want me arriving with you, then go on your way, and I'll go on mine," I said.

William laughed. "And you're going to what, waltz into Brenden like you waltzed into the fortress? That turned out so well for us the last time."

I pursed my lips, irritated and unsure of how to navigate these unpredictable waters. I sat deep in the saddle, looking for an opening to break out of the ring of soldiers, but they'd constrict the moment I tried to slip through one of the gaps between them.

A horn blew through the still woods, carrying across the forest full and deep, smooth as honey. A hush fell over our group, limbs going rigid. William's men looked to him for instruction. I searched for the source of the horn, heard a whinny and the sudden sound of over a dozen horses. Someone, or something, was going to appear over that ridge at any second.

William jerked his chin at me, hissing, "Get her out of here, Carver."

No.

I'd come too far to back down now.

I tried to break away from the encircling men. Stryder skittered out of reach, but Carver was right behind, reaching for my reins. The pounding of hooves amplified, and a line of horsemen crested the top of the ridge. William cursed. There were at least twenty of them, outnumbering us two to one, their forms dark against the sun. In one fluid motion, they descended to meet us, the horn blowing again. Bronze armor overlaid their red and gold uniforms, and a red tuft of hair shot out of their helmets. The same colors embellished the horses' blankets. One of the soldiers bore a flag with the emblem of two serpents twisting together. The flag of Brenden.

My fingers involuntarily reached for the dagger in my boot, but I pulled them back. The Brendens' expressions were concealed beneath their helmets, but the way they rode displayed intimidation. The fractured circle of Gharridans around me formed into a line. William only cast a singular glance at me before stepping in front of the line to meet the approaching riders. I'd already been seen. He couldn't hide me from them now.

The thundering hooves dug into the ground in front of us, leather saddles creaking as the men uniformly halted and aimed their savage spears at our chests. I searched the slits where their eyes were, but each only bore an expression of stone underneath the bronze mask. The effect sent a chill up my arms. My hands went cold. One Brenden broke away from the group, a vast array of colorful ranks displayed on his vest. His gaze scrutinized each of our faces.

"You are trespassing in Brenden territory." His heavy accent muddled his words. "What is your business?"

Border patrol.

My eyes flicked between the two men, wondering if William would reveal his identity. If Brenden was truly against Gharridan, this hostile meeting could turn deadly.

Othello sidestepped beneath William. "I am Crown Prince William of Gharridan, and this is Katherine Daharaway of the Kavari. We've come to seek an audience with King Arguis."

William's title did not seem to impress the Brendens' leader. His stoic face remained unchanged. "We received no word of a party arriving from Gharridan."

"It is a matter of urgency."

Suspicion radiated from the man, but he lowered the spear and lifted his bearded chin with authority. "I am General Nixon. We will escort you into Brenden on good faith to determine if you speak the truth, but I cannot guarantee you an audience with King Arguis. Nor can I guarantee that you will not be charged with illegal trespassing on Brenden soil."

William hesitated as if wanting to say more but then nodded his acceptance. The line of Brendens encircled us, and we all bunched together as they cut off any thought of escape. I eyed the strangers wearily, my mind wandering back to the last time I'd been held prisoner by Silas and his men. The fading scars that covered my wrists itched at the memory.

The Brenden soldiers never looked at us, keeping their focus straight ahead. William asked a few more questions of the general, but his answers were short and clipped, eliminating any desire to probe further. Silence hovered between us with no other conversation passing between our two parties for the rest of the day. William glanced at me several times, a thousand different frustrations begging to burst from his lips, but he wouldn't risk speaking in front of them. He couldn't. If they suspected I wasn't supposed to be with the group, that would only bring him further complications.

I found the quiet eerie at first, but the change in landscape quickly captivated my attention. The forest ended abruptly, like the edge of a cliff, and we emerged into an entirely different world. The trees were replaced by a strange plant that grew upward with multiple arms stretching out, covered in spikes like a porcupine. They littered the sandy and rocky earth along with a variety of other unusual shrubs I had never seen before. I expected the land to stay flat, but mountains rose in the distance like jagged teeth extending toward the sky, and a patchwork of hills dotted the areas in between. Everything about the environment around me screamed of severity.

Dust kicked up around the horses' feet as we rode, coating their fur and our bodies in a layer of dirt. I studied the Brenden soldiers around me as we rode. Their skin was several shades darker than my own olive shade, a rich brown that contrasted with the red of their uniforms. Most of their hair was dark and short-shaven, but a few wore braids extending down their backs over their armor. Each man wielded a deadly spear, as well as a strangely curved sword that hung from their belts. Their bows were shaped differently, but I only picked out three archers among the group. A Brenden caught my inquisitive surveillance. I turned away.

When the sun began to disappear over the distant hills, the Brendens stopped for the night, placing our group in the center of theirs. Several watchmen kept vigil on the outskirts of the camp. Whether to keep us in or others out, I couldn't decide. I laid out my bedroll next to Katherine's, ignoring William's questioning gaze. Katherine was repairing one of the latches on her quiver, her bow lying beside her within easy reach.

I frowned. Why had they allowed us to keep our weapons?

"I'm shocked it took the men so long to figure out you were tailing us." Katherine's face remained stoic, her lips pulled in a tight line.

I swallowed a laugh, cocking my head curiously. "How long did you know?"

She arched a red eyebrow. "Since the first day. I had a feeling you weren't going to take no for an answer, so I kept an eye out. It didn't take very long to spot you."

I thought I'd been so careful, but Katherine proved a difficult person to fool.

"Why didn't you say anything?"

Katherine surveyed our surroundings, ensuring none of the others had strayed closer. "Because I would have done the same thing in your shoes. It doesn't matter if you're not a Kavari, Taryn. He was your father. You have a right to be here as much as I do."

A Gharridan soldier brushed past, and we both quieted even though I wanted to ask what the plan was once we reached the king of Brenden.

If we make it that far.

The Brendens hadn't welcomed us with open arms. Entering into a city full of hostile enemies could result in our immediate deaths if William didn't play his cards right. If we ended up having to run, everything relied on speed because until we crossed the border and reentered the forest, there was nowhere out here for us to hide.

I sniffed, noticing the change in the air, and glanced down at my cracking knuckles. "It's so dry here."

"It will only get worse," Katherine said.

A howl sounded in the distance. I froze, the skin on the back of my neck prickling. Another howl answered from the opposite side of the hillside. One of the Brenden soldiers noticed my reaction and laughed, uttering a stream of fast-paced accentuated words in his native tongue. Another heard his comment and looked at me, catching my confusion.

"Desert wolves," he explained in his thick accent. "You're in no danger."

His words didn't exactly comfort me, but none of the other Brenden soldiers seemed to react to the reoccurring howls. At least we were on the inside of the group, meaning that the Brendens would be the first to be attacked. I held on to that thought.

William sat a ways off, he and Carver speaking in low voices. If the Brendens hadn't intercepted us when they did, I might not have made it into Brenden. William had been bound and determined to send me back to Gharridan. I watched his expression grow hesitant and cautious as he spoke with Carver, trying not to catch the Brendens' attention.

The secret meeting with his mother. The far-off look. His adamance that I not come to Brenden.

He was hiding something.

I didn't know how, but I could tell. Something else was going on here—something about coming to Brenden that he didn't want me to know.

Dust caked my lungs over the next two grueling days. The world around us steadily grew warmer, and I shed my cloak during the afternoon for the first time in months. When the sun fell that evening, the temperature continued to drop throughout the night, but as soon as the first rays of dawn crept across the vast sky, it once again began to rise.

The Brenden horses grew fidgety, increasing their pace and trying to race ahead.

We were close.

A massive hill rose before us, the horses picking their way up a rocky path to the top. Ever so slowly, we crested the ridge.

My breath caught in my throat.

A sparkling city spread out before us, shining like jewels in the sun. Its structures were not multi-shaped like Gharridan's but flat and boxy with canopies of curtains creating shade on the rooftops. In the center of the city lay the most extravagant building I had ever beheld. Large teardrops of gold roofed its turrets and towers that jutted up into the sky. The sunlight reflecting off the metal was nearly blinding. It must be the palace.

I shielded my eyes, gaping at its grandeur.

"Palazaar," General Nixon stated. "The shining capital of Brenden."

The horses took off down the hill in a thunder of hooves, dust flying around us like smoke. Stryder's legs surged beneath me, racing to keep up with the excited horses beside him. A low wall encased the city, its creamy bricks seeming dull against the shine of Palazaar. The gatekeepers eyed us as we approached, inspecting each of the strangers being escorted through their walls. War paint etched the skin below their eyes, and their fingers clutched the spears in their hands, ready for any sign of trouble. The same strangely curved swords that the other Brendens carried swung from their belts.

"What are those?" I asked Katherine, indicating the weapon.

She followed my gaze. "They're called sabers. Although it may look similar, it is an entirely different weapon from that of a longsword."

The guards spoke with General Nixon, their native language rolling off their tongues in long streams before they stepped aside to grant us entrance into the city. Our large company pushed its way through the bustling streets, people scattering out of the way like insects. Bright colors permeated the city, dripping into every aspect of its culture, Brenden's wealth displayed in the expensive dyes used to create all the vibrant colors staining every piece of the city. The inhabitants stared at us as we passed, growing silent and pointing out the foreigners riding in the center of the battalion. The same rainbow of colors arrayed their garments, and many of the women had their hair done up in elaborate braids intertwined with jewelry.

I examined their faces, calculating, taking everything in turn. The deeper we plunged into the city, the more lost I became, and the closer we inched to the intimidating palace, the smaller I felt. Its massive infrastructure rose above us like a mountain, its exterior carved with exquisite figures and daring statues. I craned my head back, gaping once again at the teardrops of gold encasing the roof.

"Are they solid gold?" I asked. The idea sounded absurd.

Katherine glanced around us. "Brenden's main trade is mining. Nearly every precious metal and jewel on the continent originates from here. The kingdom is wealthy enough that it wouldn't surprise me, but I doubt any Brenden would be willing to tell you the truth."

General Nixon ordered us to dismount at the steps of the palace and wait while he ventured inside. Both William's and Katherine's expressions remained calm, but tension built within me. King Arguis must be an extremely powerful man. If he really had ordered the death of my father and orchestrated the attack on Dellwyn, he might just execute us on the spot. My fingers twisted nervously into Stryder's mane as the Brenden soldiers watched us, spears easily within throwing distance.

After what seemed like a lifetime, General Nixon reappeared and descended the steps of the palace. His movements were stiff and his voice gruff as he announced, "King Arguis will see you now."

I begrudgingly let them lead Stryder away as I climbed the steep steps behind Katherine, emerging onto what looked like a massive porch. The pillars of the palace stretched high into the sky, towering above us. The golden roof orbs were not visible from here, but I marveled that their weight didn't bring the entire building crashing down. Idols lined the outer wall of the palace, separated by partitions, each having coffers of gold and offerings laid out before them. The stone statues appeared strange to me, not having faces and carved into abstract shapes, yet every few idols I found a Brenden kneeling in prayer.

We passed the threshold, stepping onto the marble floor as the doors shut behind us, closing us off from the rest of the world as we descended deeper into the building. Walking through the palace was like traversing a long hallway full of beauty and history, each corridor more exquisite than the last. The hallway opened up into a large antechamber where I got my first glimpse of what I assumed were the throne room doors. I nearly stumbled. They were coated in limestone, their surface gleaming from the sunlight that entered through a glass square in the ceiling. The detailing on the massive doors was immaculate, and the symbol of the two twisting serpents was carved into the grain. They were a wonder in and of themselves.

My stomach twisted in my gut, afraid of what this king would have to say, of this king who might have ordered my father's death.

He could be innocent.

But I needed to know. I had to be sure.

I took a deep breath, hands shaking at my sides as the guards opened the elaborate doors before us, ushering us toward an unknown fate.

CHAPTER THREE

VLADIMIR

LONELINESS PLAGUED MY soul like a disease, the confining walls of the palace threatening to crush my lungs and suffocate me. I strolled the long corridors, nodding at the guards, passing noblemen arrayed in fine robes and conversing with the council members. Yet among so many people, I still felt alone. The emptiness hollowing out my chest felt similar to the time after Michael's death. His absence made the world darker, and the air colder, sucking the very meaning out of life, but even Katherine had been here through that. Now she was gone too—and so was Taryn.

My jaw clenched as I gazed out over the bustling city below. I imagined Michael marching up behind me with a scowl on his face, asking how I could have possibly lost his daughter. One promise. He'd only asked for one promise, and I couldn't even keep that, had barely been able to keep that up until now. After everything that had transpired, it was a miracle that Taryn was even still alive.

The morning we left the queen's camp, I had noticed Stryder was missing from his picket when I went to tack Dante. A foul taste settled in my mouth as I made my way to her tent, only intensifying when I stepped inside and found her and everything in it gone. Everything except a hastily scribbled note left behind.

I'm going to look for my family.

I shouldn't have been surprised. I was the one who had asked her what she was going to do. A part of me had anticipated her departure, but not this quickly. I told myself it was probably the best thing for both her and Gharridan. Queen Adamara didn't want her interfering in the government unless she was a Kavari, and Taryn had no interest in joining our ranks. She'd forgiven her father and learned her mother's family name, and nothing tied her to the capital. She was free to leave. I just wished she had told me she was leaving. She owed me that, at least.

My fingers dug into the grout of the window ledge as frustration dispersed throughout my body. I pushed away, making my way down the grand hall and passing the vast throne room. I refused to allow my eyes to wander beyond its doors. I couldn't. The ghosts of the dead that lingered there haunted me, their faces permanently inscribed on my mind. A shiver ran down my spine. Death clung to that room like a curse, leaving me dreading the day I would have to cross that threshold again.

I found the queen in her study, signing a thick stack of documents. The chancellor hovered over her shoulder, explaining what each meant as he set it before her. I waited patiently before the desk as she finished. Winter sunlight poured in from the windows, coming to rest on the shelves of books that lined the wall behind her. Our scheduled meeting was not one I was looking forward to, and I was anxious to get it over with. Queen Adamara and I hadn't held an official conversation between the Crown and the Kavari since the day she tried to instate Mordakai.

The quill dropped into its holder, splotches of ink staining the queen's hands.

"Leave us." She shooed the chancellor away, leaning against the back of her chair and motioning for me to sit. When the door pulled shut behind the man, she met my eyes.

"We have much to discuss, Vladimir."

I dipped my head in acknowledgment.

"First and foremost is the matter of our national security."

Silence stretched between us, the severity of the matter weighing us down.

The queen arched an eyebrow. "I'm finding it difficult to discern who I can and cannot trust. Zedekiah was my closest adviser and friend. He served Gharridan for many years, always doing good for the country. I would've trusted him with my life." She hesitated. "But he betrayed us. We now have reason to suspect he may have been working with Brenden and possibly Algarar, considering their association with Gapsvar. What reports I've received from our border guards have ensured that there is no movement from Algarar, but war may be approaching. I would like to hear your thoughts on the matter."

I steepled my fingers together, mind working. This issue was one I had mulled over during every long, endless day in the saddle. I cleared my throat. "With the Algarian soldiers' interference, I fear that they have made some kind of alliance with Gapsvar. Considering their joint hatred of us, it's not unexpected, but it's still concerning. With regards to Brenden, I am interested in the report William will return with. Michael solidified our alliance with them, so why they should seek to kill him and start a war is beyond me, but their attack on Dellwyn invokes severe consequences. We don't know what motives possibly pushed them to do this, which is the most frightening aspect of this scheme."

"If Brenden was behind the murder of Michael Gallows, William will find out, and he will find out why," Queen Adamara stated.

She pulled a paper from within the top drawer of her desk. "In other matters, the royal treasury remains secure. I was fearful that Zedekiah might have relinquished it to our enemies."

My eyes scanned the records of numbers, but no entry struck me as peculiar. As the queen's adviser, he would have had access. He could've done far greater damage to the heart of Gharridan if he'd wanted to.

"Did you check into Zedekiah's personal accounts?" I asked. "Whoever hired him would have paid him an advance. Surely there is a record of it somewhere."

Queen Adamara glanced sidelong at the desk. "No, but I will have one of the accountants look into it."

"What about Zedekiah's family?"

"He had none."

My eyes shot up from the records. "What?"

She turned to look at me. "Both Zedekiah and Mordakai were orphans. They had no one but each other."

"Not even a distant relative?"

The queen shook her head.

I leaned back in the chair. If Zedekiah and Mordakai were orphans, how had they both managed to work their way up into the most powerful positions in the government? I scolded myself, knowing that I had been in similar circumstances at one time, but that was different. Michael had found me. Who had found these two?

"Another matter that requires discussion is the matter of the Kavari." The queen's words interrupted my thoughts.

My spine stiffened.

"I know we haven't agreed in the past, Vladimir, but I need to know that I can count on you."

I clasped my hands in front of me. "My allegiance is to the Crown and to Gharridan."

She eyed me. "I'm assuming that the absence of Michael Gallows' daughter implies her abdication from any place within the Kavari?"

She'd worded that question carefully. Taryn had left without warning and without explanation. She'd gotten what she wanted, and I highly doubted she would be back. Not for the Kavari anyway.

"I'm assuming that at this time, Your Majesty."

The queen's face grew very tired. "With two Kavari down now, due to Marco's incapacitation, we are in desperate need of additional forces. Considering my, shall we say, *unwise* choice in the last instatement, I would like us both to work together on this. I am aware that this is not the way it's meant to be done, but we are left with no other choice."

I swallowed, the reality of her words sinking in. Katherine

and I were the only Kavari left. Marco was no longer of any use to us. As leader, it was my job to seek out those who would train and apprentice to serve in the Kavari, but I began to fear it would have to be done the queen's way this time.

She pulled a paper from the desk and handed it to me. "I have put together a list of eligible parties that would fit the role well, although I'm afraid none are as good as Mordakai might have been, had he not been killed."

I suppressed a snarl. Mordakai would have done this country no favors.

My eyes glanced over the list, recognizing only a few names. These were not great men of valor, but mere soldiers who had moved up the ranks and a few council members possessing very little battle training.

"Our options have dwindled," the queen said.

I waved the list in the air. "I would like to discuss this with Captain Verone first, as well as receive the opinion of a few of the council members. And Katherine."

Queen Adamara looked away at the mention of Katherine's name, annoyed. "Do what you must, but I would like it narrowed down to one or two candidates before William returns."

Her words dismissed any value of Katherine's opinion.

"And I want to meet with you again before the end of the week," she added.

I nodded, my chair scraping against the floor as I stood to leave, glancing at the queen one more time. She was staring out the window with a troubled look in her eyes, arms crossed, no doubt a hundred different matters weighing on her. Maybe Zedekiah's betrayal had broken Queen Adamara down to where she was finally willing to open her eyes to everything going on around her. She'd changed. Since Zedekiah's betrayal, she had become a much more somber person.

I stepped into the empty hall, relieved the dreaded meeting was over and that it had gone better than expected. Cold and uninviting walls the grey color of gloom blurred past me. I looked without really seeing, the confines of the castle pressing down on me alongside the burden of my position.

What our country needed more than ever right now was unity. I charged myself with the mission, to gather the seams of this country and knit them together so tightly that nothing we faced could break it. We didn't know what the future held, didn't know how Brenden's actions in Dellwyn and the country's involvement in Michael's death would pan out, but if we were to survive it, we had to be united under a singular cause. Steady. Determined. Strong. As one.

I made my way through the corridors, eventually ending up outside the military offices. The guard stationed in front of Captain Verone's study motioned for me to wait. Raised voices muffled through the door, as well as a fist pounding against the desk. I crossed my arms, intrigued, and waited for him to finish.

Verone emerged a few minutes later, two soldiers trailing out behind him. I cocked an eyebrow as he glanced my way. The fury in his face dissipated, and he threw the guard a disconcerted look. In everything he did, he always remained calm. I was convinced that if we were all ever trapped inside a building that was on fire, he would stay cool and collected, calmly directing everyone to the exits. This flustered appearance was a side of him I had never seen.

"My apologies, Vladimir. I was not aware that you were waiting."

I shrugged. "No matter. What was that about?" I nodded to the two soldiers disappearing around the corner.

Verone scowled after them, his mouth drawing into a tight line. "Just a little bit of misconduct that needed to be addressed. It's dealt with now." He looked back at me. "What can I do for you?"

I noted the guard out of the corner of my eye and indicated for Verone to walk with me. Our boots echoed down the passageway, and I checked over my shoulder to make sure we wouldn't be overheard.

"What have you been able to find out about the men in the throne room?" I asked. The faces of the traitors who had rallied behind Zedekiah flashed in my mind.

Verone cast a wary eye around us. "All of the men were newer recruits, joined within the last six months."

"Who instated them?"

He shrugged. "Officers below me. None of the recruits had anything in common prior to joining; different villages were all listed on their papers."

"So we know nothing?"

"I'm not finished," Verone said. "I sent messengers to each of the villages they came from. None of the villagers had any recollection of men by these names. No person or family in those areas claimed them."

Residency wasn't always verified, mainly because there'd never been reason for a soldier to lie about it.

"Zedekiah's seal of approval marked each of their papers, though," Verone continued. "I made my way through their barracks, spoke with those that had interacted with them, but none of the soldiers seemed to know them at all. They kept to themselves."

"How did such young recruits get assigned to the throne room?" Irritation swelled in my voice.

"They were under Mordakai's instruction. Zedekiah requested their presence."

Mordakai had walked to his death that day without knowing. His brother attained what he needed from him and then killed him, never once looking back or seeming to regret his decision even though all they'd had was each other.

I took a few steps away, thinking, turning the events over in my mind. I paced back. "Verone, why would Zedekiah kill his brother?" I looked at him quizzically. "I've played that moment over and over in my mind. When you begin to really think about it, it doesn't make sense."

"I've wondered the same thing." Captain Verone stroked his chin, his bushy eyebrows lowering in concentration. "What was it he said, right before Zedekiah killed him?"

I thought back to that moment in the throne room. Tension was high as we argued over the queen's decision to instate Mordakai, but then Taryn revealed that someone had tried to murder her. Mordakai had shown only triumph leading up to that moment, but after Taryn's words, his entire demeanor had changed. Mordakai had rejected his place in the Kavari and asked that the incident be investigated.

"That there was another matter he wanted to discuss before the council, pertaining to the death of Michael Gallows."

I'd thought Zedekiah had killed his brother because he was about to betray him to the council, but I now realized that didn't make sense. Zedekiah revealed himself when he took his brother's life.

"Verone—"

"You think Mordakai may have had other information about his brother?"

"What are we missing here?" I asked, puzzled. "Did Mordakai know who his brother was working for?"

"It's a possibility."

I stared at the doors of the military offices lining the walls, then turned back to the captain. "Did you find anything when you searched Mordakai's office?"

Verone hesitated. "I don't know that they were searched, but I do know that his quarters were cleaned out."

I pursed my lips. I should have been here to ensure that a proper investigation was done. "Have his study searched as well as his living quarters. I know you've already done Zedekiah's but search it again—No, I'll search it myself. Let me know if you find anything."

We parted ways, and I made my way back to the main floor. If Mordakai knew anything about his brother's scheme, surely there would be some sort of clue hidden with his things. There was something else he had wanted to tell us. Something his brother was willing to kill for in order to keep it hidden.

I was so lost in my thoughts the page had to call my name several times, nearly holding me back to get my attention.

"I'm sorry," I mumbled, annoyed at the interruption as I took the letter from him.

I cracked the red seal, only paying haphazard attention to it as I walked, but its contents immediately brought me to a halt. I froze, eyes widening as they traveled over the words. Without a second thought, I bolted for the nearest stairwell and nearly leapt down the steps.

CHAPTER FOUR

THERE WAS A time when I considered the throne room of Gharridan to be the most magnificent place on the continent, but even with its twisting pillars, grand tapestries, and checkered floor, that room held no comparison to the throne room of Brenden. The marble floor stretched out before me in a sea of swirling beauty, its lines glistening from the sunlight streaming in through stained-glass windows. The painted glass stretched up to the ceiling, displaying a myriad of colors that shaped landscapes, portraits of knights, battles fought and won, and kings seated on their mighty thrones.

I craned my head back, trying not to gape at the architectural masterpiece encompassing the ceiling. A grand scheme of shapes and designs intertwined across it, outlined in gold and dipping in and out of the endless rows of pockets that covered the ceiling like a swathe of inverted bubbles. When I glanced back down, my gaze locked on the dais. Only five steps led to the top, unlike the fifteen that made up Gharridan's, but the throne was encased in solid gold with a script etched into the sides. King Arguis, clothed in fine linen of the deepest purple and richest blue, inspected us from his elaborate throne. An extravagant circlet of gold studded with an unnecessary number of rubies and precious stones rested on his head, and his hair was shaved almost completely to the scalp. Dark brown eyes continued to examine us as we came to a stop before him, the sound of our steps reverberating around the room.

King Arguis rose from his throne like an executioner lifting his weapon for a death blow. He stared down at us, his expression growing harder than stone as he took each of us in. My heart pounded within my chest like a hammer against steel, and I flexed my hands at my sides, resisting the urge to reach for my dagger. I felt the press of guards at our backs, their hands steady on their weapons. One word from the king, and we would all be dead.

My breaths turned shallow as the king descended the steps of the dais, lifting his chin. The guards shifted on their feet, spears prepared to enter our chests at their sovereign's direction. The king's mouth set into a thin line, eyes calculating, but then his eyes landed on the crown prince.

He broke out into a broad smile. "William!"

The king clapped him on the back like an old friend and drew him into a bear hug. "I almost didn't recognize you for a moment. Last time I laid eyes on you, you were just a lad!"

My eyes widened in shock as the entire tone of the room

shifted from intimidating to welcoming. I watched the strange king, wondering if this was some kind of twisted game.

William smiled in return. "King Arguis." He bowed. "It is an honor."

"And I see you have brought the healer with you!" The king grinned at Katherine as he stepped forward, reaching to clasp her hand in his. "Miss Katherine, I'm afraid that my daughter has been a bit ill as of late. I wonder, might you extend your abilities as a gift of good nature?"

Katherine seemed taken aback by the question. How strange it must be for her when a neighboring sovereign embraced the gift, yet her own country was repulsed by it. She threw a glance at William as if to ask for permission, but William kept his eyes on the king, jaw clenched.

Katherine offered a shallow bow. "I would be happy to help in any way that I can, Your Majesty."

The king gave her an appreciative smile before turning back to William. "We received no word of your coming, so I am having them prepare your rooms as we speak. Now, what brings you to Brenden?"

William's expression faltered as he chose his words carefully. "I am sure by now that you have heard of the death of our beloved Michael Gallows."

My muscles tensed.

This was it.

I watched closely for the king's reaction, searching for any flicker that he held blame for the murder. His jovial expression vanished, a wave of sadness that bore the weight of death overcoming him.

"I will never be able to convey the depths of our despair

when we received the news on the loss of his life. Michael Gallows was single-handedly responsible for the peace between our two great countries, and I fear there will never be a man wise enough to replace him."

Sincerity emanated from the king's voice, but I knew how expertly deceit could be crafted like truth. How a murderer could appear innocent. Nothing about the king's character betrayed any malice or evil. He displayed the exact opposite, but was it authentic?

My gaze drifted beyond him to where three figures stood rigidly to the right of the elaborate throne. One was a girl only a few years shy of womanhood. Her ferociously curly dark hair was swept up into a high ponytail, pulled taught against her face, and her throat was encased with a thick gold-studded necklace. The other two were young men who looked only a few years apart. All three were arrayed in the same cloth as the king and wore braided circlets of gold around their heads. His children. The elder boy possessed the same dark hair as his sister and father, but the younger's held a bronze sheen that glistened like burnt gold.

"I thank you for your words, King Arguis." William dipped his head in appreciation. "We traveled here to seek information of his dealings before he died. It is Queen Adamara's wish that if we work together, we might be able to discover some new insight into the matter of his death."

No accusation hung in William's voice, but the words he spoke treaded on dangerous ground. They could lead the king to believe that we already suspected his possible involvement in the murder.

"We are happy to lend assistance in any way that we are

able," King Arguis replied.

He turned, his gaze catching mine before dropping to my side. "You bear the ring of Michael Gallows upon your finger, but I am afraid we have not been properly introduced. Might I ask your name?"

My fingers twitched at the mention of the ring, feeling overly protective of the band.

"My name is Taryn Gallows."

A hush descended upon the room like a whispered secret as the king absorbed my words. His brown eyes softened, and something shifted within their depths. "Might I assume that you are the daughter of the late Michael Gallows?"

"I am."

He stared at me.

And then bowed.

Shock coursed through my veins at the unexpected gesture. William and Katherine shuffled their feet in surprise and watched the king curiously.

"Dear child—" His words cut off. "You have my deepest condolences."

My back stiffened at the display of empathy. It was too easy, too innocent, but maybe he was telling the truth. Or maybe he was involved in the murder, and it was an act of monstrosity that haunted him. An act he now regretted, and he was seeking a way to make amends for his wrongdoing.

A moment of silence fell on the throne room before the king turned to address our entire group. "I'm sure you are all tired from your journey. You will be escorted to the great hall, where you will find some refreshments while they finish your rooms. Tonight, we shall hold a feast in your honor."

My mind warred over the king's actions and my own contradicting assumptions.

"Katherine, if you wouldn't mind following me?"

Distaste hovered in William's face as he watched Katherine leave the throne room with the king. I glanced back at the three children on the dais and found the bronze-haired prince studying me, something buried deep within his gaze. He turned away, and the three of them followed after their father.

As we were escorted out of the throne room, a presence materialized behind me, and a chill marred the air. I didn't have to turn to know it was Death trailing a few steps behind me, wondering what I would do. I ignored him. I couldn't do anything until I uncovered the truth.

Each room of the castle we passed proved more extravagant than the one before it. In the grand hall, a table was set out with an assortment of crackers, cheeses, and strange fruits I had never seen before. Beside the water was a strange drink, yellow in color. I poured a glass, lifting the liquid to my lips. It was both sweet and sour, smooth yet with a kick. I poured a second glass, eyeing the other Gharridan soldiers around me. William moved forward as if to converse with me but I stepped away toward one of the Brenden guards, eliminating his attempt to speak about anything openly. His gaze bore into me from across the table. I stood quietly by myself until we were called to our rooms.

While the guards led the soldiers down a separate stairwell, William and I were escorted to the guest rooms. I thanked the servant and stepped inside, trying to quickly shut the door, but William's boot wedged into the opening and he slipped in behind me.

I threw my cloak on the enormous bed, a massive canopy encompassing the mattress.

"What are you doing, Taryn?" William asked. "I told you not to come."

"And you thought I would just listen?" I tossed him a glare. "I'm not a servant commanded to do your bidding, William. Why are you so bent on me not being here anyway?"

Something crossed William's face, an emotion I couldn't place. He turned away. "You shouldn't be here."

Every muscle in his body was tight, his jaw rigid, hands balled into fists at his sides. Something lingered beneath the surface.

I tilted my head. "What are you not telling me?"

William avoided eye contact. "It's just the stress of our countries' relations."

I turned his face to me, searching his eyes. "No, there's something else. What's going on?"

"You're not part of this government, Taryn. You wouldn't understand."

Anger churned within me. "After all we've been through, you're really going to pull that card?"

"The majority of what we went through was your fault. I never wanted to go to the fortress of Gapsvar. You're the one who dragged us up there."

"I didn't drag you anywhere," I retorted. "You left for the capital and then followed me of your own free will."

"You were heading into a death trap." He scoffed. "It's not like you left me a choice."

"You always have a choice."

William laughed. "I'm the crown prince of Gharridan,

Taryn. I've never had a choice."

I pursed my lips as his eyes met mine. A battle warred within them, but the source of the fight remained a mystery.

"Tell me what it is, William," I said softly.

He pushed past me, not even bothering to turn as he said, "Please don't interfere with matters here, Taryn. We can't afford for our countries' relations to get any worse."

William shut the door behind him, leaving an eerie silence in his absence.

CHAPTER FIVE

VLADIMIR

THE BITING COLD stung my cheeks. I wiped absent-mindedly at my runny nose. Flakes of snow collected in Dante's mane as we delved farther into the forest, and I altered our course for the third time. Flurries drifted through the air, barely covering the ground; it would help keep our tracks obscured, but I still wasn't willing to take any chances.

Through the bare branches of the intertwining trees, I could barely make out the outline of the dark cabin. No smoke rose from the chimney, and the windows were smudged with dirt and bore signs of abandonment.

I tethered Dante to a rotting post, my boots pressing softly across the snow-dusted ground. The structure of the cabin still stood sound and firm, even though from the outside it looked like the building could cave in at any moment. When I pushed against the rough wood of the door, the hinges squealed for oil as it swung inward, snowflakes drifting into the abandoned building. I pulled a dagger from its sheath and rested my other hand on the hilt of my sword as I cautiously stepped onto the dilapidated floor.

"Did you come alone?" The husky voice protruded from a shadowed corner.

In response, I shut and bolted the door behind me. "I trust that no one followed you?"

A cloaked figure emerged from the darkness, drawing back his hood, the sunlight of the windows revealing his face and catching his bushy eyebrows. I surveyed him up and down, not quite believing that he was really here.

"I'm assuming you found your brother?" I asked.

Randal Lynch wrung his hands together and glanced out the window nervously. "I spoke with him."

I arched an eyebrow. "And?"

He licked his chapped lips, eyeing the dagger in my hands. "He's agreed to come back to Gharridan."

I let out a breath.

"But he has conditions."

I stood still, waiting for his terms. "What conditions?"

He licked his lips again. "Jarrod wants guaranteed immunity and safe transport out of Gharridan immediately after he testifies. He also wants access to the court to be restricted during the trial."

I cocked my head, wondering what this situation entailed. I didn't care about the immunity; I just wanted to finally know why Michael had been searching for him all these years.

"Done," I agreed. "What is he testifying about?"

Randal shook his head too quickly. "I don't know; that's for him to say."

My eyes narrowed.

Randal rubbed his hands together. "He wants the immunity in writing, with the seal of Gharridan, but he doesn't want anyone else to know."

I crossed my arms. Granting him immunity was one thing but drawing up an official document with the seal of Gharridan—without anyone's knowledge—was another matter entirely. To grant immunity, I had to seek the approval of both the Crown and the council. The stampings would have to be witnessed.

"I have to garner the approval of both the Crown and the council to grant immunity," I explained. "At least two other people will know about this."

Randal frowned disapprovingly. "If you want my brother to come forward, you must do this alone."

My teeth clicked together, wondering what Jarrod possibly had to say that was so important. If I granted immunity to this man, and he ended up being a murderer or something worse, it wouldn't bode well for Gharridan or me. I studied Randal, deliberating.

"If I grant this immunity, I have your word that Jarrod will talk?"

"He gives you his word."

I glanced out the dirty window at the falling snow. "How soon can he be here?"

Randal shrugged. "It'll take him several weeks at least."

His arrival was still far off.

"And you're certain he will follow through?"

"I spoke with Jarrod. He's willing to talk with the immunity."

"Then send word when he arrives."

I stepped back into the descending snowflakes and mounted Dante. Getting that immunity without the knowledge of anyone else would be a daunting task and posed a high risk, but if it meant getting Jarrod to talk after all these years, it was a risk I was willing to take. This was the closest we'd ever gotten to Jarrod. Both Michael and Gavil had spent years searching for him before they were killed, but I'd never been given an explanation as to why. Whatever mystery Michael had been trying to uncover, I suspected that Jarrod Lynch held the key.

CHAPTER SIX

I FIDGETED WITH the sheer sleeves of my dress, unused to the loose, draped feeling of the cloth. It was thin enough to be translucent, leaving me feeling vulnerable. Something about sturdy, fitted sleeves provided me with a sense of security. A servant had brought me the Brenden-style dress after my bath and whisked mine away to be washed. I didn't know how much hope there was for the soiled fabric. It had held up incredibly well, but it was beyond filthy, covered in dirt and stains from several months on the road. I smoothed my hands over the foreign fabric of the new dress, its bright shade of purple fitting right in with the colorful design of the room.

I ambled to the door adjoining my guest room to Katherine's and knocked, hoping she would answer. After a moment, the door swung inward, and Katherine stared back at me. Dark circles encased her eyes, giving her an unearthly appearance. When I said nothing, she stepped aside and allowed me to walk into the room. It was every bit as elegant as mine, the canopy bed practically dripping with wealth and a plethora of pillows lining the head of the bed. My feet sank into the plush carpet as I took in the vibrant colors that filled the room with life.

"Did you tend to the king's daughter?" I asked.

Katherine's wavy mane of blood-red hair was pulled back into a loose braid that spilled over her shoulder. "I did."

When she offered no further response, I asked, "Is all well now?"

Katherine stood over the wash basin, pouring the contents of the pitcher into the bowl and splashing her face, excess water droplets dripping back to the clear pool below with little plinks.

"Nothing more than a cold; she will be fine by morning."

Her fingers trembled as she dried her face, and the cloth fell back onto the dresser, fatigue marring her movements.

"You look flushed," I observed.

She leaned back on the bed. "Just tired."

This was not the same exhaustion experienced after traveling. A deeper fatigue plagued her. "Are you physically affected when you heal someone, Katherine?"

"It depends on what ails them." She sighed. "The harder the healing, the more strength it draws from me."

She'd never mentioned that her gift possessed a negative effect, but it was logical that for something to be given, something else must be taken in return. Healing me after I'd nearly drowned couldn't have been an easy task. It would have cost her.

I crossed my arms, leaning against the dresser and changing

the subject. "King Arguis seems overly friendly."

"If he wanted us dead, we'd be dead already."

I frowned. "Do you think he would be acting like this if he was involved in my father's murder?"

"I don't know." Katherine shrugged. "But he wasn't expecting us. So if he had any plans, we've run right into the middle of them. King Arguis may appear like a buffoon at first, but I can guarantee you that he is not. Michael talked of his good nature, but he is one of the most ferocious and tactical military leaders to have ever led an army into battle. Brenden soldiers are not brutes, but they don't surrender to anyone, and they will either win or they will die trying. Why do you think Gharridan and Brenden were at odds for so long?"

Everything about my father's murder appeared very well planned and tactical. The precise ambush. The burned bodies. The assurance that there would be no witnesses. And then there was the attack on Dellwyn, a city that would have been completely lost if not for the brave soul who escaped. The crimes reeked of scheming, and I itched to know with complete certainty who was behind them. King Arguis might not have had anything to do with this. The mastermind behind the murders could be a traitor in the Brenden government like Zedekiah had been to us, but the attack on Dellwyn would not have escaped King Arguis' notice, making his involvement all too suspicious.

I pushed away from the dresser, wandering around the room. "Anything I should know about tonight?"

"Just be friendly. Act normal. If any noblemen speak to you, be courteous. If no one speaks to you, be silent and listen." Katherine smirked. "If you can understand them. If our *friend* is still alive, he will be in attendance tonight so William can make contact with him."

That was the first I'd heard of this. "And if he's not alive?"

Katherine didn't answer my question.

"William's been acting strange," I said.

Judging by the look on her face, Katherine had noticed the peculiarity as well. "I don't know what it is, since he only speaks to me out of pure necessity, but I'm guessing it has something to do with his mother."

"What do you mean?"

Katherine fumbled with the laces on her dress. She was arrayed in the same style as mine, except hers was deep blue like a shimmering sapphire. "All I know is that Queen Adamara wasn't happy about him going after Zedekiah when she strictly forbade him to. She does not respond kindly to any type of defiance against her orders, and William has reaped the consequences countless times."

No doubt she would be furious with me for being here.

If she ever saw me again.

"To an extent," Katherine continued, "I can understand her displeasure. William almost died."

I swallowed, knowing full well that I was to blame for him being in those circumstances, but whatever was going on with him went beyond the conversation with his mother.

A knock came at the door, the guards ready to escort us to the great hall for dinner.

William and the Gharridan soldiers joined us as we made our way down the hall. I never once met William's gaze as we paraded through the castle. Two massive doors swung open before us, and my breath caught in my throat. At least a thousand candles traveled down the center of a never-ending table piled high with delicacies: hot breads, meats, cheeses, sweet pastries, fresh fruit, raw vegetables, spreads, jams. I'd never seen so much splendid food in my entire life.

Soldiers stood near the edges of the table arrayed in overly decorated uniforms with red sashes stretching from shoulder to hip. Servants lined the walls every few feet with their hands clasped behind their backs. Mingling among the officers were various officials arrayed in fine linens of yellow and purple. The grand hall glowed like a giant jewel shining in a plethora of colors.

A hush fell over the Brendens, spreading to every corner of the room, as we stepped across the threshold.

King Arguis stood at the head of the table and extended his arm. "Welcome!" he bellowed. "May I introduce our guests of honor: Crown Prince William of Gharridan, Katherine Daharaway of the Kavari, and Taryn Gallows, daughter of our beloved ally and most dear friend, Michael Gallows."

My hands curled into fists at my sides, trying to hold back the bout of anger that suddenly washed over me at his words. I closed my eyes for a moment and forced calmness to waft through my emotions. He could be innocent. He could be sincere. His announcement drew every eye to me, their gazes overlooking Katherine and William. Some offered small nods of condolence as I passed, seeming to pay reverence to my father. I felt the resolve dwindling away inside of me. Maybe we had the wrong information.

The guards escorted us to the front of the table, where we were seated directly next to the king and his family. I recognized the same three children from the throne room, but the queen was nowhere in sight.

King Arguis clutched his ruby-encrusted goblet and lifted it into the air. "Might we all raise our glasses in remembrance of the great man who fell much too soon."

I stared at my glass, grinding my teeth together as I raised it to comply with those around me.

"To Michael Gallows," they toasted in unison.

The servants did not fill our plates. We passed the dishes around the table and filled our own. Some of the food was not in bowls and simply set on the table, free for the taking. Whenever an empty space appeared in the mounds or a dish ran low, a servant was immediately there with a replacement. I picked up a round, orange object and passed it back and forth between my hands, trying to decide how to eat it.

"The fruit is inside," the officer sitting next to me said with a thick accent.

"What?"

He picked up another one of the strange fruits and dug his finger into it, pulling back the outer encasement to reveal a different texture inside.

I dug my fingernail into my own and peeled back the thick layer of crust, revealing white webbing that wrapped around the hidden fruit. I pulled it apart and popped a piece into my mouth. An explosion of flavor filled my senses as the sweet juice permeated my tongue. Gharridan possessed nothing like this.

None of the conversations around me were understandable unless someone tried to speak directly to me. The Brendens hurried along in their quick, short language, laughing among themselves as they ate the meal. William seemed to know the language well and talked with the king and his sons as well as several officials seated around us. Katherine stayed quiet, but I suspected that she understood everything that was being said. The tired look in her eyes had vanished, replaced with a calm expression as she slowly savored every bite of her food.

"Do you understand what they're saying?" I mouthed to her from across the table.

She only offered a rare smile before turning back to her plate and eating another forkful.

Once dinner ended, the king clapped his hands. Everyone stood and spread throughout the great hall. I meandered off to the side with Katherine, observing the Brendens as they socialized among themselves. The hours wore long, and the conversations grew louder as the wine began to take effect. I watched William as a servant offered another glass of wine to him and the Brendens he was speaking with.

William refused the drink.

I tilted my head. William wasn't one to refuse a glass of wine. My mind flicked back to the dinner only a few hours ago, but I couldn't recall seeing William drink from the goblet of wine. He'd drunk the sweet yellow liquid, but that was all. I stepped around a bulging plant until he was in clear view, focusing all of my attention on him. He appeared at ease as he spoke with the men, but I knew better. I kept my eyes on him, catching the slight twitch in his fingers, the bob of his throat, the way his eyes kept darting around the room as if searching for someone.

He excused himself from his current conversation and meandered back to the table, picking out a few pink fruits. An official walked up beside him. I shifted slightly, walking parallel until I could see both of their faces. Neither one of them acknowledged or looked at each other, but their lips moved. They were talking to each other, but no one would notice unless they were studying them like me.

The mysterious man was short-shaven, like the rest of the Brendens, and well kept. He wasn't wearing a uniform, which meant he was neither a soldier nor an officer. Robes draped across his body in such a fashion that I couldn't tell if he was a minister or an official. The colors and dyes of his cloth were not as deep or as grand as the others. He was important, but he was not wealthy.

I squinted, trying to read their lips, but their heads kept changing angles, which made the job difficult.

"Miss Gallows." I jumped at the voice, spinning around. At the sight of the man, I quickly dipped my head in acknowledgment, composing myself.

"I am Prince Tristan," he said.

The king's son. The one with the bronze hair I had seen in the throne room. Instead of his royal apparel, he was arrayed in a special military uniform with a strange circular symbol on the shoulder. He raised his eyebrows in question.

I dipped my head forward again, uncertain of how to respond to his introduction.

"You are enjoying yourself this evening?" His accent wasn't as strong as his countrymen's. Prince Tristan offered me a goblet, which I accepted, sipping on the sweet sun-colored liquid inside.

"Yes." Katherine's words from earlier about courtesy rushed to my mind as I nodded. "Very much so. The Brenden food is wonderful."

After the meager rations I'd endured while traveling, anything that entered my mouth would taste heavenly. My gaze darted back to where William had been conversing with the man, but both of them had vanished.

"Your father was a very good man."

My fingers tightened around my glass at Tristan's words. "You knew him well?"

"I did." Tristan chewed on his answer. "He seemed to invest in everyone he met."

A pang of jealously rose within me that even this foreigner had received something from my father that I could never have. The bitterness was gone, but the wound was still fresh. I wondered if the pain of never knowing why my father left would ever lessen or go away.

"You can't have seen him very much," I observed.

Tristan shook his head, and I noticed the tight line of his mouth. His expression was so serious that I wondered if he was even capable of smiling. "Just every few years, mainly to ensure that we kept the peace between our countries. When he visited shortly before his death, I had no idea it would be the last time that I would ever see him."

The warm air around me grew icy, my body turning to stone. I stared straight ahead, clenching my glass nearly to the breaking point, my eyes unseeing as my lips formed the next question.

"My father, he visited Brenden before he died?" It took everything within me to keep my voice even.

Tristan didn't seem to notice the sudden change in me. "Yes. Several weeks after he left, we received news of his death. It was quite shocking."

I dropped my eyes, loosening my grip on the glass. "What

was he in Brenden for?"

Tristan's expression shifted. He avoided eye contact as he shrugged. "I'm not sure. I'm afraid that I didn't see very much of him. It was a short trip."

The change in his demeanor was unmistakable to me. A cover-up. If Brenden *was* behind the murder, it was no coincidence that my father had visited right before his death.

"Excuse me." I dipped my head at the Brenden prince and moved to pick up a sweet pastry from the table. My eyes roamed the room, landing on Katherine, who was watching me. She stood by herself, hands clasped in front of her. Her eyebrow lifted in question, but I turned away. If they wouldn't tell me their secrets, then I wouldn't tell them mine. William was far too reluctant to relay their plans to me. I needed to figure out what exactly my father had been in Brenden for, and I needed to figure it out before William did.

CHAPTER SEVEN

VLADIMIR

LIGHT BLED THROUGH the shuttered windows, the outside world too cold to let a breeze pass through the room. A vase of hellebores and winter jasmine sat in the middle of the table, brought fresh by a maid at the first sign of wilting in the previous flowers. The physician had hoped that the bright colors might induce a sense of cheer in the room. Across from me, Marco slumped in a chair, his vacant eyes staring mindlessly out the fogged window. His mangled beard had been shaved, but thick stubble was quickly replacing it. The clothes he wore hung loosely over his emaciated body, which was only just beginning to recover from the months of malnourishment.

"How are you today, Marco?" I kept my voice gentle.

He paid me no attention, as if I wasn't even there. His lips moved soundlessly, muttering to himself, saying things that only he could understand. Since we'd returned, I'd barely gotten more than a sentence out of him. He'd been so distraught the first week that we'd had to strap him to a chair to keep him from hurting either himself or someone else until he calmed down. He'd settled by now, and I tried to visit him each afternoon if only to sit with him in silence for a while. Even though his mind had left him, he didn't deserve to be alone. The physician checked on him every day, but there wasn't much he could do. The best insight he had for Marco was to keep him comfortable and away from anything that could trigger stress. Brighten the room, do everything possible to keep his atmosphere lighthearted.

"If it were warmer outside, I'd take you on a stroll through the gardens."

Marco never lost focus on whatever held his gaze. The vacant eyes before me had once been filled with wisdom and hope. Familiarity. I turned to the window, closing my eyes. Seeing him in this state without any hope of improvement was becoming increasingly difficult.

"There's so much to tell you, Marco." I told him about Randal Lynch and the document, how I felt like an outlaw sneaking through the castle, tricking the chancellor into leaving the room and then rifling through his papers. I watched Marco as I spoke, my voice eventually breaking.

Marco deserved better than this. He'd given his life to serve his country, done everything in his power to defend it, yet he was cursed to live in this empty state for the rest of his life. For fulfilling his duty. Anger surged within me at the injustice of it, and it took me a moment to regain my composure. When

Michael died, I'd thought that I would at least have Marco for counsel and guidance, but even he had been stripped away from me.

I stood from my seat, circling around the table and setting a hand on his shoulder, squeezing for a moment before letting go. The thud of my boots echoed in the empty room as I crossed to the door.

"Coming."

I froze mid-stride. It was rare for Marco to utter something that wasn't unintelligible. I turned, stepping closer.

"Coming." He repeated, rocking back and forth.

"Marco?" I questioned.

"Safe."

His eyes never left the window.

"Terrible." He rubbed his arms. "It's terrible."

I knelt in front of him. "What's terrible, Marco?"

He suddenly looked at me, recognition flickering.

"What they did to him."

My heart sped within my chest. "What did they do to him?"

"Dead," Marco whispered. "They killed him."

"Who killed him?"

"Don't tell them." Marco cradled his head in his hands. "It's a trap."

"Marco, it's me, Vladimir." I tried to catch his attention. "You're in Gharridan."

He lifted his eyes and stared at me, the same recognition hovering in them for a moment longer. It was as if something within him was struggling to get out but couldn't find the way.

"Coming," he said again.

"What's coming?"

But his eyes grew vacant again, and whatever sanity had momentarily surfaced sank down to unreachable depths once again. He slouched, his lips moving soundlessly every few breaths.

I waited there, hoping he would come back to me, if only for a moment, but he didn't. I stood to leave and slipped out of the room quietly. He'd said a few phrases here and there on the way back to the capital, but once we'd arrived and he had reentered a calm lifestyle, hardly any words came out of his mouth. This was the most I'd heard him speak since his rescue.

The words he had uttered could be total nonsense, yet he'd looked like he was trying to tell me something. Trying to convey a message with what little speech he possessed. I wondered what was 'coming,' and if that was what he had even meant. Maybe not all of his mind was gone. Maybe he just couldn't figure out how to gain access to it. If we could figure out how to tap into it, we might be able to free him from the prison I feared he might otherwise never escape from.

His words echoed in my head all the way back to my chambers.

Coming.

CHAPTER EIGHT

TARYN

I WASN'T SURE how much freedom Brenden would grant us within their borders, but I was determined not to stay shut up within my room or the walls of the great hall. A servant brought breakfast to my room in the morning, and the tray held twice the amount of food that I could ever eat myself. Any of the preservable food on the plate I wrapped into a napkin and stuffed into my pack. We would be returning to Gharridan at some point. Under what circumstances, I wasn't sure, so I needed to save any food that I could get my hands on in order to be prepared.

I cracked my door open and peeked out into the hall. Finding it empty, I ultimately decided to venture as far as I could until someone stopped me. Unlike the dark grey walls of Gharridan, Brenden's corridors boasted drawings painted on the bricks of nearly every wall. Some were of mountainous back-drops, some of the royal family, and others appeared to be stories told through stroke and color. One in particular caught my eye, and I stopped in shock, staring at it. A mighty gold dragon stood guard over its treasure, its talons clutching at the glittering coins possessively. Below him, standing on his hind feet, was a silver mouse. It was from a book. The book of children's stories that my mother and father had always read to me. The painting depicted the story perfectly, matching down to the most minuscule details. The tale must have come from Brenden. I kept glancing over my shoulder at the painting as I walked away, stunned to have found something so familiar in a land so completely foreign from my own.

After what seemed like an eternity of meandering, I found a set of glass doors that led into the gardens. The guards opened the doors for me without question, and I entered the veranda, feeling their eyes boring into me as I stepped onto the lawn. They may not be required to stop me, but I suspected that they would commit to memory where I had been, where I was going, and at what time.

Brenden's gardens were twice as large as the Royal Gardens of Gharridan and boasted the grandest display of colors that I had ever beheld. Each plant was unique in its own way, a different variety from anything that grew in Gharridan. Some leaves were smooth like silk, others coated with a rough texture or spiked. I wandered along the gravel pathway, inspecting each of the shrubs and constantly turning my gaze toward the walls of the castle in an attempt to get my bearings and figure out which way was east from west. Discovering whatever William's spy knew would be the challenging part. Aimlessly wandering through the castle wouldn't help much in my search for answers, but the excursion would bring me familiarity of the layout.

I turned at the sound of gravel crunching beneath several pairs of boots.

"Taryn!"

I froze as King Arguis strode toward me with outstretched arms and a broad smile pasted to his face.

"Your Majesty," I greeted him, dipping into a curtsy.

The king laughed. "How wonderful, strolling the garden at the same time. Might I join you?"

Refusing the king did not seem wise. Something about the guards standing behind him and the way he'd phrased his words left me with the impression that our meeting here was not coincidental.

I nodded, falling in step beside the king as he took off again.

"How do you like our gardens?"

"They're very lovely," I answered. "I've never seen these kinds of flowers."

"That's because your plants are too fragile!" the king said. "I don't know how you Gharridans can watch such beautiful creations die every single year. I would go crazy without them."

"I don't mind it," I said. "It reminds us of the fragility of life."

I hadn't intended for my words to bring attention to my father. Nevertheless, I found myself thinking about him. The idea saddened me, how fragile life was. How someone who was your whole world, your reason for living and breathing, your everything, was gone in a final breath. The fragility of life had stolen my parents from me. And Beva.

Wetness dampened my eyes as memories of Beva filled my mind, bringing with them a dark sadness that swelled with hopelessness.

"I wanted to talk to you about your father, actually …" the king began.

No doubt he thought the tears were meant for my father. I didn't respond, continuing in silence for the next few paces.

The king cleared his throat. "… and personally express my thanks for your father's investment in Brenden."

"I hear he united our two kingdoms," I said.

King Arguis let out a low chuckle. "You make it sound so simple, yet the alliance was a giant leap for both our countries. Brenden and Gharridan would still be at odds with one another had he not stepped in. When your father first came to meet with us, I wouldn't see him, but he wasn't willing to take no for an answer. He refused to leave the throne room unless I agreed to meet with him. Obviously, that behavior wasn't acceptable, so I had him thrown into the dungeons."

I threw King Arguis a sharp look.

He tilted his head. "But it is also very discourteous to throw a foreign ambassador into the dungeons. I felt bad for my actions, so I offered to let him go if he promised to return to Gharridan's border immediately. But, in typical Michael fashion, he wouldn't leave that cell until I agreed to have a meeting with him. I relented. We had our first discussion in this very garden, actually."

King Arguis took in the garden around him as if recalling the memory. I followed his gaze. My father had walked on this very path, maybe even stayed in the very room I was currently sleeping in.

"I'm glad he was able to unite us," I said.

"I am too." The king sighed. "I tire of war. Some men seek it out for glory, but in the end, war does nothing but cause division and destruction. Too many lives are lost on account of one man's pride."

His statement outright contradicted the premeditated attack on Dellwyn. He spoke so ill of war, yet my heart hardened at the knowledge Brenden had intentionally started a war with us. Katherine said he was the most ferocious military leader she had ever known, which meant he was the best liar I had ever met.

"In all of our talks," he said suddenly, "Michael never mentioned that he had a daughter."

I kept my head down, refusing to meet his gaze even as I felt him waiting for an answer.

"It is no easy thing to lose a father," he continued.

I crossed my arms and looked for an escape, growing uncomfortable with the conversation.

"I, too, lost my father when I was young. I never got over it. It still haunts me to this day."

His tactics raised alarm bells within me. Was he trying to make me vulnerable? Make me think that I could trust him so he could harvest more information? I hadn't come to swap sob stories with him. An iron cage formed around my heart as he wove his words together.

"My father passed away twenty years ago, yet I still remember the loss as if it were yesterday. It's strange. You can forget what the pain feels like, but you can never forget the memories. After his death, I immediately became the sovereign of this country. In a way, I wasn't given the proper time to grieve. So understand me that when I say I know what you're going through. I mean it. Hardly a day passes that I don't think about the man who made me what I am today."

I jutted my chin out. "I'm afraid the relationship between my father and I was strained. I barely saw him growing up. He was little more than a stranger to me."

The king paused, studying me. "That may be, but I am familiar with the haunted look that plagues your eyes. Whether it is of bitterness or sorrow, I cannot tell, but that is a wound that can only be healed of your own accord. It will get better, but it will never go away."

What the king saw in my eyes must be regret and sorrow. The bitterness had already been dealt with. I hadn't forgotten what my father had done to me, but I had forgiven him and put the past behind me.

A small figure stood farther up the path, two braids hanging over her shoulders.

I blinked.

Helvah disappeared.

"Whatever your relations with your father, he was a good man. He will be greatly missed."

My heart raced within my chest, and I felt my breaths quicken. Was it all lies, or was it truth?

"Thank you for your words, King Arguis." I took a few steps away. "I'm afraid that I must part ways with you here."

He bore a surprised expression at my brusqueness, as if he thought our conversation had been going rather well. He dipped his head. "I will see you later, Miss Gallows."

I dipped my head as well and scurried out of the royal gardens, desperate to get away from the conversation that the king had trapped me in. Everything about the court of Brenden confused me. I couldn't figure out how their culture worked. The king had done one thing yet was saying another. The Brendens were not just skilled warriors—they were experts at deceit.

The guards watched me as I brushed through the doors and rushed down the hall, trying to put as much distance between me and King Arguis as I possibly could. His words bounced around in my head, colliding into one another with dizzying speed. I placed a palm against my forehead. I needed quiet. The memory of the ricochet invaded my thoughts, its silver surface shining in the sunlight. Zedekiah must have been desperate if he was willing to give that up. If only we had correlated the burnt bodies to Brenden earlier. What did King Arguis have to gain by faking a false sense of peace between our countries? Even if he wasn't guilty of my father's death, Brenden had still destroyed Dellwyn. What were they playing at?

A flash of cloth rippled out from around a corner, heading down a hall I had not yet explored.

It was a navy cloak. William's cloak.

All thought of the conversation with King Arguis deserted my mind, my pace quickening as I fought to catch up with him. As irritated as I still was with William, I needed someone to talk to—someone who would understand. I rounded the corner, skidding to a halt when I caught sight of a man walking with William. It was the same man from the feast that William had spoken with covertly. I slipped behind a pillar, looking for signs of anyone else. Silence drifted down the corridor, creeping in and out of the alcoves and washing a sense of peace over me. When their figures vanished down another corridor, I traveled farther again, darting from one pillar to another, doing everything in my power to stay hidden. William glanced over his shoulder once, twice, three times, but my form lay safely stashed in the shadows. I inhaled, the dry air cracking my lips as I delved farther into the depths of the castle. The stone floor slanted downward, the air chilling as we entered what appeared to be abandoned lower floors.

The faint click of a door echoed through the passageway. My eyes flicked from side to side, looking for the room the two men had entered. Muffled voices seeped through the cracks of one of the doors, but the words were unintelligible. I glanced at the nearest door, wondering if the room could be joined to the next like Katherine's and mine. Tentatively, my fingers curled around the neighboring door handle and I gently pushed it inward, silently pulling it closed behind me. I let out a sigh of relief. A slip of light poured in from the bottom of the door. I slid down the wall, easing as close to the opening as I could without drawing attention.

"—will never admit to anything that they have done. What have you come up with?"

That was William's voice.

Another voice answered, talking about matters I didn't understand and people in court I had never heard of.

"It hasn't been easy to keep my tracks covered, digging where I shouldn't, but I've managed to get a look at the king's official documents."

Suspicion laced his raspy voice.

"And?"

"Two weeks before Michael died, the king dispatched a team of six assassins. Nothing in the document indicated what they had been dispatched for, but they did not stay within Brenden. They crossed the border."

An icy sensation traveled across my skin, chilling me.

On the other side of the wall, William remained silent.

Then he said, "Vladimir said there were seven bodies burned in the clearing."

The raspy-voiced man hesitated. "That doesn't necessarily mean anything. Assassins will sometimes have regular infantrymen with them. There could have been as many as twenty Brendens that crossed the border."

Twenty Brendens.

My father had taken down seven men, but how many had he had to fight with at once?

"There is no mistake of this?" William questioned.

"None at all."

They both remained quiet.

"What of Brenden's other plans? The attack on Dellwyn?" William asked.

"I haven't been able to decipher their strategy, but the king has been holding multiple private meetings a week with his chief of staff and war council. No one knows what they're about. They've kept the discussions under wraps, but the Brenden military has been preparing and recruiting for some unknown event over the past few months."

"Who ordered the attack?"

The man hesitated. "That is the one undeniable proof I can provide you with. This was not an instance of internal treachery among Brendens. King Arguis personally signed the documents with the stamp of his signet—including the document dispatching the assassins across the border."

I forced my eyes closed. I wanted to scream in anger, but I pressed my fist against my mouth, trying to control the emotions warring inside. King Arguis played the part well. Extremely well.

But was it him?

Zedekiah had betrayed his queen and country. It was possible that there was also a traitor within Brenden's walls, but the king could not be oblivious to the attack on Dellwyn. He had to have possessed some knowledge, even if it was only partial, and now someone needed to pay for their crimes. Brenden would not stay unscathed. Brenden would burn to the ground like the seven bodies in that clearing, reduced to nothing but a pile of bones and ash. I stood to my feet, having heard what I needed. The door shut quietly behind me, and I padded back the direction I had come, trying to remember the way.

There was no denying it. There was nothing left to question.

King Arguis had ordered the murder of my father.

CHAPTER NINE

I FOLDED MY arms across my chest, rotating in a circle as I inspected the room with a critical eye. Mordakai's office had been completely cleared out. The only thing left behind was the furniture, now covered in a thick coat of dust. I ran my finger along the desk, drawing a clean line across the wood. If anyone had tampered with the room before it was cleaned out, the evidence was long gone. I pulled out each of the desk drawers only to find them vacant, without even the remnant of a document or paper. Having his office emptied was standard protocol, but there should have been a record of where the contents were taken, especially considering the unusual circumstances of his death. My eyes roved over the desk, and I reached behind each of the drawers and into every crevice, searching for a hidden latch or drawer, but found nothing.

This discrepancy should have been discovered weeks ago. There was no excuse for it, other than that I hadn't been here to carry it out. Mordakai had known something about Zedekiah's betrayal, and someone was trying to cover it up. I left the room in defeat, shutting the door behind me and ensuring that it locked before I headed to my next destination.

Mordakai's personal rooms lay on the other side of the palace. Verone was leaning against the doorway, waiting for me. He threw me a questioning look as I approached.

"Clean," I said. "Too clean."

I pushed past him into the room—and stopped in my tracks. Everything had been stripped. No linen covered the bed. The shelves stood empty. The doors of the armoire hung wide with not even a single stitch of clothing left inside. Dim light filtered in through the grimy windows, the same thick dust coating everything it could land on. There wasn't even any ash left in the hearth.

"Where are his things?" I asked.

Verone's boots thudded methodically across the floor. "They were burned."

I spun toward him in bewilderment. "Burned?"

He crossed his arms. "One of the lieutenants searched his rooms right after the massacre. He found nothing and the guards were told to leave the room as is. When I first came to inspect the room this morning and found it empty, I had to ask about fifty different people, eventually going all the way down to the maids, to figure out what happened. The day after your group set off after Zedekiah, they were given instructions to clean out the rooms and burn his belongings."

I struggled to believe what I was hearing. "Instructed by whom?"

"That's what I would like to know. Housekeeping has no idea or records, just that it was added to their tasks. One of the maids thought it was a little strange that none of his possessions were passed on to someone else, but seeing as Mordakai had no family, she didn't think much about it."

I surveyed the room again. Even if someone had no family relations, there was clothing that could be given to the poor, books that could have been donated, utensils that could have been used. Burning it was wasteful. It didn't make any sense. Unless—

"Do you think the burning was committed because of his disgrace?" Verone asked.

I shook my head. "Not for treason. I'm sure your lieutenant did his best, but these rooms should have been turned inside out." I grabbed the post of the bed, studying the bare mattress. "Someone didn't want us to find something."

My eyes met Verone's. "Which means Zedekiah left behind a loyalist."

"What do you mean his things were burned?" Queen Adamara asked. She leaned back in her chair with a quizzical look.

"Every single one of his belongings was stripped from his rooms and destroyed," I explained. "Nothing was left behind. No clothing, no documents, no bedding. Any evidence we might have eventually discovered was destroyed. I believe there is another traitor in the capital. One who was tied to Zedekiah and left behind to smuggle out information."

The queen let out a long sigh, placing her head in her hands. Stress lines creased her face when she looked back up. "Did you check Zedekiah's rooms?"

I nodded. "I went straight there after Mordakai's. Everything there was burned as well."

The queen drummed her fingers on the desk as if trying to wrap her head around the idea. "I should have searched them myself, had multiple people inspect them. I didn't even consider that he could have left traitors behind. This whole situation should have already been taken care of, but in the midst of everything going on with the funerals and Zedekiah's escape, it, it—" She let out an unamused laugh. "I don't even have anyone to advise me on this right now."

I could tell she wasn't sleeping well. Her appearance made that obvious. She looked beaten down and utterly defeated, and I'd never seen her reveal this side of herself. Strength had always exuded from the air around her, but Zedekiah's betrayal seemed to have exposed her vulnerability.

"Have you chosen your next adviser yet?" I asked.

Queen Adamara sighed. "No. Quite frankly, I'm afraid to. I don't want to make the wrong choice, but I know that another needs to be chosen quickly."

I didn't envy her that decision. Learning to trust someone else after your trust had been betrayed was a difficult task, but I hoped that the consequences of her last choice would encourage her to consider wisely.

"Where do you suggest we start looking for this traitor?"

I straightened, taken aback that she asked for my advice first. My mind ran back and forth, taking into consideration all the evidence we'd collected so far. "Anyone he was close to in government. Any servant, scribe, or council member that he came in contact with. Zedekiah spent most of his time with you. Surely you would have a better idea than I would of who he fraternized with."

Queen Adamara nodded, liking the idea. "I'll write out a list. We can begin to question the people one at a time."

"Captain Verone and I will do what we can on our end, see what we can find out."

She smiled grimly, pulling a piece of parchment from her desk and dipping her quill in ink. "Let's get to work."

CHAPTER TEN

TARYN

THE DAGGER TWISTED back and forth between my hands. The blade was sharp to the touch. I turned it carefully. Sunlight glinted off the steel, sending flashes of light bouncing around the walls in an untraceable, chaotic pattern. Leather wrapped the hilt, worn from years of use. It would need to be replaced soon. I flipped it over again, examining the elaborate swirls and designs etched into the cross guard, the small black stones sealed into the pommel. My mother had given me the blade before I was even strong enough to wield it.

This dagger is yours to guard and protect you, Taryn. Carry it with you always. Never let it leave your side.

Her words echoed in my head, reverberating around the dark thoughts circulating within. I had always used this dagger for my physical protection, but now maybe it was time to use it for a different purpose. I swallowed, nerves and uncertainty creeping up my throat, swelling within my lungs until I thought I might choke. I looked out the open window, watching the Brendens milling about in the courtyard below.

I had to know. I had to be sure, even though my actions would warrant severe consequences, not only for me but for those around me. I had to be sure the Brendens understood this had nothing to do with my companions. It was all me. Everything. I hadn't quite decided how I was going to carry it out, but the plan was building in my mind, connecting one dot to another, trying to put all the pieces into place.

My heart hammered against the confines of my chest.

Cold sweat slid down my back.

Fear was trying to overcome me—but I wouldn't allow it such a prize.

A knock sounded at the door, and I jumped, smoothing out my skirt and trying to hide the dark secrets brewing behind my eyes.

"Come in," I called, standing to my feet.

The door swung open and William stepped inside, closing the door cautiously behind him. He was back in his Gharridan garments the same as me. I'd changed into my old dress the moment the maids brought it back. Their thorough cleaning had worked wonders on the damaged fabric, and the torn hem had been mended.

I lifted my chin, waiting for William to speak first.

"Are you enjoying yourself?" His voice sizzled with sarcasm.

I smiled. "Actually, I am. Maybe I'll join Brenden's government and make it permanent."

William's face darkened into a scowl. "You shouldn't be here."

I rolled my eyes. "Your vocabulary has been very limited since we arrived."

"I didn't come here to argue," William said. "I'm sending Carver back to the capital in the morning. I want you to go with him. Feign sickness if you have to."

"And you didn't think I would argue about that?"

"Taryn, please."

"Try to talk me out of this all you want, but you'll be wasting your breath."

William put his hands on his hips, exasperated. "I don't understand why you came."

"Why do you *think* I came?" I rebutted. "You know why."

"And exactly what do you plan on doing?"

I hesitated, eyes darting away.

William caught my misstep and cocked his head. "You're planning something."

I turned to walk back to the window, but he blocked my path. "I know that look in your eyes, Taryn. It's the same look you had when you decided to go searching for Marco. The same look you had right before I drank Beva's sleeping concoction."

I couldn't let him know what I was doing until after the fact. He would try to stop me.

I pursed my lips. "What have you discovered about my father's death?"

He made his own misstep, stumbling over the next words. "That's not what we're talking about."

I shrugged. "Isn't it? If you don't tell me your secrets, I don't tell you mine."

He searched my eyes, trying to decipher their hidden agenda. "Whatever it is you're planning, Taryn, you need to stop. Your father's death will be avenged. I'll make sure of it, but I need you to not meddle with this."

I smiled. "Meddle with what?"

Frustration tore at William as he clenched his jaw.

Two could play at this game.

"If you try to fix this yourself, it's going to make everything worse," he warned.

"I'm not trying to fix anything."

We stared at each other, locked in a stalemate, neither willing to give up our secrets unless the other gave up theirs first. He didn't trust me, didn't have faith in my judgment—he was wise not to. I wouldn't trust me either, not with what I had planned.

"Is that all?" I asked.

William shook his head, marching across the room and out the door. "Dinner is in half an hour."

CHAPTER ELEVEN

TARYN

I SAT QUIETLY and nibbled at my food, conversing politely with those who addressed me, but deep within me welled an animosity toward the Brendens. How skilled they were at their deception. Their lies. Their cunning. I found it difficult to keep the intentions of my heart from spreading all over my face and hovering in the air around me.

William's nervous eyes strayed to me throughout the evening. The heat of his gaze burned through me, the intensity of his stare weighing me down. I ignored him and hoped none of the others in the room could sense his mannerisms toward me. William wouldn't back down until he discovered what I was up to, and there was no doubt in my mind that from here on out he would have me followed. Acting quickly was in my best interest—before he discovered what I was planning.

Dinner ended, and I made a scene of retiring early to my rooms even though William wouldn't buy it for one second. I left the grand hall and moved toward the royal chambers, hiding behind a pillar just out of sight of the guards. I needed to ensure that William and Katherine both left the dinner before I ventured out into the open again. The minutes ticked by, the muffled sounds of the dinner guests drifting down the hall.

Katherine emerged first, ambling casually down the hall, but William's steps were hard and determined, his eyes darting in every direction as he crossed beyond the doors of the grand hall. He disappeared in the other direction, no doubt in search of me, but he'd be back as soon as he found my rooms empty.

I pressed my back against the cold wall, my gaze landing on Prince Tristan as he strode out of the double doors, his face set in stone. I waited until he was nearly in front of me before opening my mouth.

"Your Highness," I said.

He startled, reaching for his weapon.

"I didn't mean to frighten you," I added.

Suspicion washed over him as he looked up and down the hall. It was obvious I was hiding. "Miss Gallows, can I be of service to you?"

I swallowed, drawing the courage to force out the words and fearing that I had underestimated my familiarity with him. "I need to speak with you."

"With me?"

"Yes." My eyes darted behind him, afraid that William would appear around the corner at any moment. "With you and your father. There is an urgent matter I need to discuss with you tonight. Highly secretive. No one else must know. Not even anyone in my party." I gripped the skirts of my dress. "Is there somewhere private we could talk?"

He shuffled on his feet, eyes narrowing. "To what matter are you referring?"

Death lurked across the hall, waiting.

He wasn't going to buy it. I swallowed again, trying to find the right words. "I dare not say it out in the open for fear of—" I cut off. "It is imperative that we find somewhere private to meet where listening ears cannot find us."

I observed the shift in his expression. Something in Tristan's eyes told me he trusted me, and he slowly nodded. "Wait here for me. I will speak with my father."

Tristan slipped back into the room, and I pressed myself into the shadows. Terror clutched at me, but the war of anger boiled stronger. A prick of guilt lit my conscience. I looked up, finding both Death and Helvah staring at me, their pleading gazes trying to influence what I was about to do. I closed my eyes, pushing the images of them away.

I had no other choice.

This was the only way.

Tristan reemerged a moment later, checking over his shoulder before he grabbed me by the elbow and steered me down the hall. "Come with me."

We crossed back and forth in the palace until I had no earthly idea of where we were. The lights in the corridors dimmed, and our shadows elongated along the walls like giant monsters creeping beside us.

"Is your father coming?" I asked softly.

Tristan didn't answer but continued walking until he pulled us inside a dark study, finally releasing his hold on me. He lit several candles and torches, filling the room with warm light. A colorful tapestry covered one part of the wall with floor to ceiling bookshelves on either side of it, and a thick ladder led up to a small loft housing several other shelves. No documents littered the desk. Only a fresh set of paper with ink and a quill lay atop its shiny surface. Everything in the room was organized and immaculately clean.

The prince did not speak.

Neither did I.

I reached into the small pocket hidden within my dress, clutching the dagger firmly within the folds of my skirt.

The door opened, and King Arguis entered with a perturbed expression on his face, still draped in his royal apparel. He glanced briefly between Tristan and me before shutting the door and locking it behind him.

"What is this about?" His voice rang with authority.

I glanced between them hesitantly, stepping closer to Tristan. "Are we safe here from prying ears? Even away from the guards?"

The king eyed me curiously. "I told them to wait farther down the hall. What is this about, child?"

My heart raced.

He acted so concerned, but was it real?

My father's grave flashed before my eyes, my imagination conjuring the image of his corpse lying in the snow, pierced with his own sword, surrounded by seven burning bodies. His death could not go unavenged. This was the only way.

A vision of my father's warm smile and sparkling green eyes played before me, and I faltered. Was this what he would have wanted? My attention caught on the wide-eyed figure of

Helvah standing in the corner of the room. Her head shook, begging me to rethink this.

Vladimir's words echoed in my head.

What are you going to do?

It wasn't too late. I could leave now. Disappear.

But no.

I'd already made my choice.

I had to know.

"There's something I need to discuss with you pertaining to my father's death." I took another step closer to Tristan, the dagger firmly in my grasp.

"What about his death?" The topic seemed to pique the king's interest.

Another step. The words swirled through my mind, each syllable carefully crafted before being released. "I want to know why you ordered his death."

The air chilled around us, but there was no draft in the room. Goosebumps traveled up my arm, and I met the king's gaze, my eyes coated with venom. His brows drew together as he stared back at me while Tristan stilled with shock.

"What is this dark accusation, child?"

I whipped the dagger from concealment, too close to Tristan for him to knock it from my grasp. My arm wrapped around his throat, the edge of the blade pressed firmly against his neck.

The king rushed toward me with his hands outstretched, but I pulled the dagger tighter against Tristan's skin, forcing him to stop.

"Taryn." Tristan's voice was low and warning.

"Don't come any closer." I kept my grip tight, but if Tristan wanted the upper hand without me slicing his throat, I didn't doubt he could easily overpower me. I wasn't going to hurt him, either of them. That wasn't my intention, but this was the only way that I could know.

"What is this about, Taryn?" King Arguis' voice remained calm.

My hands shook, trying to control the emotions warring within me. "I know about Dellwyn, and I know what you did to my father."

The king tilted his head, eyes flicking to his son. "If you wouldn't mind giving us some explanation, I'm afraid that we're having a hard time following you. Perhaps it would be better to put the weapon away first?"

"No," I snapped, my fingers clenching the dagger. "This is the only way you'll tell me the truth."

I tried to keep my head straight as a million contradicting emotions flooded through me, trying to drown me. I only had one shot. One opportunity to discover the truth.

I took in a shuddering breath, barely able to keep my hands from trembling. "You bring us into your kingdom like some beloved dignitaries, yet you lie and you trick, acting like you haven't destroyed our cities or murdered my father. You tell me stories of your dying father, trying to gain my sympathy. Well, I have a story I should like to tell *you*, Your Majesty." I spit out the title between gritted teeth. "I never knew my father as you knew yours. I lived a quiet life after my father's abandonment, only to be torn from my peaceful world and thrown into the chaos of power-hungry politicians, vying for a position in the Kavari that I had no desire for—against the man they thought killed my father. But my opponent was not the murderer. It was his brother who committed the treacherous act, and when he was discovered, he left a massacre in the wake of his escape.

"We crossed the continent trying to track down this murderer, thinking that once we found him, all would be at peace. In our search, I stumbled upon a missive stating that the first conditions of a treaty had been met and that Brenden was ready. How strange, I thought, that a kingdom we were supposed to be at peace with was mentioned in this vital document and that they were ready. Eventually, we caught up with the murderer. We fought. Vladimir killed him, but before his death, he dropped a seemingly useless object in the snow. A thin piece of steel shaped like a crescent moon that had the ability to strike someone from a distance. A ricochet, Vladimir called it, choice weapon of the assassins of Brenden.

"When they killed my father"—emotion welled within my voice—"they slit his throat and pierced him with his own sword. Surrounding him in the snow were seven bodies, burned completely beyond recognition. We thought it was to conceal their identities, never connecting that Brenden ceremonially burns their dead instead of burying them.

"As if that wasn't evidence enough, we receive word of your massacre in Dellwyn, forcing us into a death-riddled war, and I learned that my father visited Brenden shortly before he was murdered and that you yourself, King Arguis, dispatched a group of assassins across the border into Gharridan."

A ragged breath tore out of me. All the words had finally been said. I'd laid it all out, stacked the evidence against them. If the conclusion I had come to was true, Tristan and his father would not be able to deny it. There was nothing for them to hide behind, nowhere for them to run.

The king shuffled on his feet, choosing his words with care.

"That's quite a journey you've endured, Miss Gallows."

My hands shook, unnerved by the calm that emanated from his deep voice. I couldn't speak. The words stuck in my throat like a thick sludge that I could neither swallow nor regurgitate. I pushed past the barrier, forcing out my question.

"I want you to tell me why." My voice was dangerous, ripping at the seams. "Why did you kill him?"

The king and his son remained silent, their eyes meeting, communicating without speech. Some sort of agreement passed between them, and I hated the tranquility that continued to permeate the king's face. He met my gaze.

"I did not order the death of your father." King Arguis' voice filled the chamber, the words poisoning the air like smoke.

Uncertainty fluttered within me, and a shaky laugh escaped my lips. "Lies will not save you, King Arguis. Only the truth. Brenden ordered my father's death."

The king lifted his chin, eyes filling with understanding. "I will tell you the truth, Taryn, the truth about Brenden, but it will not help you if you do not choose to believe it. It is true that several weeks before your father's death, he visited us in Brenden to ensure that all was well between our two countries. He mentioned talk of a treaty and wanted to confirm that we had not taken part in it. He advised us to watch our borders and to alert him should any Gharridan try to sneak into Brenden in search of sanctuary. All was well between our two nations when he left."

The dagger wavered in my grasp, my mind spinning with the possibility.

"Shortly thereafter," he continued, "one of our battalions

along the border was attacked. If our battalions had not been crossing one another's paths, it might have been weeks before we found them. None were left alive, every man slaughtered. Nothing was taken from the men, not money, not weapons, not food. All was still intact—except for one man. One of our assassins had been assigned to the battalion, and everything on him, his weapons, purse, down to the very clothes he wore, was stripped from him. We were never able to find who was responsible. Officially, it was marked as vagabonds, but we knew something greater was going on, so we enlarged our battalions and increased the border patrol. I dispatched the assassins to try to hunt down the perpetrators, mindful of Michael's last warning to us, but there was no evidence left from the attack."

Was he lying? He had to be. It was too convenient. Too well thought out.

"No," I said firmly. Death crept over my shoulder, a chilling breath against my skin, watching with anticipation. "If it wasn't you, then it was someone in your government. Someone in Brenden bought off Zedekiah. Someone in this country worked together to undermine Gharridan."

No fear prevailed in the king's eyes. "I can assure you that no one in the country would risk such an endeavor. I have never heard of this Zedekiah until you mentioned him a moment ago, Taryn. Michael is the only person from Gharridan that we have had contact with in years. Our kingdoms do not mix. Brenden is a completely self-supporting country. Why would we need your country when we already bask in so much wealth? Why would I endanger my people on such a frivolous scheme?"

"Because it's always about power," I whispered. "Everyone always wants more."

More.

Zedekiah wanted more power.

The missive.

The ricochet—

A series of tremors dispersed throughout my body, my mind trying to cross-examine every little piece of evidence. The dagger wobbled in my shaking hand, drawing a drop of blood from Tristan's throat, but I wasn't focused anymore. I wasn't prepared. In one swift movement, Tristan slipped from my grasp, the dagger clenched safely in his hands. I blinked, stunned at his quick and effortless movement.

The tip of the blade stretched out toward me, inches from my chest. I took a shuddering breath, facts and words still exploding throughout my mind. There was no question now. I would be executed, but I hadn't meant to let Tristan free until they knew that the others were innocent.

"Lower your weapon, Tristan," the king commanded.

I turned to him, a million questions blazing behind my wild eyes.

He lifted his chin. No malice enveloped his face, instead I found a shadow of pity, a whisper of remorse.

"Aren't you going to kill me?" I croaked. I'd just threatened his son's life.

He shook his head. "Taryn, if I was guilty of the crimes you've accused me of, you would have already been dead. Tristan would've ended your life shortly after entering this room. I asked him to wait."

The silent communication. I looked at Tristan curiously, tears still blurring my vision. He hadn't struggled. Hadn't fought. Had I ever been in control of the situation?

"I am going to let you go free, Miss Gallows, in the hopes that my mercy provides proof of Brenden's innocence in this matter."

I shook my head. "I don't understand. Your signet was on the papers. The orders came from you. How can you explain away your merciless attack on Dellwyn?"

Dellwyn.

If he hadn't killed my father, then why had he attacked Dellwyn?

He had to be lying.

King Arguis cocked his head, a puzzled expression enveloping his face. "Brenden made no attack on this Dellwyn. Our military has not left the country in months."

My lips parted. No. The attack on Dellwyn was Brenden. The spy had been certain. It was the main reason William had been sent to Brenden in the first place.

A commotion sounded from the back of the room, drawing our attention. With that small distraction, I shot toward Tristan, grappling for the dagger. My attack caught him by surprise, and the dagger fell midair, twisting head over end. Panic raced through my body as we both lurched for it, fingers outstretched, but I altered course and shoved into his massive form, knocking his tall frame backward. My foot slid beneath his feet, unearthing him. The force sent his head into the bookshelf, the sickening smack of skull on harsh wood resounding through the room. The contact knocked him out instantly, his body crumpling to the floor. A cry escaped King Arguis' lips as he rushed forward, reaching for his son, but the dagger had returned to its owner. I extended it in front of me, warning him to stay back even as unease slithered up my spine like a serpent.

"Taryn, what are you doing?"

I jerked to see William and Katherine standing just beyond the king. Fear laced Katherine's voice.

William's eyes were steady on mine. His sword hung ready in his hand, but he made no move to stop me. My gaze flicked to the other side of the room where the tapestry hung. Two Gharridan soldiers held it back, revealing a passageway behind it, and the presumed spy that William had spoken with lurked inside.

I swallowed, my voice hoarse. "On your honor, and on my father's grave, do you swear that you speak the truth? "

"I swear it." King Arguis' voice grew soft. "You've threatened the life of both me and my son. Why would I lie to you?"

Tears stung my eyes as I finally believed the sincerity in his.

I'd come here for the truth, and I'd gotten it, even if it wasn't the answer that I had been expecting. Zedekiah had thrown that ricochet to Vladimir at the end of his life.

Because it's always about power.

My own words echoed in my head as the pieces connected.

The missive.

The ricochet.

A setup.

King Arguis hadn't lied.

Zedekiah had.

He'd wanted us to believe that it was Brenden. Wanted us to start the war. The plan was too elaborate to even wrap my mind around, but King Arguis had spared my life, claimed that everything we had learned was false.

Death's voice brushed against my ear. *Take it.*

No. That would be the easy choice, but that wasn't what I

had come here for. It wasn't in me, and it never had been.

"This will be Northunder all over again, Taryn," the king said. "You can kill me, but you will damage your soul in the process. I will be nothing more than a body whose blood you spilled, and each of my children will become just like you, living out the rest of their days without a father."

I blinked back tears and looked beyond him to where I found Helvah standing. Watching. Fear filled her eyes, apprehension, waiting to see what I would do. She had been orphaned too. At my hand. And had I just acted like I would curse the king's children with that same fate? I felt Death's icy fingers curl around my forearm. *Take it.* Helvah gently shook her head. This was my choice. So many things in life had not been my choice, but this decision rested solely with me. I glanced at Tristan's body, beginning to stir on the floor, and then back to King Arguis.

I took a step back and lowered my dagger. "I believe you. I swear I never intended to harm either of you, but I needed to know."

The king let out a ragged breath, relief and understanding rushing over his face.

Hot tears stained my cheeks as I watched Helvah's form disappear, cursed myself for getting into this predicament.

Bloodshed wouldn't solve anything.

My eyes met William's, but I did not find relief written across his expression. There was a resolve there, and an anger.

Something in his eyes shifted.

A decision.

A choice.

Behind me, Tristan groaned. I glanced back and saw his

eyes flutter open as his left hand reached for the back of his head, coming away bloody. I heard a dull thump, turned to see Katherine fall to the floor unconscious.

William strode forward. "I told you not to meddle in these affairs, Taryn."

I realized what he was going to do and darted forward to stop it, but I was too late. William thrust his sword forward, plunging it through King Arguis' back. It hovered there for a moment before he ripped it out, and the king let out a gasp as he fell to the floor.

"No!" I screamed, rushing forward.

The king's eyes grew wide as he stared up at me, his mouth moving as his head twitched in shock. "Taryn," he gasped, "it wasn't us. It wasn't, tell them, tell them that I—that I—" His eyes glassed over. "That I love—"

Tears streamed down my cheeks as I pressed my hands over the wound, blood gushing through my fingers and soaking my dress. His lips moved again as he tried to talk, and then stilled. Horror crept across my skin.

I yelled again, shaking him. Someone pounded on the door, the guards alerted by the shouting. I looked at Tristan, who stared back in shock, slumped over but trying to crawl his way to his father.

Someone was pulling me up, ripping me away.

"Let go of me!" I screamed.

"Taryn, we have to go. *Now*."

I turned to face William. His eyes were hard, his face serious.

William had killed King Arguis.

He had killed the king of Brenden.

Someone crashed into the door from the hallway, shards of wood flying across the room. The guards would be in here at any moment.

The sincerity in the king's voice rang in my ears.

"He was innocent," I whispered, more to myself than William.

William pulled on my arm, but I pushed back. He grabbed my other arm, yanking me toward him until I was fully in his grasp and couldn't escape. "If they find you here, they will kill you."

The door splintered as someone shouldered into it again.

I swallowed hard, choosing to let William pull me after him. He had killed him. It was the only thought racing through my mind as he led me behind the tapestry and into the dark tunnel. I couldn't process much, but I could hear the Brenden spy leading the way ahead of us. I tried to think, but I couldn't. The sight of the king's lifeless body on the floor, his son watching him die …

I didn't know how long we ran for, how far our feet pounded against the sandy floor beneath us, but we were suddenly in the stables, and William was throwing a Brenden cloak around my shoulders.

"What are you doing?" I asked, noting that all of our horses were saddled.

Realization dawned on me, and I looked around, alarmed, remembering Katherine's limp body on the ground.

"Katherine," I breathed. "William—" I grabbed the collar of his cloak. "William, we have to go back!" I turned to march back into the castle but stopped at the sound of warning bells disturbing the quiet night. William led Stryder in front of me as he mounted Othello, the other soldiers following suit, but the spy was nowhere in sight. Shouts issued from the guard shack, and my eyes widened in horror.

We weren't going to make it out of here.

"He told us to leave through the north gate," William told one of his men.

The bells spread farther and farther, bouncing from one corner of the city to another. Beneath me, Stryder took off after the other horses.

I felt like I was lost in a daze, in some sort of nightmare.

I was aware of riding, but not of anything else.

The night wind whipped at my hair, slid across my cheeks.

William had killed him.

William had killed the king of Brenden.

CHAPTER TWELVE

TARYN

THE DESERT OFFERED no hiding place. Its rocky terrain spread before us with open arms, announcing our presence to the world, laughing at our feeble attempt at escape. Desert wolves howled in the night, their forms dark against the pale moonlight as they traveled across the ridges. I knew there were soldiers behind us, knew that they were going to catch us, but I never looked back. I never listened for them. All I could hear was the pounding of the horses' hooves against the cracked earth, the sound of air flaring through their nostrils, the pulse of Stryder's body beneath mine as he thundered away from Palazaar.

I still didn't understand how we'd made it out of the city, how we'd slipped through the gates unnoticed, but I did realize that this escape had already been planned. The spy must have arranged it. The missing guards, the construction on the wall that left a gaping hole to the world outside.

Even so, I found it difficult to concentrate on anything besides running. We couldn't stop, even though the horses shuddered with exhaustion, even though their coats dripped with sweat. If we stopped, we would die. The sun rose and set in a blur; the landscape dotted with hills but nothing else. The trail of dust that followed our escape swirled around us, rising in the air like a beacon, alerting our pursuers to our location.

There was no water here. The dry air chapped my lips and dried my throat. Thirst overtook me, possessed my mind, but the greatest concern rested with the horses. They would give out unless we managed to find water soon. What little was in our canteens was reserved for them while our throats were left screaming for a drop, but it only sustained them and did not completely refresh.

I glanced behind me for the first time since fleeing the walls, seeing the cloud of dust billowing in the distance but nothing more. Sometime in the night, a black line appeared across the horizon in the direction we were headed, and the temperature grew colder. The dark line rose higher and higher until I realized it was the forest. The floodgates of relief washed over me. We were close to the border, which meant we were safe. For now. Unless we crossed paths with the border patrol. I swallowed. If we could at least make it into Gharridan, they wouldn't be able to track us very far. Their military wasn't dressed for the winter, and they wouldn't last very long in our cold climate.

I hadn't spoken to William, hadn't been able to process the events I'd witnessed. He stayed at the front of the group, seeming to know where he was headed through the unending landscape. None of the other men spoke a word as we rode, not even to ask questions. The fear of being caught captivated us.

I glanced at them as we rode.

Did they know?

Had William told them exactly what he had done?

Night descended again and our company slowed, the fatigued horses nearly falling down beneath us. When we safely passed through the confines of the forest, a gurgling brook sounded from up ahead. I nearly dove straight into it.

The water tasted heavenly. Stryder gulped down gallon after gallon of water beside me, drinking so fast that he could barely breathe. I stared down at the dark stains on my hands and swallowed as the moonlight illuminated them.

It was blood.

I examined the rest of me. Blood covered nearly the whole front of my dress in various patches and crusted along the skin of my hands, sneaking underneath my sleeves. My fingers trembled at the sight, and I turned away from the water, retching into the brown grass. I reached back into the water, submerging my face and hands, vigorously scrubbing as hard as I could to get King Arguis' blood to disappear. I only wished the memories haunting my mind could be so easily washed away.

I shivered as I wrapped my cloak around me, the damp cloth of my sleeves chilling me. After un-tacking Stryder, I unrolled my bed and fell into it, the world around me fading as I succumbed to exhaustion.

We were up before daybreak the next day, having only slept long enough to replenish the strength we needed to keep traveling. We pushed the horses, and when it felt like they could go no farther, we had to push them again. Our pursuers were not visible among the trees, but they were there. They had to be. That evening the soldiers built a fire. I considered the idea a horrible one but kept my mouth shut. I didn't join them around the flames even though the temperature was dropping. My mind had finally begun to settle, and I found that I could now think clearly. I cradled my head in my hands, sick at the thought of Katherine being stuck in Brenden.

She might not even be alive.

William hadn't said a word to me yet and simply acted as if I didn't exist. I'd avoided him because I was still seething with anger, but I needed to address what had happened. The soldiers remained quiet, now conversing only in low voices and whispers. They seemed fearful of William's subdued expression, but if they wouldn't ask the question hovering over the group, then I would.

"What exactly happened back there, William?" My voice pierced the darkness as my eyes burned into him, waiting for the prince to admit to his crimes.

The soldiers glanced among themselves.

William stared into the shifting flames, bringing his gaze up to meet mine. "Exactly what you saw happen." A resolve flickered across his features. "Katherine Daharaway killed the king of Brenden."

The blood in my veins iced over, my entire body freezing as I stared at him. He met the intensity of my stare, and no remorse hovered behind his eyes. The statement was so bizarre, so unexpected, but then I felt as if the life had been sucked out of me as everything slowly came into focus.

Katherine Daharaway killed the king of Brenden.

Queen Adamara had turned down my offer to go to Brenden, specifically demanding that Katherine go instead. She sent them to Brenden because she wanted vengeance for my father's death—but she needed someone to take the blame. Queen Adamara and William hated Katherine. Before William killed King Arguis, he had knocked Katherine out. He hadn't tried to bring her into the secret tunnels with us. That was why William was so upset about me being in Brenden, why he was hiding his plans. They had planned this all along. William wanted me to believe that Katherine had killed King Arguis. If I hadn't been in Brenden, there would be no one to contradict the blame laid on Katherine. Brenden would never let Katherine leave alive. She would take the fall, and everyone would hate her all the more for it because she had started a war with Brenden.

It was ingenious.

William's dark eyes filled with a cold I had never before seen in them. He watched the emotions flit across my face, knew I'd figured it out.

Heat flared in my chest as anger surged within me. I lunged at him, striking his chest with my fists, a vicious snarl tearing out of my throat.

I hated him.

I clawed at him until he pinned my arms to my sides, dragging me away from the fire and out of earshot as I fought against him.

"How could you?" I screamed at him. He pushed me up against a tree, securing my arms against my sides.

"Lower your voice," he said through gritted teeth.

"Why, so your men won't know you're a murderer?" I snarled.

"You shouldn't have been there, Taryn. You weren't even supposed to be in Brenden, for crying out loud!" William let out a stream of curses. "You complicated everything. If you had simply waited like I'd told you or left with Carver like I'd suggested, we wouldn't even be in this situation right now."

I let out a bitter laugh. "Meanwhile, you planned to murder an innocent man and blame an innocent woman for the crime?"

William's face morphed into a deep shade of purple. "Katherine is not innocent. She killed my father."

"If that were true, then why is she still a Kavari and risking her life serving Gharridan?" I challenged. "Your father died of a sickness, William. It was not Katherine's fault. You keep looking for someone to blame when the truth is that it was simply his time to die. King Arguis was innocent, yet you murdered him anyway. You're no better than Zedekiah when he slit Beva's throat."

The vein in William's forehead pulsed, and I knew I had gone too far—but I no longer cared.

"Are you really judging me when five seconds before I killed him you were trying to kill him and his son?"

"I had no intention of hurting them," I snapped. "All I wanted was the truth, and the only way to get it was to put the fear of death within them. I let them go once I knew he was innocent."

"King Arguis was not innocent. You saw the ricochet, heard the evidence. Brenden is guilty."

"He is innocent," I said.

We'd been tracking down the wrong killer.

I moved so close to William's face his hot breath blew past my cheeks. "He didn't kill my father, William. Before my father died, he warned Brenden that something suspicious was going on. King Arguis told me that several months ago, one of their battalions was attacked. Nothing was stolen or touched, every man was killed—except for one. An assassin. He was stripped of his clothes, weapons, identity. Everything. They never found the perpetrators."

William laughed. "And you believed him? How convenient that Brenden has a perfect explanation for our exact accusations of their involvement in the murder. Brenden was mentioned in the treaty, Taryn."

I recalled the look in King Arguis' eyes when he was willing to let me kill him, and the sincerity in them when he fell to the floor. He hadn't been lying. He had no reason to. He'd said it himself. Why would he endanger his country? Incur the wrath of Gharridan?

"I couldn't act until I knew for certain, but our spy in Brenden gave me evidence, Taryn. The king's signet was on the papers. I saw them myself."

"What if the whole situation with Brenden was a setup?" I asked. "How do you know that spy wasn't part of it? King Arguis had the chance to kill me after I threatened his son, William, and he let me go. You had treason committed by your most trusted adviser. What if Zedekiah threw Vladimir that ricochet because he wanted us to believe that Brenden was responsible for my father's death?"

Something flickered across William's face.

Doubt.

It was possible. Zedekiah had betrayed us in everything else. William knew it was a possibility.

"What about Dellwyn?" William asked. "Can you explain that away too?"

"He denied it, and when you think about it, an attack on Dellwyn doesn't make any sense." I shook my head. "I don't have proof, but he was sincere," I said. "King Arguis was telling the truth." Hot tears stung my eyes. "How could you do it? How could you kill him?"

I saw the war within William. He didn't want to believe me, but he also knew that I could be right. "I was following orders."

I shoved my finger into his chest. "You are responsible for your own decisions, William, and there are consequences for your choices! You had the chance to make the right decision, to choose to do what is right, but you didn't, and now there is a country without a king and four children without a father!"

William had lost his own father. He knew that pain better than anyone.

I lowered my voice. "How can you want to become like your father when you are becoming everything that he was not?"

Hurt welled in William's eyes. I'd struck a blow. The damage was done, but he quickly replaced the hurt with a chill that could no longer be warmed. He stared back at me, inches from my face, our bodies too close together. I took a shuddering breath, trying to control my rage.

"When we return to the capital, I will announce that Katherine is the one who killed the king, and you will stand beside me to affirm that account."

I pushed away from him. "I'm not going anywhere with

you. I will not let Katherine take the blame for this, and I most certainly will not lie for you!"

He grabbed my wrist, spinning me back toward him. "If Katherine isn't already dead, she'll be dead within a day or two. Claiming she killed the king will no longer make any difference to anyone else in the world. She wanted to serve her country, and she did."

I tried to squirm away, but his grip remained firm.

"You are coming to the capital with me, whether willingly or unwillingly. I'll strap you to the back of my saddle if I have to. I don't want to do it this way, but I will do whatever I must." His was gravely serious. "Are we clear?"

He meant what he said. I didn't doubt it. All I could picture was traveling back to the castle with my hands tied in front of me, Stryder tethered behind Othello, four soldiers surrounding me. Flashes of the days spent together in captivity sent a shiver down my spine. I never wanted to be in a position like that again, and I would never get to Vladimir that way.

"Are we clear?" he asked again.

Reluctantly, I nodded, pulling free of William and moving toward the men at the fire.

"One day, you will see that this was the best thing, Taryn. It will benefit our country."

I swung back to him, unable to believe the words coming out of his mouth. "Are you blind, William, or do you not realize what you've just done?"

His brows knit together.

"You can't take vengeance on an innocent country. You did not eliminate an enemy, you created one. Whoever gave the order for my father's death is still out there, and whatever they originally set out to do is still not finished. In the midst of all that chaos, you managed to start a war with the wrong country."

A pallor lightened his flushed skin, and for the first time in our argument, I saw uncertainty shoot across William's face. I stormed back to the fire, leaving him alone to simmer over the consequences of his actions. They couldn't let Katherine take the blame for this, and I would do whatever I had to in order to stop them.

I stopped in my tracks, bending over and placing a hand against my stomach, the pain aching through me at the sickening understanding of the fate Katherine had been left to.

CHAPTER THIRTEEN

THE DAMP OF the tunnel coated my lungs, the chilly air sending prickles across my skin. My fingers grazed along the earthen walls, feeling my way through the darkness. Memories flashed before me, of Zedekiah dragging Taryn into their depths, of running blindly behind William, praying that he knew the way. The queen had obliged my request to wander through them, something that should have been done the moment I assumed the role as leader of the Kavari.

Once inside, I was surprised to find that they weren't as expansive as I originally imagined. The main tunnel Zedekiah had taken out of the throne room only branched off into an abandoned wing of the palace before continuing all the way past the outer walls, but several more ran throughout the depths of the castle, one leading away to the royal chambers, others providing quick shortcuts through the expansive halls. They were designed to keep the royal family hidden and safe in case of an emergency, as well as give them an opportunity to escape should the castle ever be breached. I wandered the tunnels nearly every day, solidifying their coordinates in my mind, ensuring that I could think quickly if something along the lines of what Zedekiah had done ever happened again.

I slipped out of the darkness, pressing the hidden door securely back into place before heading to the chancellor's office, knowing he would be inside at this time of day.

The trick would be to get him out.

I maneuvered through the kitchens, filling a goblet with wine before making my way back up the steps to the offices. The sight of the wine made me wrinkle my nose in disgust, a warm sense of anger spreading throughout my body as the liquid surfaced memories I had tried to suppress for years.

My footfalls reverberated off the stone walls as I approached his door. If Zedekiah had managed to secure a document with both the seal of Gharridan and the royal seal, then so could I. The queen's office had been far too easy—especially when I knew the guards at the door well—but the chancellor's office was another matter entirely. My original intentions had been to break into his office in the dead of night, but he possessed a fascination for tricks and puzzles. Breaking into his cabinets to forge a letter or use the seal would be nigh impossible without drawing someone's attention.

I knocked on the door and stepped inside.

"Chancellor," I greeted.

He smiled up from his desk, spectacles sitting low on his

nose. "Vladimir, how may I be of service?"

From my jerkin I pulled the documents that I had swiped from the queen's desk. "I just had a few questions about these documents before they were legitimized with your seal."

He nodded quickly, oblivious of me surveying the contents of his desk and shelves, looking for where he kept the stamp. I set my heavy goblet on the desk, hyperaware of its proximity to the chancellor.

"Now, I was unsure about the taxes on this bill."

I already knew the answer as I laid out my concerns, but the chancellor didn't need to be privy to that. Let him think I was incompetent.

He read through the document, eyes darting back and forth, then dropped it onto the desk, quickly explaining away my confusion. I nodded, pretending like everything he spoke made perfect sense.

"Would you mind approving it while I'm down here?"

He sighed, but fiddled with the knobs of the right-hand drawer and pulled out the seal of Gharridan, splattering wax onto the bottom of the letter and then marking it with the seal. Before he had a chance to replace the seal, I reached for the document, my arm tipping over the goblet and sending its contents all over the chancellor's lap.

He dropped the seal like a hot coal, muttering a stream of colorful words as I profusely apologized for my clumsiness. He waved me away dismissively and stepped into the side room, the door pulling closed behind him. The second it snapped shut, I whipped the document of immunity from my jerkin, dripped what was left of the melted wax onto the parchment, and marked it with the seal. My eyes kept darting to the door as I waved my hand over the wax, hoping the rush of air would coax it to dry faster.

"Vladimir?"

I froze at the voice from behind. The adjacent door was still tightly sealed, but I could hear the chancellor walking across the stone floor whereas I hadn't heard any footsteps approach behind me. I glanced over my shoulder, taking in the red robes of a councilman.

"Finnigan!" I greeted, plastering a wide smile across my face. "What brings you here?"

He returned the smile, but it didn't reach his eyes. My fingers tensed as I watched his gaze wander over the surface of the desk.

"Just had a matter of state to discuss with the chancellor." He cocked his head. "Is he in?"

The side room door swung open, revealing the chancellor in a fresh set of robes. I gathered the documents back into my hands, slipping the immunity onto the bottom and sliding my finger between the papers to keep the wax from sticking to both pages.

"Yes," I said. "I'm afraid I made a mess of the chancellor's robes before you arrived." I lifted the goblet from the table, a small puddle of wine that hadn't spilled out welling in the bottom.

"Ah." Finnigan glanced from the cup to the seal left exposed on the table, and then brought his eyes back to the chancellor.

"My apologies again, chancellor," I said, wincing in embarrassment. "Thank you again for answering my questions."

He nodded in acceptance, but a sour frown still marked his

face.

"Finnigan," I nodded at him as I strode past his red form.

I left them behind, slipping into one of the servants' stairwells to ensure that the wax had completely dried before concealing it back within the confines of my jerkin.

Easy.

Maybe not child's-play easy, but easier than I had expected.

When I reached my office, I locked the door behind me, moving to the cabinet where I pulled out a glob of wax to warm and unlocked the box containing the Kavari's seal. The document was done. Now all there was left to do was wait to hear from Jarrod Lynch once his brother was in close proximity to the capital. I stared at the illegal document I had created, the possible implications bombarding my mind. If Michael's intuition about Jarrod Lynch was correct, there was no harm done, but if Michael's intuition was incorrect, I stood to lose everything.

CHAPTER FOURTEEN

CROSSING A KINGDOM provided plenty of time for thinking.

And for planning.

I didn't try to escape. Didn't try to run. Even if I did, I wouldn't know how to find my way back to the capital. I traveled in silence with William and his men, my mind working during every waking hour, preparing for what was coming. William attempted to start a conversation with me, but I ignored him, refusing to even acknowledge his presence.

His irritation brought me great satisfaction.

With every passing day, my anger against him intensified. William had murdered the king in cold blood. Even if his actions were directed by his mother, he still had the choice of whether or not he was going to follow orders. William hadn't even given the king a chance to defend himself, and though I knew that even now William still doubted the truth of the king's words, I'd seen it in King Arguis' eyes. Brenden was not the true enemy.

Another enemy walked among us.

Whispers drifted among the men, and I knew that William was building his case against Katherine. The conversations were muddled and sporadic, but I was able to gather enough to know that they were tainting Katherine's reputation. When we passed through towns or villages to gather supplies, I wasn't allowed to venture in, but I sensed that there was a verbal agenda in town as well as a supply agenda. William always stayed behind with me, ignoring my glares and silent judgment.

If I wanted to get to Vladimir, I knew that I needed William to trust me. A difficult task considering that the mere thought of talking to him made me want to vomit. If I tried to break away from William and his men before we reached the capital, they would only chase me down, and I would lose my chance. I had to make William think that I trusted him.

"Your men knew, didn't they?"

William and I stood alone at the edge of the tree line, Othello and Stryder grazing behind us as the other soldiers rode back from the village. William didn't answer, his jaw set hard.

My temper rose. "Didn't they?"

He refused to meet my gaze. "They knew enough."

My next words tasted bitter in my mouth. I didn't want to say them, knew they sounded fake and unreal, nothing like me, but I had to say them.

"You really think Brenden isn't innocent."

William grew suspicious. "I don't kill people for sport,

Taryn."

You mean murder.

I swallowed.

"Maybe in the moment, I was too emotional."

William knew what I was trying to say. He shrugged, but he didn't quite believe me. I would have to do better than that.

I started interjecting little comments as we rode. Not too much, just a little. Enough to make him think that I was actually changing my mind. Enough to fool him. A wall still stood between us, the open familiarity we'd once shared no longer there, but I found myself trying to dismantle it brick by brick—even if every brick I removed was one that I wanted to hurl at him.

We were close to the capital. I could feel it. The horses stepped anxiously, eating up the ground, trying to go faster. Yet, for all their excitement, William slowed the pace and held us back. Every day up until now, we'd been pushing the horses. It didn't make sense for him to hold back at the very end. My eyes narrowed at the setting sun, realizing that William planned to enter the capital under cover of darkness. Time was slipping through my fingers.

I sidled Stryder up beside him.

"I'll do it," I said.

"Do what?" He turned to look at me,

I swallowed bitter bile. "I'll lie for you."

The horses stepped in silence, and he nodded once, pulling his gaze back ahead. "Like I told you before, Taryn, this will all work out. One day you'll see that this was the best thing for our country."

My jaw stiffened at his words. Dusk descended around us, but we didn't stop, and as we traveled into the night, the outline of the walls of the capital came into view. We used the same entrance I'd been brought through when I first came to the capital so many months ago. Darkness filled the courtyard, and my eyes darted around, looking for my chance at escape.

We dismounted, and a few stablemen approached, taking the reins and leading our horses to the stables. I glanced in every corner of the courtyard, hoping that by some miracle Vladimir would know that we were coming. William spoke with one of the guards, and I inched away from the group, trying to disappear into the blackness. I turned slowly, maneuvering toward the main entrance.

A soldier barred my path, and another came to stand beside him.

The hair on the back of my neck rose.

"It's nothing personal, Taryn. I just need to know that I can trust you first."

I spun at William's voice. The two soldiers grabbed my arms, and I tried to jerk free of their grasp.

"Let me go!" I yelled, struggling against them.

William nodded to the soldiers, and they dragged me backward, my protests silenced as we stepped onto a stone staircase. I kicked and clawed at them, knowing that William wouldn't let them hurt me, but I wasn't strong enough to overpower both of them. Instead, I went limp, forcing them to lift me up the stairs, but when my shoulders began to burn, I set my feet down and stumbled along with them. This passageway wasn't familiar to me. We avoided the main halls. I muttered at my guards and screamed for help. Eventually, one of the soldiers groaned, clamping his hand over my mouth while the other lifted my feet off the ground. They carried me like a child, my voice muffled by the soldier's dirty hand. I continued to fight them, making this task as unpleasant as possible. The soldiers finally dumped me in a room, slamming the door behind them and barring it from the outside.

I rushed the door, screaming and pounding against the wood.

"Let me out of here!" I demanded. "William!"

My fist smashed against the door again and again, and I threw my weight against the handle.

"Make sure she doesn't get out of there," one of the guards said from the other side of the door.

I let out a strangled scream of frustration. I should've known William would try something like this. Letting me go proved too great a risk for him. He wasn't willing to trust me yet.

I backed away from the door, surveying the room around me and searching for an exit. Darkness encompassed the room. I could see little more than the outline of the door and some of the furniture. If my anger hadn't provided me with courage, I might have been afraid. I squinted, trying to get my bearings. Where was I? I shuffled my feet cautiously along the cold floor, and I splayed my arms out in front of me, feeling for furniture. Drapes covered the window, blocking out the light. I crossed the room until I felt their thick cloth against my fingers. With a quick jerk, I yanked them back, bathing the room in moonlight.

The drop to the ground below was dizzying, too long of a fall to survive. No other rooms or windows were in sight. I stuck my head out the window, discerning that this room sat inside one of the castle's towers. The view took my breath away. It had to be the best one in the whole castle. The clear moonlit night illuminated and expanded the scene, showcasing the Jidero River and the jagged, snow-capped mountains rising in the distance. Looking out the window was like looking at the entire kingdom of Gharridan all at once.

I leaned farther out the window, searching for a way to climb up or down, but the stones fit together smoothly, eradicating any foot or hand holes to grab onto. I needed something to climb down. There had to be bedsheets, or a rope hidden somewhere. I turned back to the spacious room for answers and opened the nearest drawer, digging through it. It contained nothing helpful except for a few elaborate candles and a flint stashed inside. I quickly lit several of the sticks and placed them around the room.

A thin coat of dust layered the furniture like snow, and it went flying in all directions as I tore through the room. I found nothing. The room screamed of frivolity. Daring dresses arrayed in silk and lace stuffed the wardrobe, its doors barely able to contain the contents. A fancy set of hair combs lined the dresser. My feet sank into the plush rug, and I stopped, scrutinizing the room around me.

Whose room was this?

Based on the length of the dresses in the wardrobe, the inhabitant had not been very tall, and everything seemed almost childish. The richness and innocence of it all screamed of something I couldn't quite grasp, hammering at my mind. Someone of high status had lived in this room. Someone who had hardly any responsibility. The room almost seemed as if it was for—

A princess.

I spun, staring at everything. That was impossible. William was the only child of King Roldan and Queen Adamara. Or was he? I hadn't exactly grown up in the capital. Neither of them had ever spoken of a daughter. Yet everything in this room evidenced a princess, from the canopied bed covered in luxurious lace to the expensive, layered, and elegantly stitched toys in the corner. Even the small shoes were studded with jewels.

I marched over to the desk, sorting through what was mostly blank paper. A quill lay on top, the feather thinned and failing. I picked it up and found the most minuscule of initials etched into the side. *A.R.*

I meandered back to the door, looking for a way to pick the lock or escape. There was a lock on the inside, which I quickly bolted shut, and the guard on the other side grunted. If they wouldn't let me out, I wouldn't let them in. After a moment, I returned to the window, realizing that this tower was on the outer wall. No one would see me from here unless they were in the lower fields, looking directly at me, and I doubted they would be able to hear me from this height.

If I hadn't blindly assumed that William would trust me, I might not be in this situation right now. I should have tried to escape when we were still with the horses, but they couldn't keep me locked up here forever. Eventually, I would find a way out.

I kicked at the bed, angry at the world and especially at William. No one could believe that Katherine killed King Arguis … but with that thought, I caught myself. Would they? The idea terrified me. The soldiers could testify to how much Katherine wanted revenge on Michael's murder. Even Vladimir could. It wasn't a secret. With the way I'd seen other soldiers and the people of the court treat her, I doubted it would take much to convince them of her supposed crime.

Vladimir would be the only one who could see through it.

He, more than anyone, knew what Katherine was capable of, but if she wasn't here to defend herself, maybe he would give in to the lies.

I ran my fingers through my hair, mind working. I had to find a way to get out of here, but it wouldn't be tonight. William didn't appear to be coming back any time soon, so I peeled the first blanket back to avoid the dust, sinking into the silky sheets. I closed my eyes, resting while I could, and waited for the sun to rise and reveal all that the darkness had hidden.

CHAPTER FIFTEEN

◆◇◆

VLADIMIR

THE POUNDING BURST from my dreams and into reality. I startled awake, moonlight from the open window illuminating the room in a ghostly haze. The cold air accosted me as the blanket slipped from around my shoulders, exposing my bare skin. The pounding thudded again, louder this time, more urgent. I dropped out of my bed and crept toward the door, cracking it open to see who waited on the other side.

"What is it?" I grumbled.

A distressed guard stood outside the door. "Your presence is requested in the queen's study."

I froze, fear gripping me, and quickly nodded, shutting the door behind me. I pulled on my wrinkled trousers and shoved my arms through a spare tunic, grabbing my sword and belting it to my waist as I hurried out the door and down the chilly corridors. My fingers ran through my hair, trying to straighten what was no doubt a disheveled mess. The numerous thoughts inside my mind muddled together, glazed over from the sleepiness that still plagued me. I blinked, trying to focus. I wondered if it was Taryn. If something had happened to her. She'd been invading my thoughts lately. Or maybe Queen Adamara had received news from William and Katherine on their way back from Brenden.

My heavy boots echoed down the halls. I didn't pass a single soul as I made my way to the queen's study. The halls were dark, filled with oddly shaped shadows, but as I approached the double doors, light shone through from the crack at the bottom. Two soldiers guarded the entrance and opened the doors at my arrival.

I squinted against the harsh light, eyes trying to adjust from the gentle darkness.

"Vladimir, I'm glad you could come so quickly," Queen Adamara said.

She paced at the other end of the room, her thin nightdress covered with a cloak and her hair hanging loosely. I'd never seen her in such a casual state, the mere image rather disarming. Captain Verone leaned against the far wall, trying to keep from nodding off. Two council members hovered near the desk, Finnigan and Hart, but my gaze landed on the last figure in the room, who turned at my entrance.

"William." Surprise overwhelmed me.

He radiated exhaustion. Dust and mud caked his clothes, his hair and beard scraggly, but it was the look in his eyes that pulled me up short. I'd grown up with William. I knew how volatile he could become when he lost his temper, how he could drown out the problems of the world with sarcasm, and how his eyes looked when something horrible had happened.

Everything about this situation screamed that something was wrong, that something was off. I turned to examine the empty space behind me before turning to all of them again.

"Where's Katherine?"

I heard the edge in my voice, the apprehension, fear.

Queen Adamara stopped pacing, pausing for a moment before stepping closer. "That's what we've called you here for, Vladimir." She folded her hands, turning away. "Tell them what you told me, William."

My heartbeat slowed within my chest, and I leaned back against the frame of a chair, trying to steady myself.

My eyes met William's, a hundred questions burning within them. I cocked my head, the room seeming to grow smaller around me. "What is it, William?"

William glanced behind him at his mother. Something flickered across his face. Indecision? He was second-guessing himself.

"After leaving the camp, we made our way to Brenden and were intercepted at the border," William began. "The patrol escorted us into Palazaar, and King Arguis welcomed us. I was able to speak with our man on the inside. He provided evidence. Evidence that Brenden was behind Michael's death. Shortly before Michael's murder, King Arguis had dispatched a team of assassins to cross the border into Gharridan. I met with our spy there, and he produced a document with proof that Brenden had ordered the death of Michael Gallows."

My breath caught. So it was true. Zedekiah had been in

league with Brenden, and their government was trying to undermine our country. My stomach grew sick at the news, but I couldn't help but wonder: why? Why Michael? Michael was single-handedly responsible for the peace shared between our countries all these years. Brenden loved Michael. The murder made no sense.

"Everything was going according to plan, except King Arguis had an alibi for the dispatched assassins. We went to present the evidence to King Arguis and give him a chance to explain his side, but Katherine was there when the informant shared the evidence and …"

My face paled. "And what, William?"

He took a shuddering breath. "Katherine got to the king before we could."

Something unsaid hovered in the air like a foul wind. "What do you mean she *got* to him before you could?"

William met my eyes. "Katherine, she—" He licked his lips. "She killed King Arguis. On Brenden soil."

Horror engulfed Finnigan and Hart's expressions.

I immediately shook my head. "No."

I knew how hot Katherine's passion burned for avenging Michael's death, but murdering the monarch of another country, risking Gharridan's preservation in the process—no. She hadn't done this. No matter how unpredictable she could be, she would never have killed King Arguis in cold blood.

"Katherine wouldn't do that," I said.

William swallowed. "I saw her do it."

Silence hovered over us. We were already at war with Brenden because of their attack on Dellwyn, but killing the king of Brenden would ignite the eradication of the world as we knew it. Brenden wouldn't take satisfaction in simply defeating us. They would fight until they completely destroyed Gharridan.

Hart cursed, throwing his hands in the air and raving. "If this country falls, it's on her. Her selfish acts will bring Gharridan crumbling into ruin!"

My gaze flicked over to Captain Verone as Hart continued his rant. Verone's throat constricted, and he stared at the far wall, seemingly unable to think or speak.

"Brenden had already brought war on themselves," I said, turning to William. "Were you able to discover anything about what they were planning?"

He shook his head.

"Where's Katherine?" I asked, the question burning through my insides like a hot coal.

"We barely escaped Brenden, running as soon as we saw what happened." William looked away. "Katherine didn't make it out."

Katherine didn't make it out.

The words echoed around in my head. I tried to make sense of them, tried to absorb them, but when they finally sank in it felt like someone had forced a sword into my gut, wrenching out my insides. Katherine couldn't be gone. I leaned against the chair for support, the bile rising in my throat, threatening to regurgitate. No. Not Katherine. My throat went dry, my body growing cold and achy. I shook my head again, denying the facts. Katherine wouldn't do this.

"We'll have to prepare for war." Queen Adamara's voice pierced through my thoughts. "Captain Verone, how long will it take to call up our army?"

Captain Verone looked every bit as sick as I did. The revelation had left him speechless. Pity swelled through me for him. He shouldn't have to do this right now. He should be grieving, not organizing a war.

"Brenden won't attack before spring," I managed.

Everyone brought their attention to me.

"They live in the desert. They don't have the supplies to sustain a march through the winter. Not with the cold and not with the snow. They will amass their numbers, but they won't march for Gharridan until winter is gone. Expect their troops around the first of summer."

"And if they choose to brave the cold?" Queen Adamara asked.

"They won't," I answered. "But if they choose to, we will be ready."

William rubbed his eyes wearily. My gaze bore into him, willing him to say that this was all a misunderstanding.

"I'll call a meeting with the council," the queen said. "Our minds will work better once they've been refreshed, but I wanted all of you to be aware of this tonight."

At her dismissal, Captain Verone was the first to leave the room, walking as if in a trance. Finnigan and Hart followed in his footsteps, Hart still muttering about the mess that Katherine had created.

The queen's expression was merciful as she met mine, offering condolences. William brushed past me, gripping my shoulder and giving it a tight squeeze.

"William, I—" But there were no words to say.

I stormed away, the weight of the conversation pressing down and threatening to suffocate me, to ruin and destroy me. Katherine wasn't dead. She couldn't be. She was—she was like a sister to me. I'd never gone long without her. Now that Michael was gone, she was the closest thing I had to family. The only thing I had of family. I shook my head again and again as I walked, finding myself back in my room, the moon a sullen light of sadness. I stared at nothing, my mind trying to process, to understand, but I couldn't. In the end, I sat at the edge of my bed, buried my head in my hands, and wept.

CHAPTER SIXTEEN

TARYN

I SLEPT THROUGH half the day, awakening when the sun had already made its journey to the other side of the sky. I sat up in the bed and rubbed my eyes, examining the room around me. It looked different in the daylight. A child had lived here, there was no doubt about it. I ran to the window, hoping to find someone stationed down below, but the lower fields lay empty, and no guards patrolled in sight. Gingerly, I stepped onto the narrow ledge, bracing myself against the window frame. The stones chilled my feet, their surface slick. I leaned out of the window as far as I dared, breathing raggedly as the dizzying height affected my vision.

"Taryn!"

I spun at the voice, my feet slipping on the stones. The sudden movement threw me off balance, and I let out a gasp as I fell. My hands grabbed at the edge of the window, adrenaline pumping through my veins. I strained against the weight of my body as fear coursed through me and filled me with panic. Two hands grabbed my arms, grunting as they strained to lift me back into the room.

I gasped, trying to calm my racing heart as I felt solid ground beneath me again.

"Do you have a death wish?" William stood in front of me, his eyes wide with horror.

His question struck me as funny. After everything I'd been through in the past few months, maybe I did.

"You're the one who barged into the room and scared me." I brushed past him.

He followed. "If I hadn't, you'd be plastered all over the ground right now."

I frowned at the door I'd locked the night before. "How did you get in here?"

"You don't think I have a key? The guards couldn't bring you breakfast because of that."

I had been sleeping so it really didn't matter anyway, but I was annoyed I'd lost what little control I thought I had.

"Well if you would let me out of here, I wouldn't be trying to jump from the windows."

"You're not going to be locked up here forever, Taryn." The casualness of his voice nearly drove me mad. He acted like this entire situation was a minor inconvenience.

"It's only temporary, right?" I scoffed. "Give it a couple of years, until the war with Brenden is over, and then no one will care what I have to say."

William worked his jaw, trying to hold back the retort that

simmered on the surface. "I didn't have a choice."

"You always have a *choice!*" I snapped. "It may not have worked in your favor, but you had the choice to refuse to go along with this."

Torment wavered in William's eyes. "She's my mother, Taryn. What was I supposed to do? I can only go against her so many times."

I suspected the cold lingering in William's eyes was to cover the regret he was obviously dealing with. The reality of his decision appeared to weigh on him like an unmovable mountain.

"You don't have to live with this forever." My voice softened. "You can fix this; make it right."

William laughed bitterly. "And how would I do that?"

I bit my lip, placing a hand on his shoulder and meeting his gaze. "Tell them the truth, William. Be honest about what really happened."

For a moment, I thought he wanted to believe me, but the cold returned. "You know I can't do that."

I stepped away from him. "You're a coward, William."

My words stung, and he raked his hands through his hair in frustration. "My hands are tied, and if I'm going to let you go, I need you to side with me on this. I don't like it either, but it's not like Katherine didn't deserve this."

He wanted me to look the other way, act like none of this had ever happened. I might never walk freely again unless I went along with his plan. My lips pursed. That was not who I was, and I wouldn't demolish an innocent person's reputation to ensure my security. I took another step away from him.

"Then I guess you'll have to watch me rot in here."

William's gaze lingered on me for a moment, the reality of

my words sinking in. I would never give in to his demands, and that created a massive dilemma for him. He couldn't keep me trapped up here forever. I would get myself out one way or another, or someone would find me.

I raised an eyebrow. "What are you willing to do to keep your secret? Kill me?"

Hurt flickered in William's eyes, but he stepped forward. "You really think I would try to kill you? After all we've been through, I'd think you'd know better than that by now."

I fought the urge to step away from him and show weakness. He stood too close to me, the nearness reminding me of being locked in the dungeon with him in Gapsvar awaiting our executions. The bruises that had littered his face, his eyes staring intently into mine as he almost kissed me, implicating something beyond friendship might exist between us. I couldn't explain how I felt about William even now. Too much had changed too fast. Once, not so long ago, I had dared to think there might be something between us; but now, after what William had done, I couldn't even imagine that.

Except I could.

Hard as I tried to push it away, part of me still cared about William.

The thought sickened me.

Standing here, right now, I wanted to believe that William was the same person I had traversed half the countryside and nearly died with, but I had to remind myself that he wasn't.

William watched the indecisiveness that no doubt flitted across my face.

I looked away from him, taking in the room around us.

"Who did this room belong to, William?"

My words brought him out of his trance, and he took a step back, but not before I saw something pool deep within him. "It's just a room, Taryn."

I lifted my chin. "I think we both know that isn't true."

He strode back to the door, hesitating before twisting the handle. "As long as you promise to not attack the guards, I'll make sure that some food is brought up. I want to get you out of here, but the timing is up to you. I really wish you would see my side of this."

I crossed my arms. "I really wish you would see that what you did was wrong."

He left without another word.

CHAPTER SEVENTEEN

◆◇◆

VLADIMIR

WHEN DAWN BROKE across the land the next morning, I did not rise from my bed. Not that day, or the next. I lay there, staring at the tan canopy above me. My mind attempted to block out the events of the previous days, but the thoughts were deafening. They haunted me, refusing to leave me alone.

She couldn't be gone. Katherine had been there through everything with me. She had trusted me, even when she'd desired to do otherwise. I couldn't see her killing King Arguis in a blind rage. She had killed Zedekiah, yes, but that wasn't murder, it was justice . . . which meant maybe she had killed the king. Maybe she was capable of it if she knew Brenden was guilty, the way Zedekiah had been guilty.

I stopped the thought before it could progress, irritated

with myself. No. Katherine wouldn't have killed King Arguis. She was smart. She would've known the implications for our country. Going to war with Brenden was one thing, but assassinating their king in cold blood was another matter entirely—even if it was in the name of vengeance.

So why would William lie?

I squeezed my eyes shut, rubbing at my developing headache. Something about William had seemed off that night. Maybe it was the exhaustion, or the helplessness of what Gharridan was about to face, but the more I dwelled on it the more flaws I found. I sat up. How had they managed to escape when Katherine hadn't? All the soldiers had returned. Katherine was the only one missing—

Unless they had left her behind on purpose.

The idea festered in my mind, building upon itself until I thought I might burst.

I stood and dressed for the day, my movements habitual and emotionless. I gripped the edge of the wooden dresser, grinding my teeth together, trying to bear the pain, but it ripped at my insides, shredded every part of me.

Katherine was gone.

She wasn't coming back.

When I emerged into the corridor, the noise of the world resumed around me. As if nothing had changed. As if everything was as it always had been—as if Katherine hadn't left this life. I refused to meet the eyes of any that passed me. I wasn't sure where I was going, not until I found myself in front of the door to Captain Verone's office. I lifted my knuckles to knock, but they rested gently against the wood of the door, afraid to move. Eventually I twisted the cold handle, swinging the door open and stepping inside. The room felt oppressive and dark, the only light illuminating the room filtering in through the far window. Captain Verone stood in front of it, the light silhouetting his frame, shoulders sagging, head low. He didn't turn at my entrance.

"Verone?" I asked tentatively.

He ignored my presence.

I moved around the desk to stand next to him. My throat constricted as I caught sight of a hallow berry tucked into his left breast pocket. I lowered my eyes, aware that in his ancestors' country, the plant was a symbol of sorrows and honor for the dead. His focus remained fixed on the world outside the window. The world that continued to move even when for us, it seemed like it had stopped.

"The cold wind bites like a serpent today," Verone said with stoic eyes. "Always lashing out."

I clenched my jaw, trying to conjure words. "Has the queen already summoned the council?"

Verone lifted his chin. "Not yet, but as soon as she does the entirety of the capital will know of what transpired in Brenden. Word will spread quickly throughout Gharridan."

The thought sickened me. No one deserved that dishonor, least of all Katherine.

"She didn't do this." I ground out the words. "She couldn't."

Verone stiffened, his expression unwilling to betray any kind of emotion. Ever so slightly, he shook his head. "No. She didn't."

Anger coursed through my veins, lighting my skin on fire. I gripped the captain's shoulder, giving a tight squeeze of consolation before turning on my heel and leaving the room. Every step I took increased the anger in me like a pumping furnace. The thoughts flying through my mind screamed that this wasn't right. Something was wrong. I traversed the castle, searching, seeking, my gaze eventually finding what I was looking for.

William's hazel eyes softened at the sight of me, his mouth opening to speak, but I didn't listen. My palm pummeled into his shoulder, pushing him back into the study he'd just left.

"Vladimir, what—"

The slam of the door drowned out his words.

"What happened in Brenden?" I growled.

William's face darkened. "I told you what happened."

I grabbed him by the collar and shoved him up against the door. "I want the details, William! You were sent on a mission to gather evidence, but instead the king is killed and you return without a Kavari. What. Happened?" My menacing voice turned dangerous. "The only way you and your men escaped Brenden without Katherine was if you kept her from leaving."

"We didn't get to the room in time," William gargled out.

"I need a better explanation than that, William."

"Katherine was there when we heard the evidence. She left quickly. I didn't think much about it. Our spy and I were discussing our plan of action, deciding to simply bring it before the king. When we got to his study, Katherine was already there. She had him at knifepoint. I tried to talk her out of it, and we explained to the king what was going on, but he had an alibi for the evidence. I did what I could for Katherine, but she—" William faltered through his words, emotions rising within him. "She didn't believe him. She wouldn't believe him, and she killed him."

I swallowed. "That still doesn't tell me how Katherine was left behind in Brenden."

"By the time she killed the king, the guards outside the door realized something was wrong. She started fighting the guards and—and we had to run, Vladimir."

My grip on his collar tightened, pushing him harder against the door until I released him with a shove. "So you left her to fend for herself. You left her to die."

Accusation dripped from my voice like a bleeding wound.

"If I had stayed there, all of my men and I would be dead, or worse," William defended. "Katherine made her choice. I wasn't going to risk my life or the lives of my men to help her evade the consequences of her actions."

With eyes blazing, I turned away from him, trying to keep my emotions in check.

"I know you're upset, Vladimir," William started.

I spun at his voice. "I don't need your compassion, William. Your hatred of Katherine is no secret."

I counted William as a brother, but on the subject of Katherine, we had always disagreed.

The clang of bells burst throughout the castle, jolting us out of our heated argument. I ripped the door open, charging out into the hall. Queen Adamara was calling for the council to convene. I didn't want to deal with this right now.

William strode up behind me, our disagreement over.

"What is it now?" he questioned.

I didn't answer but quickly made my way to the throne room, still trying to bear the loss of Katherine. As I passed through the massive doors, I tried to force the memories of the slaughter from my mind. If I looked down, I knew all I would see was the smears of blood and bodies littering the floor.

Queen Adamara perched regally on her carved throne, eight guardsmen stationed behind her, the council seated in their chairs along the wall. William took his place to the right of his mother, and Captain Verone emerged from the corridor, standing at the base of the dais. His expression remained unreadable. Murmurs echoed throughout the room, the council members anxious about the sudden meeting. Hart scowled in his chair, but Finnigan leaned back with a curious expression.

I braced myself, unprepared for what we were about to face as a country.

I took my place to the left of the queen, and she dipped her head in acknowledgment toward me before turning to address the others.

"Captain, Kavari, council," she began. A hush fell over the listeners as she stood, filling the room with an eerie silence. I lowered my gaze, dreading her next words.

"I have gathered you here today to inform you of a most horrific event, a tragedy." The queen's sparkling blue eyes fell momentarily. "Our beloved Michael Gallows was taken from us not even a year ago. As you recall, the traitor in our midst was identified as Zedekiah, who our faithful Kavari tracked down and killed. We had reason to suspect that he was involved with another country but didn't have the evidence to prove it. I assigned my son, Crown Prince William, and Katherine Daharaway with the task of traveling to Brenden to seek out the truth, to see if Brenden had orchestrated Michael's death. While there, they found what they believed to be convicting evidence, but Katherine Daharaway decided to take the law into her own hands and avenge the death of Michael Gallows herself."

Queen Adamara hesitated, and the pain intensified within me. "I regret to inform you that she has killed the monarch of Brenden, King Arguis, and started a war that can now only be ended in bloodshed."

The silence blanketed the room until all I could hear was the ringing in my ears. They would never forgive Katherine for this. The quiet was instantly replaced with a chorus of shouts and angry yells as the council members burst from their chairs like a disrupted cave of bats. The questions and accusations flew around the room at a rapidly increasing rate.

"How could you allow this?"

"We warned that this would one day happen!"

"Why was a Radonaya allowed to join the Kavari?"

"She started a war. This will decimate our country! How do you expect us to recover?"

"She will hang for this!"

My chest heaved with the difficulty it took to keep my anger in check.

"Enough!" The queen's voice thundered through the room, bringing it once again under control. "Katherine did not escape the country of Brenden after committing her crime. She has already paid the consequence."

"Serves her right."

My eyes flashed to Hart as my hands balled into fists.

"How do we move forward from this?" a rather round councilman asked.

Queen Adamara took a deep breath. "I have been advised that Brenden will not attack until spring, but we need to gather our troops to prepare for what is to come. Those of you presiding over the various cities, send for their troops. Have them march to the capital, where we will unify before moving out to protect the border."

She continued to speak of her plans, to talk of battle tactics, but all her words ran together in my mind, muddled, seeming too surreal and palpable.

The doors of the throne room groaned as they opened, revealing a lone figure striding into the room. I dropped to a lower step on the dais, thinking that my eyes deceived me, yet Katherine ambled forward, her blood-red hair spilling over her shoulders in a tangle of knots. The remnants of a dress hung torn and ragged over her dirt-plastered body.

She was alive.

Confusion swept through the room like a fierce wind, the council members stunned to silence.

How did she escape?

Queen Adamara's chin lowered as her eyes bore into Katherine. "Seize her."

The guards behind the queen moved to take Katherine, who appeared on the verge of fainting.

I shouted, unsheathing my sword and stepping between them.

The council heated again, but now their derogatory remarks were aimed at me as well.

"Lower your weapon, Vladimir!" the queen barked.

William's eyes bore into Katherine, unable to believe what he was seeing.

I lowered my sword, but only slightly.

The queen's gaze sharpened. "Katherine has committed a crime, Vladimir, and you will step aside unless you wish to be locked up as well."

My jaw ticked.

I turned to Katherine, her face pale. "What happened in Brenden?"

Her tired, scared eyes darted between me and the council members, unaware of what was going on.

"I don't know," her voice cracked. "What are you talking about?"

"Even now, she denies it," Hart muttered.

I met Katherine's eyes earnestly. "Katherine, did you kill the king of Brenden?"

Her lips parted, horror filling her eyes, but no words came out.

"Take her away," the queen ordered.

I moved to stop the guards, but the queen warned, "You do yourself nor the Kavari any favors by resisting this, Vladimir."

Her message rang loud and clear, stopping me in my tracks.

I watched in utter helplessness as the soldiers led Katherine from the room, her scared expression pleading for help. My heart fell within my chest. Katherine hadn't denied it. Maybe she had assassinated the king.

"She must face punishment for her crime," one of the councilmen interjected.

Queen Adamara's gaze traveled to each individual in the room, her mind working. "Yes, she must."

The councilmen erupted again, throwing out various tortures and punishments. The discussion stretched on, their ideas growing more horrible with every passing minute. I shook my head, still shocked and unable to process what was happening.

"For her crimes," the queen deliberated, "she must be sentenced to death."

My eyes widened at her words and the agreement from the council members. "You can't execute her without a trial!"

"I don't find this any easier than you, Vladimir," the queen argued. "But what would a trial prove? We have an eyewitness. Any argument on her part would simply be a means to save her neck. She placed our entire kingdom in jeopardy, and now she must pay for it."

The full weight of her words bore down on my shoulders, crushing me. A trial would prove pointless. It was Katherine's word against William's. Katherine had no one to vouch for her. The people would believe the Crown, and so would the council. There was no hope for Katherine in this matter.

I turned to Captain Verone, his expression every bit as distressed as mine.

Katherine was going to die.

CHAPTER EIGHTEEN

TARYN

WHEN THE BELLS rang, I pounded against the door, demanding to know what they meant, but the guards remained silent. I ran back and forth between the window and the door, afraid of missing something happening in the yard below but also afraid of missing a chance for me to rush them if they came inside. Nothing happened on the ground below, as usual, but I watched it all the same. The bells had rung for less than a minute, but it had to mean that something important was happening.

The hours wore on, and I slumped against the door, beyond bored with having nothing to do. In the quiet, I heard the sound of boots on the stairwell. I slid to my feet, pressed flat against the door, prepared to burst out of it at the smallest chance as it opened.

William anticipated my actions, arm outstretched, pushing me back inside the room as he closed the door behind him.

But I was just as fast.

My dagger flashed forward, pressed against his throat.

"This has gone on long enough, William," I growled. "Open the door."

William flinched at the weapon, his eyes finding mine. "Are you really judging my actions when you threatened to use this blade on King Arguis not so long ago?"

His words cut deep, making me falter. The half-second distraction was all he needed. His hand clamped around my wrist, yanking me toward him until he twisted the dagger out of my grasp. It clattered to the floor where he kicked it across the room, too far to reach. I jerked my hand out of his hold, glaring at him.

"You wouldn't have used it on me anyway."

"How do you know?" I challenged, even though I knew he was right. I didn't have it in me, but my words made him momentarily doubt himself.

"When do I get out of here?" I demanded.

He leaned against the door, ensuring that I wouldn't try to open it. "I don't know."

No fight lingered in his voice or expression. A weight pressed against his mind.

"What's going on?" I questioned. "What were the bells for?"

"Council meeting."

I lifted an eyebrow.

He sighed. "My mother told the council about what happened in Brenden, and we were deciding about how to proceed with the impending war."

"Did she tell the council the truth about what happened in Brenden or the lie that you and she concocted?"

William pursed his lips. "Katherine's alive, Taryn."

My eyes widened. "What?" It wasn't possible. "How?"

He shook his head. "I don't know how, but she burst into the council meeting today half-conscious."

My chest tightened. Katherine had somehow made it out of Brenden and escaped back to Gharridan completely on her own. I swallowed at the terrifying picture that was placed in my head.

"Is she all right?"

William shrugged. "As far as I know. I haven't spoken with her."

An icy chill crept over my body, stabbing my skin like tiny icicles.

I cocked my head, fearful of William's answer. "What's going to happen to Katherine?"

Her appearance created a dilemma for William, one he might not make it out of. At the same time, hope bubbled within me. Katherine could reveal the truth to Vladimir.

William looked away. "She's going to be charged."

"With what?"

"What do you think?"

William made me angrier with every word coming out of his mouth. "What's her punishment?"

William's silence provided me with the answer, and I erupted.

"She's innocent, William!" I exploded. "You can't let them kill her for a crime she didn't commit!"

"It's either her or me, Taryn!" William burst out. "And she is far from innocent. Katherine let my father die. This is justice that should have been dealt out years ago!"

I shook my head, unable to believe what I was hearing. Neither William nor his mother cared about Katherine's innocence. They just wanted to deliver the punishment they'd desired since the death of their father and husband. I sensed William was only telling me this because a part of him knew it was wrong, but he was trying to convince himself otherwise.

"It's not like Katherine doesn't deserve it," he reasoned.

My fist swung for his cheek, but William ducked, my hand gliding through air. My chest heaved with fury, my arms and fingers trembling.

"Get out," I whispered, my voice deadly.

William watched me with surprise.

My eyes narrowed into slits as I tried to control the storm raging within me.

"Get. Out."

William straightened, gaze trained on me as he slipped out into the corridor.

I let out a deep breath, trying to close my mind to the murderous thoughts pouring through my brain. He couldn't let Katherine die. He couldn't be that heartless. Yet a small voice inside me whispered—*maybe he was.*

CHAPTER NINETEEN

VLADIMIR

MY BLOOD BOILED as the guards blocked the door to the dungeon, refusing to let me in. It was not only frustrating, but humiliating. It felt like my power and authority had been reduced to nothing, and without warning.

"I am the leader of the Kavari and so help me, you will open these doors or I will open them with your head."

The guard swallowed, throwing a nervous glance at his companion. "I'm sorry, sir, I can't. Queen's orders. No one is to see her."

I clenched my jaw, resisting the urge to slam the man's head against the stone wall. He was only following orders. There was no use making him more afraid of me than he already was. I hiked up the stairs of the dungeon, irritation building with each step that I took. The queen had no right to do this. It was unlawful. Undignified. Unjust. I couldn't nail down anything about what had happened in Brenden's palace until I spoke with Katherine.

The few people I passed scattered before me, wary of the expression plastered onto my face. I didn't wait for the guards to open the doors to the queen's study but burst through them unannounced. Queen Adamara was sorting through documents with several council members. They startled at my brusque entrance.

"Vladimir, we're in the middle of a meeting," she said.

"Why have you forbidden anyone from speaking with Katherine?" I demanded. "If she did indeed murder the king, then it is my job as Kavari to question her—she's under my authority."

The queen frowned down at her papers before setting them aside, glancing at each of the council members in turn.

"That's actually what we're meeting about at this moment, Vladimir. The council and I have decided that you need to remain out of this investigation."

The vein in my forehead pulsed to the verge of explosion.

"And why might that be, Your Majesty?" I kept my voice steady, controlling the rage threatening to overflow at any moment.

She sighed. "You're too close to this. Too close to Katherine. We fear the connection will interfere with your judgment."

"As leader of the Kavari, this country comes first before anything else, and my judgment is not allowed to be skewed on anything. Whatever my personal feelings are, they remain of no consequence. That is my duty."

The queen leaned back in her chair. "And how do we know you won't try to break the criminal out?"

I took several steadying breaths to recede my rage at her refusal to even call Katherine by her name. She suspected I would try to liberate Katherine from her execution, which was exactly what I planned on doing.

"If you're worried about my actions, then I suggest you have a guard present. Come to the dungeon with me yourself if you're that worried about it."

My words lingered in the air, and the queen and council members exchanged glances with one another.

"It would be cruel to keep you from saying goodbye, no matter her crimes." She looked away for a moment, chewing over her words before hastily scribbling a note and stamping it with her royal insignia. "You may go and visit her, but she stays in that dungeon, Vladimir, and no matter what lies she tells you, you cannot let your personal feelings interfere with your judgment. Your duty is to protect Gharridan, not your friends."

I snatched the paper from her hands, grumbling as I left the room. "I know what I swore to protect, *Your Majesty.*"

The doors slammed shut behind me, echoing off the stone around me.

When the guards in the dungeon saw me coming down the stairs, they fidgeted, gripping their spears and trying to appear confident.

I waved the paper in their faces, infuriated by having to attain permission in order to get past my own men. They glanced at each other before quickly stepping aside to allow me entrance.

"Nothing personal," I growled as I shoved past them into

the damp dungeon. A small assortment of petty criminals filled the cells. Murderers were dealt with immediately, so it was mainly pickpockets and thieves stuck down here. They shrank away from the bars upon recognizing my face.

Only one cell boasted an extra set of guards in front of it, and it was sectioned off from all the others with an iron door instead of open bars. My hope deflated. If I was going to get Katherine out of here, it wouldn't be while she was in prison. The dungeons offered only one way in and out.

The second set of guards moved their spears to block the entrance, but I simply waved the permission in their face like a flag. After a moment's hesitation, they lowered their spears and opened the cell door for me. The confined space was sectioned off into three small cells, and Katherine sat in the back of the farthest one with her arms wrapped around her knees. An ugly bruise covered her left eyebrow, and smears of dirt and grime stretched across every inch of her body.

"Vladimir?" She jumped to her feet at the sight of me, rushing to the bars. Her fingers twisted around the metal as if pleading for a way to get out.

"Are you okay?" I asked, surveying her closer.

She shrugged off my concern. "I've been in far worse places than a jail cell."

I looked at her seriously. "What happened?"

Her bottom lip trembled, and she shook her head. "I—I don't know, William, he—we got to Brenden, and everything was going according to plan. William wouldn't say much to me, but I knew he was talking to the spy and that they had found some substantial evidence that implicated Brenden's involvement."

"What happened with King Arguis, Katherine?"

Katherine's hands shook, her eyes closing. "I don't know what happened. My memory is fuzzy, but someone knocked me out. When I came to, the king lay dead on the floor, his son beside him. The Brenden guards were about to break through the door, and so I slipped into the passageway trying to find the others. I ran blindly through the tunnels, eventually sneaking my way into the stables, where I hid in the hay while I tried to figure out what had happened. The throbbing in my head became so intense that it was difficult to think straight. A battalion left the stables, and they all spoke about how the Gharridans had killed King Arguis. I hid there for two days, eventually managing to steal a set of Brenden clothes I found in a chest. After wrapping my hair, I saddled a horse and worked my way out of the city."

My eyes widened at the narrow escape she'd somehow managed. She shouldn't have made it out of there alive.

"I need to know what happened before you were knocked out, Katherine."

She rubbed her head in frustration. "William came to get me, saying that he wanted to search the king's study. We made our way there through the tunnels, but they were already in there, and when we realized what Taryn was doing—"

My head snapped up. "Taryn?"

She cocked her head. "Yes. Taryn was there. She followed us to Brenden."

I felt my chest rise and fall, but it seemed like I wasn't breathing. Taryn. I cursed myself for not thinking of it before. How ignorant could I be? Of course she wouldn't have just left knowing Brenden was possibly involved in her father's murder.

She was too determined and stubborn.

"Who killed the king, Katherine?" I asked.

Katherine shook her head, tears glistening in her eyes. "I've done everything to recall the lost moments, but the fact is they're not there. All I know is that when we burst into the study, Taryn was already there holding King Arguis at knife point."

The words hovered on my tongue, waiting to be released as I connected the pieces in my mind. "Did she— Katherine, did Taryn—"

I couldn't even ask the question.

Katherine shrugged helplessly. "I don't know. Is she not back here in the capital?"

"Katherine—" I shook my head. "She left before I was up that morning after the discussion in the tent. I haven't seen her since." My pulse quickened. "William didn't say anything about Taryn being in Brenden."

Maybe she was dead. Maybe she had killed the king, and they had—

I stopped the thought. William would have told me. He would have told me if something had happened to Taryn.

"Why are they saying that I killed the king, Vladimir?" Katherine's voice was small and shaky, her features tinged with fear.

"William is lying about something," I concluded. "And he's trying to pin it on you."

Katherine shook the cell bars. "Then get me out of here so I can speak for myself!"

If Taryn had killed the king of Brenden and William was accusing Katherine of committing the crime, he was trying to protect Taryn.

"What is it?"

"They're not going to listen to you right now," I explained. "It will be your word against William's. You don't have anyone else to verify your story."

She scoffed. "Neither does he."

I shook my head. "The guards have already verified William's claim."

Katherine swallowed. "Are they really going to execute me for a crime I didn't commit?"

"You're not going to die." My voice hardened.

"Then what are you going to do?"

I stepped away from the bars, pacing back and forth on the damp floor. The queen was set in her decision, and with her claiming that my judgment was skewed the council would never take my word for it over William's. Even if by some miracle we found Taryn, it wouldn't be enough unless we managed to get a confession from William. I needed to accomplish this legally, but I also didn't have the time to go about it that way. Katherine's life depended on it.

"Do you think the queen is trying to get more power, or does she hate me enough to execute me?" Katherine's gaze was torn as she looked up at me.

"I think it's both," I said. "But I also think William is trying to protect Taryn. I need to do some digging and speak with him."

She nodded. "Hurry."

I moved to leave.

"Vladimir—" Katherine cut off, and I turned back to her with raised eyebrows.

"Captain Verone," Her voice faltered.

I dipped my head in understanding. "I'll make sure he's able to get to you."

She nodded her thanks, and I exited the cell, going in search of William. There was no doubt in my mind that Katherine was telling the truth, but what bothered me more was why William was lying about the situation. He had to be protecting Taryn. That was the only explanation.

"—there's talk of ghosts in the castle again. Haunting the towers and milling about the corridors."

The two soldiers hushed as I approached, their expressions apprehensive. "The capital has no ghosts," I muttered, disapproving of the topic. "Where's the crown prince?"

"Haven't seen him today, sir."

I frowned, making my way toward the royal family's private quarters.

William's eyes narrowed when I entered his room unannounced, irritation flecking from his skin. "What is it, Vladimir?"

I shut the door behind me, locking and bolting it. He rolled his eyes, marching over to undo what I'd just done, but I blocked his way.

"What happened in Brenden, William?" I demanded.

He pivoted, marching back to the garments he was sorting through. "I already told you what happened."

I crossed the extravagant room, every nook and cranny oozing with wealth, my eyes glued to his, watching for any hint of a lie. "Tell me again."

"We went to Brenden. We found evidence convicting the king. Katherine took it upon herself to kill King Arguis. I know this is hard for you, Vladimir, but it doesn't change what happened."

I scrutinized his expression.

He still wasn't telling me something.

"It was just the two of you there?"

William gave me a funny look. "Of course."

I folded my arms over my chest. "Then why did Katherine say that Taryn followed you to Brenden?"

The slightest hint of recognition flickered across his face. He tried to hide it, but I had already seen it.

"You lied about that," I said. "I want to know why."

William sighed, throwing a belt on the bed. "Yes, Taryn was there, Vladimir, but I don't think telling my mother that will help anything now, would it?"

"So you didn't tell anyone?"

"No," he replied. "Seeing as she wasn't supposed to be there in the first place, I didn't think it would be a wise decision."

If he hadn't told the queen, then he didn't want her to know. William didn't trust his own mother, which was both helpful and horrifying.

"Where is she now?"

"Why does it matter?" William asked, shifting away.

I followed until I was facing him. "Because she could possibly be a witness."

"After we escaped Brenden, she took off. I don't know where to."

His eyes darted away, avoiding contact, and his Adam's apple bobbed. He was lying. I knew him too well for that. No matter the situation, those two characteristics always revealed that the truth was still hidden. He looked back to me, acting like nothing was wrong.

"I know you talked to Katherine. What did she say to you?"

"She doesn't remember everything. Someone knocked her out."

William let out a little laugh, turning away. "Yes, she was knocked out. After she killed King Arguis, the spy went after her. If I hadn't stepped in, he would have finished her off."

His lies were well rehearsed. Katherine had been knocked out, but she wouldn't have forgotten the feelings of anger and vengeance from killing the king before succumbing to the darkness.

My hands clenched into fists at my side. "Did Taryn kill the king, William?"

William's expression darkened. "Katherine's trying to pin the blame on Taryn now?"

My voice rose. "Katherine said when you both found Taryn, she was holding the king at knifepoint and about to kill him!"

"She knows you'll side with her, so she's trying to sell you a believable story, Vladimir! Open your eyes. Katherine killed the king. She chose to do it, and she can never take that back. It's her choice to live with for the rest of her life!"

Fury flared in William's face.

"Where is Taryn?" I pushed.

He shoved a finger into my chest. "I already told you that I don't know, Vladimir. If you want to find her, good luck scouring the continent. When she left, she didn't want to be found."

He made his way across the room, preparing to leave, thus ending our conversation. I swiveled on my heel, my mind working as I thought of another way to keep his attention.

"What happened between you and Taryn in the wilderness?"

My words pulled him up short, but he looked away, shrugging his shoulders. "Nothing."

His Adam's apple bobbed.

"Nothing?"

"She's the daughter of Michael Gallows," William said. "Nothing more."

Taryn had been too consumed with her own thoughts to hold a conversation on our way back from Gapsvar, but I'd seen the way William looked at her, how his gaze lingered, how he longed to say something but always thought better of it.

I strode past him. "If you say so."

He was quiet as I left, but I turned one last time before closing the door behind me. "I know you're hiding something, William, and you better start praying right now that I don't figure out what it is."

His defiance burned against me as I marched out of the room.

CHAPTER TWENTY

VLADIMIR

I WORE DOWN the carpet in my room, pacing and concocting a plan to get Katherine out of the dungeon and far away from the queen's grasp. Our options were limited. I squeezed my eyes shut, trying to sort through all the information. William lied about Taryn—that part was for certain—but what I didn't know was if he was telling the truth about not knowing where she was. If she had killed King Arguis, I couldn't see her returning to anywhere she would be recognized. I chewed on my lip in frustration.

I needed William to tell the truth.

Captain Verone was on our side, that was obvious, but I didn't know how much he could get involved without putting his position in jeopardy. I'd found him outside Katherine's cell when I returned from speaking with William. Their intertwined fingers connecting through the iron bars had quickly broken apart at my entrance. Katherine's cheeks flushed pink, but Verone remained calm as ever.

You're not dying, Katherine, I'd told her.

But even though she'd agreed to my words, her eyes had still pooled with doubt.

I sat on the edge of the bed, head in my hands, mind exhausted from running through all the possibilities.

Why would Taryn just leave? She wouldn't allow Katherine to pay for her actions, but maybe William had hidden her away and said that he would take care of it. I couldn't see Taryn running away from such a heinous act, but Taryn didn't care much about the affairs of Gharridan. Her sole desire was justice for her father and then to find her mother's family. A war was something she wouldn't have entangled herself in.

I attempted to rest, but the speed at which my mind was racing doubled, and I refused to close my eyes, afraid I might not wake up in time if I accidentally fell asleep. The moon hung high in the starlit sky when I finally left my room and ventured to the north tower. Torches burned along the stone, drowning the walls in shadows. Twice, I doubled back to ensure I wasn't followed, but I sensed no tail. When I emerged into the north tower, I took the second door on the right, finding myself in a small, dank room where Captain Verone and councilman Finnigan stood before a round table. The candles burning on the table gave their faces a sinister appearance and emitted a strange light about the room.

"Finnigan," I said, striding forward. I quickly leafed through all the information I had on him. Nobleman's son. Several years of military experience. Good-natured. Highly spoken of. He'd been on the council for years, but he wasn't the council member I would have expected to show up here tonight.

Captain Verone apprehensively glanced between each of us as if not sure what to say.

"What do you have planned?" I asked. From the look in his eyes, I knew he had something brewing.

"I'm sure Katherine told you her side?" Captain Verone questioned.

I nodded. "I spoke with her earlier. She says she didn't kill the king, and I believe her. Katherine can't confirm who was behind the murder because she was knocked out." I hesitated. "But I have my suspicions."

They eyed me curiously, and I explained Taryn's presence and intentions in Brenden. "I think William is trying to cover for her."

"Where is she now?" Finnigan asked.

"That's a good question," I answered. "William said she parted ways with them, but he's lying. Taryn wouldn't let Katherine die in her place. He has to know where she is."

"And you think she knows what actually happened?" Verone asked.

I shrugged. "If what Katherine said is true, then she has to."

"Do you think William told his mother the truth?" Finnigan asked.

"I don't know." My voice lowered. "Queen Adamara isn't exactly fond of Taryn. I can't see her overlooking the fact that the girl started a war with Brenden to simply appease her son. If anything, I think that she would be after Taryn's head."

Verone crossed his arms. "Katherine said the queen requested her to go on this mission with William even though Taryn volunteered."

I nodded.

"What if they planned to frame Katherine from the very beginning?"

His words hit like a punch to the gut, knocking the wind out of me. "What do you mean?"

"The queen hates Katherine. If she insisted the Radonaya travel to Brenden, she had a reason. There had to have been some kind of plan in place. Taryn entering the picture would've thrown off their plans, but it still provided the Crown with a perfect opportunity to legally dispose of Katherine."

I chewed on the words and felt a sinking feeling in my stomach. "It's possible. Queen Adamara was adamant about Katherine's involvement, making me wonder if they did plan to find Katherine guilty of something."

Verone's fists pounded against the table in anger. "The queen is so blind in her hatred of Katherine that she's willing to—" He cut off, unable to continue.

"Their ruse would have played out nicely," I said. "Except Katherine came back."

Finnigan stroked his chin. "If the queen is so blinded by her hatred, perhaps she needs to be removed from power."

Verone and I stared at him in disbelief over the treason-riddled statement.

I quickly shook my head. "I don't agree with many of the queen's decisions, Finnigan, but she is the reigning sovereign. Trying to remove her would ignite this country in chaos. We can't fight a foreign war and a civil war at the same time. Gharridan would be ruined."

Finnigan shrugged his shoulders, not seeming to agree but dropping the matter.

I swallowed. "We need more time."

They both nodded.

"I asked the queen for more, but she refused. She's not letting me do anything with the case because she's afraid my judgment is skewed. Finnigan, is there any way you could get the council members to grant us more time?"

He shook his head. "I spoke with them. Most of them are in favor of the queen's decision. With all the poison the queen has infected the country with these past few years about the Radonaya being a symbol of death, most of the council already believes Katherine may have possibly killed one king. Saying she killed another doesn't seem very far-fetched for them. If you petition the council, they will side against you. Only a few others besides me seem to find an issue with this."

That was what I was afraid of.

"Katherine needs a trial," I grumbled, "but unless we find Taryn, with no other witnesses it will simply be her word against William's. The council won't question William's integrity before the entire court."

I gripped the edge of the table, inhaling deeply as I prepared for my next words. Without extra time, we were left without any other options. Even with the power I held as leader of the Kavari, with the queen opposing me it wasn't enough to overturn Katherine's conviction. That would require the support of the council.

"We need to break her out," I said.

A hush fell among us even though both of them knew it was the only way to save Katherine's life.

We surveyed each other, silently asking if there was any other way.

"Let's say we figure out a way to break her out," Verone said. "What then?"

That was the tricky part.

"I don't know." I sighed. "The first objective is to get her out and then get her somewhere safe. I'll have to figure out the rest from there."

"The queen's going to know you did it," Finnigan said quietly. "You're talking about treason."

I nodded slowly, mulling over the thought. "I'm going to have to go with her until I find a way to fix this. I'm going to have to find Taryn."

Captain Verone spoke up. "My loyalty is to Gharridan, not to the Crown. I can be your eyes and ears inside the capital while we find a way to salvage this situation."

"And I'll do what I can to sway the council," Finnigan put in. "It won't be easy, but if the council sees Vladimir's persistence with Katherine's innocence, they will have to listen."

Captain Verone nodded. "All right, all we need is a plan then. We only have a few hours."

A smile twitched at the corner of my mouth. "I think I already have one."

CHAPTER TWENTY-ONE

VLADIMIR

THE LACK OF sleep wore me down, making it difficult to keep my senses sharp. I needed the right frame of mind. The gravel leading to the stable crunched beneath my feet as I went to fulfill my responsibilities. Finnigan and Verone were currently carrying out their own.

Snores drifted from grooms when I entered their bunkhouse and silently crept up to Gerald's bed, sliding a hand over his mouth and pressing a finger to my lips as he startled awake. Wild eyes stared up at me before calming with recognition. I motioned to the door, removing my hand from his mouth, and we both slipped out, leaving the others undisturbed as we ventured out into the night. Gerald held his tongue until we reached the lower fields, far away from any prying ears.

"What's going on, Vladimir?"

I scanned the darkness around us, mulling over the plan one more time in my head before I hastily explained to Gerald what I needed him to do. Fear overcame him when I finished.

"Vladimir, if they find out I helped you—"

I shook my head. "You weren't helping me. You were following orders. You were doing your job."

He swallowed, then nodded reluctantly.

At least one thing was taken care of. I let out a sigh of relief, leaning against the fence as my gaze wandered over the field of horses. Those with lighter coats shone against the moonlight, but the dark-colored horses moved about like shadows under the moon. The animals dozed, a few of their heads bobbing, their skin twitching at the insects in the night. A dapple snapped at a black horse that in turn struck out with his back hooves, but the kick was merely a warning and didn't connect with flesh.

I shot upright, squinting, afraid that my eyes were playing tricks on me as I slipped between the coarse slats of the fence and approached the dark horse. He trotted up to me but lost interest after realizing I offered no food. My fingers brushed across his smooth coat, not believing what my eyes were telling me.

Stryder.

I spun, slipping back through the fence and chasing after Gerald.

"The black horse," I sputtered. "The Adellaion, when did he get here? How?" He shrank away in trepidation. I grabbed him by the shoulders, voice sincere. "This is very important, Gerald."

He glanced around. "I was instructed to keep him out of sight. He arrived the same night Prince William returned; he wanted it kept hush-hush."

"Who was riding him? Or was he riderless?"

Gerald stuttered, "I-I'm not sure. It was dark, but it was a woman. She went into the castle with William."

My blood pulsed, mind racing. "Have you seen her since?"

He shook his head.

I whirled back toward the castle.

Where was she? She would have come to me.

Unless someone kept her from coming.

Adrenaline pumped through my veins as I tore back up the hill, combing through every possibility. I started in the guest room she had stayed in before, but it lay dormant, the interior untouched. Doors flew open and shut as I checked every other guest room, any vacant space I could think of. I questioned the few guards I trusted. None of them knew anything. I crawled through the sticky, filthy dungeon and left no stone unturned.

Maybe she isn't even in the castle, I thought.

Think. Think. Think.

The hours dwindled away, stretching dangerously close to dawn. There was nowhere else to look unless William was keeping her in his rooms. No. He wasn't that stupid, and I had been in them today. I would have seen her there or heard her or found a trace, *something*. I passed a set of guards, recognizing one from earlier. I frowned, recalling their topic of conversation, and then stopped short.

—there's talk of ghosts in the castle again. Haunting the towers and milling about the corridors.

Ghosts in the tower.

My eyes widened. No one would ever dare look there. My feet pounded across the stones, even as the first rays of dawn slowly streaked across the horizon. I charged through the door into the stairwell, winding my way up the stairs, winded when I reached the top. My unannounced presence startled the two soldiers guarding the door. I was right.

"Open it," I said.

They glanced at each other. "Can't, sir. Prince William's orders."

I didn't have time for this.

My fist met the first soldier's face with a resounding smack, sending him flying backward. I immediately went for the second soldier, and after a dull thud from the butt of my dagger, he lay unconscious on the floor as well. I unbolted the door, flinging it wide open and bursting inside. Darkness cloaked the room like a heavy curtain. I hesitated at the silence, afraid that I had been wrong.

Something emerged from the shadows.

"Vladimir?"

I spun at the voice.

"Vladimir, is that you?"

Taryn crept into the light spilling from the doorway, mouth hanging slack in disbelief.

"Taryn," I breathed, afraid I was seeing a ghost.

"Vladimir!" She rushed forward, crushing me in a hug, face buried deep in my chest. "There's so much I have to tell you, Katherine didn't—"

I grabbed her face, bringing the depths of her green eyes to meet mine. "Taryn, did you kill King Arguis?"

She bit her lip and shook her head furiously. "No."

Anticipation and dread rose from deep within me. "Then who did?"

A flash of fear crossed her face. "Vladimir …"

"Who, Taryn?"

Condemnation lit in her face. "It was William. William killed King Arguis."

I felt the blood drain from my face as the world closed in around me.

He killed King Arguis.

William wasn't protecting Taryn. He was protecting himself. Which meant—

"He planned to frame Katherine from the beginning, didn't he?"

She nodded.

The weight of her words crashed down on me like a crumbling wall. If Queen Adamara already planned on executing Katherine, nothing would stand in her way. Even with Taryn's testimony, we couldn't risk a trial right now. If the queen failed to execute Katherine, I had no doubt she would try to assassinate her. Katherine had to get out of here, and she had to get out of here now.

"Vladimir, there's more, there's—"

"You'll have to tell me later," I interrupted. "We're running out of time; they're executing Katherine at dawn. Help me pull these guards in here."

Daylight slivered through the window, illuminating the room.

We locked the men inside the room, barring the door. I relayed the plan to her as we dashed down the stairs, giving her directions on where to go and praying everyone would be in their place. That depended on Captain Verone gathering the necessary soldiers to implement the plan without word getting out.

A crowd had gathered in the courtyard where the event was to take place, and the executioner stood atop the dais with his ax, a summoner of death waiting to send souls from this world into the next. My gaze scanned the people, finding each of my men stationed in place. I caught their eyes, and they offered a simple nod in return, confirming that they were ready. I stared down at the ground, picking out the nearly imperceptible thin line of liquid trailing through the crowd. I grimaced. The chances of someone getting hurt were high, but at least this wouldn't kill anyone. I hoped.

The queen stared at me from where she and William loitered on the balcony. She arched an eyebrow, questioning why I wasn't standing with them. In the same instant, I noticed several soldiers moving at the corners of my vision, heading my way. My grip on my sword tightened. She expected me to try something. She was wise to. I rejected her gaze as I wandered into the crowd, waiting for the moment Katherine would emerge from the castle doors, forcing my tail to break apart as they followed me. I quickly found the other two men, noting their location, looking back toward the stable and counting the steps. Someone yelled behind me, the sound of bodies being shoved into one another rippling through the crowd as the queen's men struggled to reach and detain me. I smiled. I would like to see them try.

Shadows moved on the other side of the walkway—Katherine was almost here.

Ten.

Nine.

Eight.

I pushed my way toward the balcony, the queen's eyes following me the entire time.

Seven.

Katherine appeared in the shadow of the archway, surrounded by six guards.

Six.

A hand clamped down on my shoulder. My elbow jerked backward, catching the hollow of the man's neck.

Five.

I caught the gaze of the man acting as my trigger.

Four.

One of the other soldiers reached for me, another four behind him.

Three.

I drew my sword.

Two.

I nodded.

The trigger threw his torch into the garden pot. It exploded straight up in a burst of flames, raining ash from the billowing smoke. Another line of flames erupted through the crowd, shooting upward and stretching out across the ground. Screams echoed from every direction as people scrambled to avoid the fire. Chaos ensued. I barely flinched—I'd been prepared. I charged through the smoke that thickened around me, covering my mouth with my arm and coughing as I maneuvered through the onslaught. The balcony was no longer visible, but the queen's personal guard would have already rushed her to safety.

A sentinel stepped into my path to stop me. I plowed into his body, the force sending him flying through the haze in a crumple of armor and surprise. I deftly darted around the frightened people, eventually leaving gravel and finding stone as I tore my way through the castle corridors. The screams and panic faded behind me as I delved farther away. The gray walls passed by in a blur. I took two more turns, and then the final door loomed ahead of me, almost within reach, but someone stepped into my path.

I pulled up short. William's sword was drawn, face stony. "I can't let you do this, Vladimir."

"Step aside, William," I warned.

He shook his head, and I lifted my sword in response, aware of the sound of clinking armor and running feet quickly approaching behind me.

"Lower your weapon."

I tilted my head. "Tell me the truth, and I might."

"I told you the truth," he spat.

"No, you didn't, but I learned it anyway. Taryn told me everything."

William's face paled, his sword slipping in his hand.

I shook my head. "I don't know who this person is that you've become, William, but he's nothing like your father."

At my words, he lunged forward. I brought my blade to meet his, metal scraping on metal as his sword rode down to my hilt, shoving against me. I pushed back with equal force, straining with the effort, my muscles taught.

"I don't want to hurt you," I ground out.

He broke away, returning with a harder blow, but based on the sloppiness of his performance he wasn't thinking straight. His eyes lacked focus. Pure hurt and rage drove him. I feinted away from his blow, ending up on his other side and returning with a kick that shoved him backward into an approaching guard. They clattered to the floor in a mess of weapons and armor, limbs flying in every direction. I backpedaled and flew out the door, Dante sidestepping at the sudden movement, whinnying after the horses that had all left without him as I cut the lead from the post, kicking Dante's sides before my backside had even hit the saddle.

I never gave another glance to the commotion behind me or to the heavy unrest we had ignited. I just rode like death pursued me. Dante's hooves pounded furiously beneath me, eating up the ground. The orchard blurred through my vision as we tore through it, the secret door on the outer wall hanging ajar. My heartbeat hammered in my ears, my conscience screaming about the consequences of my actions, but I kept my focus trained ahead as Dante thundered into the countryside, leaving the capital and its corruption far behind.

CHAPTER TWENTY-TWO

TARYN

I WATCHED THE smoke billow into the sky as the screams from the courtyard pierced my ears, my mind drawn back to the explosion at the prison in Gapsvar when Vladimir had saved William and me from the noose. Stryder sidestepped beneath me, trying to flee the chaos building in the courtyard. My hands held steady on the oiled leather reins as I peered at the vacant doorway, waiting for Katherine's appearance.

Any time.

Any time now.

The seconds ticked by. Even in the chill air, sweat gathered on my brow.

Katherine burst from the shadows in the doorway, eyes wild. Three guards trailed behind her as she barreled toward the horses. All four leapt into the saddles, joining the other soldiers already mounted beside me. The group veered for the orchard, ready to run.

"What about Vladimir?" I asked.

"Our orders are to leave with or without him," one of the men said.

I opened my mouth to protest, but the horses around me lurched into a gallop. With one final glance over my shoulder, I heeled Stryder forward. I wasn't going to wait for William to lock me up again. The hoofbeats drowned out the yells of terror behind us. Vladimir's plan had worked. I'd thought he was crazy for waiting until the last minute, but he was right. If he had tried to break Katherine out any sooner, we would've never made it. He needed something to disorient and occupy the crowd, and he'd found it.

I just hoped Vladimir had planned enough time for him to escape.

I hated nothing more in the world than running from an enemy. We knew they were coming for us, even as the cold wind froze our lungs and the snow attacked our cheeks. I smiled at the snow, once again our savior as it concealed us from those who wished to find us. Poor Stryder, pushed too hard over the last few months, struggled to keep up with the other horses.

Every chance I had, I searched the world behind me for Vladimir, but he was nowhere to be found. The pummeling fear that haunted me hadn't left since we first set out after Zedekiah. I wondered if it ever would.

Night descended upon the landscape, dusted white with snow, but we didn't stop. Not until Katherine brought us to the entrance of a large cave, tucked away in the side of a hill and surrounded by trees. The stone walls blocked the wind and sealed in the heat of the fire the others built. I rubbed my arms, staring out into the darkness. One soldier watched the front of the cave while the other watched the back, making sure no creatures emerged from its depths.

The outline of a horse appeared through the trees, and a prickle of fear trembled up my spine. When the animal drew closer, I recognized the slumped figure on his back.

"Vladimir," I called, my boots crunching in the shallow snow.

I grabbed Dante's reins, his sides dripping with sweat. Vladimir stumbled as he dismounted, exhaustion already beginning to overtake his body. He reached for Dante's reins, but I shook my head. "I'll take care of him."

He nodded his thanks, eyes bloodshot and bleary, looking like he hadn't slept in days.

"You need to rest, Vladimir," Katherine said.

She was still shaking from the day's events.

He nodded, seeming to nearly fall asleep in the process. Katherine guided him over to a bedroll where he lay down, asleep before his head even touched the ground. Katherine spread a blanket over him before lying down as well.

"Katherine, about what happened in Brenden—"

"We need to discuss this when all three of us can talk, but I just want to know one thing." Her eyes shot to mine. "Did William kill King Arguis?"

I swallowed the lump in my throat and nodded.

Something connected in her eyes, and she lay down, her back to me. I'd slept more than necessary the past few days and took over the watch from the other guard, crouching at the front of the cave, gaze boring into the dark world around us. Even if I tried, I doubted sleep would come. It was like the entire world around us had been lifted like a fragile plate and slammed back down to shatter into a million pieces, with no hope of ever matching it back together again.

Vladimir had jeopardized his position by going behind the queen's back. The council wouldn't smile on that, and I dreaded the repercussions that would follow the act.

My fingers clutched at the chilled clasp holding my cloak together, the small weight a familiar comfort. The way things stood, I wondered if I would ever be able to search for her family.

Illdalore.

A name. The only information I possessed, the only thing to help me find them—if they even wanted to be found.

And there was still the matter of my father. If King Arguis had told the truth and Brenden was not involved in my father's death, then I had another enemy to search out. Another enemy to find—another enemy to kill.

The snow transformed into a heavy sleet that fell on us in torrents the following morning. It brought misery to our already miserable outlook, but for all its trouble, the weather also proved a blessing. The endless downfall obscured our tracks and kept distance visibility to a minimum. Anyone following would have to be within ten feet before they saw us. None of us spoke much outside of critical communication; I didn't think any of us were really ready to talk. Tension transfixed Vladimir's face as he guided us forward, eyes peeled for any sign of trouble. Whatever thoughts burrowed beneath his serious exterior, he kept them well hidden and out of sight.

Two more days of traveling passed as quickly as the first. When we stopped for the night, the soldiers milled about by the horses, leaving Vladimir and Katherine and me alone around the fire. The quiet built between us, no one wanting to be the first to open the discussion.

"Well, we're officially fugitives," Katherine said dryly. "What now?"

Hopelessness pooled in Vladimir's face. "I don't know."

"I can testify against William," I said, "if the council will agree to a hearing."

Katherine shook her head. "I doubt that will be enough, not unless William decides to tell the truth. You don't have a way to prove that you were in Brenden, and no one is going to call the queen or the crown prince's bluff. Everyone knows you left the camp before we did, and the council will think that you're lying for Vladimir and me."

Anger surged through me at William, at the sickening way he was willing to blame Katherine for his own actions.

"But isn't that the point of the Kavari?" I asked. "To keep the Crown in line?"

"This goes beyond that," Vladimir said quietly. "The queen planned to frame Katherine from the beginning. She gave the order to kill the king of Brenden."

Katherine's eyes widened. "What?"

I looked up at her, but the shock on her face quickly diminished into understanding. It surprised me that she hadn't put the pieces together until now.

Katherine shook her head. "We were already headed for war with Brenden because of Dellwyn, but why would she order such a heinous act that would seal our destruction?"

"Because she wanted to kill two birds with one stone," I said. "Avenge my father's death and kill the bane of her family with one calculated stroke."

"Someone had to take the blame," Katherine whispered. "It had to be either me or William."

Something burned deep within Katherine, an emotion I couldn't quite decipher. "You can't let her get away with this, Vladimir."

Vladimir ground his teeth together. "For now, I have to, and you have to stay out of sight. The council is not on our side. I can't risk letting you get caught until I know I can sway them. Queen Adamara won't rest until you're dead, until she makes sure that her and William's scheme has no witnesses."

The weight of the truth hung over us like a heavy cloud, smothering any hope that had arisen within me.

"What's the next move?" Katherine asked.

Vladimir picked up a dead stick, tapping it in the dirt. "Getting you out was my first objective, but before we do anything else we need to get you somewhere safe."

Katherine arched an eyebrow. "Which would be?"

Vladimir thought for a moment. "Somewhere the queen won't look and where people won't mind. Hiding you is a little difficult with your hair."

"If I can find some elder root, I can keep it colored for a

few days."

Vladimir shook his head. "Let's not worry about that unless we have to."

"We could go to Navarre," I suggested.

Vladimir considered the idea before shaking his head. "Queen Adamara knows where you're from. I don't want to risk her searching there. There's a small village wedged between the northern mountains not far from here. The people there should be able to take care of you."

"And after?" she pressed.

Vladimir's jaw clenched. "I'll have to go back to the capital. A war with Brenden approaches. We still don't know how Algarar is involved or what their plans are, and we still aren't certain who exactly it was that aided in Michael's death." Vladimir turned away. "We may never know, but we need to do everything within our power to find out."

"You seem certain the queen will let you back into the capital." A question lingered underneath Katherine's words.

Vladimir pursed his lips. "She has to."

CHAPTER TWENTY-THREE

TARYN

SOMETHING ABOUT RUNNING felt wrong. Cowardly. The idea ate away at me, kept me restless at night, bombarded my mind during the wearying days. The idea of wrongness plaguing me delved deeper than just running away, though. The entire world felt wrong, like the ground beneath me had tilted too much, and if it turned any more it would send us sprawling off the edge with our fingers desperately grasping for something solid to hold on to.

Conversation dwindled after our discussion. None of us had much to say. Katherine's face remained stoic, her hard, collected nature having returned after the fear of her almost execution. Vladimir was unreadable, but I sensed the burdens he shared with no one.

Days slipped past, blurring together and veiling the passing of time. The elements laughed at us, throwing down mixtures of freezing sleet and biting snow, keeping our spirits low and our clothes damp. Vladimir seemed confident that we hadn't been followed, but I wasn't so sure. At times I felt eyes watching me from behind, but when I turned to look there was nothing but nature.

Two weeks passed before we came to the first town, spread out across the valley floor.

Vladimir pulled the group up, jaw tense and eyes calculating.

"We don't know if it's safe to be seen," Katherine said.

"I know." Vladimir never took his gaze from the town. "But we need provisions. I'd also like to get information."

It was a risk either way. If we entered the town we might be seen, but if we didn't our food supply would dwindle.

"I'll go," Nic piped up. His curls nearly bounced on his head, earthy skin trembling with expectation. He was younger than the other soldiers accompanying us, newer to the guard. He wouldn't be as well-known or as easily identifiable.

Vladimir hesitated, glancing between all of us before deciding that Nic's call was the best. He tilted his head, clapping Nic on the shoulder. "Watch your back. Learn what you can quickly, get some food, and then get out. If you suspect trouble or are suspicious about being followed"—Vladimir pointed to the right, where the earth sloped up into a hill—"ride for that hill when you leave instead of coming for us, and we'll know something's wrong."

Vladimir's grave expression made a hint of apprehension flicker across Nic's calm features, but he quickly hid it, nodding and jumping onto his horse. The hoofbeats faded into the distance as we watched him pick his way toward town, leaving behind a trail of trampled snow.

Katherine clenched her teeth beside me. "I don't like this. One of us should have gone in there with him."

Vladimir crossed his arms, hiding the worry that I knew simmered just below the surface. "Nic knows what he's doing. He'll be fine."

Katherine muttered something unintelligible under her breath. Either she wished she was the one in town or worried about Nic's ability to be discreet.

I sat on a root and leaned against the rough bark of a tree, on the lookout for anything suspicious. The sun shone through the bare branches, casting a warm light on us that we hadn't seen in days. The horses grazed not far away on what little food they could scrounge through the snow, no doubt happy for the day's rest.

Hours passed.

Nerves clawed at my stomach. Tension seemed to stick to our small group like sweat. When the sun made its descent, I started pacing, the dropping temperature requiring me to move and warm up my body. No one left the town. Vladimir's breaths deepened, his eyes riveted on the quieting city.

"Should one of us go in there?" I asked.

No one answered.

Night fell.

I started walking again, casting a wary look toward the town every few seconds.

"You're going to forge a trail right to us with that pacing, Taryn."

I frowned at Katherine but meandered over to where she

sat by herself. She was anxious, but she hid it well. I ground the heel of my boot into the damp earth.

"Why do you do it, Katherine?" I asked.

"Do what?"

I took a deep breath. "Continue to be a Kavari, continue to serve a country that hates you."

Katherine stared at me as if trying to read my thoughts. "Because it's all that I have. It's the only thing that gives me hope."

A question lingered on the tip of my tongue, but I hesitated before continuing. "What were you before you became a Kavari? How did my father find you?"

Katherine turned away, face to the cold wind, eyes sinking deep in memory. "When I was barely a few weeks old, I was left on the steps of an orphanage. The only thing left with me besides a ratty old blanket was a scroll with the name 'Katherine Daharaway' hastily scribbled on it."

"Did you ever find your parents?"

Katherine shook her head. "People are very superstitious about the Radonaya, Taryn. I'm sure the moment my parents saw my red hair they decided to give me up. It's a miracle the orphanage even took me in, considering what I was. Thankfully the headmistress took pity on me, kept me hidden away from the others. From the time I could walk, I remember always wearing a hat or having a scarf wrapped around my head to conceal my hair even though the headmistress already left it very short. I had to fight for food among the other children, even as a three-year-old. When I was six, I got into a scuffle with some other street kids. My scarf unraveled in the fight, exposing what I was to the rest of the village. The townspeople ordered me thrown out, and I was on my own with nothing but the clothes on my back.

"I went to a nearby town and either kept my hair wrapped or caked it in mud to mute its vibrant color. I lived in the gutter, pecking my way in among the other street urchins. Fighting for food, fighting for a place to sleep, groveling to get my hands on a blessed blanket that someone had dropped. Every day was all about survival. The only thing that mattered in life was finding out where my next meal came from. I was ruthless.

"During one of the harshest winters, times grew harder, and so I found myself in a new line of work. I became a pickpocket, working for the biggest criminal in the city." Katherine laughed. "Young as I was, I was good at what I did, but the better you get, the more you do, and the more you do, the more you risk exposure. I grew too bold, and I picked the wrong pocket—the mayor's. I'd been living that life for six years by then. They wanted information about who I worked for, but he was my only source of income, so I refused to give in. They used what methods they deemed necessary to get the information, and through the process of having my face held underwater, the mud came off and revealed my identity. They dragged me to the town square, ready to chop my hand off—the punishment for thievery, and also an attempt to make sure that I would never be able to use my 'gift.'

"But unbeknownst to me, Michael had heard whispered rumors of a Radonaya from my old village and had been searching for me ever since. He'd been in town for a while, and through a set of various sources, had set his eyes on me, noticing that my head was always wrapped or that my hair was always too dirty to tell the color. He'd watched me pick pockets, watched me cheat the system. When the mayor was about to take my hand, he stepped in and stopped them, spoke with me privately, and said that he could provide me with a better life—if I was willing to work for it. A life where I wouldn't have to stress about my next meal ever again.

"Of course, I agreed. It was either that or lose my hand, and Michael offered me a fresh start. My whole life, everyone around me had either hated me or been frightened of me. Michael was the only one who ever treated me like I wasn't some kind of monster. He taught me that if you love people, they might one day love you back too. Michael gave me the home I never had but always wanted. He gave me something to live for. That, and the hope that if I protected this country, it would one day protect me back."

Her words hollowed my heart, inciting an appreciation for the simple things of my childhood that I had taken for granted. I'd never even come close to her level of hardships.

"If you had the ability to heal, why were people afraid of you?" I asked.

Katherine fidgeted. "The reason people are so superstitious of the Radonaya is because it's believed that Radonaya don't only possess the power to heal, but also the power to kill."

Her words sent a chill down my spine.

"I didn't even know I possessed the ability to heal until Michael brought me back to the capital."

I gaped. "How could you not know?"

Katherine shrugged. "I guess I was never close enough with someone to touch them. I knew people feared my red hair. I just didn't know why."

"Who was the first person you healed?"

"A soldier, about to die. I told Michael he was crazy, that I was not a Radonaya, but when I placed my hands on the man, it just—it just happened. I don't know how to explain it."

Though I'd experienced her healing abilities, I'd never seen them used on someone else. "Did you ever experience the ability to, to …"

Katherine shook her head. "I've only ever had the desire to heal someone that was wounded. There were times when I wondered if that 'ability' was what killed King Roldan, but I know it wasn't. I felt myself heal him. When I left his room that night, the king was on the road to recovery."

"Why can't William and his mother see that?" I asked. "They've infected Gharridan with this ludicrous lie."

Katherine remained silent for so long I began to question if she would answer. "When you unexpectedly lose someone you love, you look for someone—or something—to blame. If you can prove the death shouldn't have happened, it seems to somehow ease your suffering because there's still someone left behind that you can take vengeance on." Katherine's voice dropped to a whisper. "And you think that it will make you feel better."

"But something so far-fetched?" I pressed.

"It's not, really." Katherine's voice fell even quieter.

"What do you mean?"

"People fear my kind for a reason, Taryn. The Radonaya before me were rumored to use their powers to curse instead of heal."

"Your past doesn't define you, Katherine."

Her eyes met mine. "But it does undermine me."

It seemed our pasts had a way of following us, no matter

how hard we tried to shed them.

"What do the other Radonaya say?"

Katherine offered a half-hearted smile. "I've never talked to another Radonaya."

"What?"

"We're very rare, Taryn."

My face grew incredulous. "Where do your people even come from?"

Katherine shrugged. "That's what I would like to know. I've been to almost every village and town in Gharridan. I've asked and followed leads, but I've never been able to find another like me. I may be the only one in Gharridan, but if there are others they keep their identities secret."

Vladimir approached, directing all of us to head farther into the woods. We obliged and crossed to the other side of the ridge where our flames would not be seen. My conversation with Katherine pulsed through my mind as we continued to wait, the minutes ticking by as we sat around the fire.

"Maybe we should—" Vladimir cut off, unsure of how to move forward.

Something had to have happened to Nic. He'd been gone too long.

Stryder gave a low whicker before leaves rustled off to our left. Katherine had already aimed her bow at the intruder before I had time to turn around.

"It's just me," a voice called.

Nic emerged from the woods with raised hands as he eyed Katherine cautiously, aware of her deadly aim.

Vladimir lurched to his feet, scowling at Nic's ability to slip past the watch. "It's been hours. What took so long?"

Nic threw a sack of food at our feet before stretching his legs out in front of the fire. "You might want to sit down."

Katherine lowered her bow, casting a look over her shoulder and into the darkness.

Vladimir obliged, albeit rather unwillingly, and sat cross-legged in front of Nic. "What is it?" he pressed.

"I was in the shop getting supplies when I ran into a soldier that I know but haven't seen since we finished boot camp."

"You were recognized?" one of the other men hissed.

Nic held up a hand in defense. "It's all right; we're still safe. He offered me dinner and an ale in the tavern. I tried to refuse, but he wouldn't take no for an answer. If I hadn't stayed, he would have been suspicious, and I figured this was a good way to get what information we needed. There was a bard there playing his lute and singing these jolly old songs that sent your foot tapping, and the tavern serves excellent food. I actually got a little carried away. I'm thankful for the food we have, but quite frankly, it's rationed. I got a whole potato cooked to perfection with several nice pieces of tender chicken and—"

"Nic." Vladimir closed his eyes.

"Right." Nic looked down sheepishly. "Anyway, I asked my buddy what was going on, and said that I'd just returned from a station in the mountains. That was all the prompting he needed before laying everything out in severe detail."

"Which was?" Katherine's impatience showed in her voice.

"Most of Gharridan already knows. The capital sent out falcons and messengers, and word has been spreading like wildfire among the towns."

"What has spread?" Vladimir was growing every bit as impatient as Katherine.

Nic grimaced. "The capital was left in a mess after you broke Katherine out. People were hurt in the fire. Soldiers are out searching for both of you as we speak, and every Gharridan has orders to bring you in."

"Me?" Vladimir asked.

Nic nodded. "Once it was clear you helped Katherine escape and they couldn't recover either of you, the queen initiated a meeting with the council."

The hair rose on the back of my neck, my body stiffening in anticipation of his next words.

"After hours of deliberation, they finally came to an agreement. Due to Katherine's actions and your defense of her, both parties …"

Nic hesitated.

"What is it?" I asked.

He swallowed. Whatever it was, he didn't want to say it.

"The Crown and council voted unanimously to disband the Kavari."

CHAPTER TWENTY-FOUR

A CHILL CREPT through the silence, feeling like Death had entered our circle.

I shivered.

The night offered no other sounds than the beating of our hearts and the crackle of the fire.

"What do you mean they disbanded the Kavari?" Trepidation reigned in Vladimir's voice.

"Katherine has a price on her head, five hundred gold coins. Queen Adamara stripped you of your position. You're both now wanted fugitives in Gharridan."

I struggled to draw breath, feeling like all the air had been squeezed from the world around me.

"She can't do that," Katherine blurted out.

Nic shrugged. "I don't know much about the politics of

Gharridan, but the Crown and the council were in complete agreement, and there was no one from the Kavari to defend themselves."

Vladimir rose, the weight of a thousand worlds crashing down onto his shoulders. He took slow, careful steps as he paced, running a hand over his mouth.

I sat back, observing and trying to decipher everything the information meant. If Vladimir had known this would happen, I doubted he would have ever left the capital. There would have been consequences, yes, but surely nothing this severe. My hatred for William intensified. This was his fault. He had brought the death of the Kavari.

"What are you going to do?" I asked, unable to bear the stunned silence.

Katherine blinked in shock.

Vladimir eased himself down, eyes vacant as he stared into the dying fire.

"I have to go back," Katherine said, reality dawning on her face. "It's the only way to fix this."

Vladimir's expression twisted as he gave a slow and deliberate shake of his head. "No. That will only make matters worse. Step one foot back inside the capital and they will kill you without hesitation."

Katherine lurched to her feet. "We can't let her do this, Vladimir. If she disbands the Kavari, then she is becoming the very thing the Kavari were created to prevent. King Roldan's father believed one person shouldn't hold that much power."

I lifted an eyebrow. "Isn't that exactly what she wants?"

They all considered the question.

Vladimir chewed over his next words carefully before

speaking. "I don't think it's that the queen wants power. In all honesty, she's never been adequate or seemed to enjoy her position as monarch. I think in a hidden part of her, she has always blamed the Kavari for her husband's death—and this is her way of seeking revenge."

The words were dangerous, but they rang with truth.

We all looked to Vladimir, waiting to see what our next course of action was.

"This will never be fixed unless we can get William to testify about what actually happened in Brenden," Vladimir relented, "and I don't know that we will ever get him to admit it as long as his mother has her claws buried in him. She's all he has. He won't turn against her. What we need is someone on the inside I can trust, someone who can figure out a way to restore my reputation in the capital. Captain Verone and Finnigan are on my side, but I fear the queen might suspect them of helping me if they aren't imprisoned already."

"The council agreed unanimously, Vladimir," Katherine stated. "Finnigan didn't vote for you."

"Finnigan may no longer be on the council."

Nic shifted. "I could go back, work as your secret messenger."

Vladimir shook his head. "I don't think that we can do it; this may already be too far gone."

I wasn't going to just sit by and watch while everything this country had worked for was swept aside in the queen's revenge for her husband's death. Katherine and Vladimir loved and protected this country. They deserved better than this. Much better. The words left my mouth before I could stop them.

"I can do it," I said.

Their heads shot up, but Vladimir's eyes already held his answer. "No, Taryn. You're too close to this. They would never believe you."

I crossed my arms. "William doesn't know how I got out of the tower, he just knows that I disappeared. I can tell him that you forced me to come with you against my will."

Vladimir cocked his head. "He's not going to buy it."

I didn't even have enough faith in myself to accomplish this, but I would find a way. I knew William. I knew what he wanted, and I knew how his mind worked.

"I can get William to trust me, get the Crown to trust me, and I'll work to help Finnigan and Captain Verone if they need it. If I can get information, I can send you messages through them. I might even be able to get William to confess to the murder if I play my cards right."

Vladimir's pale blue eyes pierced mine, sensing the hidden meaning within my words. He was the only person who knew me better than William, and I doubted Vladimir had missed the strange looks and conversations that had passed between William and me, brief as they were.

"And what if he doesn't believe you and kills you instead?"

I swallowed. That was a possibility, but it wasn't one that I wanted to think about.

"If they think you know where we are, they'll just torture you for information and we'd end up worse than we started," he warned.

I bit my lip.

"Not if you send her in as a scurion."

We all looked to Nic as he voiced the suggestion.

Vladimir leaned forward, hope twinkling in him for the first time in days as he mulled over the thought. "She says we abducted her, and we don't tell her anything about what we're doing. To solidify it, all we'd have to do is send the Crown a message."

Katherine's eyes brightened. "Every scurion comes with a message. They wouldn't even question it."

Vladimir looked at me with expectation, asking but not daring to hope.

"It's not a question," I said. "I'm doing it."

I would do whatever was necessary to get back to the capital and clear both Katherine's and Vladimir's names. I didn't know how I was going to pull this deception off on William, but I knew that I had to do it. I knew I already possessed a part of him, which made my job easier. A touch of guilt pressed against me, but I shoved it away. William deserved whatever happened to him for what he was doing to the Kavari.

A smile touched at the corner of Katherine's mouth. "All right then. What message do we want to send to the Crown?"

The farther I traveled from Vladimir and Katherine, the more I realized how much of a suicide mission I was walking into. Why hadn't I let Vladimir talk me out of it? All I needed to do was succeed in getting William to trust me, but I feared moving a mountain might be an easier task. I had no valuable information. I'd strayed away from the fire while Vladimir and Katherine planned among themselves, deciding what their best move was and what message they would have me deliver to William. Saying farewell to them this morning had been harder than I anticipated.

I'd asked Vladimir whether I should stick to the roads or go off terrain. He'd been hesitant to answer, but eventually conceded that the roads would probably bring me to William sooner. Even though William and the queen both knew that Vladimir wouldn't be riding the roads, they would still be watched. Vladimir had stepped close, his own fear-filled eyes catching mine.

"Be careful," he'd whispered.

He'd given my shoulder a squeeze, driving home the point.

"If you feel that your life is in danger, no matter what is going on, get out of there. Immediately."

When I'd finally nodded my consent, he'd hesitated as if wanting to say more, then reluctantly lifted his hand from my shoulder, the cold air brushing across my skin in the absence of his warmth.

Now, as Stryder plodded down the road leading back to the capital, it felt strangely reminiscent of when I had first left my home in Navarre. There had been nothing to worry about back then except for where my next meal would come from. I'd never even been to the capital and was not a part of the inner workings and deceits of the government of which I was now so deeply entangled. A pang of jealousy ruptured deep within me, wishing I could somehow return to that life before everything became so complicated.

I stayed off the road at night, choosing to sleep under a blanket of stars instead of an inn. By the time I finally caught someone's attention, I'd already been backtracking for a week. I'd become skilled at detecting movement and discerning when I was being followed after having to watch my back for so long.

Dense woods surrounded either side of the road. All was still among the towering trees, but I saw the movement of a shadow to my right. Not long after, another appeared on my left. A prickle of fear ran up and down my spine as my mind strayed to the thieves that had attacked me when Vladimir first found me, but these were not thieves. Thieves would have attacked by now or given themselves away. These men were too silent, too skilled in their art. My followers stalked me for about a mile. I kept my eyes straight ahead, but from the corners of my vision, I counted two horses on my right and three on my left. Sweat broke out across my brow. Why hadn't they attacked yet, and why were they content to simply follow me?

They were waiting for something.

I kept a steady pace. A smile twitched at the corner of my lips. They were waiting for me to run. I held Stryder at a walk even as he fought against me. I would make their game painstakingly slow. I refused to allow them the pleasure of telling the queen that I had tried to run. Time ticked by, and the sun slowly crossed in front of us, arching its way across the sky as if following the path of a rainbow.

The horsemen were ahead of me now.

I heard the hoofbeats behind me, the melodic rhythm on the damp ground, but I didn't turn. I let them come. Ahead of me, three horsemen emerged and made their way from the thick forest to the road in front of me. When they reached the center of the road, the main rider turned his horse to face me, blocking the path. Stryder continued until we were barely twenty yards away, where I pulled him to a halt.

I knew they planned to arrest me; I just had to make sure I told them what I was here for first.

"Where is Vladimir?" the head rider demanded.

I lifted my chin. "I have a message for the Crown."

CHAPTER TWENTY-FIVE

VLADIMIR

QUEEN ADAMARA PLANNED to completely redesign the government of Gharridan. Whether it was a selfish desire for power or an honest distrust of the Kavari, I wasn't sure, but her actions undermined the very existence of the Kavari. Gharridan had already learned its lesson the hard way once before, and I didn't want them to have to learn it again. It seemed some had forgotten that merely two generations ago, Gharridan had been ruled by a cruel and ruthless tyrant who thought of no one but himself. The people suffered not only from the king's iron fist but also the famine and drought that wracked the land. His own servants killed him in his sleep, but they spared the life of his son, William's grandfather. The people allowed the Crown to pass to the son, but there was a catch, an amendment to the government. The

Kavari were created to back the Crown—but to also call it out. The council's role was to stay objective and act as a referee between the two parties. While the Crown still possessed the power of governing and ruling Gharridan, the Kavari held the authority to challenge it.

I knew the tyrant's reign held no memory in the minds of the younger generations, but his example was passed down and instilled in the people to remind them of the Kavari's necessity. Queen Adamara's proclamation of the Kavari's disbandment would spark dissension and unrest among the people of Gharridan—or at least, it should.

I stoked the fire, rearranging its burning contents. The only one with the power to challenge the proclamation was me, and I had no idea how I would accomplish that. I hoped that Taryn would be able to send us some insight once she got to the capital, but the thought twisted my stomach into a knot. What if she didn't reach the capital? She wasn't a Kavari, but nor was she someone the Crown could trust. I'd sent her right into the jaws of the lion. Whatever happened between her and William, I hoped it was enough for him to learn to trust her again. William would blindly follow his mother for the sake of her approval, but he wasn't a complete fool. He'd spent enough time with his father that I knew pieces of the king still lived inside the crown prince. Pieces of goodness, honesty, and hope. If anyone was to entice those parts of William out into the open, it would be Taryn.

I looked up, Katherine's intense gaze staring at me from across the fire. "I'm not going to go into hiding," she said.

A firmness and finality radiated from her tone. This wasn't a half-hearted decision. She'd thought long and hard about it, and she wasn't going to change her mind. The other soldiers suddenly seemed in need of a horse to brush or a dish to clean as they scuttled about, avoiding eye contact with either of us Kavari.

I arched an eyebrow. "If you'd like to march straight back to the capital, I'm sure the queen would be more than happy to reschedule your execution."

"Going into hiding won't solve anything." Katherine continued on as if I hadn't even spoken. "It would only prolong our problems."

"You do realize that there's a price on your head right now."

"There's always been a price on my head." Katherine scoffed. "It's no secret that half the people in the court don't want me there. They're afraid of me. Just like my parents and the people in the town I grew up in were. They always have been."

"And?" I pressed, failing to see her solution.

A smile tugged at the corner of Katherine's mouth. "I think it's about time I changed that. Ever since King Roldan's death, I've also been afraid of my ability, hiding it unless using it is absolutely necessary. It's taken me years to accept it, but the ability to heal is not a curse, Vladimir, it's a gift. A gift that should be bestowed on the people."

The plans continued to form behind Katherine's eyes as she spoke. "My ability is the very reason the queen wants me dead, the very thing that she's afraid of. I say we use it against her."

I cocked my head in consideration. "How?"

"If I want to prove to the people of Gharridan that I am innocent, I have to create evidence that I am trustworthy. What better way to do that than to bestow my gift of healing upon them?"

I sat back; unsure I was hearing her correctly. "You want to find random people who are ill and heal them?"

She rolled her eyes, thinking for a moment. "We can—we can move from one village to another. I can tend to their sick and wounded. Nothing earns someone's trust like saving a life."

"Would you even have the strength to do that?"

Katherine rarely healed others, but I knew that it sapped her own strength. She'd nearly passed out after healing Taryn those months ago, having to rest for hours.

She pursed her lips. "I can do it. Not all in one day, but if we spent even a few days in one town, I could accomplish a lot."

I stroked the rough stubble overtaking my chin, thinking. Her idea wasn't bad—it was actually a pretty good one—but I liked the idea of Katherine in a safe place better.

"It will put us out in the open," I said. "Any opposers would probably send for soldiers, and we'd be surrounded."

"That's why we watch our backs carefully."

I took a deep breath, watching her closely. "You sure that you're up for this?"

The queen's decree had finally broken something inside Katherine. She'd snapped.

"I'm tired of living like this. I need to do something."

Even if I tried to change her mind, I wouldn't be able to. I nodded, deciding to agree with her.

"Nic," I called over my shoulder. He popped up, acting like he hadn't noticed any of our conversation when he'd been eavesdropping the entire time.

"What was the name of the town we passed yesterday?"

"Hollow's Way, Sir."

"All right then, we'll start there."

CHAPTER TWENTY-SIX

TARYN

FOR THREE LONG and grueling days, I stayed imprisoned in the dungeon of the capital. I'd been shown the simple mercy of keeping my cloak. I might have frozen to death without it, the damp of the cold stone amplified a thousand times in the deep of winter, as if the chill below-ground wasn't enough for the constricting space. I hovered near the door, arms wrapped tightly around my knees, trying to preserve my warmth. I'd thought the tower restricting, but those four walls were nothing compared to this dank cell. My only company was Helvah, who seemed to be there every time I turned within the cell, but as soon as I blinked, she was gone. Her form haunted me, and I prayed she'd been spared from any fate like this.

The guards had ignored my requests to speak with William

when they'd first dragged me through the gates, and they continued ignoring them. The only interaction with others I experienced happened once a day, when a bowl of disgusting soup and a hard chunk of bread slid underneath the tiny opening in the door. The smell alone made me want to vomit. If the little cover on the opening wasn't slid back into place, I would've shoved it back out into the corridor. I turned my nose away at the soup but gnawed on the bread. I wasn't hungry enough to reduce myself to that. At least, not yet.

More than anything, I missed the warm rays of the sun hitting my skin, the openness of the countryside spreading out around me. The cage enclosing me seemed to grow smaller every day, and it took every ounce of strength within me to not go insane from the confinement. This detour wasn't part of the plan. I was supposed to give the message to the Crown and earn their trust while secretly sending Vladimir information about everything I learned. Coming back to the capital proved pointless if William and his mother simply decided to leave me to rot.

I sidled closer to the iron door, listening for the faintest plod of a soldier's boot, the barest hint of a whisper. Whenever I detected a sound, I projected my voice through the cracks in the door, demanding, "I need to speak with Crown Prince William."

Sometimes, I heard a slight shuffle in their steps, a brief pause between words indicating that they'd heard me, but most times they continued as if nothing had happened. I banged on the cell door until my fists burned with splinters, small bruises forming on the edges of my palm. I fought tears that sprung to my eyes, threatening to spill over. Wasting away down here was a fate worse than death.

On the fourth day, the rhythm of footsteps echoed through the empty dungeon, and I heard the jingle of keys outside my door, the click of a key fitting into the iron lock. I'd barely stood when the door swung open and someone jerked me out into the corridor. My numb feet stumbled beneath me as I struggled to maintain my balance, my captor pulling me forward at a ridiculous pace.

Maybe I was to be executed.

I fumbled up the stairs behind him, the small increase of light making me squint, barely aware of my surroundings except for the several corners that we turned. When he deposited me into a different room, I let out a little cry at the sudden shock of light accosting my eyes. I buried my face in the crook of my elbow, the bright sunlight like poison to my vision. The door pulled shut behind me.

They'd left me alone.

I didn't move but tried to let in the smallest amount of light to accustom my eyes to the difference. Even after a few minutes, I still found it difficult to open my eyes without squinting. My gaze swept over the room, trying to collect my bearings and figure out where I was, but all the colors around me hazed together disjointedly, and splotches of light flashed before my eyes. I covered my face again, slowly peeking through the cracks of my fingers. The room held nothing more than a wooden table and chairs and a few bookcases. I hesitantly searched out the window, trying to figure out exactly where I was. The brighter light outside stung my eyes, and I had to look out in short glances. Soldiers milled about on the ground below. This room had to lie somewhere within the guard tower.

The door flew open and I took a step back, squinting hard against the dizzying brightness. The silhouette shut the door behind them, and I stepped away from the window, my eyesight still not functioning quite right.

The figure remained silent.

"William?" I asked uncertainly.

He stared at me for a moment before striding across to the other side of the room, looking out the window.

"What's your message?"

I bristled at his brusque tone, my shoulders straightening. "You could have asked me that in my cell, but I guess a prince deems himself above visiting such places."

The color of his face distorted; his jaw tightly clenched. "I didn't know you were—" He caught himself, refocusing his thoughts. "What's the message?" he repeated.

"Nice to see you too, William. Well, I should say 'hear' you. When you've been locked in the darkness for three days, seeing anything is difficult."

"The only reason you're not still in that darkness is because you claim you have a message, but since you don't, I guess it's time to take you back."

The memory of the dank smell struck a chord of fear within me. "Vladimir instructed me to tell the Crown that he is still leader of the Kavari and that he denounces any disbandment the Crown may have tried to impose."

William crossed his arms, disinterested in the message I delivered. "Well, the message was a waste of time because whatever comes out of his mouth no longer holds any authority."

"Why?" I challenged, my eyesight improving. "Because he had the audacity to try to save an innocent life?"

William stiffened.

I knew I needed to tread carefully, but I also knew that he'd never believe I'd changed my mind overnight.

A smirk touched his lips. "Why in the world did he send you? Vladimir knew he was just sending you straight to a cell."

I shrugged indifferently. "If he hadn't released me from the tower, I would still be locked in there anyway. There's not much difference between the two cells. One is just warmer and has a better view. The warden wasn't concerned either way."

I swallowed my triumph as I saw what I'd been waiting for finally flit across William's expression.

Remorse.

Concern.

"I couldn't let you out of the tower, Taryn, not when I knew you'd immediately go prattling to everyone about what you witnessed in Brenden."

"And I wonder why I would do that."

My words silenced him, and he took a step back, really surveying me for the first time and no doubt combing over my filthy appearance. Dirt stained my cheeks as well as my clothes. I couldn't even begin to count the number of knots tangled in my greasy hair. But William had seen me in far worse states than this.

"Why did you come back, Taryn?"

My breath caught.

This was my chance.

I looked beyond William. "Because I'm tired of running."

He shifted. "Well, it's pretty hard to run inside a prison cell."

I lifted my chin. "Don't worry. I'm sure it won't be long until your mother has me executed. She seems to fancy bestowing death sentences on innocent people."

William stayed quiet for a moment. "She doesn't know you're here yet."

His words made me hesitate. This was the second time he hadn't alerted her to my presence, and I cocked my head. Perhaps William was seeking a way to get out from underneath his mother.

I said, "I don't know why. You can't care too much if you kept me down there for three days."

William's eyes met mine, and I sensed the frustration simmering behind them. He wanted to trust me, I could feel it. But he also knew that he couldn't.

"I didn't know how deep they placed you in the dungeon, but it was for your own good unless you wanted my mother to learn of your presence. And you're the one who decided to go with Vladimir, Taryn. You didn't give me a choice."

Anger burned within me, and I took a step toward him. "Neither did you."

I watched my accusation slice through him.

"Vladimir found me. He offered a way out. Do you really think I would have turned him down? I wasn't going to be your prisoner forever."

He averted his gaze, almost looking ashamed, like a little boy understanding the impact of his mistake. When he opened his mouth to speak, no words came out.

I shook my head. "Don't you dare tell me one more time that *you* didn't have a choice."

He stared at me, trying to decipher the true intentions I'd buried beneath my skin. Dark circles sagged below his bloodshot eyes.

He wasn't sleeping well.

"Why did you come back?" he asked again.

I waited to answer, knowing that my next words would be critical and either earn his trust or solidify my betrayal. "Because the Kavari are not everything I once thought them to be."

I avoided meeting his eyes.

He stood quietly for a moment before turning to leave but hesitated in the doorway, casting one final look over his shoulder. "The guard will be back for you shortly."

I hugged my arms against my chest, staring out the window and forcing back tears.

I had failed.

William didn't believe me.

And he never would.

After a while, the guard reentered and ushered me out. I grew nervous when we didn't take the same path as before. He led me to a new cell and locked me inside. This one had a tiny window at the top that seeped light. A cot was nestled in the corner, as well as a fresh basin of water on a rickety table. The door shut behind me with a permanent boom. I circled the small room and dipped my hands into the water, washing my hair and face as best I could. My fingers slithered through the knots entangling my hair, but I wondered if the strands might have to be cut. I was of no use to Vladimir stuck in here, and for a moment I wished I'd never volunteered to return.

The opening at the bottom of the door lifted a few hours later, and a tray with a bowl of steaming soup and a fresh hunk of bread and corn slid inside. I picked it up gingerly, not believing my eyes.

"I can't let you out until I know I can trust you."

William's voice was etched with pain. I hadn't failed. Hope swelled within me, and I listened to the sound of his boots thudding down the floor until they faded off into the distance. I may not have escaped the dungeon yet—but I'd gained a foothold.

CHAPTER TWENTY-SEVEN

VLADIMIR

HOLLOW'S WAY LINGERED off the beaten path, built into the side of a hill with a mountain reaching up across its back. The slanted roofs bled smoke, the wooden infrastructures solidly stacked together to insulate the warmth of burning fires inside. No walls surrounded the small city, and no one questioned our entry. Our horses plodded directly down the main street, curving around the haphazardly placed houses. A few villagers bustled about, studying us curiously, but all remained quiet and still. Peaceful. It was unlikely that news of the Kavari's disbandment had reached all the way out here yet, but when it did, the people would hopefully have a proper view of the Kavari in their minds.

Nic asked one of the villagers where we might find the healer's house, and he motioned toward the back of the village, dipping his head in respect. My boots landed with a crunch in the snow as I dismounted, handing my reins off to one of the men as Katherine and I approached the house. My fist thudded dully against the grain of the wood.

It opened seconds later, a gray-haired woman peering out at us suspiciously as she took in our travel-worn clothes.

"What do you want?" she demanded. "I have enough people in this town to take care of in winter without outsiders banging on my door."

Her blunt words momentarily stunned me, but I cleared my throat. "I am Vladimir, leader of the Kavari."

The woman drew back with surprise. She scowled, as if irritated she had to be hospitable even though she would rather not. "Well, how can I be of assistance to you?"

"I've actually come to do something for you." Katherine stepped forward, removing the hood of her cloak and sending her blood-red hair spilling around her shoulders.

The woman's eyes narrowed as she lifted her chin, taking in the sight of Katherine. "You're a Radonaya then?"

Katherine nodded.

The woman huffed, glancing back and forth between Katherine and me. She chewed on her lip before finally giving in and opening the doorway wider.

"Come in out of the cold, I suppose. Don't know that I trust the unnaturalness of your kind, but we've had a terrible sickness descend on the village the past few weeks. We could use your help."

Perhaps that was why the village looked so deserted, but no flag had flown outside the town's parameter to mark this village as cursed with the plague. As I stepped inside, the smell of herbs assaulted my senses, the sudden barrage of scents so strong and sudden that it dizzied me. A row of shelves lined the far wall, overfilled with a mismatched variety of different jars and plants shoved tightly together in order to make room for all of them. Among the herbs, I detected the smell of stew cooking and found a pot hanging over a blazing hearth, the flames filling the room with warmth.

"What sickness has overtaken your people?" Katherine asked as she surveyed the shelves.

The old woman's expression grew even more sour as she scurried about. "Fever, with a strange cough. It's hitting the children the hardest." Her eyes fell. "We've already lost several because they haven't been able to sustain their breathing."

She knelt next to a cot by the fire, revealing a small child buried underneath the pile of blankets who stirred at our voices. A pale face rolled toward us, his eyes opening for a brief moment but then shutting once again as if the task of holding them open was too great. The woman's face softened as she placed a fresh, damp cloth across his forehead. He swallowed, the action making him cough. It sounded thick and wet as if it faced a wall of resistance as it tried to force its way out. Pain scrawled across his face from the effort.

"I've tried everything I know, but it hasn't seemed to curb this monster," the woman muttered.

Katherine knelt on the other side of the cot, scrutinizing the boy's state.

"Can you help him?" The woman's eyes widened in earnest.

Katherine gently pulled back the thick blankets, taking a deep breath before placing a hand on the boy's forehead. The hair on the back of my neck tingled and rose, just like it had when she'd healed Taryn. Visually, nothing changed, but the energy in the room shifted, like the elements around us were aiding Katherine. The air seemed to grow tighter around us, tensing to see if the sickness would be released from the child's body.

After a moment, Katherine removed her hand from the boy's head. The air around me relaxed as if it had been holding its own breath.

A shiver trailed down my spine.

The sick boy's eyes popped open, the weariness evaporating. He stared up at Katherine curiously, gratefully, as if he somehow knew that she was the reliever of his pain.

"Thank you," he whispered with a faint voice.

His eyes fluttered shut.

Katherine let out a shuddering breath, eyes rising to meet the old woman's. Lines of weariness traveled across her skin as dark circles formed beneath her eyes.

"It may take a few days for him to fully recover his strength," she said, "but he will mend."

Wonder filled the herbalist's wrinkled eyes as she pulled the blankets back up over the boy. He slept peacefully, breaths steady and even.

"Are there others I can heal for you?" Katherine asked.

The grumpy herbalist rose to her feet in awe, swinging a cloak around her shoulders. A giddiness affected her steps. "Yes, there are many more. Please, follow me."

Katherine moved to follow her out the door, but I caught her arm. Her tired gaze refused to meet mine.

"Are you sure you're up for this?" I asked.

"I'll be fine, Vladimir." She slipped out of my grasp. "Let

me do this."

Katherine would overextend herself if she wasn't careful. I knew that all too well. She wouldn't stop unless someone made her.

The woman led us across the quiet street to the next home, where we were met with the wary looks of those skeptical of the Radonaya. Yet in the end, the fear for their child's life was greater than the fear of what Katherine might do to them. After their child was healed, the faces once filled with suspicion filled with hope as we left their home. I monitored Katherine as she grew weaker and weaker with each healing. She was pushing herself too hard.

When we descended the steps of the fifth home, I turned to the herbalist, speaking in a low voice. "Is there somewhere you could arrange for us to sleep for the night? Katherine needs to rest."

Katherine turned as if to protest, yet lacked the energy to even form words. The herbalist sensed the break that Katherine so desperately needed and nodded. "There's an abandoned house near mine. I think it should fit all of you."

When we moved to follow, Katherine stumbled. I grabbed her shoulders to steady her, and she leaned against my arm for support.

"Thank you," she mumbled.

A chilly draft meandered through the dusty house, but it was far better than sleeping outside in the elements. Nic had explored the town with a few of the other men and scrounged up some food to eat, and Bog started building a fire in the hearth. Katherine barely mustered the strength to eat, but I instructed Nic to make sure that she got all of it down. I walked back across to the herbalist's house, the cold wind biting at my cheeks. Her gaze met mine as I entered the room. She spooned a bite of soup into the young boy's mouth.

"Thank you for convincing the families to let her heal their children," I said.

She dipped her head. "Thank *you*, and make sure that Katherine knows we are in debt to her."

She gave me a serious glance, expression implying she wished to tell me something. "There's a town about four days' ride from here to the south. They have the sickness there as well. They would appreciate a healer, and it would be wise to not stay in one place for very long."

I'd seen the hostile glares from some of the villagers, the distrustful way that their eyes followed us as we moved through town.

"We'll leave at first light." I nodded my thanks and stepped back out, fully aware of the danger should we linger anywhere too long.

CHAPTER TWENTY-EIGHT

TARYN

THE GOOD NEWS was that William didn't want me dead. The bad news was that I didn't know how to get him to trust me from that starting point. He'd moved me to a nicer cell, though, which meant that even if he wanted to hate me a part of him still cared and didn't want me to suffer. I wasn't sure how long I would have access to that part of him, but I would milk it for all it was worth.

I sat up on the stiff cot. The thin mattress made the forest floor seem soft, but compared to the stone floor of my previous cell the cot felt like lying on a mound of cushions. I went to the water basin, but the water was disgusting after washing with it last night. The small reprieve from the dirt had been nice, but I would need to do a full-body dunk if I wanted to make any more progress. When I was through, I scooted the three-legged stool up against the wall in an attempt to look out the window. My fingertips grasped the edge of the windowsill, but I wasn't tall enough to get my eyes over the edge. I plopped down in defeat, unwilling to risk breaking my leg trying to climb the stones for a short glimpse out the window.

I'd find a way out of here soon enough—I hoped.

A knock sounded at the door, and I jumped to my feet as William entered unannounced. Distrust blazed in both of our eyes as we stared each other down suspiciously.

William ground his teeth together. "If I'm going to help you, Taryn, then you're going to have to help me."

I studied him, waiting to see what he wanted.

"I need to know where Vladimir and Katherine are."

"I don't know."

He rolled his eyes. "That's not going to help."

"I'm telling the truth," I replied hotly. "Vladimir wanted you to get his message, but he didn't want you to know anything else. They didn't tell me anything about their plans or where they were going."

Understanding flashed through William, transforming into anger as he shook his head in disbelief. "So they sent you back as a scurion."

I hesitated. "All I know is that he was trying to get Katherine somewhere safe. Somewhere she wouldn't be found. He planned on coming back to the capital to sort everything out after that."

William gripped the edge of the table. "How many soldiers went with him?"

I pursed my lips, deliberating on whether or not to answer, but he had to already know. "Five."

"What were their names?"

"I don't know."

He stared at me. "You're a terrible liar, Taryn."

"I'm not going to betray men who were only trying to save an innocent life. Look at the records and figure out who didn't show up for duty. You're the crown prince. It shouldn't be that hard to figure out."

He rubbed his forehead. "So what you're telling me is you really don't have any useful information that can help us."

"I've already told you everything that I know."

I could tell he wasn't satisfied with my answer, but he let it go.

"How did you get out of the tower?"

"Vladimir found me."

"How?" he asked.

I shrugged. "How am I supposed to know?"

"And you came running back here after scurrying away with him?" he pressed.

"We've already been through this," I argued.

"I'm just trying to figure out exactly what it is that you want."

I crossed my arms, trying to keep my irritation at bay. "Did you tell your mother about me yet?"

He rolled his eyes again. "Do you think you'd still be in this cell if I had?"

I didn't respond. I was probably safer in here than out there with Queen Adamara on the throne.

"William, do you really not have any regret over your actions?"

My bluntness caught him off guard. He chewed on his

cheek, unsure of what to say. Yet I saw the truth in his face, the bob of his throat, the twinge in his focus. Hidden there, somewhere in the far back corner of his mind—what he'd done was eating him alive.

I swallowed. "I don't judge you for what you did." The words came out of my mouth like bile. "I know you said your mother can be difficult, and her demand put you in a tight spot."

He avoided my gaze, and I begrudgingly took a step closer to him. "But I could never choose to think differently about someone if they didn't struggle with the consequences of their actions." I scuffed the ground with my toe and lifted an eyebrow. "I have to know that you're not just going to follow your mother's orders even when they're wrong simply because she tells you to do so. I have to know that you're going to do what you know is right."

He started to answer but quickly shut his mouth, thinking better of it. "If I let you out of here, are you going to run?"

"I already told you that I'm tired of running."

He still wasn't buying it, but he longed to believe me. His gaze remained fixed on my eyes. "Whose side are you on, Taryn?"

I squared my shoulders. "The only side I'm concerned about being on is the right side."

William pushed away from the table, plodding slowly toward the door. "I'll speak to my mother, and I'll try to convince her not to kill you." He stopped in the doorway. "But if she ever finds out you were there when King Arguis died, that's exactly what she'll do."

I didn't doubt it.

CHAPTER TWENTY-NINE

VLADIMIR

KATHERINE'S NOSE BLED twice a day for the next three days. Not one complaint ever left her mouth, but the toll her ability took on her body showed in every movement.

"You overdid it," I said.

Her stubborn expression encompassed her tired face. "I'm not used to healing. It will get better."

I liked her idea, but I still held reservations. I wasn't okay with it—not if it killed her. She continued to claim that she was fine, but I feared what might happen if she healed a wound that she didn't have the strength for.

The next town harbored even more sickness than Hollow's Way. Death ran rampant through the streets, touching any of the afflicted within his grasp. We stayed one day, then another.

Too long, but Katherine insisted on helping all who allowed her to. I watched helplessly, unable to do anything as her ability drained her of life. Eventually, it would take too much.

We made way for the next town. I knew I would have to return to the capital at some point, but I wanted to keep building the people's trust in Katherine for as long as we could. Our greatest weapon right now was the support of the Gharridan people.

We heard no more news of the capital. Apprehension grew in my stomach. I wondered if Taryn had made it, if William had believed her lie. Doubt rooted deep within me, fearful of what had become of her. More than once, the thought of the queen executing her flashed before my eyes, but I blocked it from my mind, unable to bear the thought that I had sent Taryn to her death. Gambling her life on William's feelings had been too high of a stake.

The third town held no sickness. The people eyed Katherine with distrust, and I quickly learned that news of the Kavari's disbandment had reached the people.

We left within the hour.

Worry persisted in my mind.

We needed news. Needed insight.

I tried to keep it from my mind, but it kept persisting.

"Bog." I sidled up beside him, speaking in a low voice. He turned to me expectantly. "I need you to do something for me."

A gleam lit in his eyes as he listened to my plan.

He departed the next morning.

CHAPTER THIRTY

TARYN

NOTHING ELSE IN the world compared to the wonderful freedom of life—even if it was only partial freedom. Shortly after I had talked with William, they released me from the prison cell, and I returned to my old room. A guard stood vigil outside the door at all hours, following close behind if I set one foot outside the perimeter. If I tried to escape, they would capture or kill me before I made it through the outer gate. I needed to work my way around the castle, but my tail hindered any sneaking. I had yet to go farther than the corridor, already irritated with the guard stepping closely behind me. Meeting with Captain Verone or Finnigan proved impossible at this point, but I was two steps closer now.

I walked in a circle around the edge of my room, weighing my options. My eyes roved around the confines of the grey walls, and I decided I was over being cooped up, even if I had to be followed. Marching over to the door, I flung it wide open and nearly collided with William. I stumbled back in surprise, heart racing. He stood regally, wearing freshly pressed clothes, his beard neatly trimmed. He wore distrust like a garment, no touch of humor in his expression.

"She wants to speak with you."

My throat constricted, completely aware of who 'she' was. He turned on his heel, and I moved to follow, latching the door behind me as he tore down the hall without glancing over his shoulder to see if I came. He hadn't spoken to me since the dungeon, even though I'd been holed up in my room for two days. Only yesterday the guard had informed me of the permission to leave my room, but I'd just left for the short stroll, not wanting to push the limits and end up having all of my privileges revoked.

We approached the queen's study and my body stiffened, every joint going rigid and making my movements sharp. What had he told his mother? And how would she respond to me? William might be willing to risk me, but I doubted his mother would.

William hesitated outside the carved wooden doors, hand clenching the curved door handle. "Let me do most of the talking."

He pushed open the doors, leading us inside the elaborate study.

Queen Adamara turned at our entrance, her deep blue eyes studying me distastefully as she lifted her chin. Her teal dress pooled around her like foamy waves, the effect making her eyes sparkle even though they held no kindness.

"My son tells me that you had a run-in with Gharridan's traitors, Vladimir and Katherine."

I harnessed all the power within me to not cross the room and slap her. The Kavari were no traitors. They loved their country.

Slowly, I nodded. "He sent me back with a message."

The queen scoffed. "Yes, I know, as a *scurion*. And he sent you to tell me that he still holds his power and denounces the disbandment of the Kavari." She lifted a piece of paper from her chaotic desk. "This document proves otherwise."

I studied the document, noting the Crown's seal as well as the seal of Gharridan lining the bottom in dried wax.

"For some reason, my son seems to think we can trust you, but I find that difficult to believe since you abandoned us in the wilderness without permission and without word."

"I needed no permission," I said. "I've sworn allegiance to no one."

She stayed silent for a moment. "Does that mean you are still considering swearing allegiance to the Kavari?"

My mouth went dry.

Whatever words I spoke next would be critical.

"To side with an outlaw would be treason."

William's skeptical gaze pierced me, still suspicious I possessed an ulterior motive for returning.

Queen Adamara tilted her head, deliberating. "Yet you seemed so close with Vladimir."

I chose my answer wisely. "He's the man who replaced my father as leader of the Kavari. Nothing more."

She sighed. "And why is it that we should allow you to stay here in the capital? What do you have to offer us?"

My heart beat even faster, breaths growing shallow inside my chest as my mind raced to find the appropriate response.

William stepped in. "She's the daughter of Michael Gallows, the great protector and friend of this country. Is that not enough?"

Her gaze flipped between William and me, trying to decipher a hidden meaning. Were it not for her son, I feared I would find myself locked up in the depths of the dungeons—or worse. I stared at her, trying to decide on exactly what she wanted.

"You may stay."

I released a sigh of relief, but her eyes snapped up, catching mine in a deadly stare. "But if I ever find out you were consorting with traitors to the Crown, the punishment will be irreversible."

I nodded.

I understood.

If she ever found out why I was really here.

Why I had really come back.

What I really knew.

If she discovered I secretly loathed her son—

She would kill me.

CHAPTER THIRTY-ONE

VLADIMIR

I CREPT THROUGH the dense trees, bending low to the ground to avoid detection. My boots sank into the mud, the world buzzing around me. Katherine and the other four men followed close behind, pressing against my back, straining to see what we all thought we had heard. A decent-sized meadow spread out before us, breaking the woods apart. Metal grated against metal with a sickening screech, hammers pinged against nails as the tents went up. Horses issued a chorus of whinnies. Shouts rang across the camp as busy soldiers bustled about, trying to finish unloading before sundown. I stared. It was a Gharridan battalion, armed and ready for war.

"Are they already preparing for the war against Brenden?" Katherine asked.

I surveyed the camp and shook my head. "They would be

amassing to the west, not the east."

"Then what are they gathering for?"

I didn't answer.

I didn't know.

Even if by some chance these soldiers were headed to the war with Brenden, they wouldn't be battle-ready. Not yet. Troops would march to the capital, but not in battle formation, not until they were close enough to join with the bigger battalions. They bore the flag of Gharridan. It flapped proudly in the winter wind, but what were they here for?

We stayed hidden, observing them, looking for any clues regarding their mission. I scanned their faces for anyone familiar, but the distance made it difficult, their features blurring together. A command tent hovered amid the soldiers, but the tent flaps never moved.

"Look, there." Nic pointed out a soldier roaming the outskirts.

The soldier in question seemed to be scanning the trees.

Bog.

I stood up, much to the protest of those around me, and moved to the edge of the forest until I was sure he could see me. It had been weeks. Bog would've had time to go to the capital and back, and we'd visited multiple other villages. But what was he doing with a battalion?

Bog caught sight of me, and he hustled away from the camp.

"What if he's sided with the Crown?" Katherine's voice rang with irritation at my rashness.

I kept my focus on the soldier as he approached. "It's Bog, Katherine."

We waited anxiously as he approached, glancing over his shoulders to see if anyone was following him.

"I thought finding you was going to be impossible." He shook his head.

I clapped Bog on the back, glad that he was safe. "Is Taryn all right? Did she make it to the capital?"

He quickly nodded. "She's fine, last I knew."

"How did you find us?" Katherine remained unconvinced that this wasn't a trap.

"We had to backtrack through a couple of towns trying to guess where you would go next."

"We?" I questioned.

Bog sighed. "Yeah, someone wants to talk with you."

I stiffened, my next words sharp and pointed. "What did you learn in the capital, Bog?"

He winced. "That's why we're here. Just come with me. He said he would explain everything to you."

Unease clawed through me at the endless possibilities of who 'he' was.

The closer we got to the command tent, the more my stomach filled with dread. Maybe Katherine was right. Maybe this was a trap. But what if it was Captain Verone? If he'd been able to escape the capital, that is. The soldiers stared at me as I maneuvered through them. Did they hate me? Were they waiting for the perfect moment to arrest me?

A guard pulled the tent flap back for me, and I slipped inside. A smiling face met me, looking up from a makeshift desk.

"Vladimir!"

I blinked as Finnigan lurched from his chair, marching over to clasp my arm.

"I was worried we wouldn't be able to catch up with you."

I shuffled my feet, confused. "What's going on?" I asked. "Why is this battalion here, and what happened in the capital?"

Darkness descended on Finnigan's face. "You've heard that the queen disbanded the Kavari?"

I nodded.

He sucked on his cheek, looking away. "Some of us council members never deemed Queen Adamara the most competent of rulers."

The same idea had crossed my mind, but I'd never voiced it. Finnigan trod on dangerous ground.

He shrugged in defeat. "She has tried in the absence of her husband, but Zedekiah poisoned her mind long before we discovered who he truly was."

"Do you think she will come around?"

The question held an underlying meaning—did he think the queen would reverse her decision about the Kavari?

Finnigan casually strolled around the desk, mulling over his next words.

Something flickered in his eyes.

Something he feared to speak aloud.

I tilted my head, studying him.

Something was wrong.

Something was very, very wrong.

"Finnigan?"

"The council and I, well, several members, have been talking among ourselves about the future of this country, how best to proceed from here. After much deliberation, we feel it is in the best interest of Gharridan to permanently remove Queen Adamara from power."

His proposition stunned me. I froze, thinking I had heard him wrong, but his expression didn't change. His face remained calm and passive as he waited for my reaction. Queen Adamara needed to be dealt with, but not like this. Forcibly removing a monarch from power? He was talking about treason. It was mutiny. She'd done nearly the exact same to the Kavari, but I planned on fixing her mistake.

"What you're suggesting would completely rip Gharridan in half."

He shrugged again. "More than it already has?"

Most likely the council members in favor had already made up their minds and planned to go through with it before there was ever a deliberation. I couldn't believe what I was hearing.

"I'm not happy about Queen Adamara's choices either, and don't doubt a different monarch could reign better," I said. "But we need to accomplish this peacefully. I can get the Kavari reinstated with time. What you're suggesting is a civil war. We can't risk a war among ourselves when Brenden will shortly be pounding on our doorstep."

"Removing the Kavari has already divided Gharridan, Vladimir. We need to make sure that the *right* monarch is in power."

I laughed, thinking he was joking. "So you're going to put William on the throne then? He would never forgive you after condemning his mother like that, nor would he participate in the madness of this plan."

Finnigan let out a long sigh. "We're not putting William on

the throne."

He was insane.

Gharridan would not sustain an overthrowing of the government.

"Then who?" My eyes narrowed. "Who could possibly be better?"

Finnigan stayed silent, pressing his palms flat against the desk.

His eyes met mine.

"You."

Time stood still, the air nearly suffocating me as a loud ringing jammed my ears, blocking out all other sound.

No.

They couldn't think—

But from the look in his eyes, I already knew.

They'd planned far beyond overthrowing the queen.

My jaw snapped tight, expression growing deadly as I stepped forward and leaned over the desk, inches from his face. "I will not pursue the throne, Finnigan. That's treason. When I took the oath of Kavari, I swore to *protect* Gharridan, not conquer it!"

Finnigan had expected my rejection. His next words slid off his tongue, smooth as honey. "Think about it, Vladimir. The people love you; the court loves you. Some may have made your life difficult when you first took Michael's position, but you have continued to prove yourself time and time again. I can't think of a more fitting king to rule Gharridan."

For a fraction of a second, his words tempted me, a vision of my life as king playing out before my mind. My judgment was better. I always put Gharridan first. Maybe things could change. Maybe this was the best way to bring about peace and restore the stability of our country.

I shook my head, forcibly removing the idea from my mind. No.

I was not meant for kingship.

That was not my calling.

This was madness.

It was insanity that the council had even dredged up this possibility.

Anger surged within me, and I shoved my finger toward the doorway. "Is that why you have a battalion of soldiers out there? To aid me in overthrowing the very government I swore to protect?"

"Those soldiers stand behind you. When presented with the prospect of having you as their king, they jumped at the chance to support you."

Disbelief engulfed me as my fury intensified. "Did you already make your intentions known to the queen?"

He shook his head. "Not yet."

"Well, at least you did one thing right," I said. "I will not be a puppet for you to place on the throne, and I will not rule as Gharridan's king."

Disappointment clouded Finnigan's features. "I was afraid you would be against this, Vladimir, but I implore you to do this for your country of your own free will."

Free will? He could not force me.

"I will not vie for Queen Adamara's throne," I repeated.

"Oh, I think you will." Confidence oozed from the words.

I lifted my chin, wary. "And why is that?"

A strange intonation coated his voice. Shivers ran up my

back as Finnigan's eyes remained steady on mine. "Because if you don't, I will kill Crown Prince William and his little friend Taryn Gallows."

His words fell dead in the tent, filling my mind. My chest constricted, feeling like the words had knocked the wind from me. The council's discussions had burrowed deeper than I ever could have imagined. He meant what he said, believed it with conviction. His passion struck me with fear.

I placed a hand on my sword. "Not if you're dead you can't."

"This is why I advised you to do this of your own free will." Finnigan smiled. "And I don't think that killing me would be a good idea. The council members in the capital are already set up to murder both her and the prince if I don't return unharmed and with your promise to claim the throne."

My breath caught in my throat as my mind sped from one thought to another, trying to comprehend the absurdity of Finnigan's proposal. Trying to work my way out of this. "You wouldn't kill William."

Finnigan raised an eyebrow. "I'm willing to overthrow the queen. Why wouldn't I be willing to murder her useless son?"

"Then why not just kill both of them?"

Finnigan's expression looked pained. "I don't think the people of Gharridan would appreciate that. They would turn on the council and completely destroy themselves. Gharridan needs to know that in exchange for Queen Adamara, they are gaining a ruler they can place their trust in—a ruler they can believe in. A ruler who actually cares for them and the throne."

I shook my head. "There are loyalists to the Crown. They won't let this go peacefully."

Finnigan shrugged. "Then that loyalty is a price they will have to pay."

All sense had left him. I jumbled through my thoughts, looking for a solution, but kept coming up short. This plan was catastrophic and only aided the agenda of the council. "What is it that you want me to do?"

Finnigan glanced over at the desk with a casual air, his composure indicating our conversation was just like any other.

I resisted the urge to wring his neck.

"You already have this battalion at your command, but I want you to amass an army strong enough to overtake the capital."

His words caught me off guard. "How?"

"By visiting the people and gaining followers. Bog has already told me of your plan with Katherine, and I think she should continue with it. You can accomplish the same thing, traveling village to village, swaying the people in your favor and recruiting troops. Once many of them hear of the injustices of the Crown, they will take up arms and join your ranks."

I shook my head. "This will never work. It will only create chaos."

Finnigan sat in his chair, leaning back. "It will work. And if you want to keep William and Taryn alive, you will not speak of this conversation to anyone, not even Katherine. You will stake your claim for the throne of Gharridan."

He could be bluffing. Were there really enough council members in Gharridan willing to assassinate William?

I swallowed.

There didn't need to be very many.

He only needed one.

He'd cornered me like an animal, caught me in a trap and left me at his mercy.

I swallowed again.

I didn't have a choice.

"What's your decision, Vladimir?" he pressed.

I licked my lips.

He'd left me without one.

CHAPTER THIRTY-TWO

TARYN

I SPENT MY days living as inconspicuously as possible. I attended dinners with various members of the court and council, strolled through the gardens as the weather allowed, exercised Stryder in the lower fields, and did everything I could to appear absolutely trustworthy. Interactions with the queen spread few and far between. She barely even acknowledged my presence in the palace. To her, I was nothing more than an annoying pebble wedged in the bottom of her shoe and not even worth the time to scrape out. William's attitude toward me stayed aloof, but his demeanor softened. Our conversations were stilted, awkward. Words passed, but a wall of distrust remained high between us, its stones and foundation remaining impenetrable. I needed to break it down, even if I had to chip away at it one tiny piece at a time.

I'd casually asked after Finnigan to the other members of the court, only to learn he had left the capital on personal business shortly after my arrival. I hoped it was his own personal business and not the hand of the queen making him discreetly disappear. Captain Verone at least was still safe. He'd nodded at me yesterday as we passed each other in the hall, the dire look on his face insinuating that we needed to talk. Last he knew, I'd escaped with Vladimir. Now I entertained the court, posing as a friend of the Crown. Surely he could see Vladimir's plan through all the deception.

With guards constantly at my back, I visited the only place besides my room where I felt like I could truly be alone.

I went to Marco.

I studied Marco as he slumped in his chair, staring out one of the large bay windows, his eyes unseeing and vacant. A dark grey curtain of dismay hung over the sky, leaking flurries that descended from the sky to coat the ground with winter. Before I'd returned to the capital, Vladimir had asked that I look after Marco, fearful of his future since the Kavari had been disbanded. I visited him every day if only to simply pass the time with him. Although he never spoke a word to me, I strangely felt like he enjoyed my company. Something inside of him still understand the comfort of another human being.

"It's snowing today." I watched his expression as I sat in the seat next to him. "It shouldn't pile too high, just enough to leave a small dusting."

His lips moved soundlessly as they always did, and I observed with curiosity, wishing that I could find a way to get through to him. A part of him still hovered beneath the surface. It had to.

"I'm Taryn, Michael Gallows' daughter," I said. "You and he were good friends not that long ago."

Every day I brought up his past life, trying to find something that might trigger him and draw him out. It might be a lost cause, but I was willing to try anything if it would help.

"Vladimir wishes he could be here," I continued, "but the circumstances are extenuating. Queen Adamara has disbanded the Kavari on the unsubstantial claim that Katherine killed the king of Brenden." My voice dropped to a whisper. "But William is the one who actually killed him. They're trying to pin it on her."

More than anything, I coveted how freely I could talk with Marco in this room. His eyes darted back and forth, lips still shuffling soundlessly.

"I'm not quite sure what we're going to do," I admitted. "Vladimir always said you possessed most of the wisdom in the Kavari. We could really use your help right now."

I half smiled as I watched him gaze at the swirling snow outside.

"Coming."

I stilled.

The word echoed loud and clear, reverberating off the glass windows. It was not timid. It held no fear or trepidation. The single word fell from his tongue full of strength and power. Marco's eyes remained unseeing, but in their depths I thought I caught a spark of clarity.

"Coming."

He suddenly grabbed my arm, and I jerked in surprise.

"Coming."

"What's coming?" I asked.

His grip tightened, chest rising and falling, and he took several deep breaths as if trying to muster the strength to speak again. His voice descended into unintelligible whispers.

"Marco," I said slowly. "I can't understand you."

His eyes reflected back at me with the most clarity I had ever seen in them. "Massacre. Northunder. Coming."

The clarity immediately dissipated, disappearing as quickly as it had come. I watched in horror as he slipped away into his own world again.

"Marco?"

He released his grip on my arm, and I shook his shoulder lightly, trying to draw his attention again.

"What's coming?"

His lips jittered as his eyebrow twitched. I frowned, intrigued but frightened of his words. The hair rose on the back of my neck, a chill seemingly hovering in the air around me. I knew it was absurd. It had to be, yet—yet he'd spoken so passionately, like for a fraction of a moment the cage of his mind had splintered open, allowing the return of understanding. Looking at him now, the cage had already repaired itself.

I stayed with him for another hour, talking again once I had regained my composure. I waited to see if he would come out of his stupor, but he never did. My fingers drummed against the arm of the chair, unable to make out the meaning of his ramblings. With a heavy heart, I left him for the day, troubled by his words. I told myself it was all gibberish, but a queasy uncertainty in my gut continued to ravage me.

Northunder.

I slowed my steps as the word triggered a memory. King Arguis mentioned that name when I had held him at knife point in Brenden.

This will be Northunder all over again, Taryn.

With everything that happened in that moment, I hadn't given it a thought since. Was it a place? A country? I ran all the information I'd learned since arriving in the capital through my mind, but it came up blank.

Massacre.

I frowned, stopping in the corridor and feeling my guard hesitate behind me. I'd almost forgotten he was there. My mind twisted around the information, deliberating on a course of action. I turned on my heel, marching through the palace to the massive library. Plush carpets filled the room with leather couches situated around them. The far-left wall held an extensive stained-glass window, the array of colors glistening like a rainbow throughout the room. Shelves upon shelves of books surrounded me, stuffed with every volume imaginable. Ladders stretched up to a vast balcony containing another entire floor of books.

I stepped farther into the room, reading the spines of books as I searched up and down the aisles. Sacred texts, *The Nature of the Wind, A Warrior's First Step.* Gharridan was rich in its literature and texts, but I'd never seen so many books in one place before. A scholar stepped quietly into my aisle.

"Can I be of service, Miss?"

His stiff brown robes fell nearly to the floor, hands clasped tightly together before him. His short stature revealed the ring of hair surrounding a circle of baldness on his head.

I dropped my hand from the shelf it rested on. "Actually, I was wondering if you had anything in the library about Northunder?"

He frowned, his serious expression turning disapproving. "The Algarian capital?"

Algarar.

My heart fluttered in my chest, and I nodded.

His frown deepened, but he led me away to a separate section of shelves, eyes passing quickly over the titles.

"Do we have any particular history with Northunder?" I pressed.

His fingers stilled along the spines and he set his judgmental gaze on me as if I had spoken a curse. I shuffled awkwardly, not sure what was wrong with what I had asked. He eventually returned his focus to the shelves, indicating a section of history books.

"I believe what you're looking for can be found in here."

He offered a simple bow, smoothing his robes as he backed away.

My eyebrow shot up in confusion.

I pulled out one of the leather-bound books, gingerly flipping through the pages. The handwritten script scrawled across the pages in short, tiny letters, making it difficult to read. So much information filled the pages that I thought I would never find it, but after a few hours of searching and reading, a few sentences in the script finally caught my attention. I devoured the words, but quickly became hopeless as I dated the events listed as occurring more than twenty-five years ago, when Gharridan and Algarar were engaged in open warfare. The book did not list any motive, but was written merely as a chronicle, stating everything in a series of facts.

The war between Gharridan and Algarar ended with the massacre in Northunder, after which the only surviving heir to the Algarian throne surrendered and Gharridan proved triumphant.

I bit my lip, wondering why Marco would bring up something that happened so long ago. If my memory served me right, this war ended before Marco ever became a Kavari, although he might have been training to become one at the time. My shoulders drooped. Marco must have somehow been involved in the war, and maybe his speech breaking through was just critical memories of a time gone by. Or, I realized, it could have something to do with the torture he endured in prison.

"History never seemed to be your strong suit."

I jumped. William loitered behind me. I glanced over the pages I had just read, looking for something more before snapping the book shut.

"William," I began, "what do you know about the massacre of Northunder?"

My question surprised him, curiosity creasing his brow. "Why in the world would you want to know about that?"

"I went to see Marco. Sometimes—" I hesitated, unsure if my words would place Marco in danger. "Sometimes he mutters things when I go and sit with him. He spoke the name Northunder and the word 'massacre' earlier."

William glanced over my shoulder at the book. "You've never heard of the Royal Massacre?"

"*Royal* Massacre?"

"That's what it's called. We were losing the war with Algarar, and my father didn't know if our country would be able to survive. Gabriel was the leader of the Kavari at that time, and your father was training underneath him. We needed a secret way to win the war, an advantage, and Gabriel set out to seek that."

"What did he do?"

William shrugged. "He single-handedly poisoned the entire palace of Algarar during a feast. Over two hundred and fifty people died, including the king, his wife, and two princes—one was the crown prince. The massacre effectively stopped the war and decimated the country of Algarar in the process. It took them over a decade to recover."

I looked down at the book, baffled.

"How did the heir survive?"

"He was in the country due to sickness. One of the princesses was supposed to be with him but must have returned, because she died in the massacre. His sickness was the only reason he survived."

The prince had returned home to find his entire family and everyone he knew dead.

"I'm assuming that's why we've never been on good terms with Algarar?"

"If someone had done that to Gharridan, I don't think I would be on speaking terms with them."

How horrible.

I pushed the pictures from my mind. "Where was Marco when all this was going on?"

"I wasn't even born yet, Taryn," William said. "This happened twenty-five years ago. Marco didn't become a Kavari for another five, so I'd assume that he was in training."

If he hadn't been a part of it, then why was Marco trying to tell me about it?

William leaned closer, caution hanging in his eyes. "Taryn, you do realize that Marco's mind is gone, that whatever he manages to say is most likely nonsense."

I placed the book back on the shelf. "I know. It probably

means nothing, but I just have this feeling that there's something there, William, like Marco was trying to communicate with me."

I could tell he thought I was crazy for considering it, but maybe that was better.

I crossed my arms, shoulder leaning into the bookcase. "Does your mother still hate me?"

"Does the sun still rise in the east?"

The ghost of a smile touched my lips, but I quickly erased it. For a moment, it felt like William and I were old friends again, but I reminded myself that he was not who I thought he was, and this was all a façade. His face looked tired, worn out.

A thought struck me. "What did Gabriel poison the Algarian court with?"

He shrugged again. "I don't think my father ever knew, didn't want to know. Gabriel never disclosed it. Whatever poison it was, the effects weren't immediate. Gabriel was already safely out of the city by the time people started dying."

A shiver ran down my spine, thinking of the catastrophic event and how far kingdoms were willing to go to ensure survival.

The thought of a poison strong enough to kill that many people undetected intrigued me. I cocked my head at William's words, looking beyond the library doors and realizing—I knew just where to look for books with information on plants.

CHAPTER THIRTY-THREE

AN ARMY LAY at my disposal.

Not as the leader of the Kavari, but as a contender for the throne.

My stomach twisted and knotted within me like a tangled rope, the damage too severe to ever reverse. I squeezed my eyes shut. This wasn't right. My mind screamed for me to change what I'd done, to reject this foolish notion, but I couldn't. Finnigan's claws had sunk too deep to be pulled out. His reach had grown beyond the capital. Finnigan's control left me powerless, but I couldn't let William and Taryn die.

In many ways, William was like a brother to me. Most of the time when I was forced to endure his presence, I wanted to strangle him, but it seemed that was a natural inclination for most people close with William. The fury over what he had done to Katherine still burned within me, and while I was shocked he had held to his lies, I wasn't exactly surprised by it.

Queen Adamara had placed the fault of her husband's death solely on Katherine ever since that accursed night. Young as William was, he had held on to that accusation with everything in him, refusing to let go. The hatred for Katherine had only grown stronger with each passing year as the disease of blame spread out into the capital and its surrounding villages. I understood more than anyone that accepting the death of a parent was difficult—and that having someone to blame made the reality easier to take—but I also knew how tough William's mother could be on him. I'd observed how she never had time for his opinions and doubted his ability to rule the throne one day. William felt like a disappointment in her eyes, and he was willing to do anything to turn that disappointment into pride—including letting someone else take the blame for his mistake.

I could only hope he would choose to repent and see the error of his ways, but William wasn't the only one subject to Finnigan's death threats. I cursed myself for having let Taryn return to the capital. Bog had assured me that she arrived safely, but I had received very little information beyond that. Finnigan had refused to tell me anything else. If I could get word to Taryn, tell her to get herself and William out of the capital, we might be able to stop all this nonsense, but if Finnigan intercepted the message—

It would have to be hand-delivered, and I wasn't sure who I could trust anymore. Katherine was out of the question. Nic would willingly volunteer, but Finnigan wasn't stupid. He would cover his tracks, keep a watch on every entrance and exit. If he'd convinced this many soldiers to reject the Crown and stand behind me, there was no way of knowing how much influence he possessed over the military. The battalion around me would favor allegiance to Finnigan, and if anything went wrong, more people than William and Taryn would lose their lives. I would just have to play along with his game a little longer.

I stopped in my tracks, boots skidding in the snow.

Or would I?

Finnigan planned to announce my desire to contend for the throne once I had amassed enough troops, but what if the troops I gathered joined under a completely different goal and pretense?

"What are you going to do?" Katherine's voice drifted from the shadow of a tree.

Finnigan had warned me not to tell anyone, but Katherine was perceptive. She would never have continued with her mission unless I told her what was really going on.

"Exactly what he wants me to do. For now."

She raised an eyebrow. "Once you start down this path, there is no going back. You either become the king of Gharridan, or you die trying."

"I'm not going to become the king," I said defensively.

"And you really think Queen Adamara and William will just forgive and forget that you tried to steal their country from them? I can tell you from personal experience that they never forget a trespass."

"I can't just let William and Taryn die."

The severity of the situation passed between our eyes, a heavy weight of understanding.

"We need to get them out," Katherine said, "but William would never believe you under the circumstances."

I lifted my chin. "If Taryn wasn't in the capital, would you tell me to just let Finnigan kill William?"

I'd thought about what her answer would be, how she would feel if the situation were even slightly different.

She looked away.

"Finnigan killing him wouldn't change anything," she said softly. "William would still die believing I was a murderer. I would hope that we could change that first."

Her well of forgiveness burrowed deeper than I ever could have imagined.

"Finnigan knows the people of Gharridan," she continued, "and how much they love you. If he wanted to overthrow the government, this is the most peaceful way to do it."

"That doesn't make it right," I said.

"I know, but you can't ask the people of Gharridan to stand behind you as their king and then rip that hope away from them."

I crossed my arms, staring at the ground. "I need to fool Finnigan, make him think I'm rallying soldiers to overthrow the Crown, but I'll actually be rallying soldiers behind me in an effort to save Gharridan. I need to persuade them to want nothing more than the balance of power within the diarchy restored."

Katherine slowly nodded. "It could work, but you would have to tread carefully. If Finnigan discovers what you're really up to, it will cost William and Taryn their lives."

"I'll speak to the men, see what they say."

"What about me?" Katherine asked.

I looked up at her. "What do you mean?"

"Do you want me to go with you or continue visiting each

village as I've been doing? Queen Adamara may have disbanded the Kavari, but in my book you're still our leader."

I stayed quiet for a moment, thinking through our options. Katherine didn't seem like it mattered to her either way. "I think going to war and accepting you as an innocent might be too much for them to process all at once. Going ahead by yourself may be a better idea. Continue building trust with the people and healing them, but don't overdo it. I'll send some of the soldiers with you for extra protection in case you run into any loyalists to the Crown. Don't stay more than a day in one town, and don't make your route predictable. No one should ever be able to follow your tracks."

Katherine shot me a condescending look.

"What?" I asked.

"You think I don't know all that?"

A smile touched my lips. "Oh, I know you know it; I just also know that you don't like to listen, so it's best to say it all again."

Katherine sighed, glaring at the camp behind me. "Where should we meet up once we've both accomplished our goals?"

"When you've done all you can, meet up in Civon. I'll have an army assembled in the lower fields to the south. If everything goes according to plan, we can sort out Gharridan's issues and already have an army prepared for Brenden."

A smile twitched at Katherine's lips. "You're only about to challenge Queen Adamara's claim to the throne. I'm sure sorting out Gharridan's issues will be easy."

CHAPTER THIRTY-FOUR

IT TOOK LESS than fifteen minutes to lose my guards. A loud distraction here, a quick turn there, down a narrow stairwell. My breaths came in heavy gasps as I listened to the silence, making certain that I hadn't been followed. I leaned my head back against the stone, victory shivering through me, even if it was short-lived. The guards' instructions would be to alert William, but they wouldn't tell him without trying to find me first. I doubted informing their boss they'd failed to do a simple job would appeal to them.

I pushed away from the wall, moving through the dusty shadows as I glanced over both shoulders. The deserted hallway stretched before me like a haunted chamber. I stepped cautiously, counting in my head until I reached the fourth door on the right. The handle twisted easily beneath my fingers and I entered the room, shoes sinking into the plush carpet as I shut the door behind me and swept my gaze around. I waited for my presence to be acknowledged, but the room held no sign of life. I swallowed. Had I miscounted? My mind jumped back to the corridor, retracing my steps in my mind. No. This was the fourth room.

"Taryn?"

The name drifted from the left corner, a dark shape forming out of the shadows of a bookshelf.

I exhaled in relief. "I was afraid you weren't going to be here."

Captain Verone approached. "I've already been here for twenty minutes. I wanted to make sure you were alone before revealing myself. Is Katherine okay?"

His last question held fear, the words too rushed.

"When I left them both she and Vladimir were fine."

He nodded. "Where are they now?"

"I don't know." I shrugged. "They sent me back as a scurion and didn't want anyone to know where to find them. I'm supposed to gather intel, try to get the Crown to trust me. What happened after we escaped?"

Verone growled. "The queen called the council and the court together for a meeting when soldiers failed to return with Vladimir and Katherine a day after they escaped. Two people were severely burned by the fire, and several more were injured in the chaos. The situation made Vladimir look bad. Everyone believed William's story, and with Vladimir taking Katherine's side, escaping and causing damage in the process, neither the council nor the court stood in his favor. When the queen brought them together and suggested a disbandment in light of their actions, everyone agreed."

I swallowed. "No one defended him? Not even Finnigan?"

Captain Verone sadly shook his head. "I do think some councilmen remain who support Vladimir over the queen, but the support for the Crown was overwhelming. Our allies did better to stay quiet instead of causing dissension. If they'd spoken out against the Crown and sided with Vladimir, I fear they may have been removed. It's better for them to secretly stay on the Crown's side until he returns."

At least there was hope.

"How many councilmen?" I asked.

"It's hard to say. I've spoken with two who have both confirmed that they stand behind the Kavari, not including Finnigan."

"Where is Finnigan?"

Captain Verone licked his lips. "He left the capital a few days ago, citing personal reasons, but I fear Queen Adamara may have discovered his loyalty."

I crossed my arms, pacing back and forth in the room. "We need to know how much support Vladimir holds before he returns to the capital, but he can't stay away for long. Brenden could begin marching toward us at any time. I doubt that I will be able to procure much sway with the council members. I should leave that to you and Finnigan. They know you better."

Verone nodded. "I sent word to all of the outposts, and they've dispatched scouts to watch the border. As soon as they detect any movement they'll send word by falcon, and we should know within a week."

"You've been in the military a long time, captain. Is it possible for us to stop this war before it begins?"

Verone's eyes grew somber. "William assassinated their king on their own soil, Taryn. There is no going back from that."

I nodded, the sinking feeling in my stomach growing stronger.

A thought struck me.

"Captain, what do you know about Marco and the Royal Massacre?"

My dramatic change of subject prompted a raised eyebrow. "As far as I know, Marco had nothing to do with it. It was all on Gabriel, although I believe your father was somewhat involved."

I frowned. "How did Gharridan feel about his actions?"

I watched as thoughts swirled behind Verone's eyes. "Some were thankful that Gabriel had found a way to end the war. Others thought his methods too harsh. His actions resulted in the death of over two hundred and fifty people—the majority of them innocents."

"And the royal who survived?"

"Dorjan. He was not more than a boy at the time."

I scowled. "How could Gabriel be so merciless as to take that boy's entire family away from him?"

My words made Captain Verone uncomfortable. "Gabriel granted the mercy of allowing a survivor, but he had always intended there to be two so that the young prince would have someone. He didn't like the idea of killing children."

"What do you mean two?"

"The sickness of Prince Dorjan was no accident, but it also befell one of his sisters. Both were transported to the country to keep away from the other heirs, fearing it would spread, but when the young prince returned, the princess was not with him.

The Crown declared she had been killed in the massacre, but …" Verone trailed off.

"But what?" I urged.

"Gabriel had spies who made certain of the royals' deaths. They swore the princess was not among them."

Twenty-five years ago.

"What was her name?"

Captain Verone's eyebrows drew together. "I'm not quite sure; it was a very long time ago, but I'm sure it's held in records somewhere."

Northunder.

"Do you know how old she was?"

He shrugged. "Maybe a handful of years older than King Dorjan."

A dangerous thought brewed in the back of my mind, one that I knew I shouldn't give any attention to, but it began to grow, twisting around the facts that Verone had just stated.

"Why are you so interested?" he asked curiously.

I shrugged his question off. "Marco mentioned it in his delirium, and I wondered if it held any context, but I don't think it does."

I moved to leave. "See how many council members you can gain, and I'll see what I can do on my end. Hopefully Finnigan will return before the week is out. Let's try to meet again when he does."

It didn't take me long to locate William. He stood in the archery fields in a rumpled soldier's uniform, his boots caked with dirt and his hair a disheveled mess. I stopped a short way from him, watching him for a moment as he nocked an arrow, judging the distance of the target and calculating the wind before lifting the bow to loose it. It flew straight and true but slightly off the mark. A smirk lifted the corner of my lips. For the crown prince, he wasn't that great of a shot. At least he knew how to use a sword. A serious expression enveloped his face, his mind focused completely on the task at hand, not hearing when I approached from behind. My feet moved softly through the grass, the other archers throwing me wary glances. I waited calmly behind him as he nocked another arrow, waiting until he drew back the string.

"Watch out for the tapestry."

His arm jerked at my voice, the arrow flying off-target and disappearing into the fields below.

Snickers drifted from the other soldiers.

William spun around, scowling. "Don't do that."

I smiled. "Shouldn't you already know how to practice with distractions?"

He grabbed another arrow, quickly eyeing his target and releasing it.

It struck off-center.

"I know you're smirking," he said without looking at me.

"At least it was closer than the last shot."

He snatched another, letting it go almost immediately.

The tip hit dead center.

"Why didn't you do that last time?" I asked.

"I never said I enjoyed archery."

He fired another shot, not paying much attention. It hit the circumference of the red dot but wasn't as direct as the previous shot. I reached for the bow to take it from his hands. He frowned, mouth open in protest, but then let it go. I nocked an arrow, surveying the target before I pulled back, closing one eye as I let it fly. It hit between William's last two, and I whipped another shaft from the barrel, letting it go in a flash.

It split William's arrow in half.

"Where were you earlier today?"

I avoided William's gaze as I drew another arrow. "I needed some time alone."

"And you had to lose your guards to get it?"

I released the string.

"You're the crown prince, William; you should know how suffocating it feels to have guards following you around day and night."

He stayed silent for another moment as I fired again. It felt good to stretch my muscles, to feel the weight and power of a bow in my hands.

"How can I trust you if you can't even stay under guard?"

I handed the bow back to him. "Trust me or don't trust me; I really don't care. I'm tired of being treated like a criminal."

Not my best choice of words, but within all the deception I was weaving together, a little bit of honesty needed to be filtered in. William set the weapon down, marching toward the target to retrieve the arrows. He returned, and I fiddled with the leather belt on my dress. "I need you to do something for me."

He surveyed me for a moment, trying to decipher if this was some kind of trick. After a moment, he replaced the arrows in the quiver and picked up his bow again. "And what might that be?"

I watched his next arrow strike the target. My palms grew

sweaty. "I need you to get me into my father's room."

He scuffed his boot against the ground, readjusting his stance. "Why can't you just go in?"

"Because it's locked."

"Then it's probably locked for a reason."

William threw me an indifferent look before returning to his archery.

My jaw clenched, back stiffening in defiance. I would get in there with or without him.

I stepped away. "Fine. I'll do it without you. Go ahead and have them prepare my jail cell again."

William placed a hand on my arm as I started to leave, turning me toward him. I became increasingly aware of the other soldiers around us and the heat from William's hand where he was touching me. I didn't like being this close to him. Not after what he had done.

"Why do you want to go in your father's rooms?"

"He's my father, William. Why wouldn't I? How would you feel if you were locked away from everything that was left of your father?"

I slipped my arm out of his grasp and marched away. As long as William continued to distrust me, I wouldn't be able to accomplish anything. I was halfway back to the castle when I sensed him fall into step beside me. We crossed the rest of the way to the front gate in silence, neither wanting to speak first.

"I have to get the key," William finally managed. "Meet me there."

For a moment, I considered following him to try and see where he would go but then thought better of it. I needed his trust more than anything.

As I stood outside my father's door, a heavy remembrance of the last time I had entered it blanketed my mind. At that point in time, I'd still hated him. Hated him for leaving me and never telling me why. I wondered what it would be like to walk in there now, if the feeling would be different. If I would feel more connected to the things of his past. I pulled on the door handle again. It was still locked, just as it had been when I'd tried earlier.

A servant carrying a basket of clothes passed me without paying any attention, as did a few maids. Boots echoed from farther down the hall, and I turned to see William striding toward me. His mouth was set in a hard line, eyes full of apprehension. He remained quiet as he placed the key into the iron lock and opened the door, stepping back for me to enter first. I squeezed past him, wishing I could've done this by myself.

The room looked the same as last time, only the dust was thicker. Light filtered in from the window above, but with the dormant hearth the room felt cold and uninviting, like a tomb full of relics from the past. I crossed my arms and shivered, surveying his belongings lying around me. I wanted to open the wardrobe, to inhale his scent, but I refrained. Not with William here. All the books were still on the bookshelf exactly as they had been, and I scanned their titles, pulling out the same book of children's stories from before. It automatically fell open to the page that held the drawing of my mother. My fingers brushed across the page tenderly, stroking the lines of her hair.

William's footsteps padded quietly across the floor toward me. His breath held as he looked over my shoulder.

"Is that your mother?" he asked gently.

I swallowed, not wanting to have to explain this—especially

not to him.

"You look just like her."

I tilted my head, staring at the portrait and noticing for the first time the number of similarities we had. Our eyes were shaped the same, our eyebrows curved up, except I knew that my left one tended to look a little cockeyed. The nose radiated the same sharpness. I wondered if the way she was smiling in this picture was the same way that I smiled, if both of our smiles held on to a piece of hope and wonder in the world.

I shut the book, placing it in a layer of dust, and scanned the titles of the other books. Not much seemed of interest to me, but I pulled down two volumes on herbology and another one that appeared to hold the script of some kind of history.

"How did you know the drawing was in there?" William asked.

I shuffled through a few pages in the plant book. "I saw it last time I was here, before we went chasing after Zedekiah."

He stood silently as I leafed through the books but failed to come up with anything significant.

"What are you looking for?"

I hesitated, unsure of how much I wanted to share with him.

"I'm interested in figuring out what Gabriel used to massacre the people of Algarar. I remembered seeing these books in here."

"Planning your own assassination attempt?"

"No, you're the expert on that."

He stiffened beside me, but I wouldn't apologize for speaking the truth. I continued leafing through a few volumes and felt his gaze on me, implying that he thought I was still on a wild-goose chase.

"If you want to take the books to your own room, I won't tell, and I doubt that anyone would miss them."

I'd already planned on sneaking the children's book out anyway.

"Thanks," I said, stacking the books together and cradling them in my arms.

I walked out the door and heard the key rattle in the lock behind me.

"There's more in the library if you can't find what you're looking for."

I turned, awkwardly catching his eyes for a moment before nodding my thanks, a sense of relief washing over me as I walked away.

He was beginning to trust me.

CHAPTER THIRTY-FIVE

KATHERINE

THE ABSENCE OF Vladimir lingered like a chill in the air, creeping into every vulnerability and leaving a trail of shivers behind. I felt his absence everywhere, touching everything—even in the companions surrounding me. The soldiers traveling with me did not fear me in the sense that they cowered in terror, but from their overly cautious behavior and wariness I knew they would never accept me as one of their own. Few people in this world had ever looked at me without judgment, and Vladimir was one of them. His presence always eased the tension. I missed that luxury.

Beneath us, the horses' hooves plodded along the hard-packed earth, creating a lilting rhythm. I fought the urge to hum a melody against the beat.

Thoughts invaded my mind, pushing and prodding to gain

my attention. What Vladimir was doing, pretending to challenge Queen Adamara for the throne, scared me. If this plan of his didn't play out perfectly, the disbandment of the Kavari would be the least of his worries. Yet councilman Finnigan had left him without a choice. We treaded dangerous waters.

Breaths surged in and out of my lungs, my blood boiling at the arrogance Finnigan dared to display. He cared nothing for Gharridan. All he wanted was a sovereign that he could control.

When Vladimir asked me if I thought he should let William die had Taryn not been involved, I would've been a liar if I said that I had never considered it. In fact, it was something I'd thought about many times. It invaded my thoughts in the middle of the night, circled my mind during the long days in the saddle. If William were gone, he could no longer vouch for himself in the matter of King Arguis. A shiver ran down my spine as the image of King Arguis' body sprawled on the ground, surrounded by blood, flashed through my mind. I could still hear the sound of the guards pounding on the study doors, the splinters of wood as they tore their way into the room—but I couldn't bring myself to condemn William. What William had done was wrong, but overshadowing that fault with another wrong wouldn't justify the situation, and I knew he was acting under the queen's orders. Zedekiah's face popped into my mind with his sickly pale skin and snow-white hair. I frowned. His situation had been different. Zedekiah deserved to die. He had no soul, no moral compass on which to stand. He was a vile, evil creature, and death had been too merciful an ending for him. While William's actions might suggest otherwise, he wasn't inherently evil, and the fault for his hatred of me lay entirely with his mother.

I wished she didn't hate me.

Something wet dripped from my nose, and I lifted a hand to catch it. Two spots of bright red blood stared back at me, their hue almost matching the color of my hair. I pulled a dirty, wrinkled handkerchief from my pocket, wiping the blood on it and then holding it against my nose. The nose bleeds were not a simple annoyance. They were terrifying. Nothing like this had ever happened before, yet I had also never healed this many people in such a short amount of time. After King Roland's death, I'd suppressed my ability, something the queen had encouraged. It took years for me to realize that his death had not been my fault, yet sometimes I still wondered if it had been. I knew little about the Radonaya. They were mysterious and rare. Perhaps continuing to heal this many people would eventually kill me.

"Lady Katherine?"

I rolled my eyes at the formal address, looking over at the guard. I'd already forgotten his name, and the word 'snout' immediately came to mind. His nose was the biggest and longest I had ever seen, sticking out from his face like a handle on a water pitcher.

I lifted my eyebrows.

"I believe the village is waiting just up ahead."

I brought my gaze forward, squinting and barely able to make out the fuzzy outline of a village in the distance. My mouth drew in a straight line. Even without Vladimir, the last few towns had been strangely friendly, but there was no telling how a town felt about the Radonaya until we entered it.

My heels tapped at Flicker's sides, urging her into a trot, and the other horses followed suit. Weariness still clung to my body, but I ignored it, pushing the exhaustion to the back of my mind and trying to find renewed strength. I removed the handkerchief from my nose, dabbing at it a few times to ensure that the bleeding had stopped. Once I was satisfied that it had, I stuffed it back into my pocket, eyes looking to the village that slowly came into focus as we drew closer.

The shops were small and the houses few, but everything here was built with great detail taken into mind. Different designs and swirls decorated the buildings, the door frames carved into pleasing shapes. I remained quiet while the soldiers conversed with several of the villagers, asking after any that required a physician. My eyes roved over the people, noting their neat dress that spoke of wealth and of the nervous glances they cast between one another.

"Ah, there is one who could benefit from the touch of a Radonaya." The man who spoke was short, his eyes flitting between us with fear. "She's been sick for a few weeks now. I-I can take you to her."

Snout nodded his appreciation, but I cocked my head in suspicion as we followed the man. Something about the mood of the town felt … *off*. I pushed the apprehension away, thankful that there was at least one person willing to let me use the power of the Radonaya on them, but I still kept a watchful look out. The house he led us to hovered at the edge of town with a spiked fence surrounding it. No grandeur graced this building, no intricate designs. Rot ate away at the wood, the left side of the house crumbling beneath the neglect.

"This is where you're keeping your sick?" I questioned.

The short man's gaze darted from the house back to me. "We didn't know if it was contagious."

Exhaustion overcame me as I dismounted, my legs wobbling. I placed a hand against Flicker's side for support. The last village sat only a day from here, and I'd healed more there in one day than I had in any other place. I'd barely stayed awake for the ride today. I made my way up the porch, the dilapidated steps groaning beneath my feet, threatening to snap from the weight. When I pressed against the door, it swung open, strangely quiet. No fire burned in the hearth. The only light came from a small window and the gaps between the planks of wood. I frowned with distaste. This was no place to house a sick person.

"Don't get too close," I warned Snout.

A mound of blankets was stacked on a lifted cot. They stirred slightly at my entrance. I knelt beside the body and dug through the blankets until I could find a face. Her eyes were closed, head tilted to the side. My fingers ran across her skin, but I detected no fever. *Strange*, I thought. I placed my palm across her forehead, my touch reaching out, trying to find the sickness. Around me, the air tightened, drawing breath. I reached further, eyebrows furrowed in concentration, but there was—

Nothing.

There was nothing.

My eyes snapped open to find the woman staring up at me, brown eyes filled with fear.

I stumbled away from her in shock, tripping on the floorboards.

"You're not—" I cut off, hearing the sound of hoofbeats in the distance.

I rushed out the door, blood pumping through my veins.

"Run! It's a—"

Snout suddenly grabbed me, twisting me around until I faced the door again. Before I could struggle against him, I felt the impact of the two arrows embedding in his back. I spun, finding the approaching soldiers outside the fence before I caught Snout as the weight of his body fell against me. I stumbled backward into the house, managing to hold my grip on Snout until the door was shut.

"Get away," Snout mumbled, struggling to draw breath as his tunic turned dark with blood. "Vladimir said—"

I saw the life draining from his face, threatening to disappear. One of the arrows had struck dangerously close to his heart.

"No!" I yelled, hearing the other Gharridan soldiers volleying back at the enemy.

I would not let him die for me.

I placed a hand around each arrow shaft. His chest barely rose and fell. Blood stained my fingers, pooled on the floor, soaked into my dress. I reached out, only to find Snout hanging on by the barest thread of life. I could feel him slipping through my fingers, and I cried out in frustration, holding on to him with all the strength left within me. Blood ran from my nostrils, trailing over my lips. The air around me grew too tight to draw breath. Colors exploded in every shade of the spectrum around me. I tried to close the wounds, but I didn't know if I could close them in time. I felt my skin grow cold, sweat dripping from my brow, strength draining from my body. So close. I was so close. A blood-curdling scream ripped out of my body as I desperately tried to pull Snout away from death, but the corners of my vision blackened, a dark contrast from the burst of color.

My arms stiffened at my sides, sight leaving me as a ringing pulsated in my ears, the darkness closing around me, squeezing away the air, squeezing away the life from me as I fought to keep him alive. The world dissipated into nothing, and I couldn't breathe, couldn't see. Darkness overcame me—

And I slipped away.

CHAPTER THIRTY-SIX

CAPTAIN VERONE VERIFIED two more council members with Vladimir, but he also discovered three in favor of the Crown. Finnigan had still not returned. His absence smelled of suspicion, and anxiety mounted within me. We only had a few allies, and with Finnigan gone, the list ran shorter. I didn't personally know the man, but Verone insisted he could be instrumental in swaying the council back over to Vladimir's side—and we needed all the help we could get.

I continued visiting Marco, but he didn't speak to me again. We just sat in silence as he stared mindlessly out the window, his words out of reach. I wanted to scream in frustration. I could tell Marco held something bottled up inside that was aching to get out. It was like we stood on opposite sides of a sandy shore, him on one side and me on the other, aware of each other's presence but too far away to communicate, the turbulent water too violent to cross. We needed a bridge in order to reach each other, but I didn't know what that bridge might be or how to build it. When Marco had spoken to me, it was like he had found a boat and was paddling toward me, struggling against the current. He would shout a few words to me, trying to get through, but then the water would carry him away again.

When I wasn't sitting with Marco, I was scouring my father's books for information about the massacre or the poison, but I continued to come up dry. None of the information within the pages seemed relevant. One of the books on plants held massive amounts of handwritten notes with different methods and concoctions for the handling of various herbs and what ailments they treated, but nothing about a poison deadly enough to kill an entire court.

I picked up the book of children's stories, mindlessly flipping through the pages, seeing but not reading. I found myself staring at the picture of my mother, unable to look away. My fingers gingerly touched the paper as if I could feel her skin once again, but I only felt the stiff smoothness of the paper. I shut the book, hand running over the worn leather of the front cover. I frowned, running my fingers over the leather again, thinking I'd imagined it, but I hadn't. The leather bowed in the middle and didn't lay flat like it should. My fingers pressed harder against it, and they glided over a little bump, the most subtle of indentions. I flipped up the front cover to stare down its edge. The center of the cover definitely had a tiny bulge. I felt along every inch, looking for any kind of hidden opening. At the base of the book, so close to the spine that I almost couldn't see it, a small, tiny slit pierced the leather, shorn so perfectly that it was almost imperceptible to the eye.

I wiggled my finger inside, the opening barely big enough for two of my small fingers to pass. They brushed the edge of a foreign object. I thought my heart stopped for a moment. It took some maneuvering and interesting angles, but I managed to work the mystery out, scraping it along the edges of the opening and wondering how someone had jimmied it in there in the first place. A piece of yellowed, folded paper rested between my two fingers, worn with age, the edges brittle. Ever so carefully, I unfolded the parchment, revealing a curved script spread across its page.

Writing this out could have me hanged for treason, but I must remove these thoughts from my head. I have no one else to share them with. I always looked up to Gabriel, but he is not the man I thought him to be. I write these words with anger; I can feel it coursing through me. He knew from the beginning what would happen when they found out, but he didn't care. This is madness. I'm going back for her. I won't leave her to die. Gabriel threatened to excommunicate me from the Kavari, but I'm willing to accept that fate. It isn't right. Gabriel may have ended the war, but it was the innocents who paid the cost. He should no longer hold his position of power. I feel I must burn these words over fear of their discovery.

I stared at the page in shock. My father had written this, but for some reason had never burned it. He'd kept it tucked away, a paper condemning him of treason. I'd never heard anything but good spoken of Gabriel, yet it appeared my father had thought differently. I read the letter over and over, nearly committing it to memory, before sticking it back into its little hole. A few flecks of the page fell away, but the center of the paper remained intact. A thought pricked at the back of my mind, tempting an idea. I tried to discount it, but as I ran the words of the letter through my mind, it became more difficult. The thought grew and began to fester until I let the book fall to the mattress and hurried through the castle to the library.

Once inside the massive room, I avoided the scholars, making my way to the back where a narrow door led to a cramped study. The historian looked up from his scroll, his spectacles perched low on his nose.

He frowned when I asked him about the massacre.

"You're going very far back, Miss Gallows."

"Could you please at least tell me what you know?" I pressed.

He sighed, motioning for me to sit on one of the wooden stools as he ventured out into the library, returning with several books. He explained everything William and Captain Verone had already touched on, but I hadn't gotten what I wanted yet. I still felt like something was missing.

"The sister of King Dorjan, what do you know about her? Do you know her name?"

The historian opened a thick book beside him and scanned the pages. "What is your interest with her?"

I shrugged. "It just seems strange that she was pronounced dead, but her body wasn't with the royal family."

"The only thing that is odd is that they never found her body. A servant claimed that she was supposed to have been with her brother, but Dorjan claimed that she had already returned. Her body was not identified in the massacre; however, many weren't. The royal family was buried in the royal tomb, but there were so many bodies that most of them were buried in a mass grave."

He placed his finger on the page, sliding it across the paper until it came to a stop halfway down the page.

"Ah, here. Djara. That was her name."

Djara.

The name sounded very Algarian.

"Do you know how old she was?" I asked.

He shook his head. "Not exactly. She was too young for Gabriel to consider an adult, but not young enough to be a child."

Twenty-five years ago.

I scooted my stool back, rising and striding away. "Thank you for your time, historian."

My stomach roiled as I left the library, and I clutched at my gut. It was just wishful thinking. I knew it was, but the idea wouldn't leave me and continued to strengthen in my mind, blocking out everything else. I squinted as I realized someone was calling my name, so lost in my own thoughts that I hadn't noticed. I turned, finding William giving me a questioning look, but I didn't want to talk right now. I hurried back to my room, flinging the door open, startling when I found that William had followed me inside.

"I'd like to be alone, William."

He ignored my request and shut the door behind him.

"You look like you've seen a ghost." William appeared concerned. "What's going on?"

I touched my cheek, realizing that my face must be pale.

Twenty-five years ago.

"Djara," I whispered breathlessly.

William lowered his brows. "What do you mean?"

"Djara was the name of King Dorjan's sister, the one they

never identified."

Confusion washed over him. "What does she have to do with any of this?"

I'm going back for her.

I stepped away from him, pacing back and forth and swiping a hand across my clammy brow. "I know it probably sounds crazy, but I just—I just have this feeling in my gut, and it won't go away."

"Taryn?"

"It's just so strange that Marco spoke about that, and with the perfect timeline and the massacre taking place in Northunder …" I trailed off. "There was always a sadness there and a hope of reconciliation, and she said they were in the north."

William stepped closer. "What are you talking about?"

I won't leave her to die.

I took a deep breath, meeting his eyes. "I think Djara may have been my mother."

CHAPTER THIRTY-SEVEN

VLADIMIR

OUR BATTALION GREW with every town we passed through, the numbers in our small army tripling, but it wouldn't be enough.

The Gharridan outpost loomed before us larger than life, like a fire-breathing dragon. Behind me rode five rows of cavalrymen followed by foot soldiers. Each man wielded a deadly blade, but I hoped our presence here wouldn't force them to resort to their weapons. We only had one shot, and this would be my great test, to see how much the soldiers of Gharridan trusted me.

The sun blazed red in the sky, an angry, glowing ball of fury as it navigated its way behind the jagged mountains. I needed an army possessing as much passion as the sun's colors and as intense as its glare.

The messenger rode out ahead of us, the white flag in his hand billowing in the wind. The fortified gate cracked open, and he disappeared inside. The message he carried made our intentions clear. The gamble was if the commander in charge of this outpost was willing to hear me out. Our battalion continued its advance, and I kept my eyes on the guards patrolling atop the wall as they watched our approach. This outpost had enough soldiers to obliterate us if they so desired, but watching an unknown army march to your doorstep was unnerving nonetheless.

When we were within a hundred yards of the wall, the front gate opened, spitting out my messenger and a rider who I assumed was the man in charge. I pulled back on Dante's reins, the men behind me coming to a stop as well. I noted the speckled horse beneath the captain, the sharp angles of his face, and his thick eyebrows. A handlebar mustache curved above his lips. His uniform was pressed, a vast display of ranks displayed across his right shoulder.

Lyle.

General Lyle.

I knew him by face and name, but that was all. I'd never dealt with him personally.

The two horses stopped before us, snow spraying up around their hooves in a cloud of white. The expression masking the general's face was unreadable. Was he friend or foe? His gaze roved over me, up and down, taking in the lines of men halted behind me.

"I was told Queen Adamara declared the Kavari disbanded." His gravelly voice grated like stone against stone.

Dante pranced in agitation.

"She did," I said.

General Lyle observed my fidgeting horse. "Then I could lose my position for even speaking to you. Everyone within the Guard of Gharridan was given orders to place you under arrest and bring you back to the capital. Alive."

"I'm sure you were."

The brisk air tensed between us as the silence lengthened, but I refused to show my hand until he did as well.

"If your position is in such danger," I ventured, "then why are you here?"

General Lyle glanced back at the outpost. "I've been in the military a long time, Vladimir. I can't profess to knowing much about politics, but I love my country. My tactics are good, as well as my perception. I have a talent for picking out things that don't seem quite right."

The unspoken message rang loud and clear.

He didn't like the orders from the capital. He was willing to hear me out.

My hope sparked.

If he believed in me, perhaps there were others who did as well.

"I'm here because I love my country too," I said.

General Lyle chewed on his lip for a moment and then raised his brows in question, waiting for my reasoning.

"The rumors of me fleeing the capital with a fugitive are true, but I only did what I had to because I believe the fugitive was wrongly accused. They were not given the time or opportunity to prove their innocence. I do not wish for any more division within our country. Only unity. And truth. And justice."

General Lyle shifted in his saddle, his mind working. "What

is it exactly that you're asking me to do?"

I hesitated, carefully weaving my answer together. "Brenden will be marching for Gharridan's borders. I need every able-bodied soldier you can spare armed and ready to march to the capital, where we will rally for battle. Brenden likely won't begin their march until spring, but we need to be ready in case they decide to brave the winter."

He eyed me, suspicion still hovering around him. "That's all?"

I took a deep breath. "I also need enough support from the Gharridan people to sway the council to my favor and reinstate the Kavari."

Now was the moment of truth.

General Lyle nodded slowly, as if he had been expecting my answer. "I see."

The wind whistled in my ears, the cold biting at my skin, but the general did not speak.

"Can I count on your support?"

He cocked his head. "If you succeed, then all is good and well, but if you do not succeed, what happens then?"

I swallowed. *Then every man who aids me will be held accountable.* General Lyle would lose his position, his career—possibly even his life.

"I think you know what happens."

His expression implied he already knew but wanted to make sure I was aware of what I was asking of him.

"I don't know you, Vladimir, but I did know Michael, and he was the wisest man I ever met. If he trusted you to take his position, then I'll trust you on your judgment of this matter. Michael would not have named you his successor without good cause and faith."

I nodded my thanks as a wave of sadness rushed over me. Doors in my life that should have remained shut were opened because of Michael.

"I can give you what you ask, but just because I am willing to take your side does not mean that everyone else is. These soldiers see themselves as servants of Gharridan, but whether they see the Crown or the Kavari as the true authority, that will vary by individual. No matter the cause, I will not ask my men to betray the beliefs they hold solidly in their hearts."

The general would support me while I was here and give me what I asked, but he could not guarantee my safety—nor the soldiers' support.

"I understand."

He turned his speckled horse back to the outpost, and my men and I followed, a wave of relief spreading through the battalion. I hid the smile that tried to stretch across my lips.

One step closer.

CHAPTER THIRTY-EIGHT

❖

KATHERINE

NO DARKNESS HAD ever held me prisoner this long. I floated in the abyss somewhere between life and death, aware of nothing. Memories were my only comfort, memories of a time long ago when I was younger and had first tasted death.

I remembered my pale skin stretched across the bones of my body, giving me the look of a skeletal creature. I remembered the pangs of starvation that clawed at my stomach. I hadn't eaten in weeks. My city was no friend to beggars. The harsh winter kept the nobles huddled inside, squandering any hope of charity. There was a feeling of the darkness closing in, of weightlessness, but my vision had distorted as I faded in and out of consciousness. I remembered opening my eyes as someone laid a heavy blanket over me, dribbling water between my lips and pressing a loaf of bread into my hand. At the sight of the food, my soul had renewed with hope, and I managed to swallow a few bites. Eventually, I had mustered the strength to crawl into the recess of a wall, fearful that if any other beggars saw my blanket and food that they would be stolen. When the sun's rays broke across the sky after days of only wintry clouds, their warmth ignited the desire for life in me. I didn't know how long I lay there for, rationing the bread to keep myself alive, but I never forgot the cold feeling of death, the despair of watching my life slip away and not being able to do anything about it— the exact way I felt now.

A sharp pain pricked my shoulder in the present, and I squirmed to get away, stilling once I comprehended my awareness to the pain. With a gasp, a rush of air filled my lungs, popping my eyes open and sending me sprawling upright. A ragged breath shuddered out of me, eyes adjusting to the dim light of my surroundings. A dark-haired woman sat beside me, soft wrinkles lining her skin. Her narrow, bright blue eyes bore into mine. I knew I should be afraid, that I should try to run, but an understanding swelled within the depths of her gaze.

A wave of nausea swept over me, and I wretched over the side of the bed, emptying my stomach of only bile. The straw of the mattress stabbed at my back as I leaned back into it, each of my limbs aching with weariness. My eyes drifted closed, and a small exhale escaped between my chapped lips.

"Am I a prisoner?" I asked.

"Only to your exhaustion."

The woman's voice sounded disinterested, bored even. I cracked an eyelid to study her, noting her plain clothing and pinned-up hair.

"What happened?" My voice cracked, my throat miserably dry. The woman reached for a glass on the table beside me and lifted it to my lips. The cold water shocked my system, awakening my senses and moistening my throat.

"You ventured into the wrong village."

Voices carried from outside, and my gaze drifted over my surroundings. The shutters were drawn tightly, explaining the dim light, but we were in a constricting one-room cottage. Fire crackled in a small hearth, a cast-iron pot hanging from a hook above it. An earthy smell permeated the air, a shelf of dried herbs next to the fire.

"I thought this town had no healer."

The woman's attention cut to the door as if waiting for it to open. "It doesn't. Not officially, but the villagers come to me when they are sick."

The voices outside quieted.

"Where are the soldiers?" I tensed in anticipation of her answer. "The one who was shot, did he—did he—"

I couldn't bring myself to say the words aloud.

She frowned, throwing me a distasteful look. "He's alive, but what you did was stupid. You'd be dead right now if it wasn't for me."

I bristled at her tone. "And he'd be dead if I hadn't healed him."

She disapproved of my answer. "You have to have full strength to save someone dangling on the brink of death. If you're already exhausted, it will kill you. Healing others drains your own energy. Your body should have given you signs."

I stared at her in shock, my limbs turning to stone. "How do you know that?"

She scoffed. "How do I know what?"

I sat up, fighting the weariness. "You wouldn't know my body was giving me signs unless—"

She cocked an eyebrow. "Unless what?"

Words left me. "Unless ..."

"Unless I was a Radonaya?"

The door burst open, banging against the back wall with a resounding thwack. "Is she awake yet?"

One of the Gharridan soldiers stomped into the room at the sight of me sitting up in the bed, but I could barely rip my eyes from the woman.

"You can't be," I whispered.

She stood, indicating that our conversation was finished, but I was nowhere done.

"She is," the woman stated. "But she needs a few more hours rest before you leave."

"Leave?" My voice sounded as if it belonged to someone else. Anger reverberated within it. I'd never even seen another Radonaya before, let alone met one. I wasn't going anywhere.

The soldier stepped closer, brows furrowed. "It's not safe to stay here."

I ignored his demands, pushing past him to follow the woman outside. The village sat on the incline below us, the woman's cottage hovering at the edge of the tree line.

"You're not a Radonaya," I accused. "Their hair is blood red."

I tripped over an exposed root in my awkward gait between a walk and a stumble. My palms dug into the hard ground, skidding along the earth and creating small abrasions running up and down my skin. I grimaced at the pain, grinding my teeth as

I pushed myself up and gathered my feet beneath me.

The woman placed her hands on her hips. "You shouldn't be outside the house."

"You shouldn't lie to me."

The woman tsked, closing the distance between us and grabbing my injured hands. I jerked back, but her hold tightened as she turned my palm upward, placing her other hand above the abrasion. I swallowed in fear, wincing. Warmth flooded my skin, a sense of energy seeming to radiate over where her hand hovered. She pulled away, and I stared at my skin. The dust and dried blood remained, but the wounds were closed. The abrasion puckered a little, like a wound that had already been healed, but nothing else evidenced the previous cut.

"Why would I lie to you?"

I gawked at her. "But your hair …" I trailed off, unable to muster an intelligible response.

Her expression morphed into curiosity. "You've never met another Radonaya, have you?"

I shook my head.

"Seeing as you are a Kavari, or were, I thought you would have come across another by now," she mused.

I noticed the other soldiers around us for the first time, shifting uncomfortably on their feet. Another wave of nausea washed over me, and I clutched at my stomach, trying to keep the bile down. When I felt steady enough to stand upright, I met her directly in the eyes.

"I've searched this kingdom high and low. I have never found another like me. Please, I need answers."

She chewed on her lip, glancing at the soldiers before ushering me back inside. I stumbled through the door, falling back onto the bed but remaining in a seated position. I doubled over as a coughing spasm wracked my body until I could barely draw any breath. The woman handed me a glass of water, which I immediately downed.

"My name is Colleen," the woman offered, still watching me curiously.

"Katherine."

"Yes, I know."

She sounded like William.

"Do all Radonayas not possess the blood-red hair?"

"No. Every Radonaya is born with it,"

"Why?"

She shrugged. "I don't know. We're so rare that it's not something you can really study."

"So you don't know why we are the way we are."

Her head shook hesitantly. "I've only met one other besides you, and she knew little more than me."

"Is she still around?"

Her head shook again.

I studied her. "You're not afraid of me. Do you not think I killed King Roldan?"

A faint smile touched her lips, her mind wandering. "You didn't kill the king, child."

My brows drew together. No one had ever spoken so confidently on the matter before. "How can you be so sure? What if I did?"

Her chin lifted. "As long as your hair retains the hue of fresh blood, you have not used your gift to harm someone."

I cocked my head. "No. Our blood-red hair is counted a symbol of death for the people we could not save."

Colleen chuckled. "It's nothing more than superstition. Who you are and aren't able to save has nothing to do with the color of your hair."

"Then why is your hair black?"

Her mouth set in a thin line, eyes growing hard. "If you've never met a Radonaya, and your hair is still bloody red, I guess you wouldn't know."

"Know what?"

She stayed quiet, as if debating whether or not to answer me. "Radonaya can do more than just heal, Katherine."

My blood rose. I stood at the edge of a dangerous revelation. "What do you mean?"

"You already know that we can give life through healing, but …" She hesitated. "We can also take it."

My eyes narrowed. "Take it how?"

"Why do you think so much superstition surrounds someone with the ability to heal?" She cocked an eyebrow. "Just like when you can feel the infection and the pain inside someone and draw it out, you can also draw the life out of them. The cost of choosing to kill someone bleeds the vibrance from your hair, leaving it dark and lifeless."

The hair rose on the back of my neck, prickling down my arms.

"What is it known as?" A tremor touched my voice.

Her face remained calm as a breezeless day. "It's called the touch of death."

CHAPTER THIRTY-NINE

TARYN

WILLIAM STARED AT me like I'd lost my mind. He had every right to. I knew how absurd the words sounded coming out of my mouth, yet I felt they held a connection.

"What?" he questioned.

I paced back and forth, thinking through my jumbling thoughts and trying to come up with a clear way of explaining. "Something you have to understand about my family, William, is that my mother hardly ever talked about her past, and when she did, it was extremely vague. I'm lucky I learned what little I did about her."

William leaned against the desk, skeptical, but nodded for me to continue.

"One of the things she would speak about was her family

in the north, and how she hoped that I would one day be able to reconcile with them."

"Algarar is not exactly north, Taryn."

I shook my head, "No, but Djara's town was called Northunder, and my mother was just cryptic enough that she might have left out the second part. I also know that she married my father twenty-five years ago."

"Which would be around the time of the massacre."

"Her last name was Illdalore. I don't know why a royal would have a surname; she also had a crest." I pulled my mother's clasp out of my pocket and showed it to William. "Do you know any of the Algarian crests?"

"I don't even know all of the crests in my own country, Taryn, let alone a foreign country's."

I pursed my lips, deep in thought.

"I thought you said your mother came from somewhere called Dalendria?"

My face fell, but I thought quickly. "That also could've been cryptic. She could've been talking about a house or a shop, a place in Northunder."

William rubbed the back of his neck. "It is strange, but it also could be coincidental."

I lifted my eyebrows. "But *this* coincidental?"

William hesitated, his breath catching. "I don't know, it's—"

He stopped, unable to procure a solid answer. There was something here. Even William couldn't ignore the pattern. The facts held every possibility.

William shook his head. "*If* it's true, then why would your father keep you and your mother hidden away in secret?"

The question deflated me as my hope dissipated, but a

thought struck me. With horror, I looked directly into William's eyes. "What if that's how he did it? How Gabriel got into the castle and poisoned everyone?" I bit my lip. "What if he used her, tricked her into helping with the massacre?"

William froze, considering the thought. "That would explain why she hid away her whole life, why no one could know about you and her. If Dorjan knew what she had done, even unknowingly, Algarar would be out for blood, and they wouldn't stop until they'd been avenged."

The longer I let the thought fester, the more it horrified me, and the more it solidified the truth in my mind. The idea became too much to process. It explained nearly everything, but it also brought unimaginable pain. I didn't have a way to prove my lineage while in Gharridan, but I wondered if I could discover the truth by traveling to Algarar. Assuming I was right, it still left the question of how Marco knew about it. My parents were so secretive that I couldn't see my father sharing this information with him, but I had to remind myself that my father had sent the missive we never recovered to Marco. The two had been Kavari together for twenty years. There had to have been some sort of brotherhood between them, a great amount of trust. Marco was the only one who could give me the answers I needed, but also the only one who couldn't.

A letter slid beneath my door, asking me to join the ladies for tea at the previous location in exactly one hour. I'd never drunk tea with the noblewomen, and I never would. I stuffed the letter deep into a drawer. The message was from Verone but written covertly so as not to attract suspicion should anyone find it. I twitched with nervousness, realizing that if Captain Verone had risked slipping that underneath my door, the matter must be urgent. I laced on my boots with fumbling fingers, wishing he'd requested to meet sooner. A path wore in the carpet where I traveled back and forth, waiting for the time to tick by. It crept tortuously slow. Not being able to stand it any longer, I left early, figuring that I might have to lose my guards even though they hadn't been trailing me much as of late.

I peeked my head outside the room, but no guards were in sight. I stepped down the hall as softly as possible to keep from alerting anyone to my presence. When I was far enough away from my room, I kept my chin up as I passed the guards, possessing the air of someone who was allowed to be there. No one appeared to be following me, so I only diverted down one corridor instead of three.

Darkness filled the room as before, but a little light filtered in through the covered window. A twinge of mustiness mixed in with the damp air. My gaze flicked to the right as a man who was not Verone emerged from the shadows.

I took a step back, drawing my dagger and facing the enemy.

"Who are you?" I demanded.

The door creaked open, distracting me. Verone entered. He saw my weapon and quickly shut the door behind him.

"It's Finnigan, Taryn."

I looked back to the stranger, his face growing vaguely familiar in the dim light. I'd never formally met Finnigan, but I recognized him as one of the council members.

"Where have you been?" I snapped, irritated that I'd been

blindsided by his presence. I shoved the dagger back into the sheath at my side.

"With Vladimir." Finnigan smiled, his expression personable and inviting.

My eyes widened. "What? Why, are they okay?"

"They're doing fine," he answered, walking closer to us. A lock of curly black hair spilled forward over his bronze skin, brown eyes bright. "Katherine is traveling from village to village healing the sick and impaired, trying to win the people of Gharridan back over to her side."

I blinked. Last I'd heard, they were trying to get Katherine somewhere safe and not leave her out in the open, but the idea sounded very Katherine. I doubted it thrilled Vladimir, but the plan was good. It would accomplish far more than staying in hiding ever would.

"What about Vladimir?" I asked.

Finnigan glanced between us. "He's going to return to the capital shortly."

"Is that safe?"

He didn't yet have the support he needed for a successful return. It was too premature.

Finnigan waved off my concern dismissively. "As soon as he has the support that he needs, he's going to come and challenge the queen. If we can convert enough of the council to his side, then we'll be left in good standing, and if Katherine can win over the people of Gharridan, that will help get her a pardon."

"Will we have enough council members to overturn the queen's disbandment of the Kavari?" I asked.

Finnigan looked to Captain Verone. "We will. I'll convince

them. The queen can't know about this, though, not until we have full support." His hands gripped the edge of the table. "Where are our current standings?"

Verone's face remained stoic. "Counting you, we've managed to make our way up to five, but that still leaves sixteen council members opposed. Most I've spoken to have been unmovable. Hart remains adamant with his position, and he'll do everything in his power to ensure Katherine is executed."

Finnigan smiled grimly. "Hart will be a problem. I'll find a way to take care of him."

I glanced between the two, wondering what 'take care of him' involved.

Finnigan continued, "We need to seed doubt for the Crown's ability to rule, level the playing field."

"How?"

Finnigan flashed a devilish smile. "I have my ways, and if some of the council members refuse to be swayed, we'll resort to leverage."

Finnigan knew the court. He knew the council, how they worked and how to play them.

"And if one of them decides to talk?" Verone pressed.

Something dark lingered behind Finnigan's eyes. "Trust me. They won't."

CHAPTER FORTY

SUSPICION LINGERED IN every corner of the outpost, lurking in the shadows and in every eye we met. The small battalion made no grand entrance, but from the looks of the soldiers, they weren't happy about us being here. I couldn't blame them. General Lyle had essentially committed treason, but if they went against him, they likewise would be committing treason.

Nic swaggered up beside me. "I think everyone in this outpost would like to kill us."

"Not all," I grumbled. "But most. Watch your back."

Wherever we stepped, it was like a wave of the sea parting before us. No one wished to get within five feet of a treasonous legion.

I sighed. "This isn't going to work."

Nic eyed the men around us. "What made you think it would?"

I glared at him. "I'll have to speak to the entire outpost tomorrow, try to convince them to at least compromise on the situation. They can't all hate me, but most of them will fear the Crown more. Their service to the kingdom pays for their livelihood."

A mischievous smile crept up the corner of Nic's mouth. "You want me to work my magic on them tonight? Convince them all how great of a leader you are?"

"I'd rather you be alive in the morning, Nic. Your 'magic' seems more effective in giving others a desire to strangle you."

He opened his mouth, then quickly shut it as he comprehended my words, his expression almost pouting.

I let out a dry laugh, clapping him on the shoulder. "Don't take it personally, Nic."

Our men dispersed throughout the bunkhouses, taking up room wherever a bed could be had. I'd warned them to only travel in groups, to never leave without another soldier of my battalion beside them. I wouldn't trust anyone in this outpost unless they gave me a reason to.

"Do you think this General Lyle will keep to his word?"

My gaze shot to the general atop the walls, overseeing our battalion's entry into the camp.

"That's something we'll have to find out."

CHAPTER FORTY-ONE

TARYN

THE WIND RIPPLED through my hair, separating the strands into a chaotic mess as Stryder thundered beneath me, eating up the ground between him and Othello with every stride. William leaned forward over the white horse, the animal's thick mane billowing out behind him. Stryder surged, pent up with excitement as we closed in on them. Three strides. Two. One. I sat up, easing up on the reins, much to Stryder's chagrin. Othello flew ahead, crossing the invisible finish line first.

A barrage of dirt sprayed around the white horse as he dug his heels into the ground, and William wheeled him around to face me.

"You let me win."

The accusation shot through me. His bad temper had been

flaring before we ever left the stables, his mind distracted and somewhere else. Distant.

I shrugged beneath his stare, brushing it off. "Stryder needed to be humbled. He can't think he's the best at everything just because of his bloodline."

William scowled.

I rolled my eyes as he trotted away, urging Stryder to catch up. I chewed on my lip, debating, then swerved Stryder in front of Othello, cutting him off.

"What's going on, William?"

He looked at everything besides me. The ground. The castle walls. The looming forest. He shook his head. "Nothing's going on."

I maneuvered Stryder up next to Othello, my leg brushing William's as my gaze bore into his.

"You should know by now that you can't lie to me. Not without getting caught."

He remained silent, finding a sudden interest in the wandering breeze.

"Is it your mother?" I asked. "I heard you arguing earlier."

He let out a hollow laugh. "You seem to have a tendency for overhearing things you shouldn't."

His eyes finally met mine, probing.

"It's not like you and her are quiet about—"

"Why did you come back, Taryn?"

His misplaced question caught me off guard, leaving me without an answer.

He leaned closer, trying to find the answer hidden behind the wall I forced between us. "There's a reason you came back. I just can't figure out what it is."

His stare burned so intensely I feared he would see right through me, see the thread of deception I had woven around his heart. I'd gained his trust, but I hadn't been able to get rid of every flicker of doubt. Uncertainty still lingered.

My mouth went dry, the close proximity and his expectant, perceptive demeanor confusing me, making me think he'd discovered part of the truth.

He pulled away, as if broken out of a trance. "I'm sorry, that was uncalled for. I don't know what came over me."

His expression cased over into the distracted air he'd borne before.

I found my voice. "Is that what your mother and you were discussing?"

He turned back as if confused, then shook his head. "No, that wasn't relevant. It's just been—" He cut off, guiding Othello back toward the stables.

My true motive has been bothering him ever since I'd returned; I'd known that, but something else had brought the sudden question to the surface.

"We've been through multiple near-death experiences together, William, if there's something going on that you want to talk about ..." My voice faded.

I saw his struggle out of the corner of my eye, the war within over whether to open up or keep whatever he was dealing with caged inside.

I'd found that I gained more of his trust when he was at his most vulnerable.

The thought sickened me.

"It's nothing I can speak of," he managed.

Guilt and regret laced his words, mixed with a twinge of

sorrow. I'd never seen him this beat-up about something. Did it have to do with King Arguis? Curiosity piqued within me, wanting to know, but I'd be stepping out of place to ask it.

He changed the subject. "Have you uncovered anything else about your mother?"

I shook my head, swiping the hair out of my eyes and tucking it behind my ear. "Not yet. I've been searching but have yet to find anything that would confirm it."

He nodded, our jilted conversation drifting into silence. I was left with a sense of dread, fearing that what he was brushing off was more serious than I cared to imagine.

CHAPTER FORTY-TWO

I T'S CALLED THE *touch of death*.

Colleen's words ripped through me, the strangeness of the superstition surrounding the Radonaya making sense in my mind after so many years. What she said was true. Why else would someone bestowed with the power of healing be so despised?

"Why have I never heard of the touch of death before?" I asked.

"Because when a Radonaya uses it, they go into hiding. People often think them dead because they chose to not heal the person, and because they disappear so suddenly."

I stared at Colleen's dark locks, several loose wisps of hair curling around her narrow face. "How long does it take for it to ..." I trailed off, unsure.

"Days," she interjected. "My hair faded to a dull red, then brown, then black, as if the strands were decaying and rotting until it transformed into the color of death."

I wanted to ask her what had happened, why she had chosen to kill someone, but I feared such a personal probe might alienate her, and I still had far too many questions to ask. Her will was strong, but nothing about her personality seemed malicious or aggressive.

"Our healing ability, it is like magic then? Where does it come from? Where do *we* come from?"

Colleen shook her head. "So many questions. All asked out of order. It doesn't matter whether or not someone believes it's magic. It just is. As for where we come from, a Radonaya can come from anywhere, but most are born in one place in particular. It goes by another name within its walls, but you would know it as the City of Iso."

I stared at her. "Iso?"

She sucked her cheeks. "You're a Kavari, girl. Surely they've taught you about that."

"Yes, I know," I said defensively. "The City of Isolation."

Most people knew about it, the city that hadn't opened up to the outside world in over a hundred years. It was surrounded by a massive wall that offered no way in except through the main gate. The city was impenetrable, and anyone caught wandering too close was targeted by hidden sharpshooters. I'd never heard of anyone surviving an encounter, and the city was simply left alone. Some maps didn't even include the city on their maps.

"Is that where you came from?"

She frowned. "Maybe. It doesn't matter where I came

from."

"But how did you get out?"

"My backstory is not up for discussion." She eyed me.

At least she was answering questions about the Radonaya, even if she refused to tell me anything about herself.

"Could my parents be there?" I'd never dared to hope, never been brave enough to look for them—until now.

Colleen let out a laugh. "Your mother is dead, child."

I stiffened at her harsh words, the breath of hope that dared to fill me snatched from my lungs. "That's quite bold of you."

Her laughter faded, eyes growing somber. "No, I suppose you wouldn't know."

"Know what?"

"The mother of a Radonaya has always died after childbirth."

I stared at her. "But why—"

The cottage door burst open, slamming against the bricks. "Soldiers are coming, Katherine. If you don't leave now, they're going to kill you."

My heart ripped within me. I needed more answers, but answers would be useless to me if I was dead. I stumbled to my feet, moving to the door but then grabbing Colleen's arms. "Come with us. I need your insight. Please."

I saw it in her eyes before the words ever left her mouth. She shook her head. "I've stayed hidden this long for a reason, and I'd rather not be caught traveling alongside someone with a bounty on their head."

The soldier pulled me out into the yard. Hooves pounded the earth in the distance, an ominous rhythm that steadily grew closer. I needed more time. I had so many questions and she possessed the answers I wanted. Answers I so desperately needed. I turned to her, struggling in the soldier's grip, my eyes desperate.

"But—"

She helped shove my weak body onto Flicker's back, face hard as stone. "Go."

"Will you be here if I come back?"

She gave no answer.

The first soldier took off, and Flicker bolted after him. I gripped her sides with my legs, my hands buried in her mane as my muscles ached from the sudden exertion. I cast one final glimpse over my shoulder, watching Colleen until the trees blocked her from view. So close. So close to everything, and now it was all ripped away from me. Ripped away like my position in the Kavari, like my home in the orphanage, like Michael. The only father I had ever known.

Flicker surged ahead beneath me. My legs tightened against her sides. I would come back.

I swear it, I thought.

I would be back.

CHAPTER FORTY-THREE

TARYN

THE THING I missed the most about my mother was her voice. Soft, like a gentle breeze caressing my skin, but firm as a fierce windstorm. Her sharp brown eyes could cut you like a dagger and draw out all of your secrets with one look. Whenever the sun fell low in the sky and the fireflies lit the landscape with a million flashes of color, she would sing to me with her deep, honey-smooth voice until I drifted off into dreams. After her death I found it difficult to fall asleep with only silence for company, all too aware of the fact that I would never hear her voice again.

My family, in the north, I hope that one day you can reconcile with them.

I remembered the sadness in her eyes as she had spoken those words, a longing that I could never comprehend, but I hoped that now I could provide the reconciliation she had so desired. Since I'd relayed my suspicions to William, I hadn't found any other evidence of her heritage, but my heart told me that there was something here. The mystery spread out before me like an unfinished dress. I had most of the garment sewn together, but there was still something missing, a piece of fabric that I couldn't locate, and I couldn't finish the dress until I'd uncovered the last piece and stitched it all together.

I leaned against the cool windowsill, the night air tousling the wisps of hair around my face. Lights flickered in the city below, soon to be extinguished as it slept for the night. Looking out on such a vast city spreading out in every direction, filled with more people than I could comprehend, still took my breath away. I'd never experienced anything quite like it until leaving my home, and the constant press of people still unsettled me. Here, in my small room surrounded by four walls, I could almost imagine that I was by myself again. That I was safe.

The door crashed open, smacking against the far wall. I nearly jumped out of my skin at the commotion, eyes going wild as I reached for my knife. A breath shuddered out of me as I realized the individual barging into the room was William.

"William, what in the—"

He took a few staggering steps, clumsily reaching for the door and shutting it gently. When he turned back to me, his smile was lopsided.

"Sorry," he slurred, stumbling forward.

He barely took a few steps before tumbling into the bed, steadying himself before sitting on it.

My mouth fell open, shocked at his audacious behavior.

"William, are you—"

I didn't need to finish the question. I could smell the alcohol from here.

I shook my head, striding forward. "No, William, you can't be in here."

I tried to remove him from the room, but he pulled his hands away, shaking his head.

"No, no, no, I came to—to talk to you."

A real intelligent conversation this would be.

"You're drunk, William." My tone hinged with irritation.

He looked up at me, the same lopsided smile still on his face, breath reeking of alcohol and golden hair in disarray. "Am I?"

I rolled my eyes.

He stood to his feet, grabbing my shoulder to steady himself. "I always tell myself that I'm—that I'm not going to drink." He waved a finger in my face. "Every year I tell myself that, but …" He lost his train of thought for a moment. "But I always need to forget. It makes it easier."

I struggled to keep my shoulder up beneath the pressing weight of his hand. "Makes what easier?"

He looked down at me, heat radiating from his body. I squirmed uncomfortably.

"But this time, I can't stop thinking about you." He pressed closer. "Those—those devilish green eyes and that sharp tongue of yours."

I took a step back, but he followed, nearly tripping until I caught him, but then I was pinned between him and the wall.

"William—"

"Why did you do it, Taryn?" he whispered, breath hot

against my cheek. "Why did you come back?"

I tried to maneuver around him, but he was difficult to move, even drunk.

His glassy eyes bore into mine, searching for secrets. "I was so angry when I went up to the tower and you were gone. That you chose the Kavari over me."

I turned my face away, the reek of alcohol making me want to vomit. "Angry that you wouldn't have a prisoner for the rest of your life?"

"No, no." William pushed away from the wall, and I exhaled in relief, grateful for the space. "Not a prisoner … Needed, I needed you to understand." Emotion overcame him as his eyes grew watery. "Every day, I see it."

"See what?"

"See *him*." William pitched forward, barely managing to keep his balance. "Nightmares, oh the nightmares. Every night. Sword. In my hands. The king, King Arguis, lying dead on the floor. I try to pull it out, but I can never change it. When she told me her plan in the tent that night, I didn't think it was possible, thought she was crazy, but I didn't have a choice. If I had disobeyed her …" He shook his head at the thought. "Who knows what would have happened?"

So he did harbor regret.

Part of him still cared enough to know that what he had done was wrong. The thought filled me with hope.

He fell forward again, but I quickly sidestepped so that he was the one crashing against the wall. "And you"—his voice grew husky—"staring at me with those judgmental eyes, saying you've forgiven me, forgotten. I know you haven't. I know there's something you aren't telling me."

I swallowed, afraid to speak.

He squinted, as if trying to find the answer written on my skin. "You really do hate me, don't you?"

I locked eyes with him, unable to hold the truth back. "Yes."

His face transformed, growing more somber. "Sometimes I think about that night, in the dungeon." He tottered over to the bed, falling back against the covers, voice growing faint, words slurring together. "And I wonder, wonder what would've happened if I—if we had—"

He closed his eyes, arm thrown over his forehead, feet still resting on the ground. After a few quiet moments, his breathing evened out, and I let out a groan, throwing a glance at the door. I couldn't move him myself, and I wondered what was worse: him sleeping here, or the rumors that would spread if I asked one of the guards for help. His face had softened, the deep sleep making him appear younger than he was as the weight of the world lifted from his shoulders.

And I wonder what would've happened if I—if we had—

I had wondered too, wondered how different all of this might be if I hadn't said his name. Hadn't stopped him. But even if it had changed, he was still the crown prince, and I was simply the daughter of a Kavari. We could never change our stations, and he could never turn his back to his responsibilities. Besides, in that moment of vulnerability there was still a side to William that I hadn't seen yet, a side I didn't like. A side that made me hate him, and it made me grateful for whispering his name in the darkness of that dungeon, causing him to draw away.

I shook the thoughts from my mind, moving his feet until

he lay crossways on the bed and then spreading a blanket over him. I wouldn't want to be him when he woke up in the morning. He'd be nursing that headache for the foreseeable future. My nose twitched in distaste, wondering how anyone could willingly subject themselves to that kind of torture. I guessed, for some, the brief hours of forgetfulness was worth the pain.

I wasn't fond of the twinge of compassion that lit in my heart. William didn't deserve it, but knowing about the remorse over his actions deflated the bitterness in my heart toward him. Part of him was still human, at least. I wiggled one of the other blankets from underneath William and settled onto the plush rug. I considered just rolling him off the bed, but with his dead weight, he'd probably end up cracking his skull. A frown creased my forehead, wondering what he'd wanted to forget so much that it had driven him to this level of drunkenness, but more than anything, I just hoped one of us would be gone before I had to deal with him in the morning.

My eyes shut, but a thought still played through my mind, repeating itself over and over.

He'd shown remorse.

Which meant it was possible for him to change.

I held on to that hope, never wanting to let it go.

CHAPTER FORTY-FOUR

VLADIMIR

A DRAFT SHIVERED its way through the room, tickling across my skin and awakening me, but my eyes remained closed. I kept my breathing even, my ears perked and listening. The door to my room was open. I hadn't heard it creak, but I could sense it in the way the room sounded, how the air suddenly grew larger with a hallway to explore instead of only four solid walls. My fingers twitched beneath the blankets, curling around the hilt of my dagger.

Silence surrounded me, nothing unusual, but I still didn't open my eyes. Though my hearing denied it, every other sense in my body told me that something was off. I would lie here, and I would wait. My breaths threatened to accelerate, but I kept them steady, refusing to alert any intruders—whether or not they were with me.

The silence shifted as a soft sound emerged.

The sound of a weapon being drawn from a leather scabbard.

My eyes popped open as I raised my dagger in front of me, narrowly catching the blade swinging down toward my exposed neck. The muscles in my shoulder and arm contracted as I fought to keep the sword from pressing my own weapon into my throat. A loud screech echoed from the metal as I drew my dagger up the length of the blade, slipping out from underneath the strike and sliding off the side of the bed.

There were three of them, three soldiers advancing toward me with drawn swords while I had nothing more than the dagger. My longsword stood unreachable at the side of the bed. I heard the whistle in the air as the closest blade rushed toward me, and I deflected it with my dagger, feinting to the left as my other hand cracked him on the wrist before bringing my leg up to kick the man square in the chest, knocking him backward. The sword clattered from his grasp onto the stone, and I reached for it, rolling onto my back as another blade missed me by a hair's breadth.

The hilt was in my hands, and I jumped upward, landing on my feet to swing my blade around where it caught metal, jarring my arm. I pulled out of it, immediately bringing the blade down onto his shoulder.

It sank into flesh.

The following scream reverberated off the stone walls and out into the corridor as he clutched at the wound, falling to his knees. The last man moved behind me. I twirled the sword around, driving it backward and hearing the man let out a gasp as it plunged into his side.

The first man scrambled on the floor to get away, but I planted a boot on his shoulder. "I wouldn't move if I were you."

He stilled.

The wounds I had inflicted were not fatal, but they would need time to heal. I'd expected something like this, but not so soon. We couldn't stay here any longer, couldn't take the risk. Footsteps echoed down the hall, and I watched as torchlight sent the walls outside my room into a sea of waving shadows. Nic flew into the room, sword raised and breathing ragged. He stopped abruptly at the sight of the bleeding men at my feet.

"Vladimir—" His voice cut off, shock resounding in it.

Blood splattered the floor, the three men grunting and moaning from the pain, clutching at their wounds.

"What time is it?" I asked.

Nic threw me a quizzical look. "What?"

"I said, what time is it?"

He must have found the question trivial, but glanced to the window. "Nearly dawn."

His eyes fell back to the men on the ground, a million questions hovering in his eyes. Several more of my soldiers entered the room, and eventually General Lyle's face emerged. He didn't seem surprised at all by the situation; instead his eyes seemed to convey that he'd told me he had no control over who held these men's allegiance.

I let out a shuddering breath, casting a look at the injured men around me before I brought my eyes back up to his.

"I want every man in this outpost dressed and standing in the courtyard in the next ten minutes."

He watched me, finding the resolve in my eyes. A calculating nod followed, and he backed out of the room.

"Vladimir." Nic hesitated. "What—"

"Drag these disgraces out into the courtyard," I instructed the men, making my way around the bed where I snatched up my sword and quickly belted it on. "Nic, go send word to the grooms that I want the horses ready for travel. We're leaving at first light."

He opened his mouth as if to protest but quickly thought better of it. "Yes, sir."

I pulled my boots on and poured water into the clay basin, splashing it on my face even as I felt a cold sweat break out on my brow. I didn't know if this was a situation that could be rectified. Men who would have fought alongside me months ago had just tried to take my life.

They tried to kill me.

I took a deep breath, snatching up my saddlebags and making my way out into the courtyard, which was already beginning to fill with men. Torches illuminated their tired, anxious faces staring back at me as I hopped onto a crate to stand head and shoulders above them. An uneasiness shifted through the group. I said nothing as they stared back at me, just kept my expression cold and blank. This division had gone on long enough. It would end now. I waited until I saw General Lyle approach, nodding his confirmation that all the men were present.

The look on my face turned ferocious.

I let it rage wildly.

There would be no mercy.

None.

"Most of you don't know me." My voice was low, yet it carried through the group with a chill. "Some of you may not even know the late Michael Gallows, who led the Kavari before me. You were told that Queen Adamara, your ruler, disbanded the Kavari because I enabled a fugitive to escape. That is true." I paused, hearing the shuffling of feet throughout the crowd. "But it is true only because I believed that fugitive to be innocent. Crown Prince William accused Katherine Daharaway of murdering the king of Brenden, sparking the war that now looms before us. At the time, there was no one to discredit his story, but we now have a witness who claims otherwise. The king of Brenden was murdered by a Gharridan, but it was not Katherine Daharaway. This witness needs to be brought before the council to hear her case and ensure that justice is dealt, but in order to do this I must hold my right as leader of the Kavari."

I gazed out over the crowd, at the sea of men hanging on my every word and waiting to either join or condemn me.

"I love this country. When I had no place to call home, this kingdom gave me one. I only want what's best for Gharridan and will do whatever it takes to ensure its survival. Regardless of what rumors may circulate, I have no wish to rule Gharridan. I never have. The only thing I desire for Gharridan is for us to be united once again and stronger than before. War approaches. It will be vile, it will be harsh, and it will be deadly. We cannot hope to win against the enemy if we are warring among ourselves."

I turned on the crate, gathering strength and courage for my next words.

"I will march toward the capital when the first rays of dawn shoot out across the sky. I do not march for power, nor to cause destruction or violence. I march to show the Crown that the people of Gharridan still believe in the Kavari and still believe in justice. The Crown and the council will not listen to my voice alone. It will take an entire nation of voices to convince them. To reinstate the Kavari, I have to prove to the queen that the entire nation wants them restored."

I motioned to Nic, and he and the others brought forth the three men who had attacked me, their wounds already haphazardly wrapped with bandages. "I am well aware that there are those who stand wholeheartedly with the Crown and wish for the Kavari to be destroyed. These three men attacked me while I was sleeping, attempting to take my life and no doubt earn the praise of their work from the queen, but they were unsuccessful."

My gaze bore into the crowd. "I could've killed them. Killed all of them, in three simple strokes. But I didn't. I chose to let them live because I refuse to kill someone simply because they don't support me. Every man has free right to choose who their allegiance lies with, and I will not be a tyrant who takes that choice from you."

The moment of truth approached.

"I ask you now, where does your allegiance lie? Will you choose to ride with me?"

The darkness lightened, brightening the soldiers' faces, the dark circles underneath their eyes amplified in the light of dawn. Nic and my men stared out at the soldiers, waiting for their response, waiting to see what they would do. I swallowed, trying to keep my hands from shaking as fear charged through me.

"I will." General Lyle stepped forward with a grave face. "I do not wish to see the country I have served these many years destroyed. We have come too far for that."

Murmurs rumbled through the crowd, and another man stepped forward, pledging his allegiance. He was followed by another, and then another until it seemed as if the entire squadron had moved forward to express their support of me. I looked to General Lyle, expressing my thanks, and he nodded one of his slow, silent nods in return. The crowd around me grew louder as they took up a chorus of chants, shouting of their loyalty as they hurried back to their barracks to gather their packs.

I stepped off the crate.

One step closer.

As soon as one weight lifted off my shoulders, another fell to take its place. If we failed and the council turned against us, each and every one of these men would be charged with treason. I couldn't let that happen. The men's loyalty sparked a chord of hope within me, and I determined to keep it burning until it was a roaring wildfire.

CHAPTER FORTY-FIVE

THE FOLLOWING MORNING I left before the sun rose to pore through history books in the library. I pulled books on Algarian history, architecture, culture, studied maps of their cities, looked for any trigger words like Illdalore, Dalendria, or Djara, but after countless scoured and turned handwritten pages, nothing useful or even remotely important jumped out at me. Nothing about Dalendria. Nothing more about my mother. It was frustrating to be so close to uncovering her past yet so far away. I knew I had reached a dead end, knew that I would have to find someone or go somewhere else to uncover more, but I refused to lose the hope that nested in my heart.

When I returned to my room, William was gone. Relief washed over me, erasing the anxiety that had been building within me at the thought of him still being there. I would have to talk to him eventually—if he even remembered anything after passing out. Most importantly, I needed William to trust me enough that he would be willing to reconsider his feelings toward Katherine. That alone was no small undertaking, and I didn't like the ideas turning in my mind, the ways I would have to go about achieving it.

I deserted my room and ventured down to the training fields. A fog lingered in the air, making my breath damp and my arms chilly. It created a ghostly atmosphere in the landscape, leaving me unable to see barely a few hundred feet in front of me. Moisture clung to my skin, and it grew sticky to the touch. No sound of weapons reached my ears. No clash of swords or smack of arrows. I shuffled through the misty air to the stables but came up short again. The stable hands milled about, mucking the stalls and watering the horses, but the crown prince was nowhere to be found.

I gave up, returning to the castle and strolling through the deserted hallways, trying to figure out how to best solidify William's trust. The remorse he'd shown would be a valuable card to play, but getting him to admit it while he was sober proved the challenge. I passed the hallway leading up into the north tower and stopped, staring at the cracked door. Ever since escaping that prison, I'd been afraid to walk near it, but I lifted my chin, choosing to conquer my fears. It could only make me afraid if I let it.

The old door creaked beneath the press of my hand, swinging open to reveal the spiral staircase it concealed. A shiver raced down my spine as I climbed the steps, my footfalls echoing softly off the surrounding stone. The memories of me kicking and screaming as the soldiers carried me upstairs circulated within me. The landing between the rooms was quiet, and I moved toward the only one I had been inside of, a current of anger washing over me at the memory of being trapped in there, of William imprisoning me. My fingers trembled as I reached for the handle. I paused, struck with fear, almost backing out, but then I opened the door. Light from the window and hallway spilled into the dim room, the patches creating a jagged pathway across the floor. Everything remained the same, as if I had never left. I timidly entered the room, my feet hesitating as they took each step.

"You can't have missed this room that much."

I jolted upright, spinning in search of the voice that emanated from the shadows. A dark form sat in a chair, gaze fixed out the window.

William.

"I—" My voice cut off, unable to form words.

"You shouldn't be here."

William's appearance frightened me. Every piece of attire he wore was black, blending in with the darkness. I stood there helplessly, wanting to leave but afraid to. He rose from his seat, the light catching his red-rimmed eyes.

Something was horribly wrong.

"Are you all right?"

He released a grim laugh, drawing his bloodshot eyes away. "Sure. I'm good. Totally fine."

His words were stilted. Disjointed.

I crossed my arms, surveying him up and down. "You're not drunk again, are you?"

He frowned. "Most of it has worn off by now. Unfortunately. Sorry, I guess you witnessed part of it."

I didn't quite know what to say, but with a look at the abandoned room around us, I began to slowly piece together what I thought might be the issue.

"You told me you do this every year. To forget."

William threw his hands in the air in mock surprise. "Oh, that's right. You don't know what today is. Why would you?" He stepped closer. "Your father hid you and your mother away for who knows what reason. You didn't even know who he was, so how would you know what today is?"

His eyes were only inches away, boring into mine, the instability of his emotions roaring like the edge of a waterfall.

I kept my voice steady, trying to keep him calm. "Then why don't you tell me?"

His mouth twisted into an unbelieving smile but then turned down into mockery as he whispered, "Why would you care, Taryn? We both know you'd rather be with Vladimir and Katherine right now, traipsing who knows where across the country, fulfilling your own agenda. On the way back from Brenden, you made it very clear how much you hated me. How much you despised me. The memories are still a little fuzzy, but I'm pretty sure you told me the exact same thing last night. I doubt that's changed in the last few hours. Although I can tell you're trying very hard to hide it."

I didn't dare move, didn't breathe as I tried to procure the right words. "I told you why I came back, but you can choose to believe whatever you want. Or are you still incapable of making your own decisions?"

His face hardened at my accusations. "Get out." He brushed past me as his dark form moved over to the light of the window.

"You also told me something last night," I bit back.

He paused.

"You told me that you see King Arguis' face in your mind every day, haunting your dreams, that you regret what you did."

I watched him try to hide it, but from the look on his face there was no denying that what he had thrown at me last night was true.

His back turned to me. "I said get out."

I ground my teeth together, wanting to leave, wanting to abandon him in his own misery, but I couldn't. I had to gain his trust, and as much as the deceptive thought in my mind sickened me, I knew he was vulnerable right now. I felt like a vulture, circling its prey over and over, waiting for the opportune moment, but if I didn't hold my ground, the Kavari might never be reinstated.

The soft carpet indented beneath my steps as I crossed the quiet room, keeping my breaths steady. I placed a tentative hand on the midnight fabric of his shoulder and drew his attention back to me. "Tell me about today, William. I want to understand."

Emotions warred within him, bursting to get out but also desperately trying to stay inside. A haunted look shadowed his features, his eyes filled with torture. He worked his jaw, gaze shooting to the window. I waited beside him, afraid to move as I wondered whether he would finally let me in or continue to push me out.

"Today would've been her eighteenth birthday."

The words dampened the room like a judge ordering a death sentence.

I stilled.

"Whose birthday?"

William's breathing evened out. "My sister's."

The untouched dresses meant for a young girl, the gathering dust portraying years of abandonment. I was right, a princess had lived here. But William had never mentioned a sister. William gripped the edge of the windowsill. My heart leapt out to him.

"I'm sorry," I said. "I never knew."

My arms wrapped around him, and his hot tears silently wet my shoulder as he leaned against me. William had never been this open, this vulnerable.

Several minutes slid by before I dared to ask, "What happened?"

He pulled away as if embarrassed, moving to sit on the edge of the bed. "Adelaide had issues from the moment she was born." He sniffed, wiping his runny nose. "Always pale, always tired, always under the weather, but she fought to never give up. She tried her hardest to do whatever everyone else could do, even if it wasn't feasible."

"Were you close?"

William remained quiet for a few moments. "She followed me around everywhere. It was annoying, really, until we learned how great of a team we made. My mother accused me of corrupting her, saying that Adelaide never got into trouble before I took her under my wing, showed her how to get away with things. But unlike me, Adelaide showed restraint and never took things too far, always caring too much about everyone else but not herself.

"One day, she got really sick, really tired. She didn't leave her rooms and stayed in bed for days to rest." The ghost of a smile touched his lips. "I was a little irritated because we'd had an escapade planned for the kitchen, but two guards came for me in the middle of the night, said that my mother sent for me. The whole way there, I desperately tried to think of every horrible thing I'd ever done. Many came to mind, and I was scared out of my wits over which one my mother had discovered, but that wasn't why she had sent the guards after me."

William's voice fell flat, emotionless. "When I walked into the room, I found my mother and father sobbing over my sister's bed, their faces broken."

I held back tears.

"There was no warning." His gaze grew distant as if transported back in time. "A maid was sitting with her and realized that she had stopped breathing. The doctor thinks it was something internal, something we couldn't see, and then she was just, she was—"

She was gone.

William trailed off, unable to bring himself to say the words. I sat beside him, gripping his shoulder, trying to convey my condolences. There was no room for words, only understanding.

William shifted beside me and looked down at his hands. "The doctor had told her to take it easy, to be careful, but I led her all over everywhere, tiring her out instead of letting her rest and trying to find a way to cure whatever was ailing her."

My breath caught in my throat.

This was William's truth.

"She was good, with the most tender heart, like my father. She deserved better. I should have found a way to save her."

"William, it's not your fault."

A humorless chuckle escaped his lips. "How would you know? Everything else is."

"William—"

He stood, striding to the door.

I stared, eyes wide, and hurried after him into the hall where I pulled him back. "It's not your fault."

He half sat on the ledges of one of the stained-glass windows, ignoring me. "Yes, it is."

I grabbed his cheek and pulled his face back to mine, staring into his glistening hazel eyes. "No, it's not."

I waited to release my next words, wanting them to take effect. He unwillingly held my gaze, not wanting to believe.

"There's nothing you could have done. It was out of your hands. You can't blame yourself, and you can't change the past."

Tears sparkled in his eyes. "But what if you could? Would you do things differently with your father?"

I swallowed, his words striking dangerously close to the heart. Even though I still didn't understand my father's abandonment, I would give anything to go back to that moment right before he walked out our door for the last time, to tell him that I loved him, to tell him that I was sorry.

I swallowed again, shaking my head. "You can't." My voice cracked. "You have to move on."

He stared back, absorbing my words, as if he wanted to believe me, but I feared that he wouldn't. Sincerity burned within me, begging him not to blame himself for this, to not torture himself forever. He lowered his gaze to my hand, still resting on his cheek, and then brought his eyes back to mine. The vulnerability clouding his face was raw and rampant. My breaths grew shallow as his Adam's apple bobbed, his eyes locking with mine, but all I could do was stare back. The next moment, his lips were on mine. Warm. Gentle. Soft. His fingers wove into my hair, his other arm twisting around my waist, drawing me closer. And I was—I caught a quick breath, the realization catching me off guard—I was kissing him back.

It was wrong. Wrong on so many accounts. I tried to convince myself that I hated him. I knew I hated him, but it didn't seem to matter in this moment. I needed William to trust me, but I grew suddenly afraid that I wouldn't be able to trust myself. I couldn't pull away from his embrace. Didn't want to. William was too fragile, too vulnerable, and a rejection at this point might drive him further away than I ever had before. Internally, I recoiled at the treachery of who I was being, who I had become. I told myself it was different from how William didn't have a choice. It was. I didn't have a choice. Not in this matter. Did I?

We broke apart and stood there staring at each other as if unsure of what the other was thinking. I couldn't move, didn't remember how to move. What we'd done could never be undone, unfelt, forgotten. A sense of sanity suddenly returned to William. He slowly rose, gently leaving a kiss on my forehead before treading down the staircase. His footsteps reverberated off the walls, continuing to echo in my mind long after they faded away. I leaned back against the cold wall where William had left me standing in the shadows of the hallway, the memory of the kiss lingering on my trembling lips.

CHAPTER FORTY-SIX

I DID NOT speak for three days.

The cruelty haunted me, to be so close to everything I had ever wanted only for it to be ripped away again.

Yet it seemed that had been my fate for my entire life.

My parents.

Gone.

My home in the orphanage.

Gone.

The privilege of serving a country I love.

Gone.

Michael.

Gone.

The only other Radonaya I had ever met.

Gone.

Would Vladimir be next?

He was the only person I had left besides Verone, but I wasn't even sure that I still had him. I'd always held him at arm's length, afraid of losing him and afraid that my reputation would bring him disdain within the court. I didn't want anyone to suffer the disgrace I continued to endure.

I closed my eyes as the sun warmed my skin, my body swaying with the lilt of the horse beneath me. Verone's kind face swam before my mind, his embarrassment of his scar, the objections of his age, but I'd found that the men my age were unable to relate to the hardships I'd endured. There was always a lack of connection. Not that there had been many. With the superstition surrounding me, most of them stayed as far away as they could, but there were still the few that were curious.

Verone had never treated me as a curiosity, nor as a creature to be feared.

My thoughts pulled away from him, mulling over the fragments of information Colleen had provided. I lifted my hand, once thinking it to be insignificant, but the hand possessed the power to heal.

And kill.

The idea horrified me. Had I ever been close to taking someone's life and not realized it?

My hand shook beneath my scrutiny. I feared the power lying just beneath my skin. I'd always thought there were so few of us, but how many Radonaya walked among everyone else, their changed hair giving witness to the darkness they'd succumbed to? Maybe my people had always surrounded me, and I'd simply been looking in the wrong places.

The mother of a Radonaya has always died after childbirth.

The words sank into me like a stone into a river. Her statement hadn't pained me, it simply solidified a fact that I'd known in my heart to be true long ago. But those words haunted me more than anything else she'd said. Were we created? Chosen? Did we all come from the same bloodline, or was our existence completely at random? Why would the birth of a Radonaya bring the death of their mother?

I'd always assumed that I'd been abandoned at the orphanage because of my red hair, but maybe I'd been brought there because I truly was an orphan. The questions circulated in my mind, endless riddles for which I had no answer.

The City of Isolation.

It was the one tidbit of information she'd uttered that left me a trail to follow.

The Radonaya *did* come from somewhere.

The City of Isolation was impenetrable, but based off my and Colleen's existence, someone had gotten out. And if there was a way out—that meant there was also a way in.

CHAPTER FORTY-SEVEN

TARYN

DINNER WOULD BE in the grand hall this evening. I splashed cool water on my face and watched the droplets sprinkle back into the basin like drops of rain. Nausea ripped at my stomach over the thought of seeing William again. I'd been avoiding him ever since our encounter in the tower, and he hadn't sought me out. My anxiety didn't stem from the kiss or even from William himself; it stemmed from the hatred I held for myself over what I was doing to him. Playing him, capitalizing on his emotions and trust when I could still barely stand the sight of him. Any friendship we held would be lost once he discovered my betrayal. Yet I also hated the part of myself that still wanted to trust him, wanted to believe the way I felt toward him was real. Hard as I tried to convince myself otherwise, I knew that I still cared for William.

The pain of hurting him still pulsed through me even after everything he had done.

I flung open the wardrobe, the sudden motion blowing my hair over my shoulders, and stared at the few articles of clothing I'd managed to collect since being here. It wasn't much. A few day dresses and two formal gowns. A frown creased my forehead at the sight of the uncomfortable fancy dresses with their itchy lace and tight bodices. I chose a deep indigo with enough fancy stitching to be dressy, but comfortable enough to be practical.

A knock came at the door and my breath faltered, terrified at the thought of William standing on the other side. I couldn't face him. Not yet. I moved silently across the floor, timidly cracking open the door.

But it was only a page.

He offered me a sealed note, and I nodded my thanks.

I didn't recognize the handwriting scrawled across the fresh parchment. Apparently the queen had placed an order for a formal gown to be made on my behalf, and the dressmaker requested my presence to attain the proper measurements. I rolled my eyes. This was a jab from the queen. A mockery of my inexperience with the ways of court. I lifted my chin. Two could play at this game.

I swung my cloak around my shoulders and stuffed the letter into my pocket. If I hurried, I could get it over with before the dinner and it would prevent me from accidentally running into William on castle grounds.

The cold air in the courtyard stung my cheeks, whipping through my hair as I slipped through the main gate without the guards so much as questioning me. I glanced over my shoulder

once, then twice, but no one followed. William, it seemed, finally trusted me, and even though no one should recognize me,
I still pulled my hood over my head, leaving my face in shadows.

I wended my way through the streets, attention focused.
The dressmaker's shop lay in one of the more run-down areas
of the city. The Mudblocks, they called it. The weight of my
dagger hung reassuringly at my side and I kept my hand hovering over the hilt, wondering if I should have brought a second
weapon. While the capital wasn't overrun with violence, under-
ground gangs still perused the streets, dealing under the table,
taking care of dirty work, and staying off the city watch's radar.

The heels of my boots clicked along the cobblestones, the
leftover slush coating the hem of my dress. I avoided eye contact with those I passed, maneuvering through the merchants
selling wares and the messengers running back and forth
through the alleys. Carriages clattered by and people scattered
to get out of their way as the horses charged up the cobblestone
street.

My gaze roved from one side of the street to another,
searching every window and swinging sign for the dressmaker's
name. When I finally saw it, the shabby sign hung lopsided off
the building, the paint faded and cracked. I frowned. This didn't
quite feel like the queen's taste.

A tall, burly man stumbled into me, knocking me out of the
street and into the alley.

"Sorry, miss."

Before I could turn to look at him a hand clamped over my
mouth and an arm of iron fastened across my waist. A muffled
scream escaped my lips as I bucked against the man, trying to
loosen his grip. My elbow slammed into his stomach but only

produced little more than a groan. I wiggled against him, reaching for my dagger, fingers barely grasping the hilt, pulling it from its sheath. I swung my hand wildly, the blade finding skin. His hold relaxed. I stumbled forward only to be spun around by the burly man who had plowed into me. He grabbed both my wrists, twisting the dagger from my grasp. I leaned against his weight, bringing my legs up to push him away, but the other man grabbed my waist again. Out of the corner of my vision, I caught sight of a third figure.

Panic overcame me, searing through my veins, transforming me into a savage creature that lashed out with a deranged ferocity.

But I couldn't get away.

They picked me up like a sack of wheat, arms pinned to my sides, legs firmly clamped together. A dirty hand distorted the strangled noises desperately trying to claw their way out of my throat, trying to scream for help. The devastating feeling of helplessness washed over me. Fear crept up my spine. We were plunging farther into the alley, the world around me darkening. They didn't laugh, didn't say anything. They just carried me to who knew where without another soul noticing.

My heart hammered against my chest like a drum, eyes wide as I searched for some kind of identification on any of the men, but their clothing was plain and dark, the raised hoods of their cloaks casting their faces in shadow. My body tilted as they carried me up three steps, and I watched as the archway of a doorway passed over me. They deposited me roughly into a wooden chair, jerking my hands behind me and fastening a series of quick and hardy knots. I bit my lip, the terror of the memory of being Silas's captive flooding me as the bonds were fastened around my feet.

My chest rose and fell as I stared beyond the men to a fire blazing in the hearth. Planks of the floor were missing, others riddled with holes. Cobwebs decorated the corners and beams. Besides the chair, the only furniture in the room was a splintered table. One of my captors dropped my dagger into the center of the floor in plain sight.

"That will be all."

I jerked at the new voice, issuing from another room in the building. Its owner hovered in the frame of a doorway leading into darkness. He tossed something to the burly man, who snatched it easily from the air, the jingle of coins abruptly stopping. Without another word my abductors slipped back into the alley and vanished from sight.

I tried to even out my staggering breaths, tried to appear calm, but I couldn't deny the panic that burned within me as the man emerged from the shadows.

"Taryn Gallows, is it?"

I studied his face, trying to memorize exactly what he looked like. "What do you want?" Despite the fear coursing through me, my voice remained solid as the city gates.

He held my gaze, expression contemplative. "I haven't been able to reach Vladimir, so I had to come up with a way to lure you outside the castle grounds."

My eyes narrowed.

The shop.

"That letter didn't come from the dressmaker, did it?"

The man frowned. "I was afraid you might catch on. The queen would never order anything from the Mudblocks."

He was wrong. She would if she were trying to insult me.

"Why am I here?"

He crossed his arms. "Because we had a deal, and Vladimir hasn't delivered."

Vladimir didn't seem like the type to get involved in street gangs or petty business such as this. "I don't clean up Vladimir's problems."

"But you do want to defeat the Crown."

I stilled. What had Vladimir meddled with? I squirmed in my seat, trying to get more comfortable. "I'm listening."

He walked farther into the room, eyes wary and distrustful. "I need you to obtain something for me."

I cocked an eyebrow in impatience. "What?"

"Vladimir promised a document of immunity for my brother, Jarrod Lynch. He needs it before he can testify."

Jarrod Lynch.

The name rang with familiarity, scratching at a memory locked within the cages of my mind. My brows lowered in concentration. A document of immunity? The night I went with Vladimir to visit Gavil before he was murdered flashed before me. Gavil said that my father had been looking for Jarrod Lynch for years, and that he'd finally managed to track down Jarrod's brother.

"You're Randal Lynch," I said, recalling his name. Vladimir must have made some kind of deal with him before he left. "What is this about? Why was my father searching for your brother?"

"Vladimir didn't ask questions."

"I highly doubt Vladimir was abducted and then tied to a chair."

His face grew taut. "Do you want to stop the Crown from

taking over Gharridan or not?"

I quieted. "What are you offering in return?"

"Once the immunity possessing all three seals is in Jarrod's hands, without the Crown or council's knowledge, he will come forward and he will testify."

"Yes, he'll testify," I said. "But testify about what?"

"That's what you will find out when he comes forward."

I didn't like this. He didn't want to tell me what he was doing, and I questioned if Vladimir had really agreed to these preposterous terms. All of this could be a trap, an attempt to grant immunity to a dangerous criminal, but whatever Jarrod was testifying against might be worth being left in the dark for. If my father had spent that many years looking for the man and Vladimir was willing to offer him immunity, then he held or knew something critically important.

"When do you need it by?" I asked.

Randal scrunched his face in concentration. "I'll give you three days."

My stomach dropped. Three days? I didn't even know how to begin going about obtaining this complex of a document, but I didn't have a choice.

"Done."

He studied me. "Do I have your word? Because if you don't deliver, Jarrod will disappear again. This time forever."

I didn't hesitate. "You have my word."

He nodded. "There's a cabin on the east side of the Jidero. Leave through the western gate, pass through the lower fields until you come across the three stumps. You'll come across two birch trees along the tree line. Follow them into the forest, and they will lead you there. Three days. Before sunset. This is your last chance."

He doused the fire with a pitcher of water and then walked behind me, slicing through the ropes. "I'll leave you to untie your feet. Don't follow me."

He disappeared into the alleyway, and I tore into the ropes binding my feet, snatching up my dagger and then bursting out the door. My eyes searched wildly up and down the road, but he was nowhere to be seen. I clenched my dagger tightly in my hand, skirts a disheveled mess, my heartbeat quickening again.

I hurried back the way I'd come, eyes scanning every direction for an approaching enemy. I had no idea how I was going to get that document, but an overwhelming feeling of dread warned me that something terrible would happen if I didn't.

I was still shaken from the ordeal when I stumbled up the steps of the palace.

"They're waiting for you in the grand hall, Miss Gallows."

I glanced up at the guard, confused.

Dinner.

Dinner.

I'd forgotten, and I was late. Very late. I took a deep breath, following the guard down the hallway and trying to calm my racing heart. All eyes turned to me when I entered. They stared at me like a noble who had been shamed. Heat rushed to my cheeks unbidden at the sudden attention of everyone seated at the table. Mud lined the hem of my dress. There had to be splotches of dirt all over the fabric, and I knew that my hair was knotted and tangled.

Courtiers, nobles, and officials filled the table, dressed in their formal attire with gold dangling from the women's ears and the men wearing richly dyed colors. Only one seat remained empty, and I nodded in thanks as one of the servants pulled the seat out for me, the legs dragging noisily across the polished floor. My smile was stiff as I sat, smoothing out my skirts beneath me as if nothing were out of the ordinary. A heat radiated from my left, and I felt Queen Adamara's eyes burning into me like wildfire. I deliberately avoided her gaze. I knew I should greet her, but I couldn't bring myself to look into that judgmental face. All around me, the chairs creaked as the attendees shifted uncomfortably in their seats. I lifted my eyes and briefly caught William's gaze on me from where he sat several chairs down, next to his mother. He lifted an eyebrow, apparently quite perturbed at my appearance. My gaze flitted away.

A massive roasted pig perched on a silver platter in the center of the long table with a concoction of dried herbs and delicacies surrounding it. My mouth watered at the sight of it, the sweet smell of its meat overpowering my nostrils. Idle chatter eventually picked up around the table until it drowned out the quiet that had befallen when I entered. I kept my eyes riveted on my plate as I was served and then focused on eating, not engaging in conversation with anyone else around me.

Eventually, my gaze darted around between bites, taking note of Captain Verone and picking out councilman Finnigan seated farther down the table. As I chewed on the tender pork in my mouth, the wheels of my mind continued to turn, drowning out the voices around me. I doubted Captain Verone could discreetly get me the document of immunity, but I'd bet anything that Finnigan could. He seemed to have a heavy sway and pull within the government. Vladimir might have even already discussed the document with him. I shook my head. No. Randal stated he didn't want the Crown or council knowing—but I didn't have a choice. I couldn't get it on my own, and Finnigan was the only one I could trust.

When the food dwindled away and our bellies grew full, Queen Adamara rose from her seat, signaling the end of dinner. She moved gracefully through the double doors to the adjoining chamber, and everyone proceeded to follow. I stifled my frustration, not realizing the evening had more scheduled than just a dinner. William hung back from the doors intentionally, and I knew he was waiting for me, but I started fussing with the sleeve of my dress to deter him. He could only stall for so long before running out of excuses to follow the others. Once he passed out of sight, I fell into step beside Finnigan, tapping him on the shoulder and slowing my pace, indicating that we needed to talk.

Everyone else had already cleared the room, and we sauntered slowly toward the doors.

"I need your help procuring something." I spoke quietly, barely glancing at him.

His eyebrow lifted.

"Vladimir needs Jarrod Lynch to testify against the Crown, but Jarrod wants something in exchange. Full immunity, certified with all three seals."

Finnigan's eyes widened, surveying around us to make sure our conversation wasn't being overheard. "What is this about, Taryn? Full immunity is no small pardon."

My mind worked quickly. "My father searched for Jarrod for years. Vladimir finally managed to track him down, and he possesses something that will help him reinstate the Kavari. He needs it by the day after tomorrow and without alerting anyone else in the court to its creation."

Finnigan's expression soured. "That would've been difficult for even Vladimir to obtain."

"If he doesn't get it, he doesn't testify."

"Did you speak with Vladimir?"

"No." I shook my head. "I-I met with Jarrod's brother this afternoon."

Finnigan appeared skeptical. "Are you certain this is legitimate? Because if I grant immunity to the wrong man—"

I knew the implications, but I also felt that there was something here.

"I am. A man named Gavil told us about this man before he was murdered. Whatever information he holds, it's critically important."

We crossed through the doorway and into the next room.

"I'll see what I can do."

Finnigan strode away as if he didn't even know me, occupying a spot at the edge of the room. I shouldn't have approached him in public, but time was of the essence.

I took in my surroundings, unsure of where I was supposed to be or what I was supposed to do, but I opted to rest in one of the sitting chairs positioned by itself. A few conversations struck up around the room, but most of the gathered individuals remained hushed. Maybe I wasn't the only one who hadn't realized more than dinner was involved this evening. Expectation hung in the air like a sharp fragrance, as if everyone was waiting for something exciting to happen. I squirmed in my seat and once again caught William's gaze. He seemed to have taken notice of the apprehension in the air as well, and his brow creased in worry. I didn't know whether that reassured me or made me more nervous. He studied me, a million questions falling across his eyes before he tore his gaze away. I found myself wondering what was going through his mind.

Queen Adamara reclined in her cushioned chair for a while, observing the scene around her with sharp looks before eventually sitting up straighter. I unintentionally straightened my posture as well.

"I would like to thank you all for your attendance this evening, and for your support of the Crown," she began. "We deeply appreciate your service to our country, but with joy also comes sorrow, and I'm afraid that I must share some most dreadful news with you." Her voice became morose, expression faltering for a moment. "You all know of the horror Katherine Daharaway committed in Brenden, how she was sentenced to death, and how Vladimir decided to betray Gharridan by aiding a fugitive. His actions left me with no choice but to disband the Kavari."

My fists clenched, nails digging painfully into my palms.

"We've wasted far too much time and used too many resources in an attempt to track them down, and yet still have not managed to locate Vladimir since his disappearance." The queen's attention landed on me. "Until now."

My pulse raced, my mouth growing dry as the air tightened around me. No. They couldn't have Vladimir. Not now. Not when we were so close. I risked a look at Verone, but his eyes remained steadily on the queen.

"We received word from one of the western outposts that Vladimir has been making his way across Gharridan, stealing troops from our military and amassing his own army in an attempt to secure the Crown for himself."

My fingers trembled. It was a lie. Vladimir would never do such a thing. Avoiding bloodshed at any cost would be his top priority.

Everyone leaned forward, eager to hear the queen's next words.

"It is an act of treason and punishable by death. I brought you here tonight to inform all of you that we have sent our own forces out to meet him and destroy his little rebellion in the night. Anyone caught conspiring with him will be executed."

Executed.

Vladimir had no reason to suspect that the Crown would attack him outright. My gaze caught William's. His ghostly face and rigid stature suggested he was just as distressed as I. She couldn't do this. Queen Adamara was raving mad, attacking her people and trying to kill an innocent man who had only ever spent his life serving Gharridan, and all for revenge on a woman who wasn't even responsible for her husband's death.

"Our troops should be meeting his rebellion on the battlefield even as we speak."

My eyes widened in shock as the realization hit me, the color draining from my face.

Vladimir was going to die.

If he wasn't dead already.

CHAPTER FORTY-EIGHT

VLADIMIR

THE SOUND OF thousands of traveling horses and soldiers grated across the countryside. Whinnies echoed between the rows of men as hooves thundered like an ominous storm. Shouts rose above the noise. Wagons creaked in protest underneath the weight in their beds. It seemed as if the entire Gharridan army was marching to the capital. Dante pranced with agitation beneath me, uncomfortable with the constant barrage of those around us.

"It's only going to get worse," I warned him.

We'd marched to two other outposts, gathering overwhelming support of the troops from each, and two villages had offered their able-bodied men as well. Those who couldn't provide soldiers offered other gifts such as supplies or food, but while many of the people we met backed the Kavari, not all held us in such high esteem. Many still hated Katherine and thought the Crown to be right in all.

The sun descended lower into the sky, and I signaled the troops to stop for the night. The more soldiers we amassed, the more we slowed. It wasted precious time, but we would reach the capital within the week. Katherine had still not returned, though. I closed my eyes, hoping that no ill had befallen her. We'd agreed to meet up outside of Civon, but we'd passed through there two days ago. Sending her off alone had been a grave mistake. For all I knew, Queen Adamara had already captured her and had her executed.

A group of hunters split away from our main group as each soldier began their part of setting up the camp. The hunters would be out late into the night. Our caravan would have frightened any wildlife farther into the woods. I doubted they would manage to come back with much during the hours of darkness, but anything was worth trying at this point. I took my time with Dante, brushing away my thoughts like the dust on his coat. There was still so much to do. So much planning that hadn't even been discussed yet.

Amid the usual clamor, another sound twinged at my ears, something out of place. I walked to the edge of the tents, squinting against the shadows that accompanied twilight. A dark line broke the crest of the nearest hill, approaching us with a thunder of hooves and clatter of armor. My insides twisted. Open warfare was the last thing I wanted.

"Form a line!" I yelled, drawing my sword and setting forward from the camp. Hundreds of boots scurried behind me as men dropped what they were doing to unsheathe their swords and fall into formation. The impending army slowed, and although the light was dim, I noticed that none of their weapons were drawn. One of the horsemen broke away from the pack, drawing closer while the others stayed behind.

He stopped just beyond the edge of camp.

"Vladimir?" the man called out, his eyes searching the darkness.

My weapon fell to my side, and I stepped forward, not daring to believe it. But I saw the grin spread across his face.

"Melvin!"

I ran out to meet him, clapping him on the back as he dismounted. "What are you doing here?"

He let out a groan as his feet smacked against the ground, and he reached out to grip my arm.

"Captain Verone sent me on a special mission," he said with a wink.

I lifted an eyebrow. "Along with all these soldiers?"

Melvin glanced behind him. "Verone didn't send them out; I've been gathering them. A hundred and fifty strong, all in favor of Gharridan and of supporting the Kavari."

My gaze swept over the columns of cavalrymen behind him in shock. "What about the queen? Has she heard of our coming?"

News of mini armies popping up all over Gharridan would travel quickly.

Melvin frowned. "Not when I left, but I'd be surprised if she hadn't gotten wind of it by now. You're too large and too close to the capital to escape notice any longer."

That was what I feared. "I want to get in there without taking any lives."

Melvin's lips pursed into a thin line as he quietly said, "Accomplishing that would require a miracle, my boy."

I glanced at the men backing me to make sure none of our conversation had been overheard, and then motioned for them to stand down. "We have a hundred fifty men joining our ranks. Make sure they're supplied with whatever they need."

Melvin's eyebrows rose as he watched the men march past us and filter into the camp. "How are you keeping all of them fed?"

"We've sent messengers ahead to towns and asked for extra supplies. Most of the men have been hunting, bringing in what game they can, and the villagers have been quite generous with their offerings."

But the rations were dwindling.

"It's because they know they stand behind a good man." Melvin leaned in close to my ear. "I need to speak with you in private, Vladimir."

I gave a curt nod and motioned for him to follow me as I returned to my tent ahead of the mass of intermingling confusion that was our new arrivals. Smoke twisted through the air from the fires around me as the scent of cooking soup dispersed throughout the camp. Melvin slipped through the worn flaps of my tent, the unbothered expression he'd plastered across his face instantly vanishing.

"I trust you with my life, Vladimir, but I have to know, what do you plan on doing if this doesn't pan out?" His eyes pierced mine. "What will bringing an army to the capital's doorstep accomplish?"

I grimaced. "We're going to be at war with Brenden. It's not an if, but a when. At least this way, part of the army will already be gathered, and I need to have the support of the people of

Gharridan behind me in this."

"Do you really think that Queen Adamara is just going to let you waltz into the capital with an army at your back?" Melvin questioned. "She'll take that as a quest for power and combat it with everything she has at her disposal."

"I know." I ran a hand over my face in defeat. "But I need to be able to march into that throne room without bloodshed. The council will be more inclined to listen if I have the support of the people at my back."

He looked at me seriously. "You can't do this without bloodshed, Vladimir."

"I will find a way," I snapped.

I shut my eyes in apology, taking a deep breath. "I didn't have a choice, Melvin. Finnigan wants to be rid of the queen, and he threatened William's and Taryn's lives to get me to follow through with this."

His eyes narrowed with distaste. "Finnigan betrayed you?"

"Finnigan betrayed Gharridan. His interests are only selfish right now. He can't be trusted."

Melvin ground his teeth together, deep in thought. "You're going to have to have allies on the inside who are willing to let you in."

A smile twitched at the corner of my lips. "Do you think you might be able to help me with that?"

He scowled. "I'm all but a fugitive now, thanks to you."

"Well, at least now you get to join our band of outlaws." I smirked. "Captain Verone is still loyal, but I'm not sure which council members he has been able to sway. I'm going to ride ahead tomorrow, try to meet with him and figure out a plan of action."

Melvin nodded, opening his mouth to speak, but a sudden commotion echoed from the edge of the camp again, followed by an explosion that shook the ground beneath my feet. Our eyes locked, fear crinkling at the corners. I went flying out of the tent. Heads ducked out of tent flaps all around me in confusion. Others ran past.

That was when the first flaming arrow flew into the camp, finding its mark on the top of a canvas tent. The fabric quickly caught flame. Another arrow descended on the tent next to us.

Horror crawled up my throat.

We were supposed to have more time.

My feet pounded against the earth as I drew my sword, running blindly toward the direction that the arrows had come from.

"I need archers!" I yelled, watching as the number of flaming arrows multiplied, igniting the tents all around us like a forest fire. The devouring flames ate their way through the coarse fabric, stretching as far as they could in search of new victims. I quickly realized my sword was of no use and sheathed it, snatching an unwatched bow from the ground and grabbing several arrows from another soldier. I scrutinized the darkness, trying to determine where the arrows were coming from. Woods surrounded us on all sides. The attackers were shooting from the trees. A flame suddenly ignited out of nowhere in the distance, and I nocked an arrow, focusing on the light. If I could find the source of the flame, I could find the archer.

The flaming arrow barreled over our heads, but I kept my eyes peeled for where it had come from. Another light ignited in the darkness, and I quickly released an arrow, its fletching whistling in the air. My nimble fingers quickly sent two more after it, rapid-fire, as I adjusted my aim slightly with each shot.

One of my arrows found its target.

The spot remained dark.

Six more archers flanked me. I pointed out into the darkness. "Watch for the light and fire at it!"

I left them in charge, racing along the edge of the camp, flames and smoke billowing from every direction, men shouting, horses whinnying in fear. I coughed as the smoke invaded my lungs, choking me. More archers passed by, and I jammed my finger toward the enemy.

"Take them down!" I ordered.

A soldier stood dumbfounded, staring at the flames, his eyes wide and mind frozen. I picked up a bow and shoved it into his hands.

"Start firing!"

I didn't wait to see if he listened but continued charging down the line. Men worked with blankets to quickly put out the flames. Hoofbeats pounded near the edge of the woods. Too many. I drew my sword, finding General Lyle's face among the soldiers. He sent me one of his nods, drawing his sword along with his men.

"Ambush!" I yelled to the men around me. "Form a line! Weapons at the ready!"

The stampeding battalion rolled toward us like a monstrous wave threatening to wipe us from existence. I raised my sword with the men around me, flames glinting off the steel of the blade as we charged forward to meet the enemy. Despair clung to my lungs. I had never wanted this, never wanted bloodshed, but as swift as a flowing river, the blood was about to run.

CHAPTER FORTY-NINE

TARYN

ONLY ONE COLOR dominated my vision as I stormed down the hall after Queen Adamara dismissed us. Red bombarded every corner of my mind, preparing to explode within my senses. Anger. Fear. Revenge. The emotions swirled within me, overcoming my self-control. My fingers trembled, hands shaking at my sides.

Everyone had left the room at the same time in a flurry of footsteps, but one set of boots followed me all the way back to my corridor.

"I didn't know anything about this, Taryn; this was the first time I've heard about any of it, same as you."

The anger within me boiled over like a rupturing volcano.

I spun, slapping William across the cheek as hard as I could.

The sound of the impact ricocheted off the walls around

us in the resounding silence.

"There are men out there tonight, William, *your men*, that will die on a battlefield that shouldn't even exist! Are you so blinded by bitterness and hatred that you would be willing to sacrifice the lives of the people of Gharridan for your own vengeance?"

My words seethed with hatred. His hazel eyes avoided mine as he worked his jaw where I'd struck him. The skin flared pink.

"If Vladimir dies tonight, his death is on you. The only reason he left with Katherine in the first place is because you wrongfully accused her of the murder of an innocent man!"

"I didn't know he was innocent!" William growled.

"But you *did* know that Katherine was," I spat. My chest heaved with indignation as I crafted my next words. "You will *never* be king of Gharridan, because by the time your mother gets through with this country, there won't be anything left to rule! Truth is what brings unity, William. Lies do nothing more than destroy, and divide, and completely ruin everything they touch. Gharridan cannot come back from this."

I let my words sink in. Whatever trust I'd managed to procure with him was long gone, but I would never regret my words. I'd had enough of dancing around the issues, pretending like I'd forgiven him, acting like everything was all right. I didn't want to forgive him. Didn't want to be around him—didn't want to even look at him.

William's face twisted in pain; my words had gutted him.

I was glad.

I wanted my words to echo inside his mind for the rest of his days, haunt him whenever his thoughts grew quiet, and linger with his spirit long after his soul left his body. He would never learn any other way.

His lips parted.

No words came.

"You're nothing but a coward, William."

I didn't wait to see his reaction. I didn't want to ever see his face again.

The door to my room slammed behind me, barring William from my presence. I took a deep breath in an attempt to calm myself, fingers still shaking as I began to count the minutes out loud, willing the time to crawl faster. It dragged on like a stubborn old mare dragging her feet, made worse by my counting. I'd caught Verone's attention before leaving the room, and he had caught Finnigan's. We needed to talk, and we needed to talk now. After a painstakingly slow five minutes, I left my quarters again, the hallway now devoid of William.

An eerie silence plagued the castle, ghosting through each corridor I traveled down, but I couldn't tell if the chill creeping up my arms was real or if it was my heightened senses playing tricks on me. I was the first one to arrive in our meeting place. Only shards of moonlight from the small window lit the room. I sank against the far wall, anxiety shredding me like a dagger. There had to be something we could do, some way we could help Vladimir or warn him, but if what the queen said was true, it was already too late.

A few minutes later Finnigan and Verone entered the room at the same time. I strode forward, leaning forward over an old table, my fingernails digging into the wood.

"Did you know about this?" I hissed. My eyes bore into Verone like those of a ravenous wolf.

He scowled at my words. "You dare assume that I would

put Vladimir in that kind of danger? I was in the dark, just like you."

"What is this matter about him trying to place himself on the throne?" I pressed.

"It's not true."

"What?" Finnigan snapped.

Verone shook his head. "That's what the queen wants us to believe, but we had a rider return from one of the outposts the battalion visited. Vladimir is gaining the people's trust by trying to get Gharridan to unite. He has no desire for the throne."

Finnigan's hands curled into fists, eyes taut. "You're certain?"

Verone nodded. "I know Vladimir. He would never do such a thing."

"But the queen is still about to slaughter him and all his men," I said.

"He won't be alone," Verone interjected. "I knew he was getting close, so I sent Melvin and a battalion out to meet him."

"What was your last contact with Vladimir?" I asked.

"I haven't had direct correspondence with him since he left." Verone shrugged. "Everything I've learned has been third-party."

"But the queen knows," I observed.

Finnigan crossed his arms. "If you didn't know about this, Verone, do you mind explaining to me how there is a Gharridan army about to destroy Vladimir and his men, yet the captain of the guard knows nothing about it?"

"Not a word of this was spoken to me," Verone said defensively. "Nothing about this ever crossed my desk or went through my ranks. The queen would have had to pull from elsewhere, unless she had someone to retrieve the soldiers right from underneath me."

The breath hitched in my throat—or unless she questioned his loyalty.

My eye shot up to his, suddenly growing wide. "Captain Verone, you have to go."

Both he and Finnigan threw me a strange glance.

"If she managed to procure an army without your knowledge and without consulting you, that means she doesn't trust you or knows something about you that you don't think she knows. As captain of the guard, you may not have accompanied this mission to wipe out Vladimir, but you would have been informed." I swallowed. "Your life is in danger."

Captain Verone's dark face paled in the moonlight, the realization hitting him like a stone wall. "She had me issue an order for one of the battalions to be transferred to the western border, but if someone tampered with the orders before they went out—"

Finnigan's eyes darted around suspiciously. He grabbed Verone by the arm. "Did anyone follow you here?"

Verone opened his mouth, fear penetrating his face when no words came out.

"We all have to go." I rushed for the door, flinging it open.

Footsteps echoed from down the corridor, the clink of armor growing closer.

Finnigan shoved me forward into the hallway, voice deadly. "Run."

I took off without looking back, feet pounding against stone as I lifted my skirts and dashed through the halls like a madwoman. Captain Verone and Finnigan ran close behind me, but our pursuers had picked up their pace. I prayed they wouldn't catch us. When we reached the first branch in the corridor, I felt a sudden breeze as Finnigan and Verone each split down separate passageways, but I continued straight ahead. Heart racing. Lungs screaming. Fear pulsing through my veins.

It was a setup.

The dinner.

The talk.

The revelation.

It was all a setup.

My feet slapped across the floor as I heard the clatter of the soldiers' armor reverberating through the halls. A burning sensation filled my lungs as I pumped my arms, pushing myself as fast as I could through the dark corridors. The rustle of armor amplified.

They were getting closer.

A side door emerged on my right and I quickly barreled into it, tumbling down the staircase until I found myself in the servants' quarters. They jumped back in shock, wide eyes watching me with curiosity. I tried to ignore them as I cut through the sea of black-and-white uniforms, making my way to the other side of the hall. They didn't stop me, and I wondered if my quick passing even gave them time to register my face. I didn't look to see if the guards had followed, but I knew that if the queen suspected me, I needed to make sure I was in my room.

The stairwell at the other end of the servants' quarters loomed before me and I crept up the steps, cracking the door and looking both ways down the hall trying to figure out where I was. Once I regained my bearings, I scurried my way through the castle until I reached my room. I shut the door behind me, yanking my dress from my body. Less than a minute passed before a fist pounded on the door.

"Just a minute!" I called, trying to disguise the panic in my voice as I threw a robe around my nightdress.

My bare feet padded across the rug, shaking fingers grasping the door handle and then swinging the door inward.

I squinted against the torchlight, pretending the sudden brightness bothered me as I forced my expression to appear quiet and confused. Three guards stood outside the door in full armor, hands tightly gripping the hilts of their swords. No friendliness exuded from their faces, and I stayed still as the central soldier peered over my head and into the room as if looking for someone.

"Can I help you?" I asked.

Trying to hide how out of breath I was seemed like trying to conceal a fire.

The guard frowned upon finding my room empty. "We're looking for Captain Verone, Miss Gallows. Have you seen him?"

I cocked my head as if in thought. "Not since the dinner. Is everything okay?"

His eyes grazed over me, searching out a lie, but he didn't find what he was looking for. "Yes. Sorry for disturbing you, Miss."

I nodded, slowly shutting the door behind me. I sank against it as a sea of emotions crashed over me.

She knew.

The queen knew.

Captain Verone had been discovered.

I would probably soon be discovered too.

Vladimir was under attack—if he wasn't dead already.

We lost.

Nothing.

It had all been for nothing.

I covered my mouth, muffling the cry that ripped from my throat as tears streamed down my cheeks, shoulders shaking with despair.

CHAPTER FIFTY

VLADIMIR

DEATH SURROUNDED ME like a cloud, suffocating me like the smoke rising from the burning canvas of the tents. Its powerful smell overwhelmed me, drove me mad. The metallic taste of blood hovered in the air, and I tasted sweat as it poured down my brow and across my face, its salty flavor out of place with the horror surrounding me. Blood coated the length of my sword, flames glinting off the last few bare patches of steel. Every time I turned, I found another blade raised to strike, another face roiling with anger. My sword grew heavy in my hands, muscles heaving with exhaustion. Man after man, sword after sword, one cry of defeat after another. I barely managed to defend myself. My consciousness screamed at me as I swung the weight of my sword around, driving it forward into a man's chest, felt the weight of his shocked body hanging on it and then the weightlessness as I drew the weapon out of him.

The savage beast that was War raged around me. I hated him more than anything.

I doubled over and retched what little my stomach held, disgusted with myself over the scene around me, before turning to meet the next foe—but these men were not foes. The men I fought were living, breathing Gharridans, men I had fought alongside—men I had fought *for*. The division in our country had tunneled so deep that we had found ourselves here on the battlefield destroying one another. I didn't want to do this. All I had wanted was to avoid bloodshed.

The next warrior fell, and I felt the anguish burn within me. But they would kill us if we didn't kill them first. My knees grew wobbly and weak like my stomach, but the opposing side was dwindling.

They had not anticipated our numbers.

"Drive them back!" I barked at the men gathered around me. Our attackers began to look for their fellow countrymen, realizing their lack of numbers and that they would soon be surrounded, realizing they had lost. One by one, they turned tail, running back into the safety of the forest, fleeing for their lives. When my men attempted to follow, I held an arm out, stopping them.

"Let them go," I ordered hoarsely.

The night was dark, but with the fires still blazing I could see the apprehension scrawled across their faces. If any of the enemy survived, the threat remained.

"I want a line of you at the ready in case they return for a second wave; the rest of you start gathering the wounded. Save who you can—no matter which side they are on." I sensed their hesitation. If their own countrymen had betrayed them, they weren't considered worth saving. But my eyes bore into them. "I mean it."

The gritty smell of War—wounds and blood and sweat—hovered in my nostrils as I found my way through the remnants of what had once been a camp. The fires had nearly destroyed everything; where once a tent had been pitched, a charred patch of earth and heaps of ash and burnt canvas lay in its place. With each step, my heart hung heavier in my chest, threatening to sink me into my sea of agony. It took everything in me to keep from collapsing to my knees. Bodies lay strewn about the bloodied ground. Some still screamed in pain; others remained completely silent. I felt bile rise in my throat, dry heaving as I quickened my pace across the earth.

Their blood was on my hands. I'd traded their lives for Katherine's. Taryn's. William's. Who was I to weigh the value of one person's life above another? *All* life was valuable. Precious. Irreplaceable. I'd wanted to lead these men to defend their country, but instead I had marched them to their death, engaged them in what I feared would be an endless war.

I raked my hands through my damp hair, pulling at the strands in frustration. I thought I could outsmart Finnigan, thought I could stay one step ahead, thought I could unite this country. I was a fool.

"Vladimir!"

I jerked to the left.

A soldier ran toward me, waving a hand for me to follow him.

"Quickly!" he gasped.

I flew after him. The soldier backtracked through the camp, abruptly stopping before two battered soldiers kneeling next to an injured man on the ground.

I staggered in shock, stomach plummeting when I saw who held their attention. I pitched forward, swallowing as I found my way to my knees beside Melvin. Blood soaked his clothes, a rip in them hovering over his abdomen where he had been pierced by a sword. The blow didn't warrant immediate death, but his body would never survive the devastation.

His ragged breathing grew louder as I leaned closer, coming into his line of vision.

His hand grasped mine. "Vlad—" He coughed with a gut-wrenching wheeze.

"Shh," I whispered. "Save your breath. You're going to be all right."

I choked on the lie.

Melvin took a deep breath, trying to gather the strength to speak. His eyes locked with mine, gaze burning into me. "No, you listen to me," he rasped. "Do not let this country fall, Vladimir. It has stood strong for too long to tear itself down."

I dipped my head in acknowledgment. "I will restore Gharridan, Melvin. I promise you."

He squeezed my hand, eyes tormented with pain. "Whatever you have to do—" He coughed. "Whatever it costs, whoever's life you must take, you unite this country, Vladimir, and you make it stronger than it ever was. If anyone can do it, it's you."

I nodded and squeezed his hand back in affirmation, his skin already a sickening shade of grey.

His breaths shallowed, but he never took his gaze from me.

"Vladimir, you, you—"

His mouth was open to deliver his next message, but it remained that way as death stole his final words. The light left his eyes suddenly, and they turned vacant. His hand clasped in mine went limp. I lowered it gently to the ground as my shoulders sagged, tears descending from my eyes as I slid my hand over his face, closing his eyelids.

I bent my head, succumbing to the grief that washed over me. Melvin deserved more than this.

Melvin hadn't cared about sides, hadn't cared about our country's differences. All that Melvin had ever cared about was justice, and he didn't even get to live to see Gharridan united once more. His last glimpse of his beloved country had been the most torn he had ever laid eyes on. A sob wracked my body as I knelt over him, my heart broken as I lost another of the greatest men I had ever known. A man who believed in me. A man who fought for me. A man who always wanted what was best for me.

My fingers dug into my hair. If I had figured out Zedekiah's plan before all of this happened—if I'd helped Katherine escape but stayed in the capital—

I lifted my head, realizing that what it would take to restore Gharridan couldn't be done without bloodshed. Melvin wanted me to unite this country, but I no longer felt like that was possible.

I gently crossed Melvin's arms across his chest, placing his war-stained sword in his hands where it would be buried with him when they laid him to his final rest.

The ground wobbled beneath my feet as I stood, surveying the chaos around me. This battle was uncalled for. It should never have happened—just like everything else we'd gone through since Michael died. Melvin's death and the death of all the men in this battle lay solely with one person. Anger surged within me.

Do not let this country fall.

It was already crumbling between my fingers, but I held on to what was left, determined not to let it dissipate into the wind with everything we had already lost. I might not have been able to unite us, but I vowed to do whatever was necessary to save us.

Whatever it costs.

I moved through the camp, finding where the wounded were being organized in the few tents that hadn't been scorched. One of the soldiers assisting saw me and approached.

"Sir?" he questioned.

My gaze flicked over the wounded men bearing injuries both minor and fatal. "I need to speak with one of them. One who is lucid."

The soldier caught my meaning, disappearing into the first tent for a few moments before darting into one and then another. His head poked out of the third tent, motioning me inside. I ducked through the flap, making my way to where the soldier stood before a man lying on a mat. An abrasion covered his side and a nasty wound in his leg kept him from walking, but if he avoided infection, he would heal. He would live to see another day—unlike Melvin.

At the sight of my seething expression, his already pale face turned whiter. Fear emanated from his eyes like a cornered prey.

I squatted beside him. He was young. Didn't look like he could have been in the army for more than a year or two.

"You know who I am." I kept my words calm, even.

He nodded.

"If you want to survive, you're going to answer my questions."

It wasn't a request.

He swallowed.

"Whose orders were you under?" I asked.

His gaze flit from mine to the soldier standing behind me. "The queen's."

I grimaced. "How did you find out we were coming?"

"I don't know, but someone alerted the government. The queen called our regiment up a few weeks ago."

"What were the orders?"

He licked his lips. "We were told you were amassing your own army, planning to overthrow the queen and take Gharridan, and we were sent to make sure it didn't happen."

"Is she planning a second attack?"

"Not that I know of. Sir."

Truth hovered in his gaze. He had no reason to lie.

I chewed on my lip as I rose to my feet, marching out of the tent.

Grace had been extended too far.

Queen Adamara was trying to destroy this country.

I refused to let that happen.

My gaze swept from side to side, looking for any familiar faces. I grabbed two soldiers I'd talked with last night and asked them to bring me eighteen other men, with instructions to assemble outside the command tent, which by some miracle remained intact.

My mind worked quickly as I glanced among the destroyed

rows of tents, trying to gather my thoughts to figure out what I needed to accomplish. There was much to do and far too little time.

There is never enough time.

When I reached the tent, the men were already crowded inside, their faces nervous yet expectant. I briefly rubbed my forehead, exhausted but trying to still appear in control in front of them. They needed to see strength, not weakness.

"Queen Adamara sent Gharridan's own men—your comrades—to attack us. To kill us, because she suspected us of being a threat."

They glanced between one another uncomfortably.

"I don't know what is going through the queen's mind or what has possessed her, but this insanity cannot continue. Let me be clear—I have no desire to take the throne. I only wish to restore the justice that Gharridan seems to be lacking, but I *will* remove her if she will not give up this ludicrous endeavor. I want all of you to pair up and ride out to the ten remaining cities and villages that we've yet to reach. Tell them what happened, tell them of the slaughter and bloodshed, speak of our hope for unity. Emphasize that I harbor no wish to sit on the throne of Gharridan. I want you to ask for their help, to join us at arms and restore their country alongside us."

I paused, letting my words circled the room as I took each of them in.

One of the men swallowed, tentatively asking, "What happens to Queen Adamara if we restore justice?"

What would happen? There were crimes she needed to answer for.

I took a deep breath. "That decision will be discussed between the council and the Kavari, and then will be ultimately decided by the people."

I raised my eyebrows, asking for their consent.

They all nodded in agreement.

"Good." I stood straighter. "We will reunite outside the capital in two weeks' time. It's crucial that you're not late. Queen Adamara needs to see that we have the backing of the Gharridan people."

Once they left, I headed back to the infirmary to help where I could.

I suffered no external wounds, but I doubted I would be so lucky next time.

Next time.

This was not the end of our battles with Adamara.

The war had only just begun.

CHAPTER FIFTY-ONE

TARYN

I CONFINED MYSELF to my room over the next few days. I didn't eat. Couldn't eat. The thought of food made my stomach roil. Someone knocked once, and William identified himself, but I didn't answer. His face would only make me angry. The carpet wore down where I paced back and forth, anxiously waiting to hear from Finnigan or Verone—but also terrified of hearing from them. Fear and despair infiltrated my mind, tortured me. Vladimir was dead.

Vladimir was *dead*.

Verone might already be in chains, and there was, there was nothing I could do. I couldn't hide in my room forever, but I also doubted that I could endure the weight of this palace after everything that had transpired. Eventually, I would be found out.

I should run away—run away and never look back. I chewed on my fingernails, letting myself linger on the idea. I never asked to be part of any of this, yet I'd buried myself so deep it seemed I would never see daylight again. My saddlebags peeked out at me from underneath the bed. I could do it. Pack my few belongings, go out for a ride and never return. There was nothing left for me here. I wasn't a prisoner. Not yet. I still had the free choice to leave.

My teeth ground together.

I still have free choice.

But would leaving be the right choice?

I knew the answer and cursed myself for wanting to be so selfish. I wasn't that girl anymore, the girl who would run off on her own at a moment's notice. I had an obligation to make the right choice. It was the only thing in my life I still had control over.

Helvah looked at me from across the room, tears staining her cheeks, accusation in her eyes. My choices didn't affect just me but those around me, and I had forever altered her life.

No. I would stay, and I would fight.

I changed into a fresh dress and slipped down the hall, making my way toward Marco's room. A silence permeated the castle, as if Queen Adamara's revelation had chilled it to the bone.

Marco sat in his cushioned chair, gaze fixed on the bay window like it always was. He didn't acknowledge my presence as I slipped into the chair beside him. Rain streaked the windows, running down in little rivers as if Gharridan itself were crying over Vladimir's death. The oppressive gloom of the weather dampened the tone of the room.

"I'm afraid I have some terrible news for you, Marco," I

choked out.

Maybe there was still some hope to grasp, yet I could find nothing to hold on to.

The next words refused to come. I doubted I would be able to utter them anyway.

Marco turned to me, his eyes lined with clarity. "Who are you?"

I straightened a little, wiping the tears from my face, encouraged by this new question.

"I'm Michael Gallows' daughter."

His eyes pooled with suspicion, then softened, mouth opening several times in succession but never uttering any words. I stayed still and silent, trying not to distract him from whatever he was preparing to say.

He focused on me. "Coming."

"What's coming, Marco?"

The brief clarity revealed the battle warring within, but the only word he managed again was, "Coming."

"Marco," I began carefully, "what happened in Northunder? Do you know what happened to Princess Djara?"

His head tilted back and forth as if in a trance. "Massacre. It's terrible. Safe. Coming."

The window regained his attention, the lucidity vanishing.

I pursed my lips, distraught. Marco might have information about my mother, something that would help me know how to find her family. Over the past few days of isolation, it had plagued me, and the more I continued to think about it, the more firmly I grounded myself in the belief that my mother was Princess Djara. My father would've worked closely with his predecessor, Gabriel. He could have easily met my mother during their ambassadorship in Algarar. Why she had left was unclear, but maybe she hadn't agreed with the war her family had waged. Maybe my parents had fallen in love, and my father warned her and was able to save her life.

It was a possibility.

Slumping with disappointment, I left Marco's room and wandered the halls, if only to give my carpet a break. I didn't think it would appreciate several more hours of me wearing over the same path again and again. No one paid me any attention as I wove my way through the crisscrossing corridors, admiring the tapestries and paintings but not really seeing them. It helped me memorize every nook and cranny within the castle walls. Sitting still was not an option. I had to keep moving, had to keep seeing things, had to keep my mind off the fact that Vladimir was—

The corridor opened up into an open-air balcony. Finnigan leaned against the marble railing dressed in a dark tunic; his dark, curly hair was pulled back into a low ponytail away from his darkly bronzed skin. The gardens below captured his attention. My steps faltered for a moment, tripping on the stone floor. I hesitated, my eyes catching his and asking if it was safe to stay and talk.

He glanced around for a second before turning away and dipping his head in the most imperceptible of nods. I approached, standing several feet away and admiring the luscious gardens below. Most of the beautiful plants had morphed into fruitless brown twigs for the winter, but spring was coming. Spring was close.

"It's a bit chilly today, is it not, Master Finnigan?" The balcony lay empty except for us, but I still feared the threat of listening ears. "Do you think those practicing on the training fields are cold?"

Finnigan lifted his head. "I'm sure if it was too difficult a day the captain would pull them back. He knows what's best for the men and should be doing a good job with them today."

Hope fluttered through me. Captain Verone wasn't in a jail cell—he was still captain of the guard.

Finnigan shifted away from the railing. "I'm afraid I must depart. I've had pressing papers tearing at me all day and must return to them. Might I suggest you not tarry long in the winter air, Miss Gallows? I'm sure the hearth in your room would keep you much warmer."

Strange words.

His head tilted, expression implying a deeper meaning.

The document.

He'd gotten the document.

And it was in my room.

"Yes, Master Finnigan."

We parted, heading our separate ways. I tried to keep my stride steady as I hurried back to my hall. Finnigan had done it. He'd gotten the immunity. I flung open the door and barred it behind me before dashing to the hearth to investigate. It didn't take me long to find it, stashed beneath a book resting on the mantel.

The paper felt crisp and fresh as I quickly skimmed its contents. It outlined the clear immunity of Jarrod Lynch. He would be ineligible to be tried for any crimes and was placed under both the protection of the Crown and the Kavari. To deny this immunity or break the agreement was considered treason. All three seals lined the bottom of the parchment.

I chewed on my lip, questioning the credibility of the Kavari's seal since they'd been disbanded, but I'd done what I was told. A smile crept across my lips, offering hope. Maybe Jarrod Lynch's testimony would be the answer to all our problems. I rolled the document up, stuffing it in my pocket before grabbing my cloak to vacate the castle grounds.

Randal was waiting for me.

A drizzle still descended from the sky, but it was little more than a light sprinkle dotting the bare flesh of my hands. That, along with the thawed snow, created a damp, muddy ground like quicksand that Stryder's hooves sank deep into. Leaving the castle induced danger, but circumstances had left me without a choice. It was a risk I would have to take. If Verone was still in command, surely I was safe for now.

I scanned the edges of the forest while keeping a close watch on my back. The birch trees appeared like tall ghosts in the mist, beckoning us closer. My eyes dragged over my shoulder but never found any followers. The white trees stretched infinitely into the forest, leading us farther and farther away from the capital.

The cottage sat still, silent. Not even a whisper of life hovered in the windows. Water splashed around my feet when my boots hit the mud, soaking the hem of my skirt. I looped Stryder's reins over the post and he pawed the ground in agitation, dampening his winter coat. I approached the cottage, but the front door burst open before I could reach it.

"Do you have it?" Randal's voice rasped.

I pulled the paper from the security of my cloak and extended it to him. His hungry eyes surveyed the paper with a ravenous appetite, snatching the immunity from my hands. He nodded, checking each and every paragraph.

"It's all there. Everything you asked for," I said.

"Good," he said greedily. "Very good."

I lifted my chin. "Could you give me an indication of what this testimony is about?"

He scowled. "I already told you; you must wait to hear along with everyone else."

I didn't like being left in the dark.

"There's a council meeting scheduled for the morning," I said. "Do I have your word he will be there?"

"He'll be there."

Something cracked in the woods.

A dead branch?

An animal?

Randal's wild gaze jerked to mine.

"You said that you came alone."

Fear slithered up my spine as my gaze bore into the shadowy trees. "I did."

Randal took off, shoving the document of immunity into his shirt as he disappeared around the corner of the house. Within seconds, I jumped on Stryder's back, steering him around the house and over Randal's tracks to imprint nonsense into the mud and erase any sign of the man.

A whinny echoed through the mist.

I dug my heels into Stryder's sides. He flew underneath me, bolting through the trees at breakneck speed. Mind racing, heart pounding, I guided him around the trunks, desperate to reach the edge of the forest and for Randal Lynch to get away. The thunder of hooves built behind us, and I felt the blood drain from my face.

Just a few more strides, just a little longer, but the adrenaline exacerbated the fear within my body. I didn't know these woods. I hadn't lived in them, hadn't grown up in them. I urged Stryder faster, the wind slapping at my cheeks, stinging my skin until it went numb, cloak billowing behind me. The forest abruptly slanted downward. Stryder's hooves sucked in and out of the mud sickeningly as he tried to slow down, but his front hoof caught in the slop and he nearly fell to his knees as he struggled to regain footing. The unexpected lurch sent me tumbling to the earth below where I landed with a hard slap on the ground, knocking the air from my lungs. Stunned, I lay flat on my back, staring up at the interweaving branches of the trees. I couldn't move, couldn't talk. Air finally rushed into my lungs. I stood to my feet, staggering, but it was already too late.

Eight horses surrounded me.

Four arrows aimed at my heart.

Gharridans.

My eyes darted among them, a river of relief washing over me when they came to rest on Finnigan.

"Finnigan," I gasped. "What's going on? You nearly scared me half to death."

But even as the words left my mouth, I knew something was off.

His eyes.

They were dark.

Cold.

Dangerous as a raging ocean.

My heartbeat slowed within my chest as I took in the other men, their hostile expressions, their weapons.

Fear.

Fear spread through my veins, growing in strength.

"Finnigan?"

Goosebumps spread across my arms.

The hair on the back of my neck rose.

He looked at me, and I did not know him.

No emotion touched his face as he flicked his wrist, and the soldiers descended on me like vultures to a corpse.

CHAPTER FIFTY-TWO

OUR ARMY SAT at the capital's doorstep. A half day's ride would find us at the city gates. Bedrolls spread out in every direction, the last remnants of the tents separating the rows of men. Soldiers milled about with purpose, preparing for the confrontation that lay ahead. A feeling of hope warmed the camp, but along with the hope there lingered a sense of dread. I saw it as it crept into the men's minds, displayed across their faces, etched itself into their movements. What happened tomorrow would either unite their country or destroy it. The heaviness of the thought threatened to crush me, but I had more pressing matters to deal with before dawn.

We still needed to formulate a plan.

I brought several high-ranking officers into my war command. None possessed the qualities to replace Melvin, but they were good men with sharp minds.

I rubbed my head as we argued around my wobbling desk in the command tent. For the past few hours, we'd been hashing out every possible point of action. How we would get into the capital, what the outcome might be, how many lives the mission might cost us. There was no end to the deliberations.

"Do you think any of the guards at the gate would be on our side?" one asked with trepidation.

I shook my head. "If they haven't joined us by now they've sided with the Crown. Even if they did support us, acting on their own to help us would only result in their certain death before we could even get through the gates."

His gaze fell back to the creased map along with the other men's, seeking out solutions that were not to be had. No route we considered avoided bloodshed.

"Are there no—" The officer hesitated. "No hidden entrances that we could explore?"

The idea had already crossed my mind. I chewed on my lip, staring at the map where I knew the entrance I'd first brought Taryn through was and also where the secret tunnels led out to far beyond the capital walls. I shook my head. "If there were, they wouldn't be big enough. Most would only be wide enough for one, maybe two men to enter at a time. Once they discovered where we were filtering in from, it would be a massacre. We'd only have one man to meet ten, twenty, there's no telling how many. We'd be trapped."

I examined the faces around me. Most were stone, some still lingering deep in thought, but I could see and feel the hopelessness buried deep underneath their skin. I had no assurance to offer. Our minds were battered, our ideas shot.

"We'll reconvene later this evening," I announced.

They glanced between one another. I knew it unwise to put off the war council meeting when the plan of attack was scheduled for the next morning, but I couldn't take another minute of this. I needed to clear my head. If we chose wrong and our men died, their blood would be on our hands—on my hands.

The men left quickly, and I sighed once I was alone again in the tent. Doubt trickled through all of my plans, disrupting any progress, and worry clawed at me as the fear of failure ripped at my mind.

A sliver of light shone on the ground as the tent flap pulled back.

"Yes?" Irritation laced my voice.

I didn't want to be disturbed right now. I needed to be able to think.

"I thought you'd sound happier to see me."

I spun, my bewildered eyes locking on the woman in the doorway with blood-red hair flowing down her back.

"Katherine?"

A smile twitched at the corner of her mouth. I crossed the tent in two long strides and crushed her in a bear hug.

She chuckled, her muffled voice saying, "I didn't think you'd be that happy."

I stepped back, staring at her and thinking this had to be a trick. I crossed my arms. "When you didn't show, I was worried."

"So was I."

"You don't know how much it means to see a friendly face." I smiled but sensed an uneasiness behind her expression.

"What happened?"

She shook her head. "You first. I think the matters here are more pressing."

I walked her through everything that had happened, relaying Melvin's death and our current conundrum of how we could get into the capital without more bloodshed.

She stared at the map; eyebrows lowered in concentration. "I see the predicament," she mused. "Do you think we could go in with just a few men and clear my name with Taryn's testimony?"

I quickly shook my head. "Everything else aside, it would be Taryn's word against William's. The council would never choose her word over the crown prince's, and after what I've done and what has happened here, we would be arrested immediately. The queen won't let us just saunter into the throne room."

Katherine frowned. "That wouldn't solve our Finnigan problem either. We need to get William and Taryn out of there."

"As long as he still thinks I'm claiming the throne, he won't harm them."

"But the second he finds out you aren't …" Katherine's words trailed off, and I grimaced.

"I know."

I needed to get a message to Taryn before Finnigan uncovered my plans, but I didn't think the queen was stupid enough to leave either of the secret entrances unguarded. Sending someone through the front gates would be just as difficult. In this time of uncertainty everyone passing through the gates would be heavily questioned, and sneaking into the palace was another matter entirely. I couldn't run the risk of one of my men being caught.

"How did your work go?" I asked Katherine, studying her tired face for any change.

She smiled, but it didn't reach her eyes. "The people have a new reason to gossip about the Radonaya. It wasn't without incident, but we are all here. I'll give you the details another day. We need to nail down our plan of action first."

I nodded. If I tried to listen now, I wouldn't retain anything she told me anyway.

Simply knowing she was safe provided me with more assurance than she would ever know.

I only left the tent for one brisk walk, returning immediately to pore over the map again and again, searching for solutions where there were none. If we had some way to grab the council's attention and get them to listen to us, it might work, but we didn't. We needed leverage. Darkness descended, but I still hadn't reconvened the war council. I couldn't. Not until I had something better to offer them.

"Sir Vladimir?"

I lifted my head at the voice. "Yes?"

One of the soldiers stepped inside. "Someone approached the outskirts of the camp and is requesting to speak with you. I believe they're a messenger."

My brows drew together. "From the capital?"

The soldier looked equally confused. "No, they—they said they're not from the Crown, but that they needed to speak with you immediately. That it was urgent."

The hair on the back of my neck rose.

The idea smelled like some sort of trap.

"Send him in."

He departed, and a few moments later, the flaps of the tent parted. A young woman entered, her tan dress frayed and worn from intense travel. Dirt was smeared in her dark skin and hair, and her sharp brown eyes flashed at me like daggers.

"You don't look like a messenger," I accused as I moved to the other side of the desk. I kept a ready hand on my sword. "What is your name?"

"Darya." She lifted her chin, mouth set in a thin, humorless line. "You're a hard man to find, Vladimir."

"It's difficult to stay in one place when your own country wants you for treason." I examined her again. "It appears as if you've been traveling for a long while. Who sent you?"

"Marco."

A chill traveled up my spine and sunk deep into my bones.

I stilled, eyes locked on hers. "Marco isn't even coherent right now."

She bit her lip. "I know. I heard about him in the capital. Before that, I thought he was dead."

My head tilted. "Why did he send you?"

With a glance over each shoulder, she reached into her brown cloak, withdrawing a missive wrapped in a leather wallet. It fell to the desk with a soft thud.

One corner was torn on the scuffed leather. Deep indentions marked the edge of the opening.

I studied it before peering at her suspiciously.

"What is this?"

She shrugged indifferently. "I don't know, but Michael gave it to Marco before he died, and Marco nearly forfeited his life to ensure that it reached your hands."

My eyes dropped back to the worn leather, disbelief coursing through my system.

No.

It couldn't be.

That letter was long gone.

We'd sacrificed everything to find it.

I swallowed.

Yet here it was, within my grasp.

"When did Marco give this to you?" I questioned.

Her thick eyebrows arched. "He and my father were close, and I've worked for him before. He trusts me. Marco passed through Fenville on his way back to the capital. Sought me out and handed it over to me, said it was a matter of life and death that I get it to you. Marco was afraid he was being followed or would be apprehended. He instructed me to wait two weeks before following him, so by the time I reached the capital he was already captured, Mordakai was murdered, and you had gone after Zedekiah. I'd been waiting in the capital for months when I ventured to the outlying towns to try to find you. Shortly thereafter, I'd heard of your return, but when I got back to the capital, you had already run off with Katherine. I've been nothing more than a sitting duck since then, biding my time and taking on piddly work—until your soldiers rode into town two days ago looking for volunteers to join your army." She crossed her arms. "Like I said, you're a hard man to find."

My eyes bore into the missive. Hope dared to rise within me. I never thought we would see it again. Michael gave his life trying to obtain it—Marco sacrificed his life to protect it. So many people had died trying to preserve whatever was written in that letter. Maybe it held our solution to this impending war.

Coming.

Marco's words during his brief moment of clarity echoed in my head.

Safe.

Had he been trying to tell me that the missive was on its way?

Coming.

My fingers picked the missive up gingerly as if it might disintegrate into dust. I unfolded the leather encasing the missive and flipped it over so I could read the inscription. The letter wasn't long, and I found myself reading faster until I suddenly reached the end. When I did, I nearly fell over from shock. I ventured back to the beginning of the letter, reading it over and over again, my eyes unable to comprehend what they were reading, thinking they had made a mistake, thinking I had misunderstood.

I had not.

My chest rose and fell as my breaths grew deeper, angrier, filling my body with fury. My blood boiled beneath my skin as my hands began to shake with outrage. The letters on the parchment mixed together until I could no longer focus on the page.

"Sir?" Darya asked, but her voice sounded far away, as if I were in a dream.

I wished I was in a dream.

This was no dream.

It was a nightmare.

A nightmare far worse than anything I could have imagined.

I heard myself call for Bog. His head poked through the entrance, and I focused on his narrowing gaze.

"Yes?" The change in my demeanor concerned him and frightened Darya.

I folded the missive, securing it inside my tunic, unwilling to part with it. My eyes bore into his as I tried to keep the storm warring within me at bay. My words came out harsh and demanding.

"Summon the war council."

CHAPTER FIFTY-THREE

❖

Taryn

COLD RADIATED THROUGH the silent stone, seeping through my skin and delving straight down to the bone. The ethereal light drifting down from a tiny slit in the rock provided my only comfort. Daylight bled through the small opening, telling me that the sun had risen less than an hour ago, but no one came for me. The muscles in my legs ached. A crick disturbed my neck. All night I'd paced. Paced until I couldn't stand anymore. Paced until my mind couldn't process any more information. I wrapped my arms around myself protectively, leaning against the back wall of my cell and biting my lip, trying to come to terms with the truth.

Finnigan had arrested me.

He'd betrayed us.

I'd never seen the man harbor any love for the queen, but

there was no other explanation—he'd betrayed us.

And he could have been lying about Captain Verone. Maybe he had also been arrested. It wouldn't matter. There was no hope for either of us now.

Finnigan knew everything.

A creak echoed through the eerie dungeon. I jumped to my feet, recognizing the sound of the outer gate, and my fingers twisted around the bars on the door, desperate for a glimpse of what was going on. Boots marched. Their thud against stone ricocheted off the walls, sounding as if an army was moving to greet me. I took a step back as a key fiddled around in the lock and the door swung open. Six of them. There were six guards.

"We're here to escort you."

Hope fluttered in my chest.

I recognized that voice.

He was one of the guards that regularly patrolled the corridors.

"Glen," I said cautiously. "What's going on?"

My eyes adjusted from the light dripping in through the outer door. Glen avoided eye contact, but not in a hostile way—in a way that said he didn't want to do this and was only following orders.

"The prisoner is to be taken before the queen."

Prisoner.

But prisoner was better than a corpse.

When he hesitated to remove me from the cell, I willingly ventured to stand between them, letting them lead me out of the darkness. They left my hands untied but kept a tight grip on the hilt of their swords. Even though their steps stiffened with tension, I sensed they held no fear of me escaping. They were correct. Maybe there was hope. Maybe I could talk my way out of this, but I couldn't lie to myself. I had no alternative.

My feet plodded slowly, terrified of what was to come, of what the queen would do to me. I searched every corner we rounded, every alcove cloaked in shadow, for William. If anyone could help me, it was him, but considering our last conversation had consisted of a slap and reprimand, I felt even that small twinge of comfort slipping away. A pang of guilt shot through me. I'd already used William countless times, and as much as I still hated him for his actions, I hated myself more for allowing myself to do that to another human. I was done. No more manipulation. No more twisted games.

Terror struck within me as we turned another corner. They weren't taking me to the queen's study or a room with a small audience—they were leading me to the throne room. The council—

The council meeting.

Jarrod promised he would testify today, but was his brother even still alive?

The massive doors loomed before me. If only their beauty signified an entrance into heaven and not an entrance into hell. Anxiety twisted around my heart, constricting my lungs and making me feel like I was drowning at the bottom of the ocean. The doors swung open, granting us entrance onto the checkered marble floor. I surveyed the columns that twisted up into the ceiling and felt oddly reminiscent of the last time I had entered this room. I had entered here intending to invoke the right of a Blood Vier, to lay claim to a position in the Kavari that I held no desire for in order to prevent Mordakai from attaining it, but Zedekiah had killed him, laying siege to the throne room in an attempt to take over. My eyes fell to the spot where Zedekiah had struck down his brother, the section of wall where his sword had pressed against my throat. I shivered, remembering the sharpness of the steel against my neck, the trickle of blood running from where it had begun to split the skin.

Queen Adamara watched us from her elaborate throne. The carved horse that made up the back of the chair, propelled upward in a rear, somehow looked more savage than it had before, as if it would come alive and trample me beneath its hooves. William stood to the right of his mother, face carved with disdain. Members of the council lined the walls in a wave of red garments. A sea of blood. I spotted Finnigan immediately, dressed in his council robes, dark eyes scrutinizing my every movement.

No one uttered a word.

When I caught sight of Captain Verone, shackled at the foot of the dais, I had to hold back the tears, the despair.

My feet grew wobbly, breath hitching as I finally came to a stop before the steps of the dais. The queen's condescending face leered down at me. Tension hung in the room like the silence before a storm, the world waiting in anticipation of the pouring rain and flashing lightning. I expected a crack of thunder to emit from Queen Adamara at any moment. The silence stretched on and on like an endless road. Maybe speech had left them, but I knew that everyone in this room, except the queen, feared to move so much as a finger.

"Taryn Gallows." Queen Adamara uttered the name with distaste. It echoed throughout the chamber like a curse. "From the moment you set foot inside the capital, you have worked tirelessly to tear this kingdom apart."

I stayed silent.

"At the urgency of Vladimir, you set to disrupt the decision regarding someone who had already been chosen to lead the Kavari, and while it exposed the traitor in our midst I cannot help but assume your motives were not pure."

Heat flared in my chest. "My motives were—"

"I am speaking!" The queen lifted a hand, silencing my defense. "You have disobeyed nearly every order ever given to you, and you came back to the capital claiming that you sided with the Crown and had revoked all association with the Kavari."

I swallowed.

Her eyes blazed. "Councilman Finnigan revealed your true intentions yesterday, exposing you and Captain Verone as allies of the treasonous Vladimir, claiming that you support his usurpation of the Crown. Is this true?"

"Finnigan is equally as guilty," I ground out. "He plotted alongside us."

"So you admit to treason," she mused.

"No," I retorted. "Vladimir never expressed any interest to me about overthrowing the Crown."

The queen lifted her eyebrows humorously. "Then, pray tell, why is there a Gharridan army sitting at my doorstep with Vladimir at the head?"

"Maybe because you unjustly disbanded the Kavari and marked him as an outlaw."

I knew Vladimir. He held no desire for the throne. He had only ever wanted what was best for Gharridan and for his people. He wouldn't risk unnecessary bloodshed.

"He aided and abetted an enemy of Gharridan."

I closed my eyes in frustration. "Katherine is innocent!"

"Says a girl who knows nothing of the situation."

Anger trembled through me, wanting to tell the truth, but without Vladimir and Katherine here to back up my story, they would never believe me. William would deny it, and the council would consider my words a feeble attempt at a pardon. Unless William chose to come clean, it was my word against his.

The queen settled back, calming her temper. "Finnigan was trying to gather more intelligence from you and Verone."

I noticed she omitted the title from Captain Verone's name.

"He only gave you up when he learned that you had secured immunity documents for a known traitor of Gharridan—Jarrod Lynch."

"I do not believe that he is a traitor," I said.

"And why would a lowly village girl have any insight on the matter?"

Her words were meant to sting, but I brushed them off. "He said that he has evidence of treason within Gharridan. He wouldn't come forward without guarantee of immunity."

Queen Adamara leaned forward dangerously. "You meddle in matters that you do not understand."

"If he was a traitor, then why was my father the only one looking for him for the past ten years?"

A bitter smile formed on Queen Adamara's lips. "Because I asked him to."

Her words hovered in the air, daring me to challenge them.

"The matter was kept quiet to preserve the Crown from appearing weak before their enemies. This Jarrod Lynch that you speak of in such high regard, *Miss Gallows*, plotted to kill my children years ago when he worked as a physician for the royal family. Michael discovered his indiscretion, but Jarrod fled and managed to evade capture for the past decade. This man, who my husband and I trusted with our lives, betrayed that trust. He attempted to destroy us, and threatened to take away from us the very people we loved most."

Her voice broke on the last words as if the memory had grown too heavy to bear.

I didn't move.

Was it true?

Had she really commissioned my father to secure Jarrod Lynch, and I had just granted him immunity?

William had never mentioned anything about this attack, but I couldn't ever remember mentioning Jarrod's name to him. That matter had always stayed between Vladimir and me. I met William's eyes for the first time. No surprise encompassed his face. What emotions burned behind them, I couldn't tell, but he held no remorse for me. His mother discussing the matter seemed to solidify the betrayal he feared from me.

Something twisted in my brain, telling me that the situation was all wrong. When we'd first spoken with Gavil, he'd said that Michael had wanted him to testify against treason in Gharridan, but if Queen Adamara's story was true, there was no testimony, only Jarrod's attempt to escape.

"It's not possible." My voice barely rose above a whisper. It sounded weak, pathetic, like someone who had lost but still held on to the unrealistic hope of winning.

A dry laugh escaped her throat. "Whether you believe it's possible or not, it's the truth, and there are those who will testify to it."

With her words, I knew it was over.

I had nothing left to defend myself with.

I'd been tricked. Betrayed. Twice.

Jarrod Lynch wasn't coming. He'd gotten his immunity. He was probably halfway across the country by now.

"The question remains, what do we do with you now? Captain Verone obviously must endure the humiliation of a public trial where he will be sentenced to hang, but you, on the other hand, are a danger in and of yourself. You've caused more damage in a few months than one should cause in a lifetime, and the fact that you're a Blood Vier makes you even more deadly. People might wish to show mercy for the sake of your father."

Her finger tapped on the wooden arm of her chair. Once. Twice. Three times—like the ticking of a clock winding down until the next strike. One eyebrow arched intricately, and the whole room held its breath, waiting to see what she would decide. Her head cocked to the right.

"Perhaps we should see what our future king has to say on the matter. William, what should be done with the traitor?"

No.

William hid his shock well, his eyes surveying the attendants of the room before coming to rest on me. He swallowed as he tried to avert his gaze, but he was trapped.

My distaste for William momentarily faded as I desperately wished for him to bestow mercy. Yes, I had used and betrayed him, but I knew that he cared about me, and those feelings wouldn't snap with a single betrayal. They would linger, and he would either lash out with mercy or vengeance. The room around me swelled with anticipation, waiting for William's verdict.

His gaze turned sidelong at his mother when he spoke. "It's not for me to say."

She frowned. "One day when you're king, William, there won't be anyone to make decisions for you. Your weakness shows."

He flinched at her words, but he didn't bring his eyes to mine again.

"Taryn Gallows is a traitor to the Crown, and to Gharridan," the queen continued. "She deserves the punishment bestowed to prisoners of equal crimes."

Mercy appeared to have left me.

I trembled at her next words, my body growing faint.

"Taryn Gallows, for your crimes you are hereby sentenced to death."

Helvah's presence materialized at my side, but I couldn't look at her. My gaze flicked over the queen's shoulder to a figure lurking in the shadows with greedy fingers reaching out, a grin splayed across his face.

Death, it seemed, had finally come for me.

CHAPTER FIFTY-FOUR

VLADIMIR

THE ARMY COVERED the landscape like a dark cloud, an approaching storm equipped with rolling thunder and flashing lightning, full of unmatchable power. Behind me came the sound of thousands of soldiers marching in strict lines toward the capital of their country, ready to challenge the Crown. Heat flared in my chest, a sign of the anger still burning deep within me. The outer walls climbed higher and higher before our eyes, appearing more foreboding than ever before. Once, not long ago, these walls had given me the assurance of belonging and protection—of home. Now they stood as nothing more than a picture of injustice and betrayal.

My gaze roved over the top of the wall, marking each of the arrowslits, aware of the eyes that were no doubt watching us. I didn't know what their tactics would be. What their plan of attack was. Captain Verone wouldn't fight us, but I didn't know how much longer he could keep up his ruse. The captain of the guard couldn't ignore an army on his doorstep without revealing himself.

"Now would be the time to have a plan, Vladimir."

Anxiety radiated in Katherine's voice, her attention fixated on what lay beyond the city gates.

"There's no other way in," I said. "I had Nic scout out the hidden entrances last night. Both are heavily guarded. Even if we overtook them, the castle would be alerted to our presence."

"Right, well, I'm sure the front gates will welcome us with open arms."

"I'm working on it," I grumbled. "I just have to get someone's attention."

I motioned for the army to halt just outside of firing range. The walls loomed above us like a monster, the jaws of its entry gate clamped tightly shut. Behind me, the rows of foot soldiers and cavalrymen stretched out endlessly. I needed every one of them to still be alive at the end of the day. Getting inside the city gates and what would happen once we crossed the threshold was unknowable. I was gambling with far more than I was willing to lose. I spun Dante around, weighing the options in my mind.

"Vladimir."

I caught Katherine's gaze. She read my expression, sensing something dangerous brewing within my mind. Something she knew she wouldn't like. General Lyle rode in line beside her, each watching me expectantly, waiting for instructions.

"Stay here."

I tapped my heels against Dante's sides, wheeling him toward the city gate before taking off in a canter. I didn't have to turn around to know that Katherine's stare would be wide, her face coloring into a shade of red as vibrant as her hair. I'd hidden my plan from Katherine because she would never have gone along with it. Dampness clung to the ground, so no dust rose from Dante's path. The rhythm of his stride thrummed in my ears, keeping steady with the beats of my heart. I meticulously calculated my distance from the top of the wall as we approached.

Twenty more strides.

Fifteen.

Eight.

Three.

I eased Dante up, his hooves digging into the soft earth just over a hundred yards from the city gate, easily within range of the archers. They could shoot me, right here. End all of this—or make me a martyr.

A strong breeze flipped my cloak over my shoulder and ruffled my hair, winding between the dark locks. I kept my eyes peeled on the guard tower window, looking for signs of movement, knowing someone would be watching. I transferred my reins into one hand, reaching for my sword and pulling it out of its sheath in a painstakingly slow movement. It offered the soft sound of metal scraping over leather. I raised the weapon, holding it over my head, facing it upward to the sky.

Go slowly, I warned myself.

Twisting the hilt between my fingers, I flipped my sword upside down, leather still firmly in my grip. My arm extended completely out, sunlight rebounding off the gleaming steel. A raised sword stretched toward the sky created a signal that we were about to go to battle. An upside-down sword meant more than just we came in peace. The silent message would be received loud and clear.

I've come to bargain.

The breath caught in my throat. Dante stood still beneath me. Every soldier on the wall could see me, see what I was doing, what I was asking. They could not deny me this right.

The rays of the sun beat down on me like a searing iron, drawing sweat from my brow. Around me the world remained silent, a whisper of impending destruction floating on the wind. I did not smile, did not change my expression. I kept my chin held high, arm locked in place. When enough time had sufficed for them to have made a decision, I lowered my sword, replacing it in its sheath. No movement issued from the walls, no sounds of creaking gears, no decision from the watchtower. It would not be instantaneous. They would have to send a messenger to the castle. Deliver the news. Deliberate—and then return.

I kept one hand on the hilt of my sword, one on the reins. And waited.

The wood groaned in protest, hinges squealing as the massive safeguard opened wide enough to let a lone rider pass through. I kept my breaths even, trying to control my rage as Finnigan rode through the gates on a grey horse, red robes flapping behind him. Chin lifted, eyes cold, his gaze never wavered as his horse sauntered toward me. The grey halted several feet away from Dante, hooves leaving deep impressions in the soil.

"That's quite an army you've built." Finnigan's voice rang with approval.

"It takes a lot of men to overthrow a kingdom," I lied.

He chuckled, surveying the landscape beyond me. "That is why you're here, then? To lay your claim to the throne?"

A question hung in his words.

A test.

He knew something.

"Yes," I answered.

Finnigan leaned forward, crossing his arms across the saddle. "Interesting considering that every report I've garnered boasts the exact opposite—that you have no desire to rule Gharridan."

My hands twitched.

"I came to bargain with the queen." I knew the words I spoke were critical. "I will not risk bloodshed to overthrow this kingdom, there's—"

"The queen is occupied." Finnigan's voice grated against stone. "She's just sentenced Taryn Gallows to death."

My breath caught, gaze flicking to the opening in the gate. "What for?"

He shrugged. "Does it matter? I told you what would happen if you disobeyed my orders. You're reaping the consequences."

Heat swelled within me, fire in my veins.

I kicked Dante forward, removing the missive tucked inside my pocket and handing it to him. "Read this."

Suspicion wavered in his eyes as he took the leather, roving over its contents.

"We can take down the queen," I continued. "There's no need—"

"I don't want the queen taken down," he growled. "I want her extinguished, and I want you sitting on the throne." He handed the missive back to me. "This gives all the more reason."

I ground my teeth together. Finnigan didn't care about the contents of that letter, didn't care about its implications. All he wanted was a monarch to control—a puppet.

"Finnigan—"

He sat up in the saddle and cut me off. "Here's what's going to happen. I'm going to ride back through the gates, tell the keepers that you've agreed to the queen's terms and have been granted entrance into the city. Your army will ride through the city streets. Fight or don't fight, it is of no matter to me, but you *will* lead a battalion into the throne room. You will present this evidence to the council, and you will claim rule over this country."

His words struck like a serpent's bite, full of venom, sharp as the edge of a knife, letting them hover between us before continuing. "You don't know who is with me or who is against me. Take one step out of line, and I will take the life of the Blood Vier and the crown prince. Take a second step, and I will eliminate your little Radonaya. Moving against me will only grant them certain death."

I resisted the urge to shoot a glance at Katherine.

"Are we agreed?" Finnigan pressed.

I wanted to wrap my fingers around his insolent neck, prevent him from ever making another threat, but instead I gave him a curt nod.

"Good." His smile never reached his eyes. "We will be waiting for you."

The grey horse spun around at Finnigan's command, trotting back to the gates. Once he passed through, they quickly shut behind him. I cantered back to Katherine and the war council, face hard.

Katherine's gaze bore into me, expectant.

"Vladimir?" General Lyle questioned.

"Pass it back through the ranks," I ordered. "They are opening the gates. We will march into the city, but no blood is to be shed. Do not attack the soldiers within the city. Defend yourself only if you must. Stay in the streets as silent watchers, keepers of the peace. Remain in formation."

"They're going to open the gates?" General Lyle's words fizzled with doubt.

"Yes." I studied the gatekeeper's tower, wondering how great an argument currently raged within the walls.

"This is a trap," he objected.

"Most likely," I agreed, "but Finnigan is helping us get in and we don't have any other options."

"Vladimir," Katherine hissed, demanding my attention.

I leaned over so only she could hear. "When we get to the throne room, *do not* let Finnigan and his men anywhere near Taryn or William."

Her lips pursed as she nodded.

She didn't like this.

Neither did I.

My orders rippled back through the lines of men, repeated over and over again as they passed from one battalion to another. Confusion wafted over the soldiers, but there was no time for explanation. We waited, the walls of the city seeming to grow even more silent. I gripped the pommel of my saddle. Finnigan getting us inside the city was not a given. He might fail. Yet even as doubts swarmed my mind, the gates began to groan, their wide girth swinging outward, beckoning us with a welcome into the security of the capital.

Dante stepped forward, leading the army. Two guards flanked me, and several others watched my back closely. The shadow of the gate fell over me, casting us into darkness. My eyes roamed over the city, searching for anything out of place. The streets lay empty, silent as a ghost town. No children wandered. No merchants traded. Every shutter was tightly drawn.

It was too off, too easy.

Yet into the belly of the beast we crawled. The line of soldiers stretched out behind me as we wove our way through the streets. No soldiers greeted us, not even a sight so simple as a bleating goat. The hoofbeats echoed off the cobblestones, reverberating through the empty capital. The guard tower door remained shut. No archers appeared over the wall. We delved farther into the city. Quiet. It was too quiet. Only ten lines had passed the city gates.

"Something's wrong." Katherine's voice rang with warning.

I turned to address her, caught sight of the archer hidden on the rooftop.

The glint of the arrowhead.

The lives of my men flashed before my eyes.

I yelled.

Arrows whistled.

An explosion rocked to the right of me, the world filling with splintered wood, broken stone, and smoke.

Another explosion to the left.

Flames erupted.

My ears rang.

Dante bolted beneath me, thundering through a cloud of smoke. I felt him swerve, felt myself fall to the cobblestones, the rough surface ripping my clothes, rattling my bones. I couldn't hear, couldn't see. Dizziness assaulted me as the smoke billowed. I lay stunned, then rolled over, trying to get my bearings as I cursed myself. I knew Gharridan's tactics, should've expected a show like this. I struggled to my feet, coughing in the smoke, the ringing in my ears making it impossible to think.

A soldier emerged from the smoke, swinging his sword.

My blade was still in its sheath.

There wasn't enough time.

An arrow struck his chest clean through the ribs and drove him to the ground. Katherine emerged from the smoke with blood plastered across her arm and soot in her hair, another arrow already at the draw.

My ears teetered in and out of ringing, and I heard the clash of steel on steel.

I shook my head. "There wasn't supposed to be bloodshed."

I saw men lying on the ground, scattered horses galloping wildly.

Katherine grabbed my arm and brought my shock back under attention. "If you want this to end, we go to the throne room. Now."

Something in her eyes restored the sanity in me. I nodded, regaining my clarity. A few more soldiers materialized in the smoke, which we either evaded or struck down. These were

Gharridans, once my own men. I shouldn't be forced to kill them.

Six of my loyal men found their way to me, and Katherine led us forward, slinking into dark alleyways and drawing us away from the fighting. The streets would be crawling with soldiers, but Katherine picked her path with adept precision, her sharp gaze keeping a lookout, leading us up to the palace grounds. This was her element—she'd had to learn it well to survive.

A stampede of footsteps pounded from the right, and Katherine's arm shot out across my chest, forcing me against the alley wall. I held my breath as each of our bodies pressed flat against stone.

I glanced down at Katherine's tunic. "Where's the blood from, Katherine?"

"Not mine," she whispered.

I could see a tear in the fabric and knew she was lying.

The footsteps faded, and Katherine scurried to the next connecting alleyway. The ringing continued to fade in and out of my ears as the city streets slanted upward, bringing us closer to the palace. My back and arm ached from where I'd hit the cobblestones, but I was more concerned about the state of the soldiers I had left behind. We'd climbed high enough to where I could get a glimpse of the city gates—or where the gates were supposed to be. Smoke spread out in every direction, masking whatever destruction the soldiers of the city had wrought. Another explosion rocked the ground, shooting ash and rubble into the sky.

"Don't look back, Vladimir. Keep moving."

Katherine pulled me along, the six soldiers trailing closely behind us as the palace wall grew nearer. I had no plan to get inside. Most of the queen's soldiers would be preoccupied at the main gate, but in broad daylight guards would still be milling about as a second defense. We were still in the city, but we reached the end of the alley, far off-center to the palace entrance.

"Now what?" I muttered, growing frustrated.

Katherine pushed ahead as if I hadn't spoken, approaching a thick belt of ivy, fingers trailing carefully along the green branches.

"Ivy isn't strong enough to hold us," I snapped.

"No." She threw me an irritated look, grunting as she grasped something, hand disappearing into the foliage. "But this is."

Hidden behind the dense ivy, thick metal spikes had been driven into the wall, just wide enough for a hand to grab or a foot to rest on.

"How—"

Katherine smiled mischievously. "Had to sneak in somehow without anyone knowing."

I scowled. Her creation of this secret makeshift ladder was dangerous. It offered undocumented entry to the castle grounds to anyone who discovered it.

"Don't worry, Vladimir. No one would find it unless they knew exactly where to look for it."

I knew it would take a well-trained eye to find any of the spikes and a further level of intelligence to realize that each of them was connected for a common purpose, but it was still reckless.

Katherine shimmied up the wall first, pointing out the spikes to each of us as we grasped for the next rung. The metal left a stain of rust on my hand, my muscles complaining as I pulled myself upward. We heaved over the wall, dangerously dropping down into the gardens far away from the castle gates.

Katherine held a finger to her lips as she skulked around the bushes, using the hedges and tall plants for invisibility. Her eyes darted in every direction, seeking out danger. I could see the smoke from here, rising farther and farther until it tainted the blue sky. Another small explosion drifted to our ears. Whoever died today, their blood would be on my hands.

No one occupied the gardens. The castle would be on lockdown, the staff and nobles safely tucked away into secure locations. Most of the soldiers would hover near the city gates, expecting the enemy to attack from there. The castle rose above us, but there was still a stretch of open land between the garden and the stone walls.

"There's a supply entrance just to the left." Katherine was out of breath as she leaned against the thick trunk of a tree. "I don't know if the guard will be stationed on the inside or the outside. You'll have to make a run for it. I'll cover your back."

I surveyed the door, uncertainty gnawing at my insides. I motioned for the six soldiers to follow me, taking a deep breath as I broke for the castle wall at a dead run. Air whistled past my ears as my feet fled across the grass. I heard the arrow, didn't have time to turn, but it suddenly averted course, struck from the air. I saw it fall with another arrow impaled through its wood. A moment later, there was a yell as an archer plummeted from the castle wall. We were almost within reach. I barreled around the corner, plowing into a surprised guard and tackling him to the ground, wrenching him inside the supply entrance. His head slammed against the stone, rendering him unconscious as a barrage of shouts traveled along the castle wall at the missing archer.

"Move!" I yelled at Katherine as she sprinted toward the door. Once they figured out where we'd entered, they would be here in moments.

She tumbled through the door, never missing a beat as she hurtled up the stairs and into the main corridors, leaving us scrambling up the stairs to catch up with her.

"How do you know the council is gathered?" Katherine asked as we ran.

"Because Finnigan said that they were."

Taryn's sentence would have been issued in the throne room.

Katherine scurried into an alcove, checking to make sure no one was watching our movements.

We turned several more corners, avoiding the guards, knowing they were coming for us. I glanced behind at my little six-soldier army. Our success depended on how many soldiers guarded the queen. Finnigan barely managed to get us into the city walls, but I begrudgingly hoped he had a far better plan once we entered the throne room.

I was depending on it.

CHAPTER FIFTY-FIVE

TARYN

THE GUARDS WERE dragging me back to my cell. At least the execution wasn't immediate, but sitting in a cell waiting on an impending death might be worse. They'd bound my hands behind me, the rough ropes taking me back to horrible memories of when William and I had been abducted. Faint red scars still lined my wrists where the skin had chafed so many months ago. I swallowed, my feet stumbling to keep up with the guards' jerky and aggressive movements.

So this was how it would end.

"Hold up."

I winced at the voice, glad that I was unable to turn around and look him in the eye. He shouldn't be here. He'd made his choice in the throne room.

"Orders are to take her straight to the dungeons, Your

Highness."

"There's been a change of plans."

The grip on my arms tightened. These guards wouldn't give me up without a fight, not without an official order. The one on my left reached for his sword, but a fist suddenly flew into my peripheral vision, decking the guard to my right and sending him sprawling across the floor into unconsciousness. I lurched at the sudden freedom felt on my right arm, turning just in time to see the hilt of William's sword find the skull of the other man. The sudden release of weight sent me scrambling for balance.

"William," I growled, taking in the two guards. They'd be awake within seconds.

He lifted an eyebrow. "Oh, I'm sorry, would you rather have gone back to a cell? I can arrange that."

I scowled.

He grabbed my arm, pulling me out of the main corridor and down a deserted staircase.

"You're welcome, by the way."

"You could at least untie my hands."

William smirked. "That's okay. I actually find it keeps up the charade."

I fiddled with the ropes in my hands, the awkward angle of my body only making it harder. William felt me wiggling and stopped, stepping behind me to undo the knots. I couldn't see his face, but I sensed the change in his demeanor, the subtle switch from humor to tension.

"Is it true?" Disappointment rang in William's voice. His fingers stilled. "Did you really grant Jarrod Lynch immunity?"

I was glad my back was to him. Glad I wouldn't see the hurt.

"I didn't know he threatened you. His brother swore he would testify about treason."

William went back to work on my bonds, staying quiet for a moment. "Why didn't you tell me you were digging into this? If you had just been honest—"

"You mean like you were honest?"

The ropes fell softly to the floor. Fury blazed through me as I turned to him. He clenched his jaw, expression hard.

"Don't act like such a saint, William. I know who you are. You've shown me over and over again."

I scurried down the last few steps, reaching for the door handle, but he grabbed my arm and spun me around.

"What are you doing, Taryn?" His eyes bore into mine, searching.

I knew what he meant, but I sidestepped the question. "Avoiding an execution."

"I mean it," he warned. "Is everything you said, everything that happened—" The words caught in his throat. "Was it all a lie?"

I swallowed, wanting to be anywhere but here. He knew, he had to, but he wanted to hear it from my own lips. For the first time in a long time, I spoke truthfully, voice singed with contempt. "It doesn't matter, William. You made your choice. You sent your own men to their death. That's something I can't ever forget."

He dropped my arm and took a step back. Sensed the truth in my words.

A boom echoed through the stone walls, briefly shaking the ground beneath our feet. We stared at each other for a moment, confused, before exiting the stairwell and clambering for the nearest window. The archway gave us a sprawling view of the city. Smoke rose from the city gates like an ominous cloud, blocking half of Vladimir's army from view. A second explosion rocked the streets, sending another plume of smoke into the air filled with dust and rubble. My eyes widened in horror.

"No! What are they doing?" I exclaimed.

William's shock equaled mine yet lacked concern. "Vladimir is trying to overthrow the kingdom, Taryn. We can't just let him waltz through the gates."

I stared at the destruction, shaking my head as a wave of helplessness washed over me. "No. Something else is going on here, William. Vladimir would never do that."

He stiffened beside me. "You don't know Vladimir as well as you think you do."

A leather sheath hid inside his tunic, just within reach. I yanked his dagger from him, stepping back defensively. "If you won't do anything, I will."

"What are you going to do? Make them all shake hands?"

He snatched at my wrist, but I darted away.

"Taryn," he warned. "If the guards catch you they'll take you straight to a cell. You have to get out of here."

I shook my head and stood my ground. "I won't leave them to die."

My steps were cautious as I walked backward, the dagger extended in front of me. When I reached the first turn, I tore down the hall, looking for the fastest way to reach the chaos at the gates. I veered sharply to the right—and ran directly into Finnigan.

Before I could even step back, his hand twisted painfully in my hair. I kicked and clawed at him, nails stripping flesh, dagger flailing, but he wrestled the knife from my grasp and pressed it against my throat, stopping my struggle.

"Many thanks," he muttered. "Just saved me a trip downstairs."

Four guards stood behind him.

William rounded the corner, and a soldier blindsided him before he could reach for his sword, shoving the prince against the stone wall. William grimaced at the impact, unable to shake the guards who held him back. Finnigan forced my hands behind my back, retying them with a chain. I flinched as the rough metal scraped across my skin. The dagger repositioned from my neck down to the small of my back, tip pressing firmly but not forcefully. One wrong move would send the blade shooting up between my ribs, striking me directly in the heart.

"Why did you betray us?" I asked.

He ignored me.

"Was the document of immunity a fraud too?"

Finnigan laughed. "Oh it was real, but I didn't procure it. Found it rifling through Vladimir's things. Seems you weren't the first person Jarrod petitioned for the document."

I lowered my brows. "Vladimir already had it?"

"You don't really think I could have gotten this document so quickly and on my own, do you? I caught Vladimir tampering with the seal in the chancellor's office after spilling a glass of wine all over the chancellor's lap. Obviously he was up to something. Anyone who knows Vladimir knows that he doesn't drink wine. Or any kind of intoxicating drink."

I struggled against my captor. "But why are you doing this?"

"Enough with this nonsense." Finnigan's hand sliced

through the air. "Now here's what's going to happen. We're re-turning to the throne room. If you give any indication that I have a dagger at her back, William, I will drive it through her heart without hesitation. If you"—Finnigan turned to me—"try to wriggle free from my grasp, try to escape, try *anything*, one of my men will slice William's royal neck."

He glanced between us. "Are we understood?"

"Finnigan—" The touch of the dagger cut off my words.

William struggled to catch Finnigan's eyes, his face still buried in stone. "What's going on? Why are you doing this?"

Finnigan smiled, his hand on my shoulder guiding me back toward the throne room. "Because Gharridan is about to crown a new king. We wouldn't want to be late for the ceremony, would we?"

I kept my steps even.

Vladimir would never claim the throne.

He didn't want it.

But someone else wanted him to have it.

And he would kill whoever he needed to make it happen.

CHAPTER FIFTY-SIX

THE COUNCIL CHAMBER lay empty, confirming my suspicions that Taryn had been condemned in the throne room. The question was whether or not the queen and council were still gathered there. The explosion at the city gate could have kept them deliberating, and they could easily have gone into their own lockdown, making it nearly impossible to reach them. But that seemed unlikely. The queen would think she was still in control, that the battle was confined to the city gates. She wouldn't force herself into hiding until the last moment.

Katherine crept along the corridor in front of us with an arrow always on the string, prepared to strike anyone who dared attack us. Avoiding the guards was becoming increasingly harder. They traveled in the stairwells, barreled down the corridors, caught sight of us in the windows. If we didn't reach the throne room soon, we might miss our short window of opportunity. I kept my sword drawn, trying to control the anger swirling inside me and to not think about what would have to happen. Everything depended on the council being gathered, on the council listening to reason, but I had no control over how they would react. Whatever resulted could spark riots. A civil war. A bloodbath. The possibilities were endless.

We were close now.

Katherine sucked in a deep breath, nodding an affirmation to me before rounding the last corner. We followed on her heels, and the entrance to the throne room appeared before us. Two guards stood stationed outside the doors, arguing with a man escorted by a soldier. Surprise washed over their faces at our presence, momentarily freezing them in shock before they reached for their weapons.

"Don't even think about it," Katherine warned, arrow pointed at the closest man's neck.

"Open the doors," I demanded.

Their hands still gripped the hilt of their swords, ready to defend, but they hadn't drawn for fear of Katherine's arrow.

"You can join us," Katherine bargained. "Vladimir is bringing evidence before the council. I know you two, and you know that Vladimir would never betray his country. I suggest you hear him out before forfeiting your lives for something you don't yet understand."

Her bow creaked as indecision hovered in their eyes.

"What kind of evidence?" The man escorted by the soldier arched an eyebrow at us inquisitively.

I shifted on my feet, studying him and the burn along his

arm. A faint familiarity hung over him, but I couldn't place his face.

"Come in and find out for yourself," I said. "The entire kingdom needs to hear this."

The worried guards exchanged glances, minds made up. They stepped away from their post, curious to know what was going on but not willing to take responsibility for whatever happened.

I composed myself before flinging the massive doors wide open. "Barricade them behind us."

I flew into the room like a windstorm, cloak billowing behind me. I heard the bolt slide into place, securing us inside, and several pairs of footsteps following me. Shouts of surprise echoed from the front of the room, bouncing off the walls of the large chamber. My throat constricted when I saw Taryn at the steps of the dais, hands tied behind her back. Finnigan idled directly behind her. William stood just beyond them with two guards close by, close enough to catch him with a dagger if needed. Katherine would have to watch them and make sure they stayed alive.

Fear hovered in the council members' eyes as I passed them. They looked ready to flee. My murderous gaze kept them in place.

"Everyone," I said calmly, "will remain seated."

The red-clothed council glanced at the door that had been barricaded behind us, closing off their only hope of escape. Most of them wouldn't be armed, and no Gharridan soldiers were stationed here to protect them. I noted the queen's personal guard standing behind her. Four of them. Weapons drawn, ready to defend her.

But not for long.

For the first time, I caught a flicker of fear in the queen's face.

Strange.

"What is the meaning of this?" she demanded.

Her guards tightened their grips on their swords.

My pace slowed, dragging as it stopped a few feet before the first step of the dais. I turned, catching the gaze of each of the council members, marking the expressions on their faces, memorizing them to discern how they would change.

"Vladimir," one of the council members probed carefully. "What is the meaning of this? What is this army trying to invade our city?"

I smiled grimly. "I set out to overturn the queen's disbandment of the Kavari after she condemned an innocent person to death, but I'm afraid I come bearing far more important business today of a most pernicious nature."

A heaviness filled my words, an irony, as if anything could be more crucial than the first matter I had discussed.

"And what business might that be?" Finnigan's voice fell solid in the quiet room.

I sensed the expectancy in his voice, the reminder of what it was he wanted me to do and the consequences I faced if I did not follow through with his instructions. Taryn's eyes bore into mine, piercing my soul for the information I was about to share. Warning lingered in their green depths, trying to tell me something, but I already knew. I wished she didn't have to endure this.

I retrieved the missive from my inner pocket, unfurling it for all to see. "The last time I spoke with Michael Gallows," I began, "he was in search of a high document that left the capital containing details of treason and the possible terms of a harmful treaty."

Everyone's attention remained riveted on me.

"Michael intercepted the missive, confiding its whereabouts to a man named Gavil, who is now dead. Marco was on his way to the capital with the letter when he was abducted and then subsequently tortured to a state where his mind is no longer capable. We thought the document lost, but Marco had suspected foul play, and he handed off the letter before his abduction. That letter was finally delivered into my hands last night, and I hold it before you today."

They all leaned forward expectantly, waiting for my next words.

"And what is in this letter?" a councilman asked.

I turned back to the queen, wanting to see her face.

"A bargain of treason containing evidence that convicts Queen Adamara of the death of Michael Gallows."

CHAPTER FIFTY-SEVEN

◆◇◆

TARYN

I HEARD THE air rushing in and out of my lungs, felt the warmth of it as it escaped through my lips, but I held no memory of breathing. The entire throne room's attention was fixed on Vladimir, but like a congregation hearing a clamorous distraction, every eye turned with trepidation toward the queen. She lounged on her carved throne, immovable, lifting an eyebrow as she absorbed Vladimir's shocking statement as if it were nothing more than a land dispute.

The blood drained from my face, leaving me a pale shell, my legs wobbling beneath me.

Was it true?

A deep, humorous laugh escaped from her throat as if Vladimir had just delivered the punch line of a joke. "Pray tell, Vladimir," she managed between chuckles, "what manner of statement is this?"

"Yes," Hart grumbled. "That is a bold accusation."

No one knew how to react.

Vladimir's statement was jarring, and the queen's response was absurd.

"What is written within this letter?" a stout councilman asked.

Vladimir's face remained stoic, eyes hard as stone. He stretched out the missive to read, and the council members all leaned forward in their chairs with eagerness. Gaze downcast, Vladimir's eyes roved over the words like an executioner declaring a death sentence.

King Dorjan, Ruler of Algarar and Sovereign of the Southern Kingdom,

Gharridan agrees to the terms laid out for the treaty of Northunder. Upon receiving this letter, Michael Gallows will have been eliminated per the first conditions of the treaty, and we will move on to the second conditions. When they have been met, we will continue to the third conditions, and the promised land will be given into the possession of Algarar. Once Mordakai has claimed his position as leader of the Kavari, Gharridan will quickly fall under the Crown's control. Zedekiah will make his way toward Captain Dugal, where you may continue filtering your troops through Gapsvar. Hold steady until Brenden has been coaxed into warfare. Gharridan and Brenden will ultimately destroy each other, leaving Algarar to claim sovereignty over all.

Gratefully,

Queen Adamara, Ruler of Gharridan and Sovereign of the Central Kingdom

The words fell like an arrowhead embedding into bone—suddenly and with unimaginable, unforgettable pain that seemed like it could never be quenched. Heat rushed through me, stoking the flames within me as my chest constricted with the effort of restraining it. I felt the hatred and anger that had festered in me for so long flare up as I turned my blazing eyes on Adamara, reveling in her royal apparel and golden crown.

It wasn't Brenden.

Wasn't some invisible enemy.

It was her.

It was Adamara.

All along.

She killed him.

Queen Adamara killed my father—ordered his death. Traded his life to fulfill the terms of a dirty treaty with our enemies.

The storm in me exploded, bursting throughout the throne room.

"You!" I screamed, lunging against Finnigan's restrictive hold. The tip of the knife pressed deeper into my back in warning, but I didn't care.

I continued to fight against him.

"Not yet," Finnigan whispered in my ear, struggling to keep hold of me.

The words only fanned the flames burning within me.

He knew.

He *knew*.

I looked skyward to stare at the ceiling of the throne room. Death hovered there, trembling with anticipation, preparing to strike, smiling at Finnigan's words—words I had whispered not so long ago. Whispered in the forest near my father's grave as I determined to bring his killer to justice. Death did not forget.

He would not leave empty-handed today.

The queen sat poised on her throne, indifferent to the turn of events.

One of the council members with a thick beard strode toward Vladimir, wrenching the missive from his hands to read it with his own eyes. He stared at the page before displaying it for all to see, pointing out the Crown's seal stamped on the bottom in dried red wax.

"Is this true?" he demanded, his wild expression boring into the queen. Several of the other council members had come to examine the letter for themselves as well. I glared at Queen Adamara with hatred, yearning for vengeance.

She gave no indication of defending herself, of trying to clear her name. Instead of looking like a cornered animal, she stared at all of us with disinterest, as if this accusation was the most natural thing in the world.

"Mother?" William's voice rasped. I could see his emotions spiraling into turmoil.

There was nothing for her to fall back on.

The proof lay here before us, blindingly obvious.

Queen Adamara shifted in her chair, one arm propped up on the arm of her throne, fingers dangling in the air.

"I do not deny it."

Her words lingered like a chill in the air.

So cold.

So unfeeling.

I gnashed my teeth at her indifference, hot tears stinging the edges of my vision. "How could you?"

The words scraped across my vocal cords like sand, rough and painful. She turned to me lacking any compassion, any sympathy—any remorse. A darkness whirled in her countenance and consumed her soul.

"Because the queen is no stranger to murder."

The new voice traveled across the checkered floor, its owner hidden halfway behind a pillar. I'd seen him slip in with Vladimir and his men. I was sure of it.

The queen noticed him for the first time, squinting in annoyance.

Her back went rigid.

"This man is a known fugitive," she declared, sitting up in her seat as if she still held any authority.

The man emerged from the pillar's shadow, pulling a folded piece of paper from his vest and waving it at the queen. "This document of immunity cancels out any warrants issued for my arrest."

My breath caught.

Jarrod Lynch.

His bald head glistened in the light, stark eyebrows arched in a sharp curve. The closer he came, the more I saw the resemblance between him and his brother. A burn covered the entirety of his right arm, leaving the skin scarred and withering.

"That document was obtained through a dirty transaction. It holds no power here."

Vladimir faced the man. "What is this you speak of?"

Finnigan pushed me down a step, and I became increasingly aware of the knife's harsh pressure. "All in good time," he said, bringing the room's attention back to himself. "However, there will be plenty of time to testify against the queen later. I believe that Vladimir's news is not the only reason he came before the council today."

The tip of the dagger inched through the fabric of my clothes. Vladimir's eyes shot to me, recognizing the pain scrawled across my face, and I realized—

I was Finnigan's leverage.

"Don't—" I managed before Finnigan broke skin. I gasped at the pain.

"Vladimir comes before the council today to claim the throne of Gharridan. After learning of the queen's treachery, I can't help but imagine that you all would agree."

Vladimir started to protest, but I gave a sharp shake of my head, grimacing as the knife ventured farther. Blood gathered at the back of my dress.

William looked between Finnigan and Vladimir as if unsure he had heard them correctly. His position on his mother remained unclear. From his expression, I knew he didn't agree with her actions, but this discussion didn't just harbor concern for his mother. Finnigan's actions affected more than Adamara—this was William's throne they were talking about.

"Who stands with me?" Finnigan prodded. "Who stands behind removing this treacherous excuse for a queen and instating Vladimir as king?"

The breath hitched in my throat, all the pieces falling perfectly into place. Finnigan hadn't been recruiting council members to help reinstate the Kavari. He'd been garnering their support to place Vladimir on the throne.

"I do." One of the council members stood, looking distastefully at the queen. "I will not support a traitorous ruler."

"I do as well."

An influx of council members rose one at a time across the room, standing in favor of Vladimir. Only four remained seated, taking in the progression of events around them, not yet ready to cast their lot. Finnigan hadn't managed all of this support himself. The letter had made some of them turn their backs on the queen. Next to his mother, William's face paled. If the council turned against them, they had no place to go. I wanted to see the queen burn, watch the flames devour her along with her crooked throne. William was getting everything he deserved because of his choices, but that didn't make this situation any less shocking or terrifying for him. If the council pushed this, he would lose everything.

"Enough." Queen Adamara rose from her throne. "This is treason. Vladimir won't live long enough to claim the throne. None of you will. Guards!"

At her command, the hidden door in the wall burst open, a mass of soldiers spilling through onto the dais, taking up positions behind the queen. Finnigan stepped back in shock, dragging me with him. Tears pricked at the edges of my vision as the pain from my back swelled with the unexpected movement. With a flick of her hand, two of the queen's guards quickly grabbed Jarrod, muffling any of the words that he uttered.

"Give me the girl," the queen warned Finnigan, "or Vladimir dies."

Finnigan's fingers dug into my arm, unwilling to part with me. If the queen got her hands on me, I didn't stand a chance. I was Finnigan's only leverage. Katherine had moved next to William, and I suspected she was there to protect him.

"No," Finnigan snarled.

I heard the whistle through the air, felt Finnigan's sudden backward jerk as the arrowhead scraped across flesh. His hold evaporated on me as he stumbled backward, clutching at where the arrow had grazed the front of his chest. My moment of freedom was brief as one of the queen's guards yanked me toward the throne, pulling me behind it to stand by Jarrod. Vladimir moved to intercept me, but a wall of soldiers and blades quickly stopped him. Finnigan doubled over on the floor, blood pooling around him from the wound.

"I would make your next decisions carefully, Adamara," Vladimir warned, his sword hovering out in defense.

She lifted an eyebrow. "You think this wasn't already planned?"

A sly smile tugged at the corner of her lips. "I never intended to have you in the throne room so soon, but I did mean to have you here. While your missive and Mr. Lynch are an unexpected surprise, they only make me feel less guilty for what I've prepared to do."

Vladimir remained aware of his surroundings, his attention darting around us. "And what might that be?"

Adamara sighed dramatically. "How horrible, the people of Gharridan will say, Queen Adamara tried to secure the country, but the Kavari became greedy. Vladimir marched on the capital to take the throne, full of such a thirst for power that he murdered the entire council, and the queen barely escaped with her life, barely scraped together the pieces of a dismembered nation."

The room fell quiet, the reality of her words dawning on those present. Many of the council members stood in panic; others remained frozen to their chairs, gripped with fear. My eyes flashed to their belts. They were not armed. The council members were scholars, critical thinkers, noblemen, bookkeepers. They were not warriors. A few of them may have learned the craft, but they were far outnumbered by the ones who hadn't.

They didn't stand a chance.

The queen swept toward the hidden entrance. "Kill them all."

"No!" I yelled. I tried to wrench free of my captor's grasp, but he only pulled me along behind the queen.

William's expression was a mix of anger and confusion. His mother grasped his arm. "You will witness this, to testify on what happened. You've done it before, and you can do it again. These men are trying to steal your throne, destroy this country. They deserve far worse."

William's eyes strayed to me.

"Keep your focus on the task at hand, William, and I will keep her safe. You *will* do this for me."

I was as safe with her as I was with a starving bear. He couldn't dare agree to this, but I reminded myself that he'd done it before. He'd subjected Katherine to the same fate.

"Don't listen to her, William, you're better than this!" I pleaded, but I was quickly whisked away.

Cold steel pressed against my skin as I watched the hoard of soldiers prepare to descend upon Vladimir and the council. It was too big of an onslaught. A wave of nausea rushed through me as I focused on Vladimir's pale blue eyes, strangely reminiscent of when Zedekiah took me hostage. The darkness overcame us, the closing of the door sealing us in.

I went numb. The dampness of the tunnel set in, suffocating me. The wound on my back ached. Perspiration dotted my brow, and I felt the blood running down my back. The fabric of my dress felt like rough bark. I didn't understand why the queen had taken me instead of leaving me to die with the others, unless it was to make sure William fulfilled his duty. I wanted to ask, wanted to pester her, but it took all of my energy to keep moving.

The queen's path differed from the one Zedekiah had led me down. She strayed to the left, the tunnel steadily climbing upward instead of down. We began to spiral around and around. Even in the darkness, the repetitive motion and pain made me dizzy. I leaned dependently on my guard, trying to keep my feet from slipping out beneath me. I needed to get back to the throne room, needed to save everyone in there. I almost laughed at the thought. How would I, wounded and hands tied, be of any use to them, or even be able to get to them?

A mechanism clicked, and sunlight suddenly blinded us, searing in from the opening of the tunnel. The colors of my vision fractured, distorting within my mind as the pain in my back ebbed, every step riddled with agony. I vaguely recognized our surroundings, realizing we were in the hall outside Adelaide's room, passing the window where I had kissed William not so long ago.

Had he known about this plot?

The guards forced us—I turned, realizing they'd dragged Jarrod along too—into Adelaide's room, and everything was the same as I remembered it, coated in a layer of dust. This tower of imprisonment and torment. My guard held me near the window, and I sagged against his armor, struggling to remain strong.

"Secure the door," the queen ordered.

If she was certain she would win, it seemed odd to barricade herself inside.

"The country needs to think I fled from Vladimir's attack."

She'd been crafting this for months.

When the soldiers found the council and Kavari slaughtered in the throne room, they would go looking for the queen. She wouldn't leave this room until they assured her it was safe. I stared at the soldiers, studying them. They wore Gharridan uniforms, but there was something about their eyes, their mannerisms, the way they carried themselves.

These men were not Gharridan.

Several posts and furniture were placed before the door to lock us safely inside. I swallowed. There was no other escape, and she wasn't going to let me walk out of here alive.

"You think anyone will actually believe you?" I spat. "There's proof that you murdered my father."

She rolled her eyes. "Oh yes, what's more believable? That I killed the leader of the Kavari, or that Vladimir, whose Kavari were disbanded, gathered an army to take the throne and murdered the entire council to secure it, trying to kill the queen in the process?"

I turned to Jarrod. A bruise was forming over his left eye. His gaze locked on the queen, filled with both revulsion and admiration.

Why was he still alive? Why was *I* still alive?

She turned to us, light from the window illuminating her golden hair, glinting off the gold of her crown.

I wanted to rip it from her head.

Her steps were slow and calculating as she sauntered over, eyes slier than a serpent. "Did you *really* think that useless document of immunity would protect your life, Jarrod? You've evaded me for far too long. No piece of paper would hold up between you and death."

Jarrod didn't respond.

The queen cocked her head. "After all these years, what finally gave you the *courage* to show your face, to try and testify? You were never anything more than a coward before."

My eyes narrowed at the familiarity between them. This man hadn't threatened the life of her children, but he wasn't just a physician. He was something more.

"Who are you?" I asked.

"Jarrod Lynch." He grimaced. "I used to be the personal physician of the royal family, and we became very"—he hesitated—"*very* close."

The queen chuckled, an amused smile breaking over her face. "Only a fool would believe a woman would reciprocate anything for you."

Shock coursed through my body.

Understanding.

"You had an affair?" My head pounded. I didn't know how deep the stab wound was, but I was losing too much blood. I felt weak as I battled the pain.

Jarrod shrugged his shoulders, bemused. "It was more than an affair. Adamara promised me many things—promised me half the kingdom. The vile woman had me wrapped around her finger so tightly I would've done anything for her." He licked his lips. "Once she knew for certain that I was at her mercy, she began speaking of things—horrible things involving treason."

I glanced between them angrily. "Like the planned murder of my father?"

Jarrod Lynch shook his head slowly, never taking his gaze

from the queen. "No. Something far worse. I knew what was at stake, but I agreed to it, thinking that the queen was as attached to me as I was to her. I was a fool. Adamara already had everything expertly planned out—even had someone to blame—she just needed me to execute it."

"And more should have been blamed," the queen growled.

Her gaze on Jarrod turned deadly.

"What did she do?" I asked, my eyes darting back and forth between them with apprehension.

What could be worse than murdering my father? Worse than pinning the murder of a dozen council members on an innocent man?

Jarrod lifted his chin, staring down the queen defiantly. "She used me to poison someone, blamed the death on the inexperience of a young Radonaya." He looked at me. "Your *beloved* Queen Adamara plotted and carried out the murder of her husband, King Roldan."

His words gutted me, piercing directly to the heart. They left me stunned to silence, unable to breathe.

I looked incredulously at Queen Adamara, convinced this must be a sick joke, but no denial rested in her eyes.

She had the audacity to grin, lifting an eyebrow. "You seem so surprised."

King Roldan.

Katherine's inability to explain his death.

The hatred for the Kavari and Radonaya.

The blood in my veins froze—Jarrod Lynch spoke the truth.

Queen Adamara had murdered her husband.

Nausea bubbled within my stomach. I struggled to keep

from retching. "How?"

"It was easy," she recalled. "Although it required much research beforehand. After your father showed up with that Radonaya, I had to figure out how to assassinate my husband without arousing suspicion, had to find a poison that Katherine couldn't heal. Fate sided with me, bringing me the knowledge that a Radonaya's power was useless against Mors Secunda. All I had to do was find a patch. Its strange effects that heal you before later bringing death upon you strengthened the story that Katherine chose to let him die."

Katherine.

Forced to take the blame for someone else's twisted plans.

"Why?" I cried out in anguish. "How can you live with yourself?"

Fury burned in the queen's eyes. "Why?"

She stooped low, coming within an inch of my face. "*Why?*" she repeated, drawing out the word. "Because my husband stood for Gharridan and the wretched Kavari, and both of those parties destroyed my world and murdered my entire family."

Silence echoed in the room.

Confusion wafted through my thoughts, not understanding, not finding reason, but then—

Realization overcame me, insignificant words William had spoken so long ago in the midst of a blizzard howling like a ravenous wolf, his words returning to my mind, connecting.

My parents first met when she came here seeking asylum after her kingdom was overthrown.

I gaped at her, mind spinning as I stared at her in bewilderment.

She lifted her chin, seeming to know what I was about to reveal.

The treaty of Northunder.

Marco had said something was coming.

That there was treason.

That it was terrible.

Marco knew.

He knew who Queen Adamara was.

Where she had come from.

I was wrong.

My mother had said that her family was in the north, but I was wrong.

She was not from Algarar.

My mother was not the princess they never found.

"You're her," I whispered. My words resonated with fear, chilling me. "You're Djara."

The words fell like an anvil.

Princess Djara lifted her chin—and smiled.

CHAPTER FIFTY-EIGHT

VLADIMIR

THE QUEEN'S GUARDS outnumbered us five to one. To think we had any sort of chance was foolishness.

"Vladimir?" Katherine stretched out my name, her voice tilting upward in a question. She knocked an arrow, waiting for the signal.

"Start firing and don't stop!" I commanded.

The first arrow loosed, finding its mark in the approaching soldiers.

Fear spread through the council members like wildfire.

"Get behind me!" I yelled, intending for them to escape through the doors, but the queen's soldiers were already running for the exit, circling back to surround us. Katherine picked off the queen's men one by one, but she didn't have enough arrows for every soldier, and they would reach us before she ever emptied her quiver. The council members who still remained loyal to the queen broke away, hoping their devotion had earned them mercy, but there would be none.

My eyes darted from the tapestries to the floor, to the pillars, seeking out any semblance of a weapon for the council members to defend themselves with. Eight soldiers couldn't defend them against an army of fifty. These were not soldiers of Gharridan. After years with the military the discrepancies were obvious to my well-trained eyes. These soldiers were sons of war, bred for violence in the land of Algarar. They were not here for prisoners. They were here for blood.

I caught sight of the pots of oil used to replenish the torches along the wall.

"Boss?" one of my men questioned.

I indicated the jar of oil. "We fight with fire. Organize the council members. Don't let them surround us."

William plowed ahead of the Algarian soldiers to reach me first, his sword arched in a death blow.

I caught the strike, the force behind his swing jolting my arm.

"William, don't do this," I advised.

He heaved his arms back, bringing down his sword again in response. I easily parried it, deflected another blow, and then shot forward for his quick regroup, my muscles tensing as our steel clashed and his blade slid down to my hilt. Our eyes locked momentarily. A battle warred within him. I shoved against his weight, pushing him far enough away to get a few words in.

"Hear me out."

His eyes were full of anger when he attacked me again. I

brought my sword up quickly, blocking his blows one after the other as I circled him and fought to keep my ground. I didn't have time for this. I had an entire council to protect. He feinted right, raining down on me again and again. If he offered me a fatal strike, I had no choice—I would have to take it.

"William!"

Katherine's arrows whipped around me, sinking into flesh. Two of my other men were engaged in combat with the Algarians.

"I have nothing to say to you!" William roared, slicing at me.

"Listen to me!" I yelled.

He ignored my words, barreling toward me in a rage. This time I moved forward, striking quickly enough that he lost several steps. The blades locked again, our faces inches from each other. Sweat beaded on William's brow.

"You come to our doorstep with an army to claim the throne, and you want me to listen to you?"

We broke apart, and I ducked his sudden strike. When it swung around, I unsheathed my dagger in a flash, catching the blade, sparks flying off the metal.

"I have no desire for the throne," I ground out. "This is a trap, and you're playing right into Finnigan's hands. I didn't come here for this!"

"Then what did you come here for?"

A crash echoed through the room as one of the oil pots smashed against the floor, the fluid spreading between the line of soldiers. A spark fell to the floor, and I jerked away, covering my eyes. The heat seared my back, flames shooting up from the oil like a geyser. It drove the Algarian soldiers apart, separating them and evening the odds between my men and theirs. Katherine drew her dagger, bow rendered useless in the close proximity. Another oil pot crashed on the other side of the flames, separating our opposing sides again. If the fire could keep the soldiers from rushing us all at once, we might have a chance.

I ducked as William's blade whistled overhead, close enough that the wind of its current rippled through my hair.

"I came here to save Gharridan," I bellowed. "Your mother killed Michael Gallows for heaven's sake, hear me out!"

He faltered for a moment, and I caught it, the faintest flicker of doubt. He knew this wasn't right, knew there was more to what was going on here, but he wasn't willing to accept it. Not yet.

"You should be asking yourself why your mother has a battalion of Algarian soldiers—our enemy—defending her. They were in Gapsvar also, were they not? These men fighting, their comrades are the same ones who tried to execute you and Taryn."

When he struck again, the ferocity in his attack had died out, and his motivation petered out within a few passionless blows. He looked around him, seeming to notice the soldiers in the room for the first time, the subtle differences in our appearances, the varied fighting techniques. His wavering eyes met mine, suddenly unsure.

"If your mother sentenced the entire council to death and murdered Michael, do you really think she's going to let Taryn live?"

He let out several heavy breaths, his resolve lowering with each one. Fear sparked across his face. An understanding.

His weapon lowered.

"Just this once," he said hoarsely, and turned to strike the nearest Algarian soldier.

I bravely turned my back on him, delving into the fray and taking the enemy by surprise. They hadn't expected William to turn on them, to leave the duel so willingly. The council members huddled behind the flames, hurling anything they could find at the soldiers. One still clutched a pot of oil protectively, not wanting to part with it until the last moment. Another pot crashed into one of the soldiers, drenching him, a stray flame lighting him up like a bonfire. The fires drove the enemy back from the entrance, and the council members inched closer to escape.

But the Algarians still swarmed us, and dread rose within me as I met blade after blade, another weapon waiting with every turn. Katherine fought on my left and William on my right. The Algarian numbers never dwindled and hopelessness took root within me, but even the toughest plants could be killed if there were enough weeds to choke them out of existence.

CHAPTER FIFTY-NINE

◆◇◆

TARYN

I STARED AT the queen, at Djara, my world still reeling from her revelation. Tears stung my eyes. My heart gaped open at the gut-wrenching truth.

"How did no one ever know?"

"You think you deserve to know the truth?" She leered at me before composing herself. "You don't, but forcing you to take this to your grave without being able to warn a single soul is torture enough, and I can't tell you how refreshing it is to finally speak the words after all these years."

She stood and trailed her finger along the length of her daughter's dresser. "When I first came here, I told them my kingdom was destroyed, but I just swapped Algarar's name for an unknown land across the sea. I was away with my brother Dorjan when that devil Gabriel and his apprentice Michael Gallows came to our capital displaying hopes of peace—but it was all lies. They poisoned the entire castle. Only a handful of servants survived."

Her voice broke, hesitating before she continued. "Both of my parents, my three older brothers, my two precious sisters …" Tears glistened in her eyes as she named them off. "Two uncles, three aunts, countless cousins, they were all gone. Just like that. Murdered. They didn't even have the chance to say goodbye." A tear slipped down her cheek. "Now it is offhandedly remembered as the Royal Massacre, as if it held no significance beyond any other casualty of war."

A pang of empathy unwillingly welled up within me. One night, one hour, and she'd lost everyone. Everything.

Except her brother.

"Gabriel had to do something drastic in order to end the war," I challenged.

Fire blazed across Queen Adamara's eyelids. "Do not speak his name to me as if you understand. You know nothing of the atrocities of war. The smell of death in the streets, weeping widows, children screaming for their parents, fear of how we would feed our armies, take care of them. A mass execution was not the answer. Gharridan ripped apart our entire kingdom. The massacre *devastated* Algarar. We've only completely recovered in the past few years, and that is just outwardly. We will never recover emotionally."

I shook my head. "I still don't understand how you infiltrated Gharridan, or why."

I cringed at the thought of entering her twisted mind more than I already had, but I needed to know. I grew lightheaded, felt my face pale. Whether it was from the news or the loss of blood that continued to trail down my back, I didn't know.

The vulnerability she showed slipped back behind her hard gaze. "After the massacre, we needed a way to retaliate, but our entire chain of command had been wiped out. When Dorjan became king, he spread rumors of my death in case there was still a plot against the throne of Algarar. Once no one knew of my existence, we began to plan. We knew that defeating Gharridan head-on would never be enough. It had to be personal, and the best way to completely destroy a country is from within. We also knew that Gharridan's crown prince had yet to be betrothed, and Dorjan was convinced that I could turn the eye of any man. So for three years, I trained to rule the kingdom of Gharridan, to overthrow it, and when the time came, I entered Gharridan from the east and rode for the capital, claiming asylum from a destroyed nation. King Roldan was so sympathetic, so full of compassion and open arms. It didn't take long to woo him, to claim his heart—a beautiful, broken girl with nothing left to her name. It was only mere months before we exchanged vows at the altar."

I shook my head in disbelief. "That was nearly twenty years ago. Why wait so long to enact your revenge?"

"Because I needed power." The queen sneered, stepping toward me. "And I needed an heir. I had to make sure this country trusted me completely."

"Before you murdered your husband and took his place."

Jarrod laughed. "She tried to kill me the moment she learned the king was dead."

The queen ignored him. "Nothing more than a nuisance."

"But I still managed to escape and return," he added.

Tears sprung to my eyes. "You murdered my father."

"Of course I did," she snarled. "From the moment I set foot in Gharridan, your father never trusted me. He was always sticking his nose where it didn't belong. He never once believed Katherine was at fault for my husband's death, and he suspected something was going on between me and Jarrod but couldn't find any evidence to prove it. He kept looking. I knew I would have to get rid of him before moving forward. I wanted him dead for his involvement in the massacre, for all of the pain I suffered because of him and Gabriel."

"You don't want vengeance," I said. "You want annihilation."

The queen shrugged. "Why not?"

"You intentionally started the war with Brenden," I breathed. "The attack on Dellwyn—"

"Never happened," she snapped. "I needed a reason to send William to Brenden. A reason for him to kill their king and leave Katherine to blame. Why send more of my Algarian brethren to die in a war when Brenden could obliterate Gharridan for me, thereby weakening both our neighboring nations?"

She fixed her fiery gaze on me, taking a few steps closer. "For twenty long years, I have waited to see my family avenged, to see this kingdom burned to the ground, decimated beyond repair. I have longed to see the Kavari ripped from power, hanging from a noose, to see the brilliant country of Algarar bask in all the glory she deserves."

The queen grew condescending. "And maybe I won't be able to see it from this throne, but I have seen the beginnings of it. Brenden marches at your border, ready to strike. The Kavari will cease to exist. If your father hadn't bred you—if you hadn't shown up claiming the right of a Blood Vier, meddling in affairs that were none of your concern—Gharridan would already be destroyed. They've been shown the mercy of time that they did not deserve."

She grabbed me by the hair, yanking me back until I stood before the window. The edge of Vladimir's army stood outside the city walls, volleying explosives back and forth but not yet engaged in open warfare where sword would clash against sword.

"I want you to watch as this kingdom crumbles to the ground." She leaned in close to my ear. "I want it to be the last thing you see."

My heart hammered in my chest as Adamara's grip on my hair tightened, pushing me closer to the window's ledge.

A thunder of footsteps echoed in the chamber outside the door, shouts coming from the halls.

The queen froze at the sound, fear growing wild in her eyes as someone pounded against the door. It was too soon. They shouldn't be looking for her yet.

She motioned to Jarrod's guards. "Throw him out the window."

I ripped my arms from behind me, having wiggled with the chain enough that I managed to slip my hand out, and crashed into the guards dragging Jarrod away, disorganizing them. My fingers grasped for a weapon, but there were too many of them. A boot shoved into my ribs as Jarrod fought against them, struggling to get away, to stay alive.

The wooden doors splintered behind us.

Several soldiers rushed the barricade, trying to hold it closed, but whoever was on the other side would break through at any moment.

A dagger flashed in my vision and I jerked to the left, the weapon sliding off course and down my arm, drawing blood. I stifled a cry of pain. Queen Adamara swung at me again, and I stumbled backward, feeling for anything on the ground that could be used as a weapon, rolling over, tripping one of the guards and causing him to lose his grip on Jarrod. Jarrod hung halfway out the window, his body sprawled across the opening like a spider, trying to avoid falling to his death. The dagger bore down again, lodging itself into the wood directly by my head. The queen wrenched it free, but not before I'd grasped the hilt of the dagger as well. The injured muscles in my arm burned as I fought to hold on to it, struggling to use my weight to pull the queen down with me, but she was stronger than she looked. The pain in my back screamed, pleaded for mercy. I lurched to my feet, fighting for control over the weapon.

Malice filled Adamara's eyes as she drove the dagger toward me. I pushed back equally as hard, our eyes darting between each other and the dagger as we fought over who would arise triumphant.

The doors burst open, splinters and furniture flying across my peripheral vision. Blade crashed against blade. Bodies hit the floor. Boots thudded, but I couldn't tear my gaze away from the queen's.

Adamara grimaced. "My only regret is that your father's death did not come directly from my hand."

I felt the hilt of the dagger turn in her direction. I groaned, panicking as I realized I was losing control of the weapon.

The dagger thrust upward.

Blood shot across my face. The sickening sound of steel piercing flesh hovered in my ears. I reeled with shock. Warm blood poured across my hands, seeping into my dress, the moisture pressing through to my skin.

Queen Adamara's eyes widened, gasping as I pulled the dagger out of her gut. She stared at me as if unable to believe what was happening. Her body swayed for a moment, stumbling two steps backward before collapsing to the ground.

The world seemed to slow around me as if in a dream. My eyes filled with horror as I stepped back, staring at her body splayed across her daughter's floor. Blood covered her elaborate dress, more of it spreading farther down her skirt by the second. A yell reverberated through the room, and William rushed past me, kneeling at her side, crying out for her and lifting her into his arms. So much blood. Her eyes stared lovingly up at her son as her lips moved soundlessly, unable to utter whatever words of farewell she wished to offer. William clutched at her, unwilling to let her go, pressed his hand against the wound, sobbed her name over and over, begged her to stay with him. Her head lolled, looking up at her son, reaching her bloody hand up to caress his face. To convey what her voice was unable to share. Her body shook as a line of blood escaped the corner of her mouth.

William broke as he held her, still trying to stop the blood gushing from her wound, spreading out onto the floor like an infection. Adamara choked, gurgling before she suddenly stilled. Her bloodied hand fell slack at her side, eyes dimming as her soul departed from her body.

I watched in horror, frozen, before looking down at my bloodstained hands. My pale fist opened, releasing the dagger. It fell to the floor with a clatter, thick with blood. A tremor overcame my hands as I took another step back, looking behind me to find Vladimir standing with his men, looking as equally stunned as I.

Blood.

There was so much blood.

Death stood over Adamara, his black eyes smiling at me. He dipped his head in goodbye before vanishing along with her soul.

William clutched at his mother, rocking back and forth with her in his arms.

Blood.

Blood was everywhere.

I let the reality seep into me like the blood adorning her dress, let it torture me, stared at the lifeless body on the ground. The queen of Gharridan was dead, by my hand, and she would walk this earth no more.

CHAPTER SIXTY

THE FLAMES IN the hearth danced to a silent song, twirling this way and that, playing with one another. So full of life, so energetic, yet all it would take was a splash of water, one smother of a blanket to extinguish them into nothing—just like a life. I shivered, remembering the feel of Death's eyes on me as the queen and I grappled with the knife. I could still sense his chilling smile as Adamara bled out on her daughter's floor, the possessiveness with which he'd bundled her in his arms. Death had not visited me again since. Maybe he never would. I hoped not. The mere thought of him sent a trail of goosebumps running down my arm.

I clutched my cloak tighter around me to ward off the cold. Even the heat of the fire was not enough to singe off the memory.

You should be happy.

The thought struck like poison.

Happy.

I'd avenged my father's death. I'd gotten what I wanted.

But it had cost.

I had never taken a life before.

Adamara orchestrated the death of my father, murdered her own husband and who knew how many others, was willing to murder the entire council. She tried to destroy the kingdom itself—and she'd had every excuse. But it didn't make her right. Her actions, no matter what motivation spurred them, were vile, which was why I couldn't understand the hollow, twisted feeling in the pit of my stomach that haunted my conscience. Or the guilt that shadowed me.

Maybe it was because of the memory burned into my mind of William clutching his dead mother against his chest, the tears spilling from his eyes.

That was the last clear memory I had. Everything after was a blur.

I remembered blacking in and out from loss of blood and pain as Vladimir spirited me away, half carrying and half supporting me down the stairs. At one point, Katherine was the one guiding me, taking me back to my room where six guards were stationed outside. Whether it was for my protection or the kingdom's, I wasn't sure. I remembered bells ringing, horns sounding. Katherine materialized again at some point, her cold fingers pressing against the wound on my back—and suddenly I was drowning in the Jidero River again, the weight of the water pressing against me, the inability to draw a breath, the fear of knowing I was about to die—and then it was all over. The pain in my back slipped into a dull throb. Katherine reached for my bloodied arm, but I pulled away. It wasn't deep. The vicious cut from Adamara's blade would heal on its own, and it was a scar I didn't want to erase.

I was left alone. Numb. Speechless. I didn't know how to move, and I didn't want to. I watched the sun rise and descend over the next three days, ignoring the food that was brought to me, welcoming the blankets that were pulled over my shoulders to keep me warm.

I was afraid.

Afraid of what was to come.

I let thoughts of every imagination and every hard realization entertain my mind, toy with me. Torture me.

A knock came at the door, and I jerked with fright, hating myself for reacting to the smallest of sounds like a spooked horse. What would they do to me for killing the queen?

The door inched open hesitantly, and Vladimir peeked his head inside the room.

I remained quiet, crossing my arms and staring into the flames of the hearth.

He shuffled across the floor in a slow rhythm, coming to rest beside the mantel. My gaze wandered to him, taking in the dark circles beneath his eyes, the tangled mess of his dark hair. His posture wasn't regal as it usually was, but slumped, beaten down like a ship that had weathered a massive hurricane.

"We managed to stop the bloodshed," he said. "We rang the bells and blew the horns, flew the black-and-white flag that called for a cease fire."

I wondered what all the sounds had meant. I nodded. "That's good."

Far too much blood had been spilled.

"But our armies are still separated," he continued. "We don't have room for all of them in the city, and I'm not convinced it's a good idea for the two parties to intermingle yet."

I swallowed, kicking at the carpet. "How bad was it?"

"It could have been worse." Vladimir shifted on his feet. I could feel the hesitance in his voice. "Hundreds are injured, and we don't have an exact body count, but thankfully after the explosions the armies stayed divided and didn't go past more than volleying rubble at one another."

I nodded again, incapable of any other response.

"Will they charge me?" my voice cracked.

He shook his head.

Whether it was the truth or simply to reassure me, I wasn't sure.

I fought back tears. "Where she came from, who she was … how did no one ever suspect?"

"I think Michael did," Vladimir confessed. "Around the time King Roldan died. Suspected enough to have Jarrod hunted down. Maybe he didn't know the extent of the crimes, but he may have known that he and the queen were having an affair. That was probably when he began to suspect Adamara and why he never fully trusted her judgment after the king's death."

"All those years …" I trailed off. The queen's entire life had been built on a lie.

"Zedekiah knew," Vladimir said.

I threw him a questioning look.

"He tried to tell me. In the woods where we killed him. They were his last words: *You don't know who she is, do you?* At the time, I thought he had been referring to either you or Katherine. It never crossed my mind he could be referring to the queen."

My eyes narrowed. "But why?"

"I've been piecing it together over the past few days. He wanted us to attack Brenden, wanted us to start a war with them to further weaken us. That's why he threw me the ricochet. I think they wanted us to suspect Brenden sooner, but they struggled to plant a hint without raising suspicion. I didn't connect the burnt bodies with the assassins until after I'd seen the ricochet. I've wondered if Zedekiah had meant to leave a ricochet at the sight of your father's death."

I'd chased Zedekiah down to avenge my father, but far worse things had been working behind the scenes.

I bit my lip. "How's William?"

Vladimir didn't answer.

"Does he hate me?" The question grated against my insides.

Vladimir stared at the fire. "He doesn't want to see you right now. Or me."

William had watched me kill the queen, and even though she had committed horrible atrocities, she was still his mother.

"Is he going to be okay?"

Vladimir's throat bobbed, flames reflecting in his pale blue irises. "I don't know. I don't know what he's going to do. William is in a very precarious and volatile state right now, and truth be told, I'm worried. He's had the foundations of everything he believes, everything he was taught, everything he thought he knew ripped out from underneath him with nothing left to stand on. If he doesn't choose the right advice and counsel, he's going to fall, and Gharridan with him."

And my betrayal only aided it.

I swallowed. "Will he take your advice?"

"William thinks I tried to steal his throne and take over his kingdom."

"But you did that to protect him," I interjected.

Vladimir shrugged. "I don't know what William is going to believe or what is going to happen to this country when the people find out that their monarch was a lie."

"I hope the Kavari is at least allowed to help smooth tensions out."

Vladimir swallowed, his face dotted with hopelessness. "Taryn, I don't even know if the Kavari still exist. William may ascend to the throne, but until everything can be sorted out and the truth comes to light, Gharridan is under the control of the council. They summoned William and me to a meeting this morning. After deliberating for over six hours, we barely managed to come to an agreement on anything. Five of the council members were killed in the throne room, leaving sixteen to decide the fate of Gharridan."

I shivered at the thought, wondering what they would tell the kingdom, fearing the truth would cause the most harm. I rubbed my arms, seeking warmth from the fire. The silence stretched between us, filled only by the crackling flames.

"You do realize that if you hadn't killed her, she would have killed you."

I closed my eyes, fighting tears, my mind a swirling sea of emotions.

"I just—" I cut off, unsure of what I was trying to say. I could still see the blood covering my hands—Adamara's blood. "The more I think about it, the more I realize I'm no different than her."

Vladimir's dark brows lowered as I continued.

"I could have easily been her. Someone took my family from me. I wanted my vengeance. I thought about killing King Arguis, Vladimir. I went to his study to find out the truth, but if it had turned out he was the one behind it, I might have, I don't know if—" I struggled for the words. "Revenge coursed through me like a poison. And I came back and deceived William. Deceived William and the court just like Adamara deceived the entirety of Gharridan. We both lost someone we loved. I was willing to go nearly as far as she did. I can't—How am I any different from her?"

Vladimir crossed his arms, face shadowed by the dancing flames. "Because you chose to let go."

I shook my head, but he turned to stand in front of me, grasping my shoulders and catching my eyes. "Adamara clung to bitterness like a disease. It had been festering in her for over twenty years, and she never let it go. Right or wrong, I cannot be the judge over her motivations for her actions, but you chose to *forgive*, Taryn. You spared the king's life. You set aside your quest for revenge, untangled yourself from the bitterness, and you let go."

I swiped a tear from my cheek.

"What happens to us in our lives is out of our control. We could no sooner dictate our circumstances than we could touch the stars. The only thing we possess control over in our lives is how we react to those circumstances. How we *choose* to respond to them. You could have chosen to desert me when I first sought your help in solving your father's murder, or when I made your existence known to the council, but you didn't. You chose to stay. You could have easily abandoned me and Katherine when the queen disbanded the Kavari, but you didn't. You could have chosen to hate your father for the rest of your life, but you didn't. You chose to forgive him. You chose to *let go*, and that was a liberating freedom that Adamara was never able to experience because of how *she chose* to respond to the situations around her. Was what happened in Algarar horrible? Yes. Did she have every right to retaliate? Again, yes. It doesn't, however, mean that her decision about how she would live her life was the right one. She had a husband and children who loved her, a kingdom that adored her, but she let the festering bitterness steal any promise of a peaceful future she might have had."

He was right.

"But I still killed her."

I focused on him, standing so close, a flicker of dark emotions warring within him.

Vladimir's arms dropped to his sides. "Taking a life … it's not something I ever desire to do, and I wish that I didn't have to. Sometimes, in dreams, nightmares, I can still see their faces watching me, the realization of their fate hovering before their eyes. It never gets easier, never feels justified, but I have to constantly remind myself that failing to do my job could cost someone else their life. When I am forced to kill, it is either in the name of justice or to protect the life of another."

His sincere gaze met mine. "Take heart that you did not set out to take her life in hatred, Taryn, because that is something you could never forgive yourself for." Tears glistened in his eyes, and I sensed that he spoke from experience. "You were defending yourself. We all saw it. That knife was going to either enter you or Queen Adamara, and the queen knew good and well that she had a chance of losing when she pulled that dagger on you."

But I still killed her.

The memory haunted me, tainted my thoughts. How did people live with themselves, knowing that they had taken another's life? I let the tears silently slide down my cheeks, trying to reassure myself but finding no solace. I couldn't take back what I did. It could never be undone. The crime was permanent, the damage irrevocable, but even if I was given the chance to change it, I wouldn't. One of us was destined to die in that tower, and I wouldn't tempt fate thinking I could make the outcome better by going back.

She made her choice, I thought.

And it was the deadliest mistake she had ever made.

CHAPTER SIXTY-ONE

THROWN FLOWER PETALS drifted down around me like a sprinkle of rain, dancing in the air before finding a place of rest on the checkered floor. To any beholder, it was a magical, beautiful sight—but instead of petals, all I could picture was ash falling from the sky, coating the inhabitants of the throne room in the destruction of their own country. The bodies pressed in around me, shoulder to shoulder, the massive room unable to hold another soul. Anticipation and excitement wavered in the air. Heads darted in and out of the crowd, trying to catch a glimpse of the central aisle left clear for the new king to ascend to his throne. I felt the bones of my dress squeeze against me, the overwhelming heat of the masses suffocating. I struggled for air, wanting to be any-where but here.

I did not attend the queen's funeral. Vladimir had advised against it, and I had not pushed it. I wasn't prepared to face William today. The last time I'd seen him was when I was pulling a dagger out of his mother's gut.

Gharridan still lay in shambles. Jarrod had testified before the council, but they had yet to reveal all to the country. The council wanted William crowned first to attain a small measure of peace before unloading the explosive bomb of betrayal on all the country's citizens. How it was to be executed would be at the discretion of the new king and the council. I almost wondered if they wouldn't just bury it to keep the peace—but the people deserved to know.

A cheer rose from the end of the hall as the doors swung outward, traveling along the length of the crowd. The volume was deafening, filling every part of my senses as they clapped and cheered for their monarch-to-be. Kingly garments arrayed William, a long, elaborate purple cloak trailing on the ground behind him with exquisite stitching. Everything that touched him testified to the regency of a royal, but it was the expression etched into his face that broke me. Gone was the prince whose voice dripped with sarcasm, who did anything to not take something seriously, who did everything he could in order to please his mother. The man that walked before me now harbored an expression of coldness.

An air of duty.

The weight of burden.

His face remained harsh and stoic as he traveled the road to the throne—once his mother's, now his. There was not a glance to acknowledge the presence of his people. He kept his expression straight ahead, focused on what was to come. Sympathy and hatred for him warred within my heart, fighting for dominance. He would have to come clean with the council about what really happened in Brenden, especially now that they knew Katherine had been completely exonerated in the king's death.

I didn't hear or pay attention to what was said. Most of it was elaborate speech, highly decorated words that were beyond my comprehension. More of a lyrical tribute to our ancestors and the history of our country than anything that had to do with William's actual reign. It didn't interest me.

When the coronation came to an end, they lifted the golden crown and placed it upon William's head. He turned back to the crowd, and the cheers before were nothing compared to what reverberated off the walls of the throne room now.

I could feel Vladimir's presence behind me. He'd stayed silent through the entire ceremony.

"Will they let him continue to rule once they know the truth?" I asked.

"I don't know." Vladimir's breath brushed across my ear.

William sat on the throne, his expression never changing as he stared out over the exuberant crowd. He saw me. I know he did. There was a slight pause in his sweep of the room, but he merely continued on as if I didn't exist.

"But William has far bigger problems to deal with besides trying to keep his throne."

"What problems?"

"A messenger bird flew in before the coronation. Several Brenden battalions were spotted crossing the border into Gharridan the day before yesterday. The central army is not but a few days behind them."

War loomed closer than I had thought.

I swallowed. "How many men from both our kingdoms will die because of the queen's deception?"

Vladimir's voice grew rough. "Too many to count. They have a personal vendetta with William."

This wasn't something that could be sorted out with negotiations. William assassinated their king. The Brendens were out for blood.

"What do we do?"

Vladimir glanced up to where William sat on the dais. "We wait and see what our new king allows us to do."

I followed Vladimir's gaze to where the son of a king slayer sat in a throne he wasn't prepared for, ruling a kingdom that might deny him, and facing a war that no one in this country was prepared to win.

"Long live the king!"

The thunder of voices boomed around us, swallowing the new ruler with their cheers.

END OF BOOK TWO

EPILOGUE

THE SCRAPE OF steel against whetstone filled the chamber, a slow, monotonous rhythm, each swipe followed by another. A man leaned forward in a chair, firelight reflecting off the bronze of his hair as he worked the thin metal disk within his hands. Dark clothing arrayed him like a cloud of shadows, blending into the dim room. A circular pattern decorated the right shoulder of his uniform, the stitching barely discernible as it was colored the same shade as the cloth. A coldness hovered around him, a hardness carved deep within his heart, and his eyes never strayed from the task, remaining focused, impenetrable.

"Prince Tristan."

The voice issued from the door, a hesitance in its tone.

The disk slid across the tool, never breaking rhythm.

Boots brushed against the stone floor, coming to a halt before the prince.

"What news?" the prince asked.

The methodic scrape of metal pulsed throughout the room.

"Our spies report that William was crowned king of Gharridan, and that there is unrest centered at the capital."

The prince stopped mid-swipe, the sudden silence deafening. The corner of his mouth twitched with displeasure, the only indication of emotion within his face. He set the whetstone aside, tilting his head as he examined the metal instrument held securely between his fingers, turning it this way and that to inspect every aspect of the disk.

"And what of the queen?"

"No specifics could be attained, only that she is dead and William has replaced her as monarch."

The prince placed the disk on the wooden table before unrolling a leather sheet filled with various weapons and vials, each held securely by a leather tie or belt. He slipped the disk into an empty compartment and pulled out an arrow tip, scrutinizing the sharpness of its edge.

"Perhaps the new king always had plans of killing more than one royal."

The prince stood and crossed the room, surveying a wall lined with bows before selecting the one with the finest craftsmanship, the hardiest materials. His fingers slid across the smooth wood, the heavy draw weight indicating a powerful blow.

"You have other news you wish to share?" The prince's voice sliced through the air like an ax.

"His Majesty asked for you, when you planned on joining the troops."

The prince fastened his scroll of weapons to his belt before sliding daggers into empty sheaths concealed within his dark clothes and fastening a quiver to his back. Black paint outlined his eyes, and he tied a scarf around his head, hiding his bronze hair and masking his face in shadows.

"Tell my brother I will join him."

The prince crossed the room, but hesitated in the doorway to look back at the messenger. The flames of the fire ignited the gold flecks in his eyes.

"But not until I've killed the king of Gharridan."

Acknowledgments

I feel like the end papers of a book should just have the words 'thank you' chaotically printed all over them to show an author's gratitude—but it still wouldn't be enough. If you've made it this far, made it halfway through this series, thank you. Like, a thousand times. Writing and publishing is terrifying because you pour years of yourself into something that people either may or may not like. To everyone who has bought, read, requested in libraries, or left reviews of *The Blood Vier*—a million times thank you. I love you guys.

As always, thank you mom for supporting me in every way and for reading my books over and over and over (you may have read them more than me). I wouldn't be where I am today without you.

To my Aunt Debbie, thank you so much for your valuable feedback and support.

To my sister Donna, thank you for putting up with the eighty million texts I send you almost daily, and the endless blurbs and random book things I'm always asking your opinion on. Thank you for supporting me in literally every way and always being willing to listen to me drawl on about my books and the writing world for hours and hours. I'm sure it's not always interesting, but you haven't told me to shut up. Yet.

Caitlan, my Instagram writing and publishing buddy(one of these days we'll finally meet in person), thank you for being so supportive and for always being there if I need anything. Writing is a lonely world and having someone else who understands it and lives in it makes it so much easier to bear. Thank you for helping me figure out formatting issues, gushing over books, and for all the messages (especially the ones that are sent in all caps).

To my absolutely AMAZING and CRAZY TALENTED cover designer Fran, THANK YOU so much for the glorious masterpieces that are the covers for both *The Blood Vier* and *The King Slayer*. You blow me away every single time and I always scream and freak out for at least ten minutes straight whenever I first see them.

Thank you to all my friends and family for your support and to the amazing God that I get to serve every day.

To you, the reader, I hope that you've fallen in love with these characters as much as I have, and thank you for coming on this journey with me.

Christy R. Harrill is the book-loving and anything medieval fantasy obsessing author of the *Blood Vier* series. She lives in Oklahoma where she enjoys hiking with her dog Hank and devouring every book she possibly has time for. Christy loves winter, and still hopes to attain the dream of getting snowed in with four feet of snow one day. She thinks that the only good thing about summer is wearing sandals, and has a weakness for buying pretty notebooks—even though she already owns far too many blank ones at home.

For more information, please visit Christy at
christyrharrill.com
Or follow her on Instagram and TikTok
@christyrharrill

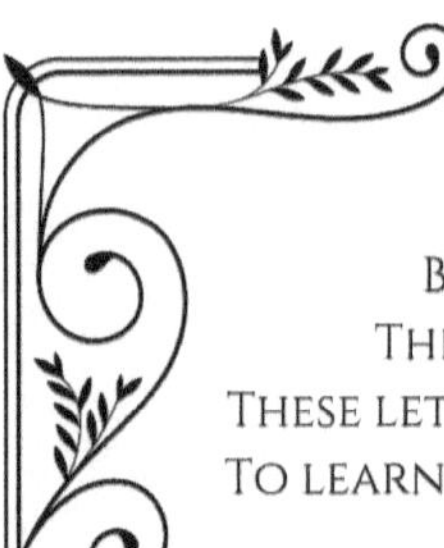
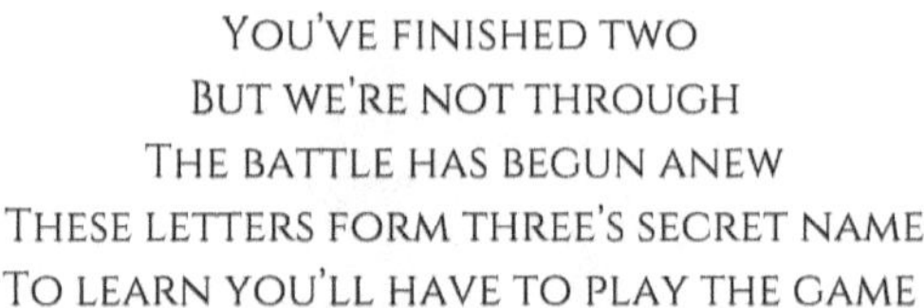

You've finished two
But we're not through
The battle has begun anew
These letters form three's secret name
To learn you'll have to play the game

34.2.1.1
45.14.1.4
61.12.7.5
72.17.2.1
131.9.8.7
162.11.6.2
182.2.5.3
195.29.6.5
215.8.3.1
223.3.2.3
239.6.12.2
279.7.5.3
315.22.8.5
347.15.9.5
402.20.7.2

LEAVE A REVIEW

If you enjoyed reading *The King Slayer*, please consider leaving a review on Amazon, Goodreads, or Barnes and Noble. Reviews help authors find more readers like you.

www.ingramcontent.com/pod-product-compliance
Lightning Source LLC
Chambersburg PA
CBHW031236310726
48971CB00004B/1044

THE EXCURSION

A THRILLER

T. O. PAINE

DARK
SWALLOW
BOOKS

Published by Dark Swallow Books
www.darkswallowbooks.com

Library of Congress Control Number: 2022915979

Paperback ISBN-13: 979-8-9866958-0-8
Hardcover ISBN-13: 979-8-9866958-1-5
eBook ISBN-13: 979-8-9866958-2-2

"It's not the strongest of the species that survives, nor the most intelligent. It is the one that is most adaptable to change."

\- Charles Darwin -

CHAPTER ONE

CHARLY

Before the summer sun set over the cabin, before my cousins disappeared into the woods, and before Amanda found the raccoon tail, I never wanted anyone to die.

No.

That's not true.

I wanted Amanda to die, but we were just children, kids running through the forest, playing my dad's game. Saying crazy things like *I wish you were dead*, and, *When I grow up, I'm going to be a millionaire*. You can't blame me for the things I said to my cousin. For wishing she would die. Like so many, I was thrust into this world, into the arms of two random people I assumed would take care of me forever, but who failed. They left me to survive on my own, dragging my neurodivergent brother with me everywhere I went. I had no choice. As it turns out, I was the only sane one.

If only I could go back to that summer. Back to before everything fell apart. We were little animals back then, taking everything to the extreme. Fight or flight and everything in between. We said crazy things. We did crazy things. We played my dad's game, but I never *really* wanted Amanda to die. I just wanted to win. And, by the way, she didn't die. In fact, she became a millionaire.

And why am I thinking about her while driving across town in the dead of winter?

Because of my mother. She's beckoned me for what I hope will be the last time.

I'm on my way to her assisted living center.

My tires jostle over a seam in the pavement, and my cell phone bounces on the passenger seat. Snow slides off my Ford hatchback. I took a shortcut through suburbia to avoid the traffic on Interstate-25, but I shouldn't have. Orange and black signs block the road up ahead. They're doing construction the day after a major snowstorm.

Only in Colorado.

My mother left a voice message yesterday. She said if I visited her, she would give me the cabin. It's her fault I can't get Amanda out of my head. I hadn't thought about that place in years, and now everything's swept over me like a tidal wave. I turned eleven that year. My brother, Jacob, my cousins, Amanda and Cam, and I . . . we played my dad's game.

And there it is—my real worry. My dad got the cabin in the divorce. If my mom is offering me the cabin, maybe she's talked to him. Maybe he's come back.

And, what will I do if he has?

A pothole opens up before me and I jerk the wheel to dodge it, narrowly missing the curb. I straighten the car out just in time to lurch to a stop at a light.

What *will* I do if Johnathan's come back?

I've been practicing my speech for eighteen years, telling myself I would never speak to him again, never call him "Dad" out loud again, plotting ways to get even with him for abandoning us. The thought he might have returned has me twisted in knots. As much as I hate to admit it, a part of me wants to hug him. The insecure little girl who watched him drive away at the end of that summer, never to see him again . . . she wants to hug him.

Then, the thought of him embracing me makes my stomach turn.

He promised he would come back, and he never did. Eighteen years is too long.

No one in this world keeps their promises.

Everyone lies.

Especially my mom.

The light changes, I round a corner, and a construction worker flips his flag to STOP. My tires slide on the black ice, and I stop a few feet before him. He looks down the road as if I'm not here. I wait, my hands on the steering wheel, looking directly at him. He's bundled in multiple layers, a red scarf hiding his face. Tan leather gloves. Black leather hiking boots. It's freezing out there.

I close my eyes.

It will be cold in the assisted living center.

It will be colder still in my mom's room.

She's in hospice.

I open my eyes and stare at the worker.

He has his entire life ahead of him, and he's spending it in the cold, holding a sign.

My life is ahead of me, too. And what am I doing with it? I'm unmarried, living with my younger brother in a two-bedroom apartment, waitressing at the closest place that would hire me. I've come far since I turned sixteen.

Since my mom left me no choice but to live on my own.

I've actually done very well for myself. In many ways,

life's been easier for me than my mother. After the divorce, Dad left her forever, and the drugs and alcohol took over. It began with Bloody Marys on Sunday mornings and ended with needles in her arms, or worse. I'm not sure. After I turned sixteen, she stopped paying the rent, and Jacob and I had to find our own places to live. I remember finding brochures for her, begging her to go to meetings—begging her to stop.

And now, it's come to this.

But I've made my peace with her death.

I swear. I have made my peace. She played with fire for too many years, and now she's facing the final burn. Stricken with every cancer and disease known to man, she has endured enough. We've all endured enough. Jacob won't see it, but it's best we let nature take its course. It breaks my heart, but I did everything I could do for her. And, I've made my peace.

The worker flips his sign to SLOW, I hit the gas, and my decrepit Ford Focus moans. The front wheels spin on the ice before catching a patch of pavement, launching me forward. The roads are mostly clear, and I make good time after exiting suburbia. The sun has arrived in a blazing fury this afternoon after yesterday's snowy onslaught. Such is life in the Mile High City. We're closer to the sun than most places, but that doesn't always make it warm.

The assisted living center resembles a run-down bowling alley. Maybe it used to be one. The single-story building creeps across the parking lot, its asphalt shingles glistening where the snow has melted, sparkling in the sunlight. There are no windows in front, only a single set of double doors.

Those doors split the world in two.

For those checking in, they separate the before and the after.

People come here to die. It gives me chills.

I buzz in and convince the staff my name is indeed Charly Highsmith. Joan Highsmith's daughter. A half-awake nurse directs me down the hall to her room.

After today, I swear, I'm never coming back. And, after today, I'm going to take charge of my life.

Through the doorway, I see her sitting upright in her bed, her eyes closed, her body buried in one of those rough hospital blankets. Baby puke beige. As I enter, she opens her eyes and gestures toward a chair by the window. "Have a seat, Charly. I'm glad you're here."

Handprints and other smudges catch the afternoon sun attempting to shine through the paned glass. A pale green curtain ends halfway down the wall where an old radiator begins. I don't think the radiator has worked in years.

I hate the cold.

"I can't stay long," I say. "Jacob's waiting for me. What's this about the cabin? Did you talk to Johnathan?"

She averts her eyes. Smooths out a wrinkle in her blanket. "No. I haven't seen him."

"Your message said I could have the cabin, but it's not yours to give. What's going on?"

"The keys are in that box by the window."

A jewelry box sits on the windowsill next to pictures of her when she was young. An ornately framed picture shows Jacob and me holding hands when we were little. He must have been about eight. It was taken before our last summer as a family.

"Bring me the box, and I'll find them for you. You don't have to stay, even though I *am* dying."

The box contains cheap gold earrings, necklaces, plastic buttons, a couple of old pictures from a photo booth, and a bent syringe the nursing staff must have mistaken for a sewing needle. A few keys are buried at the bottom.

"Give it here," she says. "And sit. Please. We need to talk."

I'm about to explain again that I can't stay when her eyes well up. She holds her hands out for the box, but when I hand it over she doesn't have the strength to hold it aloft, so she lowers it onto her lap.

I sit. "What do you want to talk about?"

She rummages around, pulling out keys as she finds them, not looking at me. "I want to tell you about your father. Oh, I shouldn't feel this way. I haven't talked to him since the divorce." She holds up a keyring with three keys attached. "Here. These are the ones."

She's lost her mind. "Mom, what's going on? You can't just give me the keys to *his* cabin."

"Yes, I can. I think—yes. It's part of his estate. You might as well have it now."

"What? His estate?"

"Because of the trust fund." She shifts her gaze to the window. "The papers came yesterday. Here, take these." She hands me the keys. "The papers are on the floor over there."

It's unbelievable.

Something from my dad, after all this time. I mean, something from Johnathan.

I snatch up the legal-sized envelope and take it to the window. The return address references a law firm I've never heard of before. It came from St. Louis. I pull the papers out, and halfway down the first page, there's an amount typed in bold. It's more than one and a half million dollars.

My heart drops.

I gape at the amount.

"Is this a joke?"

"No. There's nothing funny about this." She clears her throat. Coughs.

I teeter on the verge of a nervous laugh. The paper says I will receive the money when I turn thirty. That's only a couple of years away. Jacob and I will be set. I won't need to waitress anymore. Could I quit sooner than that? Probably not. My savings aren't what they should be. I've slowly depleted that windfall I had a few years ago.

There's so much to think about now. It's so much money, but—these papers came from Johnathan. He's still alive. The money is one thing, but the fact he is still alive, and the fact that he thought of me . . .

I don't care about the money.

I want to know where my dad is.

"I'm so happy for you," she says. "I wish I could be there when you get the money. I'm so sorry for all the things I—"

"Don't start that again, Mom. I told you last time, you don't have to apologize anymore. I made my peace with"—she's going to die in that bed—"with you, last time."

"Please sit back down. There's more you need to know."

My hand brushes the radiator when I pull the chair closer to her bed, and it burns. The heater works after all. "Where's Johnathan?" I sit and rub the back of my hand, but it only worsens the pain.

"The reason they sent the papers is . . ." She covers her eyes.

"What? What is it?"

"Right after the papers came, a lawyer called. Your father had a heart attack last week, and—"

"And?"

"And he passed away. I'm sorry."

CHAPTER TWO

RANDALL

Randall Thorne doesn't spread his *experience-of-a-lifetime* brochures across the table. He doesn't hang posters of hunters clad in camouflage suits sneaking through the Congo Basin. He doesn't polish the barrel of a Remington 7600 hunting rifle—to make it shine, to use it as a prop, to pass it around the room hoping someone will fall in love with its power.

He doesn't do any of these things because he doesn't have to.

Randall knows how to sell an excursion with words alone. He knows what to say and how to say it. He practices his pitch in the bathroom mirror, shouting. Prepping his voice. When he strides into the vacant bingo hall, he pulls lint off his stormy gray suit, and he tells himself, *I am the greatest.*

I am in control.

I will win.

The stage invites him up the steps to the lectern, but he stays below, standing between the long tables, gracing the thick red carpet with his presence. Only around ten tycoons are expected today. This hall is too large. Overkill. He moves the tables at the front closer together. He needs to make his pitch close and personal.

He closes his eyes.

I am in control.

"Is this the place?" a man shouts across the venue, a Southern drawl pulling on his words.

Another man walks into the hall behind the Southerner. Then another. These two are plainly dressed in rugged button-down cotton shirts, slacks, and cowboy boots. Rural millionaires. They stay close to the Southerner, flanking him on each side.

"Yes," Randall says. "Please come up front and take a seat."

"Why we in this bingo place?" the Southerner asks.

"For discretion. This is an exclusive opportunity. Please, please, take a seat."

Others enter through the doorway, passing by the bingo hall proprietor. He stands off to the side. This is not the greatest venue in Denver, but it will do. Long tables sprawl across the floor. Bright lime and aquamarine chairs blend with the clown-red carpet, giving the place an old Las Vegas feel. Hotel conference rooms work better, but they're expensive, and too many hotels keep records. The proprietor took the cash wad with a smile earlier this morning, no questions asked.

It will be as if Randall was never here.

Two women with designer handbags and steep stilettos head toward the stage, followed by a man with curly hair in a blue silk shirt and black leather vest. His vest does little to mask his well-defined chest, and his curls shine beneath the fluorescent light. Too much product. He glances from side to side, then settles his eyes on the women's rear ends as they walk. He looks like a croupier, except his watch is worth tens of thousands of dollars. Randall could smell the man's money before he entered. He's the perfect client. Young, rich, and dumb.

A round-bodied gentleman shuffles in next. Time has taken his hair, and he has the pasty complexion of old money. Overweight and soft, he pauses to take a breath, places his hand on a table, and wipes his forehead. He'd never survive the hunt.

"Everyone." Randall waves. "Welcome. Please, take a seat. We have one hour until the hall opens for bingo, so let's get started."

The Southerner sits at the front, joined by his two compadres.

"What brings you to Denver?" Randall asks him.

"You. I missed it when you came through Dallas last month. Had an emergency with my daughter."

"Oh, well, thank you for making the trip up here. Are you staying through the holidays?"

"Yep."

"Excellent."

The two women take a seat on Randall's right, and the curly-haired man slips in behind them. A straggler rushes into the hall and sits by the round man. She wears a hemp rope adorned with a rough-hewn rock hanging around her neck. Her sandals look like Birkenstock knock-offs, and she carries a notebook. Hippie. She should not be here.

Randall walks up to the curly-haired man and extends his hand. "I'm Randall Thorne."

"Barry Rockwell." The man stands. They shake hands.

"Barry Rockwell? Is that Bartholomew Rockwell?"

"I prefer Barry."

"Yes, of course, you do. I know your family. Well, I don't *know* your family, but—let's say I'm aware of your lineage."

"Isn't everybody." Barry gazes at the floor as he retakes his seat.

"You're in the right place, Barry. What I've got to offer— it's exactly for someone like you." Randall flashes his knowing smile and steps before the group.

All eyes go to him.

They're his.

He raises his hands. "Greetings. My name is Randall Thorne. Welcome. Welcome to the first day of the rest of your life." He cocks his head and looks at everyone from the corner of his eye. "That is, if, after my presentation, you think your life is still worth living."

CHAPTER THREE

CHARLY

I tell myself it sounds worse than it is.

My dad is dead.

I tell myself it doesn't matter. It shouldn't matter. I've spent over half my life without him already, so nothing has really changed. I stopped calling him "Dad" years ago. His name is Johnathan. A man named Johnathan promised he would come back for me one day, but he never did.

And now, he never will.

It's water under a broken bridge.

Soon, my mom will join him. I made my peace with her impending demise again earlier today. I couldn't wait to get out of the assisted care center. As soon as she gave me the keys to Johnathan's cabin, I grabbed the trust fund papers and left for the last time. Sitting here, stopped at a red light, I realize I'm about to be a real orphan. I've always felt like one, but now it's really going to happen.

I don't know what to do.

Maybe there is nothing *to do*.

An awkward feeling of freedom takes over, and I pull into

the Appleton's Wine and Spirits parking lot. I shut the engine off and march inside. Standing there, dead center in the wine aisle, the bottles stare at me like lemmings on a cliff.

Jacob probably wonders why I'm not back at the apartment yet, and I don't have a good answer. Not yet. I pulled into the liquor store for a reason, but it's been months since I had a drink. Hell, it's been years, but if ever there was a day for it, today's the day.

Johnathan is never coming back.

The tile floors are covered in black spots where price stickers fell, stuck, and gathered dirt. I doubt anyone has ever mopped this place. The ceiling is yellow, and the coolers in the back look like elevators to hell.

Unlike my mother, I've never had a problem with drinking. Back in my teens, I only did it to fit in with the guys. To make sure I had a place to sleep. I'm never going to go back to that life. Never. I'm only here to buy something nice to celebrate the news of my trust fund.

Right?

Or am I here to begin the mourning process? Drown my sorrows.

Either way, I'm buying some wine. That's final.

Hundreds of bottles line the shelves. Maybe thousands. Reds and whites, each label bragging about its vineyard. California. France. To narrow it down, I decide on red, but there are still too many to choose from.

The liquor store owner watches me from behind the counter. He smiled when I entered as if we were old friends. Did I remind him of my mom? She undoubtedly frequented this place. She frequented all the liquor stores in Denver, but other than her eyes and chin, we don't look alike. I have Johnathan's sandy blond hair—though it's getting darker every year—and his height. I'm somewhere north of five foot, ten inches.

My mom is a dark little mouse.

We're nothing alike.

I pick up a bottle of red wine at random and head for the counter.

I'm not like her. Drinking and drugging her entire life.

Wait.

Not her *entire* life. She had to take time off to give birth to Jacob and me, and she didn't drink when we were little, unless I repressed those memories. I was barely eleven when the divorce happened, and I know she was drunk then. If she drank when she was pregnant with me, it had no effect. I turned out fine. But Jacob didn't. I've always wondered if his damage occurred in utero or if he was genetically predisposed to autism.

Damn her addictions.

And damn Johnathan for leaving.

Damn him for not coming back before dying. For lying. For saying he would return and—I put the wine on the counter, and the glass clacks loudly. It almost broke. The clerk grabs it by the neck and turns it over, looking for the bar code.

I don't know him, and he doesn't know me. He must have been staring at me out of boredom. He wears a permanent grin, like he keeps a map of the path to nirvana in a cigar box or something.

How annoying.

I wish I knew nirvana. Peace. I haven't known peace since my dad left. He left because of my mom's problems, but he could have stayed for me.

Why wasn't I enough?

"Will that be all?" the clerk says.

"I think so." He retrieves a brown paper bag from beneath the counter. "Wait. Can I get a bottle of whiskey also?"

"Sure." He steps aside so I can see the shelves behind him. "Which one?"

"That one there with the black label. I don't really care."

He rings it up, puts it in the bag, and I pay.

The last rays of the day's sunlight dance across the parking lot, illuminating my poor old hatchback. She has always run fine, but the dents and dings from hail and road rocks have taken their toll.

I throw the bag of booze onto the passenger seat and head for home.

It's time to tie one on.

CHAPTER FOUR

RANDALL

Seated in the front row of the bingo hall, the hippie girl breaks his flow, raises her hand, gripping her pen as if it's mightier than the sword. Randall can smell her from where he stands by the stage. Garbanzo beans and grain. She smells like an animal. Like prey.

Bartholomew Rockwell, on the other hand, is a hunter. A wealthy hunter. Old money. He sits next to the girl. The others—the Southerner from Dallas and his two cronies, the two women with their designer handbags, the round-bodied balding man—they all have potential, but Barry . . .

Ah, but Barry has the perfect combination of ego and money.

"As I was saying," he says as if speaking to Barry alone, "no one here has lived a life worth living, because no one here has experienced an excursion with Zaroff Enterprises." Randall paces before the group, changing direction and retracing his steps, keeping his eyes on his primary target. "No one here has proven they have what it takes to hunt like a god. To overcome. To adapt. To—"

"Excuse me." The girl waves her pen.

"Please, hold your questions until the end."

She glowers at him.

Hippie.

Randall gathers his composure and continues. "To adapt means to behave as we truly are. We are hunters. From the dawn of time, we hunted. Before we built feedlots and slaughterhouses, we hunted. It's in our DNA. Over thousands of years, we rose to the top of the food chain, surpassing the skills of every other animal. Fulfilling our destiny as—"

Beep, beep, beep.

A robot vacuum cleaner emerges from beneath the stage directly in his path. It spins toward him, bumps into Randall's ankle, then moves toward the group. Its motor whines, and dirt crackles against its rollers.

"—our destiny as the kings of the earth's kingdom."

"What was that you said?" the Southerner asks.

The vacuum cleaner reverses direction and heads back toward Randall. He steps to the side and waves to the bingo hall proprietor, still standing like a cardboard cutout at the back of the room. "Hey, can you attend to this?"

The proprietor whips out his cell phone, taps the screen, and the vacuum cleaner comes to a stop.

"Now docking," its robotic voice says.

The proprietor puts on a smile. "I apologize for that. It would appear the cleaning crew wants to hear what you have to offer."

He is not funny. Randall's neck burns.

The machine spins a three-sixty and retreats beneath the stage.

"You're wrong." The hippie is waving her pen. Her nostrils flare. "Humans are no better than any other animal.

Just because we're the smartest animals, it doesn't mean we should kill the others."

Her freckles look like fish food flakes. Randall wants to crush them and sprinkle them into a Piranha tank. Watch the fish eat. Watch them devour her weakness.

"You're absolutely right—we *are* the smartest animals. We evolved to become the kings of the earth. Like it or not, we must accept this for what it is."

"But, we don't *have* to hunt to be fulfilled." The rock hanging from around the girl's neck would fit nicely in her throat. It's just big enough to get stuck in there. It would cut off her oxygen and shut her up. She needs to shut up.

Bartholomew—Barry—shakes his head at the girl, clearly struggling to hide his annoyance with her interruption. He's interested in Randall's sales pitch. This is good.

Randall clears his throat. "We are hunters. I'll say it again. We *are* hunters." He slaps his chest. "The great crime is, until now, you've never had the opportunity to prove it." He scans the group. "I doubt many of you have what it takes. Though you're genetically hunters, without what I have to offer, you'll never know what it means to hunt. You'll never experience the true feeling of supremacy. The rush of looking over a kill unlike any other." He turns away, looks toward the ceiling. "You are hunters, certainly, and many of you have gone on many hunting trips, but you were merely traipsing around the woods with some run-of-the-mill rifle, hunting down weak, insignificant animals."

The hippie girl shifts in her seat. Writes in her notebook.

"Anyone can shoot the neighborhood squirrel with a BB gun." Randall eyes the round man. "Anyone can hunt down a commonplace deer. An elk. An antelope. Simple prey. Some of you may have upped the ante and gone for a predator. A mountain lion. A polar bear—"

The hippie girl stands. "Polar bears are endangered."

"No, they're not," Barry says.

She looks down at him, her neck flaming red. "Yes, they are. You can't just go around killing endangered animals to prove you're a man or something."

"I don't have to prove anything." Barry smirks. "I've already got more heads on my wall than will fit."

"Miss," Randall steps forward, "I'm going to have to ask you to leave."

An elderly couple stroll into the hall, bingo cards in hand.

"I'm not going anywhere," she says. "Hunting is murder."

Randall strides toward her, puts his hand on her shoulder, leans in, and whispers, "You're absolutely correct. How would you like to go hunting, just you and me?"

Beep, beep, beep. The robot vacuum surges to life from beneath the stage.

The hippie shoves Randall's hand off her shoulder. "Get away from me."

He grasps her hand. Her fingers feel like dry twigs. So easy to break. He hadn't noticed until now, but her face is gaunt. Her cheekbones are as thin as her fingers. So breakable. She's probably a dry, dirty vegan—weak and malnourished. Not fit to survive.

The vacuum cleaner runs into Randall's shoe.

The proprietor isn't standing in the doorway anymore.

Randall lets go of the hippie girl's hand and kicks the machine. It changes direction and heads toward the two women. They clutch their designer bags and lift their feet.

The Southerner stands. "This is ridiculous."

His compadres rise, flanking his sides.

The elderly couple with the bingo cards stop halfway to

the stage. The old man grasps his partner's arm. "What's going on here?"

Randall's cell phone plays "Hail to the Chief."

Shit.

It's Mr. Dawson, his boss. The head of Zaroff Excursions. "I'm so sorry, everyone. I have to take this. I'll be right back."

The hippie girl yells something about Inuit tribes in Alaska.

The Southerner mock-salutes Randall and passes the elderly couple on his way to the exit.

Randall steps behind the stage. "Hi, Lance. Listen, I'm in the middle of—"

"How many have you sold?"

"None, yet. I've got this one gentleman, a Rockwell, he—"

"How many came?"

"Seven or, no, six. One is an activist, and another one is leaving right now. Listen, I really need to go."

"You've got to make a sale. The location can't be empty over the holidays. We've got to fill it."

"Dammit, Lance. I'm doing my best."

"I don't have to remind you what will happen if you fail, do I?"

"No, sir."

"Don't make me come to Colorado. I'm not in the mood to go hunting this year."

"I understand, sir."

Randall pockets his phone and rounds the stage in time to see the Southerner and his pilotfish exit the hall. The proprietor hasn't returned, and the vacuum cleaner is trapped beneath the tables, bouncing off chair legs like a Plinko chip.

Randall's got to make a sale.

His brow has heated up.

Two months ago, Mark Hodgkins missed his quota in South Africa. He went on a special hunting trip with Lance and never came back. There's no way Randall is going to let that happen to him. If anything, it will be the other way around.

"You're a murderer." The hippie girl stands on her toes, thrusting her face toward Barry's.

"And, you're a bitch." His calm words cause her mouth to drop open.

Randall reaches into his pocket, slips his hand through the slit in the fabric, and grasps the handgun strapped to his thigh. "Everyone, calm down."

"We're out of here." The two women gather their handbags and stand.

"Please, wait," Randall says. "I have more to tell you. Everyone, please. Take your seats, and let me explain."

"No, thank you," says the taller of the two women. "Like, we came looking for a Christmas gift for our husbands, but this is too weird. We thought, maybe . . ." She glances around, taking in the bingo cage, the red and green flags hanging from the ceiling, the red carpeting. "Maybe—"

"No way," the other woman says. "He's creeping me out."

Randall's fingers tighten around his pistol. They have no idea how quick he could be. How dead they could be.

The vacuum cleaner clears the table legs and heads toward him.

"You're in big trouble, buddy." The hippie waves her notebook in the air. "You can't legally take people into the woods and hunt polar bears."

"We don't hunt polar bears," Randall yells.

"What?" The balding man cups his ear and points at the vacuum cleaner. "I can't hear what you're saying with that thing running around."

"*I can't hear.*" Randall mocks the man using a high-pitched voice. "*I can't hear. I can't hear.*" He pulls out his pistol and shoots the vacuum cleaner. Pieces fly over the carpeting and smash into the man's shins. The two women scream. The hippie drops her notebook and runs for the exit.

Barry tips his head back and laughs.

Everyone except Barry leaves.

Bartholomew Rockwell is so perfect, despite his greasy curls.

He's the one.

"Hey, what kind of gun is that?" Barry asks.

Randall stows his pistol and rushes over to him. "It's a simple weapon. Don't worry about it. You're obviously an accomplished hunter. Let's book your excursion now."

"Whoa, not so fast." He steps back. "I'm interested, but—it's interesting, sure, but your whole, we're-the-top-of-the-food-chain speech—I don't know." He shakes his head. "I'm sorry. I'm not buying anything today."

Randall rubs his chin and mutters, "I may have been wrong."

"What was that?"

"You seemed very accomplished before now, but . . . I'm not so sure you could handle it."

"I can handle anything, I'm just not going to buy anything today. Not like this."

"Okay, another day perhaps. But wait, let me make you a deal before you go. Half off if you book your excursion between Christmas and New Year's. Here." He hands Barry a business card. "Please, call me when you get your courage back. That's got my personal number on it."

Barry looks at the card, then glances at what's left of the vacuum cleaner and grins. "You're one crazy son-of-bitch, you know that?"

"Give me a call when you're ready. I promise, one day, you'll look back on this decision as the single-most defining moment of your life. The moment you decided to prove you're not only a man, but a god amongst men."

CHAPTER FIVE

CHARLY

The lights in my kitchen are off, but I can see well enough to put my bag of booze on the dining table and empty my pockets. Two of the keys Mom gave me match each other, and the third is short and rounded. It probably opens the boathouse. It's strange to think I own a lake cabin now.

I pull the wine and whiskey from the paper bag and place the bottles next to the keys on the table.

I sit.

Jacob's bedroom door is closed. His laptop blares through the walls. He's undoubtedly lying on his bed, watching YouTube videos in the dark. He likes to watch people play video games more than play games himself. Playing games makes him anxious. I love him so much, I wish he could experience peace without turning off the world.

I take the cap off the whiskey and raise it to my lips. Wait. I'm not my mother. I'm not desperate. I can be civilized about this. Instead of glugging it down, I grab a water glass from the dishwasher, some ice from the freezer, and make a respectable-looking drink.

The first sip burns my throat.

I swallow my spit until the heat goes away, then I take a bigger gulp and slam the glass down. It spills. My eyes water. As the euphoria hits me, I become Inigo Montoya from *A Princess Bride*. I've been in the revenge business for so long, I don't know what to do with my life now that Johnathan is dead. All the things I planned to say to him don't matter. I'll never get a chance to make peace with him.

I take another drink.

It goes down smooth.

What am I doing?

Once again, I'm not my mother. She would down the entire bottle and go buy another. Or, she would take her pain pills and fall asleep. Or—heroin, or crack, or whatever else she could get her hands on. She always ran from her problems. Chicken or the egg. Did Johnathan leave because she became an addict, or did she become an addict because he left? There's no excusing him, either. He said he left for work, but he never came back. Who does that?

A coward. That's who.

I stare into my glass.

I'm not a coward. I raised Jacob from the time we ran away . . . mostly.

I'm a fighter.

I'm not my father.

I'm not my mother.

I have a life. A good life.

I have my art. It relieves my pain. Over the years, you might say I've gotten better at painting, but I don't share it with anyone. Recently, I've switched to capturing the scenery of the city and the mountains. The paintings I did before, during my teens—they're disgusting. They're a montage of dudes, booze, and a desperately random life. Memories of Grant, one of my boyfriends from that sordid time, crowd into my head. I remember leaving him in the middle of the night—drunk and disoriented. I had so much angst back then.

Now, I have a good life. I have my own apartment with one and half million dollars on the way. I have Jacob. Christmas is coming.

Our tree stands in the living room corner next to the glass sliding door. We decorated it last week, but we keep the lights off most of the time. The flickering bothers Jacob. I understand, and I don't let the darkness bother me.

I take another gulp. The whiskey doesn't burn as much now, and I refill my glass.

When the money comes, I'll feel like a winner. My dad loved winners. That's why he invented the game we played that summer. Amanda, Cam, Jacob, and I, running through the forest. In some way, I never stopped playing the game. I never stopped competing with Amanda. According to the internet, she's on top of the world. She appears to have a great life.

I have a good life.

Condensation forms on my glass and runs down my hand.

I have a good life but . . . do I?

I take another drink and stare at the keys to the cabin.

My apartment suddenly seems smaller. Darker. Lonesome.

Sounds from Jacob's laptop penetrates the walls. People arguing over video games.

My glass is mostly empty.

I don't remember drinking it all.

My mother would go ahead and finish the bottle.

I'm not my mother.

"Jacob," I yell. "How are you doing?"

"I'm fine. I'm watching PewDiePie."

"I want to go on a trip for Christmas. Are you okay with that?"

"No. I want Christmas here."

I go to his door. "How about New Year's?"

"I don't know. I don't like to go places. I like it here."

"Well, think about it. Are you hungry?"

"No."

I'm energized. I grab my laptop from the coffee table and find Amanda on Facebook. Cam, too. I message them both. While I wait for their responses, I dump the last of the whiskey into the kitchen sink and watch as it swirls down the drain.

Cam messages back, *I'm in.*

Amanda messages back, *You're in luck. A business meeting was just canceled, so I'll be able to pry myself away from work. I'm in.*

That's it then.

We're going back to the cabin. We're going to reunite. Make up for lost time.

We're going to have great lives.

CHAPTER SIX

RANDALL

By now, Randall ought to have found the best dry cleaners in each major city where Zaroff Excursions conducts business, but Denver's has always eluded him. The Royal Clean on 17th Street seemed like a good choice. It seemed like they might know what they were doing. But when he hangs his charcoal herringbone suit—his favorite—in the backseat of the company sedan—a jet-black Lincoln Continental, also his favorite—and tears the plastic away, a piece of blue lint falls from the sleeve. He pinches it, smells it, throws it on the ground, and wonders if the imbecile inside bothered to clean the suit at all. He'd love to take that man hunting.

But there's no time.

Lance meant it when he said the cabin can't be empty over the holidays.

Randall's prep bag lies on the backseat of the Continental.

A rope. A knife. Adrenaline. Everything he needs.

Driving down Colfax Avenue, Randall is reminded of the first time he came to the Mile High City for work. The streets lined with dirty snow. The red and green Christmas tree lights hanging haphazardly over smoky tavern windows. His pride. He recalls the cabin hidden high in the Rocky Mountains— the cornerstone excursion site for Zaroff. It's where it all began. He guided hunting trips from the cabin during the holidays at the tender age of twenty-seven, cementing his greatness within the organization.

Now, at forty, with less than a week before the end of December, he risks losing his reputation as the best guide— the best hunter—unless he can sign a client tonight. Lance threatened to come to Colorado if he failed. His boss threatened to take Randall on a hunt. What a joke.

He continues to cruise down Colfax Avenue, thinking . . .

Ah, the irony. This is all Lance's fault. He has become stupider and lazier with each sales event. Those leads at this last one—how did an animal rights activist get an invitation? That kind of thing should never happen. And it won't. Not once Randall is in charge. Let Lance come to Colorado. He has no idea what he's in for.

The "G" in the neon sign for *The Singer* looks like it burned out in the 1970s. He drives around behind the bar and parks in the dark end of the lot, one tire sinking into a pothole, the passenger side up against a chain-link fence.

Feeling the weight of his years following that sudden initial rise, the monotonous, demeaning crawl toward the top without fulfilling his destiny—he needs a drink.

And a client.

With New Year's only two days away after tonight, hope is all but lost.

Before he can get out of the car, his phone rings.

"Randall Thorne here."

"Hey, is this the guy from the place? The hunting trip? This is Barry Rockwell. You gave me your card."

"Yes, yes. Hello, Barry. Mr. Rockwell. How are you?"

"I'm great. Look, I thought about what you said, and I'm willing to take you up on that deal."

"That's wonderful."

"My calendar is free near the end of January, so—"

"Oh, you won't want to wait until then. The format, the entire experience, it's changing next year, and between you and me, it's not going to be as good."

"Huh? How?"

"First of all, corporate is raising the fee, and—right. They're raising the fee, and I wouldn't be able to give you half-off then, like I promised."

"I see."

"They're also adding some restrictive rules and regulations." The words roll off his tongue free and easy as if they were true. "Next year, the experience will be great, but it won't be the same. It's sad, really. The rush. The thrill of the ultimate kill. The achievement—it just won't be the same, but it's not too late. I have one spot left right before New Year's. What do you say?"

Snow gently falls from the evening sky, melting the moment it hits the windshield. Glistening beneath the parking lot lights.

"It's tough. I'd planned on taking this babe on a trip over New Year's Eve."

"We can complete the excursion in two days. Just you and I, together, gods in the wild. I'll have you back in time to kiss her under the mistletoe. I promise."

"Can she come along?"

"No. Absolutely not. For quality assurance, we adhere to a strict set of rules. It would dilute your experience, and we demand a high amount of discretion. You must come alone, and you must tell no one."

"Okay." He pauses. "Two days? I don't know. That's cutting it pretty tight. New Year's is Friday."

"I've got to say, Mr. Rockwell, I find it disturbing that you would let a woman stand between you and your last chance at the greatest blood-thumping experience of your life. Especially when you can have both."

Randall waits. He counts down in his head. Five. Four. Barry gets five seconds to think. After that, the silence must be broken. The sale must be made. Three. Two.

"Okay," Barry says. "I'll do it."

"Great. One question. At the presentation, I heard you say you've been on several big game hunting trips. I assume you won't need a training session."

"Correct. I'm an advanced hunter."

Braggart. Unbecoming. Minor failing, though. He's so good. So wealthy. The perfect client. "Okay, then. I'll make the arrangements and call tomorrow with the details."

Randall hangs up. He knew it. He knew Barry was the one when the arrogant young man strode into the bingo hall last month. He just knew it.

This changes everything.

He's going up to the cabin after all, but there's little time.

He needs to arrive at the cabin by tomorrow so he can set everything up.

The snow continues to melt on impact. He steps out of his Lincoln, locks the door, and strolls across the parking lot toward *The Singer*.

He has everything he needs to guide an excursion this week—his prep bag, his hunting apparel, a client.

Everything he needs, except for the most important part.

The prey.

CHAPTER SEVEN

Dad pulled the car up to the cabin and shut the engine off.

Jacob and I opened our doors and jumped out.

"Wait for us," our mother said.

The July sun beat down, but the cool mountain air refused to be abused. Compared to the stale air conditioning we'd suffered through for the last three hours, it was literally a breath of fresh air to leave the car. Jacob and I ran onto the porch and stood in the shade beneath the awning.

Our parents pulled the luggage out of the trunk and came to the door.

"Hurry, Dad." Jacob held up his Transformers watch. "Hurry, Mom. You said we'd be here at four. We have one minute left. One minute."

Dad unlocked the door to the cabin, and we ran down the hall to the closet.

Board games.

Mom and Dad continued around the corner into the dining room by the french doors, then headed up the stairs without saying a word. They'd been so quiet lately. The car ride had lasted forever. I couldn't wait to get the games down. Light streamed in through the french doors, but it didn't make it to the hall closet where Jacob and I stood. The darkness made the cabin seem cooler than it was.

"Chutes and Ladders?" I asked.

"No." Jacob gazed up at the closet, his lower lip slightly twitching.

"Don't start playing anything," Mom said from the top of the stairs. "We're going to eat dinner as soon as your cousins arrive."

Our cousins. Amanda and Cam. I couldn't wait for them to come. New blood. Playing games with my brother could get so boring. He almost always lost unless he was hyper-focused or got lucky. Amanda, on the other hand, usually won. She was the same age as Jacob, eight, and I was the oldest at ten. Still, she almost always won. I should have been able to beat her at everything, but for some reason, she always had a golden halo around her head.

Cam, well . . . he was just a kid. Quiet. A little creepy, maybe. His parents divorced when he was in first grade. For the longest time, I thought it was the divorce that sent Cam into weirdo-land, but he might have been born that way. Like Jacob, but worse. If not born strange, then it was his mom who screwed him up. She gave him a cat to replace his dad after the divorce. It was a divorce cat. Cam blamed the poor thing for his parents' break-up.

Jacob stared up at the board games on the top shelf.

"Candyland?" I suggested.

"No."

I stepped into the dining room, grabbed a chair, and pulled it to the closet. "Checkers?"

"No."

"Chinese Checkers?"

"No."

"C'mon, Jacob. Pick one before they get here. If Amanda gets to pick, she'll ruin everything."

"Why do all the games start with 'C?'"

"They don't. They—oh. You're right. Wait, Monopoly doesn't."

"I like that they start with 'C.' 'C' is for cookie."

"Then pick one." I got up on the chair, and it wobbled until I steadied my feet.

"I can't pick, Charly. I can't pick only one."

"Why?"

"Because they all start with C."

"But they don't." I reached for Monopoly, and the front door opened. Amanda and her mom, Aunt Janice, strutted inside, followed by Cam. They must have picked him up and brought him because his mother, the divorcee Aunt Meg, wasn't with them. He wore his Cleveland Browns sweatshirt and a deadpan face. What a dud. My dad hated the Browns, and so did I. We were a Broncos family.

"Where are your parents?" Aunt Janice asked.

"Upstairs."

"Candyland," Amanda said, running toward me. "I want to play Candyland."

She bumped into my chair and I slipped off, pulling the Monopoly box down as I fell. Green houses and red hotels bounced on the floor. My butt landed on a particularly sharp playing piece. The cannon.

Without hesitation, Amanda climbed onto the chair and reached for Candyland.

Her mom took a step backward onto the front porch. "I can't stay. Tell your parents I said hello, and I'll be back

Sunday morning. Got it?"

"Yes."

Cam stared down at me. His uni-brow was coming in nicely, and his left eye twitched once. I held my hand up for help, but he didn't take it.

"Candyland," Amanda repeated.

"No." Jacob retreated into the dining room. "It starts with 'C.' I want to play Monopoly. Monopoly."

Amanda leaped from the chair, gripping Candyland with both hands. "No way, freak. We're playing this."

I stood.

Jacob ran to the other side of the dining table.

She put the game on the table and opened the box.

"Charly?" Jacob's lips twisted when he said my name. "Help. I don't want to play Candyland. I want to play Monopoly."

"Shut up, freak." Amanda unfolded the game board.

"Stop calling him that," I said.

She turned, her raven hair swinging off her shoulders, her eyes locking on mine. "Make me."

"That's it. I'm telling." I headed for the stairs.

"You're in trouble now, Amanda." Jacob stiffened his spine. "Charly is telling on you. You're in trouble now."

CHAPTER EIGHT

RANDALL

The door to *The Singer* is three inches thick and made of solid wood. Sour-smelling beer poisons the air. Three old men clad in sweatshirts sit huddled in the far corner where the bar bends toward the bathroom, nursing their beers and grumbling. Couples sit at tables, glasses clink, a cacophony of voices compete with Led Zeppelin on the sound system. A young, bearded man sits at a two-top near the front door, arguing with an attractive woman. His cheeks are red, and she stirs her drink with a little red straw. Randall walks past them on his way to an empty barstool at the bar.

"This seat empty?"

"Be my guest," says a man wearing a teal, waterproof hoodie. Something from one of those outdoor sports stores. REI, maybe.

"What'll it be?" the bartender asks.

"Top shelf, whiskey. A single." Randall notices the hoodie man's drink and regrets not seeing it before he ordered his whiskey. The man's drinking a beer. Heineken. He has *some* class. "My name is Randall."

"Tyler. Nice to meet you."

"What brings you here, Tyler?"

"Nothing." He takes a drink of his beer. Glances away. "Just needed a drink, I guess."

"Me too."

Tyler's bottle has but one swallow left. Randall doesn't recognize the logo on Tyler's hoodie. It's a nice garment, new but not extravagant. His hiking boots have no scratches, and his hands are pale and smooth. Clearly, his mother combed his hair for him this morning.

"Here ya are." The bartender places Randall's whiskey on the bar.

Tyler glances at the shot.

"Can I get one for my friend?" Randall asks.

Tyler holds his hand up. "No, thanks. I'm sticking to beer tonight." His bloodshot eyes say otherwise.

"No," Randall retorts. "I insist."

The bartender pulls a shot glass out of nowhere and begins to pour.

"So, Tyler, what is it? Work or women?"

"What?" He finishes his beer, and the bartender replaces the empty mug with a whiskey shot.

"Work or women? What's got you sitting here tonight?"

"Oh, that." He glances up at the ceiling. "Women, I suppose."

"What's her name?"

"There's no one at the moment."

Randall raises his glass. "Then you're a free man, like me. Cheers."

They clink glasses and down the whiskey. The alcohol burns Randall's throat, but he doesn't react. It's been a while since he's had the hard stuff.

Tyler puts his shot glass down on the bar, slow and careful, his expression unaffected by the burn.

"Two more," Randall says.

The bartender nods.

"Thanks," Tyler says. "I—what was your name?"

"Randall."

Tyler glances at the floor. "Nice shoes. What are you selling?"

"You're very astute, young sir. I am indeed a salesman of sorts."

Tyler rolls his eyes.

"Look, I'll be straight with you. I can see you're an intelligent, perceptive person. You would do well on an excursion, you know."

"An excursion?"

"Yes. I sell guided hunting trips—excursions, if you will—but they're unlike anything you've ever heard of."

"I'm not a hunter."

"Oh, no?"

"No." He rubs the rim of his shot glass. Stares at it.

"We're all hunting for something, right?" Randall locks his eyes on Tyler's. "We all want something. Right?"

"I suppose so."

"If you don't mind my saying, you look like you've stopped hunting for what you want. Like you've given up."

"I wouldn't say that."

"What are you looking forward to then? What plans have you?"

"I've got plans." Tyler leans back on his stool.

"Here ya are," the bartender says.

Randall puts a fifty on the bar. "Keep them coming, kind sir." Tyler begins to open his mouth, but Randall has him on the hook. "Sure. You say you have plans, but this time next year, what will you have done? What will you have accomplished?"

"Hey, I appreciate the drinks, but—"

Randall grasps Tyler's wrist. "Do you see that woman over there by the door?"

Tyler peers past him. The bearded asshole she was arguing with when Randall entered the bar has left, and she sits alone. "Yes."

"The one with the red straw in her drink?"

"Yes."

"Attractive, isn't she?"

"Yes."

"Go talk to her."

Tyler makes a half-cocked smile. Looks away. Shakes his head. "No. Not tonight."

"You can have her. In fact, you can have anything you want. That's what I'm trying to tell you. That's what excursions are all about. Go on one excursion with me, and you'll never hesitate to hunt for what you want again. Look at her."

Tyler's head lolls to the left. He squints, trying to focus on the woman.

Randall deftly takes the whiskey intended for him, lowers it below the bar, and pours it on the floor.

The woman notices Tyler gawking at her and averts her eyes. She sips from her tiny red straw, her lips pursed tight, her hair tied in a messy bun. She's the perfect bait. Her eyes swim in the dim light, scanning the bar for something worth her attention. Something other than Tyler.

"What do you think?" Randall says. "You like her, right?"

Tyler takes a drink of his whiskey. "I guess so, but I'm

not a ladies' man. I'm not looking for a one-night stand. I want someone I can settle down with."

"Tired of being alone?"

"Yeah." He finishes his shot. "I was seeing someone a few months ago. Sarah. We were together for about two years."

"What happened?"

"She said she we grew apart." He raises his shot glass. "She complained about my drinking, but I had it under control. I have it under control."

The bartender whips out a bottle of whiskey and refills their glasses.

"I can't believe I let her brother live with me." Tyler shakes his head. "Once he got back on his feet, he moved out, and she was gone." He turns his head toward the woman seated at the two-top by the door, then closes his eyes.

Again, Randall dumps his own shot out on the floor and loudly puts the glass on the bar as if he had just finished it. "Go talk to her. I'll come with you." He puts his hand on Tyler's shoulder. "I'll be your wingman."

"I—"

"Here." Randall slides Tyler's shot toward him. "Drink up. Let's go."

Tyler leans forward, rests his arms on either side of the shot, and stares into the glass. "Something has got to change," he mutters. Slurs his words.

"What's that?"

"Something has got to change. I can't go on like this. She . . . Sarah . . . I can't live this way."

"Listen to me." Randall stands. "You've got nothing to lose."

Tyler drains his shot, slams it down, and turns toward the

woman. "Okay. Let's do it."

Randall follows him to her table, hanging back a little. A good wingman.

"I noticed you sitting alone," Tyler says.

The woman glances up from her glass. "And?"

"And . . ."

"Well?" she asks. "What do you—"

"He wouldn't stop talking about your eyes," Randall interrupts. "I apologize if we disturbed you, but I had to make him come over here. He wouldn't shut up."

She gazes up at Tyler. "Is that true?"

Her eyes are light brown and deep. Wells of amber. Randall was right to compliment them. They are her best feature. Good breeding. He gives Tyler a nudge.

"That's right," Tyler says, shoving his hands in his pockets. "Even from over there at the bar, I could see them. They're beautiful."

She pulls out her cell phone and swipes the screen. "I haven't heard anything like that in a while." She frowns at the screen and swipes it again. "That son-of-a-bitch."

"I'm sorry I bothered you." Tyler turns to go.

"Wait." She swipes the screen again, wrinkles her nose, and begins tapping the screen with her thumbs. "What's your number? I'll text you, then you'll have mine."

Tyler stands there for a moment, stupefied.

Randall taps Tyler on the back. "Where's your phone?"

Tyler pulls his phone out and gazes at the screen. He's clearly too inebriated to make sense of what he's seeing. The drunken fool must have double-vision by now, so Randall takes it from him. "Go ahead, miss. Send your message."

"I'm Chrissy, by the way." She taps her phone, stands, and points the camera lens at Tyler. "There." She taps the screen again, and the flash goes off. "My boyfriend's going to hate this."

Randall holds up Tyler's phone. "We got it. Thank you."

"Yeah." A smile takes over Tyler's face. "Thank you."

She shoves her phone into her back pocket and heads for the ladies' room. "Don't mention it. I'll see you around."

"Should we wait for her?" Tyler asks.

"No." Randall slips Tyler's phone into his pocket and pulls out his wallet in one motion, then strides to the bar. "We need to go before she comes back and changes her mind." He throws some cash down for a tip, turns, and motions toward the front. "Let's go."

CHAPTER NINE

CHARLY - THEN

The door to my parents' room was cracked open. I put my hand on the brass doorknob and peeked inside. Downstairs, Amanda was torturing Jacob. Making him play Candyland. Calling him a freak. This was my chance to get even with her. It was never fair that she always got her way. I was going to tell on her. I wanted her grounded.

The doorknob was cool compared to the summer heat outside.

"Joan," Dad said, "when are you going to stop?" His voice was calm but firm.

I took a deep breath.

"It's starting to affect how you treat the kids," he said.

"I only take these to help me sleep. I'm fine."

"But you dozed off in the middle of breakfast this morning."

I opened the door. "Mom. Dad. Amanda's calling Jacob names."

"They're here already?" Mom asked.

"Aunt Janice just left. She said she'd be back Sunday. You

have to come now. Jacob is having a meltdown."

"We'll come after we finish unpacking." Dad closed a dresser drawer. "Now go."

"But Amanda is making us play Candyland. She won't let us play Monopoly."

"Go," my mom said. "You don't have time before dinner to play any games anyway."

"But—"

"And close the door behind you." She waved me away.

I pulled the door closed and walked down the hall. My parents had put my suitcase in the bigger bedroom, probably because I was the oldest. Jacob's suitcase was in the room across from mine. This left Cam and Amanda to share the fourth, smaller bedroom, unless my parents allowed them to stay in the basement. That was unlikely, though. There was nothing down there but dust, cobwebs, and an unfinished bathroom.

When I hit the bottom of the stairs, Jacob was sitting on the floor between the kitchen and the dining room, and Cam and Amanda were at the table with the Candyland board spread open between them. She picked up a card.

"What are you doing?" I asked.

Amanda didn't turn to face me. "We're playing Candyland. C'mon."

Cam frowned at the board.

Jacob shook his head. "Candyland starts with 'C.'"

"Shut up, dill-wad." Amanda drew another card.

"Be nice to him. My parents are coming. I told on you. You're going to be grounded for the weekend."

She whipped around and squinted at me, her pointy nose centered between her delicate, dark freckles. "You're lying. I think you're lying."

"No, I'm not."

"Prove it."

"Yeah," Cam said. "Prove it."

"Candyland starts with 'C.'" Jacob sat in the corner, clutching his knees to his chest. Tears streaming down his face. "The letter 'C.'" He rocked back and forth.

I ran to the stairs. Mom and Dad would have to come now. At the top, my dad's voice boomed down the hall. "Dammit, Joan, you've said that before. It's going to kill you."

"Leave me alone," she shouted.

"Look at your sister. Do you want to end up like her?"

"I—"

I ran to their room and thrust open the door. It banged against the wall.

"What now?" Mom stood by the dresser in the corner, her hands held out. Her summer dress clung to her thin frame, a lemon-yellow sail with no wind. "What do you want?"

"Jacob's crying," I blurted. "He's on the floor, and Amanda won't leave him alone."

Her face was red. "We said we'd be down in a minute. Tell her to leave him alone."

"I did."

"Charly," Dad said, his voice cold as ice, "go play until we're finished talking, okay?"

"But they're playing Candyland, and Jacob doesn't want to."

"I promise we'll come help as soon as we can." He folded a pair of jeans and laid them on the bed. "Okay?"

"Promise?"

"Yes."

Amanda was going to get it now. When Dad saw Jacob rocking on the floor, he'd ground her for sure. She deserved worse, but it was a start. Then it would just be the three of us.

"Green," I heard Jacob say.

I cruised down the stairs.

"Okay," Amanda said. "You can be green."

Jacob was sitting next to Cam. He picked up the green Candyland token and placed it on the board.

"What are you doing?" I asked.

"Playing Candyland." Jacob grinned. "It starts with 'C' and 'C' is for cookie, and that's good enough for me. Right, Amanda?"

"Right."

The Monopoly mess cluttered the floor by the closet. "But—"

"Sit down, Charly." Amanda patted the seat next to her.

I wanted to rip that sly smile off her face.

"Amanda won Candyland the last time we played," Jacob said. "Last time when we were at home after we watched *Ice Age*. And she won when we played on Christmas break."

I moped into the hall and began picking up the Monopoly pieces. I couldn't believe she was going to get away with this. It was like she bribed him with cookies or something.

"Aren't you going to play?" Amanda asked.

"No."

"Then would you mind putting our bags away? They're by the front door."

"Get them yourself."

"And cat starts with 'C.'" Jacob grinned. "How's your cat, Cam?"

"He's gone."

"Where'd he go?"

"He went away."

"Where? Where did he go, Cam?"

"Nowhere. He's gone."

"It's your turn, Jacob," Amanda said.

My mother screamed something from upstairs, and we all jumped when a door slammed. I wished Jacob was still rocking on the floor so Amanda would get in trouble. I put the top on the Monopoly game, stepped up onto the chair, and slid the box onto the top shelf.

My dad came down the stairs. "How's it going, gang?" He saw me in the hall. "It looks like everyone's getting along now, having fun?"

"We are, Uncle John." Amanda shifted in her seat to face him. She put on her goody-two-shoes smile.

"She's lying," I said.

"It doesn't look that way to me." He smiled. "Who's winning?"

"Amanda," Jacob said. "She won last time, too, after we watched *Ice Age*. And the time before that. She's going to win again today, and Cam has a cat."

"No, I don't," Cam said. "Not anymore."

"Listen"—my dad pulled out a chair and sat next to Amanda—"Charly, come over here."

I stood next to Jacob.

"What is it, Uncle John?" Amanda beamed.

"I had an idea for you kids tomorrow. How would you like to play a game? A big game. Outside."

"Like what?" I asked.

"In the woods?" Cam lit up.

"Yes."

"What kind of game?" Amanda put her hand on my dad's wrist.

"Like a treasure hunt. I haven't worked it all out yet, but I think I can set it up around lunchtime."

"Is there a prize?" she asked.

"That's the best part. There's an ultimate prize."

"Clear the table." My mom descended the stairs. "I'm making dinner." She put her hand on the wall and kept it there, letting it slide along as she ambled into the kitchen.

"Game over," Jacob said. "Clear the table. Amanda is ahead, so she won again. She is going to win tomorrow, too. She's going to win the big game. She's going to get the ultimate prize."

No, she's not.

CHAPTER TEN

RANDALL

Outside *The Singer* bar, the temperature has dropped twenty degrees, but it's not too cold to snow. Billowy flakes float down onto the concrete. Randall walks to the corner of the building, away from the neon lights in the windows, and checks over his shoulder to see if Tyler follows. Like reeling in a half-dead fish, Tyler's right behind him.

"How was that?" Randall asks. "How do you feel?"

"I—great." Tyler spreads his arms. Takes in a deep breath. "I feel great."

"That was a rush, right?"

"Yeah."

"I've got more where that came from. That was nothing."

"What do you mean?"

"When I held up her phone number, and you saw it, you felt powerful, right? You went after something you wanted, and you took it. You exercised your power, and now you feel great. You just said so yourself."

"I did. I do."

"Are you adventurous enough to feel more power? More?

To feel it right in the palms of your hands?"

He sways. "How?"

"This way." Randall heads around the corner toward the back parking lot. "I have something in my car you need to see."

"Wait." Tyler attempts to take a step forward but stumbles back, catching himself against the building.

"Let me help you." Randall grasps his arm and leads him around back. There are no lights hanging above the lot, forcing them to move cautiously past the cars in the dark. Tyler's feet bounce off each other and scrape against the pavement as he stumbles forward, relying on Randall's grasp for balance.

"My car's back there."

"Where?"

"Back there, in the corner." Randall's black Lincoln Continental sleeps in the dark about ten yards away. No one is around.

"Wait." Tyler pushes Randall's hand off his elbow. "I changed my mind. I'm done for the night. I've got to go home."

Randall grabs him by his jacket collar and pulls him toward the Lincoln.

"Stop it." Tyler pushes Randall off. "What are you doing?"

Spunk. The drunk has some spunk. This will not do. Randall lets go of him. "I apologize. I got excited. Trust me, when you hold it in your bare hands, you—you'll see. The power."

"Hold what?" Tyler's voice is loud. Too loud.

"Allow me to show you the gun we use on excursions. You're going to love it."

"I told you." He staggers to the left. "I'm not a hunter."

Randall grabs him by the collar again and pulls him off balance.

Tyler attempts to push Randall away, but Randall expects this. He pulls Tyler to the right, then the left. "You've had too much to drink tonight, my friend. If nothing else, you'll need me to give you a ride home." He keeps Tyler off-balance until they reach the car.

Tyler leans over. Rests his hands on the trunk lid. "I just want to leave. I think I'm going to be sick."

"Move." Randall motions for Tyler to take his hands off the trunk. "The rifle's in here." Randall pops the lid. "See?"

"No. I don't see anything."

"Really? It's right there. Take a closer look."

Tyler lowers his head into the trunk. "Nope. Nothing. I——"

Randall plants one hand on the back of Tyler's neck and shoves him into the compartment. Tyler's fancy hiking boots leave the ground and flail as Randall holds his shoulders down, pressing his chest against the spare tire.

"Hey!" Tyler manages to roll over and, lying on his back, kicks wildly.

Randall nearly takes a hiking boot to the face. "You neanderthal." He shoves Tyler's knees away from him and the idiot rolls after them deeper into the trunk.

Tyler twists his upper body and reaches back for the edge, but Randall slams the lid shut before he can grasp it.

"Let me out." Tyler beats against the lid.

Randall struts around the side of the Lincoln and opens the backdoor. He removes a black hood, two zip ties, and one leather glove from his prep bag. He puts the glove on his right hand. Tyler continues to strike the trunk lid, but no one can hear him. They're too far from the bar, and no one is around. He checks his pocket for Tyler's cell phone, and it's still there. The drunken fool never asked for it back after that woman texted her number. Nothing can go wrong now. Nevertheless, there's no time to dilly dally.

Randall leans over the trunk. "If you promise to calm down, I'll let you out."

"Ah!" Tyler yells. Hits the lid.

"That's not calm."

"Okay. Okay. I'll stop."

Randall pops the trunk and cracks Tyler in the jaw before he can make a move. Randall hits him again and again until he covers his face with both hands, then Randall slips a zip tie around his wrists. Blood drips from Randall's leather glove, and he quickly stows it in his jacket pocket before his stomach sickens from the sight.

"Why?" Tyler screams.

"Because you're weak." Randall punches him hard in the stomach. While Tyler tries to catch his breath, Randall zip-ties the drunk's feet together.

"Why are you doing this?"

"*Why are you doing this?*" Randall mocks. "*Why are you doing this? Why are you doing this?*" He pulls a roll of duct tape out of the trunk's side compartment and rips a piece off. "There are two types of animals in this world. Predators and prey." He punches Tyler in the face once more before taping his mouth shut. "Guess which one you are."

Tyler lets out a muffled scream. He sounds like a baby rodent caught in a trap.

Randall forces the black hood over Tyler's head. His prize secured, he stands up straight, leans back, stretches his arms out wide, and inhales. Falling from the sky, snowflakes appear in the darkness as if by magic, landing on his face. Melting on impact.

Tyler moans.

What a crybaby.

Randall slams the trunk lid shut and rushes around to the driver's door. He's taken longer than he should.

A noise comes from the side of the building, just out of sight. He took too long indeed, but no matter. Everything's under control. He walks past his car and strides to the back of the building. He stands in the shadows with his shoulders pressed against the wall.

The clacking of high heels approaches, and she comes into view, passing by him on her way to the far end of the lot. It's the woman from the bar—the bait with the red straw.

He moves after her, slipping his hand into his pocket.

She stops next to a small car parked in the corner of the lot opposite Randall's Lincoln, well-hidden between a giant SUV and a brick wall, and searches her purse for her car keys.

"Greetings, miss."

She startles, the whites of her innocent eyes flashing his way.

He marches forward.

She fumbles for her key fob. Drops it on the ground.

"Please," Randall says, "don't be scared. It's me. From inside."

She kneels to retrieve the fob and looks up at him. Squints. Puts her hand on her chest. "Oh, you scared me."

He holds out his hand, and she takes it, pulling herself to standing.

"Where's your friend?" she asks.

A muffled noise comes from his Lincoln. Dammit.

She peers past him, her face now as white as her eyes.

Randall slips his hand through the slit inside his pants pocket, unsnaps the strap, and grasps his pistol. "He had to leave."

"Oh." She presses the fob button, and her car doors unlock. "I'm looking forward to calling him. I—" Her voice shakes beautifully, like the trill of an eagle. She stammers. Tells Randall to have a good night. Opens her door and turns her back on him to get inside the car.

If only Randall could take her hunting.

But he already has Tyler.

Pistol in hand, he glances back at the bar.

Not a soul in sight.

She settles into the driver's seat.

He presses the muzzle to the side of her head and pulls the trigger.

CHAPTER ELEVEN

CHARLY

Snow blasts through the mountains, driven by an unforgiving wind. I guide my Ford Focus over Vail Pass, barely able to see the car in front of me. The day started out beautiful, but once Jacob and I hit the freeway, the blizzard began. Nonetheless, we're doing it. Only two days until New Year's Eve. This year, we're going to spend time with what little family we have left, even if it kills us.

We set out early this morning, but not early enough to avoid the weather. I wonder if Amanda and Cam beat the snowstorm and arrived at the cabin already. The downfall hasn't started sticking to the freeway yet, but it's heavy. I switch the radio off to focus on the road. Jacob says nothing. He sits in the passenger seat, his back erect like a tongue suppressor, intent on analyzing each and every snowflake as it explodes against the windshield.

At this angle, his face reminds me of Dad's. Johnathan's. Now that Johnathan has passed on, should I think of him as "Dad?"

Jacob presses his feet against the floor as we head into a

sweeping corner. A daunting cliff lies on the other side of the guardrail. His fingers work his fidget toy like ducks fighting over a slice of bread. His toy is some kind of rubbery fish. He has a vast collection of fidget toys, but this is his favorite. He's twenty-six years old and hates it when I call his fidgets *toys*. They're a part of his therapy, and I should choose my words more carefully, but I often slip up because, to me, they are toys. I don't mean to insult him.

I glance over.

He has an unwavering innocence that gives me strength when I need it most. It makes me grateful to be his sister.

The snow splattering against the windshield must be driving him crazy. Too much stimulation. I ease my foot off the gas and cruise into a turn. The back end drifts ever so slightly toward the edge as we round the corner. About ten minutes ago, a fleet of snowplows came in the opposite direction. A sign above the freeway flashes, CHAINS OR SNOW TIRES REQUIRED. I have neither, but we should be able to make it to the cabin before they close the freeway.

I can't wait to get there.

I can't wait to see Amanda and Cam. Find out what they've been doing. Tell them about Johnathan. About the trust fund.

Jacob hasn't blinked in ten minutes.

"Are you okay?" I ask.

"No."

"Is it the snow? Is it too much?"

"No. Yes. No."

"Huh?"

"I don't want to go to the cabin, Charly. I don't want to anymore."

"Why not?"

He blinks slowly. "Charly. Please. Can we go back?"

"No. It's too late. Why don't you want to go?"

"I've been having flashbacks. I don't want to see Cam. You invited Cam."

"I had to. It's a reunion. Come on, we're going to have fun. You, me, Amanda—and Cam."

"Cam is evil."

"No, he's not. He's strange—he *was* strange, but I'm sure he's grown out of it. He was never evil."

"Remember his cat?"

"Yeah, but that was a long time ago. Kid stuff."

"He killed his cat, and he hates me."

"He doesn't know you. Not anymore. And you don't know him, either."

I press on the brakes and turn toward the off-ramp. We slide sideways, slipping near the guardrails. My heart jumps. Feather-tapping the pedal before the anti-lock brakes kick in, I regain traction, and Jacob squeezes his fish with both hands, his knuckles turning white. The anti-lock brake system always scares him.

We stop at the light, and Jacob stares straight ahead, doing his avoiding thing. He won't look at me now that I refused to turn back. It's so annoying when he behaves this way. "Cam doesn't hate you. You're fine. Everything is going to be fine."

"What about Mom? She's not fine."

The light changes.

"Let's not talk about her."

I gun the car, and we accelerate across the intersection.

"She gave you the keys to the cabin," he says. "She gave you the cabin. I know what that means. She's close to dying, isn't she?"

"She's had a rough life. You know that. Besides, she didn't leave us the cabin. It was Johnathan."

Shit.

Why'd I say that?

Now is not the time to have a deep discussion, but he'll have a meltdown if I don't tell him. He has that look on his face. Oh, God. It would have been so much easier if we'd made it to the cabin, and settled in with our cousins first.

"Johnathan?" he asks. "Dad?"

"What?"

"Did Dad leave us the cabin?" He picks at his fish. "Who was it? Mom or Dad? You said it was Mom, then you said it was Johnathan. Johnathan is Dad. He's Dad. Did he come back? Did he?"

"No. He didn't. He—" I tighten my grasp on the steering wheel. "He died."

CHAPTER TWELVE

We sat at the picnic table on the deck overlooking the boathouse and the lake. A summer weekend in the mountains. The chill mountain air gave way to the sun's rays only when the breeze dropped, briefly warming us up. All of us except for Cam. He had disappeared into the forest's shadows shortly after breakfast. The moment my dad said for us to meet in an hour to talk about the game, Cam was gone.

Now, an hour had passed, and neither my father nor Cam was here. Only Jacob, Amanda, and myself. I picked at the weather-worn picnic table, pulling off slivers of wood. Jacob looked uncomfortable in his sweater. He was hot. Or, cold. Definitely itchy. He sipped from a glass of orange juice he'd saved from breakfast.

"It's gonna be a piece of cake," Amanda said.

"You'll win." Jacob pulled on his collar. "I could try, but—"

"I know." Amanda swept her hair back. "I've won a lot of scavenger hunts."

"He didn't say it was a scavenger hunt," I said.

She lowered her chin. "Whatever it is, I'm not worried."

The french doors opened. My dad stepped onto the deck. He wore a thick red and brown shirt. A flannel. It didn't suit him. He only ever wore clothes like those when we went camping. It was like he dressed up for Halloween.

"Where's Cameron?" he asked.

"He's in the woods," Jacob said. "He's hunting."

"Hunting?" Dad walked to the handrail.

"I think he's just wandering around," I said. "Maybe he got lost."

"Cameron," Dad shouted. "Come here. We're all waiting for you."

The breeze picked up and blew through the pines.

Cam appeared near the lake. He stood there wearing the same sweatshirt he'd worn yesterday. The stupid Cleveland Browns football team. "I'm coming."

"Great." Dad sat next to Amanda, opposite me.

Cam plodded past the boathouse, across the lawn, and up the steps onto the deck.

"How are you guys?" Dad asked. "You're going to love this."

"I'm hot." Jacob scratched at his chest.

Cam sat down, and my dad winked at him.

Amanda gave Cam a look. "What were you doing out there?"

"Nothing."

"He was hunting," Jacob said.

"No, I wasn't."

"Okay," Dad said. "Enough. Listen, here's what we're going to do. This afternoon, we'll meet back here at two o'clock. I'll give each of you a clue and—"

"Why can't we start now, Uncle John?" Amanda asked.

"I need time to set the game up. I haven't made the clues yet."

"What do we get if we win?"

He put his hand on Amanda's wrist. "Be patient."

"I don't understand." Jacob fidgeted in place. "What do we have to do?"

"The goal is to follow the clues until you find the ultimate prize."

"What's the prize?" I asked.

Dad looked at the forest. "You'll see. I'll tell you when the game begins."

"I can't do this," Jacob said. "Amanda is going to win anyway. I don't want to do it."

I nudged him. "It's okay. You can come with me. We'll do it together."

"What kind of clues are you making?" Amanda asked.

"You'll see. Don't worry, it's going to be fun. One clue will lead to the next, and to the next, and ultimately, you'll find the ultimate prize."

My mother threw open the french doors. "What a wonderful morning." Her robe opened, revealing her black silk pajamas. She waved a glass of orange juice over the deck.

Dad had spared her only the briefest glance, then returned his attention to us. "Does everyone understand? Two o'clock. Meet back here?"

"What are you plotting?" My mom stepped to my father's side and put her hand on his shoulder. "What are you up to?"

"We're going to play a game for a prize," Jacob said. "An ultimate prize. Amanda is going to win, but I'm going to try. Charly and I are going to try."

"It's nothing, Joan." Dad's eyes had become tired. "Go back inside."

"Why?" She drank from her glass. "I can have fun, too." She swayed, her hand still on his shoulder. "I'm not—"

He grabbed her glass and brought it to his nose. "Jesus Christ. It's not even ten in the morning."

She jerked away from him, her face reddening. "We're on vacation."

"Please. Go inside."

"Fine. I'll do the dishes." She listed over to the doors, fumbled with the handle, and stumbled inside, spilling her drink. Watching her was a punch in the gut. The faint smell of vodka hung in the air. Maybe I just hadn't been old enough to pick up on her drinking before then, but at least for me, this morning marked the beginning of the end for her. I don't think I ever saw her sober again.

Not until she checked into the assisted living center.

My dad heaved himself to his feet. "Does everyone understand? Be back here at two?"

We all nodded.

A crash came from inside the cabin. Metal clanged. I thought my mom had dropped the muffin pan or something, but another crash came. And another. I pictured her beating the refrigerator with a baking sheet.

My dad rushed inside.

"I hate it." Jacob stood. "I hate that noise. Make it stop."

CHAPTER THIRTEEN

CHARLY

It's slow going up the tight and winding mountain road. The blizzard makes it slower. Jacob and I left the freeway about an hour ago. The unrelenting snow engulfs us, and I begin to press my luck. I hit the accelerator on the short straightaways and ease off in the corners. The midday sun shines somewhere on the other side of those clouds but fails to break through.

Jacob scrunches his face. Closes his eyes.

We need to get to the cabin as soon as we can.

Oh, no. Here it comes.

He's about to have a meltdown.

I shouldn't have said anything. If only we could have made it to the cabin before I told him Johnathan had died. Having Amanda and Cam around to support us might have softened the blow.

He sits upright in the passenger seat, staring at the windshield. Watching the snowy onslaught.

"It's going to be okay," I say.

He shakes his head. His fidget toy bounces onto the floor,

and he begins pulling on his fingers.

"Take a breath. It's going to be okay."

He knocks his knees together. Reaches for the door handle.

"Stop." I grab his elbow. "You can't get out. We're moving." The front tires turn, but the car slides straight ahead. Slush splashes against the undercarriage. The rubber grips the road, and we veer to the left. I pull on his arm, but he shakes free of my grasp. "Jacob, please."

He lets go of the handle and puts both hands on the dashboard, his chest heaving. His eyes locked on the torrential snow.

I straighten the car out and say nothing. The windshield wipers moan, struggling to keep up. They slap the ice gathered on the edges of the glass. I lean over the steering wheel, squinting. The sign for Inspiration Peak flashes into view, and we nearly miss the turn. The wind whips across the two-lane mountain road, deepening the drifts on each side. The tires slip, I ease off the gas, and Jacob breathes like a beached whale, staring out the window, knuckles as white as the winter squall.

He's not going to make it.

My throat tightens.

I need to relax. This is not that bad. I've driven in the mountains on snowy days hundreds of times. We're going to be okay. It's only a few more miles to the cabin.

Once we're there, everything will be okay.

"Stop watching the snow," I say. "It's too much stimulus. Try closing your eyes."

"It's not the snow."

"What is it? Johnathan?"

He nods.

"I'm sorry, I shouldn't have said anything, but you shouldn't be surprised. You knew he was never coming back. It's just permanent now."

"Why don't you ever call him Dad? If he's dead—now that he's dead, shouldn't you—"

"No. Dead or alive, he's not—I'm not going to call him Dad. Not ever. And it doesn't matter anymore, anyway. He's dead." My face flushes.

I'm about to cry.

But I never cry.

Ever.

Jacob stamps his feet, picks up his fidget toy, and throws it at the windshield.

"Stop it," I plead.

"Dad's dead. Mom's going to die. She's going to leave. You're going to leave."

"Stop it!"

"You're going to leave me again, aren't you, Charly? You're going to leave me, aren't you?"

"Look at me."

"No."

"Stop looking at the snow, and look at me."

"I want out." He slams his fist into the windshield. "Out!"

The wind gusts, blowing snow over the hood. I can't see the road's edges. "Calm down. Use your toy."

"It's not a toy," he screams.

"Hang on, okay? I bet Amanda and Cam are already at the cabin. I bet they've started a fire. Think about how much fun we're going to have. We can have cocoa."

He pulls his knees to his chest. Rocks back and forth. "They can't be in the cabin. They don't have the keys." A tear escapes his eye and runs down his cheek. "You said Mom gave you the keys. You have the keys. Dad's keys. Dad is dead."

"Calm down. You're going to be fine. Here's the plan. We'll get to the cabin, unpack, have dinner, and go to our room. We'll keep the lights low, and you can watch videos on your phone while I talk to Amanda and Cam."

"All you care about is them." He wipes his nose. "You only care about Amanda. I don't want to watch videos. I want to go home. You want to keep going because you're jealous. You're jealous, Charly. You want something someone else has because you're jealous."

"Jealous of what?"

"Of what Amanda has. You don't think I know, but I do. I'm not stupid."

"I know you're not stupid. I love you, but—I'm not jealous of her. I just want to spend New Year's with family for once. We haven't seen them in forever. I want to reminisce and relive our childhood."

"You're jealous. You're jealous of everything Amanda has. She's a millionaire." He turns toward me. "I want to go home, Charly. Let's go home."

Jacob's wrong. I don't care about Amanda's big executive advertising position in New York. Her wealthy boyfriends. Her looks. Her money. Jacob doesn't know about the trust fund. When we cash in, we'll all be millionaires.

"Cam is evil." Jacob refocuses his attention on the windshield. "I want to go home."

"You need to let it go. Cam is not evil."

"But, his cat—he killed his cat. He'll kill me. He said so."

"When?"

"When we were little. He said so."

"That was a long time ago. Let it go."

"No. I want out, Charly. I want out. Pull over." He grabs

the steering wheel.

I hit the brakes.

The car spins out of control. He won't let go of the wheel. I pry at his fingers, but his grip is firm. My foot slips off the brake and hits the gas pedal. We speed toward the mountainside.

Jacob promised he would behave before we left home.

I pump the brakes and close my eyes.

We should never have left.

I should never have trusted him.

We crash into the mountain.

Stopped, I watch the snow whirl over the windshield in sweeping spirals. The passenger-side hood and side mirror are demolished. The wind whirs like a jet engine. The mountain blocks Jacob's door from opening, but he pulls on the handle anyway, repeatedly hitting the unlock button. He pushes on the door, but he can't open it. He's trapped.

The blizzard envelops us.

We're trapped.

"Oh, no," he says. "Oh, no. Oh, no. Oh, no."

"Calm down." I put my hand on his shoulder and he jerks away. "Everything's going to be okay. Let me see how bad it is." I open my door.

"Don't leave me. It's cold out there. You'll freeze. If your body temperature drops below ninety-five degrees, you'll die of hypothermia within two hours. You'll freeze to death, Charly."

"Relax. I'm not going to freeze to death. I'll be right back. Here, I'll leave the engine running so you'll have heat. Promise not to touch anything?"

"Yes."

I don't believe him. I love him, but he always runs.

The snowbank has swallowed the passenger side. The fender is crushed beneath the drift. We're not going anywhere.

I step into the middle of the road and gaze down the hill. Ice crystals form inside my nostrils. I'm not dressed for this. Snow slips into my sneakers and begins to melt, soaking my socks. My tongue stings. My eyes water in the wind. The frozen air is unbreathable.

My cell phone signal is weak but alive.

I try to call Cam, but he doesn't answer. His phone goes to voice mail.

I hesitate, then call Amanda. She's going to think I don't know how to drive.

She doesn't answer, and her phone goes to voice mail.

There's no break in the sky. The clouds own it.

Snow swirls around me.

The cabin lies somewhere on the other side of this hill, but it is still miles away.

We're stranded.

Jacob watches me from the car.

It's only a matter of time before he tries to run.

CHAPTER FOURTEEN

"They're getting a divorce," Amanda said. "You know that, right?"

"Shut up." I seethed. "They are not."

Yelling came from the kitchen. Cam, Jacob, Amanda, and I sat at the picnic table on the deck, listening. My dad had gone inside when we heard Mom drop a pan. She needed help, but now—nothing but yelling.

I looked away. Beyond the boathouse, ripples on the lake made their way to the shore and struck the sand.

"It's okay, Charly." Amanda drew my attention back to her. She narrowed her eyes. "You can come live with me. My house is bigger than yours anyway. We have an extra room."

"They're not getting a divorce."

"Whatever."

Cam stood and headed toward the stairs.

"Where are you going?" Amanda asked.

"Back to the woods."

"Why?"

He didn't answer.

Jacob squinted at the sun and took his sweater off. "Amanda is going to win the prize. She's going to win."

"No, she's not." I stood.

Amanda grinned. "You don't have a chance, Charly. I already have a plan."

"She has a plan." Jacob flung his sweater on the table. "Amanda is a winner with a plan."

"Stop it, Jacob."

"He's right. I have a plan, and I'm going to win. There are winners and losers, and I'm a winner."

I wanted to rip the freckles off her face. Put her in her place. But the right words didn't come. Jacob was just being Jacob. I never understood why he liked her, and I still don't. Anger swelled inside me, and I turned toward the cabin.

"Aw, don't go, Charly. Just because I'm a winner doesn't mean you're a loser. Not exactly."

My dad had left the french doors unlatched. I slammed them behind me and ran up the stairs. I needed a plan for the game. Amanda didn't win at everything, and she wasn't going to beat me. Not this time. I needed an edge. I—

Before I could reach my room, my parents' voices coursed down the hall like blood from a torn scab. They were still arguing. I heard Dad say my name, but I couldn't make out the rest. My mom yelled back at him. I crept past my room and rounded the corner toward theirs.

"I don't understand." She spoke like she had something stuck in her throat. "Is it me? Because of me?"

"No," he said. "Not—no. Maybe. Not really. It's my work. If I go and do this, we'll be set for life."

"How often are you planning to come back?"

"At least once a month. Maybe more. I promise."

Silence.

"Joan," he said, "I'm worried about you and the kids."

"What do you mean?"

"When did you start drinking in the morning?"

"I'm fine."

"When I go, you'll have to stop. You'll need to take care of them."

"How are you going to break the news? Charly's going to be crushed."

"I'm taking her canoeing at lunch. I'll explain it to her then, and we can talk as a family with Jacob later."

I waited.

She didn't respond.

"Joan, are you okay with this?"

"Canoeing with Charly? On—on the lake? I suppose so."

"No. Are you okay with everything else?"

Footsteps sounded inside.

I backed away from the door.

"It might be good." Her voice wavered. "It might be good for you to go away for a while. I mean, for us."

The footsteps got louder, and I turned away. It sounded like my father was coming toward the door.

I sprinted down the hall.

What did she mean, *good for us?*

I didn't want Amanda to win the game, and I didn't want Amanda to be right about my parents. Divorce. I vowed to keep both from happening. Dad said he would come back every month, but—how could it be *good for us?*

How could it be good for anyone?

CHAPTER FIFTEEN

I shut the engine off despite the dropping temperatures outside. We ran the defroster for an hour, but ice crystals still cling to the upper corners of the windshield. The blizzard has intensified. I can no longer see the hill up ahead.

"We will die in two hours if our body temperature drops below ninety-five degrees." Jacob holds his fidget toy to his chest. "I read about this. We will die. I don't want to freeze to death, Charly."

"We've got to save gas. There's only a quarter tank left."

"What if it won't start again?"

"It will start again."

"I'm cold. I want my sweatshirt. We're going to die." He leans over the dashboard, his shoulders rising toward his ears. Tense. "Let me out."

I knew he wouldn't sit there forever, trapped with his door against the snowbank. "If I let you out to get your sweatshirt, will you stay calm?"

"I won't run if that's what you mean. I won't run."

He's said that before.

I open my door. The wind slaps me in the face. I grab Jacob's hand, and he crawls over the gearshift. His foot knocks my soda out of the cupholder, and he apologizes.

"Leave it," I say.

Together, we trudge through the snow to the back of the car. The sun has begun its descent behind the mountains, darkening the sky. The blizzard has nearly filled the hole I dug behind the tires earlier this afternoon. My effort was in vain. The front end is buried so deep in the snowbank, there's no way I could get us out. Someone will have to pull the car with a chain or something. The nearest tow truck places didn't answer my calls, and only one took messages. I'm hoping they call back soon, but they probably won't. With all this snow, I'm sure they're all busy.

I could call the police, but this isn't an emergency. Not yet. Besides, I don't trust them. They'd only call a tow truck and give me a ticket for reckless driving. That's the last thing I need. Worse, they might look up my record.

I push snow off the hatchback and open it.

Jacob stands there, staring at his suitcase.

"Hurry," I say.

"Will you open it? I hate the sound the zipper makes."

"Fine."

I agree, the zipper's *skritch* is annoying, but for Jacob, the sound is all but unbearable. He didn't fold his clothes. He pushes the wads around, searching for his sweatshirt.

A raccoon tail falls out, bounces off the bumper, and hits the ground.

"You still have this?" I ask.

"Yes. Of course, I still have it. I kept it."

I pick it up. The tail has lost some hairs near the severed end, but the rest is full. Brown and black stripes, soft to the touch. "Is it really the same one?"

"Yes." He finds his sweatshirt and struggles to put it on over his coat. "I always take it with me. It's good luck. Amanda gave it to me."

"I know." I throw the tail back into his suitcase and shut the hatchback.

Jacob heads for the driver's door. "I want to show it to Amanda. She'll like that I kept it. Right? Right, Charly?"

"Yes, I suppose so."

"She gave it to me because I was a winner."

"You *are* a winner. You don't need a tail to—wait. Look." A gigantic black SUV emerges through the blustery snow, coming up the hill the same way we did. I wave my hands. I'd think it was a military vehicle except for the shiny chrome grill. It's too nice for the army. The headlights pierce the falling snow, and the windows are so heavily tinted, I can't see the driver, but he must see me because he pulls over.

Jacob frantically pulls on the door handle to my car. "Charly. It won't open. Hurry."

"Hold on."

The SUV's passenger side window opens. When I see the woman inside, I realize the SUV is a Humvee. It must be worth tens of thousands. She's about my age, and her platinum blond hair is done up in a braided mohawk. She has full-on lip gloss and heavy mascara. Her green eyes are striking, and I wonder if she's wearing colored contacts. She smiles as if we're old friends. "Like, wow. Your car is really stuck."

"Why are we stopping?" The man in the driver's seat leans over the steering column. His curly hair is drenched in product. It shines. His broad shoulders bury the steering wheel. "We can't help them."

"We only need a push," I say. "Or, a pull."

"Charly. Hurry." Jacob pulls on the door to my car. It won't open. The auto-locks must have kicked in when we got out. I grab him by the arm and pull him over to the Humvee.

"We've got to keep going," the Humvee driver says. "We're expected."

Jacob pulls his arm out of my grasp and repeatedly bends his knees, bouncing up and down.

"Does he have to go to the bathroom or something?" the woman asks.

"No." I turn to him. "Jacob. Stop it."

"She's wearing too much makeup," he says. "She wears too much. She's a raccoon. Or a bandit. A bandit raccoon."

"Shh." I put my hands on the woman's door. "Can you help us get our car out?"

The man revs the engine. "No. We don't have time to pull you out. We're on a schedule."

"I'm sorry." The woman extends her hand. "I didn't introduce myself. My name is Kennedy McCallister, and this is Barry Rockwell." She winks as if I should know who they are. "Apparently, we're late for this thing he's doing."

He shifts into drive, and the engine lets out a low grumble. "Someone else will be along soon. There's nothing we can do for you."

"Barry, stop. We can't just leave them here."

"Yes, we can."

There's no sky. It's a whiteout.

"I'm not riding with strangers." Jacob bounces. Bends his knees. "Since the eighties, over five-hundred hitchhikers have been murdered. Over five-hundred."

The man leans toward Kennedy. Gazes at Jacob. "Is he all right?"

"He's fine." I wrap my arms around myself. "It's just cold out here."

"I'm not riding with strangers," Jacob says.

Sometimes, when he's nervous or scared, Jacob resorts to quoting things he knows, and he knows a lot. His statistics are usually accurate. I don't want to be murdered a mile from here by these strangers any more than he does, but we have no choice. Though, thinking about it, the odds aren't bad. Five-hundred murders over three decades. That's a pretty small percentage. My bigger concern is how "Barry" looked at Jacob. He doesn't seem very understanding, if not downright hostile. Stupid jock. "Could we get a ride?"

"He thinks he's smart, doesn't he?" Barry says. "Tell me. Since the eighties, how many hitchhikers murdered the people picking them up? Why should we risk giving *you* a ride?"

Jacob squints. Lowers his chin. "Less than half the murders—"

Kennedy puts her hand on Barry's shoulder. "Barry, baby, we can't leave them out here."

"But they're weird. Look at that car. Look at him. They're not going to like it if we show up with unexpected guests. It might screw up the whole trip. Come on, babe."

"Oh, please. You're only going hunting."

"No. I told you, it's not only hunting, it's—it doesn't matter. We're leaving them here and that's final."

"We can't do that." She hushes her voice. "If we leave them here, and they don't make it, and it gets out that we left them . . . what if someone tweets about it?"

Barry pulls her close and whispers something in her ear.

I search my pockets for my cell phone, but I don't find it. I must have left it in the car. "Jacob, give me your cell phone." He does so, and I hold it up to the window.

Click.

"What was that for?" Kennedy asks. "Barry. She took our picture."

"Shit." He slams his hands on the steering wheel.

I've never met anyone before now who could scowl and smile simultaneously. If Kennedy has never had Botox, then she's an alien. "Will you take us with you now?"

"You didn't have to do that." She scowls. "We were going to help you."

Barry unlocks the doors. "Get in."

"C'mon, Jacob." I open the rear door.

"No." Jacob steps away.

"Get in, you bonehead." Barry honks the horn.

Jacob puts his hand over his ears and takes another step back. "He's going to kidnap me, Charly. He's going to kill me."

"No, he's not."

"I'm going to count down from ten." Barry revs the engine. "Then I'm leaving, with or without you."

Jacob's face twists. He jerks to his left as if to run, but the wind slaps him in the face, and he stops.

I wrap my arms around him and whisper, "If we stay, and our body temperature drops to ninety-five degrees, we'll freeze to death. If we go with them, we have a sixty-eight percent chance they won't harm us. You said so yourself. Which is it going to be?"

". . . Eight . . . Seven . . ."

"Don't leave me, Charly."

"I'm not going to leave you."

". . . Six . . . Five . . . Four . . ."

"Which do you want to do? Stay or go?" I whisper.

"I'll go."

"Okay. Close your eyes, and I'll help you get in. Everything's going to be okay."

I open the door.

Jacob climbs in and looks out the back. "He's got guns, Charly. Oh, no. He's got guns. Look."

Two gun cases lean against a stack of black suitcases beneath the back window.

"I told you to close your eyes."

"He's got guns, Charly."

"It's fine. She said he was going hunting."

Barry hits the gas, and snow flies up behind us, covering the back window.

CHAPTER SIXTEEN

RANDALL

There's nothing more annoying to Randall than begging.

Let me out of here, they say.

Why are you doing this? they ask.

If you let me go now, I promise not to tell anyone. I just want to see my family again. And on, and on, and on . . .

Thinking about it makes him sick, and now he must listen to it once again.

He trudges through the snow, making a path from the cabin down the hill toward the lake. It wasn't snowing when he arrived last night, but it is now. An angry blizzard hit this afternoon. It was nice to sleep in, but he jerked awake when he remembered he hadn't untied the man from *The Singer* bar. Leaving his mouth taped shut for too long will weaken the man's spirit, not that Randall cares. He cares only about the quality of the hunt. He should have removed the tape and zip ties last night, but it was late. He was tired. He barely had the energy to drag the drunken loser down the hill and into the boathouse before crashing on the couch.

The man is right where Randall left him, lying in the fetal

position in the middle of the cage. Passed out.

It's late afternoon, and the sun has dipped behind the mountains to the west. Randall goes inside the boathouse and flips the light switch. The lighting is abysmal. The wind blows cold air through cracks in the walls. He saunters over to the workbench and looks out the window. When he takes over, he's going to renovate this place.

He turns and does a mental inventory. Everything is still here, undisturbed—the red and blue kayaks against the far wall, the canoe, the green metal file cabinet, the stack of packing crates, and the slew of garden equipment in the corner—hoses, rakes, rags, rusted shovels.

And the cage.

He takes out his cell phone and types in the security code for the electronic padlock. The lock on the cage door unlatches, and Randall grabs a garden rake on his way inside. He jabs at the man's ribs with the handle. "Wake up."

The man moans.

How pathetic.

Randall pulls the hood off the loser's head.

The loser struggles. Tries to free his hands and feet, driving the zip ties more deeply into his broken flesh. Dried blood cakes his wrists. His ankles.

"Your name is Tyler, right?"

The man groans through the tape and flails to free himself.

"Hold still." Randall rips the duct tape off the loser's lips.

"Help!"

Right. They always yell *help*, too. *Help. Help. Oh, help me . .*

Randall cracks the rake's handle over the man's back. "Shut up. Your name is Tyler, right?"

"Help me."

"What's your damn name?"

"T—Tyler."

The man's eyes are so bloodshot, Randall wants to put the tape over them. Hide them from view so he doesn't get sick. He gives the man a swift kick in the gut. "Tyler. That's what I thought it was." Taking the rake with him, he steps outside the cage and shuts the door.

"Help me."

"*Help me,*" Randall mocks. "*Help me. Help me.*"

Tyler sits up and scoots toward the door. "Please."

The electronic padlock makes a satisfying grinding noise after Randall latches it.

"Why are you doing this?" Tyler asks.

"You'll see." He pulls out his phone and opens his notes app. "All right. How tall are you?"

"What?"

"How tall are you?"

"I don't understand."

"I have some standard questions I have to ask, and you have to answer. How tall are you?"

"How long are you going to keep me here?"

Randall's neck heats up. "Forever, if you don't answer my questions."

"I—"

"How tall are you?"

Tyler pulls against his bonds.

The zip tie cuts into his wrists.

Fresh blood runs over his hands.

It's so disgusting, just like his eyes. Two pools of maroon-colored disease.

Tyler begs, "If I answer your questions, will you let me

go?"

"I'll take your ties off. How's that? Let's start with that, shall we? How tall are you?"

"Five foot eleven."

"Weight?"

"One-eighty."

"Age?"

"Twenty-eight."

"How fast can you run?"

"What?"

"Do you run? Do you exercise at all?"

"Please. I won't tell anybody—"

"I know," Randall yells. "I know. If I let you go now, you promise not to tell anyone. Blah, blah, blah. How fast can you run? Have you ever run? Did you participate in track in high school? Anything?"

"No."

"Did you play any sports?"

"No!"

The wind howls. Snow rushes into the boathouse from beneath the door. "You've got those fancy hiking boots, but I bet you've never gone hiking. I'm putting you down as 'lazy ass' for physical attributes. That's accurate, don't you think?"

"No. Please. Why are you asking me these things?"

"For the excursion. Remember? I'm taking you on an excursion."

Tyler looks around the boathouse. Confused.

"Look," Randall says. "It's getting cold in here. I'm going to skip to the end. Let's see . . . oh, I think I know the answer to this one, but I'll ask it anyway. Have you ever *gone* hunting?"

"Let me out of here."

"I'll take that as a no." He swipes the screen. "All right. I think that will do it." He stows his phone in his breast pocket.

Tyler shakes with rage.

It's not good. Randall needs the loser to save some energy for later. "Come. Sit over here with your back against the wall. I'll cut your hands free now."

Randall retrieves a box cutter from the workbench.

Tyler scoots over and sticks his wrists through the bars.

Randall bends over, and his back pops. He loses his balance and grasps the cage to steady himself.

"Careful," Tyler says.

"Shut up." He shoves the box cutter's tip beneath the zip tie and thrusts upward. The plastic snaps and Tyler screams as the blade cuts deep into his arm. Randall pulls it away and watches the blood run down.

His stomach lurches. He wants to vomit.

"Oh, God," Tyler moans. "Why the hell did you cut me?"

"*Why the hell did you cut me? Why the hell*—oh, stop your whimpering." Randall tosses the cutter onto the workbench and grabs an oily cloth from the floor. "Clean yourself up with this. I'll be back." He stands up straight and folds his arms over his chest as he turns to go. "For the love of Darwin, it's freezing in here."

"Wait." Tyler wraps the cloth around his arm. "What about my feet? They're still tied together."

"Oh, right. Lie on your back and put them closer so I can reach. If you kick me, your arm won't be the only thing I cut."

Tyler does as told, tears streaming down his face, blood running down his arm. He's so gross. So disgusting. His blood is sickness filled with bacteria and weakness.

Randall severs the zip tie, and Tyler jumps to his feet, holding his arm. The cloth is soaked with blood and dripping. "Here." Randall averts his eyes and throws Tyler another one.

"It's not enough. My bleeding won't stop."

Randall rummages through the file cabinet until he finds a roll of duct tape. He tears a piece off and shoves it into the cage. "Here. Fix yourself and get some rest."

"Wait. Don't go."

Randall opens the door and takes a couple of steps into the blizzard. He can't see the cabin through the torrential squall.

"Wait," Tyler screams. "Stop. Stop. Stop."

"*Wait. Stop.*" So, so pathetic.

Randall turns and pulls his collar tight around his neck. The whipping wind isn't deterred. Snow pelts his face, melts and runs down his neck. "You want the light left on?" he calls in through the doorway.

Tyler stands at the cage door, holding his arm. "Yes."

Oh, look. Tears. He deserves to die. He's so weak.

They all deserve to die if they can't survive the hunt. If they're not strong. If they're not men.

Even Ronald?

Wasn't Ronald a man?

Randall covers his eyes. His hand is cold to the touch. He turns his face toward the arctic maelstrom.

It snowed the morning Ronald died, just like now.

Did Ronald deserve to die?

Your brother?

Randall turns around. Tyler is the same height, the same weight as Ronald, and he has the same pathetic look in his eyes. But he is not Ronald. But Ronald liked hiking. Ronald would have liked Tyler's boots.

No. It had to be done.

Randall blinks. Wipes his face. Shivers.

"Help," Tyler yells. "Somebody, help me." He stamps his

feet.

"No one can hear you."

"Help. Help. Help."

"We're miles from everywhere."

"Help."

"*Help.*" Randall pulls his collar toward his ears. "Calm down. You're going to bleed out if you don't calm down."

Tyler screams. His arm is so revolting. Bloody, sick, and diseased.

An approaching car sends shivers down Randall's neck. It's coming up the drive on the other side of the cabin. No one should be here.

Tyler lets out one final scream, slumps to the floor, and blubbers. He sniffs and blubbers like all the others. "*Help me. Help me.*"

Randall strains to hear the approaching car. A brown sedan flashes between the cabin and the firewood at the top of the hill. Lance threatened to come to Colorado, but that was only if the cabin went unreserved over the holidays. Randall has a client—Barry Rockwell—but he isn't supposed to arrive until later tonight. Why would Lance come early?

Unless . . . the car is not Lance.

"Please, let me go."

"Shut up." The engine shuts off. Whoever is here has parked. They're staying. "Get some rest. You need to save your energy."

"Why? What are you going to do to me? Am I going to die?"

Randall flips the switch, the light goes out, and he closes the door.

CHAPTER SEVENTEEN

CHARLY

Jacob sits next to me in the backseat of Barry's Humvee, wringing his hands and glancing backward at the hunting rifles. The interior reminds me of a lounge in Las Vegas. Two-tone beige and brown leather seats. Video screens mounted inside the headrests. Rugged, stain-resistant carpeting.

"Over 39,000 people died from gun-related injuries in the United States last year."

"Stop it, Jacob." I reach over and touch his wrist. "We can talk about gun control another time."

"I don't like guns, Charly. I don't like them."

"Can you shut him up?" Barry asks.

Jacob's fish fidget is on the floor of my car, and my car is buried in a snowbank several miles back. Once Barry and Kennedy take us where they're going, I'll call for a tow truck, and the first thing I'll do is get Jacob's fidget back into his hands. "Close your eyes and relax. We'll be out of this soon."

The sky continues to dump snow over the mountains. There's no end in sight.

Kennedy turns in her seat to face me as Barry powers

over a hill. Hoop earrings swing from her ears, matching her necklaces and rings. Her bleached blond hair is in a braid, spotlighting her slender face, and she has a wide, gleaming smile. "So, like, what do you do, Charly? For work."

"I'm a server in a restaurant, but I'm also an artist. I mean, I like to paint."

"Have you done anything I might have seen?" Kennedy asks. "Do you post your work online?"

"No, my paintings are personal. But someday—"

"She's a waitress," Barry mutters.

My eyes meet his in the rearview mirror. He has way too much product in his hair. He must have added some to his eyebrows too, and he undoubtedly uses nose clippers daily. I don't know what it is with rich people, always worried about their looks. When our trust fund matures, I'm not changing. Sure, it will be nice not to worry about the bills, and we can get a better place—a house, maybe—but I'm not going to become pretentious. A lot of people deserve that money more than I do. I'm going to be a charitable millionaire. "My job is only temporary. I have a trust fund coming due soon."

We hit a bump, and Kennedy bounces, giggles, and turns in her seat to face me. "That's great for you. I'm a fashion influencer. Maybe you've read my blogs."

"I doubt it. I'm not into fashion much."

She glances at my waist. My shoes. "Are you on Instagram?" She holds up her cell phone. "Here's my profile. See? I have one hundred twenty-eight thousand followers."

"That's amazing," I say. "Good for you."

She shifts her body, faces front, and gazes longingly at her phone.

We hit another bump, and the wind whips snow over the windshield.

Jacob opens his eyes and slams his hand down on the leather seat. He's shaking.

"How much farther is it?" I ask.

"I want to get out," Jacob says. "I want to go home."

Barry spins the wheel and hits the gas, powering through a turn. "I'm not playing the 'are we there yet' game. We'll get there when we get there."

The Humvee feels unstoppable despite the weather. This jerk could have pulled my Ford out of the snowbank. "Where are we going?"

"It's a lodge," Kennedy says. "Right, hon?"

"The hunting guide called it a cabin, but you're right. I'm certain it's more like a lodge. It had better be nice with what I'm paying."

"I hope so. I hope there's a lot of things to take pictures of. I'm going to post everything. Ooh, maybe it will be rustic, do you think? Like, wagon wheels on the walls and creepy black and white pictures of settlers and things?"

"You can't do that. Post. You're not even supposed to be coming with me, and now I have to figure out how to explain these two."

"Coming with you? Hunting? I know I'm not going hunting. There's no way I would go into the woods, but—"

"No, on the trip. Look, when we get there, let me do the talking. If I have to pay extra, then so be it. We'll be fine as long as you stay out of the way."

"Out of the way?" Her voice tightens. "What do you mean? I'm not staying out of the way."

Jacob shakes his head and kicks the back of Barry's seat. "Slickhead."

"What was that, you little cretin?" Barry shifts down. The engine grumbles. The Humvee slows down.

"He's a curly-headed slickhead with too much money." Jacob kicks Barry's seat again. "Look at his hair. He thinks he can tell people what to do because he has too much money. He's a slickhead."

"Stop it, Jacob," I say.

"Is he retarded or something?" Barry asks.

"No. He's autistic. He's sensitive to things. You know, you could try being sensitive to others."

Jacob raises his voice. "I'm sensitive to slickhead assholes."

"Jacob, please." I lean forward. "How much longer is it until we're there?"

Kennedy slaps Barry's shoulder. "Look at me. Do you think I'm staying in our room the entire time you're out hunting?"

"No, babe. Once the hunting guide and I leave, you can do whatever you want."

Jacob drives his shoes into the carpet. He shakes. His anxiety is escalating. This can't go on much longer. One of his feet slips and kicks Barry's seat again.

"Goddammit," Barry says. "Get him under control."

I reach into my pocket and realize I left my phone in the car along with Jacob's fidget. "We need to go back. I don't have my phone."

"That's not happening." Barry shifts gears again. The engine revs. "The sun is almost gone."

"But, I need to call a tow truck and tell them where to bring my car."

"They're closed by now. This is a one-way trip."

Kennedy frowns at her phone. "I haven't had a signal for miles. Will there be WiFi at the lodge?"

"Don't count on it."

"Jacob, do you have your phone?" I ask.

He pulls it out of his pocket. "I don't have a signal either."

I lean in between the front seats. Barry smells like a men's clothing store. "You'll have to take us back at some point tonight. We left our bags in the car."

"Like I said, it's a one-way trip. I'm not going anywhere after we arrive. Not in this weather. Not in the dark. I'm not going to risk running off the road and getting stuck like some idiot."

"What are you saying?" My neck tenses. "Are you kidding me? This thing can go anywhere, and those floodlights across the top of the cab could light up a stadium."

"He's a slickhead, Charly. A slickhead."

"And you're a bonehead," Barry says. "Isn't there some way to shut him up?"

"If you're so afraid of getting stuck in the dark," I say, "then why don't you turn back now while there's a tiny bit of light left? The deeper into the mountains we go, the less chance a snowplow will come. They'll be too busy with the main roads for days. If you don't turn back now, we might be stuck out here forever."

"Is she right?" Kennedy asks. "Forever?"

"Don't listen to her. This thing can go anywhere."

"No, I think she's right," Kennedy says. "I want to go back now. I should never have agreed to this. If they don't have WiFi at the lodge, I'll be ruined."

Jacob stammers, "I don't have internet, Charly. I don't have internet."

I take his phone, put it on the console between us, and grasp his hands. I hold them together. "It's going to be okay. We'll figure something out."

I wish I could disappear. I let go of his hands and wish I

hadn't trusted him not to run away. If he hadn't tried to get out of the car, we wouldn't have run off the road. This trip is a disaster. I don't know what I was thinking.

"There it is," Barry says.

I strain to see out the windshield. The wipers sweep back and forth, obscuring my view, only giving me glimpses of what's ahead. Tire tracks leading up a hill. Two sedans parked next to a snowmobile. One black. One brown. Beyond that, a blue tarp tent covering a pile of firewood stacked high. The tarp waves in the blustery wind, battling the whiteout, threatening to fly away.

Barry shifts gears, and we climb. A two-story cabin emerges on our left. Massive log walls with a long, covered porch. It's rustic like Kennedy hoped, but it is not large enough to be called a lodge. It's a cabin. It's my family's cabin.

My cabin, now.

The Humvee slips to the side. Barry corrects course by spinning the wheel to the right, and we slide in next to the brown sedan. It looks like my cousin Cam's car. It has a dent in the passenger door, and the passenger side mirror is missing. I remember seeing pictures of it years ago when Cam posted on Facebook that he'd finally been able to afford something. Next to it, snow cloaks an elegant black sedan. I'm not sure what kind it is, but it's nice. Maybe a Cadillac. Or a Lincoln.

"What do you think?" Barry shifts the transmission into Park.

"I don't see any hot spots." Kennedy taps her phone. "And I don't have a signal."

"No, what do you think about the place?"

She keeps tapping on her phone.

"Come on, babe. Stop it. You can live without the

internet for two days."

"No, I can't." Bolts of fire shoot from her eyes. "I can't."

He leans toward her, puts his hand on her cheek. "Come on. I'll make it up to you. When we get back to Denver, I'll take you shopping."

"He's a slickhead." Jacob kicks Barry's seat. "A slickhead with too much money. Money isn't happiness. He thinks he can buy people's happiness."

Barry glares at Jacob in the rearview mirror, his lips mouthing obscenities.

I stare out the window. The cabin looks so different in the winter. The wind whips snow flurries over the porch, sweeping them against the front door like ghosts trying to break inside. The windows above the awning are barely visible. I remember sitting at the end of the hall, looking out over the mountains that summer. "Is this the right place? Are you sure this is where your hunting trip is?"

"Yes," Barry replies. "All of you stay in the car until I come back." He reaches for the door handle.

"Wait," Kennedy says. "I'm coming with you."

"No, you're not. You're not supposed to be here." Barry glances back at Jacob and me. "None of you are supposed to be here."

"This isn't your cabin," I say. "There's something wrong."

"You're damn right there's something wrong. You're not supposed to be here."

"Why can't I come in with you?" Kennedy asks.

"Let me go inside first and explain. I'm sure it'll be okay." He rubs his thumb and forefinger together. "I'll pay extra if I have to."

"He's a slickhead," Jacob says. "He's going to use money

to get his way. Dirty slickhead."

"If no one else was supposed to be here," Kennedy looks out her window, "then why are there two cars parked over there?"

"I don't know." Barry scratches his forehead. "I think the black one belongs to the guy who sold me the trip, but— maybe the other one belongs to a helper. Like a Sherpa."

"No," I say. "That's not a Sherpa's car."

"You're right." Kennedy turns to Barry. "Those people can't afford cars."

I lean forward. "It's my cousin Cam's car. This is my cabin."

"Cam?" Jacob presses his forehead to the window. "That's Cam's car?"

"Yes."

"I don't want to see Cam. He's evil. I want to go home, Charly. I want to go home. Now."

CHAPTER EIGHTEEN

CHARLY - THEN

I did my best to keep up with Dad, but his paddle strokes were strong. He sat at the back of the canoe, propelling us forward. The canoe veered left, so I paddled left. It veered right, so I paddled right. The water slapped the hull. The smell reminded me of a freshly mowed lawn but more bitter than that. I struggled to keep the canoe's nose pointed toward the lake's center.

"Good job, Charly. Keep us straight."

"I'm trying."

The boathouse shrank behind us. While I paddled, I plotted. The game was this afternoon, and I couldn't let Amanda win. I'd spent the morning in my room trying to come up with a plan. She had a plan. I had nothing. Every idea I came up with had me cheating. I kept picturing her tied to a tree while I raced across the finish line.

I couldn't do that. I couldn't tie her to a tree. Could I?
No.

Not that I wasn't strong enough. I was bigger, older, and smarter, but it would have gotten me in trouble. It had never made sense how Amanda always got whatever she wanted. For a long time, I believed she was the cheater, but I could never prove it. She always had help.

To win the game, I needed an edge. I needed a plan, and I needed my dad's help.

"This is good." He pulled his paddle out of the water. "We can stop here."

The canoe slowed down, drifted forward, and I tucked my paddle under the seat behind me. Ripples in the lake brushed up against the canoe, gently rocking us, and Dad stowed his paddle. He opened the cooler. "Here, have a sandwich."

"What kind is it?"

"Salami, I think." He looked at it with suspicion.

"No, thanks."

"Why not?"

"I'm not hungry."

The others were probably sitting at the picnic table this very minute, scarfing down peanut butter and jelly sandwiches with soda. After Dad returned from the forest this morning, setting up the game like he'd promised, he kept me from joining them by insisting we go out in the canoe. "I'll eat something when we go back. Before the game."

He sniffed the sandwich and returned it to the cooler. "Okay. Me too."

A breeze swept over the water, raising the hairs on my neck. I should have worn something warmer than a tank top. Puffy white clouds cushioned the sky. The sun beat between them as hard as possible, but the mountain air refused to warm up.

"Charly, there's something I want to talk to you about."

"The game?"

"No. Don't worry about the game."

"Did you finish setting it up this morning?"

"Yes, almost. Listen—"

"What are the clues like?"

"After this trip, I'm going to be traveling for work."

I already knew this, but I didn't want him to know I knew. I couldn't let him know about my eavesdropping. I turned away. Gazed at the water. "I don't want to lose."

"Did you hear what I said?" he asked.

"I hate that Amanda wins at everything."

He shifted his weight, and the canoe rocked slightly. "I know. Don't let her get to you."

"But—"

"Don't worry about the game. This is important. I'm going to be gone a lot over the next year or two, but I'll come back every month. I promise."

"A year or two?"

"Yes, but I'll come back. I promise."

"Why are they making you go?"

"They're not making me, honey. It's an offer I can't refuse. They need me."

I needed him, but I couldn't worry about this right now. I needed to beat Amanda more. "What are the clues like?"

"You really want to win the game, don't you?"

"Yes."

"Because of Amanda?"

"I want the prize, too. What is it?"

He glanced back at the cabin. "It's the ultimate prize, but I don't have it yet. It's something you don't have." He chuckled. "It might be something you don't want."

I wanted it—whatever it was—as long as Amanda didn't get it.

"It's not a big deal," he said, pulling his paddle out from beneath the seat.

"Wait. Whoever finds it wins, right?"

"We need to head back. They'll be waiting for us."

"Wait." I had to try. "Can you help me win? Can you tell me where the clues are?"

He put his paddle in the water. "No. You know I can't do that. That would be cheating." He pulled hard, and we spun around. "Grab your paddle. It's time to head back."

I faced forward, stabbed the water, and stroked, trying to line us up with the boathouse in the distance. He couldn't see my tears, but I hoped he could feel my fury. I stabbed the water again.

"Charly? Are you okay?"

"Yes." I paddled hard, thrusting the canoe forward.

"You don't need to cheat to win," he said. "If you try hard, you can beat her."

"No, I can't. She always cheats. Someone always helps her. It's not fair."

"Let's see how the game goes. I'll keep an eye on her, and if you need my help, I'll be there."

"Promise?"

"Yes. I promise."

I rested the paddle on my lap and wiped my face. I loved my dad so much. He would make everything okay. He said he would help me.

As we neared the shore, I saw Cam and Jacob on the lawn, throwing a football. Amanda sat with her back against the boathouse. She had a notebook and a pen, and when she saw us coming, she stared at me for a second, then wrote something down.

"Jacob, come help us," Dad called. "You too, Cameron."

Jacob bounded toward the shore, and Cam came shuffling down the slope behind him. They grabbed the canoe's tow rope, and Dad paddled until the back swung out and hit the shore.

I stood, and the canoe wobbled, so I grasped the side to keep from falling out. Slowly, I lowered myself back onto my seat.

"Hold on, Charly," Dad said. "Let me steady it."

He jumped into the water and held the craft still.

I stood and put one foot in the water.

Cam and Jacob heaved on the rope and pulled the canoe out from under me.

I tumbled into the muck. My hands sunk into the sand, and my head went under. Green sediment—slick, slimy, and gritty. It ran up my nose and down my throat. I stood, shaking my arms and coughing. The water in my ears tried to block out Amanda's laughter but ultimately failed.

"I'm sorry," Jacob said. "I'm sorry, Charly. I'm sorry. I'm sorry."

Cam continued pulling the canoe onto the shore without Jacob's help, then threw the rope down.

"I thought you were going canoeing," Amanda cackled. "Not swimming." She stood, both arms pressing her notebook against her chest.

"Charly needs a towel." Jacob took off running toward the boathouse. "A towel. I'll get a towel."

"Stop," Dad said. "Jacob. Stop." He labored up the shore, forcing his feet through the shallow water. "No one's allowed in the boathouse. You know that. Go to the cabin if you must."

Jacob stopped.

"I'm fine," I said.

"Ha." Amanda beamed. "Fine. Yeah, you've never looked better. You should take baths more often."

"Amanda," Dad said. "That's enough."

"Why can't we go into the boathouse?" Cam asked.

"Because you're not allowed." Dad shook the water from his feet and glanced at his watch.

"But, I need something to cut with. You said—"

"Just hold on." Dad shot him a look. "We have less than an hour until the game. Let's all meet on the deck then." He turned toward the boathouse. "Cameron, come with me."

I shook the water from my feet and wiped my face.

Jacob headed for the cabin.

Amanda stood, grinning at me.

"What are you looking at?"

"Nothing." She turned to go, still clutching her notebook. "Absolutely nothing."

"What were you writing?"

"It's my plan for the game. You're going to lose."

A cloud crossed in front of the sun, and a shadow fell over the boathouse. I'd missed seeing where Cam and my dad went, and I didn't care. The shadow consumed me, and I shivered in my wet clothes. I had less than an hour to create my own plan, then I remembered my dad's promise.

He was going to help me win.

I had nothing to worry about.

CHAPTER NINETEEN

CHARLY

Kennedy waits for Barry to return from the cabin for twenty minutes before she loses her cool. She jumps out of the Humvee and heads for the front door, kicking her way through the snow.

I've spent the last twenty minutes convincing Jacob we don't need to go back to our car tonight. This is our cabin. Once we explain everything to the hunters, they'll leave, and we can worry about going home later. We can relax. Jacob can hide in one of the bedrooms and desensitize. I'll reunite with Cam and Amanda. It looks like Cam is already here. His dented, brown Chevy from the eighties sits crooked between us and the black car.

"I want to go home," Jacob says. "I don't want to see Cam."

"For the last time, Cam isn't evil. You watch. Once we get reacquainted, you'll like him. I bet he'll give us a ride to our car when the snow lets up."

"He's a cat killer."

"Oh, stop. Look, Kennedy left the door open. We need

to go inside and close it. Can you stay right behind me?"

He nods.

I get out of the Humvee, and he follows me inside.

Somewhere beyond the hall, past the dining room, Kennedy is yelling at Barry. I'd be angry, too. He dragged her up here so he could leave her in the cabin while he hunts. Their relationship seems raw, like they don't know each other very well.

"I want to go home, Charly. It's loud in here. The raccoon-eyed woman is loud in here."

"I know, but we can't. Let me straighten everything out, and I'll take you to one of the bedrooms where you can relax."

In her haste, Kennedy tracked snow inside. We follow her trail down the hall to the closet and open the door to hang our coats. The board games are still there. Monopoly. Candyland. Not much has changed. Then, I see the kitchen. Stainless steel appliances and a granite countertop greet us. The dining room table is at least six inches thick. It's maple or oak. I'm not sure which.

The french doors haven't changed. Their foggy glass panes still separate the cabin from the deck. The lawn. The lake. The forest. But the curtains are new. They're made of thick burlap and completely hide the doors when closed. A wagon wheel chandelier lights up the dining table.

The place appears desperately rustic. Just what Kennedy wanted for her blog. Pictures.

Two deer heads bookend a moose above the fireplace in the living room. A fire cracks and pops and heats the dry air. A furry rug hides the floor beneath two leather couches surrounding a coffee table made out of a barn door. A silver tray sits on the table, presenting a bottle of Scotch.

Kennedy stands over Barry with her hands on her hips.

"Well? What's it going to be?"

Barry, seated nonchalantly on one of the couches, crosses his legs and sips from a snifter. He turns his attention to the man in the hazy gray suit seated on the couch across from him. "That depends. When are we leaving on the hunt?"

The man takes a drink. His beard reminds me of Wolverine's from the X-Men—Jacob loves X-Men—except for how neatly he's trimmed it. Not a whisker out of place. Hints of gray lie low in his sideburns, giving his age away. Forties, maybe. "We'd agreed to go first thing in the morning, but that was before you broke the rules."

"Not that I want to," Kennedy says, "but if I did, why couldn't I go hunting with you? Is it because I'm a woman?"

"No, babe." Barry smirks. "It's nothing like that."

The bearded man turns toward the dining room. Puts his Scotch down. "Oh, Christ. Who are they?"

Jacob crowds into me, pressing his body against my back, and I grasp his hand. He whispers, "Where's Cam?"

"Those are nobodies," Barry says. "They were just leaving."

"No, we weren't." My back stiffens. "This is our cabin."

"Mr. Rockwell." The bearded man stands, rising off the couch like an evil deity. He's easily over six feet tall, and his voice resonates throughout the cabin. Something about it makes me want to do whatever he says. "You have put the entire experience at risk with all these people. The hunt is off."

"No." Barry slams his drink onto the coffee table and stands. "Let's work something out. These people aren't my fault. Here." He reaches into his pocket. "I can fix this."

"Slickhead," Jacob blurts out. "He's a money slickhead."

Barry pulls out his wallet. "I'll pay for the mistake, and everyone can leave as soon as the road clears."

"Like, I'm not going anywhere," Kennedy says.

"Not you, babe. Them."

"We're not going anywhere either." I squeeze Jacob's hand. "This is our cabin."

The bearded man pulls on his suit jacket, straightens the creases, smiles, and crosses the room. He holds out his hand. "Greetings. My name is Randall Thorne, and you are?"

"Charly Highsmith." Compared to mine, his hand is a frying pan.

"Oh, you're Miss Highsmith. Of course. I've been expecting you."

"You have?"

"Yes."

"Wait. You met Cam, didn't you? I saw his car outside. Where is he?"

"He's in the basement with the other one. I needed to talk with Mr. Rockwell in private, so I requested they wait down there."

"Other people are here?" Barry asks. "You were going to charge me for her *and* them, but you're hiding more people in the basement?"

"Please, Mr. Rockwell. You misunderstand. I did not invite anyone other than you. They're all here because Miss Highsmith invited them. Because she thinks she owns this cabin. I assure you, I did not break the rules. You did."

Barry's face tightens. "Rules or no rules, we're going on the hunt tomorrow, right? I haven't come this far to—I didn't drive all the way up here for nothing."

"Please," Randall raises is hand. "Exercise some patience."

"I do own this cabin," I say.

"No." Randall lowers his voice. Looks me in the eye. "My

organization owns this location. We purchased it years ago."

"No. My father owns it. He gave it to me as part of a trust fund."

"Do you have paperwork indicating such?"

"Not with me, but here. I have the keys." I head toward the front door to prove my case. The cabin must have been listed in the trust or my mother wouldn't have given me the keys. This Randall person doesn't need to know the trust hasn't matured yet.

"Charly." Jacob tugs on my shirt. "Wait."

"Stay there," I say.

He backs away from Randall. He has that look in his eye. He bounces, bending his knees over and over. "Jacob, stop moving. Stay right where you are, okay?"

He nods.

"Promise me you'll stay right there."

"I promise, Charly. I'm not going to run."

Randall follows me into the hall. "You're wasting your time. We change the locks after each experience. Company policy."

I open the door, and the wind slaps me in the face. The larger keys don't fit the lock. I try the small, rounded key, though I'm sure it unlocks the boathouse. It doesn't fit either.

Is this my cabin?

The updated kitchen. The couches. The moose head. These don't seem like things my father would have bought. According to my mom, he never owned anything "rustic." Maybe he did sell it to this man. But if so, why would my mom give me the keys?

Oh, no.

I knew it wasn't her cabin to give away.

She made a mistake.

"Come." Randall waves his monstrous hand. "It's freezing out there. It appears there's no end to this blizzard."

I close the door behind me and follow him down the hall.

"Now that we've established rightful ownership of this location," he says, "let's discuss the logistics of your departure."

"I'm not leaving."

He turns on me and lowers his chin. "Ah, but you *are* leaving, Miss Highsmith. One way or another. You're leaving."

CHAPTER TWENTY

CHARLY - THEN

"Has anyone seen Cameron?" Dad asked.

He stood on the deck, gazing over the lawn into the forest. He'd showered since our canoe trip, and his aftershave stung my nose. Medicinal. Toxic. I never liked it. I always wondered if my mother ever liked it.

She was in their bedroom, taking a midday nap.

Amanda and Jacob stood next to me by the picnic table, waiting for the game to begin. She had put on a pair of red hiking boots and strapped a bag around her waist. I couldn't tell what she had inside it, but I guessed it was her plan and some snacks. Jacob scratched at his chest. He'd put his itchy sweater back on despite the afternoon heat.

After falling in the water, I'd only had time to change into some dry clothes and eat lunch—a leftover peanut butter and jelly sandwich. I didn't have time to create a plan, but I didn't need one.

Dad had promised to help me win the game.

"Has anyone seen Cameron?" he asked again.

"I saw him," Jacob said. "By the boathouse. I asked him

where he was going, but he was running. He was running, and he ran that way, into the woods."

"How long ago?"

"I don't know." Jacob cocked his head. "Seventeen minutes?"

"Dammit." Dad lowered his head.

"Someone will have to find him," Amanda said. "He was angry about not being allowed in the boathouse. He's probably hiding."

"We'll go get him," I said. "C'mon, Jacob."

I pulled on his wrist.

"I don't want to, Charly."

"But, we can't play the game without him. C'mon." I pulled again, and Jacob relented. He followed me down the stairs onto the lawn. "Where did you see him last?"

"He went that way." Jacob pointed to the trailhead on the eastern side of the lake.

Amanda bounded down the stairs and ran in the direction Jacob was pointing. "I'll find him. You stay here, losers."

"Jacob." I grasped his hand. "Hurry."

He jerked away from me.

"Fine. Stay here."

I ran after Amanda. Thick pines loomed over the trail, sticking their branches in my face. We'd only been to the cabin a few times, so I hadn't explored the forest much, but I knew this trail split into others. Some climbed a ridge, and others ran around it. Ahead, Amanda came to a fork in the path and went right, ascending the ridge.

I stopped, not sure whether to follow her.

As she disappeared over the top, something down the path on my left cried out. I jumped. The sound was too sharp to be a baby and too loud to be a bird. I ran toward it, following the winding trail, weaving through the trees.

The cry came again. Pitiful and sad.

A brown shape appeared through the trees, and I halted. Ducked down. Listened. With one hand on the ground, I held still and listened.

My heart pounded.

Was it a bear?

Slowly, I pulled a branch down. Cam stood there wearing his stupid Cleveland Browns sweatshirt and holding a stick. He glanced around, then knelt down out of sight. The crying came again, and this time, it was followed by a high-pitched chitter.

"Hey." I stood and walked toward him. "You're missing the game." He didn't look up. Instead, he rammed the stick between the bars of a wire cage, and again, the cry came.

He had trapped an animal.

"Hey, stop it," I said. "What are you doing?"

"Watch this." He jammed the stick into the cage again. A raccoon jumped and shrieked.

"Stop it," I shouted.

"Why?" He jabbed the raccoon again. "It's funny."

"No, it's not." The poor thing desperately limped around the cage. It was small, not like a baby, but like the runt of the litter. And it was hurt. Maybe sick.

"Yes, it is. It's just a stupid animal."

I stepped forward. "He's not stupid."

"He is too." Cam stood. "If he wasn't, he wouldn't be in that cage. Look at how he moves around."

"I think he's sick. There was probably food in there. He was just hungry. Let him go."

"You like stupid animals, don't you?"

"What do you mean?"

"Like your brother."

"Shut up. Jacob's not stupid."

"He is too. Just like this thing." He bent over, rammed the stick into the cage. "And so are you."

The raccoon tested the cage bars with his paws.

"Let him go."

"No." Cam dropped the stick and knelt next to the cage.

The raccoon chittered.

Cam reached into his pocket and pulled out a knife. Not a butter knife. A hunting knife.

"What are you doing?"

He lined the knife up with the raccoon and closed one eye like he was aiming a gun. "What's it look like I'm doing?"

"Stop, or I'll tell on you."

"Go ahead." He grasped the door latch. Raised the knife.

"Where'd you find that?"

The raccoon backed himself into a corner and hissed.

Cam slowly opened the door.

"Charly?" Jacob's voice came from somewhere behind me. "Charly, where are you? Charly?"

"Jacob, go back. Get out of here."

"Dad said to find you. Where are you? I am supposed to find you."

"Go away."

Cam shook the cage, throwing the raccoon off balance. "Come here you stupid animal. Stop moving."

"Let him go." I rushed forward. I couldn't let this happen. I couldn't let Jacob see this.

Cam grabbed the raccoon by his tail and pulled him out of the cage.

The raccoon swung up and tried to go for Cam's arm. Tried to bite it but missed.

Jacob stepped from behind a tree.

Cam flung the raccoon onto the ground and buried the knife in its back. Blood spurted onto his Cleveland Browns logo. He let go of the knife and jumped clear of the animal as it screamed and twisted and tried to run. The knife stuck straight up like a flagpole.

"It's his cat," Jacob yelled. "It's just like his cat."

The poor thing made a gurgling noise, and collapsed.

Jacob had turned red and was squinting hard as if he thought he could stop the tears from coming.

Cam laughed. Pointed at the carcass. Kicked it.

"Stop," I screamed.

Jacob put his hands over his ears. "It's like his cat. He killed his cat again. He killed it, Charly. Make him stop."

CHAPTER TWENTY-ONE

CHARLY

Jacob had promised not to run. With the blizzard raging outside, Cam and Amanda in the basement, and Kennedy and Barry in the living room, he had been unable to sneak away.

Thank goodness for small favors.

I breathe a sigh of relief when Randall and I reach the end of the hall and see Jacob there, standing in the kitchen entryway, bending his knees, bouncing up and down. I need to convince Randall the cabin is mine and get Jacob into one of the bedrooms upstairs so he can escape these people. There's not much time before he has another meltdown.

Barry and Kennedy sit snuggled together on the leather couch by the fireplace. "I'm sorry, babe." He caresses her chin. "If you really want to leave, we could find a way, but I have to stay. I have to do this."

"No," she says. "I know how important this is to you."

"You have no idea. If I don't this, I'll regret it forever."

I follow Randall into the living room.

"Please," Randall says, "have a seat." The timbre of his voice compels me to do whatever he says. I don't like it, but I sit on the couch anyway. "Would you like a drink?" He sits next to me. His cologne is clean. Velvety.

"No, I'm not in the mood."

"Very well. I have an idea for your departure."

"Hold on. Just because I can't prove I own this place doesn't mean you own it. Do *you* have proof?"

"Like yourself, I don't have it with me. I would have to contact my employer."

"What about the hunt?" Barry says. "We're still going on the hunt, right? I paid a deposit. You owe me."

Randall stands. His voice booms. "I owe you nothing." He puts his hand in his right pants pocket and holds it there. His fingers move. A nervous habit, I guess. "You put everything—everything—at risk when you invited your significant other. I should send you out into the cold right now." His neck blazes red.

"No, wait." Barry forms a hard smile. "Let's work something out. I told you. I'll pay extra for her."

Slickhead.

Randall strokes his beard. Tugs on his chin.

"Let's leave, baby." Kennedy stands. "We're obviously not wanted here. This guy gives me the creeps, and there's no internet. I can't survive without the internet."

"Is she some kind of imbecile?" Randall asks. "She can't survive?"

Barry pulls out his wallet. "Here. How much will it take?"

Randall waves his hand. "Put your money away."

"Yeah, don't give him any more money." Kennedy grabs Barry's wrist. "Let's go."

Barry puts his wallet away. "I told you." He speaks in an angry hush. "I have to do this."

"Wait," Randall says.

"No." Kennedy tugs on Barry's arm. "We're leaving. Now."

"She needs to be quiet." Randall eyes Barry's wallet. "She—"

"No, I don't. You can't tell me what to do."

"Mr. Thorne." Barry trembles, his face turning red. "She doesn't speak for me."

Randall slowly pulls his hand out of his pocket and gestures toward the stairs. His eyes are stone gray. Reflective. "Come, Mr. Rockwell. Let's go upstairs and, as you say, *work something out*. In private."

"What about us?" I ask. "My brother and I need a room."

"What about you?" Cam steps out from behind the burlap curtains near the french doors.

Jacob jumps. Terror contorts his face, and he backs into the kitchen.

"Cam, wait." I rush to Jacob and grasp his arm.

Randall rises off the couch.

Cam is wearing a thick, woolen sweater that matches his raggedly combed hair.

"It's good to see you," I say. "What were you doing behind the curtains?"

Randall crosses the room. "Yes, tell us. What were you doing? You were supposed to remain in the basement with your sister."

"She's not my sister," Cam says coolly. "She's my cousin."

I go to him. We embrace. It's like hugging a tree. His sweater scratches my chin, and he smells earthy. "When did you get here?"

"Earlier this afternoon."

"And Amanda came with you?"

"Yes."

Barry crosses the room. "Am I going on an excursion or not?"

Randall shakes his head at Cam. He straightens his jacket and turns toward Barry. "Let's discuss it upstairs."

"What's an 'excursion?'" I ask.

"Never you mind," Randall says. "I'll address you and your brother after I've spoken with Mr. Rockwell."

Kennedy slumps down onto the couch as Randall and Barry head for the stairs. "It's what he calls the hunting trip. Not the best name for it, I don't think."

"What are you hunting?" I ask. "Deer?"

Randall pauses at the base of the stairs. His had grasps the railing, and his voice is thick. "Never you mind what we're hunting. You won't be here very much longer."

"Yes, I will."

I watch as he and Barry climb the stairs. I don't like this man. His suit and commanding swagger don't impress me. This is my cabin. Not his.

I go to the basement door and open it. "Amanda? Are you down there?"

"Charly? Is that you?"

Her hair, still black as night, comes into view first, followed by the bridge of her nose, her chin—her chest. It's been years, and the years have been kind to her. She's buxom, but trim. Her skin has a youthful glow. When she reaches the top, we grasp each other's elbows and stare into each other's eyes like old friends. Her dark freckles are gone.

"It's so good to see you," she says.

"You, too."

"What's with that guy with the beard?"

"Don't worry about him. There's a misunderstanding is

all."

"Great." She takes me by the hand and pulls me to the dining table. "Sit. I want to hear everything. I know you've had it rough."

She has no idea.

Cam turns away. Faces the french doors. Gazes through the glass into the night.

Kennedy pulls out her phone and frowns at it.

"Tell me about the streets." Amanda focuses on me from across the table. "What was it like being homeless?"

"I wasn't exactly homeless. I . . . let's talk about you. Is what I've seen on LinkedIn true? Are you some kind of big advertising exec now?"

"Marketing, and yes, I suppose so." Her eyes fall to half-mast. "I've done well. After college, I met the right people, worked hard, and voilà—I'm the head of the distribution channels in all of North America and Europe for MediaRight Limited. But, do you want to know a secret?"

"Sure."

"The higher up you go, the easier it becomes. I never have to lift a finger except to give a little advice to my employees here and there. I'm making more money sitting here doing nothing, talking to you, than I've ever made before. It's called passive income."

"That's amazing."

She smiles. "Isn't it? Once you have millions, the interest compounds, at least, that's what my financial advisers tell me."

"Wow. When my trust fund matures, you'll have to help me in a couple of years."

"Trust fund?"

"Yes. I'm going to be a millionaire, too." The news hits her between the eyes. She squints for a split second. I'm not certain if it's envy or fear.

"Watch out." She clasps her hands. "It's nice, but it can be lonely. When did you find out about the fund?"

"Only a couple of weeks ago. Dad made a lot of money after he left us, and he recently died, so—"

"Oh, no. Not Uncle John. Did you get to see him?"

"No."

She shakes her head. "I can't imagine growing up without my father. Poor Uncle John. And, what your mom put you and Jacob through . . . it was deplorable. How did you survive it? Homeless and alone."

"I'd rather not talk about it."

"I understand." She grasps my hand. "But, I'm so intrigued by your story. After you ran away, I only heard random bits of news from my mom. How did you find Jacob? How did you get off the streets? We all thought you were going to die. The stories we heard—the drugs, the men?"

I pull my hand away.

I want to tell her I survived something no one else could. I want to tell her I saved Jacob on my own, but that's not the truth. Someone helped me once. I feel like a little girl thinking this, but it's not fair. All through life, everyone helped her, and they did it all the time.

She's had it so easy, sitting here, glowing.

I deserve to glow.

"Charly, are you okay? I didn't mean to pry." She glances away. "I know, when we were kids, I wasn't always the nicest to you."

"I'm fine."

"I'm really only curious. We drifted so far apart after your parents divorced. I wish I could have been there for you more, but I didn't know."

"You didn't know, or you didn't care?" I bite my lip. I shouldn't have said that.

She slowly shakes her head. "Some of both, I suppose."

"It's cold out there," Cam says to no one, still staring out the french door windows.

"Amanda, I invited you and Cam here to reminisce about the good times, not dwell on the bad. We had good times, didn't we?"

"Remember when we did the magic show for Cam's sixth birthday?"

"I can't believe we didn't get in more trouble for catching that rabbit on fire."

"At least it wasn't real. But the top hat was." She laughs. "He loved it."

"Cam?" I turn toward the french doors. "Do you remember that?"

He doesn't move.

"Cam," I say, louder, "how have you been?"

He slowly pivots away from the windows. "I've been well."

"After New Year's," Amanda says, "let's get together more often. I've missed you."

"I've missed you too. And Jacob—" I don't see Jacob. I call his name, and he doesn't respond.

I go to the kitchen.

He's not there. "Jacob?"

Amanda stands. "What's wrong? I didn't even know Jacob came with you."

"He was in the kitchen a moment ago. I swear. Cam, did you see him leave?"

"Yes."

"What? When? Where did he go?" I glance up the stairs.

Cam turns toward the french doors. Looks out the windows. "I opened the door for him when you went to the basement. He seemed . . . unsettled."

"You what?" I run past him and swing the doors open.

The blizzard greets me with icy teeth. The crystals snap at my throat. "Jacob! Where are you?"

Footprints weave across the deck, disappearing over the edge where the stairs begin.

"Jacob. Come back!"

CHAPTER TWENTY-TWO

Cam kicked the dead raccoon in the head one last time. Blood ran over the animal's side, pooling near Cam's feet, the knife still sticking out of its back.

Jacob was long gone. He'd run toward the cabin after witnessing the murder. I doubted he would ever be the same, and he never would be.

I charged toward Cam. "You sick—"

"What?"

He reached for the knife, but I got there first and pushed him down. His backside hit the ground hard. I kicked his hip, and he rolled over, reaching for the raccoon. "Why did you kill it? Why?" I kicked him again but missed.

He grabbed the raccoon and stood. The knife fell out of the animal's back and tumbled onto the ground.

I lunged forward.

He swung the carcass, and the bony fur struck my face.

I stumbled and missed wrapping my arms around Cam's waist. My knees hit the ground hard, and I planted my hands to keep from slamming my face into a tree.

"What's wrong with you?" Cam stood over me.

Raccoon blood ran down my cheek. "Me?"

"Yeah. You."

I got to my feet. Wiped my face. "You're sick."

"No, I'm not. I'm a trapper." He grinned. "Like a mountain man. Watch." He placed the raccoon on the ground and began sawing its tail off. "If I could, I'd make a hat."

"Jacob was right. This is like your cat, isn't it?"

His face flushed red, and he pointed the knife at me. "No, it's not. You don't know anything about my cat."

"Everyone said you killed it, and you did, didn't you?"

"Shut up, Charly."

"You did, didn't you? You did. You did."

"Shut up, or—"

"Or what? You'll kill me too?"

"No." He went back to sawing on the tail. "I loved my cat."

"Then what happened to it?"

"Nothing." He pulled on the tail, and it snapped off. A fisherman posing with a prize catch, he stood and held the tail high in the air, grinning.

"You're disgusting. I'm telling."

I marched toward the trail. "Jacob?"

No answer.

When I returned to the cabin, Jacob was sitting on the deck with his back against the railing, rocking. I couldn't blame him—the knife, the look in Cam's eyes when he stabbed the raccoon. The blood. It was all too much.

"Where's Cameron?" Dad asked.

"He killed a raccoon," I said. "Did Jacob tell you what he did? He killed it for no reason."

"No, Jacob hasn't said anything. Where did you see

Cameron?"

"I've got it." Cam came running around the boathouse, waving the tail in the air. "I've got it. Here." He bounded up the steps and handed it to Dad.

"Cameron, I asked you to bring the cage. What happened?"

"He stabbed it." Jacob stared at the forest. "He stabbed it with a knife, Dad."

"Cameron? Is this true?"

Cam averted his eyes. The blood on his sweatshirt had already begun to dry.

"Where'd you get the knife?"

"It wasn't dead yet, like—you said it would be dead in the cage, but it wasn't, so I killed it."

Dad placed the tail on the table. Glanced at his watch. "Let me have the knife."

Cam put the knife on the table next to the tail.

"Okay," Dad said, "we will talk about this later, but"—he paused and looked at each of us in turn—"everyone remember. No one is allowed in the boathouse. Ever. Got it?"

We nodded.

"What happened?" Amanda ascended the deck.

"I found Cam," I said. "I found him first."

"Good for you. I didn't try. I changed my mind and explored the woods. I know all the trails now." She patted her bag. "I know how I'm going to win."

"I wouldn't be too sure." Dad raised his eyebrows. "It's a challenging game."

She sauntered over to the table. "What's that?"

"Everyone"—Dad waved his hand over the tail—"I asked Cameron to bring this to me."

Amanda curled her lips in disgust at the severed

appendage.

A lump grew inside my stomach.

Jacob stood and came to the table.

Dad picked the tail up and tried to cover the protruding bone at the base by smoothing the fur over it. "This is the ultimate prize. To win, you must be the first to find it."

I couldn't believe it. Cam hadn't been lying. My dad *had* asked him to kill the raccoon. For a prize. A stupid prize. "It's gross."

Dad eyed me. "I told you that you might not want it, remember? Out on the lake?" He chuckled. "But trust me, it's special. You can't get these just anywhere."

"He killed it," Jacob said. "Like his cat. Like—"

Cam slammed his hand down on the table. "Shut up."

"Calm down, boys," Dad said. "What's done is done. It doesn't matter now."

"But, you told him to kill it." My anger was reaching a fever pitch. "Why?"

"No, I thought it would already be dead. I wanted him to bring the cage back with the raccoon inside it, but like I said— it doesn't matter now." He attempted once again to smooth the fur over the exposed bone. "I have an old rabbit's foot your grandfather gave me. Would that be better?"

"No," Cam said. "I want to use the tail."

"I just want to play the game." Amanda tapped her bag. "I'm going to win, so let's get it over with so we can go swimming."

I grasped the table. I wanted to flip it. No one cared that an animal had died, except maybe Jacob, but even he had come out of his trance and looked excited.

"Charly?" Dad's eyes were cool. "Are you going to be all right?"

"No."

"Care Bear, please." He softened his voice. "Hunting is a part of life. People have made clothes out of things like this tail for centuries. Are you okay if we use it as the prize for the game?"

"Fine." I folded my arms. I'd always hated it whenever he called me Care Bear.

"Jacob?" Dad gazed in his direction. "Are you okay with it?"

He nodded.

Dad held up the tail. "Okay, give me twenty minutes, and when I come back, the game will begin."

"Where are you going?" I asked.

"He's going to go hide the prize." Amanda tipped her head back. "It's obvious."

Cam got up from the table and watched my dad cross the lawn. He studied Dad's path. It wasn't going to help. Once Dad entered the woods, there would be no knowing which trail he took. The only way to find the prize was to follow the clues.

Amanda unzipped her bag and pulled out a piece of paper. She'd drawn a map instead of looking for Cam earlier. "Uncle John should have just given the prize to me now. I'm going to find it first."

"Amanda will win." Jacob grinned. "She always wins. She has a map and a plan. Amanda will win."

No. She won't. Not this time.

My dad promised.

He promised he would help me win when we were canoeing.

Amanda sat there with that smug look, gazing at her map.

I sat across from her with nothing to worry about.

CHAPTER TWENTY-THREE

CHARLY

I can't believe I let Jacob out of my sight. It was only for a moment while I reunited with Amanda. The impressions of his footsteps in the snow are deep and dark and disappear down the deck stairs. The sun fell behind the horizon an hour ago, but thankfully, it took the blizzard with it. There's over a foot on the deck, maybe two, and more below, covering the lawn between here, the boathouse, the lake, and the forest. It's a frozen wasteland.

"Charly," Amanda shouts from inside the cabin, "come back inside." Cam stands next to her in the doorway, staring over me into the forest. "You'll freeze to death."

"That's why I have to go. I've got to find Jacob."

She turns the outdoor light on. At the bottom of the stairs, Jacob's footprints lead up the hill toward the cars.

"Wait," Amanda says. "At least let me get your coat."

Jacob promised he'd stay in the kitchen, but this is my fault. When he reaches a certain anxiety level, I know better than to trust him. It's not intentional with him, like it would be with most people.

Amanda disappears into the cabin, heading for the hall closet.

Cam stands in the doorway. I don't want to be mad at him, but he let Jacob go. He held the door open for him. He probably thinks Jacob has gotten better since childhood. I thought Cam would have gotten better too, but now I'm not so sure.

"Here." Amanda returns. Steps outside. Hands me my coat. "I'd come with you, but—" She glances up at the sky.

"It's okay. I understand. It's dark out here." I pull my coat on and head for the stairs. "I'll be right back. I'm sure he didn't go far."

Jacob's tracks run around the cabin, past the firewood and the snowmobile, and stop at the black car. The Lincoln. It looks like he tried to get inside because the snow is packed down by the driver's door.

It's locked.

He didn't stop there. His tracks go to Cam's beat-up Chevy, then to the Humvee. He was trying to find somewhere warm. It *is* freezing out here. My ankles feel it the worst. Snow is matted to my pant legs, making the denim stiff and heavy, and my shoes never had a chance to dry.

Jacob's tracks leave the Humvee and run past the front porch. He went down the other side toward the lake. I stop at the boathouse to see if he tried to go inside. It's pitch black by the door, so I kneel and touch the ground to determine whether he stood there, packing the snow down.

He didn't, and it's a good thing because we're not allowed in the boathouse.

I laugh to myself.

That was Johnathan's rule from when we were kids. The boathouse was always off limits. But he's dead now, and technically, it's my boathouse. Technically, this place is mine, despite what Randall Thorne thinks.

Randall Thorne.

Who is he, really?

I step away from the door, and the dim starlight shows Jacob's tracks heading toward the forest. "Jacob?" I don't want to go out there. Not in the dark. "Jacob, come back! I'm sorry. I know there were a lot of people inside, and you got over-stimulated. Just come back, and we'll go upstairs."

Nothing.

There's nothing but the calm hush of a fading winter wind as it pushes through the trees.

"Jacob? Are you out there?"

The chill air seeps into my bones.

"Hmmph."

The sound came from behind me. I spin around. Gaze at the boathouse's black outline.

"Hmmph."

There it is again. It's coming from inside the boathouse.

"Hello?" I call.

I wait.

No response.

The wind blows my hair over my face. Freezes my eardrums.

I wait.

"Hello?" I say again.

Did I really hear something?

Slowly, I sneak up to the window next to the door. It could be an animal. A fox or a raccoon trapped inside. Or— no. It didn't sound like a bird. I cup my hand against the glass and peer inside.

A faint light shines in from the window on the other side,

illuminating a workbench, but it's not enough for me to see anything else.

"Hmmph may. Peese, hmmph may."

That wasn't a fox or a raccoon. It sounded like, *Please, help me.* But I can't be sure. Not with the wind in my ears. Not with my heart pounding in my throat. My hand trembles as I grasp the doorknob. The cold brass sends chills up my arm. If it's locked, I have the key. I *think* I have the key. Randall said they changed the locks to the cabin after every hunt. He didn't mention the boathouse.

The knob turns.

"Is someone in here?" I ask. "Jacob?"

Something grasps my shoulder from behind, and I scream. I spin around and flail, and I hit Jacob in the face.

He stumbles backward into the snow. Falls to the ground. Sits up.

"Jesus Christ, Jacob. You scared the hell out of me."

Behind us, the wind sucks the boathouse door closed.

"I'm sorry, Charly. I'm sorry."

I help him stand. "You're freezing."

"I'm sorry, Charly."

"It's okay." I circle him, brushing the snow off. "I wish you could stay put once in a while."

His face scrunches.

"C'mon." I take his hand and pull him toward the cabin. "We need to get you inside before you freeze to death."

"If my body temperature drops below ninety-five degrees for two hours, I'll die of hypothermia."

"I know. Come on. Where'd you go?"

"I had to run."

"I know."

"I don't like that man."

"The slickhead?"

"No. The other man. I don't like him. The tall man with the beard." He pulls his hand away from mine and stops. "I don't like the slickhead, either. And I don't like Cam. Cam is evil. They're all evil, and—"

"Calm down."

The wind gusts at our backs.

He shakes like tinsel tied to a fan.

I wrap my arm around him and hold him steady while we trudge up the hill to the cabin.

A tear streams down his cheek.

The wind weeps with him.

The wind says, "*Hmmph may.*"

"Did you hear that?" I ask.

"No."

CHAPTER TWENTY-FOUR

Randall has allowed Barry to sit on the only chair in the room. Randall sits on the bed. He's explained Barry's excursion, and as he did so, one thing became exceedingly clear—Miss Highsmith and her family must leave the cabin. One way or another, they must leave.

Tonight.

He can't risk losing Barry as a client. He can't risk his boss coming to the cabin and finding all these people. Lance would never stand for this.

"Then I think you understand," Randall says. "Yes?"

"Yes," Barry says. "Again, I'm sorry I brought Kennedy up here with me. I didn't think—"

"Stop. It's okay. She will never know the true spirit of the hunt, correct?"

"Correct."

Randall stands and strides to the window. He pulls the curtain back. The upstairs master bedroom faces south, overlooking the awning, the cars, and the driveway. "The snow has stopped. As long as it doesn't begin again, our plan to extricate everyone from the cabin tonight should work."

"Thanks for this, Mr. Thorne."

"Randall. Please." He turns and holds his hand up. "From now on, call me Randall."

"Of course, Randall."

Barry's teeth couldn't be whiter. He's the perfect client. Young, dumb as a fencepost, and full of . . . fluids. Disgusting fluids. But incredibly wealthy, and wonderfully gullible. And most likely connected to more young, dumb millionaires looking for ways to spend the old money they've inherited. Barry is the perfect customer to focus on when he takes over Zaroff Excursions. He needs to make sure Barry has the time of his life.

He opens the door and motions for Barry to take the lead. Barry raises his chin and strides past him into the hallway. They descend the stairs.

Cam, that unkempt creep, stands by the burlap curtains, staring out the french doors. His counterpart, the raven-haired snoot, Amanda something, sits at the dining table, tapping on her phone. Randall rounds the corner and sees Kennedy sitting by the fireplace, also tapping on her phone. She lies back on the leather couch, her legs crossed, her feet draped over the armrest.

Barry goes to her. "Hey, babe. Sorry I took so long. What are you doing?"

"I can't connect. Why isn't there any WiFi in this place? I was going through my pictures, looking for something to post as a kind of retro thing on my blog. Look at this. Remember when we were young, and Justin Timberlake brought sexy back? He's canceled now, you know."

"Where is Miss Highsmith?" Randall asks.

"What?" Barry asks his idiot girlfriend. "Justin's not

canceled, is he?"

Louder now, Randall repeats, "Where is Miss Highsmith?"

"We call her Charly," Cam mutters without turning away from the doors.

"She left," Amanda says.

"Good." Randall steps over to the dining table. Amanda seems to be the sanest of the group. She is the only one who hasn't complained or demanded anything since arriving at the cabin. "That will save me time. Now, you all must leave."

"Good," Kennedy says.

"Not us, babe." Barry puts his hand on her knee. "You and I are staying. The hunt is still on."

"Why?"

"I'll explain later," Barry says. "It'll be okay."

She glares up at him.

"Yes, yes. You two are staying, but the rest of you must leave. Now. Did"—Randall glowers at Cam—"did *Charly* take her brother with her?"

Cam turns away from the doors. Faces Randall. "No. She didn't *leave*, leave. She went to look for him."

"What? Where? What do you mean?"

"Out there." Amanda points at the french doors. The doors that lead onto the deck. The deck overlooking the boathouse. The boathouse with the cage and the whiny hiker wannabe. Tyler, that pathetic drunk, sitting there bleeding his disgusting blood all over the place.

Randall winces at the thought.

He rushes to the doors. Shoves Cam aside. It's too dark. He can't see the door to the boathouse. There are no lights on inside. That's good. Maybe Miss Highsmith and Jacob didn't see anything.

Amanda shifts in her seat. "What's wrong?"

Randall straightens his jacket. Forces a smile. Attempts to put his hand on Cam's shoulder to apologize, but Cam steps backward into the kitchen. "I'm sorry I nudged you. I—" Cam cringes like a cornered animal.

Randall backs off.

"What's the problem?" Amanda asks.

"There is no problem," Randall replies. "Other than the fact that you are all still here."

Utterly unperturbed, Amanda gazes at her polished nails one at a time. "Our car won't make it down the mountain in this snow."

"Barry has agreed to forge a path down the mountain with his Humvee for you to follow. He'll take Miss Highsmith and her brother back to their car, then drive to the nearest town. You'll make it down the mountain just fine. I have no doubt."

"Even if Cam's beater could make it"—Amanda stands up—"Charly won't go for it. There's no way she's leaving."

"Why not?"

"She's hard-headed. Always has been. She said this place is hers, and if that's true, she's not going to leave without a fight."

"She has no ammunition for a fight." Randall shoots his cuffs. "She admitted she has no proof of ownership. She will leave, and you along with her."

"I'm not going." Cam resumes his position by the french doors. Stares into the night. "I'm glad Charly invited us here. There are some places I need to see again before I leave. Out there. In the woods."

"I'd like to stay also," Amanda says.

Randall resists the urge to reach into his pocket. Slip his

hand through the slit. Grasp his pistol. He could end this now. There's too much talking. Too much weakness spewing from their mouths.

Ah, but Barry is too important.

This excursion is too important.

He turns away from Amanda.

Barry snuggles with his Kennedy on the couch. He whispers in her ear. He tickles her. She giggles. Insufferable, but he has no choice but to suffer them.

"Did you hear me?" Amanda asks. "I said I'd like to stay. I'm interested in what you're up to."

There's too much talking.

Barry tickles Kennedy harder.

She clucks like a chicken.

There's too much clucking.

These people must leave.

"Mr. Thorne?"

Through force of will, Randall focuses on Amanda. "What I'm *up* to? What business could that possibly be of yours?"

Barry plays Kennedy's ribs like an accordion, and she screams in elation.

"Stop tickling her," Randall demands. The two of them blink at him, drunk on their stupid games.

"I was talking to him"—Amanda points at Barry—"about his 'excursion.'" She narrows her eyes. "I want to go on an excursion, too."

"No." Pressure builds in Randall's head. "You wouldn't like it. You'd never survive it."

"You'd be surprised to know what I've survived." She stands and smiles and tilts her head back. She draws Randall in. It's both exciting and threatening. A tingling he hasn't felt in a long time creeps up his thigh.

"Let her go with you," Kennedy says, curling into Barry, still laughing.

"Barry!" Randall shouts. "Mr. Rockwell. Please, stop fondling your imbecile girlfriend."

"Imbecile?" Kennedy sits up straight, pushing Barry away.

"And, you." Randall glares at Amanda. "Get your things and leave."

"I will not. I'm going hunting with you."

He marches to the french doors. Shoves Cam out of his way again.

"I'm going into the woods tomorrow," Cam says, "and you can't stop me. I did something out there. I . . . I left something out there a long time ago, and I've got to find it."

"You're a moron, and you're all leaving. Tonight."

"We're not going anywhere," Amanda says. "This is Charly's cabin."

Randall unlatches the doors and pushes them against the wind. The frigid air embraces him, but it does nothing to temper his rage. He wants to go on a hunt, too. Right now. He wants to kill them all.

He steps onto the deck, and the wind blows the doors closed behind him. He will find Miss Highsmith and her retarded brother. He will make them leave immediately. One way or another. Either with Barry or with the way of the world. With the way of the strongest and the fittest. The way evolution cleanses the gene pool at the hands of an ever-adapting king such as himself. He will hunt them down, and they will leave, or he will kill them.

He is the king.

He flies down the stairs. Stops at the bottom. Stands in

the cabin's shadow.

Two shapes are making their way toward him, trudging through the snow.

They're coming from the boathouse.

It's them.

He reaches into his pocket, slips his hand through the slit, and grasps his pistol.

The wind howls.

Then, the wind moans.

"*Hmmph may.*"

CHAPTER TWENTY-FIVE

Without a doubt, something is in the boathouse. It sounded like some suffering animal, but I can't hear it now. Not over the wind. Not over Jacob's sobbing. His hand is like ice, and he moans. We've got to go inside before things get worse.

The sun has gone down and taken any semblance of warmth with it.

The cabin looms over us as we trudge through the snow toward the deck stairs.

I should never have thought Jacob would stay inside with so many people there. He was only out of my sight for a minute, then he was gone.

Speaking of gone, my feet have gone completely numb. Once I warm up, I plan to ask Randall about the noises in the boathouse. I wonder if he's had problems with animals hibernating in there. I wonder if what I heard *was* an animal. It sounded like someone pleading for help. But that makes no sense. Why would someone be in the boathouse? I can't imagine it has much heat, and the noise I heard—it was unhappy to say the least.

It was more than unhappy.

It was desperate.

Someone stands just inside the cabin on the other side of the french doors. I wave, but the silhouette doesn't wave back. It's probably Cam. That's his station. He probably can't see us in the dark.

"Stop, Charly," Jacob says. "I don't want to go inside. I don't want to."

"We have to."

"He's evil. See?"

"That's only Cam."

"Not him." Jacob points at the bottom of the stairs. "Him."

Someone moves in the shadows.

"Who's there?" I call.

Randall emerges from beneath the eve. He raises his left hand, keeping his right in his pocket. "Miss Highsmith. Where have you been?"

"I had to find Jacob. He's freezing."

Randall steps in front of the stairs, blocking our way. "Yes, I know, but tell me. Where did you go?"

"Nowhere. Look, we need to go inside."

"He's evil," Jacob mutters.

"Shh." I tighten my grip on Jacob's hand.

"Out there?" Randall points toward the boathouse. "By the boathouse?"

"Please, can we get by?"

"Did you go inside the boathouse?"

"My brother will be frostbitten if we don't go inside."

"Frostbite occurs when the temperature falls below freezing," Jacob says. "It causes skin damage. Charly, I have skin damage."

Randall presses his lips together. "Where did you find him?" He jerks his head toward the boathouse. "There?"

Jacob tries to let go of my hand, and I squeeze hard, but not hard enough. He breaks free, bends forward, and rushes past Randall. He clambers up the stairs to the deck on all fours. I chase after him, but Randall puts his hand on my shoulder. He stops me in my tracks. The weight of his hand is astounding. I struggle to step onto the first step. Jacob reaches the top and sprints toward the cabin. Twisting, I free myself from Randall's grasp and step backward up the stairs.

Jacob is right.

There is something evil about Mr. Thorne. He reminds me of my first boyfriend, Drake.

Drake used to beat me.

"Go," Randall says. "Go inside then." He motions for me to leave.

I run up the steps.

Jacob has already gone inside.

The french doors hang open, and the wind parts Cam's hair on one side. He stands there, motionless. A blank look on his face. I rush inside and close the doors behind me before Randall makes it to the deck.

"Are you okay?" Amanda asks. "We were worried about you."

"Where's Jacob?"

"He's over there." She points at the living room.

"What's wrong with him?" Barry passes by me on his way to the kitchen.

Jacob sits with his back against the wall by the fireplace. A log crackles, sending embers into the air. Fortunately, the embers turn to ash and die before landing on his shoulder.

"I told you," Kennedy says. "He's one of those people on

the spectrum. I've read about it." She lies on the sofa, her arms draped weakly at her sides. Her braided blond mohawk has loosened, but her hair still looks fantastic.

I go to Jacob. Take him by the arm. "Let's get you upstairs. You've had enough excitement for one night."

"Kennedy," Barry calls from the kitchen. "Come here. Let's do this."

"Be right there. Can you pour me a glass of wine?"

Jacob and I head for the stairs.

"Wait, Charly," Amanda says. "Aren't you going to have dinner with us?"

"I don't know. I might come back down."

The french doors open, and Randall steps inside. "Miss Highsmith."

I'm not talking to him now. The way he kept asking about the boathouse outside—it gave me the heebie-jeebies. And his heavy hands . . . I don't trust him at all. He's hiding something in the boathouse, and he won't tell me the truth about it. I'm sure of this. I'll have to go back out there later to find out for myself.

"Her name is Charly," Cam says. "*Miss Highsmith* sounds weird."

I pull Jacob up to the stairs.

"Charly," Randall says. "I'm not finished with you."

I ignore him. There's nothing he can do to me.

This is my cabin.

CHAPTER TWENTY-SIX

My perception of time has changed over time. When I was younger, one minute took an hour. Especially when I was waiting for something.

And, we were all waiting for something.

We sat at the picnic table on the deck, waiting for Dad. He left to hide the raccoon tail a few minutes ago. Amanda put her map back in her bag and rested her elbows on the table. She smelled like flowery strawberries, and I wondered when she'd started wearing perfume.

Jacob and Cam sat across from us.

A breeze cooled my neck beneath the insistent afternoon sun. Earlier, my mom had slipped off to her room for a nap. I assumed she was still there, and I doubted she would get up before the game began. Probably not before dinner.

It was a great day for the game. When the early morning clouds had disappeared, the temperature had risen. Sweat glistened on Jacob and Cam's foreheads. That kind of thing would have driven me crazy. Boys don't mind sweating or smelling bad. Or farting. I knew Jacob wouldn't change out of his sweater, and I doubted Cam would take off his Browns sweatshirt until Sunday.

They were disgusting.

"What did it sound like when you killed it?" Amanda asked Cam.

He grinned. I'd never seen him so happy. "Like a girl."

"What do you mean?" she said.

"Like a girl," he repeated. "It had a high pitch and screamed like a girl."

"Boys scream too," I said. "I think the raccoon sounded like a little boy screaming."

Amanda turned to me. "I killed a mouse once, and it barely made a noise. Have you ever killed an animal, Charly?"

"No," I said.

"Charly killed a spider for me." Jacob wrinkled his lip. "It was on my blanket. She killed it dead."

Amanda drummed her fingers on the table. "Spiders aren't animals. They don't count. You've never killed anything, have you, Charly? Is it because you're afraid?"

"Spiders are arachnids." Jacob used his matter-of-fact voice. "And, arachnids are animals. So, spiders are animals."

"They still don't count." Amanda kept her gaze on me.

"I'm not afraid," I told her.

"Is everyone ready?" Dad was hustling up the lawn.

"Yes," Amanda shouted. "I'm ready."

He joined us at the picnic table, his red and brown flannel shirt unbuttoned to reveal a blue T-shirt beneath. He had sweat on his forehead, and he didn't wipe it off. "Okay. I spent the morning hiding enough clues so each of you will have a chance at finding at least one. The clues are written on white pieces of paper, and I left them near the trails, so don't wander off the beaten path, got it?" We nodded. "Whoever finds the raccoon tail first wins. Got it?"

"Amanda's going to win," Jacob said. "She always wins."

I nudged his shoulder and glowered at Amanda. I couldn't help myself. She grinned at me, and my lips tightened.

We stood, and Jacob walked around the table. He leaned over and whispered in my ear. "You're not going to leave me, are you, Charly?"

"No," I whispered back. "Not as long as you keep up. Promise you'll keep up?"

"Yes."

Dad saw Jacob whispering. "Also, I want all of you to promise you'll play fair." He shifted his gaze to Amanda. "Do you promise?"

I nodded.

"Yes, Uncle John," Amanda said.

"Cameron? Jacob?"

"Yes."

"Okay." He shook his head and raised his hands. "Well? What are you waiting for?"

Amanda bolted for the stairs.

Cam ran after her.

I waited until they'd both made it out of earshot.

Dad stood there, not saying anything. He'd promised to help me, and now was a great time for him to tell me where to find the first clue. Or where he'd hidden the tail.

But he didn't say anything. He just stood there.

"Are we going?" Jacob asked. "Shouldn't we go, Charly?"

I winked at my father and took Jacob's hand. He'd find me later in the forest.

We sprinted toward the woods and crossed the trailhead in stride. The trees' shade engulfed us, and the temperature dropped. Shadows crisscrossed the trail. Up ahead, Cam's brown sweatshirt flashed between the branches and bushes. I couldn't see where Amanda had gone. Jacob ran behind me, and before long, he breathed heavily. I stopped and turned around at every bend in the trail to check on him. To make sure he didn't fall too far behind.

Cam's sweatshirt took a sudden turn and disappeared. When I got to where he had changed direction, there was no fork in the trail. He must have bounded off into the trees.

I looked around for a clue. Spotting white pieces of paper against dark green pine needles and bushes should have been easy, but I hadn't found a single one. Dad had said he left the clues close to the trail, but Cam had run off into the wilderness, leaving the beaten path.

What an idiot.

Jacob caught up with me and stopped. He put his hands on his knees and gasped for air. "Slow down, Charly."

"No. We have to keep going."

I took off.

"Wait," he said.

I ran to the next fork and waited for him. There were no footprints in the hard-packed dirt, so I couldn't tell which way Amanda had gone. Assuming she'd found a clue and taken it with her, our best option would've been to follow her. One clue was supposed to lead to the next.

"Charly." Jacob panted like a dog. Sweat trickled down his cheek. He shouldn't have worn that sweater. "Wait. I can't keep going."

"Why not?"

He sat on the ground, rubbing his leg. "I have a cramp. Ooh. My shin hurts. I have shin splints. I—"

"Get up. We have to go."

"I can't. Shin splints happen when the muscles don't have room to flex. I can't go or they'll flex, Charly. They'll hurt more."

I grasped his arm and pulled. "Stand." He stood on one foot and leaned into me. His breath smelled like wet paper. "We need to find a clue. I'm going to run ahead and look for one, okay?"

"Okay. Run ahead."

"Follow me."

"I can't."

"You have to. You promised."

"No. It hurts."

"At least try. Hop if you have to. I'll be up ahead."

"Don't leave me."

I ran down the path, scanning the trees for clues. Nothing. The trail forked again, and I went left. I should never have offered to play the game with Jacob tagging along. The trail forked yet again, and I ran back to check on him. I kept doing this, over and over, telling myself it was good to double-check the trees for clues, but each time, Jacob made more excuses. He said he couldn't run on his leg. He said there were too many rocks on the path to dodge. Too many needles on the trees.

He said his chest hurt.

Of course his chest hurt.

That's what running does.

I ran ahead again, leaving him farther behind than before.

A high-pitched *squee* broke over the ridge ahead. It might have been a bird, but it sounded like Amanda. And it sounded happy. I took the next fork toward the sound and sprinted hard. She might have collected all the clues by now. She might have found the prize. I hadn't seen a single piece of paper yet because of Jacob. Doubling back every few minutes had cut our progress by half. It wasn't fair. While Amanda followed her map, crossing off the trails as she went, I'd had to babysit Jacob.

I listened, but the *squee* didn't come again. The trail emptied into a field that stretched over a hill. Amanda wasn't there, and I hadn't seen Cam since the beginning. This was a dead end. I turned back to find Jacob and planned on getting rid of him. I wanted him to go back to the cabin. I couldn't do it anymore. Until I was certain Amanda had won, I needed to keep trying.

"Jacob?" I called.

He didn't answer.

The trail branched in three directions, and I didn't know which way I'd come. The sun hung to the south, so I knew the direction back to the cabin, but I didn't know where Jacob had gone.

He had promised to keep up, and now he'd gotten lost.

I should never have believed him.

I took a deep breath and hoped Amanda had gotten lost. I hoped she'd misread her map.

All I needed was one good clue.

I turned in a circle, searching the forest for the white papers.

Why hadn't my dad given me a hint before the game began?

He'd promised to help me, and then he said nothing before the game began.

Nothing.

Why hadn't he come to me?

And, why had Jacob disappeared? I'd promised to take him with me on the game only so he would come. Dad was counting on me to watch over him, but I wanted to win. I didn't have time to go chasing after him.

A *squee* cut through the trees. Amanda, celebrating.

The trail before me branched in three directions.

One toward Amanda's *squee*.

One deeper into the forest.

And one toward the cabin.

CHAPTER TWENTY-SEVEN

RANDALL

Randall sits on the leather couch by the fireplace, suffering from a headache, sipping Scotch and waiting for Miss Highsmith to come back downstairs.

The liquor has a bite. It's a blend, and it's not the best.

He wipes his lips.

The fire crackles.

Everyone should be gone by now, but they wouldn't listen to him. They kept whining, and complaining, and coming up with weak excuses.

Too dark, Barry said.

I'm hungry, Kennedy said.

I'm not leaving until I get my own excursion. Amanda was the worst. Who does she think she is?

Randall takes a sip.

Everything has gone to hell. Everyone should have been following Barry's Humvee down the mountain by now. Instead, Barry is in the kitchen bickering with his harlot. Miss Highsmith and her brother are hiding upstairs like cockroaches. Amanda sits at the dining table, staring at him.

Plotting. Trying to come up with a way to get her own excursion.

Women make the worst clients.

Who does she think she is?

It's almost too much to bear.

Randall takes another sip of his inferior Scotch.

If only Ronald was here. He could make them all go away. He could convince them to leave. Everyone loved him. They always wanted to do what he said. They all thought he was harmless, but he wasn't.

He . . .

The pressure builds inside Randall's head. His temples throb. He must stop thinking about his brother. It never helps. Ronald was weak.

Ronald had to go.

Everyone here must go.

"This isn't working." Barry's voice carries from the kitchen. "It's not sharp enough."

"It's a knife, isn't it?" Kennedy is unbelievably stupid, even for a woman. "Knives cut, don't they?"

"I think it's for cutting butter or something." Barry isn't the sharpest tool in the shed, either. "Not raw steak."

Randall stands and faces the fireplace. The flames dance, and the logs pop, but he can still hear Barry and Kennedy's incessant chatter. He closes his eyes and hears his parents' incessant chatter. Their arguing. Ronald tried to keep the peace but—Ronald. Always trying, always behaving like a child. Always hopeful. Ronald never understood; you can beg the boars not to fight over slop, but at the end of the day, they're still boars. They will eventually eat you alive if you let them.

Is that what happened?

Was Ronald eaten alive by boars?

No.

It had to be done.

For the sake of Darwin, it had to be done.

"What's the water for?" says Barry in the kitchen.

"Pasta," Kennedy says.

"We're making steak and pasta?"

"There's nothing else."

"I saw lettuce in there. Why don't you make a salad?"

"I don't have anything to chop it with. The knife is gone."

"Are you sure you didn't move it somewhere? I swear it was here when we arrived."

"For the last time, I didn't touch it. I checked the dishwasher, the drawers—everywhere. It's gone."

"Mr. Thorne," Barry yells. "Can you come here a second?"

This must end. They must stop their arguing. They must all leave. Tonight. Whatever their reasons for staying—too dark outside, too snowy, too hungry—it doesn't matter. One way or another, they must all leave.

"Mr. Thorne?" Barry calls.

Randall's head throbs.

"We lost the knife. Do you have another one?"

Randall doesn't have a knife, but he has a gun.

CHAPTER TWENTY-EIGHT

CHARLY

"Lie down," I say.

Jacob lies on the bed, and I cover him with blankets before closing the door. We're in the first bedroom off the hall. The one I stayed in as a child. The bed frame is constructed of rough-sawed pine and resides next to a matching dresser and desk. There's a notepad and pen on the desk. It's more like a hotel room now. All it's missing is a Bible.

"I'm cold." Jacob pulls the blanket up to his chin. "I didn't want to come here, Charly. You made me come here, and it's too cold in here."

"You agreed to come, but then you changed your mind halfway up the mountain. We wouldn't have crashed the car if you hadn't tried to get out. Then, you ran away. I know coming here has been stressful, with the storm and everything, but what's really going on?"

"Cam is evil. That man is evil. The slickhead is evil. Everyone is—"

"No one is 'evil.' We've all had our problems, and we've

all acted badly in certain situations. Cam's not evil, he had a rough childhood, just like us. He just dealt with things differently than we did. His parents' divorce messed him up too." I step over to the desk and sit in the office chair. "I'd hoped he would be less strange by now, but we've got to give him a chance. Mom said he's gone to therapy. We haven't even talked to him yet."

"He does horrible things, Charly."

"No, he did some horrible things when he was little, but I'm sure he's gotten better." I hope he's gotten better. We all did bad things growing up, but that's how we learn. If I'd been held accountable for the mistakes I made as a child and on into adulthood, I'd have never become the person I am today. Cam deserves the same forgiveness."

"He kills animals, Charly. Animals."

I rub my hands together to warm them up. "We were kids. We all made mistakes."

"I'm cold."

"I know."

"Cam is mean. He calls me 'freckles.'"

"What?"

"If I don't do what he says, I'll end up like Freckles. Freckles was his cat, Charly."

"I know. When did he call you 'freckles?' Tonight?"

"No."

"When?"

"Never mind. I'm not staying here. There are too many people. I want to go home."

"They're all downstairs. You're safe."

"They could come anytime. I want to go to the car. I want to go home." He pulls out his cell phone. "I want to watch videos."

"Do you have a signal?"

"No." He shakes his head. "I want to go to the car. I had a signal in the car. I could watch YouTube if we went to the car."

Jacob might be right. If we went back to the car, we'd be close enough to civilization to get a signal, and I could call a tow truck. Later, we could come back here with all our stuff and find out what's in the boathouse. This is our cabin, and I want to know what's going on.

Someone knocks at the door.

"I told you, Charly." Jacob scoots back against the headboard. Sits up straight. "I told you someone could come."

"Who is it?" I ask.

"It's me." The door opens.

Jacob pulls the covers over his head.

"Hi, Cam." I follow his eyes to the bed. "Jacob isn't feeling well. He's over-sensitized. He doesn't do well in groups."

"I understand," he says. "I've been to therapy."

"Oh." I meet his gaze. "How have you been, otherwise?"

"Good. Look, I want to catch up, but there's a lot of confusion downstairs. Randall still wants us to leave tonight. He wants us to follow Barry through the snow, and he wants you to come down so he can talk to you."

"We're not going anywhere."

"I want to go to the car," Jacob says from beneath the blankets. "I want to go home, Charly."

"No, this is our cabin. We came to spend New Year's Eve with Cam and Amanda, and that's what we're going to do."

Jacob jerks the covers off his head. "We didn't come to spend it with that slickhead or that man. Why can't we leave?"

The truth is, we could leave, but I'd be haunted by the noises I heard outside the boathouse. Besides, it's the principle of the thing. Randall doesn't own this place. He can't force us to leave. Why is he so determined to push us out into the frozen wilderness? "Cam, I need to talk to Jacob for a minute. Can you tell everyone I'll be down soon?"

"Sure." He turns to go, then stops. "Oh, I almost forgot. They're trying to cook dinner down there, but they're having problems. Do you remember seeing any knives when you came? That guy swears there was a carving knife on the counter earlier, but it's gone now. He said he doesn't have anything to cut with."

"I want to go to the car," Jacob says. "I want to go now."

"I never went into the kitchen." I stand. "Jacob, did you see a knife?"

"He's a slickhead, Charly. A slickhead who wants a knife. He could buy a knife if he wanted a knife. I don't. I want to go home."

The mention of food has my stomach aching. We haven't eaten in hours. "Cam, can you ask them to make enough for us?"

"Sure."

I watch closely as he leaves. His ratty hair and stained shirt scream same-old-Cam, but he's not as aggressive as I remember. He moves into the hall, taking slow, measured steps, and descends the stairs.

"Jacob, you need to calm down."

"I need my fidgets."

"Everything is in the car."

"I want to go to the—"

"I know, but we're not going to the car. It's too cold to spend the night out there. This is our cabin, and we're staying.

We're spending New Year's Eve with Amanda and Cam, and that's final." He scrunches his face. "Let's talk about the problem. The real problem. Is it Cam, or is it all the people? If it's Cam, you need to find a way to forgive him."

"It's both. Cam is evil. The people are evil. You're being evil."

"No, I'm not. I'll try to make everyone leave except for Cam and Amanda, but you have to promise to calm down and stop running away."

"I need my fidgets." He pulls on his fingers. His eyes dart to the window.

"Okay. I'll see what I can do. Maybe I can convince Barry to take me to the car, but until then, do you promise to stay in here?"

"Don't leave me, Charly. You always leave me. Remember when you left me?"

"I left you once." Heat courses up my neck. It's been years, but he'll never let it go. "Only once." I go to the door. "Promise me you'll stay this time. No more running away." I can't believe I'm asking him to promise again, but I have no choice. It will be okay. There's only one way out of the cabin from here. He'd have to jump out the second story window to run.

All I have to do is keep an eye on the bottom of the stairs. "Do you promise?"

He nods, then pulls the covers over his head.

I pull the door closed behind me.

No one is going to tell me I have to leave.

Not Jacob.

Not Randall.

Not the noises coming from the boathouse.

I'm staying, and I'm going to find out what is going on.

CHAPTER TWENTY-NINE

RANDALL

Cam comes down the stairs and steps awkwardly off the last step.

What a cretin. His gaze crosses over the dining room, ignoring Amanda who's seated at the table, past the kitchen entryway, and settles on the french doors leading to the deck. He undoubtedly wants to stand by the burlap curtains and stare out at the forest again.

Randall stops him. "Did you give Miss Highsmith my message?"

"Do you mean *Charly*?"

"Ah, yes. Charly." Randall's throat tightens. "Did you tell *Charly* she must leave tonight?"

"Yes, I told her, but—I'll let her tell you herself. She'll be down in a minute. She wants dinner." He heads for the french doors. "Hey, are you guys making enough for everyone?"

Amanda looks up from the dining table. "They are."

Barry calls from the kitchen. "We could if we had a knife."

He and Kennedy are fumbling around in there,

attempting to make dinner when they should be leading everyone down the mountain in his Humvee.

Idiots. They're all stunted idiots.

"Will you forget about the damn knife?" Kennedy asks.

Randall passes by Amanda on his way to the kitchen. She smells like lilacs in the Spring. She follows him with her eyes.

"Have you ever done this before?" Barry asks Kennedy as Randall steps into the kitchen entryway.

"What?" Blink blink. A deer in headlights. So ridiculously vapid.

"Cooking."

She laughs. "Not really. You?"

"No." He chuckles. "Me neither."

Silver spoons.

The two of them obviously grew up with servants. Not like Randall. Not like Randall and Ronald, fending for themselves every day. Searching for rye crackers in the couch cushions. Smearing stale bread with the rancid peanut butter found stuck to butter knives in the sink. Slurping half-eaten cans of kippers stolen from their father's side of the bed while he slept. They grew up hunting for their food in that cramped, two-bedroom house, and they survived. Well, Randall survived. No one spoon fed him like these silver spoon, bitching babies.

Kennedy puts her wine glass on the counter, pivots, and hefts her bottom up. She sits there like a dim-witted child, swinging her legs. Stupid. She's so profoundly stupid, and now she's drunk. She leans forward, grabs Barry's shirt, pulls him to her. She locks her legs around him and they kiss.

It's sloppy. It's disgusting.

Still standing in the kitchen entryway, Randall senses motion behind him and turns. Miss Highsmith is descending the stairs on the other side of the dining room. He turns back to the groping couple by the stove. "Get control of yourselves," he tells them. "Cooking won't be necessary. You'll be leaving soon."

Kennedy pulls her lips off Barry's. "Not until after we eat. I'm starving."

"Watch out, babe." Barry turns a knob on the stove. "It's gonna get hot in here."

Kennedy giggles and reattaches their wet, slippery lips.

Randall wheels from the spectacle. "Miss Highsmith," he says. "Please, come here."

"How's Jacob doing?" Amanda asks. She stands and follows Miss Highsmith.

"Excuse me," Miss Highsmith says, and Randalls steps aside so she and Amanda can enter the kitchen. "He's better." She turns abruptly and eyes Randall. Who does she think she is? She's tall for a woman, but Randall still towers over her. He towers over everyone, in one way or another. "This is our cabin," she says, "and we're not leaving. Not tonight. Not tomorrow. Not—"

Randall raises his hand. This woman's eyes betray no fear. This confidence could be a natural part of her, or it could have come from something she knows. Something she could use against him. Something she saw in the boathouse. "Where did you go when you were outside?"

"To look for Jacob."

"No. Tell me exactly where you went."

"Why?"

Barry extricates himself from his loathsome girlfriend's limbs and drops a steak onto a skillet, then turns a knob on the stovetop.

Kennedy hops off the counter and refills her wine glass.

Randall stares down his nose at Miss Highsmith. "Why won't you answer me?" His neck tenses. "I asked you outside, and I'm asking you again. Where did you go?"

"She told you," Amanda says. "She was looking for Jacob. Where did you find him, Charly?"

"I followed his tracks to the cars out front, came around the side, went down the hill toward the lake, and there he was, okay?"

"Down the hill?" Randall asks. "By the boathouse?"

Miss Highsmith turns toward the stove. "Is there enough for Jacob and me?"

"I think so," Barry says. "We have six steaks."

Randall walks into the kitchen and puts his hand on Miss Highsmith's shoulder. "Did you go inside the boathouse?"

"No." She jerks away.

"Look at me." He fills his chest and locks his jaw. "Did you go inside the boathouse?"

She doesn't respond. Instead, she steps into the kitchen entryway and looks toward the stairs, then the french doors.

"If she did, she'd tell you," Amanda says. "Right, Charly? You don't lie, do you? You've never lied, or cheated, or done anything wrong. Right?" Her lips curl. "Have you?" She takes Randall's arm in one hand. "Relax, Randall. Can I call you Randall?"

Her touch threatens to derail his question. He must know what, if anything, Miss Highsmith saw. If she hadn't seen anything, she would have answered *no* immediately. But, if she did see Tyler, moaning like a wounded seal—locked up in the cage—would she tell him? Here, in front of all these people?

Probably not.

Her half-wit brother might have also seen Tyler, but he wouldn't lie. He couldn't. He has mental issues. People like that can't lie because they lack the mental strength to do so. Perhaps Randall should question him.

He gently removes Amanda's hand from his arm, holds onto her fingers, then lowers them to her side. "I have something I've been working on for my organization in the boathouse. It's top secret, and I've been charged to keep it as such. I simply need to know if Miss Highsmith or her brother happened inside and saw it. If so, I'd be obliged to have them sign a non-disclosure agreement."

"Oh, why didn't you say so?" Amanda brushes her hair back. Smiles. "It's just business. Charly? Did you go inside the boathouse?"

Miss Highsmith turns around and stands there, blocking the kitchen entryway, hesitating to answer.

"Please." Randall's head throbs. The cheap Scotch he drank earlier backfires inside his brain. "Answer her."

Cam appears behind Miss Highsmith in the entryway. Gazes into the kitchen over her shoulder. She doesn't see him. In fact, Randall had forgotten he was out there. The man is incomplete. He's an example of why evolution is so important. Survival of the fittest. He is a neanderthal on the outside and a cretin on the inside.

Miss Highsmith jumps, startled by Cam's presence.

"It's started snowing again," Cam murmurs. "The road's going to be getting worse."

Barry's steaks sizzle in the pan, popping and crackling.

"Tell us, Charly." Amanda hasn't given up. "Did you and Jacob go inside the boathouse?" She leans toward Miss Highsmith. "What did you see in there? What's the secret?"

Miss Highsmith doesn't respond. The way she looks at Amanda intrigues Randall. He has difficulty reading her. He definitely can't trust her. He senses hatred in her. A great reservoir of hatred hidden behind a poker face. She's not going to keep secrets from him. He won't allow it. Whether or not she speaks the truth is another thing. He must act as if she did go inside the boathouse.

He can't let her get away with this.

Kennedy pours herself another glass of wine.

"Stop it." Barry takes the bottle away from her. "You've had enough. You're leaving."

"What? Why?"

"Something's not right." He takes in the room. "That knife shouldn't be missing."

"I don't understand."

"I can't do this with everyone here. Someone's got that knife, and—I'm going on the hunt no matter what. Look, everyone can follow me down the mountain like Mr. Thorne asked, then you can go with them. Let's finish cooking, eat, and then you can get the hell out of here."

"No," Randall says. "No one is leaving."

"What?" Barry scowls. "Why not?"

"I'm okay with that," Cam says. "It's still snowing out there."

"Me too. I want to stay." Amanda steps closer to Randall. "Where did you get those cufflinks?"

"What do you mean no one is leaving?" Kennedy takes a drink of her wine. "Barry apparently wants me gone now."

Her imbecilic voice runs like acid over Randall's brain. He needs a break. "Excuse me," he says, motioning for Charly to move out of his way so he can step into the dining room. He wipes his forehead. The french door windows reflect the dining table. The living room windows reflect the fireplace. He cannot see outside, but he trusts the neanderthal's observation. "If the snow continues, there may be too much on the road by the time everyone has eaten." He turns around and faces the group. "I wish for all of you to stay the night."

"No," Barry says. "They should leave now before it snows more."

Randall struggles to keep his voice down. "Everyone is staying."

Kennedy grasps Barry's arm. "If you don't want me here . . . I want to leave now, too. It's only snow."

"No!" Randall raises his hands. "No one leaves, you drunken imbecile."

Kennedy turns toward the hall closet, lowers her chin, and closes her eyes.

"Hey," Barry says. "Don't talk to her that way."

Randall sighs. Squeezes his temples.

"I wasn't going anywhere anyway," Miss Highsmith says. "This is my cabin."

"I'm staying, too." Cam straightens his back. "I want to go for a walk in the woods."

"There might be too much snow for that," Amanda says.

"I don't have a choice. I'm going for a walk in the woods tomorrow no matter what. It's why I came." The moron never blinks.

Miss Highsmith glares at Amanda. "Are you staying?"

Amanda steps near Randall, practically brushing up against him. Lilacs in the Spring. "That depends. Other than freezing in the woods with Cam, is there something fun we could do?"

"I'm certain you'll think of something." Randall eyes Kennedy. She sips her wine. "It's settled then. No one leaves the cabin tonight."

"Shit." Barry grabs a spatula and shoves it under the steak. Tries to flip it, but it's stuck.

Randall opens a drawer and retrieves a set of tongs. He rips the burnt steak from the pan and holds it in the air. "Don't worry. We have more." He pictures pressing the hot side against Miss Highsmith's face. Deforming her dispassionate features. Her cheeks. Her lips. Her chin. She's the reason there's no peace right now. She's the reason for the pain in his head. It's not the blended Scotch.

It's the risk of losing everything.

He can't allow her and her brother to leave.

Not tonight.

Not tomorrow.

Not ever.

"I'm not staying here tonight." Barry stomps his foot. Puts his hands on his hips. "You can't make me."

Randall drops the steak into the pan, raw side down. A ball of smoke flies into the air. He places the tongs on the counter and motions for Barry to come closer. Barry does so, and Randall speaks under his breath. "You're staying. You paid to be here, and that's what you're going to do. You paid to experience the power of a Zaroff excursion, and that's what you're going to get. Besides, I need your help. We have a lot of hunting to do."

CHAPTER THIRTY

Amanda wasn't yelling *squee* every time she found a clue because she was excited. She did it to drive me mad.

And it worked.

I chased her, swerving along the bending trail, dodging the trees. I knew better. I knew I should have gone back to the cabin and searched for Jacob. He'd fallen farther and farther behind since the game began, but I couldn't help myself.

I wanted to win.

But I hadn't found a single clue.

The trail led me between two boulders twice my height. They had once been one boulder. I imagined a massive lightning strike splitting it in two. Coarse and cracked—I dragged my fingertips over the surfaces as I passed in between, and finally, on the other side, I spied a piece of paper hiding near a log. I lunged for it, but Amanda surged out from behind a tree as though she'd been waiting for just this moment and snatched it up. She smiled. Held the clue in the air. "Another one. That makes four for me. *Squee.* How many have you found?"

"What's it say?"

"Like I would tell you. Have you found any clues?

"We're"—I gasped for air—"doing fine."

"We're? You and who else?" She made a show of looking around her. "The last time I saw Jacob, he was limping away like a baby."

"His leg hurts. Did you see which way he went?"

She pointed in the cabin's direction. If he went that way, I'd be in trouble for sure. I was supposed to be watching him.

Amanda stuffed the clue into her bag and pulled the zipper shut. "I think I know where the prize is. Where are your clues?"

"Jacob has them." I turned to run. "I've got to find him. We're close to winning, too."

"No, I don't think you are. You might as well give up."

I ran back between the boulders and headed for the cabin. I needed to get there before Jacob complained to Dad.

Dad.

If I could find him, he could help me, and I would still have a chance. The trees blurred. I pounded through the forest, no longer searching for clues.

Footsteps sounded behind me. "Charly, wait. Stop."

I turned, and Cam came running up. "What?"

"You have to help me." He held a knife in one hand.

I took a step back. "Help you what? I have to go."

"No. I have a plan. Help me catch a raccoon, and I'll let you win."

"Have you seen Jacob?"

"He went that way." Like Amanda, Cam pointed in the cabin's direction. "I think he gave up."

"Thanks." Time was running out. Jacob had definitely

gone back to the cabin. "I've got to go."

"No." Cam grasped my arm. "You have to help me. I have a plan, but I can't find the cage. I need it to trap a raccoon. If you help me, and we catch one, I'll give you the tail. Then, you can say you found the prize and win."

"That's stupid. Let go of me. What are you going to trap it with? Do you have any food?" I pulled my arm away.

"No."

"Do you know how to set the trap on the cage?"

"No." His upper lip begins to shake. "I'll figure it out. Won't you please help me find it? I'll give you the tail."

"No. I'm not helping you kill another raccoon. I'm going to win fair and square."

With help from Dad, of course.

"Charly," he called as I sprinted away. "You're going to lose if you don't—"

I ran out of the forest and onto the lawn at full speed. The lake stretched out beneath the blue sky, as still as still could be. Not a boat in sight. The boathouse's windows were dark and lifeless, hidden from the sun beneath the eves. I sprinted up the hill toward the deck and carefully opened the french doors to the dining room. I didn't want to wake Mom, assuming she was still asleep upstairs.

"Dad?" I said in a hush.

Nothing.

I tip-toed through the cabin until I was sure he wasn't there. Neither was Jacob. Back on the deck, I gazed at the lawn. The forest. Somewhere out there, Amanda was zeroing in on the prize, and I was stuck here looking for my brother. I resented him for this. I wished he'd never been born.

Dad had forbidden us from going inside the boathouse, but this was an emergency. I was losing.

The boathouse door creaked when I opened it. Dust thrust up into the light cast from the window above the workbench. I almost sneezed. My eyes adjusted to the darkness. The canoe lay before three kayaks against the far wall. Tackle boxes and fishing poles. A shovel and a rake. A raccoon trap.

Maybe I should help Cam.

No.

He was sick.

Dad wouldn't have fallen for it anyway.

It would have been cheating. It wouldn't have been fair to the others, but none of this was fair to me. It was all Jacob's fault. He held me back, and it wasn't fair. My entire life— *Charly, can you watch Jacob while I go to the store? Charly, I'm sorry, but I can't take you to soccer practice because Jacob has a doctor's appointment. Charly, don't invite more than two friends over at a time. You know how crowds upset your brother.*

I needed to find Dad and explain it to him. We needed to start the game over, this time, without Jacob.

"Charly? Are you in there?"

Someone was coming. I was caught. Caught in the boathouse.

Hot energy surged down my legs. *Run. Run. Run.*

"Charly?" Jacob called.

Thank God.

"Jacob, it's you." I closed the boathouse door behind me and stepped into the sunlight.

He came limping across the lawn.

"Where were you?" I asked.

"Were you in the boathouse, Charly? You're not supposed to be in the boathouse. No one is supposed to go into the boathouse."

"I was looking for you. Why'd you leave?"

"You left me. Why do you always leave me?"

"You're too slow."

"I have shin splints." He hobbled over near the boathouse and sat on the ground. "It hurts."

"Get up. We have to go."

"No. I quit. I can't do it."

"Yes, you can. C'mon. I can't leave you here."

"Why not? You left me everywhere else."

"Dad said I had to watch you. Now, get up."

"Stay and watch me, then." He grasped his leg. "Stay with me."

"But . . . the game." A distant *squee* sounded through the trees. "Please, Jacob, won't you try?"

CHAPTER THIRTY-ONE

CHARLY

Shiny wooden chairs, cloth napkins, and sparkling silverware surround the dining table. The wagon wheel chandelier illuminates the dining room, making for a pleasant atmosphere, but the food—yuck. My steak is black on one side and pink on the other. I doubt Barry has ever been in a kitchen before. It was nice of him and Kennedy to try, but my food is almost inedible. And worse, with the snow coming down hard again, I don't think I'll be able to convince them to leave tonight. They've become too comfortable here.

Amanda takes delicate bites of her salad, pulling the lettuce off her fork with her red lips, her polished nails shimmering beneath the chandelier, her eyes playing with Randall's attention. He sits at her side. She always gets what she wants. She didn't only come here to find out about me, about my troubled teen years. Maybe it's the disappointing food, or the fact that I'm suddenly starving, but I'm feeling raw toward her. It's not fair. She didn't come here to reunite as much as she came to rub her perfect life in my face.

Cam stands by the french doors, staring out the windows.

He can't possibly see anything out there. He didn't come here to reunite with us either. He appears to be reliving some memory triggered by staring outside, but there can't be much to see. Snow covers the trees. Ice covers the lake. The boathouse below is buried and smothered in darkness. I wonder if the sounds I heard are still happening. *Hmmph may.* Before dinner, I almost snuck outside to listen but thought better of it.

I'll get my chance.

Randall was so suspicious, repeatedly asking Jacob and me if we had gone to the boathouse, I didn't dare make a move. His story about keeping a top secret project in there is bogus. If it was top secret, why would he even mention it?

"Oh." Amanda eyes my steak. "You got one of the bad ones."

I turn my fork, and charcoal chunks fall onto my plate. "Beggars can't be choosers."

It's true. I didn't realize how hungry I was until we sat down. Steak, spaghetti. Salad. Not salad, actually. More like a pile of lettuce and one ripped-apart tomato. Barry didn't have a knife to chop the salad with. In fact, we don't even have steak knives.

"Cam," Barry says. "Are you going to join us?"

The burlap curtains hang motionless on each side of Cam as he stares into the darkness.

"Cam? Did you hear me?" Barry puts his fork down. "Is it still snowing out there?"

"I'm not sure," Cam replies. "I think so."

"It doesn't matter"—Barry directs his attention at Randall—"we're still going on the hunt, right?"

Randall dabs his mouth with his napkin. "Yes. Nothing will stop the hunt."

"What are you hunting, anyway?" I ask. "A polar bear? A snow owl? Won't all the animals be hiding from the blizzard?"

"The blizzard? Oh, no." Kennedy raises her wine glass, guiding it toward her lips. "Won't that be dangerous? I don't want my Barry to get buried." She sips her wine, and a maroon bead dribbles down her chin. "He's my ride."

"Danger is part of the experience." Randall folds his napkin and places it on his lap. "And no, we're not hunting polar bears or owls. We have plenty of native prey for tomorrow's excursion."

"What kind of native prey?" I press.

Fire flashes in Randall eyes, but no one else seems to notice.

"Nothing is going to stop the hunt," he says. He's obviously not going to answer me, so I stop asking. It's not worth it. Tomorrow, the blizzard will subside, they'll go on their hunt, and then they'll leave. It feels like I'm giving up, but if I bide my time, I'll get my chance to find out what's in the boathouse. I only hope I can wait.

Cam approaches the table. Sits down. "Can someone pass the wine?"

Kennedy reaches for the bottle but misses.

Barry hands the Merlot to Cam.

I wonder how many glasses Kennedy's had and whether this is normal for her.

"Thank you." Cam fills his wine glass, and Randall scoots his glass toward the bottle.

Cam fills Randall's glass.

"Amanda, when did you and Cam arrive?" I ask.

"Not long before you. A couple of hours, I suppose."

"Did you have a chance to look around outside?"

"No. Why?"

"Just curious. When I was looking for Jacob, I heard some strange noises down by the lake. I wondered if you had seen anything."

Randall stabs his salad with a fork. "I arrived yesterday and walked the grounds as always. I heard nothing out of the ordinary."

"What about your company's top secret project?" I ask. "Is it noisy?"

"Project? Oh, in the boathouse?" He laughs. "No, it's not noisy, but I'm curious. What exactly did you hear?"

Not so fast. I'm the one asking the questions now. He's trying to turn the tables on me.

Kennedy takes another sip of wine.

Amanda uses her fork and fingers to tear off a piece of steak.

Cam shifts in his seat when our eyes meet. "What about you?" I ask. "Did you go down by the lake? By the boathouse?"

He averts his eyes. "I'm going into the woods tomorrow. I have no reason to go to the boathouse."

"Correct," Randall says. "The boathouse is off limits." He sounds like my dad. "In fact, no one has any reason to leave the cabin."

"What if we do?" Cam asks.

"If you leave and go to the boathouse, you'll need to sign a non-disclosure agreement, like I already said."

"And, if we don't sign it?" Amanda tilts her head.

"How should I put this . . ." He places his frying pan hands on the table. Looks in my direction. "Then you'll become acquainted with my organization's law team. We take our trade secrets very seriously."

The burnt part tastes better than the raw, but I can't eat

much more steak. Too black. Too rough. The spaghetti's not much better. Over-boiled and slimy, it slides off my fork before I can get it into my mouth.

"Why the interest in my project, Charly? Are you sure you didn't see something? Do you need to sign an NDA?" He refers to the agreement the way a priest opens the door to a confessional. Sitting there, all smug—he's the one hiding something. "How about your brother? Did he see something?"

His devilish beard masks his dimples. He's laughing at us on the inside. Jacob might be right. Some people might be evil, and if so, this man leads the list. The feelings I'm getting now . . . I see nothing but evil. Signing his NDA would be like signing my soul over to the devil. I lean forward. "I already told you. We didn't go to the boathouse."

"Are you certain?"

"Yes, but I'm planning on going there later. Jacob doesn't do well in groups, so I thought we'd spend the night down there."

"Is that why he didn't come down for dinner?" Cam asks.

"Yes."

Randall's neck has turned beet red.

"Is the boathouse heated?" I ask.

Randall tightens his grip on his fork. "You cannot go there, and no, it is not heated." He stands. "Trust me, if the project were not top secret, I'd have asked everyone to sign the NDA and given a tour, but that's not the case. Signing the NDA is a last resort if someone accidentally happens to wander inside the boathouse." He leans forward. Puts both hands on the table. "From this moment on, no one goes near there. Understand?"

Everyone nods except me. He's running a scam. He said

his company takes people on hunting adventures, but he's acting like he works for the CIA. Without a doubt, he's lying, and someone—or something—is trapped in the boathouse. No matter what I say at this table, he's not going to come clean.

"Miss Highsmith," he says. "Do you understand?"

I nod.

Amanda gazes up at him with a smirk on her lips.

Cam stands. Picks up his plate. "I'm finished."

"Me, too," I say. "But, I need to take some food to Jacob."

Barry looks at Kennedy. "I guess we should clean the table."

"Oh, yes." She slides off her seat and stands with the help of the table. The wine bottle is empty. "Anyone want more wine? I'm getting another bottle."

"Haven't you had enough?" Barry asks.

It's my parents all over again. Arguing about alcohol in the cabin.

Cam returns from the kitchen and sits down. "Oh, I should have brought the wine. Sorry. Can you get me some?" He turns. Glances at the french doors. "We're snowbound for now. There's nothing to do but drink."

I scoop the last of the spaghetti onto a plate and add some salad to it. "I'll be right back."

When Jacob sleeps, he sleeps deep. He never admits this, always complaining he is fatigued from being woken up, but I've seen him sleep through some major disturbances. Still, I tip-toe into the bedroom and put his plate on the nightstand. Puffy snowflakes fall outside his window. A draft seeps through the panes.

Randall said the boathouse has no heat.

I head back to the dining room.

At the bottom of the stairs, I see Amanda slip into the basement. She closes the door behind her. I didn't think she'd be sleeping down there. With all her flirting, I thought she'd already convinced Randall to give her the upstairs master suite.

Cam sits at the dining table with Kennedy.

Both their wine glasses are full.

Kennedy slouches with her elbows on the table.

"Wait a minute," Cam says. "You saw a carving knife when you came in, but then it was gone?"

"I don't know." She slurs her words. Waves her hand in the air. "Barry said he saw it."

Something slams in the kitchen.

It sounds like Barry is trying to do the dishes by himself.

"You didn't see it, did you?" she asks.

Cam sits up straight. "No." He takes a drink of his wine. "I'm not into knives." He sees me standing at the bottom of the stairs.

I quickly cross the room as if I never stopped moving. "Where's Randall?"

"I think he's in the basement," Kennedy says.

"Yeah, he went down there right after you went upstairs." Cam swallows more wine and makes a sour face.

"I'm tired." Kennedy drains her glass and puts it down. She glances at me, and her eyes begin to close. "Did you take a knife out of the kitchen?"

"No."

"What?" Barry shouts from the kitchen.

"Nothing." Kennedy rests her head on the table. Lowers her voice. "I don't know why I came here with him. He thinks he's some big tough hunter guy, but he acts like a child most of the time."

"How about Amanda," I say. "Have you seen her?"

Kennedy lifts her head. "I think she's in the basement."

Cam looks around. "She is?"

I don't say anything. Amanda batted her eyes at Randall all evening, then snuck into the basement behind him. She's up to something. She wants the master bedroom, but it's more than that. I shouldn't judge her, but it's hard when my competitive streak keeps flaring up. I'd hoped things had changed since we were kids. Softened. I'd hoped this reunion would be us laughing at the crazy things we did when we were young, but her actions and her holier-than-thou attitude—I feel like I'm being thrust into playing my father's game all over again. Consumed by my desire to win.

This feeling isn't fair to her or me. We've all changed, but nonetheless, I've got to know what she's up to. What are they doing down there?

Kennedy stands. Sways. "Why don't you like her?"

"What?" I ask.

"Why don't you like Amanda? There's so much friction between you two."

"That's not true."

"If I didn't know better, I'd say you hate each other."

"Whatever gave you that idea?"

Cam heads for the kitchen. "I'm getting more wine. It's going to be a long night."

Kennedy puts her hand on her belly. "I've got to go to bed."

"I don't hate Amanda."

She stumbles toward the stairs. "Like, whatever you say. I just don't want to be around when you two get into it."

CHAPTER THIRTY-TWO

RANDALL

The note reads, *Meet me in the basement after dinner for a night you won't forget.*

Amanda slipped the note into Randall's hand right before they sat down to dinner. She wants to give herself to him, and it's no surprise. He *is* the ultimate male specimen, after all, but he doesn't have time for fun.

Barry's hunt is tomorrow.

It will go as planned.

Amanda stands in the dimly lit hall by the basement bathroom, her legs begging him to lift her skirt and enter her like a lion. But he can't. He dare not. The others sit at the dining table upstairs, chatting their worthless heads off.

Barry's hunt is tomorrow.

Barry's hunt is a stepping stone toward destiny. Toward taking over Zaroff Excursions.

Randall will evolve.

He will take over. He will lift the organization. Improve the processes. The infrastructure. He'll take each location to a new level, starting with this cabin and its rundown basement.

His wealthy clients will love him for the renovations, and word will spread. He will replace the basement's lighting. The two bedrooms and the bathroom, obviously done on a budget, with their white walls, hollow brown doors, cheap brass doorknobs—he will replace everything.

He strokes his beard. The Scotch he drank earlier eased his headache, and though not a drinker, he wants more. It's going to be a long night. He pretends not to notice the curves of Amanda's breasts behind her blouse. He raises the note. "Why did you give me this?"

"So you'd meet me in private, silly."

"What did you mean by 'a night you won't forget?'"

"Oh, that was just to get you down here. Wait. You didn't think I wanted to"—she averts her eyes, attempts to hold back a grin, and fails—"you didn't think I was hitting on you, did you?"

"Of course I did. Why else would you give me this? What do you want?"

"I want you to take me on an excursion. I want to go hunting with you."

"Sorry, but I cannot help you. It's not the kind of hunt you think."

She steps forward. "Oh, it is." She puts her hand on his chest. "You see, I'm an accomplished hunter. Tomorrow wouldn't be my first rodeo."

He pushes her hand away. Ignores the swelling in his groin.

She smiles like a demon.

He needs to either rest or have another shot of Scotch. "I will not be taking you with us. You and the others need to go to bed."

"I can pay the fee. It's not an issue. In fact, given the short notice, I'll add ten percent as a bonus for you."

"Absolutely not. You don't know what you're demanding."

"I know what's in the boathouse." She titters. "You're funny. An NDA . . . ha! There isn't an NDA that could protect your company from that sort of thing. False imprisonment isn't a trade secret."

"Shh." He grabs her arm and pulls her into the bathroom. Shuts the door.

"Hey," she shouts.

He swings her toward the shower.

She spins around. Rubs her elbow. "You didn't have to do that."

"Shh. The others might hear you. Be quiet."

"No. Not unless you take me with you tomorrow."

"How do you know what's in the boathouse?"

"Like I said, tomorrow wouldn't be my first rodeo."

"You've commissioned an excursion with us before?"

"Yes. You see, I have a primordial need to be a hunter. A true hunter. I want to be the best version of myself. Feel the power. When it comes to life, I want to win."

She knows the sales pitch, but she can't possibly know what's in the boathouse except—she listened when he questioned Miss Highsmith. She has gone on an excursion before. She's presumptive and aggressive and confident. Solid, the way a woman ought to be. "I cannot take you."

"I'll pay you twenty percent above the fee. Under the table. You can keep it for yourself."

"I don't have the resources for two hunts tomorrow."

"Take me on Barry's hunt. I don't mind sharing."

"It doesn't work that way. If this isn't your first rodeo, then you know the rules. You know each hunt is an individualized experience."

"Can't you make an exception?"

"No. There are consequences for breaking the rules. Do you realize you broke the rules by inviting me down here?"

"How so?"

"If you'll recall, after an excursion, you're to never speak of it again. If you wish to try again, you must contact our office. I'm assuming you failed or you wouldn't be so eager."

"I didn't fail." Her cheeks redden. "We were distracted. The guide misled me, and we ran out of time."

"I doubt that, but it doesn't matter. I cannot take two people hunting on a single trip. You'll need to contact the office and schedule your own hunt. I am pleased you wish to retain our services again, but I cannot help you."

She brushes her hair back. Raises her chin. She shows courage, inviting Randall into the basement to be with her all alone. If it weren't for the others upstairs, he'd end her now. It's a shame, really. He could use the extra money, but it's a short-term opportunity at best. She's not wealthy. Not old-money wealthy, like Barry. She most likely does not have old-money connections. Barry is the real deal. He's the future of Zaroff Excursions.

She's a woman.

And she broke the rules. There are consequences.

She's as good as dead.

"Please, take me on an excursion," she implores. "I'll sign anything your little business wants. I won't break the rules again."

Little business, she says. Conducting excursions in over eleven countries worldwide is not a little business. "I don't know who led your excursion, but I'm guessing he was new. I'm not. I'm one rung from the CEO, and"—Randall puts his palms together—"do you know what the CEO did the last time someone broke the rules? The last time someone threatened to expose us?"

The smile leaves her lips. She shakes her head.

"How would you like to spend some time in the boathouse?"

"I'm not afraid of you."

"You're so sure of yourself." He glances at her feet. Her waist. Her hands. Her face. "Did you take the knife?"

"What?"

"The carving knife Barry was asking about. Did you take it?"

"No."

"Are you certain?"

"Yes. Why?"

Behind her, the shower curtain bears a sullen floral pattern and hangs from a rusty, chrome-plated bar. A stack of white towels rests on a vanity between the shower and the toilet. He hasn't checked the vanity in a long time, but it's unlikely there's anything in there he could use to tie her up. The plastic curtain doesn't have the thickness to suffocate her. It would rip.

He'll have to knock her out.

Hide her body in one of the bedrooms.

He takes a step forward.

"What are you doing?" she asks.

"Are you certain you didn't take the knife?" He looks at her hands.

"Yes."

"Are you certain you want to go on a hunt tomorrow?" Randall raises his hand, threatening to strike her. Takes another step forward.

She holds her ground. "Yes. I'm certain."

Her courage excites him. It's a real shame. She has great genetics. To his surprise, the human race would be better with her in it, but there's too much at stake. Barry is the client of the future. Not her.

He makes a fist.

Someone yells from outside the bathroom. "Hello? Amanda? Are you down here?"

Amanda opens her mouth.

Randall is quick to cover it. He swings around behind her and pulls her close. Her ass feels good against his groin.

He whispers, "Say one word, and I'll snap your neck."

"Hello?" the voice calls again.

He presses his hand hard against her lips. His fingertips dig into her cheek. "Get in the shower and shut the curtain. Don't say a word. Do you understand?"

Amanda nods.

He removes his hand.

She steps into the stall, but she doesn't close the curtain.

"Amanda," the voice says, "I saw you come down here."

"It's Charly," Amanda whispers.

"Shh. Be quiet."

"No. Not unless you take me with you tomorrow."

"Two people cannot hunt one animal. Now shut up."

She looks to the ceiling. Runs her tongue over her lip gloss. "Maybe you could put someone else in the boathouse. You know—for me."

He pulls the curtain closed. "Stay there, and for the good of man, shut the hell up."

"Amanda?"

Randall opens the bathroom door.

Miss Highsmith stands at the bottom of the stairs, barely

visible in the dim light. She's a whore on a street corner.

Charly.

That's a good name for a whore.

She steps forward and attempts to peer past him into the bathroom.

He senses Amanda's gaze upon his back. She must be peeking through the curtains. The insolence. The bravery. Her lilac perfume. He steps into the hall and pulls the door closed behind him.

The whore yawns and stretches her arms over her head. "Have you seen Amanda? I wanted to tell her goodnight."

"Her room is upstairs." Randall doesn't believe her. Miss Highsmith didn't come down here to say goodnight. She's snooping. "I haven't seen her."

"Are you sure?"

"Yes. Tell me, how long have you been down here?"

"Huh?"

"In the basement." His throat tightens. "When did you come down here?"

"Just now."

"Very well. Let's go back upstairs." He reaches for her arm.

"Where's Amanda?" She pulls away. "I know she's down here somewhere."

"Miss Highsmith. I'm not asking you. I'm telling you."

"Amanda?"

The sound of water comes from the bathroom.

The whore narrows her eyes and smirks.

Randall wants his gun in his fist. He wants to reach into his pocket, unstrap it from his thigh, and shoot that smirk off her face. Ah, but then he'd have to kill Amanda as well, and that would be a shame. He'd also have to murder everyone upstairs. It would be a massacre and a mess. The carnage would traumatize Barry and put the future of Zaroff Excursions at risk.

His hand trembles. He puts it in his pocket.

"Sounds like someone's in the bathroom," she says.

Randall looks at her hands. He scans her pockets and her pant legs, looking for a bulge. Someone took the carving knife. He must be careful. These people aren't as innocent as they appear. Not all of them are sheep headed for the slaughterhouse.

One of them is a wolf.

One of them has a carving knife.

The bathroom door opens.

Randall spins around.

"Hi, Charly." Amanda dries her hands with a towel. "Going to bed?"

CHAPTER THIRTY-THREE

Sleep doesn't come. I toss and turn like a child the night before the first day of school.

It's not the floor's fault.

It's not Jacob's snoring.

It's Amanda.

I can't shake the image of her standing in the basement bathroom, drying her hands, looking over Randall's shoulder. They met in the basement and—why were they in the bathroom together? Were they having sex?

What's wrong with Amanda?

Whatever she's up to, she's not going to get away with it. I hated how they shooed me upstairs to bed like a child. They're in on something together. She probably knows what he's hiding in the boathouse.

I roll over. Pull the blankets over my ears.

Jacob's snoring reminds me of the noise outside the boathouse. It flaps softly like a child's blanket in the wind. Maybe that's all it was. Maybe it wasn't an animal crying. It could have been a blanket, or a pump in need of oil, or an old

TV. A radio. A top secret project. I'm exhausted, but I must consider the possibility that Randall is telling the truth.

No. No way. He's evil.

He's like my first love in life, Drake. Drake hit me, but does that mean he was evil? Or was he just troubled?

I'm driving myself crazy.

Jacob snores again.

I look at the window.

It must be past midnight.

I look at Jacob.

He had a rough day. It's easy to forget how important his fidget toys are to him. Everything we have is trapped in my car miles from here, buried in the snow. I wish we could leave. Put all this behind us. I wish we had never come. I wish I could sleep, but the noise inside the boathouse won't stop bouncing around inside my head.

Hmmph may. Peeese, hmmph may.

There's only one way I'm going to get any rest.

I quietly put on my jacket and shoes and carefully open the door so as not to wake Jacob. I wish I'd worn hiking boots, but I don't own any. I've always been partial to canvas flats.

Guttural, animal noises come from across the hall. Barry and Kennedy's room. It's been a long time for me, but when I picture Barry having sex . . . he's just not my type.

He's a slickhead.

At the end of the hall, I hear glasses clinking downstairs. I tiptoe down the steps until I can bend over the railing and spy the dining table.

Randall and Cam are sitting there, drinking. The wine bottles are empty, and the Scotch is nearly gone. They laugh and clink their shot glasses together. Cam must be drunk. He's grinning ear to ear.

Randall says, ". . . and the gentleman dropped his gun and ran, screaming, all the way back to the cabin. I yelled, 'Come back. It's only a raccoon.'"

Cam guffaws. Slaps his hand on the table and slams his shot back.

Randall pours him another.

There's no way I can sneak past them.

Back in the hallway, Kennedy moans behind her bedroom door. I hope their lovemaking doesn't wake Jacob. If he finds out I left him alone, I'll literally never hear the end of it.

The windows at the end of the hall overlook the awning above the front door. It's the only way out. I open the nearest window, and crystalline, icy snow rushes in, instantly freezing my face. I thrust my legs outside and slide out after them. But when I attempt to plant my feet on the awning, they slip out from under me and I begin sliding down it in fits and starts—arresting my descent, then losing traction and dropping another six inches down before I roll onto my stomach and, with everything I have, scramble back up the awning and grasp the window jamb with both hands. After hanging there and panting for a minute, I pull myself up and breathe a sigh of relief.

That had to have been noisy. Someone might have heard my flailing.

I peer into the hall.

It's empty.

A big part of me longs to climb back inside, but that's not an option. Slowly, I reach up and pull the window closed.

The wind stings my neck.

There'd better be something good in the boathouse.

Raising my left elbow so I can see, I scan the accursed awning I've just scaled. About five feet away, the awning butts up against a stout-looking downspout. All I need to do is shimmy over there, grab it, and slide down it like a fireman.

Still gripping the window jamb for all I'm worth, I shimmy. I make progress, but not quite enough. There's a gap between the end of the jamb and the downspout. When I reach for the downspout, my chest contracts. The cold air burns my lungs. This is more exercise than I'm used to. More excitement. I try to catch my breath and consider going back inside, but my hands are aching and the awning is only getting icier. I'd never make it.

The only way out is down, so, doing what I can to swing toward the downspout, I launch myself at it—and, after losing enough elevation to send my stomach into my throat, I get my frozen hands on it. Wrapping it in my arms, I shoot down at about twice the speed I'd fantasized I would until my feet slam onto the porch deck. Pain courses up my legs with the impact, but thanks to the adrenaline rush, I barely feel it.

I hold still, hoping Cam and Randall didn't hear me over their boozing inside.

This is stupid.

What am I waiting for?

Whether they heard me or not, I need to get out of here.

I'm off the porch and trudging through the snow, hoping there's nothing buried beneath the drifts that will trip me up. A few hours ago, I traipsed around the cabin searching for Jacob, leaving a trail, but I can't see it in the dark.

The porch light comes on as I round the corner.

The snow is deeper on this side.

The north side.

The dark side.

I make it to the backyard and lift my knees high, forcing my way down the hill, past the deck. They don't seem to be chasing after me, but I assume they are, and I push on. My shoes fill with snow. My calves freeze. I can't go any faster, but I try, and I nearly fall down. It's like running in quicksand.

When I reach the boathouse, I put my back against the wall. My chest heaves. My lungs burn. For a moment, I thought someone had followed me down the hill, but there's no one up there. Other than a faint light escaping through the french door windows, the deck is dark.

I'm safe for now.

"Hello?" A broken voice comes from inside the boathouse. "Is someone there?"

It's a man's voice.

"Please, help me."

A light bursts to life behind me. Turning, I see the glow comes from above the french doors. Fluffy snowflakes fall and settle on the deck. The picnic table's silhouette hides behind the railing and reminds me of a bug's skeleton. It's like the bugs we studied in middle school before I dropped out.

"Please?" the voice says again. "Is someone there?"

The french doors open.

I've got to hide.

I grasp the doorknob to the boathouse, attempt to turn it, but it's locked. I twist hard, and it gives a little, but not enough. Placing one foot on the wall, I twist and pull on the door. The weather-worn wood flexes, the door pops open, and splinters of wood bounce on the floor. The latch is mostly broken now. I slip inside and pull the door closed behind me. There's just enough wood left in the jamb to hold the door closed.

Moonlight pushes through a window on the opposite

wall, exposing a workbench.

Everything else is blanketed in darkness.

"Who's there?" the voice asks.

"Where are you?"

"Over here. There's a light switch by the door. Please, help me."

The floorboards groan as I feel my way through the dark to the workbench. I don't dare turn on the lights for fear Randall will see them from the deck. Frost covers the window above the bench, obscuring the moonlight.

It's freezing in here.

"Please. Are you going to let me out?"

"Hold on," I say.

I run my hands over the workbench, feeling for a flashlight, a lighter. Matches. Anything. I find a hammer, some screwdrivers. A toolbox. I open it, remove the top tray and discover a small flashlight hiding in the bottom.

I switch it on, turn around, and—oh my God.

There's a cage.

Randall has locked a man in a cage.

The man stands, grasps the bars, and shakes the door.

"Stop it." I rush to him. "They'll hear you."

"I want out."

"Shh."

"I'm dying."

He shakes the door again.

A padlock bounces outside the latch, noisily banging against the iron.

I grasp the bars. "Stop it."

He lets go and backs away before I can get the light on him.

The cage isn't small. It could hold several people. The

thick black bars stretch toward the ceiling. I shine the light on the padlock.

"Who are you?" he asks.

There's no combination dial or keyhole. "I'm Charly. I'm going to get you out of here." I pull, but the lock doesn't give. A red circle lights up in the center. I press it with my thumb. Nothing happens. There are no buttons, dials—nothing. It's completely smooth. "I don't understand."

"You'll have to break it with something," he says. "It's electronically controlled. He unlocks it with his cell phone."

"Who? Randall?"

"Huh?"

"Was the man's name Randall?"

"I don't know. Maybe. Yeah, I think so."

I shine the light on him. A blood-soaked rag hangs from his forearm. He's got a shiner beneath his left eye, and his lower lip is split. His skin is puffy and pale. I can't tell how long he's been here, but he looks like he might be right. He looks like he's dying.

"Please, help me."

"What happened?"

He rubs his head. "I don't know. One minute, I was having a drink in a bar, and the next thing I knew, I was locked in a trunk. When I woke up, there was this guy, and—he beat me up. He locked me in here."

Randall did this. He must have. "What did the man look like?"

"Tall. Really tall. Big hands. He wore a suit or like a fancy suit jacket. His hair is dark, and he has—"

"A beard?"

"Yes."

It's Randall. No doubt. He lied to us, telling us he had a

top secret project when he really had a man in a cage. Is this what human trafficking looks like?

The poor man steps backward and lowers himself to the floor. He sits with his legs crossed.

"Why is he doing this?" I ask.

"I don't know."

His head hangs down. His chin touches his chest. His shoulders droop, and he cradles his bandaged arm with his free hand. The floorboards are stained red, but it looks to me like his bleeding has stopped.

I swing the flashlight over the room, cringing at the thought of the light escaping through the cracks in the walls. The interior is somewhat like I remembered. The kayaks are still here. The canoe. A few life jackets. A metal cabinet near the workbench. There's a thick blanket on the floor next to the cabinet, and I grab it. "Here."

"Thank you, but it's too late." He shivers. "I'm going to die."

"No, you're not. What's your name?"

"Tyler."

I grasp the lock. "It's going to be okay, Tyler."

"It's no use. You can't open it. I'm going to freeze to death in here."

CHAPTER THIRTY-FOUR

CHARLY - THEN

Despite Amanda's most recent victory cry—*squee*—the game was not over. Despite my brother's ailing leg and my dad's disappearance, I was not giving up. There had to be a way to win.

Jacob sat slumped against the boathouse, rubbing his leg. "You can't leave me here, Charly. You can't."

"Isn't it any better? We don't have time for this."

"It hurts. It's shin splints."

I raised my voice. "We have to go back and find the prize now. I'm not going to lose."

"Amanda always wins. She will find the prize first. The raccoon tail is the ultimate prize. Not everyone has one, but Amanda will. She always wins."

"Only because you let her."

"No, I don't. She always wins because she's Amanda."

I wanted to open the boathouse door, shove him inside, and lock it. I wanted to leave him there until I could find the prize and win the game. "Don't you want to win? Don't you ever want to win?"

"I guess. You know what the doctor says. It's hard for me."

"You can do it. Here. Let's see how bad it is." I bent over and rubbed his leg. He yelled in pain. "Okay. Can you make it back into the woods where Dad can't see you? If he thinks I left you alone, I'll get in trouble."

"It hurts to walk."

"Here, let me just—" I rubbed his leg again.

"Ow. You're hurting me."

"Doesn't it feel better?"

"I guess so."

"Good, c'mon." I grasped his arm and helped him to stand. "You can hide while I go find Amanda."

"But I saw Cam in there." He shook his head. "He didn't see me. I saw him, and he had a knife."

"Don't worry. I won't let him find you." Jacob gingerly took one step, then another. I pulled on his arm as we crossed the lawn. By the time we reached the trailhead, he almost walked normally. "Is your shin better?"

"Kind of."

We dropped into the shadows and followed the trail. "Do you still want to wait while I go ahead?"

"You're leaving me?"

"Yes. That was the plan. I—not really. I'll be right back. I just need to find Amanda and beat her to the prize. You can hide."

"What if Cam sees me? He had a knife. Why did he have a knife, Charly?"

"He wants to cheat by killing another raccoon and taking its tail. He thinks he can fool Dad into believing he found the prize." I stepped off the path and headed for the largest tree in the area.

Jacob followed, dry needles crunching beneath his feet. "Don't leave me, Charly."

"It's okay. He won't see you behind here."

"Look," Jacob shouted. "There. There. There." He pulled away from me.

"What?"

He fell onto his hands and knees and reached into a bush. "I found one."

I joined him on the ground and snatched the piece of paper away from him.

Behind the house of boats, where one hundred years ago, a mountain man gave a donkey named Rags a box of oats, you will find the next of these notes.

Jacob snatched the paper back, and I stood. Amanda might have already found the raccoon tail. I could picture her holding it up in her greedy little hands. If we went back to the boathouse, she might come out of the woods and win before we could read the next note. But, if I found her first, I could take the tail away from her.

"I did it. I did it. I found a clue." Jacob stood, beaming.

If I took the tail away from Amanda, she'd tell on me, but we had no time.

"Charly," Jacob tugged on my arm, "let's go."

"Not that way."

"What?"

"Let's go find Amanda. We have to stop her."

"But the clue is this way. The boathouse is this way. I can do it. I found this clue. I can find the next one. I know where it is. Please, Charly? There is a box behind the boathouse. A wooden box. There are a lot of things behind the boathouse, but one thing is an old box. It might have those oats in it from a long time ago. A donkey named Rags ate oats." He stood tall, waving the paper in the air.

I couldn't say no. "How's your leg?"

"It's better." He marched back onto the trail. "I'm going to find the next note."

"Fine, but let's hurry before Amanda finds the prize." I followed him out of the woods, glancing over my shoulder. Any second, I just knew Amanda would come running behind us, shrieking with victory, but she didn't. Jacob ran behind the boathouse, favoring his leg, half-skipping every other step, and he was right. Behind the boathouse, we found another clue inside an old wooden box.

My dad was nowhere in sight.

I still wanted his help.

He had promised, and then he had left.

Jacob read the clue, then handed it to me.

A boulder named Stew fell off the mountain and broke in two. If you follow the trail and stay to the right, you can visit Stew, and under the log on his left, you'll find your next clue.

"Let's go, Charly." He took off for the forest, limp-running. "Let's go find Stew."

I ran after him. "Jacob, wait." He crossed the trailhead into the forest's shadows. "Jacob, wait. It's not there. I know where Stew is, but—"

"Me too." He didn't stop. "Me too, Charly."

"Wait." I grabbed his arm. "The clue is gone. It isn't under a log by the boulder anymore. Amanda already took it. I was there." He stared at me as if I had spoken in a foreign language. "There's no point in going there. The clue is gone."

"But, I found the clue. This clue. She hasn't found them all. I want to find the next one."

"I already saw her find the next one. I think she *has* found all the rest. It's too late. We can't win by searching anymore." I caught my breath. "We need to find her, or we have to—we need to bring back a raccoon tail." Maybe Cam's plan wasn't so stupid. If we helped him catch a raccoon, he'd give us the tail. It would be cheating, but we were out of options. If we found Amanda and took the tail away from her, she'd tell on us, but with Cam's tail, we could say we had the real one. It would be hard for Dad to know who had cheated.

"I can find another clue, Charly. I can. I'm sure I can." Jacob had never been so driven to do something in his entire life. He bounced like his leg had stopped hurting.

"There's no time. Let's help Cam catch a raccoon."

"No. I don't like Cam."

Snap.

"Shh." Someone, or something, had stepped on a stick. "Did you hear that?"

Jacob turned pale and nodded. He held up the clue. "A boulder named Stew—"

"Shh." I snatched it from him. "Someone's coming."

CHAPTER THIRTY-FIVE

Randall rests his hand on the french door handle, gazing outside. His nerves took over for a second there, but he's okay now. Earlier, sitting with Cam at the dining table, he'd heard a noise—a loud crash—come from out front, but nothing was there when he checked the porch. It could have been the wind, tearing a branch from a tree, or some poorly placed firewood falling off the stack. Or someone trying to escape.

It had sounded like someone was on the roof, so he stepped off the porch and gazed up at the cabin. The darkness hid the upper floor, but his instincts had told him something was wrong. He rushed back inside and switched the deck light on. But—curiously—no one was out there, either.

His instincts are never wrong.

He rubs his beard.

The moonlight reflects off the snow, painting the landscape a light blue.

He strains to see the boathouse.

The night air slowly moves across the desk and into the cabin, wrapping itself around his legs. His torso. It chills him.

The boathouse is buried, and more snow is on its way. Feathery snowflakes fall and settle on the deck at Randall's feet. Someone is down there. He can feel it.

"What's going on?" Cam asks.

Randall calms himself and remembers the task at hand. He has Cam right where he wants him.

"Is there any more Scotch?" Cam asks.

Randall closes the doors and turns around.

Cam holds up an empty bottle.

"Yes, one moment." Randall strides into the living room and throws another log into the fireplace. Embers fly. The dry wood crackles. He opens the liquor cabinet and retrieves a fresh bottle. More cheap stuff. "Here we are." He returns to the table, sits across from Cam, and opens the Scotch.

Cam pushes his shot glass forward.

Randall fills it to the brim.

"Thank you."

This is going well. The mop-head is already slurring his words.

"So," Cam leans over the table, propping himself up on his elbows. "That's it? You just take them out in the woods and hunt. How is that so—how is that so special?"

"It's not just to hunt. It's to fulfill one's primordial survival needs. I orchestrate each client's excursion to make sure they feel like predators. I make sure they feel the power. You'd love it."

"I don't know. Is it big game? There's not much up here like that. Mostly mountain goats."

"It's the biggest game known to man. That's where the power comes from. The calm before the storm as you track the prey through the trees. The exhilaration of the chase. The smell of fear as you close in, and finally—*bang!*"

Cam rocks back in his chair. Terror streaks across his face, and then, realizing everything is okay, he laughs like a moron.

"Would you be interested in going on an excursion sometime?" Randall asks.

"No. I don't think so." He sips his drink. "I'm not a hunter. I kind of had a thing with animals when I was little. I—" He glances at the french doors. "One time, I was here, actually. With my cousins."

"Amanda?"

"Yes. Her, and Charly, and Jacob."

"If you don't mind my saying, the four of you don't seem very close. Tell me, do you spend much time together?"

"No. Not with Charly. I see Amanda more. I don't live too far from her." He swirls his shot glass. "We sometimes eat together, or have lunch."

"Tell me about Amanda."

Cam grins. "You like her or something?"

"No, nothing like that. She intrigues me, is all. She seems very driven."

"She is. She is amazing. Nothing gets between Amanda and what Amanda wants. I do my best to stay out of her way."

"What do you mean?"

He sniffs his drink. "This is the best Scotch I've ever had." He takes a sip.

Moron.

"How does she always get what she wants?" Randall inquires.

"I don't know. It's complicated. She doesn't back down from anything. She's—it's best to have her on your side, if you know what I mean." He licks his lips and gazes at Randall. "You look like you're driven. Successful. This place is a lot nicer than when I was little. You must be making bank with your excur—your excur—your hunting trips."

Randall straightens his cuffs. "I do well. I'm fulfilled. More?"

"No." Cam places his hand over his shot glass. "I've had enough."

"How about you? Are you fulfilled?"

"Oh, I get it. You want me to go hunting. I know a salesman when I see one."

"Guilty as charged. But, honestly—are you fulfilled?"

"I don't know. I think . . . no. I mean, is anyone?"

"I am. Let me take you hunting sometime."

"Like I said, I had a thing with animals. I don't like to hurt them." He averts his eyes. "Not anymore."

"Anymore?"

"When I was a little kid . . ." His eyelids droop. He looks down at the table. Clasps his hands. "I guess you could say I hunted when I was little. I—I didn't know any better."

"What did you do?"

"I hurt animals." He grips his shot glass. "I shouldn't be telling you this."

"Why did you hurt the animals?"

"I don't know."

Randall pulls Cam's glass from his hand and drags it across the table. "I think I know."

"They weren't like people. I didn't know they had feelings. I was just a kid."

"What animals did you hurt?" He fills Cam's glass.

"Squirrels, mostly. And . . ." He scrunches his face. "We had a cat."

"And, you hurt the cat?"

Cam downs his shot. Exhales hot air. His breath sickens

Randall. This is good. The moron has lost control of his tongue to King Alcohol, the truthmaker. "I don't want to talk about this anymore."

"Ah, but pets aren't much different from prey. You shouldn't feel bad. We forget that we're all animals. We love our pets, assign emotions to them, and like you said, we fool ourselves into believing animals have feelings. We forget we're all animals. We forget that it is natural to chase, attack, and kill."

"I don't know," he slurs. "I don't know if that's right."

"Did you kill the squirrels?"

"Sometimes."

"How?"

"I had a knife." He flushes. "Oh, God."

"What is it?"

"The blood."

"From the animals? You cut them with your knife?"

"Yes."

"It's okay." Randall takes a sip of his shot. "Speaking of knives, did you see the carving knife in the kitchen earlier?"

Cam glances at the kitchen doorway. "No, I don't—do you think I took it?"

"No, no. Not at all."

"I don't need a knife. I don't hurt animals anymore."

"Why did you hurt them when you were little? Why do you think you killed the squirrels?"

"It wasn't only squirrels." He points at the window. "Out there, I killed a raccoon."

"Why?"

Cam shoves his glass toward Randall.

Randall pours.

"My therapist says it was my parents' fault. She says I was

angry over the divorce."

"Do you think that's the reason?"

"Yes." He takes the shot glass and twists it like a radio dial, staring at the liquor. "That raccoon was the last animal I ever hurt. I need to see where it happened, like visiting a cemetery. I need to tell it I'm sorry. My therapist says I need forgiveness. My parents' divorce wasn't my fault, but that raccoon . . . that baby raccoon . . ."

Psycho.

Psycho moron.

This man spent the afternoon staring out the french doors because he killed a raccoon a long time ago. A worthless raccoon. What a crybaby. What a moron. "I can help you."

"How?"

"Your therapist is wrong. The best thing for you is to embrace your survival instincts. As a child, your instincts told you to kill. This is natural. We're closer to who we really are when we're children. You weren't angry because of the divorce. You were angry because you had no outlet for your instincts."

"I don't know if that's right."

"You're a strong hunter, Cam. I can tell. Trust me, I've taken hundreds of men hunting, and we're all the same. You don't need a raccoon's forgiveness. You need to embrace your inner self. You need to hunt."

"No." He sits up. "I—"

"How did it feel when you killed the raccoon?"

"Horrible. I stabbed it in the back and—oh, the blood."

"And you killed again, didn't you?"

"No. Never."

"Ah, so you held it all inside." Randall taps his fingertips together. "Hmm . . . you held all the guilt inside. You invented emotions around the raccoon, and you held onto them. It was self-serving, Cam. The raccoon should have been the victim, not you. You invented emotions around your cat as well, didn't you?"

"Shut up. Don't talk about Freckles."

Freckles.

Randall struggles to keep from laughing out loud. The cat's name was Freckles, for Darwin's sake. "When you killed the raccoon—when you stabbed it—at that moment, how did it feel?"

"Shut up."

Randall raises his voice. "Did you kill your cat?"

Cam slams his hand on the table. His lips stiffen. "It felt good, okay? It felt good when I stabbed the raccoon. Okay?"

"Yes. It is okay. You see? You don't need to beg forgiveness to rid yourself of guilt. You need to hunt again. The proper way. Like a man. You were only a child with a knife, acting out. You had no one to teach you." Randall stands. "Get your coat."

"What?"

"I'm going to set you free, my friend. We're going hunting."

"Now?" Cam stands. Wavers.

"Yes. Come with me." Randall rounds the table and puts his hand on Cam's shoulder. "I have everything we need in the boathouse. Flashlights. Guns."

"But," he licks his lips, "I—your secret. Your top secret project. I don't want to sign anything."

"The NDA? Don't worry about that." Randall smiles. "I trust you. You won't have to sign anything. You only have to come to the boathouse with me. Now."

CHAPTER THIRTY-SIX

The cold has penetrated my skin and stiffened my muscles.
My bones will be next. The deadening pain has already crept
into my ankles and fingers. Randall has turned the boathouse
into a prison. Once more, I rub my thumb over the padlock
on Tyler's cage. I shine the flashlight on it. The surface is
smooth, and a red ring glows in the center.

The damn thing is impenetrable.

"It's no use." Tyler sits slumped in the back corner. He's
wrapped in the horse blanket I found for him, shivering. "I'm
as good as dead."

There's a pinhole on the bottom of the lock big enough
for a paper clip or a thumbtack. Maybe I can reset it. Maybe
it will pop open. "Shh. I'm going to get you out of here."

"I'm tired."

I go to the workbench. "Just hang on. I have an idea."
There are a couple of screwdrivers. A small saw. Some string.
A nail too big for the lock's pinhole. A toolbox full of rags,
reeking of gas and oil.

Tyler moans.

I shine the flashlight around the boathouse. The kayaks—one red, one blue—lean against the back wall by the canoe. I'd hoped to see a tackle box and find some fishing lures, but no luck.

"Go for help." Tyler lifts his head. "You're going to have to leave and get help."

There's nothing to reset the lock with. If I had a tire iron or something, I could wedge it into the lock and break it open. "I don't want to leave you." A shovel and two rakes stand in the corner nearest the door. Age has stolen the varnish from their wooden handles, making them cracked and splintery. Frail. There's a stack of coiled hoses on the floor and an empty flower pot.

No tire iron.

I bet there's one in Cam's car or in one of the other cars up by the firewood.

A shadow moves past the ice-covered window.

I drop to the floor, and the flashlight slips out of my hand. It shines straight up, illuminating the ceiling.

The boathouse glows.

The door handle turns.

"Hide," Tyler says.

"I am."

I grab the flashlight and feel for the power switch. My freezing fingers don't want to cooperate, and it slips out of my hand again.

The door opens a crack, then stops.

"Here, let me help you." Randall's voice sounds gentle, but he speaks with such command. "Come. You're about to embark on a great adventure."

I grasp the flashlight, and my thumb finds the button.

I press it as hard as I can.

The light goes out.

The door opens.

I scoot backward, then roll onto my side and crawl toward the kayaks in the dark.

"Right in here," Randall says.

"Where? I can't see."

Cam?

That sounded like Cam.

I pull myself across the floor, dragging my knees, and bump into a kayak.

I freeze.

"Here," Randall says, "let me get the light."

I slip in between the kayak and the wall.

A light comes on above, and the boathouse comes to life.

My eyes burn. Cold air rushes in through the door. My frozen fingertips scream in pain. The icy chill snakes its way into my bones. I hold my breath. I can't let it out for fear Randall will see it. He'll wonder why puffs of smoke come out of the kayak.

"What's that?" Cam asks.

"That's your new roommate," Randall replies.

I shouldn't, but I can't help myself. I've got to see what they're doing. I exhale through my hand and peer around the kayak. I'm behind the cage. Behind Tyler. It's a decent cover. Randall and Cam stand by the door across the room.

Cam steps to the side, nearly falls down, then stumbles forward. How much did he have to drink with Randall?

"Help me." Tyler lifts his head.

Randall grasps a shovel from the corner.

Cam gazes stupidly at Tyler. "Help you? What are you doing in there?"

Randall steps behind Cam. He spins the handle and bends

his knees like a baseball batter. "He's having the time of his life."

Just as Cam turns toward his voice, Randall cracks him in the head.

Bright blood sprays in an arc from Cam's face.

Randall steps forward, ready to hit him again, but Cam goes down.

I jerk back, out of sight.

"Ooh," Cam moans. "Why?"

"*Why?*" Randall mocks. "*Why? Why me? Poor me? Why are you doing this? Let me go. Please, let me go.*"

"Please," Cam begs.

Slumpf.

"Ah." He screams in pain.

Slumpf.

It sounds like Randall is kicking him.

Slumpf.

I take a peek, and I'm right. He'll break Cam's ribs. Maybe he already has.

Slumpf.

Randall pulls a gun out of his pants pocket. Points it at Cam's head. "Hold still."

Cam lies in the fetal position. Blood pools near his cheek.

"You're disgusting, you moron." Randall pulls his cell phone out of his other pocket with his free hand and taps the screen with his thumb. The cage's lock unlatches, and Randall removes it from the door. "Get inside." He kicks Cam in the stomach again.

I want to scream.

Cam lies there, bleeding.

Randall pulls the door open and puts his foot on Cam's hip. He pushes, forcing Cam to roll onto his back. "I said, get inside."

Tyler tries to stand as if he is going to make a break for it, but Randall raises his gun in an almost leisurely fashion. Tyler freezes.

Cam rolls over and crawls into the cage.

I smell my mother. Whiskey. Cam is drunk, and Tyler doesn't smell great either. I don't know why Randall has them locked up. This is not the "top secret" project I imagined his organization hid in the boathouse. I wonder if there *is* an organization. I wonder if Randall is some kind of sicko serial killer who lured that slickhead, Barry, here to kill him along with Tyler.

And now, the sicko has Cam.

But why the cage?

Why all the stuff about taking Barry on a hunting trip?

It doesn't make sense.

Cam coughs, and blood trickles down his chin.

Randall, watching Cam, hitches his breath, swallows, and looks away. He gags. Clears his throat. "You disgust me." He shuts the door to the cage.

"How long are you going to keep us in here?" Tyler asks.

Randall places the lock on the door and latches it. The red circle flashes once and dies. He returns his gun to his pants pocket and turns away. It's strange how he carries his weapon like a wallet. Or a cell phone.

I need to get my hands on his cell phone. It's the key.

If I waited for him to return to his room and fall asleep, I could sneak inside and steal it, but there's no time. Tyler is about to pass out, and Cam—poor Cam. He might have internal bleeding.

I need something to break the cage open with.

A tire iron.

I need Cam's car keys.

"Why?" Tyler mutters. "Why are you—"

"*Why?*" Randall says, pitching his voice up an octave. "*Why are you hurting me? Why are you doing this?*"

"I thought we were going hunting." Cam wipes the blood from his cheek. "You said we were going hunting."

Randall laughs. "Oh, we are. Don't worry."

He opens the door to leave.

Cold air rushes across the room.

"Rain or shine. Or, in this case"—Randall looks up at the sky—"snow. Don't worry. Nothing is going to stop us from hunting."

A wall of frigid air hits me. It rushes into my lungs. It becomes a tickle in my throat.

I swallow.

My eyes water.

I cough.

Randall spins around.

Cam looks at Tyler. Confused.

The tickle doesn't go away. Instead, it turns into an ache. I hold my breath, but the pain is too much. The pressure builds. I cough again, and Tyler covers his mouth.

"What was that?" Randall asks, stepping forward.

"I'm catching a cold." Tyler coughs. "I'm going to die if you leave me in here."

Randall narrows his eyes. He focuses beyond the cage. He's looking right at me.

Oh, God. I swear—he's looking right at me.

Tyler coughs again. He scoots to his right, but I can still see Randall. He coughs again, this time into his fist.

Randall reaches into his pocket and pulls out his gun.

The winter wind howls.

CHAPTER THIRTY-SEVEN

The sound came from the trees behind Jacob. He stood there staring at me, frozen. I hadn't meant to scare him when I heard the noise. I only wanted him to be quiet. I put my finger to my lips and motioned for him to come near me.

A rustling noise—a pine needle-crushing noise—came from the trees, and Jacob turned to face it.

"It might be Amanda," I whispered. "She's trying to sneak past us without using the trail."

He nodded.

"If it is her, we've got to take the raccoon tail away from her, okay?"

"What if she doesn't have it, Charly? What if—"

"Then she wouldn't be trying to sneak past us, would she?"

He shook his head.

"What's wrong?" I asked.

"It's cheating, Charly. Taking the tail. Isn't it cheating?"

"Shh."

The rustling turned into the sound of pounding footfalls,

and Cam emerged from the branches, tromping. His eyes on fire, his chest heaving. The knife in his hand gleaming. "You guys have to help me. I found a raccoon and chased it, but it got away." He looked back the way he'd come. "It's somewhere back there. C'mon, we can catch it. Maybe we can trick it into the cage, but we'll have to surround it. Help me, and I'll give you the tail. I promise."

Jacob shook his head.

"How far is the cage?" I asked.

"Not far." He took a step toward us.

Jacob backed away.

That disgusting, salty-boy odor emanated from his Browns sweatshirt. Ick. "C'mon, I'll give you the tail. I promise."

"Why don't you keep it?" Jacob asked. "Why don't you want to win?"

"I only want the raccoon."

"We'll do it," I said.

"No," Jacob yelled. "I can find another clue. I can. I can. We don't have to cheat, Charly."

I grasped his arm. "We don't have a choice."

"Let go, Charly." He broke free and tried to run, but I grabbed his shirt.

"*Squee.*" Amanda came running through the trees. "*Squee.*"

Jacob stopped pulling away.

"Look at what I've got, losers." Amanda raised her tight little fist. She had found the tail.

I let go of Jacob and leaped toward her, reaching for the tail. She moved out of the way, and I missed grabbing it by inches. I tumbled to her feet, grabbed her ankle, and pulled until she fell backward. Like a demon, I clawed my way up her waist.

That tail belonged to me.

"Stop it, Charly." Jacob pulled on my shoulders. I fell off her, and my hip hit the ground. My heart raced. My pulse beat inside my fingertips. I pounded my hands into the dirt. I couldn't let Amanda return with the tail. She was always showing off to my dad. That tail belonged to me. It was all that mattered. I wanted my dad to be proud of me—not her.

Me.

I had to have the tail.

"You're crazy," Amanda said. "Look at you." She stuffed the tail into her bag and zipped it shut. "You've lost it. You're crazy."

"Don't say that." Jacob came to my side. "Crazy's not a nice word. My therapist says people aren't crazy. They just have problems. You shouldn't call people crazy, Amanda. It's not nice."

I stood. Seething. "You cheated."

"No, I didn't."

"You kept all the clues for yourself. No one else had a chance."

"That wasn't a rule." She shook her head. "No one said I couldn't keep the clues."

"It wasn't fair," I said. "We have to play again."

"No, we don't." She wiped her hands off on her pants. "I'm going to go show Uncle John I won and then go swimming."

I stepped toward her, and her eyes widened. She put her hand on her bag. She knew I could reach her before she could run. She knew I wouldn't let Jacob stop me again.

She curled her lips. "You're acting crazy because your dad doesn't love your mom anymore. They're getting a divorce, you know. That's why he's leaving. That's the real reason. I overheard them talking yesterday."

"Shut up," I shouted. "That's not true."

"What?" Jacob asked. "Why did you say, Amanda?" He turned toward me. "Why did she say that, Charly? Why?"

Amanda took a step back.

"Give me the tail," I said.

Jacob put his hand on my arm. "Divorce? Why did she say Mom and Dad are getting a divorce? Is Dad leaving?"

"He's not leaving, and she's not winning." I pulled away from him.

"But, she always wins."

"Not this time. Not after I tell Dad how she cheated."

"She didn't cheat," he said. "I know the rules. Dad told us the rules, and she didn't cheat. He didn't say we couldn't keep the notes we found. She didn't cheat, Charly."

I spun toward him, my heart on fire. "It's your fault. You pretended your leg was hurt so I wouldn't have time to find the clues."

"No, I didn't. I had shin splints."

"Shin splints don't go away like that." I spun back toward Amanda, my eyes burning. Tears coming. "Did you tell him to fake it? I bet you did. I bet that's how you cheated."

"Hey, Charly," Cam said, "it's okay. I have a plan. If you help me catch a raccoon, I'll give you—"

"Shut up, Cam." I charged toward Amanda. "Give me the tail!"

She shook her head and darted into the trees.

I ran after her.

I couldn't let her win.

I couldn't let her take my dad's love away from me.

CHAPTER THIRTY-EIGHT

CHARLY

I learned to choose my battles a long time ago. Fight or flight. When I was in my teens, I ran away from Jacob. The responsibility. I couldn't care for him, and I didn't believe his autism was real, but I was wrong. I should have stayed with him. I should have fought to take care of him. Knowing when to run and when to fight can make all the difference in a person's life, and right now, I'm fighting not to cough.

I don't know how much longer Tyler can cover for me. Every time I cough, he coughs.

Randall isn't buying it. He's pointing his gun at Tyler.

Slowly, I slide farther behind the kayak so Randall can't see me, but he can still hear me.

Cough.

Fight or flight.

Cough.

I can't take him on. He's too large. His hands are monstrous.

I can't run, either. He's blocking the door.

The situation has seized me. Frozen me. I had sensed

Randall was evil—Jacob had said so from the beginning—but locking Cam and Tyler in a cage? Who thinks they can get away with something like that? It's so cruel, especially with no heat in the boathouse. I saw plenty of cruelty when I lived on the streets, but this goes deep. It's premeditated.

Randall is more than evil.

He's psychotic.

I've got to get Tyler and Cam out of that cage, wake up Jacob, and run.

I've got to take flight.

The tickle in my throat returns.

I cough.

Tyler covers his mouth and coughs.

Randall glares at him.

"I'm getting sick," Tyler says.

"*I'm getting sick*," Randall says in a whiny voice. "*I'm getting sick.*" He lowers his gun.

"Let us out," Cam says.

"*Let us out.*" Randall mocks. "*Let us out.*"

Tyler coughs again.

I hold my breath.

Randall stows his gun in his pocket and steps outside the cabin. Gazes up at the sky. "Getting sick is the least of your worries. You should be concerned with getting some sleep. You're going to need it later."

"Wait," Tyler says. "Don't go. We need a heater. We're going to freeze to death."

"You have a blanket. I think you'll survive." Randall flips the light switch and closes the door behind him. His shadow moves past the frosted window.

He's gone.

"You've got to go for help." Tyler sounds weak.

"How?" Cam asks. "We're locked in a cage."

"Quiet," I say. "Let's make sure he's gone."

"Who's there?" Cam asks.

I turn the flashlight on and come out from behind the kayak.

"Charly. How'd you—"

"Are you okay, Cam?"

"No." He puts his hand on his ribs. "He kicked the shit out of me."

I hurry around the cage to the boathouse door.

I pause.

I listen.

I look out the window.

"Get us out of here," Cam begs.

"She can't," Tyler says. "There's no way to open the cage."

"Shh." I twist the doorknob and slowly open the door. Randall's tracks lead toward the cabin and disappear in the darkness beneath the deck. "Okay. We're good."

"Close the door." Tyler sits there, shivering.

I check, but there's no way to lock the boathouse from the inside because I broke the latch when I came in earlier.

I go to the cage. Tug pointlessly on the padlock. If only I could get Randall's phone. Tyler stands. His hair is a mess, and the dark purple bruise on his face seems to be getting bigger by the minute. In another setting, at another time, he'd be okay-looking. Kind of cute. He has a boyish quality about him. An innocence.

I need to get Randall's phone.

Tyler steps up to the door of the cage. "Go for help. Go get the police."

"I can't," I say. "It's been snowing all day. I'd never make it all the way down the mountain, and even if I did, Randall would've come back here by the time the police came. He—"

"Just break the lock." Cam shrugs. "It can't be that hard."

He's right. There's got to be something in here I can use, but I already searched the boathouse once. There was no tire iron, or ax, or anything heavy enough. I swing the flashlight around the room again, vainly searching for something. Anything.

"Hurry," Cam says.

"Do you have a tire iron in your car?" I ask.

"I don't know." He reeks of whiskey. "I haven't had a flat tire in a long time."

"Give me your keys."

He checks his pockets. "I don't have them. I must have left them in my room."

"What?" I can't believe this. "Why?"

"I don't like things in my pockets jabbing me."

"Get a phone and call for help," Tyler says.

"There's no signal here. I barely had one when I ran off the road, and I was miles away from here."

"How far?" Tyler asks.

"At least halfway down the mountain." I pull on the padlock again. Dammit. I let it rest against the bars. "I wish you had your keys, Cam. I don't dare go back to the cabin. Randall will catch me for sure."

"Take the snowmobile," Cam says. "I parked by one when I got here. It was next to this stack of firewood. I checked it out, thinking I would take it into the woods to find where I—where we played the game. The keys were in the ignition."

"Are you sure?"

"Yes."

I don't trust him.

But that's just me.

I don't trust anyone.

Especially men.

Cam was many things growing up, but he wasn't a liar. That doesn't mean he's not lying now.

My chest aches. The cold air attacks my lungs. It's causing damage with every breath I take.

Cam has no reason to lie about the snowmobile, but if I get caught taking it . . . no more flight. Only fight.

"Go," Tyler says. "Take the snowmobile to the nearest town and get the police."

"No. There isn't time. I have a tire iron in my car. And my phone, but it's probably dead by now. I'll grab the iron and come back."

"You'll get caught if you come back."

My jaw tightens. "My brother is in the cabin with that lunatic. I'm not leaving him here without coming right back."

Tyler's eyes soften. "Okay. Just go."

I race to the door.

"Wait," Cam says. "Take something with you. A weapon or something. What if Randall catches you?"

He's right. I shine the light around the boathouse.

"Over there." Tyler points. "Did you check that cabinet?"

A green metal cabinet rests in the shadows next to the workbench. I should have checked it before, but it was out of sight, and I was out of my mind. Inside, I expect to find whips and chains. Spiked collars. Torture devices. Instead, spray cans of black shoe polish line the top shelf. The second shelf holds paint, brushes, stirring sticks, and—there it is. A box cutter. I put it in my pocket. Two walkie-talkies lay on the third shelf, next to a stack of black hats. Wait. Those aren't hats. They're hoods.

A pile of bulky straps lay on the cabinet's floor. I pick one up.

"That looks like an ankle bracelet," Tyler says. "Like what they use for house arrest."

My mother used to wear these. She once cut one off her leg. I remember it because she told me she used a coping saw. She said she was *coping* with her addiction. It wasn't funny. "Why do you think—"

"Leave it. Just go."

I head for the door.

"Wait." Cam grasps the bars. "Close the cabinet."

My heart races. My head spins. I'm not thinking clearly. I do need to cover my tracks. I close the cabinet and put the flashlight back on the workbench. I'm lucky Randall didn't notice it was missing before.

Outside, the wind has died, but the snow lives on. Trudging up the hill from the boathouse, I attempt to follow Randall's tracks, but the blizzard has obliterated them. I stick to the shadows, avoid the deck, and walk around the side of the cabin. Cam's car sits next to a stack of firewood, like he said. There must be enough wood here for two winters. It's heaped haphazardly beneath a makeshift shed—thin poles bent beneath a ragged blue tarp. The snow is about to bring the whole thing down.

The snowmobile sits half protected by the tarp. I brush snow off the seat and get on. The engine will be noisy, so once I start it, I've got to get the hell out of here.

My hands are numb.

The seat is wet.

There's no key in the ignition.

Dammit.

There's no key in the little glove compartment.

There's no key.

Cam lied.

"I need you to get off the snowmobile now, Miss Highsmith." Randall's commanding voice chills the air. "Oh, wait. I'm sorry. Cam said you like to be called *Charly*."

I freeze. I'm afraid to move. I'm afraid to turn and look at him.

"Charly. Please, get off the snowmobile."

Fight or flight? I've got the box cutter, but he's big. Worse, he's psychotic. Worse than that, he's got a gun in his pocket.

"Charly?"

I turn and face him.

"Don't be scared," he says. "What are you doing out here? You promised to stay in the cabin."

"I just wanted to look around."

"Is that so?" He takes a step forward. "Are you sure that's all you wanted to do? You know, it's after midnight." He raises his hand. Motions toward the cabin. "Come inside, now. You must be freezing."

"No."

"Okay, well, I'm freezing, and I've had enough of your lies. Why is it I can't trust anyone?" He wipes his face. "It's to be expected, I suppose. You promised to stay in the cabin, and you didn't. You told me you didn't see anything in the boathouse, yet you snuck out there just now. Why would you do that?"

"I didn't go there. Honest."

"Ah, but you did." He waves his hand. "I watched you walk up the hill."

He's got me. Maybe. "Okay, you're right. I was down by the lake, but I didn't go into the boathouse. I don't know anything about your top secret project."

He wraps his arms around himself and squeezes. "It's freezing out here. Let's go inside and talk about it."

"Go ahead. I'll be there in a minute."

He lowers his arms.

He lowers his chin.

He pierces me with his eyes.

"That's not good enough, Miss Highsmith." He reaches into his pocket. "I must insist you come with me now."

"No, thanks." I can't take my eyes off his pocket.

"That wasn't a request. It was an order."

I shiver.

Snow gathers on my jeans.

I put my hand in my pocket.

He nods toward the cabin.

I wrap my fingers around the box cutter.

CHAPTER THIRTY-NINE

CHARLY - THEN

I lost.

It was unbelievable, but . . . I lost. Amanda ran ahead of us, parading the raccoon tail for all the forest creatures to see. For my dad to see. When we exited the trees and crossed the lawn, Dad stood on the deck, cheering Amanda on.

Where had he been?

He'd promised to help me win.

I slowed to a walk, suddenly aware of my aching legs. I'd been running through the woods for over two hours. Searching for clues. Checking on Jacob. Searching for the raccoon tail.

All for nothing.

I lost.

Amanda skipped up the deck steps, gleefully ascending to her victory.

Jacob ran to catch up with her.

"Congratulations, Amanda." Dad handed her an envelope at the top. "You did great. Hurry up, everyone. Let's all sit at the table while Amanda opens her award."

Last in line, last in life, I followed Cam up the steps.

"I thought the prize *was* the raccoon tail," Cam said.

Dad placed his hand on Cam's chest, stopping him at the top. "It is. Amanda gets to keep the tail, too." He held out his hand. "I know you took the knife from the boathouse again. Can I have it, please?"

Cam lowered his chin and pulled out the knife. Slowly, he placed it in Dad's palm.

"We'll talk about this later, Cameron."

We sat at the picnic table, and Dad stood at the end like a sea captain addressing his crew. "Wait, Amanda. Don't open the envelope yet. I want to say a few words." I rolled my eyes, and dark clouds rolled across the sky. "While everyone made a valiant effort, Amanda's preparation ultimately brought her victory. Her map made her routes through the forest efficient, and she rarely left the trails. Cam, you spent most of your time off the trails, and Charly—you retraced your steps up and down the same paths, over and over, wasting precious time."

"I had to keep going back for Jacob because he couldn't keep up."

"How did you know I left the trail?" Cam asked.

"I was in the forest, making sure no one cheated."

So, that's where he'd been. Spying on us. He hadn't been at the cabin when I looked for him because he had lied to me.

He never planned on helping me.

My heart sunk.

It wasn't the first time he'd lied. And it wasn't the last.

"Can I open it now, Uncle John?" Amanda asked.

"Yes."

She grasped the envelope and tore it open without taking her eyes off me. The sound of the paper tearing made Jacob twitch, and when she pulled out the hundred-dollar bill, I twitched.

"That's too much," I said. "How can you give her so much?"

"It's all right, Care Bear." He smiled at me like everything was okay. "I'm going to be making more money soon, and I wanted to make this day memorable."

"That's a lot of money," Jacob said. "You have the tail, so you won. You always win, Amanda. You can buy a lot of games. You can buy six games for one hundred dollars. What are you going to buy?"

Cam sat upon his knees and leaned over the table toward Amanda. His eyes gleamed. "Can I have the raccoon tail?"

"No." Amanda laid the money on the table. "Jacob's right. The tail belongs to the winner."

"Right." Dad raised his hands. "Everyone, give the winner a round of applause. Congratulations, Amanda."

Cam slid back onto the bench and faked a clap. Jacob and Dad put their hands together, wildly celebrating. The sound was deafening. I felt a headache coming on. Amanda grinned. I wanted to throw up. She laid the tail on the table and stroked the fur. I wanted to shove it down her throat. Watch her gag and choke.

"Jacob," Amanda said, "you're right. The winner is the one with the tail, and guess what?"

"What?"

"You're a winner." She tossed the tail across the table.

Jacob caught it and sat up straight, grinning, holding the filthy thing in his hands.

"It's not fair," Cam complained.

"You're a fine one to talk." I lowered my voice. "Do you think the raccoon you caught thought what you did was fair?"

He turned red. "I didn't do anything."

"Enough," Dad said.

Cam slammed his hand on the table and narrowed his eyes at me. "You're just mad because you lost. If you'd helped me catch another raccoon, you would have won, but you wouldn't listen." He looked up at Dad. "You said whoever came back with a raccoon tail would win. It didn't have to be the same one. It would have counted."

"That's not quite right, Cameron." Dad rubbed his forehead.

"All you want to do is kill animals," I said. "You're a real creep."

"Enough." Dad's voice had thickened.

"But—"

"Enough, Charly."

Jacob gazed at the tail. I'd never seen him so happy. "It's okay, Charly. It's okay. I won. Amanda and I won. We're winners."

"We have to play again," I said. "We have to play again tomorrow. It wasn't fair. She cheated."

Dad walked around the corner of the table and stopped behind me. "We can't do that, Care Bear. The game is over. Maybe—"

"No. It wasn't fair."

"Yes, it was." Amanda unzipped her bag and put the money inside. "You never had a chance against me. You're just no good at games, Charly."

"Amanda always wins," Jacob said.

"Oh, yeah?" I turned around. "Please, Dad? Please? Jacob can help you set up the game for tomorrow. He can hide the raccoon tail and—"

"I don't know . . ." Dad put his hand on my shoulder. "If he hid the tail, he'd know where it was. Then he couldn't play."

Amanda stood. "Charly doesn't want him to play. She wants him to hide the tail and tell her where so she can cheat."

"That's not true."

"Then why don't you want him to play?"

I stood. Placed both hands on the table. Leaned toward Amanda. Her smug face. Her little bag with her money and her map. "Because he's too slow."

"I'm not slow." Jacob's lower lip quivered.

I immediately regretted what I'd said, but it was too late. "I didn't mean it that way."

"Charly." Dad took his hand off my shoulder and shook his head.

"You heard it," Amanda sneered. "She thinks he's slow. She thinks he's too stupid to win."

I slapped her. My palm burned as I withdrew my hand.

She hit me back, and I lunged over the table.

We tumbled onto the deck.

I pulled her hair, and my dad pulled me off her, but he didn't pull me far enough. He wasn't fast enough. I kicked, and my foot connected with her chin. Her head rocked back, and my other foot hit her in the throat.

She began to cough.

I hadn't meant to kick her so hard, but I didn't regret it. I wanted her dead.

"Stop it." Dad put me down and turned me around so my back was to Amanda.

Tears flooded my eyes when I realized what I'd done.

The clouds hit a breaking point.

Rain burst from the sky.

"I'm sorry, Care Bear, but I have to ground you for the rest of the weekend."

"What about her?"

Dad gazed at Amanda, then wiped the rain from his forehead. "I can't."

"Why?"

"You hit her first."

Unbelievable.

I turned the other way.

Jacob held the raccoon tail against his chest with both hands, protecting it from the rain like it was a baby.

The rest of us covered our heads.

"Amanda always wins," Jacob said. "I'm a winner, too. I have the ultimate prize. It's mine." He lowered his head and walked toward the french doors with heavy feet. "I'm not slow, Charly. I'm not slow."

CHAPTER FORTY

We didn't own a snowmobile growing up, but I'd ridden one plenty of times. Before the divorce, we took weekend trips to the mountains. One time, my mom and Jacob stayed home while Dad and I went with someone from his work. That trip has always stuck in my mind because I awoke early one morning to the sound of the snowmobiles starting. My dad and his coworker took off into the woods and returned just after the sun came up. He thought he could sneak away and return without me knowing, but he failed at that. At first, I panicked, then I waited. I wasn't used to being left alone at that point in my life. But, over time, I got used to it.

Especially after the divorce.

It's hard to see in the dark, but the snowmobile I'm sitting on has green stripes and a digital dash. The seat is as hard as ice. It's been a long time, but I know I could drive it if it would start. I should be miles from here by now, but Cam lied. He said the key was in the ignition, but it's not there.

"Miss Highsmith," Randall says. "It's cold out here. For the last time, come with me." He stands between me and the cabin. "Do you need help getting off the snowmobile?"

I shake my head.

He pulls his hand out of his right pocket. The one with the gun. He motions toward the porch. "Come. Now."

I tighten my grip on the box cutter. He's not the only one with a concealed weapon. If he makes one move, I'll cut him. "No, I'll come inside in a minute. I'm reminiscing about when my father used to take me on rides. You go ahead."

"We both know that's not going to happen." He steps forward. Offers me his hand. "Here, let me help you. I wouldn't want you to trip and fall in this snow."

"Okay," I lie.

"Good girl."

I lift my hand, but before he can grasp it, I slip off the seat and run in the other direction.

"Halt," he yells.

The snow catches my feet, and I almost fall as I slog down the driveway.

"Come back here."

The snowdrifts reach my waist. I change direction, but the snow is deep no matter which way I go. I pull it toward me like I'm swimming. I crawl on top of it, but my knees sink. I resort to lifting my knees ridiculously high and relying on gravity to pull me down the hill.

I tumble.

I fall down.

Randall's heavy hand comes down on my shoulder.

He's got me.

I roll onto my back and slash his thigh with the box cutter.

He screams. Covers his wound. "You whore. You stunted little whore."

I swing the knife again, but I miss.

He steps back, covering his wound. Blood—red-black blood in the dampened moonlight—runs through his fingers. He reaches into his pocket with his other hand, keeping his eyes glued to mine.

I sit up and lunge forward, knife first. The blade slices into his slacks. He jerks his hand out of his pocket and hits mine. The box cutter goes flying into the air. With all my strength, I grab his wrist and push him over.

He falls like a tree.

In an instant, I'm on him. I straddle his waist.

He reaches for my throat.

I reach back and punch his bloody thigh.

"Ahhh," he yells.

I punch him again, and my fist comes away soaked in blood.

"I'm going to kill you," he says.

I jam my hand into his pocket and feel for that gun, but it's not there.

He smacks me across the face.

I don't understand. I know he has a gun. He pulled it on Cam in the boathouse, and he put it in his right pocket after locking the cage. He put it in *this* pocket, but it's not there.

I thrust my hand in deeper and pull out a set of keys.

He grabs my elbow and throws me off him.

I tuck my elbows in and roll down the hill.

He shouts something I can't understand.

I get to my feet.

He comes bounding toward me with his arms outstretched, his hands ready to rip me apart. He's an avalanche coming down the mountain.

I duck and punch him in the thigh with everything I have.

He goes down.

I run back up the hill, his keyring in hand, heading for the snowmobile.

He yells something at me again, but I can't hear him over the blood pulsing in my head. The wind in my ears. My ragged breath burning my throat.

I reach the snowmobile and search the keyring for the snowmobile's key. It's got to be here. The first one is too big. Dammit. He's coming. I skip the next key because it's also too big. The wind changes direction and blows snow crystals into my eyes. Any second, he's going to come up behind me and—

I wipe my face off and slide the next key around the ring.

Too big.

He yells, and I look over my shoulder, down the drive, and there he is, clawing his way through the snow.

The next key fits.

The dash lights up. LCD. It's a nice machine, but the engine doesn't start.

"You're dead," he shouts.

I pull on the choke knob and try again. The engine roars then sputters, but it doesn't die this time.

"Stop."

I press on the gas and turn the handlebars, narrowly missing the firewood.

He steps in between me and the top of the driveway.

I hit the brakes and stop less than twenty feet before him.

Snow clings to his pant legs, pulling his slacks tight. His gray suit jacket has come unbuttoned, and his dress shirt is matted with snow in places. His neck is red, and he fumes behind his black beard. He holds his right hand out to his side like an Old West gunfighter.

I rev the engine. He's not going to stop me. I need to get to the road. To my car. To my cell phone.

He rocks his shoulder back and pulls out his gun. His magical gun. Where the hell was it when I needed it? When I searched his pocket?

He takes aim, and I hit the gas.

The gun goes off.

The snowmobile lurches forward.

His shot misses me, and he jumps out of my way.

I fly down the hill, standing on the runners. I lean hard and force the machine to turn onto what I think is the road. There's so much snow everywhere, and it's so dark. The headlight helps, but its beam is narrow. I can't see the road's edges without turning the handlebars.

I can't believe it.

I got away.

The snowmobile jumps and jerks, bursting over moguls built by the wind. Heavy snowdrifts burden the road. I accelerate. Jacob is sleeping upstairs in the cabin. I've got to get help and return to him before Randall does something horrible.

Before Randall locks him in that cage.

CHAPTER FORTY-ONE

RANDALL

Randall limps down the stairs into the basement. He remembers seeing Amanda go up to her room on the second floor while he and Cam—mostly Cam—drank earlier. But he can't be too careful. Miss Highsmith had a box cutter. Someone stole the carving knife. No one is to be trusted. Amanda might have come back down while he was outside. She could be in the basement right now, looking to persuade him to take her on a hunt. He already told her no, but she is persistent. Driven. Annoying.

She is an alpha female, but she's no match for him.

He checks the basement bedrooms before limping into the bathroom.

Blood drips from his thigh onto the white tiled floor.

Miss Highsmith had a box cutter.

The *prey* had a weapon, and it stabbed him.

He pulls a first aid kit from the vanity cabinet and sits on the toilet lid. He rips open his slacks. Exposes the wound. The pain is not bad. In fact, there are moments when the throbbing is pleasurable, but it's also unnecessary.

He should never have allowed the prey to stab him.

Worse—she got away.

His wound gushes with fresh blood, and a bubbling in his stomach threatens to turn into an eruption of partially digested steak and Scotch. He burps. Swallows. Places a bandage over the injury and tapes it in place. He looks away.

The prey had a box cutter.

She must have found it in the boathouse.

Someone messed up.

Big.

This location wasn't properly cleared after the last excursion. The organization is going to hear about this. Lance is going to lose his job, and—this is good. Randall can use this to his advantage. He will take over the organization. First, the carving knife in the kitchen. Then, the box cutter in the boathouse. When he takes over, this sort of thing will never happen again. He'll put a new policy in place, enforce it with an iron fist, and reap the rewards for his foresight. He will be rewarded.

He wiggles his fingers. They all work. His hand stopped bleeding while he was on his way to the cabin, and it doesn't need a bandage. Fortunately, his tendons weren't severed when he backhanded the box cutter out of that whore's hand.

That whore.

If she hadn't had that cutter, he'd have drawn and quartered her by now. It wasn't his fault. The fact is, he survived despite someone else's negligence. He survived because he is the fittest, but . . . maybe he is getting a little soft. He can't remember a time in recent history when he needed to worry about the prey attacking him.

No.

This was an anomaly.

Prey run.

Predators attack.

A small red spot appears on the bandage over his thigh. He watches it. It gets bigger. A blob of alcohol-laden bile creeps into his throat, and he swallows it back. The red spot grows, then slows, and stops. He puts a small bandage over it so he won't have to see it again.

He stands.

Tests his leg.

Pain shoots into his hip, then subsides. It only hurts when he moves.

Miss Highsmith couldn't have gotten far. The organization never leaves more than a gallon of gas in recreational vehicles for this very reason. Once, years ago, a crafty one somehow made it back and nearly escaped on a motorcycle. Randall put the one-gallon-of-gas policy in place. Without him, the organization would have gone out of business long ago.

With him as the leader, Zaroff Excursions will flourish.

But first, he's got to deal with this mess. The good news is, he doesn't have to worry about Miss Highsmith. She'll run out of gas and die in the cold. It's actually good she escaped. Less cleanup. But, the others . . .

Tyler—he's locked in the cage. He's as good as dead. Barry will have his hunt.

Cam—he's also locked in the cage, but it's against the rules to hunt more than one man at a time. Either Barry will need to pay for a second excursion, or Randall will need to find another client. Fast.

Jacob the moron—he is not quality prey. There's no point in locking him up with Tyler and Cam. It's best to kill him in his sleep.

Kennedy—she will leave with Barry after his hunt, unaware the others have gone missing.

Barry—he will have his excursion and discreetly tell his important friends. Randall will sell excursions to several highly motivated, wealthy snob-boys at twice the regular fee. The board will love him. They will oust Lance, making Randall the leader of the organization. It's long overdue.

Amanda—she must be sleeping upstairs. It's after two in the morning. If she wakes up, she'll wonder where Cam has gone. They were sharing the room. Randall doesn't have much time. She needs to die right after he takes care of Jacob the moron.

He ascends the basement stairs, closes the door, and ignores the pain in his leg as he rushes to the second floor. He switches on the hall light and listens. Jacob and Miss Highsmith's room lies across the hall from Kennedy and Barry's. Randall's room is farther down, across from the bathroom. The master suite is farther yet, facing the windows above the awning. Amanda insisted on sleeping in the nicest room, and now she'll pay for it.

He cracks open Jacob's door. On impulse, he reaches into his pocket, opens the slit in his slacks, and grips his pistol but—no. A gunshot would be too loud. He pulls his hand out.

He'll have to smother the moron.

Light creeps into the room, exposing a path to Jacob's bed.

Randall's palms tingle with excitement.

Hunters can move without making a sound, and Randall is a hunter. He's the best.

He crosses the floor.

Slowly, he pulls the blanket off a pillow. He picks the pillow up and pulls the blanket off Jacob, but—it's not Jacob.

It's another pillow.

He pulls all the blankets off. Throws them on the floor. Drops the pillow. Rushes to the other side of the bed and looks beneath it.

Jacob isn't here.

The moron must have left while Randall was outside with Miss Highsmith.

Randall goes to the window. Looks out.

The moron escaped, but he won't last long. Not in those unforgiving woods. Not in those frigid temperatures.

Randall has nothing to worry about.

Mother Nature will dispose of Jacob for him.

CHAPTER FORTY-TWO

CHARLY

My neck muscles ache. I strain to keep my chin up, my head down, and my face behind the snowmobile's windshield. The snowy road winds down the mountain. The windburn on my forehead is tremendous, but I don't dare slow down. Randall could be on his way after me right now. All he needed to do was get his hands on the keys to Barry's Humvee. That is, assuming I have the only snowmobile.

Either way, I hope he's coming after me.

I hope he isn't doing something to Jacob.

When I left our room, Jacob was sleeping soundly, unaware of who and what Randall Thorne was. He sensed from the beginning that Randall was evil, but he didn't know about the cage.

I didn't know about the cage.

The terrifically horrible cage. The spray cans of black shoe polish. The black hoods. The ankle bracelets. Who is Randall Thorne? What are those things for? All I can think is he buys and sells humans. Human trafficking. But to what end?

The road bends, and I lean hard into the turn to keep from sliding off the mountain.

If it's not human trafficking, then maybe Randall is a simple murderer. A patient murderer. One who lures people into the mountains with the promise of an unbelievable adventure, then locks them in a cage. He plays with them like a cat, torturing them with the hoods and ankle bracelets. Then he kills them.

The low-fuel light flashes.

As much as I don't want to, I slow down. My car must be around one of these corners. It's been about half an hour since I left Randall bleeding on that hill. It's been an eternity since I left my car. I can't see either side of the road. It's only when I turn the handlebars that the headlight illuminates the sides, and I nearly crash every time I take a look.

I hope I didn't miss the car.

I slow down more, and my face thanks me. I sit up, and my neck thanks me. My cheeks burn with that strange, cold-hot feeling common in sub-zero temperatures. I slow down even more and tuck a hand between my legs.

The headlight catches something on the side of the road.

I hit the brakes.

Thank God. It's my car. It's a miracle. The blizzard buried every part except the driver's side windows. I jump off and leave the snowmobile running with the headlight on so I can see.

My pink fingers appear as if they're about to crack.

I pull my sleeves over my hands and dig, occasionally glancing back the way I came.

Randall's coming for me. I can feel it.

When I've cleared the snow from the bottom of the driver's door, I open it a few inches and slip inside. My socks are soaked, and my feet feel like they will rot away soon, but it's good to be out of the wind. What a relief. I'm alive, but my phone is dead. I plug it into the charger and try to start my car. The lights come on, and the phone begins to charge, but the engine won't turn over.

What was that?

The back window turns yellow.

Headlights approach.

I grip the steering wheel for no reason. I'm not going anywhere. I'm trapped. I turn the key again and again. The engine whines and moans, but it won't come alive.

The *chug-chug* of the approaching car gets louder.

Desperate, I search the glove compartment for something to protect myself with. Why didn't I pick up the box cutter when I had the chance? My glove compartment is almost empty. I don't even have pepper spray.

The vehicle's headlights reflect in the side mirror, momentarily blinding me.

The *chug-chug* stops.

A car door slams.

I duck down. Attempt to hide beneath the dashboard.

Tap, tap, tap.

I hold perfectly still. If it's Randall, he's here to kill me. If it's a stranger, they can wait. I need time for my phone to charge so I can call for help.

Louder now—*tap, tap, tap.* They're going to break the glass.

If it was Randall, he would have broken the glass by now. He would have pulled his gun and shot me in the head.

"Hey, open up."

It's useless. They know I'm in here. They can see my breath.

Slowly, I sit up and pretend to look for something on the floor.

My phone is at one percent.

Tap, tap, tap.

I crack the window.

A man in a denim sheepskin jacket peers inside. His jacket hugs his round shoulders and cradles his thick neck. His collar covers his ears. Dark brown eyes, a wide nose, and a double chin. "Hey, looks like you got caught in the blizzard. How long you been here?"

CHAPTER FORTY-THREE

Randall will not allow the moron's disappearance to deter him. If Jacob Highsmith left the cabin, he can die of hypothermia along with his sister. There's no time to look for him now. Randall has a new plan. He has adapted.

The plan is simple.

Kill everyone except Barry and Kennedy.

Then, take over Zaroff Excursions.

Nice and simple.

Ah, but it's not quite that simple.

It could be . . . but why not jumpstart his ascension to greatness with some extra cash? Amanda offered to pay him an extra twenty percent on the side for her own excursion. After she's satisfied, he can collect payment and take her on another excursion. Just him and her. The mongoose will eat the snake, and the jackal will eat the mongoose. It's the natural order of things.

He rushes down the hall, barely limping. Already, his leg feels better. He's so strong. He ducks into his room and puts on a clean pair of slacks. No one ever needs to know the prey stabbed him. That Highsmith whore. No one ever needs to know she got away.

He gently knocks on Amanda's door. "Amanda."

Nothing.

He knocks again . . . and again, nothing.

If Amanda is not here, if she took off with Jacob, if Barry and Kennedy took them in his SUV . . . Randall knocks louder. He wipes his face. He's sweating. It doesn't make sense. He only drank two shots with Cam, but his hand smells like liquor and—*ugh*. Blood. It smells like blood. No wonder he's becoming anxious. Paranoid. Sweaty.

The prey stabbed him, and now he smells like blood.

"What do you want?" Amanda calls from deep in the room.

He opens the door. "I want to offer you an experience you'll never forget." He enters. Remembering the carving knife, he stops short of her bed. It's not safe to get too close.

She switches on the bedside lamp and sits up, not bothering to pull the blanket over her chest. Over her silky green negligee. Her breasts. "I knew you'd see it my way."

"Don't patronize me. It's unbecoming."

"I didn't think you had the resources to take me on an excursion."

"I don't, but things have changed."

She combs her fingers through her raven hair, letting it fall to her side. Letting it come to rest over her left breast. "Is that so?"

"This isn't a done deal. I'm only here to make you an offer. There are conditions."

"Shoot."

"First, you must follow the rules to the letter. We allow one hunter at a time. Therefore, you mustn't tell anyone in this cabin about this, and you're not going with Barry, so don't ask. Second, after your hunt, you mustn't approach the prey. Our services include field dressing and carcass disposal. You'll receive your trophy later. And third—"

"What about pictures?"

"Absolutely no pictures. You'll leave your cell phone in the cabin."

She pouts.

"And third, we leave in an hour."

"An hour?" She glances at the window. "It won't be light out."

"It will be by the time we reach the starting point. From there, you'll have four hours to prove you're a hunter before we return. That is, assuming you remember your weapons training from your first excursion. I don't have time to teach you today."

"I remember it."

"Okay, then. Payment. You offered to pay the regular fee plus twenty percent to me. You'll pay both as soon as we find an internet signal after the hunt. I prefer Venmo. The payment is not contingent on whether your hunt is successful or not. Do you understand?"

She averts her eyes. "I do."

"And, you'll leave immediately afterward, so we need to put your things in your car before we go."

"Okay, but I still can't be ready in an hour." She bends her knee, and the blanket slides off her leg, exposing her thigh. She trails her finger over her hip. "Wouldn't you rather hunt later in the day?"

"No. We don't have time for that. It's already unorthodox for me to conduct two excursions in a single day. I'm making Barry wait until later. So, either you and I leave in an hour, or—"

"Or what?"

"Or, you leave now."

She glances at the door. "Where's Cam?"

"He drank too much and passed out downstairs. I left him in a bedroom in the basement."

"We came together." She covers herself up. "If we leave now, you'll have to help me get him to the car."

"This is your last chance. If you can't be ready in an hour, you'll miss your chance. Is that what you want?"

"No."

Randall takes a step forward. "Then what's it going to be?"

"Why are you limping?"

"My leg fell asleep." He puts his hand in his pocket. Slips his fingers through the slit. "What's it going to be?"

"Fine. I'll get ready."

"Excellent." He turns toward the door. "Wear something warm. It's hostile outside."

CHAPTER FORTY-FOUR

I'm sitting in the driver's seat of my front-wheel-drive Ford Focus, shivering. The entire passenger side is buried under three feet of snow. The burly man in the denim coat outside my window will not leave. I've tried waving him off, but he keeps asking if I need his help. I don't trust him. He keeps asking why I drove a snowmobile out here in the middle of the night, and I won't tell him. I don't need his help. I need to charge my phone and take the snowmobile down the mountain to where I can get a signal.

Suddenly, my car's lights dim, then shut off. The battery is dead. I grab my phone, but the screen is too dark to read. It's in battery-saving mode. I hold it up to the driver's side window, hoping to use the light from the snowmobile, but the man's body blocks it. His face is cast in darkness. I lean forward and squint at my phone. It has one percent left, and now that my car is dead, it has stopped charging. I turn the key in the ignition, something under the hood clicks, the dash lights flicker, and panic sets in.

I need to calm down.

I turn the key again and again until the lights won't come on at all.

The car battery is completely dead now.

The snowmobile's headlight shuts off.

It was low on gas, but I thought it would idle longer without running out. I thought I'd have enough gas to make it farther down the mountain.

Reality sets in.

I'm dead if I stay here.

I *do* need the man's help.

"Open up, missy. Let me help you." The man's breath casts a cloud on the glass.

"Hold on." I open the door against the snow as far as I can and squeeze out of the car.

"Why'd you shut it off?" He takes a step back. "You should keep the heat on."

"Could you give me a jump?" He glances at my waist. "My battery is dead."

"I don't think so, but even if I could, you ain't going nowhere. You're snowed in." He's wearing a pair of tan leather work gloves and a black Colorado Rockies ski hat. He talks like a local. A Colorado mountain man. He pulls his hat farther over his ears and rubs his hands together. "It's too stinking cold out here. C'mon. It's warm in my truck."

The diesel smell melts the ice crystals in my nose. "Could you tow me? I really need to get to a town."

He looks at the sky. "What are you doing out here in the middle of the night, anyway?"

I don't have time to explain Randall. Describing the cage and the fight—how I stabbed him in the leg—would only lead to questions. I've got to get back to Jacob. "My brother. He's sick. I came to call for help, but my phone's dead."

"Where is he?"

"He's back at our cabin."

"So, you come out here on that snowmobile?"

"Yes."

"If it was such an emergency, why'd you stop? Why didn't you take that thing into town?"

"It was low on of gas, and my phone was in my car. Do you have a phone?"

"Nah, but I got a radio in the truck. C'mon."

"How about a phone charger?"

"Why would I have a phone charger if I ain't got a phone?" He strides to the driver's side of his truck and shouts over the hood, "You coming?"

"I only need to use your radio. I'm going to stay here until help comes, okay?" The wind whips my face with snow.

"Okay, but if no one answers the radio, I can't leave you here." He opens his door, and the dome light comes on. He's a large man, probably in his forties, but he has a round, boyish face.

I open my door and step up on the running board. The cabin smells like the inside of a dance club. A desperate blend of body spray and perspiration. I hop inside. The hot air flowing through the vents feels good on my hands, but my fingertips burn. My cheeks feel rosy at first, then they burn. Thawing out hurts.

He climbs inside, closes his door, and hits the power locks.

"Why'd you do that?" I ask.

"What?"

"Lock the doors."

"Sorry, it's just a habit, I reckon." He puts the truck in drive. "Hold on, now."

"Wait." I put my hands on the dashboard. "I only wanted to use the radio."

"It's right there." He guns the accelerator. "You can try, but nobody's going to pick up this time of night."

I grab the receiver and press the button. "Hello?"

The speakers squawk.

"Hello? Hello?" Snow streams over the hood. We pass the snowmobile. "Stop."

"No can do. We gotta get out of here before the snow gets worse. Look at how it's coming down."

"Where are we going?"

"I got a place up the road. Maybe your phone will work when we get there."

"My phone." There's nothing but a snow cloud in the side-view mirror. I can't see my car. "I left it. We need to go back."

"Sorry, no can do."

"My luggage is back there, too. Please?"

"We can come back at sun-up, that is, if it stops snowing. I ain't stopping now. I don't want to get stuck like you did."

A chill hits me. I rub the backs of my arms. "I wouldn't have left my phone if I'd known you were going to take off like this."

"Don't fret. It's going to be okay," he says. "I don't bite."

I wonder.

"What's your name?" he asks.

"Charly."

"Mine's Hector. Nice to make your acquaintance."

"Yeah. Thanks."

"How sick is your brother?"

I picture Randall entering our bedroom back at the cabin. He pulls his gun and aims it at Jacob's head. "Sick. He's very sick."

"Well, us getting stuck out here and freezing to death ain't gonna help him. Let's go to my place and see if we can call someone from there. Got one of them old landline phones in the kitchen."

Hector accelerates around a bend. The snow blocks the truck's headlights and streams over the hood. The clouds block the moon's glow. The sky is black. Hector's face glows in the dashboard light. His broad nose. His double chin. His eyes focused on the road.

A new blizzard has officially begun.

"How long you been up here?" he asks.

"What do you mean?"

"You don't live up here, do you? I think I would have seen you around before."

"No. We're here on vacation."

"So, when did you come up?"

"Yesterday."

"Well, you picked a hell of a time." He powers over a hill.

As we descend the other side, I glimpse snowmobile tracks along the road's edge. Unless Randall had another snowmobile, they must be my tracks. No one else would have been out here after three in the morning.

"We used to get snowed on like this every year, especially when I was younger. Now it only happens once or twice a year. Ain't that crazy?"

"What's your house like? I mean, is there a room for me?"

"Yeah, don't fret none." He slows down. Turns off the road onto a driveway. "I got several guest bedrooms." He presses on the accelerator, and we climb up a short hill.

The cabin—my cabin—looks down upon us.

I put my hand on his shoulder. "Wait. Stop."

"What's the matter?"

I need to warn him. "That's your house?"

"Yep. Has been for years."

"When was the last time you were here?"

"A few days ago. Why?"

I can't let Randall lock him in the cage with Tyler and Cam. "Stop."

"No can do."

I squeeze his shoulder. "You have to."

He presses on the accelerator. "If we stop on this hill, we'll get stuck for sure."

"It doesn't matter. You've got to stop the truck."

"No, I don't." The engine roars.

"You don't understand," I yell. "See those cars? Someone else is here."

The light comes on over the front porch.

Randall.

"Stop," I scream. "There's a man here. He's locking people in cages. You—"

"Oh, so you know about that." He spins the wheel, guiding the truck toward Cam's car.

Everything collapses around me. The blizzard has plowed its way into my heart. I freeze from the inside out. Ice cold blood courses through my veins, making every movement slow. Painfully slow. I try the door, but it's locked. I jerk on the handle until I think it's going to break. I hit the power lock, but nothing happens. The child locks are on.

I grab the steering wheel, and the truck swerves.

He hits the brakes, and we slide to a stop in front of the cabin.

As if I were an annoying black fly, he backhands me and pulls a gun out of his jacket. "I was hoping we wouldn't have to do it this way."

Blood trickles down my cheek. He's cut me. I hadn't noticed his pinky ring before and—his accent. His Colorado mountain man accent.

It's gone.

"Open the glove compartment, please." He points the gun at my head.

I do as he says.

"Good. Now take out that zip tie and place your wrists through it."

A silhouette crosses the porch and steps in front of the truck's headlights.

The falling snow—a crystalline curtain swept by the wind—obscures the figure.

"Fasten the tie, missy."

Randall emerges from the gale and stands before us.

"Hurry." Hector presses the muzzle of the gun against my cheek.

Blood seeps into my mouth.

I bind my wrists together while Randall watches.

CHAPTER FORTY-FIVE

CHARLY - THEN

An hour after it had started, the afternoon rain stopped. The sun shooed the clouds away and centered itself in the sky. Everyone ran out of the cabin and headed for the lake.

Everyone except for me.

Amanda wore a green swimsuit that made her look like a fat frog.

Cam and Jacob wore swim trunks. Neither took his shirt off.

Jacob cast his eyes down when he ran by me. He was still angry that I'd called him slow. Amanda ignored me, too, because of our fight. She pranced past me as if I didn't exist. I hung my legs over the deck and opened a crummy coloring book. There was nothing else to do here. I missed my paints. Grounded for the weekend, I opened the book and watched the others from above.

Amanda laughed as she charged into the lake, turned, and splashed Cam.

It wasn't fair.

I was too old to color. Dinosaurs and Friends. A T-Rex

and a pterodactyl smiled at each other on the cover. It was ridiculous. I wanted to do real art. I wished I'd brought my paint set from home. I wished I could go into the basement and paint on the walls with real paint and real brushes.

Alone.

I took out a black crayon and doodled on the edges. Amanda's black hair. Her black eyes. Her black heart. My drawing was good, but it needed something else. I found a red crayon and drew horns on her head.

The breeze carried Jacob's laughter onto the deck. I couldn't understand why he liked her. Why did anyone like her? She was always so rotten. I mashed the crayon into the page—into her face—and it broke in my hand.

Jacob tentatively stepped into the lake, bent over, and scooped water toward Amanda, attempting to splash her, but she was too far away. They giggled. He liked her and hated me. I hadn't meant to call him slow, but it *was* his fault. I could have won the game if it hadn't been for him.

I found another red crayon and put an "X" through Amanda's face.

The doors creaked behind me. "What are you drawing?"

"Nothing." I turned the page before Dad could see it.

He sat next to me and dangled his legs off the deck. "Are you okay?"

I said nothing.

"Sorry. That was a stupid question." He looked over the property, beyond the lawn. Beyond the lake. "I didn't want to ground you, but you can't start fights like that."

I picked up a purple crayon and began coloring a dinosaur.

"Care Bear?"

It was a stegosaurus. The one with fins on its back. I

traced the black lines with the crayon, then filled in its body.

"Okay," he said. "You don't have to talk. I came out here to tell you my new job is starting sooner than I thought."

I switched to a yellow crayon.

"They want me to—"

"I'm not mad about losing," I said.

"You're not?"

"No." I filled in the dinosaur's fins, shading each one differently. Light yellow. Dark yellow. Half and half.

"What is it then?"

"I'm mad at you for lying. You said you'd help me win, but you didn't."

"What do you mean?"

"You promised." I colored the dinosaur's face red. "You said you'd help me, but when I came for help, you weren't here. You let Amanda win."

"No, I didn't. I—"

"Yes, you did."

"No, I . . . I didn't know how important it was to you."

"But, you promised."

"Hmm." He pinched his chin. "I remember saying I'd help if Amanda did something wrong, and she didn't."

"Yes, she did. She cheated. She kept the notes to herself."

"That wasn't against the rules."

I closed the coloring book and stood.

He grasped my wrist. "Please, Care Bear. I'm sorry."

"You were supposed to give me a hint or something." I shook my arm, but he wouldn't let go.

"Please, sit down."

"Why does she get everything? Why did you give her all that money? Do you like her more than me?"

"Of course not. Let me explain." His grasp was firm. He

wasn't letting go until I sat, and I didn't want to leave.

I wanted to hurt him.

I wanted to make him feel like I felt, but I didn't know how.

"Listen," he said, "you can't go through life comparing yourself to other people. It will only make you miserable. Does that make sense?"

"No."

The french doors groaned.

He let go of my arm.

My mom stood there, leaning against the door frame, a glass of wine in her hand. "Dinner will be ready soon." Her voice sounded like mud. "Will you call the kids in?"

"Why doesn't it make sense?" Dad asked.

"John, did you hear me?"

"I heard you."

She leaned to her right, then stepped out of sight, heading toward the kitchen.

Dad stood and put his hand on my shoulder. "You can't go through life hating the Amandas of the world. It will only cause you pain."

"Why can't we play the game again? I want another chance."

"It's too late."

"How about tomorrow?"

"No."

"Why?"

"Because I'm leaving tonight."

"Huh? What?"

"For work. I'm leaving for—remember what we talked about in the canoe?"

"When are you coming back? When are we coming back

here?"

"I don't think we'll be coming back this summer."

"Why not?"

He lowered his gaze. "I'm going away for work, and I'll be gone a lot, but I promise I'll be back for your birthday."

My birthday wasn't for three months. I'd been planning it all summer. "But—"

"It's time for dinner," Mom shouted from inside the cabin. "John, did you call the kids?"

His neck reddened, and he yelled, "In a minute."

Jacob came up the stairs. "Were you calling me? I was swimming. Not swimming. I was walking in the water because it was too cold, and I don't know how to swim."

"Go inside and tell your mother we'll be there in a minute." Dad turned, put his hands on the railing, and yelled, "Amanda. Cameron. Come inside. It's time for dinner."

Beyond the lake, beyond my dad, the ink-blue horizon cradled the mountains. He turned toward me, and he towered over me, and that was the moment. I didn't know it at the time, but that was the moment he became an effigy of deceit. A pillar of dishonesty. A coloring book filled with blank pages. Extinct dinosaurs. "I promise, Care Bear. I'll come back as soon as I can."

I put the coloring book and the crayons back in the closet.

We ate dinner.

He packed his bags.

He hugged me goodbye.

I was only ten years old.

I went to bed and fell asleep.

He haunted my dreams that night, his ghost promising he would come back as soon as he could.

But, he never did.

CHAPTER FORTY-SIX

CHARLY

Hector jerks me out of his truck. He pulls on my zip tie. My wrists twist and burn. I shouldn't have put it on so tight, but he'd watched so closely. Never blinking his bulbous brown eyes. Randall had also watched, glaring at me through the windshield.

Hector pulls me toward the cabin.

I stumble over the snow.

Randall raises his hands. "What are you doing here, Hector?"

"I'm saving your ass." Hector pulls me between them. "Look what I found."

The cabin's lights are on upstairs.

Amanda's room.

I don't know why she'd be awake this early. The sun's not even up yet, but maybe she can hear us. I open my mouth, and Randall slaps me hard. "Shut your mouth. We'll have none of that." Blood trickles down my cheek. Randall has reopened the wound Hector gave me with his pinky ring. It tastes bitter.

"Let's get her inside," Hector says. "I'm freezing."

"No, not in there. This way." Randall heads around the corner. "We'll put her with the others."

Hector pulls me.

The zip tie cuts into my wrists.

I'm a cow headed for the slaughterhouse. My face stings. My feet ache. The falling snow is relentless. Another inch has come down in the last five minutes.

There is no escape.

Randall leads us toward the boathouse. Toward the cage. He favors his left leg every few steps. The cut I gave him didn't go as deep as I'd hoped. "Allow me to ask again, what the hell are you doing here, Hector?"

"You know why I'm here. *He* sent me."

"Everything is under control."

"Is that so?"

"Yes."

"Then why did I find her with a snowmobile halfway to civilization?" He jerks on my zip tie again. The plastic pinches. "Those cars out front. How many others are you letting run around rampant?"

"There's only three. Or four, and I'm not letting them run around. Everything is under control."

"Bullshit. You've really screwed the pooch on this one."

"You oughtn't talk to me that way."

"Don't get all high and mighty."

"I—"

"You know what your problem is, Randall? You think you're better than everyone else." Randall stops suddenly, and I bump into Hector. He's like a wall. A big fat wall. "Lance was right about you."

Randall turns around. His eyes blaze. The snowflakes

landing on his beard get lost in the tangle. "What does Lance say about me?"

"Ask him yourself." Hector gazes upward, curling the corners of his mouth. "He'll be here soon."

"What? Why?"

"Because he had a feeling you screwed up, and he was right. This location wasn't supposed to be used for another three months."

"I didn't screw up. He did. He's running this organization into the ground. This place wasn't properly cleaned after the last excursion. Weapons were left out. She found a knife and—"

"You let her escape," Hector yells. "The location wasn't cleaned because no one was supposed to be here."

"When is he arriving?"

"As soon as he can. He got stuck in Texas, so he sent me. You know, I was supposed to be on vacation. I had to fly into Denver from Cincinnati, and First Class was taken. Do you know what they give you to eat in coach?" Randall begins to open his mouth. "Pretzels. All they give you is pretzels." Hector shakes his head. "You asshole. You've really done it this time."

"I told you. Everything is under control. Once we lock her up, you may leave."

"No way. I'm a part of this now, whether you like it or not. You know how he is. I'm not going to let him blame me for what you've done. How many did you say are here? Three? Four? We've got to get rid of them before he arrives."

"I already have a plan." Randall gazes at me. "I don't need your help."

"Is that the place over there?" He gestures toward the boathouse and pulls on my wrists.

A sharp pain shoots up my arm.

"Yes," Randall says.

Hector pulls me past Randall, and we descend the hill.

Randall opens the door to the boathouse and flips on the light.

Tyler sits slumped in the far corner of the cage, and Cam jumps to his feet, pulling the blanket they were sharing with him.

"Are you okay?" I ask.

Tyler looks up. His face is bruised black and green. He was sleeping, or . . . he was dying.

"Shut up." Hector pulls on my zip tie. Slings me toward the cage door.

My body bangs against the bars, and Cam drops the blanket. He steps near me. The whiskey hasn't left his breath.

Tyler leans forward and grabs the blanket. Pulls it over himself. Coughs.

"Is he okay?" I whisper to Cam.

"I said, shut up." Hector pulls his gun out. Points it at me.

Randall shuts the door and takes out his cell phone.

Tyler moans.

I glare at Randall. At Hector. They're going to pay for this. I'm not running away again. I'm not going to leave Jacob again. When I escape—and I will escape—I'm getting even. Randall and Hector will spend the rest of their lives in this cage, if I don't kill them first.

The electronic padlock on the cage door clicks and drops open. Randall puts his phone back in his pocket. All I need is a way to remove that lock after they leave. I need Randall's phone, but the chances of getting it are incredibly slim. Between the three of us—Cam, Tyler, and myself—we ought to be able to get out of here if they leave us alone. But they might not. This might be it. Maybe they're here to kill us.

My stomach knots up at the thought, and my shoulders tense. I lower my chin and close my eyes. I will not let them kill us.

I will not let them kill us.

Hector waves his gun at Cam. "Back away from the door."

Cam complies.

Randall removes the lock and opens the door.

Hector stows his gun and shoves me inside.

Randall locks the lock.

I kneel next to Tyler. "Are you okay?"

Tyler nods.

"*Are you okay?*" Randall mocks me. "*Are you okay? Are you okay?*"

Hector grins.

"Of course, he's okay," Randall says. "He's faking it."

"No, he's not," I say.

Randall rolls his eyes.

"Now what?" Hector asks him, blinking.

"Now, you can be on your way." Randall gestures toward the door.

"I'm not leaving. You need help. Just look at this mess."

I put my hand on Tyler's forehead. He has a fever. "He's sick."

"Shut up." Hector's double chin shakes.

"He's a drunk with a hangover," Randall mutters. "That's not a fever. It's withdrawal. He's faking everything."

Cam rushes the bars. "You can't do this. When are you letting us out?"

"It won't be long." Randall puts his shoulders back. Shoots his cuffs.

"It better not be," Hector says. "We don't have much time before Lance arrives."

"When did you talk to him last?" Randall asks.

"A few hours ago."

"And he was in Texas?"

"Yes."

"Then we should have all day." He turns away toward the door. "That's enough time."

"What are you going to do with us?" Cam shakes the bars. "Are you going to kill us? Is that it?"

I go to his side. "Wait."

Randall opens the door to the boathouse. A snow flurry spins over the threshold.

"I'm exhausted," Hector says.

"Fine. You can stay." Leaving the door open to the storm, Randall strides across the room and opens the cabinet. "You can sleep in one of the rooms in the basement, but you've got to be quiet." He picks up the walkie-talkies and returns to Hector. "I don't want you to wake the others. Here, take this. You're going to need it later."

They step outside the boathouse.

"Stop," I scream, thrusting my hands through the bars. "Aren't you going to take these off? I can't feel my fingers."

They turn around and shake their heads.

Snow falls at an angle, gathering at their feet.

Randall reaches inside, flips the light switch, and closes the door.

It's cold in here.

Very, very cold.

CHAPTER FORTY-SEVEN

Randall waits on the front porch for Hector to go to his truck and retrieve his overnight bag. It was completely unnecessary for Lance to send Hector, but sometimes plans must change. Uninvited guests with box cutters and carving knives—plague, famine, disease—Lance . . .

Sometimes plans must change.

Now that Hector is here, he can use him to end this excursion. This miserable week. There's no shame in accepting help. Not when you're the one in charge. By the time Lance arrives later today or tomorrow, this location will be spotless. Randall will report his success to the board, and Lance will look like a fool for sending Hector. He'll look like a fool for coming to the cabin.

He'll look like a fool.

"Where am I sleeping?" Hector asks.

"Be quiet." Randall opens the door to the cabin and ushers Hector inside. "Go down to the basement."

Randall glances at the heavens before closing the door. Bring it on, Mother Nature. Your little blizzard isn't going to stop Randall. He has a plan. He's the best.

They descend the stairs.

Hector lugs his bag into the basement.

It's quiet down here.

Randall checks the first door on the right. The bedroom is empty. He checks the other bedroom. It's empty too. "You can take this one."

Hector plops his overnight bag onto the bed. "I'm getting sick of this shit. I shouldn't have had to come here. I was on vacation."

If Randall was as heavy and out of shape as Hector, he'd feel the same. Hector isn't fit enough to survive. Not like he used to be. "Then you shouldn't have come."

"I had no choice. But this"—he makes eye contact with Randall—"this is the last straw. After this, I'm through."

"That's your decision." Worm bait. To quit is to die. "But, I want you to know, it's not my fault you're here. Lance insisted I make quota by conducting an excursion before the end of the year. He sent me to this location. I don't know why he told you we weren't using it anymore."

"You fucking moron."

"Watch your language."

"He didn't send you here. He sent you to the other place. The one out East, past Denver."

"No. He sent me to this cabin."

"No. He sent you to the cabin *in the plains*. Why would he send you up here in the middle of winter?"

"Because this place has never been empty over the holidays."

"You know what your problem is? You don't listen anymore. The cabin out East is the new hotness." He unzips his bag. "Yeah, you've worked here forever, but things change. You need to learn to adapt."

Randall's blood boils. "And you need to learn to shut your mouth." Hector is right, though. Things are changing. In fact, Hector has no idea how much things are changing. He wants out of Zaroff Excursions? So be it. "I *have* adapted. Your coming here has changed everything. It's given me an idea for a new plan."

"Please. Do share." He pulls a pair of pajamas out of his bag and tosses them on the bed.

Homer Simpson adorns his pajama bottoms.

How fitting.

Fat slob.

"Tell me," Randall says, "what else did Lance tell you about this excursion?"

"He said you sold it to some rich kid."

"Right. I need you to take that rich kid hunting."

"What?" Hector puts his shoulders back. Lifts his chin. "I don't do hunts anymore."

"You said you'd help."

He takes his jacket off and pats the gun strapped to his side. "I said I'd help you clean up the mess you made. Nothing else."

"We're running a business here. You need to guide again. Did you bring a prep bag?"

"You know I don't do that anymore. Lance sent me to check on you and fix anything you broke, and you broke a lot."

"Did you bring a prep bag?"

"Yes, I think there's one in the back seat of my truck. I haven't touched it in over a year, so I don't even know if it's got everything not."

"Do you think it has the adrenaline in it?"

"Probably. I always carry one in case, but hold on. I'm not doing this. It's too late."

"How so?"

"How many of the others know about this rich kid's hunt? What did he tell them?"

"Nothing."

"I doubt that." Hector unbuckles his gun strap and lays the holster on the nightstand. "While you're conducting the excursion, I'll take care of the others. As soon as you return, you can send your client—what's his name?"

"Barry."

"Right. The Rockwell kid. You can send him on his way without letting him back inside the cabin. Then, you can help me with the bodies." He wipes his forehead and pulls the covers off the pillow. "God, what a mess."

"You don't understand. We have an opportunity to do so much more here. I just need you to take Barry hunting."

"What are you going to do while I'm out? Execute everyone? That's not your style. You're always taking them out, one at a time, traipsing through the woods like some goddamned Robin Hood. We don't have time for that."

"You're not entirely wrong, but I wouldn't put it that way if I were you."

"What are you going to do?"

"While you're with Barry, I'll be guiding another excursion."

"I knew it. You want to go traipsing through the woods—"

"It's true. I am a hunter, not a murderer. But it won't be like that. In any event, I'm not asking you. I'm telling you. You must be Barry's guide."

"No way." He shakes his head. "No. It's against the rules.

One hunt at a time. If Lance catches you—"

"Lance doesn't matter. If we do this, he's as good as gone. We'll show the board how much his leadership has cost the organization. He'll look like a fool. He's the one who made up the rule—"

"He made up all the rules, and he's not going anywhere. What the hell are you talking about?"

"Lance is a fool. Do this for me, and I'll make sure you have anything you want when I'm in charge."

"You?" He laughs. Puts his hand on his belly. "In charge?"

"Yes." Randall takes a step forward.

"You're delusional."

"And you lack vision."

"How about this." Hector points at the door. "We go upstairs, send everyone to their maker, take care of your caged friends, and then get the hell out of here."

"How about we sit tight until Lance arrives. Then we can all discuss what happened last summer."

Hector glances at the nightstand. He glances at his gun.

"Don't bother." Randall reaches into his pocket. Grasps his pistol. "Don't you think we can work this out? Don't you want to go on one more excursion?"

"Why Barry? Who are you taking?"

"Trust me. Barry is the easier of the two. The other one is a woman."

"How will we coordinate? How will we keep from accidentally shooting each other?"

Randall pulls the walkie-talkie he took from the boathouse off his belt. "Do you still have yours?"

"Yes."

"We'll report our location to each other during the hunt.

It'll be fine."

Hector sits on the edge of the bed. Puts his hands between his knees. Stares at the floor.

Randall relaxes. He's got him. He knows why Hector wants to quit. Last summer, Hector panicked. He had just finished guiding a woman lawyer on a successful excursion when she had a change of heart. After killing her prey, she was overcome with guilt. This often happens with women. They're so weak. She turned on Hector. He disarmed her. He took her gun away, but he couldn't take away her license to practice law. She broke the rules in the NDA. She threatened to sue the organization.

She threatened to sue *him*.

He panicked.

He shot her.

Hector was in the process of burying her body when Randall arrived for the next excursion. The problem was, she wasn't only a lawyer. She was Lance's lawyer and long-time friend. Randall backed Hector up a few weeks later when Rachel went "missing." Randall convinced Lance there was no sign of Rachel or any deviance from standard Zaroff practices when he met up with Hector that day.

Then, he promised Hector he would never say a word.

But, things change. It's not too late to anonymously tip Lance off to the location of Rachel's shallow grave.

It's not Randall who needs to adapt.

It's Hector.

"A woman?" Hector asks.

"Yes. An arrogant, litigious woman."

Hector raises his eyebrows.

"Trust me." Randall sits down on the bed next to him. "Of the two, you want Barry. He's a piece of cake. He knows his way around a gun. He's completed several big game expeditions."

"I said I'd never do another one. I—"

"And you'll never have to. Do this one, and I promise, you'll never have to guide another client."

"After you take over."

"Right."

"You're an asshole, you know that?" He gazes at the floor. "If Lance finds out I helped you break the rules, he'll have me killed."

"If he finds out about Rachel, he'll have you killed. Which option looks better?"

"What about the people upstairs?"

"That's the beauty of my plan. We'll have less cleanup to do. After we come back, Barry will leave with his girlfriend, and you and I will only have Miss Highsmith to worry about."

"What about the woman you're guiding?"

"After she pays me, there will be a hunting accident."

"I see." He cocks his head. "You know, Miss Highsmith said she went to her car to get help for her sick brother. What was she talking about?"

"Ah, yes. Her brother. Jacob. He won't be a problem."

"How so?"

"He's a retard. He shouldn't have lived as long as he has. Sometimes I worry natural selection is failing us."

"An actual retard? You know that's not the term now."

"Have it your way. He's *slow*. Is that better?"

"Yes." Hector lifts his head. "You know, my wife has a brother with Down syndrome."

"Your wife is dead."

Hector returns his gaze to the floor.

"Listen," Randall says, "this Jacob is nothing to concern

yourself with. We could leave now, and he'd wander around in the forest until he died. In fact, he might have already done that." Randall stands. Walks to the door.

"Are you limping?" Hector asks.

"It's nothing. I cut my leg."

"How?"

"Don't worry about it. Worry about Barry. Give him his excursion and leave with his idiot girlfriend before Lance arrives. I'll take care of everything else."

"What are you going to tell Lance?"

"The truth. You came to check on me. Things weren't going well, so you took over. You gave Barry his excursion and left. I won't say anything about Rachel. Promise."

Hector shakes his head. "I guess I'm damned if I do, and I'm damned if I don't."

"That seems to be the case, but if you think about it, one option is a lot less work than the other." Fat slob. "If you do what I ask, you'll be out of here sooner. Fewer bodies mean less work. You can be back on vacation in no time."

"And we've got to finish before Lance comes."

"Yes."

"So"—he glances at his pajamas—"no sleep."

"Correct."

He sighs. "Okay, but if something goes wrong, I'm telling Lance everything."

"Me too. I think he's always wondered what really happened to his lawyer friend. Poor Rachel."

CHAPTER FORTY-EIGHT

Mom put the cake in the oven and sat at the kitchen table. Last week, I made sure she sent the birthday invitations to my friends and called my cousins. This was going to be the best party ever. Six guests in total. Seven, if you counted Dad. I couldn't wait to see him.

Three months had passed since we were all together at the cabin by the lake.

He promised he would come for my eleventh birthday. He was on his way.

I laid out the Littlest Pet Shop napkins. Pink and blue—they matched the plastic knives and forks. The plastic tablecloth. The streamers and balloons. The wrapping paper on Jacob's gift to me. The one he'd placed at the head of the table next to my mom's gin and tonic.

She folded her arms over the table and put her head down. The next time I turned around, she was asleep.

I went into the living room to look out the window in case someone was arriving early. You'd never know it had already snowed once this fall—a warning shot that winter was on its way. That was life in Denver. I loved our house here. It was the best house in the best place I had ever lived. Unlike the mountains, the snow always melted within days. My science teacher said Denver got more sunny days than Florida, and I believed her. Back then, I believed a lot of things.

Jacob sat in his room upstairs, waiting for the party to start. I'd promised to tell him when people arrived. He didn't like crowds, but he'd promised to come down as long as he could sit next to me. He wasn't happy that I'd invited Cam.

I stood at the kitchen table. "Mom?" She didn't answer. I touched her arm. "Mom, wake up." She raised her head. Her eyes at half-mast, her thin neck straining to hold her skull straight. "Mom?" She belched and picked up her gin and tonic. Her breath smelled like tomato soup and gasoline. "I'm not feeling well." She stood, bracing herself with one hand on the table. "I need to lie down."

"But, my party is in an hour."

She stumbled to the stairs. "I'll come back down then."

"But—"

The phone rang.

"Can you get that?" she asked.

"But—"

She disappeared up the stairs.

It was just as well. Given a choice, I'd rather have her asleep in her room than embarrass me at the party. These afternoon naps had become a normal thing since Dad left. I couldn't wait to tell him about it. I couldn't wait to see him.

The phone rang again.

I ran into the living room and picked up the receiver. "Hello?"

"Charly, honey, is your mother there?" It was Aunt

Janice.

"Yes. I mean, no. She's taking a nap."

"How about your father?"

"No, not yet. But he's coming."

"Tell your mother I'm sorry, but Amanda can't make it to your party today. She won her Judo match this morning, and I promised to buy her a new Judogi if she did. We're going shopping."

"Oh."

"We'll come by later and drop your present off, okay?"

"Okay."

It was just as well. Amanda was not my favorite cousin. Given a choice, I'd rather have her out shopping than suck up all the attention at my party, bragging about her Judo match. My friends were still coming. Cam would be here.

And Dad.

"Oh, and Cam can't make it, either. I talked to your Aunt Meg, and she said he was grounded again."

"For what?"

"I don't know. He's been in trouble a lot lately."

"Oh." I always hated talking on the phone. Especially with old people.

"How have you been doing?"

"Okay."

Silence.

Aunt Janice waited on the other end. I could hear her breathe. She wanted me to say something else, volunteer some dirt so she could gossip. So she could tell Amanda how good she had it. But I wouldn't say anything. I had no dirt to give. She wanted me to say something bad about school, or Jacob and his autism, or my mother, but everything was going fine.

Just fine.

"Well, give my best to your dad when you see him, okay?"

"Sure."

"And call me if you need anything."

Not in a million years. "Okay."

I hung up, and smoke drifted in from the kitchen.

The cake.

I raced to the kitchen and opened the oven. A black cloud enveloped me, seared my eyebrows, and rose toward the ceiling. The oven mitts didn't fit, so I used them like hand rags to pick up the pan. I pulled it out of the oven and put it on the kitchen table. The My Littlest Pet Shop tablecloth began to melt. I lifted the pan up, but it was too late. The plastic stretched and broke, leaving a gaping hole in the tablecloth and marring the table.

The cake was black.

My theme colors had been pink and blue, but now they were black.

Everything was black.

My party was ruined.

CHAPTER FORTY-NINE

CHARLY

I remind myself that people change. That people *can* change. Some are stronger than others. Given the right opportunities, support, and a little luck, they can use their strength to make the right choices in life. Hard choices. It wasn't easy for me, but I turned my life around after everyone left.

I did what my parents couldn't.

I changed.

And if I could do it, so could Cam. I always believed that for him, but after tonight, I think I may have been wrong. Before Randall shut the light off and left us in the cage, I swear Cam smiled. It could have been a frustrated grimace. A smile-to-keep-from-crying smile, but I'm not so sure. I want to believe he isn't the crazed raccoon torturer I knew as a child. I want to believe he grew out of it, but . . . that smile.

I watch him.

He stands in the far corner with his back to Tyler and me, staring out the window. He's barely visible in the dark.

Tyler sits on the floor by the kayaks, his face bruised and broken, his chin against his chest. I reach under his blanket and feel for his hands. The zip tie wrapped around my wrists makes it awkward, but I want him to know I'm here for him. "It's going to be okay. Just hang on a while longer, and I'll get us out of here."

"I'm not that bad." He finds my fingers and lifts his head up. His hands are warm.

"What do you mean?"

"We need to get those cuffs off you."

I pull away. "What do you mean, you're not that bad off?"

"I wanted Randall to think I was dying." He stretches his back. "I was hoping he would come inside the cage to check on me long enough for one of us to run out. I didn't know he'd have someone with him."

"So, he was right? You were faking it?"

"No. Not exactly. My face *is* killing me." He touches the bruise beneath his eye and winces. "But, I'm not *dying*."

"I don't understand. You had a fever."

"My skin gets hot when I drink too much." He scoots away from me. "Come here. Let's get those cuffs off you. There's a rough spot where the bar has rusted."

I rub my zip tie against the spot. "So, Randall was right. You're not so much sick as you are hungover."

"He's smart. He didn't fall for my act at all."

"How did he know you'd been drinking?"

"We were drinking together. We met in a bar last night."

My hands slip, and I scrape my wrist on the bar. "Ouch."

"Careful. Here, relax your arms." Tyler's touch is gentle. Warm. He rubs my tie against the rust for me, sawing through the plastic. "Randall bought me drinks until I passed out. The next thing I knew, he was beating me up and locking me in here."

"Why?"

"I think he's going to hunt me for sport."

"Oh, my God. Hunt you? Like an animal?"

"That's ridiculous." Cam stands in the corner, keeping his back to us. "If he wanted you dead, he would have shot you by now."

"How do you know?" I ask.

"Does Randall seem like someone who wastes time, messing around with people?" Cam's voice is thick, and he slurs like he's still a little drunk.

"Actually," Tyler says, "he does. He spent time tricking you into coming here, didn't he?"

"He—"

"It was the same way, wasn't it?" I say.

"No." Cam's voice tightens. "I didn't pass out from drinking."

Tyler stops rubbing my tie against the cage. "But he did get you drunk. Did he promise to take you hunting with him, too?"

Cam doesn't respond, his silhouette as still as the night sky outside the window.

"Answer him, Cam." I'm done with his attitude. I'm done with Cam's aloof, look-at-me-staring-out-the-window bullshit. It's time we got everything out on the table. "Answer him. Did Randall promise to take you hunting?"

"Yes."

"And it worked. Is that because you still like to hurt animals?"

"I have a plan to get us out of here."

"Answer me, Cam." I stand. "Do you still torture animals?"

He turns toward me. "If you'll listen to my plan, we can get out of here."

"No. Not until you tell me what you've been up to. I don't trust you."

"What is she talking about?" Tyler asks. "What animals?"

"When Cam was little, he killed a raccoon right in front of me. He was only nine years old, and he stabbed it with a knife. Right in front of me."

Cam approaches. He tightens his lips.

I stand my ground. "He also had a cat named Freckles."

"Don't talk about Freckles."

"Why not?"

He steps even closer.

I test my zip tie, but the plastic is only worn halfway through.

"If you listen to me," Cam says, "I think I can get us out of here, but it will take all of us working together."

"What about Freckles? Why don't you tell Tyler what happened to Freckles?"

"That was a long time ago."

"I don't care what he did." Tyler reaches up and grasps my elbow. "We need to get out of here. I'm telling you, Randall is saving us for something. Oh, God. He's going to kill us. He's going to hunt us down and kill us. He—he was just waiting for his friend to come."

"Which friend?" I ask. "Hector or Cam?" I narrow in on Cam's face. If he smiles at the wrong time, if he makes any strange expressions—I want to see it.

"What are you saying?" Cam asks.

"Why were you drinking with Randall in the first place? I saw you guys downstairs in the dining room. You seemed like old friends."

"There was nothing else to do. If you haven't noticed, we're snowed in. There's a blizzard out there."

"Why didn't Randall beat you like he did Tyler?" I lean in, going nose to nose. "There's not a mark on you."

"He kicked the shit out of me. Almost literally. I think he broke my ribs."

I jab him in the side with my finger.

He doubles over in pain. "Ah."

I only heard Randall kicking him from my hiding place behind the kayaks. I didn't see what was happening. They could have been putting on a show for Tyler, or Tyler could be in on it with them, but that wouldn't make sense. Cam and Randall didn't know I was hiding behind the kayaks.

Still, I'm not ready to trust Cam.

I take another step back.

Cam holds onto his side like I hurt him.

"Why did you lie about the snowmobile?" I ask.

"What?"

"You told me the keys were in it. You also told me you left your car keys in the cabin. Who does that? Who leaves their keys in a cabin full of strangers? Unless they aren't—"

"I do," Cam says. "I did. I left my keys on the nightstand upstairs out of habit, and I wasn't sure about the snowmobile. I told you that. Look, we probably don't have much time. If you listen to my plan, we can get out of here."

"Listen to him," Tyler pleads.

"No. He lied to me once tonight already. Because of him, Randall caught me trying to take the snowmobile. It was like he knew I would be there."

"I didn't know he—how could I have known where he would be?"

The boathouse door flies open, followed by a cloud of swirling snow.

Followed by Hector and Randall.

CHAPTER FIFTY

CHARLY - THEN

Using the mitts, I dumped my charred birthday cake onto a plate and grabbed the frosting from the refrigerator. No one had to know. I'd come up with an excuse for not serving it later. For now, I needed a place to put the candles.

Eleven candles.

My birthday party was going to happen no matter what.

I didn't want to disappoint my dad.

"What happened?" Jacob stood in the doorway. "Where's Mom? Is the party starting? You said you would tell me when the party started. I was looking at a book, and you said you would tell me when the party started."

"The party hasn't started." I glanced at the clock. My friends would be here any minute.

"Where's Mom?"

"She's napping." I dolloped frosting onto the cake and spread it.

"Why did she make a black cake?"

"She didn't. She—can you shut up?"

"No. You know I can't shut up. Doctor Jellison said—"

"I don't care. Here, shut up and help me put the candles on."

"Eleven candles." He took a striped blue birthday candle and stuck it in the middle of the cake. "You're eleven today, Charly. Eleven candles."

"I know."

"Eleven candles."

"Keep putting them in. I'll be right back."

I ran to the living room. Looked out the window. Our cul-de-sac had plenty of places to park, but no one was there. I sat on the ottoman and waited.

And waited.

"Are you coming back?" Jacob called from the kitchen.

"Yes, as soon as someone gets here."

But no one came.

Thirty minutes passed, and no one came.

Jacob strolled into the room carrying a rubber toy. He sat on the couch and played with it, rolling it over his fingers, over and over.

An hour is an eternity to a ten-year-old. After a while, I realized the same was true for an eleven-year-old.

Me.

I had turned eleven.

Happy birthday to me.

The toilet upstairs flushed. Mom must have gotten up to go. Now, I hoped she stayed up there.

"Are you still having the party?" Jacob asked. "You can still have the party. You can have some cake. You can open my present. We can sing."

I bit my tears back. "Let's do it later when Dad comes."

"He's not coming. He never comes. He says he is going to come, and then he doesn't. He says he has the weekend off, and he will come, and he will take us somewhere. To the zoo, or to the arcade, or somewhere. Then he doesn't come."

While Jacob rambled, I sat there, staring out the window. I had never felt more alone. I stood and wandered into the kitchen.

He followed me. "We can still sing Happy Birthday, Charly. You can open my present."

"Not until Dad comes."

"Then I'm going to my room. I'm going to look at my book."

"Okay."

He stared at me blankly, then glanced at the stairs. "Do you want to come with me?"

"Why?"

"Will you come with me, Charly?"

"Why?"

"Because of Mom." He frowned and looked down.

Last week, she fell asleep in his bed by accident. When he pulled the covers back, he thought she had died. He sat in the corner, screaming, until I heard him and came inside. It took me all night to calm him down. "Okay. Follow me."

I loved this house. We had three bedrooms upstairs, one for each of us, a big living room with a big window on the main floor, and an unfinished basement where Jacob could watch TV, and I could paint on the walls. Jacob's room was the first one on the left, and his bed was empty. "See? It's okay. She's not here."

My mom had made it back into her room after going to the bathroom after all.

Jacob sat at his desk and picked up his book.

I went to my room and sat by the window. The neighborhood stretched out toward the mountains in the west. Most houses here were the same. My friend, Claudia, lived two blocks away. Her house was the same as mine. I thought we were friends. Of everyone I invited, I thought she would have come.

I watched the intersection, hoping my dad would come soon.

My stomach grumbled. I didn't want to make noodles and butter by myself again, so I went to my mom's room to see if she was awake. The smell made me lose my appetite. Dirty laundry and dishes. Glasses with orange pulp stuck to their insides. Pizza crusts with hardened cheese. Empty bottles and cans.

Her blankets lay in a heap on the floor by her bed.

Her mattress was barren.

I checked the closet, and she wasn't in there either.

As I turned to go, something pink, and something—the same thing—blue, caught my eye. There, neatly stacked on her dresser next to an empty vodka bottle, lay the birthday invitations to my friends. Untouched. Unsent.

I raced to my room.

Pulled the covers off my bed, and there she was, asleep.

I screamed at her.

She woke up, wide-eyed.

I screamed for her to get out.

She covered her face. Rolled over. Fell onto the floor.

I went to the window. Slammed my hand against the wall. Wiped my tears away.

Somewhere out there, Dad was caught in traffic. He had to be.

Or, he missed his flight.

Or, his boss wouldn't let him leave work to come home.

Or . . . he didn't love me anymore.

CHAPTER FIFTY-ONE

Hector and Randall march into the boathouse. The wind follows them in. Snow flurries fly across the floor and leap into the cage. Randall already has his phone out when he reaches inside and flips on the light. He taps on the screen, and the padlock drops open just as Hector reaches for it.

Randall pulls his gun out. "It's go time."

Hector opens the cage door. "One word from any of you and you're dead."

"You first." Randall gestures with his gun for Cam to come out.

"Where are we going?" Cam asks.

"Oh, that's *it*." Hector glances at Randall. "Shoot him. I said one word. We still got the other one."

Randall grasps his gun with both hands and closes one eye. Aims it at Cam.

"All right," Cam says. He exits the cage.

"Stand over here"—Hector points to a spot on the floor—"and hold your hands out."

Cam does as requested, and Hector punches him in the

face for it.

"No," Randall says. "Hit him in the ribs."

Cam attempts to back away, but Hector is too fast. He lands a hard punch, connecting with Cam's torso.

Cam doubles over, coughs and falls onto the floor.

Hector quickly fastens a zip tie around Cam's wrists, binding his arms together in front of his body.

"Do you still think I'm faking it, Charly?" Cam coughs and moans and coughs again.

It's hard for me to see him in pain, but I've got to hold onto my instincts. It was a real punch, but I think Cam knew it was coming. He and Hector and Randall could have planned this. Cam has been acting strange since we reunited yesterday, and he lied to me. The snowmobile. His car keys. His obsession with staring out windows. Too strange, even for him. It's like he is a plant in an audience for a salesman on stage.

"Okay," Hector says, "it's your boyfriend's turn."

Randall waves his gun. "C'mon, Tyler."

Tyler puts his wrists together in front of his body and slowly leaves the cage.

Hector closes the cage door and locks it. He puts a zip tie around Tyler's wrists and pulls it tight. "Which is it with this one? High or low?"

"High."

Hector balls his fist and strikes Tyler's chin. Tyler's head snaps to the side, and Hector hits him again in the opposite direction.

"Enough." Randall strolls over to the cabinet.

Hector pulls his gun out and directs Tyler and Cam toward the boathouse door. The winter wind *whooshes* in, ghosties spin across the floor, and a fresh chill enters my bones. "Where are you taking them?"

Randall opens the cabinet. "Hunting. Like I promised." He grabs a spray can of black shoe polish, a couple of hoods, and two ankle bracelets.

"I don't believe you," I say.

"Would you like to come with us so you can see for yourself?" Randall walks over to the door and puts the polish on the floor.

"No. But, I still don't think you're taking Cam hunting." Cam stands there, shaking like a frigid chihuahua. "Stop it, Cam. The charade is over. Stop acting like a victim." I'm testing him. I need to know if this is an act.

Randall kneels down. "Hold still." He fastens an ankle bracelet around Cam's leg.

"What's that for?" I ask.

Randall ignores me. He fastens the other one around Tyler's leg and stands up.

"See?" Cam yells. "See, Charly? He's taking me with them with this thing on my leg. I have nothing to do with this."

"Prove it," I say. "Please, I want to believe you."

Randall picks up the shoe polish and points it at Tyler.

"No." Tyler puts his hands over his face. "Please."

"Put your hands down. Don't be such a baby." Hector points his gun at Tyler's head and looks at Cam. "Don't move, or I'll shoot him."

Randall sprays Tyler's face until it is completely black and puts a hood over his head.

"Oh, God," Tyler says. "It stings. It's getting in my eyes."

"*Oh, God,*" Randall mocks. "*Oh, God. Oh, God.*" He hands the polish to Hector and grabs Tyler's zip tie. "*It stings. Poor me, it stings.*" He leads him outside.

Hector points his gun at Cam with one hand and aims the

shoe polish with the other.

Cam shakes his head, and he squints, and before Hector can press down on the spray nozzle, Cam raises his arms and loops them over Hector's head. He pulls the fat man's face close to his and bites his ear. Hector screams and drops the polish. He drops his gun. Blood runs down his neck.

Cam holds onto him, gnashing and chomping, trying to bite through the man's thick double chin.

Through the doorway, I see Randall struggle with Tyler. Hector's screaming startles him, and he loses his grip. Tyler takes off running toward the cabin, disappearing into the snowy darkness with his hands bound together. Randall rushes back inside the boathouse.

"What do you think now, Charly?" Blood spews from Cam's lips. He goes in for another bite.

"Help." Hector flails, trying to get Cam off him.

Randall turns green. Swallows. He pulls a black box out of his jacket pocket and presses a button. Cam's ankle bracelet activates, and he goes down, shaking violently, taking Hector with him. The electrical noise muffles their cries for help. Randall lets go of the button and leans down. He hits Cam in the ribs with one hard jab and frees Hector.

"That son of a bitch bit me." Blood runs down Hector's neck.

Randall looks away. "Go after the other one. Get out of here." He convulses. "Go, now."

Hector picks up his gun and staggers out of the boathouse with his hand pressed against his head. He looks both ways, then heads toward the cabin.

I grasp the cage door and shake the bars.

Randall makes Cam stand and sprays him in the face with the shoe polish.

Cam holds still.

When Randall is finished, Cam fixes his eyes on mine and stares at me while Randall places a hood over his head. "Charly," he says, his voice muffled, "tell Jacob I'm sorry. Tell him I'm sorry I called him Freckles when we were kids. I always felt bad about that."

I was wrong.

Cam wasn't in on it.

He never met Randall before yesterday.

He had a plan to get us out of here, but I wouldn't listen.

Randall pulls on Cam's zip tie. Leads him toward the door.

"Tell Jacob I'm sorry."

Randall pulls Cam into the blizzard.

Into oblivion.

"Wait," I say, shivering. "What about me?"

"What about you?" Randall asks. "Do you want to go hunting, too?"

CHAPTER FIFTY-TWO

RANDALL

Randall pushes Cam in the back, not too hard, but hard enough to make the moron stumble through the snow. Dawn is breaking over the forest, revealing the blizzard's damage. Branches hang low, burdened by ice and snow. The trails are gone. Buried. It's going to be a rough day, but Randall is ready.

"Wait," Hector calls from behind them. "He's stopped again." Randall turns, sees Hector tug on Tyler's wrists, pulling him forward. Tyler stumbles a couple of steps through the deep snow, then pulls his hands free and bends over. Coughs. His hood inflates like a balloon.

Randall blinks and glimpses Ronald in his mind's eye. Tyler looks the way Randall's brother did that day. Ronald's last day alive. These visions keep coming to him lately. It must be the lack of sleep. He blinks again, and it's not Ronald. Ronald wasn't a sick drunk like Tyler, but they have the same build. The same hiking boots. An expensive jacket.

Randall blinks a third time.

He shakes the memory from his head.

Tyler remains bent over, his back rising and falling with

labored breaths. Hector—that fat slob—isn't much better. He stands, wearing his poor man's denim jacket with his hands on his knees just above the snowdrift.

"Give him a rest, then head that way, but not too far," Randall says. "He needs his energy for the hunt. I don't want it to be too easy."

"We're already breaking the rules. Why don't I stay with you?"

"Absolutely not." Randall raises his voice above the wind. "You go on the east side of the lake, and I'll go on the west. We can't risk shooting each other."

"I don't think mine's going to make it."

"He'll make it. Use the adrenaline shot in your prep bag; that's what it's for. Remember to give it to him before you get Barry. Oh, and I know it's been a while for you, so don't forget to give him the knife."

Hector straightens up. Grasps Tyler's zip tie. "I know how to do it."

"Wait." Randall unzips his prep bag and pulls out a walkie-talkie. "Let's test this."

Hector pulls his out. "Breaker. Breaker." In horrific unison, Randall's walkie-talkie squawks, "*Breaker. Breaker.*"

"Good," Randall says. "Any sign of Lance, you tell me."

"Why are you so worried all of a sudden? You said he couldn't have made it here from Texas overnight, right?"

"I'm not worried. I don't worry."

"Then why do you want to know if—"

"Your hunt might run long, and Lance is a liar. You don't know if he was actually in Texas when you spoke to him, do you? You are aware of how cell phones work, right? He could have been anywhere."

"I guess."

The wind rushes in from the west, hitting Randall in the face. It's okay. It's better this way. The wind is at Hector's back, and that fat slob needs all the help he can get.

They part ways.

"Move." Randall shoves Cam.

"How much farther?" Cam asks.

"Not much."

"I don't feel good."

"I don't care."

"Can you take my hood off? I'm going to throw up."

"*Can you take my hood off?*" Randall mocks. He hits Cam in the back of the head. "Feel that?"

"Ow."

"Worry about your head, not your stomach. Your weak stomach isn't going to save you."

To comply with the excursion manual, Randall must pull Cam through the forest another mile and a half. In this weather, with the sun coming up and the threat of Lance arriving early, there's no way they'll be going that far.

Another broken rule.

Ah, but rules are meant to be broken. Adaptation requires it.

Cam stops abruptly. Tips his head forward. "*Agh-gha.* I'm sick."

"You're faking it." Randall pulls on the moron's zip tie. "Keep walking."

Cam retches. Brown liquid leaks through his hood. Syrupy bile appears on his neck and runs down his chest.

Randall's stomach rolls. "You moron." He continues pulling Cam forward. "Why didn't you warn me?"

"I did."

"*I did. I did.*"

"I—"

"Shut up. I don't want to hear another word. Moron."

The snow isn't as high around the base of the trees. Randall weaves his way under the branches, choosing the path of least resistance. Cam moans each time they change direction. "Oooh. Oooh,"

"*Oooh. Oooh. Oooh, poor me. Oooh.*"

"Please. Take my hood off. I can't breathe."

"*Please, take my hood off.*" Randall stops. Cam's vomit poisons the air. "*I can't breathe. I can't breathe.* Shut up, you baby. Your cousin stabbed me in the leg, and you don't hear me whining."

"Who? Amanda?"

"Shut up, moron. We're here."

Randall has found the perfect tree. Not too big. Not too small. No branches at the base to get in the way. Perfect.

Cam gags. "Just shoot me. I can't take any more."

"Don't worry. All in good time." Randall slips the prep bag off his shoulder and shoves Cam's back against the tree. "For the love of Darwin, you're a mess. Nothing so disgusting deserves to survive."

Cam convulses. Fresh stomach syrup runs down his neck.

It's all Randall can do not to puke, himself. Randall steps back and pulls a rope out of the prep bag. It's new and incredibly thick. The kind used to lash boats to docks. "Hold still."

He lashes Cam's waist and legs to the tree, winding the rope down to the ground.

Cam convulses again.

Randall uses his fingertips to pull the moron's hood off. Despite Cam's weak stomach, the shoe polish has held up well. His blackened face reminds Randall of the Blue Man

Group in Las Vegas. He misses Vegas. When he's in charge, he'll set up a command center there and run excursions remotely.

He can't wait.

Cam swallows.

There's something stuck to Cam's cheek. It's black, like his face. A piece of burnt steak, maybe. What a moron.

Randall takes a hunting knife out of the bag and cuts Cam's zip tie, freeing his wrists. "Listen carefully to everything I have to say." Cam's eyes are at half-mast. "Are you listening to me?"

"Yes." Frothy spit bubbles form on Cam's lips.

"You are the prey. You will be hunted. You *do* have a chance to live, though no one ever has."

Cam licks his lips. Rubs his wrists. Looks down at the massive rope running across his waist, binding him to the tree.

"Which is your dominant hand?"

"What?"

"Let me put the question in terms you can understand. Which hand do you wipe your ass with?"

"My left, but I'm right-handed."

"Of course you are, moron." Randall grasps Cam's right hand and pulls it backward behind the tree where Cam won't be able to reach it with his left hand.

"Ah, stop. You're going to break my shoulder."

"*Ah, stop. You're hurting me.*" Randall takes a new zip tie out of his pocket and fastens Cam's wrist to the rope. He steps back in front of Cam. "*Ah, stop. You're hurting me.*" He takes Cam's left hand and places the hunting knife in it.

"I'm not left-handed."

"I know. It should take you about an hour to cut through the rope if you don't drop the knife."

The knife shakes in Cam's hand. He glances at his feet.

"Don't even think about it. The ankle bracelet is way too strong. You'll never cut through in time."

"You're a psycho."

"Look, let me give you some advice. Be careful not to drop that knife. If you do, we'll find you right here later, and you'll be dead. One shot. But, if you can cut yourself free, I suggest you run that way. If you try to run to the cabin, you'll run into us on your way there, and you'll be dead. Understand?"

"You won't get away with this. I'll escape and call the police."

"*You won't get away with this.*" Randall chuckles. "Do you know how many times I've heard that? Do you know how many times I've 'gotten away with this'?"

"I know these woods." Cam saws on the rope. "I'll escape. I'll make it back to the cabin and tell everyone what you're doing."

"What makes you think there's anyone still alive at the cabin?"

Cam ignores him. He feverishly slices at the rope.

"You're all alone out here, little rabbit." Randall looks to the sky. "You're going to die."

Cam doesn't look up. He keeps sawing away.

"Apparently, you weren't listening, so I'll say it again. If you go back to the cabin, we'll find you, and you'll be dead. You should go west so you don't accidentally run into your cage buddy and get shot. That is, if you ever cut through the rope. You're holding the knife all wrong, moron."

"I'm going to kill you."

"Ha," Randall laughs. "That's rich." He turns his back. "Enjoy the hunt."

Randall trudges through the snow with purpose. He has no worries. Hector should not have suspected Randall was worried about Lance's arrival. Randall doesn't worry. Ever. He never worries because he is a man of action.

Let Lance come.

The sky turns blue where it meets the mountaintops while the remaining stars hang onto their perches high overhead. It's going to be a terrific hunt. A tough hunt in this snowbound wasteland, but a terrific one. The weather is already cooperating. The snowfall has diminished to a few flakes here and there.

Randall pushes on toward the cabin.

Not far to go now.

He hopes he won't need to kill Kennedy when he arrives. He hopes she's still asleep in her bed. But, if she's not, and if she opens her mouth again, spewing nonsense about her online presence, her insufferable Twitter followers, he might have to kill her just to keep his sanity.

No.

No matter what happens, he cannot kill her.

It would ruin Barry's day.

Randall must follow his plan.

Hector and Barry will hunt down Tyler, return to the cabin, and Barry will leave with his imbecile girlfriend intact. Happy as a clam. Randall will guide Amanda on her hunt. She'll shoot down the mysterious, black-faced man, pay Randall his fee, and he'll send her on her way.

To Hell.

When Mr. Lance Dawson arrives, he'll see Randall has everything under control. Moreover, Randall has a wonderful surprise planned. An excursion. He and Lance can hunt together like old times. There's prey in the boathouse, and it will be easy peasy because Miss Highsmith is a member of the weaker sex. Sure, she has spunk, but she doesn't have the carving knife. Hector would have found it if she did. She'll go down like a deer in headlights.

There's absolutely nothing to worry about.

Once she is dead, Lance will be so consumed by the thrill of the kill, he'll never see it coming.

Easy, peasy.

Randall will place a rifle in Miss Highsmith's cold, dead hands. He'll call the cleanup crew. He'll explain to the board how Lance stupidly distracted him during the hunt. How Lance's weakness as a hunter allowed Miss Highsmith to surprise them. How she stabbed Randall in the leg, took his rifle, and shot Lance.

No worries.

Easy, peasy.

Say hello to the new president of Zaroff Excursions.

The cabin comes into view.

Miss Highsmith's brother is the only loose thread, and he's probably frozen to death by now. He's a bigger moron than Cam. It must run in their family.

"Ah, and isn't that the way?" Randall mutters, stepping onto the porch. "Bad genetics thin the herd as much as I do."

CHAPTER FIFTY-THREE

"Who's out there?" I ask.

I rub the zip tie against the iron bar. Against the roughest spot I can find.

Outside, something brushes up against the boathouse. It's not the wind. The sun has come up, and the snow has stopped falling. On any other day, the quiet solitude of the mountains draped in fresh snow would comfort me. It would remind me of Christmas mornings as a child when I hadn't a care in the world.

But this is not any other day. I can't feel my feet. The boathouse's wooden floor is frozen solid. I've got to get out of this cage.

The noise comes again.

The zip tie snaps, and I take the plastic band off my wrists. If it weren't for the cold, my skin would be sore where the tie has torn into it. Pale light seeps in through the window above the workbench. The noise came from that direction. Someone is out there. Another noise comes, this time from the far wall. Whoever it is, they're moving around the boathouse.

More noise.

Scraping.

Bumping.

Then silence.

The front door rattles.

I picture Hector standing outside with his gun. His Colorado Rockies ski hat. His denim sheepskin jacket. His bloody double chin.

Cam bit him good.

My cold breath floats in front of my eyes.

The door opens a sliver.

"Who's out there?" I ask.

"Charly?"

"Jacob?"

The door cracks open a little more. "I was scared, Charly." Jacob peeks inside. "I'm sorry I ran away. I promised not to run away, and I ran away."

"It's okay. Come inside, quick."

"We're not supposed to go inside the boathouse. The evil man said not to go inside the boathouse. Randall said."

"Just come in here and—"

"He said the boathouse is off limits. That means I can't come inside."

"Come in here before he catches you." Jacob opens the door wider. Looks up the hill toward the cabin. He's holding a plastic grocery bag. "Quick. Get in here."

"No."

"Do it before he comes."

Jacob tightens his grip on his bag and crosses the threshold. Thank God he's wearing his coat. He must have been alone downstairs at some point because his coat was in the hall closet. His pants are stiff, and clumps of snow cling to his pant legs. "Close the door."

"The boathouse is off limits, Charly."

The wind blows the door shut behind him.

The noise makes him jump, and he rushes to the cage.

"You need to go for help," I say.

"I didn't eat the dinner. I'm hungry." He glances at the workshop window. "It's time for breakfast, Charly. I'm hungry."

"I'm sorry. We'll eat later, but first—"

"Where did you go, Charly? I woke up, and you were gone. You left me alone. You promised never to leave me again. It was like the shelter."

"I know. I'm sorry." If I can keep him calm enough to find Amanda, she might be able to do something. The amazing Amanda. Of course, she will be able to help us. All of my jealousy—my anger, my intense desire to surpass her in life, my longing for Dad to look at me the way he did her the day she won the game . . . None of that matters now. "I'm so sorry I left you. I wanted to get our things from the car."

"Did you get my fidgets?" He rubs his hands together.

"No."

His eyes dart toward the door. "I'm sorry I ran away."

"It's okay."

"I didn't want to, but you left, so I left. I hid in the slickhead's car."

"You what?"

"I heard the snowmobile. It was loud. I didn't like it, but it left, and I fell asleep." He shakes his head. "It was cold, Charly, but then a car came. Not a car. A truck. It was loud, and I looked at it."

"I know. I—"

"He is evil, Charly. So evil. I saw him come out of the cabin and hit you. He hit you like Drake used to hit you. He hit your face."

"I know." I touch the spot where Hector's pinky ring cut my cheek. Where Randall slapped me and reopened the wound. He did it in front of Jacob. I would have tried harder to escape if I'd known Jacob was hiding in Barry's Humvee. "How did you get inside Barry's car?"

"The back door was unlocked. I didn't lock my side when I left his car yesterday."

"Were his guns still in the back."

"No. I'm glad they weren't. I don't like guns. Why are you in there?"

"I'm locked in here." I grasp the cage bars. "You see that I'm locked in here, right?"

"Yes. It's obvious." He lifts the padlock. "This is keeping you inside. You don't have to tell me you're locked up, Charly. It's obvious. I'm not slow."

"I know you're not. I need you to go get help. Is Randall in the cabin?"

"I don't know." He pulls on the lock. Wrinkles his forehead.

"Did you see his friend when you woke up in Barry's SUV?"

"Who?"

"The heavy man with the truck."

"No. I didn't look out the window." He pulls on the lock again. "Where's the twisty? Padlocks are supposed to have a twisty with numbers."

"Let go of it. It's impossible to open." I reach through the bars and grab his arm. "Please, go find Amanda."

"No. I can rescue you myself." He lets go of the lock. "I

can rescue you, Charly. I made a plan."

"No, you can't. You need help."

"I'm not slow, Charly." He raises his bag. "I can rescue you myself. I have a plan, and I have this."

I want to scream, but I manage to keep my voice down. Slowly, I say, "Go to the cabin and find Amanda."

"Randall is evil, but I'm not afraid of him anymore. I'm not afraid."

"You're right. He is evil, and he's mean. Listen, you need Amanda's help. I don't think Randall is in the cabin, so you should be able to go there and wake her up."

He gazes at the grocery bag. "I don't need her help, Charly. All I need is this."

"Please, go. Tell her Cam left his car keys in their room. Tell her Randall is evil, and he went into the woods. There's not much time. Tell her to take you to the nearest town and get help."

"Why did he go into the woods?"

"He took Cam hunting."

"He was supposed to take Barry hunting. Barry said so. Barry said it was going to be an experience of a lifetime. I wanted to go."

"Hurry. You don't understand. He took Cam hunting. I think he's going to kill Cam." I shouldn't say this, but I can't take it anymore. "I think he's hunting Cam."

Jacob scrunches his face.

Now I've done it. He's going to panic. He's going to run away.

I shake the bars, the cage door rattles, and he covers his ears. "Go get Amanda!"

"Stop it," he screams. "Stop it."

"Go."

"I don't need her." His face turns red. "I can save you myself, Charly. I want to win for real this time. Myself. Amanda always wins. You were right. She cheats. She always gets help. I don't want her help. I don't want to cheat." He heads for the door. "I know what to do. I'm not slow."

"Jacob."

"I'm going to stop him, Charly. He's evil."

"How? How could you possibly? You're too afraid."

"I'm not afraid of him." He steps outside and opens the bag. "I have this." He raises his hand, and the morning sunlight dances on the carving knife's silver blade.

"You took it."

He nods.

"Jacob. Bring it here."

He shakes his head.

I've never seen that look in his eyes before.

It's confidence.

The blade gleams.

The wind slams the door shut between us.

"Jacob," I shout. "Come back."

CHAPTER FIFTY-FOUR

CHARLY - THEN

No child should ever see their parents cry. It scars them. Seeing tears flow from the people who are supposed to be strong, who are supposed to take care of you, feed you, clothe you, and tell you everything will be fine even when it's not—those tears destroy hope.

They destroyed me.

In the weeks following my eleventh birthday, my mother's tears took away all security I'd ever known. *Welcome to the rest of your life, Charly.* She was in her bedroom, talking on her cell phone. Him again. Her sobs bounced down the hall and settled by my doorway, unnerving and unwelcome. Sad.

I lay on my bed, staring at the ceiling, trying to digest my breakfast.

"Charly, can you come here? Your dad wants to talk to you."

"No," I shouted.

"Please?"

"No."

He can rot in hell. He didn't come for my eleventh

birthday. He didn't even call me on my birthday. He didn't call for two weeks, and by then, I'd moved on.

He was dead to me.

If he wanted to talk, he could visit us.

She appeared in the doorway. "Yes, I'll tell her." She dropped her cell phone into her robe pocket and sat on my bed, tomato juice in hand. I had decided not to go to school today, and I didn't care what she had to say. I wasn't going.

I rolled away.

The birthday present Jacob gave me rested on my nightstand. A makeup mirror. Someday I'd use that mirror, I supposed. When I grew up. I didn't want to start painting my face now. I wanted to go into the basement and finish painting the horse picture I'd started at the beginning of summer. My mom wouldn't bother me if I were down there.

"I have bad news," she said. "Your dad and I wanted to tell you together, but—why won't you talk to him?"

"Do you mean *Johnathan?*"

"Charly. He's your father. He had to go away for work." She sipped her juice. "You know that."

"Just leave me alone. I'm not going to school today."

"That's not why I'm here, but you can stay home if you want."

"I can?" I sat up and pulled the covers over my knees.

She took my hand. "Your father and I are getting a divorce." Her ash-gray cheeks hung beneath her unblinking, bloodshot eyes. "He doesn't want to be with us anymore."

No.

This was not happening.

I jumped out of bed. Pointed my finger at her. My body shook. "He doesn't want to be with *you* anymore. This is all your fault."

"I know." She cast her eyes down. "We're going to have to move."

"What?"

"Without him, we don't need this big house."

This was not happening.

I had moved on, but—my birthday was one thing, but divorce? It sounded so permanent. I'd started thinking of him only as *Johnathan*, but deep inside, I thought he would come back someday. I thought we would make up.

"We won't be able to afford to stay here after the divorce." Her eyes watered.

"I hate you."

"Don't say that." She stood and spilled her juice on my bedspread.

I knocked the glass out of her hand and ran into the hall. "This is all your fault."

"Charly."

Without thinking, I raced to her room and shoved the dirty clothes off her dresser. I kicked her slippers—the old maroon ones with the holes over the toes—and they flew into the air, and they bounced off the wall, and I screamed.

A half empty bottle of gin sat on her nightstand, but that's not what she had mixed with her tomato juice. I dropped to the floor and peered under her bed. Nothing but more dirty clothes and bottles. Empty bottles. I slung them behind me, enjoying the sound they made bouncing off her dresser.

"Come out from under there," she said. "What are you doing?"

I stood and threw a dark green bottle at her head but missed. The bottle smashed into a print of the Bronco's Mile High Stadium by the doorway, breaking the glass and destroying the frame.

"Stop it," she yelled.

"No." I grasped the gin off her nightstand and held it like a club.

"Put that down." Never a big woman, she seemed smaller now. Frail and afraid of me for the first time in my life. She backed into the hall.

I blew past her and ran down the stairs. Out the front door. Across the lawn. Into the street. Bottle in hand, the cool autumn air rubbed me the wrong way. Today was gray. The neighbor two houses down paused to look at me before getting in his car. A sparkling blue sedan. He started his engine.

"Charly," Mom shouted from the doorstep. "Get back in here."

"No. I'm never coming back. No one wants to live with you."

The neighbor backed into the street and turned in my direction.

Mom strode down the steps, her robe flying up behind her. "Get back in here, or you're grounded."

"I'm running away."

She charged forward. "How? You don't have any money."

The neighbor pulled up in front of me, leaned over his steering wheel, and motioned for me to move. I'd seen him before. He was an adult, but he wasn't old. He had tight, curly brown hair and dimples. Not gray hair or wrinkles. Not like my parents. I could go with him.

"I don't need any money."

The neighbor honked his horn and rolled his window down.

As I ran to him, I glimpsed Jacob standing inside our

house. He watched from the living room window. A portrait framed in white trim. A suburban dream about to die.

"Is everything okay?" the neighbor asked, glancing at the bottle in my hand.

"Get away from there," Mom said.

"I—" I couldn't speak. I dropped the bottle, and it shattered on the pavement. The fumes rose into my nose. My nostrils stung. My face flushed, and I ran, but I didn't run away. I ran toward our house. Jacob no longer stood in the window. I needed to tell him what had happened. I couldn't leave it up to my mom to explain things. Not the way she had told me about Johnathan.

We're getting a divorce. He doesn't want to be with us anymore.

I ran across the lawn, and she reached for me, and I slapped her hand out of my way. Somewhere inside, she still had a bottle of vodka. I didn't want to forget that. I wanted to smash it.

I found Jacob in his room, sitting in the corner with his back against the wall. "Are you leaving, Charly? Because if you're leaving, I can come with you. I have a suitcase, and I don't have to bring everything. Not everything will fit, and I don't have to bring it all."

His damn raccoon tail hung from the curtain rod, centered in the window for the world to see. I glared at it. It reminded me of Amanda. The game. The lie. The day Johnathan said he would help me win. And, if he had helped me win—if he had helped me . . . none of this would have happened. The fighting. The drinking. The divorce.

The broken bottle of gin.

If he had helped me win, the emptiness wouldn't have come.

The resentment.

I hated Amanda. I wished she were dead.

Jacob sat there, pulling on his fingers, turning his knuckles bright red. "I don't have to bring everything, Charly. I can leave my toys. I don't need to bring my rubber ducks."

"We're not going anywhere." I knelt next to him. "*I'm* not going anywhere."

"But, I heard you—"

"Mom and Dad are getting a divorce."

"I heard that, too. And, I heard you yelling. And, I thought you were leaving in that car. Leaving with that man. The shiny blue car with that man. You were leaving."

"No, I wasn't." I put my arm around him. "Don't worry. I'm not going to leave you."

"Promise?"

"Yes. I promise. I will never leave you."

CHAPTER FIFTY-FIVE

Randall stands on the porch, walkie-talkie in hand. He stands on the precipice of another hunt. Another kill. The beginning of a new era for Zaroff Excursions. As long as Lance doesn't show up early, everything will go according to his plan.

If not, he'll adapt.

He checks the time on his cell phone. Cam should have almost cut through the rope by now. Soon, that moron will be bounding through the snow, trying to escape. Randall can't wait to hear the crack of Amanda's gun. The resounding echo bouncing off the mountains, breaking the chill morning air.

He can't wait to watch Cam go down at the hands of his own cousin. It makes him smile.

"Randall," squawks the walkie-talkie, "where are you?"

He presses the push-to-talk button. "I'm at the cabin. Where are you?"

"Mr. Rockwell and I are heading up into the trees now," Hector says. "We just passed the lake."

"Did you go east?"

"Of course we did." The speaker hisses through sporadic

static. These things were bought on a budget. "Any sign of Mr. Dawson?"

"No." Randall glances at the cars, then the driveway. "None, yet. How much farther do you have before the two-mile minimum?"

"Not much. Another fifteen minutes or so."

"Carry on, then. Make sure you abide by the rules."

"You're the one breaking the—"

Randall hooks the walkie-talkie onto his belt. Hector is not going to listen to him. Not the way a subordinate should. It won't be long now. Soon, he'll be Hector's boss, and Lance will be out on the street. Everything will turn out fine as long as Lance doesn't arrive early. As long as he doesn't arrive before the excursions are over.

Randall gazes up at the second story windows.

As long as he isn't already here . . .

Frost covers the glass. Despite what Hector said about Lance flying in from Texas, he could be inside the cabin right now. Lance has been known to do things like that. While Randall is the type of hunter to march bravely into the wilderness and kill his prey, picking them off one by one, Lance would rather hide in a blind and wait for the prey to come to him. It's a lazy way to hunt, in Randall's view. A coward's way.

Randall slowly opens the front door and steps lightly down the hall. The dining room. The kitchen. The living room. All clear.

He checks the deck. The windswept snow lays undisturbed, its weight pressing on old posts. The railing sagging. This place is falling apart.

In the upstairs hall, he pauses outside Jacob's door. The simpleton might have come back. Now would be a good time to tie up this loose end. With Kennedy presumably passed out in the bedroom across the hall, he could quietly knock Jacob out and take him to the boathouse.

No.

The boy weighs too much, and Kennedy might hear Randall hit him.

Smothering the simpleton with a pillow would be better. Let him die in that bed. But, one scream, and Kennedy would wake up. Amanda would hear it, and everything would go to hell.

He cracks Jacob's door and peers inside.

No matter. The simpleton hasn't come back.

Randall closes the door, gingerly walks down the hall, and gently raps on Amanda's door.

"It's time," he whispers.

He waits.

He raps on her door again. "Are you ready?"

"Yes. Almost."

"Meet me in the kitchen. Remember to bring all your things. You're leaving immediately after we're done."

"I know," she says in a hush.

Ah, but she doesn't know. She doesn't know where she's going after the excursion. It makes him smile.

A noise comes from the hall.

Randall spins around.

No one is there.

He rounds the corner and stops outside Jacob's room. The door is closed. He can't remember if he left it open or closed. Behind him, footsteps sound inside Kennedy's room. He turns. Faces her door. More footsteps come. She's awake and moving around. Down the hall, a door closes. Amanda is on her way.

A noise comes from behind him.

Someone is inside Jacob's room.

It must be Jacob, but it could also be Lance.

He rushes downstairs as quickly and as quietly as he can.

Barry did a horrible job with the dishes. The pan he used to cook the steak rests on the drying rack, but it's smothered in grease. The forks have spots, and wilted lettuce clings to the salad bowls. There are no knives.

"I'm ready." Amanda appears in the kitchen entryway, blocking Lance's view of the deck, suitcase in hand. She's wearing a puffy green ski jacket, fluffy white gloves, and a surprisingly rugged pair of jeans. "These are the best boots I had. I hope they're okay."

"They'll do." He assumes her Uggs—or whatever fancy-brand footwear she's wearing—will make it through one day in the wilderness. "Come. We need to go."

"Wait." She puts her suitcase on the floor and unzips her jacket partway down, exposing her cleavage. "I haven't eaten."

He opens a cupboard and takes out a box of breakfast bars. "Here. We can eat on the way."

"About the fee . . . you know, the extra twenty percent?" She taps her chin, then circles her finger right above her chest. "I was wondering if I could pay that another way."

"You'll pay the full amount." He pushes her aside and enters the dining room. "You can Venmo me."

"Hey, what's the rush?"

He stops.

On the deck outside the french doors, someone has disturbed the snow. Tracks lead from the stairs to the doors. Randall came in through the front door. He checks the handles, and they're firmly latched. There's no snow on the dining room floor. No water. Someone came inside this way, but who? And how long ago?

"What's wrong?" Amanda asks.

He grasps her wrist and pulls her toward the hallway. "We have to leave."

"Wait." She grabs her suitcase.

Kennedy reaches the bottom of the stairs—that stupid imbecile—and blocks their path. "Where are you guys going?" She puts her hand on her forehead. "What time is it?"

"We're going to the boathouse," Randall says.

"Isn't it that way?" She points behind him. "Out there?" Amanda zips her jacket up.

"It is," he says, "but there's too much snow on the deck. We don't want to slip and fall down the stairs." He steps forward. "Now, please, excuse us."

"Wait." She squints. Wrinkles her nose. "Where's Barry? I thought he went hunting with you?"

"You don't look well." Randall puts his hand on her shoulder. "You should go to your room and pack. You must leave the minute Barry returns."

"No. I—" She sways. Giggles. "Hmm. I guess I am a little hungover. Where's Barry?"

Where's Barry? Where's Barry?

It's all Randall can do to not mock her out loud.

Stupid imbecile.

He pushes her shoulder, turns her toward the stairs, and forces her to walk. "An associate of mine, an expert guide, has taken Barry on his excursion. I wanted only the best for him, and he's getting it now."

"Oh." Her hair smells like peaches, cream, and rotten grapes. "Wait. I thought no one could go in the boathouse. Amanda, you can't—"

"Miss Nichols has signed the NDA. As it happens, she

has business reasons to see the project. Her company is affiliated with mine."

"It is?" Amanda asks.

Randall stops. He lowers his chin, closes his eyes, and pinches the bridge of his nose.

"I mean, it is," Amanda says. "It does. My company has worked with Randall's organization for years. I didn't realize it when we were talking yesterday, but—"

"It's confidential." Randall opens the box of breakfast bars and hands one to Kennedy. "Here, eat this and go pack. Barry will return soon."

Kennedy frowns at the bar. "You want me to eat this?"

"Go pack your things."

"I wanted to go hunting with him"—she holds her phone up—"and take some pictures for my blog. He snuck out."

"You were never allowed to go with him." Randall's temperature rises. "You weren't supposed to be here at all, remember? Trust me, you don't want to interfere with his hunt."

She sniffs the breakfast bar. "Which way did he go?"

Her idiocy reaches a new high.

Randall's heart thumps in his chest, and not in a good way. Not in the way a hunter's heart beats nature into submission. It thumps like he's being chased. Like he is the prey, and this he does not like. He does not like Kennedy's relentless stupidity. She thinks she could wander into the woods and find her boyfriend despite the snow. Despite the frigid wind. Despite Randall's primordial desire to wrap his fingers around her throat in the name of Darwin's genius and squeeze.

And, squeeze.

And—

"We need to go." Amanda takes Randall by the elbow.

Somewhere upstairs, a door slams shut. There shouldn't be anyone up there but—the tracks on the deck.

Lance or Jacob.

Which is it?

Randall fixes his eyes on Kennedy's face.

Amanda squeezes his arm.

Kennedy wrinkles her nose. "Why does she have a suitcase?"

"Cam and I decided to leave later today," Amanda says. "I didn't want to forget it, so I'm putting it in our car on the way to the boathouse. That's the real reason we're going out the front. C'mon, Randall." She pulls on his elbow.

"Wait." Kennedy puts her hand up. "Which way did Barry go?"

Randall jerks his arm free of Amanda's grasp. Glares at the stupid imbecile. "You will stay here." Calm. Randall must stay calm. He pictures his gun firing. The peace it brings to kill something. Calm. He must remain calm. Barry is the quintessential client, and Kennedy—as much as she deserves to die—is Barry's lovebird. His pet. She cannot be harmed. "Listen carefully. If you get in the way—"

"If I get in the way, what?" she sneers. "What are you going to do?"

"If you get in the way—"

Amanda grasps Randall's wrist. "We've got to go now." She pulls him past Kennedy, and they stride down the hall. "It was nice meeting you. Have a safe trip home."

They step onto the front porch.

The wind whips through the trees in the distance.

Randall reaches into his pocket.

His gun is still strapped to his leg.

The biting air invades his nose. His lungs. It's bitter, but his gun is sweet.

Compared to the wind, his gun is warm.

Comforting.

It's comforting to know his gun is right where it should be. Right where he needs it.

He slips his fingers through the slit and caresses the trigger.

He lets the wind inflate his chest.

Part of him hopes Kennedy goes looking for Barry.

The fun part.

CHAPTER FIFTY-SIX

I would never have believed Jacob took the knife if I hadn't seen him holding it. He's afraid of knives. He's afraid of the noise the garbage truck makes on Mondays. He's afraid of plastic wrap because he once saw a movie where a serial killer used it to suffocate people. He's afraid of the dark, and he's always been afraid of knives.

Until now.

That look in his eye before he left the boathouse . . .

I've waited so long for him to show some confidence in life. In anything. And now that he has, I'm terrified. The years of therapy have finally started to work. He appeared more sure of himself than ever, and it couldn't have come at a worse time.

I sit in the corner of the cage, shivering from the cold. The boathouse door hangs crooked in its frame. The wind beats on the door's weathered wood, challenging the broken latch. It barely holds. Dry snow whirls outside the window. I fold my arms over my chest and pray for warmth. I pray the sun will conquer the cold and penetrate these walls before noon arrives, but I know it won't be so. I've never gotten what I prayed for without doing something myself, and there's nothing I can do.

I'm destined to freeze to death.

The ice on the black iron bars glistens.

The red circle on the electronic lock mocks me.

The knob to the boathouse door turns.

I jump to my feet.

Jacob?

The door opens.

It's not Jacob.

Someone in a ski hat with fluffy white tassels and a fur-lined leather coat steps backward into the boathouse and shuts the door. "Kennedy?"

She spins around. "Charly, what are you doing in here?"

"Help." I rush to the cage door. "You've got to stop Jacob. Did you see him out there?"

"No." She hugs herself and rubs the backs of her arms. Her coat is designer thin and matches her gloves. "What are you doing in there?"

"Hurry. You've got to stop Jacob."

"Not until you tell me what's going on."

"Your boyfriend's out hunting with Randall, and—"

"I know. I was on my way to look for him, but the wind— I had to come inside." The walls shake like an airplane taking off. The wind rages on. "I'm going to find him and go hunting with him."

"You don't want to do that. They took my cousin and this other guy. I think they're going to kill them."

"What?" She steps closer. "What are you talking about?"

"I don't have time to explain."

She lifts the electronic padlock. Pulls on it. "It looks like you might have plenty of time."

"Okay, I'll tell you, but then you've got to go find Jacob, okay?"

She nods.

"Randall locked me in here with Cam and this other guy. Then, he and his friend took them hunting. I think Barry went with them. Did he ever tell you *what* he came here to hunt?"

"Um, what do you mean? Like, which animal?"

"Yes."

"Uh . . . no." Her eyes go to the ceiling. "A bear or a mountain goat, maybe. Like something big."

"Like a man?"

"What?"

"Your boyfriend came here to hunt humans."

She backs away. "No. No way. Barry wouldn't do that."

"He's doing it right now, and my brother is out there trying to stop him. He's got a knife. Please, you've got to go find him."

"I don't believe you." She chuckles nervously. "This is some kind of joke, right? Barry put you up to this." She pulls her phone out and takes a picture.

"It's not a joke. Look." I press my face against the bars and point to the cut on my cheek. "Randall's friend gave me this."

"I—Barry wouldn't kill anyone. He's a dumb jock, but that's too far."

"How do you know? You haven't been dating long. What did he tell you about this trip?"

"Not much. He was really excited for it. He did say it wasn't going to be like other trips he'd been on but, honestly, I didn't care. I assumed he was hunting deer or elk or something."

"He's out there right now hunting my cousin. You've got to believe me." I point at the cabinet. "Look in there."

She crosses the floor and opens the door. Picks up an ankle bracelet.

"They put one of those on Cam's ankle and shocked the shit out of him. It's like a Taser."

She takes a black hood off the other shelf. Holds it up.

"They put that over his head," I say.

She drops the hood. "Your brother has a knife?"

"He took the carving knife. He's lost his mind."

She examines the ankle bracelet. "We need to find Barry and straighten this all out."

"No. You have to—"

"Hold on. I think I can get you out of there."

"No, you can't. There's no way. There's nothing to break the lock with, and you can't pick it. It's electronic. Please, go find Jacob."

Kennedy places the bracelet on the workbench. "It's not all electronic. It's got to have a tumbler."

"A what?"

"You said Randall locked you in there, right? How did he unlock it?"

"With his phone."

"But"—she opens the toolbox—"the lock mechanically opened, right? There's a motor inside it that turns the tumbler." She takes a tiny screwdriver out of the toolbox and works on the ankle bracelet.

"What are you doing? How do you—"

"All we have to do is activate the lock. Trick it into opening." She removes a plastic panel from the ankle bracelet and exposes a green circuit board. "There. I just need to short this part."

"How do you know what you're doing?"

"I don't. Well, like—I kind of do. My parents made me get an electrical engineering degree out of high school." She ruffles through the toolbox. Finds a wire. "I wouldn't say I know what I'm doing, but I'm not afraid of this stuff."

"I thought you were a fashion influencer."

"I am." She gathers up the ankle bracelet, the wire, and a pair of needle nose pliers. "Engineering jobs are boring." Her lip gloss shines. "Online influencing is a lot more fun. I have so many followers on Instagram. And Twitter."

I shouldn't have brought it up.

She hangs the ankle bracelet on the padlock and lowers her head. Gazes at the circuit board. "Stand back and don't touch the bars."

"Careful," I say. "That thing can paralyze you."

"I know." She holds the pliers up. "These rubber handles will protect me."

I step back.

She uses the pliers to touch the wire to the circuit board. A blue spark lights the room, the bracelet jumps off the lock, Kennedy's arm jerks back, her face tightens, her necklace leaps off her throat, bounces into her face, and the pliers go flying.

A motor whines, and the padlock drops open.

It's unlatched. It's a miracle.

The lock is unlatched.

"Are you okay?" I ask.

She nods, wide-eyed and stunned.

I reach through the bars and remove the padlock.

The door scrapes the floor when I open it.

And just like that, I'm free.

CHAPTER FIFTY-SEVEN

My sweet sixteen was anything but sweet. The only good thing about it was finally becoming an adult. I didn't need to worry about my mom disappearing for days at a time anymore. I was old enough to be on my own. She had been gone for three weeks this time. The longest yet, but I didn't care. We didn't need her.

We needed money.

I needed a job.

It wasn't like I went to school every day anyway, and Jacob was getting better at being alone in the apartment. A few hours of work a week and a paycheck. That's all I needed.

The Tasty Freeze sat across the street from Larry's All-Stars Gentleman's Club. Red, white, and blue stripes studded with stars surrounded Larry's name in neon, and the marquee read, "Topless Dancers. Foxy Girls. Now Hiring 18 and Up." Movie-sized posters of half-naked women bordered the entrance. A liquor store with torn beer advertisements in its windows sucked on the club like a leech. Only three cars were in the parking lot at two in the afternoon. Mom wasn't sitting beneath the liquor store window this time, but I hadn't expected to see her there. She'd moved on from the hard stuff to the harder stuff months ago. Meth, crack, crank—I didn't know which, and I didn't care.

Jacob and I were going to live on our own from now on.

I stepped off the sidewalk and checked my makeup in the side-view mirror of a dented Chevy. It was from the seventies or before. The mirror was cracked but usable. The bruise under my eye couldn't be seen through my base. Just a little touch-up to be safe, and the Tasty Freeze manager wouldn't notice. If he did, I'd tell him I fell down the stairs. A cliché for sure, but believable because of my age. I wasn't some old battered wife.

Just a battered girlfriend.

The clock outside the bank read 1:58 p.m. I was right on time.

A sign inside the Tasty Freeze read, "Now hiring, 16 and Up."

Perfect. It was still there.

After turning sixteen last week, I submitted job applications all over the place, but I had my heart set on the Tasty Freeze. Filling out the applications was the highlight of my birthday. I didn't have a party. Drake and Jacob were there, and that was all. Of course, Jacob stayed in his room until Drake left, so he wasn't *really* there. It's not that they don't get along with each other. It's that Drake likes to surprise people. He likes to hide around corners or in closets, and he likes to jump out and yell, "Boo." I thought it was funny at first, but Jacob never did.

Then, Drake hit me.

It wasn't all his fault. He scared me, and I reacted. Technically, I hit him first.

I approached the counter, trying to get Drake out of my head. I needed to concentrate. "I'm here for an interview."

The Tasty Freeze girl nodded and cruised down the hall, running her hand along the soft-serve machine as she passed. Oily onion ring and stale french fry smells hung in the hot air. My stomach growled. I pictured the look on Jacob's face if I could walk in carrying a bag of greasy goodness. He loved the Tasty Freeze as much as I did.

She returned from the back. "He's interviewing someone else right now, but it shouldn't be long." Her eyeliner was about to run. "Have a seat, and I'll call you when he's ready." Her red and white outfit—her Tasty Freeze smock, hat, and slacks—fit well. I wondered if they had my size.

I took a seat in the nearest booth.

Fifteen minutes passed.

I watched the clock.

I needed to return to the apartments before three.

Drake was expecting me.

I picked up the napkin holder and checked my makeup in the reflection. It wasn't the first time he had hit me. Drake was a walking cliché. He was a bully boy taking out his childhood trauma on everyone around him. But I loved him. He needed me, and it felt good. He needed someone to take his abuse out on, someone to hit, and I needed him. We met when Mom moved us into a low rent apartment east of downtown so she could afford to keep drinking. He lived across the courtyard. At twenty-four years old, with his own place, he was a dream.

Johnathan never came back.

Before long, Drake and Jacob were all I had.

"Did you want something?" A gangly guy stood next to my table.

"No, I'm waiting to see the manager for an interview."

"Oh, I meant, did you want something to eat while you wait?"

"No, thanks," I lied. I did want something, but I had no money.

I tilted the napkin holder to catch the light better and saw the bruise. Shit. My base was fading. I put the holder down and closed my eyes. If I didn't get this job today, weeks could go by. I'd already borrowed too much money from Drake. He'd get angry if I asked for more.

"Hey." The Tasty Freeze girl appeared behind the counter. "He's ready for you now. Go down the hall toward the bathrooms and wait outside the backroom door. I'll come let you in."

The door at the end of the hall opened before I got there, but it wasn't the Tasty Freeze girl. It was my competition. She was my height, and her red shirt matched the Tasty Freeze napkins. My mom's black blouse was too tight across my chest. She smiled at me as we passed each other, and for a moment, I wanted to meet her. She seemed so friendly. So nice.

I felt like the night of the living dead. Black and bruised.

"This way," the Tasty Freeze girl said, motioning for me to join her in the back room. "He's in here."

I followed her past a walk-in freezer, and we entered an office.

The manager stood up from behind his desk to greet me. "Please, have a seat."

"Thank you."

"Charly, is it?"

"Yes."

"I'm Jack. Nice to meet you."

"Yes. I mean—nice to meet you too."

"Let's see." He held up a piece of paper and quickly ran his eyes over it. "I have your application right here. It looks like this would be your first real job."

"Yes."

"You can relax." He smiled warmly. "I just have a few questions for you."

"Okay."

"First, tell me about yourself."

"Okay. I've lived—I live a few blocks away, so I'd be able to get here on time. I love the french fries here, and I've been cooking for myself and my brother forever."

"No. Tell me about you. What do you like to do?"

"I don't have any hobbies, I . . . I like to read." The lie came tripping off my tongue. I don't know why I said it, but it sounded good, like something people say. My hobby was painting art, but I never talked about it. Not even with Drake.

He waited for me to say more, but I had nothing. He stared at me, and I stared back, the anxiety creeping up my back like a python. Finally, he broke eye contact and looked at my application. "You put here that you like to bake cakes."

Another lie.

I barely remembered filling out the application. At the time, I had already filled out so many, I'd started putting down whatever popped into my head for hobbies and interests. I didn't think people actually read these things.

"Yes. I love to bake."

"Baking takes time. Why do you want to pursue work in fast food?"

"I love the french fries here."

"Yes, you said that already."

I leaned forward. Put my arms on his desk. "Please, I need

this job. I'll work hard, I promise."

He gazed with purpose at my arms. They were clean. No tracks. Then, he focused on my face. "Did you have an accident?"

"No." I sat back. "Yes. I live on the second floor and tripped down the stairs the other day. It's not a big deal."

He picked up my application. "Your address is at Windcrest Arms. You're right. That isn't far away, is it?"

"No, it's not."

"It's right up there off Bradford, right?"

"Yes."

"They've been having a lot of trouble up there lately. The police go by all the time." He gazed at my cheek again and shook his head. "I'm sorry. Right now, I need someone a little more experienced, but I'll tell you what, come back in a few weeks, and if I haven't found anyone—"

"But I need a job today."

"I'm sorry."

I stood. "Please."

He came around his desk, opened the door and called up to the front. "Missy? Can you hear me?"

"Yes," the Tasty Freeze girl shouted.

"Can you get an ice cream cone for Charly here?"

"No, thanks," I said.

"Are you sure?"

"Yes."

I couldn't get out of there fast enough.

The hallway was a blur.

I stepped out onto the curb and covered my face.

My hands smelled like grease and disappointment.

I shoved them into my pockets and crossed the street.

Why had I wanted to work there in the first place?

That girl looked so stupid in her Tasty Freeze outfit—her red and white smock, her cheap hat, her thin white slacks.

I wiped the tears from my face, smearing my makeup.

I didn't want to work at the Tasty Freeze anymore. It was disgusting. They wouldn't have paid me enough anyway. Jacob and I needed more than minimum wage. We deserved better. I deserved to make a lot of money.

I tilted my head back, sniffed, and read the sign outside Larry's club. "Topless Dancers. Foxy Girls. Now Hiring 18 and Up." I knew from Drake that strippers made a lot of money. With the right eyeliner and blush, I could have passed for eighteen. But the truth was, I couldn't even hide a bruise.

The clock outside the bank read 2:50 p.m.

Shit.

I was going to be late.

Drake was going to be angry.

CHAPTER FIFTY-EIGHT

The hardest part of guiding an excursion is holding back, watching the client muddle their way toward their prey, one naive step at a time. Randall experiences physical pain when a client misreads the landscape and moves in the wrong direction. His head throbs when a client shoots their weapon haphazardly and misses the target. His neck tightens, and his breath constricts when a client forgets to cock their rifle before trying to fire it.

But work is work, the money's good, and it's for a greater cause. Mankind. Eliminating the weak.

Amanda, with all her courage and confidence, is no different. As she plods through the snow ahead of Randall, her ass looks good in those jeans, but her gait is all wrong. The way she carries the rifle he gave her, slung over her shoulder like a handbag. It's all wrong. She claims to have done this before, but she failed last time, not only because she's a woman but because she's *too* confident. *Too* aggressive, charging through the woods like a Black Friday shopper looking for an Elmo.

Randall can't take it anymore. It's usually important for him to let clients think they're awesome. It's good for referrals, but Amanda won't be referring anyone after today. He doesn't have time to watch her wander around anymore. His boss could be on his way into the Rockies right this minute. "Wait."

Amanda stops. Her rosy, wind-burned face glows against the snowy hillside. "What?"

"Shh. Look at this." A pool of brown liquid stagnates in a footprint. It smells like last night's steak disaster.

"Is that blood?" she asks.

"No. It's vomit. Look, there." He points to another, smaller pool several feet away.

Amanda heads in that direction.

Randall follows. He places his hand on her shoulder and presses down. They kneel. "See this divot in the snow? It's a footprint. And there's another."

"It went that way," she says.

"Right. It's probably hiding on other the side of this ridge."

She stands and marches up the hill with abandon. She doesn't weave, keeping cover behind the trees when possible. She doesn't respect the prey's ability to sense her approach. No. Not at all. She is not a hunter.

But Randall is.

He spots the prey near the ridge's top. "Amanda."

She turns.

He points.

She raises the rifle.

Randall rushes to her side and reaches for the gun, but he's too late.

She fires and misses.

The prey runs up the hill, pushing its way through the snow.

Her eyes light up, and she lumbers forward.

"Cock it," Randall yells. "Pull the lever."

She does. The next bullet enters the chamber with a satisfying *clunk*. She raises the rifle, and he reaches for her shoulder, but again, he's too late.

She fires and misses again.

The prey stops. It turns its head toward us. Its face a black oval in the whirling white wind.

Amanda didn't steady her feet before firing. She didn't wait for *the moment* before squeezing the trigger. Randall's throat constricts. His muscles tense as if he's holding the rifle. As if he can hit the brakes on this runaway car by slamming his foot against the passenger side floor. This could go on forever, or worse, the prey could escape.

"Dammit." She takes off up the hill, stepping in the prey's footprints.

"Amanda, halt. Stop. Take your time. Take aim." Randall scrambles after her.

The prey nears the ridge's top. If it makes it over the other side, all will be lost.

Randall pulls the ankle bracelet remote out of his pocket and presses the button.

The prey—Cam, that's its name—stumbles. Its leg shakes, and it goes down. It yells. It moans.

Amanda stops, takes aim, and this time she doesn't miss.

The bullet shreds Cam's coat, hitting him in the arm. He lies on the ground, shaking and shouting, but he's too far away. The wind swallows his pleas, and he claws his way up a tree trunk, attempting to stand.

Randall reaches Amanda, leans in close, and whispers in

her ear. "Breathe. Take your time. You only have two bullets left."

The gunshot rings out.

Cam's head snaps back. He falters, stumbles away from the tree, and collapses.

Once a man, now a pile of meat.

Amanda lowers the gun. She grins from ear to ear, her eyes on fire.

"Well done." A snowflake lands on Randall's nose. He wipes it off and realizes more are on their way.

"I've got to see this."

"No." He grabs her elbow. "You're done."

"But, I—"

"Clients are not allowed to see their kill up close. You know the rules."

Her eyes blaze.

"You'll receive an anonymous trophy at a later time. Come with me now. We need to return immediately."

"Okay." She loops the rifle strap over her shoulder. "I'm done."

"When we get back, we'll drive down the mountain until you find an internet signal. Then you can Venmo me your fee."

"What if my cousin's car won't make it in the snow?"

Randall hadn't considered this, but he instantly adjusts his plan. "I have a snowmobile."

She hesitates. "Oh, okay."

Randall turns to go. The snow falls heavier now. They need to return to the cabin. He wants his money.

Amanda stops. Turns around.

"What are you doing?" he asks.

The raven-haired whore takes off up the hill toward the

body.

"Halt." He runs after her, but she's too quick. "Don't." His wounded thigh aches with each pounding step. The cut threatens to open. It slows him down. She increases her lead, swerving to hit the lower spots in the snow between the trees.

This is not good.

Randall presses on, but he can't catch up with her. He's too late.

She kneels before Cam's corpse. Rubs his face. Shakes her head and rubs his face with both hands.

She stares at the black shoe polish on her fingers.

She screams.

Randall approaches her from behind. "I told you not to—"

"Why?" She stands and pulls the rifle off her shoulder. Aims it at Randall.

At this range, she wouldn't miss. In fact, she could hit him anywhere she wanted. "Put it down."

"Raise your hands."

"I love it," he says. "Do you feel it? It's in your eyes—the thrill of the kill, the ascension up the food ladder. You've done it. You're the best. You can relax now. Please, lower the rifle."

"No! You—it's Cam. You made me kill my cousin!"

"I did not make you do anything. It's the natural order. You did what you were supposed to do. You're a survivor."

"Not like this. I didn't want to do this."

"You insisted on having an excursion today." He hunches his shoulders. "What was I supposed to do?"

"Not my cousin." She glances at Cam's body. "Oh, no. I'm a murderer, and—the police. They're going to think I had a motive because I knew him. We're related. There's a connection. They're going to arrest me for murder. I told people we were coming here this weekend."

"Stop your worrying. It's so unbecoming." He reaches into his right pocket.

"Raise your hands."

"We'll take care of everything. People go missing in these mountains all the time."

She lowers her head and closes one eye. Her rifle shakes in her hands. "Raise. Your. Hands."

It's comforting to know his pistol is still strapped to his thigh. "It's okay." He pulls his hand out of his pocket. "It's only my cell phone."

"What are you doing? Put it away."

"I'm recording the GPS coordinates for the cleanup crew." He looks at the sky as if he can see satellites through the clouds. "Now, give me the rifle. You were never here, and neither was your cousin."

"But, Charly and Jacob. They know I'm here."

"Don't worry about them. By the time the cleanup crew arrives, it will be as if they were never here either."

"No!" She pulls the trigger.

The gun clicks.

She forgot to cock it after shooting Cam.

What a shame.

She pulls the trigger again and again—*click, click, click.*

Randall grabs the rifle by the barrel and slings it into the trees.

She leans forward, bends her elbows, and balls her hands into fists.

Such spunk. Such a delight.

She amazes him, and he'd love to end her life right now. He'd love to feel the thrill of the kill the same as her, but he can't do that. He doesn't want to do that, but how he'd love to shoot her in the head and step upon her bleeding body, king of the world. He'd love to, but it wouldn't be wise. Not yet.

She hasn't paid him yet.

She charges forward. Her head burrows into his abdomen, and he falls backward onto the snow, laughing. He shoves his phone back into his pocket, pulls the pistol off his thigh, and buries the muzzle in her ear. "Get off me."

"No." She sits up, straddling his hips, and punches him in the nose.

A stinging sensation surges inside his nostrils.

Suddenly, this isn't funny anymore.

Randall grabs her wrist with his free hand and pulls her upper body close to his. The shoe polish on her hands smells like diesel. Her warmth is a welcome reprieve from the onslaught of snow falling from the sky. He shoves his pistol into her mouth. Fear replaces the fire in her eyes. She goes from wolf to sheep in an instant. "Get off me."

Slowly, she slides to the side, and they stand together.

He keeps hold of her wrist. "Try to run, and I'll kill you." All the fun is gone now. He no longer wants the thrill of the kill. He wants his fee plus twenty percent, and he wants to be done. "March." He motions toward the bottom of the hill. "Go."

She does.

"Don't fall down."

"You're not going to kill me."

"That depends on whether you try another stunt. I'm not so sure you're a survivor after all."

CHAPTER FIFTY-NINE

Hammer in hand, I burst out of the boathouse, blast through the snow, and spring up the deck stairs. Kennedy comes trudging behind me, carrying a screwdriver like a dagger. We couldn't find any box cutters in the boathouse. I lost the only one when Randall and I fought.

I won that fight. I could win another.

I pause outside the french doors. Fresh footprints. Someone recently came this way. It must have been Jacob. The sky is heavy with gray clouds. Another blizzard is coming. My bones may never thaw.

"Wait for me." Kennedy reaches the top of the stairs.

"I am."

In my rush out of the boathouse, the hammer seemed like a good choice. Now, it seems clunky. Heavy. Randall Thorne is a big man. He towers over everyone. What am I going to do? Hit him in the knee and run? "Give me the screwdriver."

Kennedy looks at it like she's never seen one before. "What are you going to do?"

"If Randall is in there, I'm going to stab him." I lay the

hammer on the deck and hold out my hand.

"Maybe we should chill." She hands me the screwdriver. "We can act like nothing has happened, then surprise him."

"He locked me in a cage. He knows I'm less than happy with him. He'll never fall for it."

"Oh. I guess you're right."

I put my hand on the door handle.

Kennedy puts her hand on mine. "Stop. Let's run. Let's go to Barry's Humvee."

"No, I have to find Jacob. I think he's inside."

"I don't want to go in there, Charly. I'm scared."

"I'm not running away again." I pick the hammer up and hand it to her. "Follow behind me. If Randall is in there, I'll stab him in the leg where I cut him before." My eyes burn, my nostrils freeze, the tip of my tongue stings, and I don't care. I'm going to kill Randall Thorne. "You come in behind and hit him with the hammer. Try to hit him in the head."

"I can't do that." She lowers her chin. "I've never hurt anyone before."

"What about Barry? Don't you want to save him?"

"I don't know. I—you might be right about him. He was really excited about his hunt. He could be a bad guy—a serial killer or something. I just want to go home."

"Fine. While I'm taking care of Randall, you find the keys to Barry's car." I put my hand on her shoulder. "Then we'll find Jacob and go. It's the only way." Her emerald eyes have yellow streaks. Her blonde hair sticks out in all directions, whipped by the wind. "Are you ready?"

She nods.

I slowly open the door and peer inside.

No one is in the dining room.

Kennedy closes the door behind us.

It's good to be out of the cold.

Hector. I forgot about Randall's friend, Hector. If he's in here somewhere, we'll be outmatched.

The fire in the living room went out hours ago.

Kennedy follows close behind me as I enter the kitchen.

No one is there.

"I've got to check the upstairs for Jacob. See if you can find Barry's car keys in your room."

"What if Randall is upstairs?"

"I'll go first."

The upstairs hall is empty. I open the door to Barry and Kennedy's room, screwdriver at the ready, and no one is there.

Kennedy searches for the keys.

In my room, Jacob's covers are heaped on the floor. I check under the bed to no avail.

He's not here.

My chest swells at the thought of him traipsing through the forest with a carving knife, searching for Randall. He's not a fighter. That's my job.

I step into the hall. Kennedy is still searching for the keys. "Find anything?"

"No." She comes out. "He must have taken them with him."

"Okay. Let's go." I make a beeline for Amanda's room. She's probably still asleep. Pride sticks in my throat, and I swallow it down. I need her help. "Amanda? Are you in there?" I crack the door. The scent of her perfume—flowers in Spring—wafts into the hall. "Amanda, wake up."

Her suitcase is gone.

Cam's bag sits in the corner, unzipped, and—like he told me—his keys rest upon the dresser. He wasn't lying about that much. I swear to myself I will apologize for not trusting him. I should never have accused him of working with Randall. Somehow, when I find him, I'll make it up to him before the guilt turns into shame.

I grab the keys.

"Where is she?" Kennedy asks.

"I don't know." I hold the keys up. The key to Cam's Chevy is obvious. "Let's find Jacob and get out of here."

"What about Amanda? You won't leave your brother, but you'll leave her?"

"If I know anything, it's that my cousin can take care of herself. I heard her talking to Randall in the basement last night. She's got him wrapped around her finger by now. She'll be okay."

A part of me wants Randall to hurt her. The jealous, shameful part. After suffering in the shadow of her success all my life, I—I need to find Jacob first. Then I'll help her.

"Are you sure about Amanda?"

"If Randall planned on doing something to her, he would have locked her in the cage with us. Let's go."

We race down the hall. My confidence builds. Randall and the others are still out hunting. They must be. We're going to get out of here alive. I descend the stairs to the basement. "Anyone here?" The bathroom is empty. "Jacob? Are you hiding?"

No one responds.

The first bedroom is empty.

Kennedy hits the bottom of the stairs, and we go into the back bedroom. There's a suitcase on the bed and a Colorado Rockies ski hat on the floor. It's Hector's. I rifle through his suitcase, looking for something I can use. A gun. A knife. Anything.

But there's nothing.

"Let's go," Kennedy says. "Let's take the car and go for help."

"No. I'm not leaving without Jacob."

"We can come back for him later. Let's go so we can call the police."

"No."

"Please, I just want to go home."

"I'm not running away again."

"Well, I am." She rushes me. Her head hits my abdomen. I fall backward onto the bed, unable to catch myself. Hector's suitcase hits the floor with a *thud*. She peels at my fingers, prying Cam's car keys free. They fall onto the floor, and she beats me to them. "No!" I fall off the bed reaching for her.

She races into the hall.

I run after her.

She flies up the stairs.

My empty stomach cramps and I bend over in pain. I hope she won't be able to unlock Cam's car and start it, but then I remember how she broke me out of the cage.

Kennedy just isn't as dumb as she seems.

CHAPTER SIXTY

CHARLY - THEN

When we first moved into the Windcrest Arms apartments, Mom promised things would turn around. She'd just gotten a new job. Dad had agreed to send us money each month as part of the divorce. She went to a student-teacher meeting for Jacob and talked as if she were genuinely concerned about his education. She said Jacob and I wouldn't have to share a bedroom for long because living in this sun-worn, cracked-concrete jail cell apartment complex wasn't for us. Not the new us. She promised we would move back into a house by the end of the year.

Our future was bright.

So bright, she bought a bottle of wine to celebrate our first day at the apartments and never stopped drinking it.

I met Drake the next day.

Nineteen years old, tall, long-haired, independent—a dream come true.

A year passed before Drake and I started dating. By then, Mom had plowed through five jobs and stopped trying. Sometimes, she would go out late at night and come back with a fist full of cash, stumbling and smelling like gin and strawberries. The boys at school were shorter than me and stupid. Drake wasn't. He had his own apartment, and he invited Jacob and me over whenever my mom was out of control. He always let us stay the night. I dreamed of marrying him and moving into a house together. A house like the one Mom had promised.

Drake said he liked the idea.

Our future was bright.

Now, standing outside his apartment two years later, my makeup running down my face, terrified that I'm late, that I told him I'd be here at three o'clock and wasn't, that I didn't get a job because he hit me, because he bruised me—I'm not looking forward to the future.

Worse, I needed his help. I needed his money for groceries.

I pounded on his door.

He didn't answer.

My fist ached, but I pounded anyway. "Are you in there?"

He didn't answer.

"I'm sorry I'm late." I tried the doorknob, but it was locked. "Please don't jump out and scare me."

Silence.

I was nearly a half-hour late. He must have become mad and gone to my apartment. I left Jacob alone two hours ago, and if he let Drake inside—

I raced across the courtyard, dodging the empty cans and fast food wrappers—the Tasty Freeze take-out bags, the broken liquor bottles, the cigarette butts, the cracks in the concrete. A desperately clean smell came from the communal laundry room. The familiar stain on our apartment door crept up from the welcome mat like ivy.

I reached for the doorknob.

My hand shook.

I hesitated.

Listened.

No yelling or fighting came from inside.

Still, fear gripped me by the throat. This wasn't the plan. I was supposed to have gotten the job at the Tasty Freeze without Drake knowing. In a few weeks, when we'd saved enough, I was leaving him forever. Jacob and I were leaving Windcrest forever. But now, with no job and an empty stomach . . . I should have gone inside Larry's Gentlemen's club. A place like that probably employed tons of underage strippers. Thinking about it on my way back today, I'd chosen a stage name: Care Bear. In honor of my dad.

Johnathan had always called me that, and I'd always hated it.

I should've gone inside Larry's Gentlemen's club.

At least I'd have a job. A way out.

But take my clothes off? In front of people?

No.

Never.

This Care Bear could never do that.

I threw the door open wide. "Drake? Come out. I know you're hiding in here somewhere. It's not funny."

He wasn't in the hall closet. I checked behind the couch. The bathroom. There was nowhere to hide in the kitchen, so I grabbed a carving knife off the counter. He couldn't have hidden in my room, either, not with Jacob there.

One place left.

I went to my mom's room. Flipped on the light. "Drake?"

Thin dresses, holey leggings, socks, underwear, and high heels littered the floor. Cheap plastic necklaces. A book rested on a cardboard box by her pillow and comforter on the floor. She'd sold her bed and dresser last month. It had only been a matter of time before she either disappeared or came for her stuff. She'd disappeared, and so had Drake.

He wasn't here.

My shoulders relaxed, and I lowered the knife.

My mom had been piling our mail in the corner of her room. Most of it hadn't been opened, so I scooped it up, put the knife back in the kitchen, and went to my room.

"Hi, Charly." Jacob sat on his bed with his back against the wall. "I thought you were going to Drake's. Staying at Drake's tonight. Are you staying here?"

"Yes. Have you seen him today?" I dumped the mail at the foot of the bed.

"No. I don't like him. You know I don't like him. He's getting meaner. Meaner, Charly."

"I know." Ads for bar-b-cues and tents and windows and home-remodeling made up most of the mail. I sifted through it. An envelope with an orange stripe reading *Final Notice* caught my eye. It was from Windcrest. Inside, there was a date.

Two days from now.

"What's wrong, Charly?"

"Nothing."

I read the letter. Windcrest was giving us two days to move out. If we didn't leave, they would notify the authorities. Apparently, this was the fourth notice. The rent hadn't been paid in over three months.

I read it again. "Jacob, we have to leave."

CHAPTER SIXTY-ONE

CHARLY

Cam's beat-up Dodge is smothered beneath three feet of snow. I stop chasing after Kennedy when I see her fail to open the door. She glances back at me, drops her hammer on the ground, and starts digging with her hands.

The trees at the end of the driveway shiver in the wind. "Jacob?" He doesn't answer. I check inside Barry's Humvee. He hid in here all night, but he's not there now. This leaves only one place for him to hide. The forest. Deep in the forest. "Move over." I kneel next to Kennedy and pull snow away from the door.

"Why are you helping me?"

"When we find Jacob, we'll need a way to get out of here. I want to know if this piece of crap will start."

We open the door far enough for Kennedy to slip inside, and she sticks the key in the ignition. She can't take off without me because of the snowdrift behind the car. We have more digging to do. If the engine starts, we'll make a runway to the drive and use gravity to pull us down the hill.

The motor whirs like a stuttering robot. It turns over, but

the engine doesn't catch. "Stop. You'll wear the battery down."

"But, we have to get out of here."

"Stop." I put my hand on her shoulder. "The sun is breaking through the clouds. Maybe it will be warmer by the time we find Jacob. I think the engine is too cold to start right now."

She rests her head on the steering wheel and sighs.

"There's a chance Barry *is* a good guy," I say. "If we find him, maybe he'll take us in his SUV. It's probably the only car here that can make it to the highway."

She shakes her head. Sobs.

"Kennedy, I need your help. My brother has lost his mind."

"I hate him."

"What?"

"Barry. I hate Barry. Why did I come up here? Why did I trust him? I'm so stupid when it comes to men."

"You're not stupid." I help her out of the car. "It's not your fault. You can't trust anyone. Especially men."

"I wanted to leave after we got here, but I had to listen to him. He promised he'd connect me to some of his more influential friends online, and I fell for it. Then he wanted me to leave, but it was too late."

It begins to snow.

"Here, take your hammer." I tighten my grip on my screwdriver. "Same plan as before. I stab him, and you come in for the knockout blow."

We make our way past the boathouse and head west into the forest.

Dark clouds cover up the sun.

"We're never going to find him," Kennedy says.

"Maybe not, but I refuse to sit in the cabin and wait for Randall to come back. The only thing we have going for us is the element of surprise."

"I don't know if I can do this. What if he ambushes us?"

"We're going to be okay." I wish I knew that was true. With every passing minute, the snow increases its intensity, working to blind us. The chill drills into me, and the innocent snowflakes nip at my hands. Prick my face. Kennedy produces a breakfast bar from her jacket, and we split it. The nuts taste horrible. They're stale, and the dried fruit bits are rock hard, but I'm so hungry, it doesn't matter.

Randall's overbearing voice breaks through the snowstorm.

I grab Kennedy's arm and pull her down. We crouch at the base of a tree.

"For the last time, shut up," he says.

We huddle against the tree trunk and listen.

"No. I'm not paying for this." It's Amanda. "You didn't deliver. You made me a murderer."

Kennedy makes a tiny, strangled sound in her throat and inches around her side of the tree.

"What do you see?" I ask.

"He's—oh, my God."

"What?"

"He's got a gun pointed at her." She ducks back, her eyes wide.

I lean around the other side.

She's right. Randall has a pistol pointed between Amanda's shoulder blades, and he's marching her toward the lake.

"I will report this," Amanda says. "You won't be able to cover up two murders."

"*I will report this.*" His high-pitched voice is irksome. "*I will report this. I will report this.*"

"You'll never get away with it."

"What I am and what I am not capable of getting away with is none of your concern. I think you're underestimating the situation."

She stops walking.

He shoves the muzzle up against her neck. "Move."

She turns around. "You won't do it." She puts her hands on her hips and leans forward. The wind gusts, whipping her raven hair like a battle flag. "I told everyone where I was going for New Year's Eve. I posted it on Facebook. Everyone knows where I am."

"I don't have time for this." He points his pistol at her and pulls the trigger.

Light flashes.

Her head explodes.

The gunshot rings through the trees.

I duck back behind the tree and cover Kennedy's mouth.

She screams through my fingers.

The winter wind howls.

My heart thumps.

Amanda is dead.

It's over. Game over.

The wind takes my breath away and dies.

A squirrel chitters in the branches above.

Kennedy pushes my hand off her lips and gasps for air.

"Be quiet," I beg.

"Is she—is she dead?"

"Who's there?" Randall's voice echoes through the trees. "Who said that?"

CHAPTER SIXTY-TWO

RANDALL

"Who said that?" Randall asks again.

Ah, but he knows.

He *thinks* he knows. That imbecile wouldn't listen. He told her to wait in the cabin until Barry returned from his excursion, but she didn't listen. He points his pistol in the direction of the weak woman's voice. Her whimpering came from the trees not far away. "Come out, Kennedy. You imbecile."

Snow flurries spin out of control, swirling across the forest floor, merging with the falling snow. A new blizzard is upon him. He squints. Raises his pistol. Steps into the wind. "I know you're there." He glances back at Amanda's body. Blood drips onto the ground. He gags. He closes his eyes and lowers his weapon. Her blood, it's so . . . so disgusting. It's full of bacteria. And worms. He swears it's full of gray worms. He wipes his hands on his pants as if he has her blood on them, then realizes he doesn't. He doubles over. Vomit lurches into his throat, and he swallows it back.

He struggles to breathe.

In the name of Darwin's genius, he hates blood.

He licks his icy lips, again and again.

Steady now.

Inhale. Exhale.

He lets the moment pass. He pictures Amanda's face exploding. That part, despite the blood, *was* pleasing. Pulling the trigger was a climax. Better than sex. He wanted to revel in it for a while, but Kennedy—if it is her—had to follow him. She had to ruin the experience, that stupid imbecile.

He stands up straight. Swallows. Sniffs. Points his gun at the trees. "I know you're there. I can smell you."

Is it whispering he hears, or is it the wind?

Is she talking to herself or someone else?

"Come out now, or I'll start firing. I don't have time for this."

He waits.

Counts to ten.

Then, he fires his gun into the branches just above the whispering. As much as he'd like to make another kill—rid the planet of another flawed animal—this is Barry's day. She's his lovebird. The best outcome has Barry driving happily down the mountain, hand in hand with Kennedy. Just a happy couple returning from a few days' vacation in the mountains as if nothing happened.

Kennedy emerges from the branches, stepping high over the deep powder. She sees his pistol and keeps coming. She wears a ski bunny hat and a fur-lined coat and wields a hammer.

And she looks ridiculous.

Randall lowers his gun.

"Where's Barry?" she asks.

"*Where's Barry?*" Randall mocks. "*Where's Barry?*"

Maybe five feet away, she stops. Raises the hammer.

"Put that thing down," he says. "Your boyfriend is fine." He stows his gun in his pocket. "See? I'm not going to hurt you, although you should have stayed in the cabin like I asked, but now that you're here, we can return together. Barry should be back soon, if he isn't already." Randall looks to the sky. "Everything is going to be fine."

"Nothing is fine," she yells. "You shot her. You shot her in the face."

"Oh, her." He glances back at Amanda's carcass. "That was an accident."

"No, it wasn't, you liar."

Somewhere in the trees beyond her, a branch snaps. "Who were you talking to?"

"You're a liar."

More noise comes from the trees, but it has moved. "Who's there?"

"It's no one," she says.

The wind gusts, sweeping snow off the ground and swirling it around Kennedy. He can't see her face. More noises come. "You're the liar. I heard you talking to someone."

"No, I—"

Randall's walkie-talkie squawks. "Hey, you there?"

He takes it off his belt. Presses the button. "Yes. Go ahead."

"We're done. Heading back now."

"Got it. Any deviations from the plan?"

"No, not a one."

"Good." He returns the walkie-talkie to his belt.

Kennedy stares at him, hammer still raised. Her wrist shakes.

"See?" Randall smiles. "I told you. Everything is going to be fine. Barry is headed back to the cabin now." He gestures for her to follow him. "Please. This way."

"No." She takes a step forward.

"You can't be serious." Randall shakes his head. "Put that thing down, and let's return before the blizzard buries us alive."

She says nothing. Takes another step.

The wind pelts Randall's neck with ice.

She's not listening to him. She's thinking incoherently. She could walk away from this alive, but instead, she's going up against him. The alpha male. He can't take it anymore. "Put it down, you stupid imbecile."

"Don't call me that."

"You airhead. You imbecile. You're not fit." He pulls his gun out.

A voice comes from the trees behind him. "Kennedy. Run."

Randall spins around.

Something hits him in the forehead. It's hard, and it hurts. Whatever it was lands on his foot.

A screwdriver?

Someone threw a screwdriver at him?

When he looks up, Miss Highsmith is in his face. She pushes him in the chest. His feet are wedged beneath the snow, causing his legs to bend, and he inadvertently fires a bullet into the sky.

Miss Highsmith steps on his chest and reaches for the gun but misses.

"Get off me." He grabs her ankle.

She shakes it free and heads for Kennedy.

Randall sits up. Wipes his forehead.

It's not possible. Miss Highsmith escaped the boathouse. She escaped the cage. Somehow, she unlocked the lock.

It's not possible.

He stands, and like the imbecile she is, Kennedy throws the hammer at him.

He dodges it easily.

"Hurry." Miss Highsmith takes Kennedy by the hand, and they begin clomping through the snow, clambering up the hill in the wrong direction. Back the way Randall had come. Away from the cabin.

Imbeciles.

There's no time for this.

He takes aim at the base of Miss Highsmith's neck, fires, and misses.

The women duck into the trees.

He chases after them. They're no match for him—this is true—but his leg aches, and the blizzard won't relent.

But it must.

It will.

He is more powerful than this blizzard.

He is more powerful than Mother Nature.

CHAPTER SIXTY-THREE

I stood in our bedroom, holding onto the eviction notice with both hands. Shaking. Not only had my mom abandoned us, but she'd left us nowhere to live.

"Can I read that?" Jacob asked. "Can you tell me what it says? It must be bad, Charly. You're frowning."

"No, I'm fine. It's just that—we have to move out. Tomorrow."

The notice gave us two days, but I didn't want to risk staying any longer than I had to. The last thing I needed was the police coming early and finding us alone. We'd already fought off Child Protective Services once. I doubted we could do it again.

Jacob shook his head. Scrunched his face.

I put my hand on his knee.

He jerked his leg away.

"It's going to be okay. You need to pack your things."

"Why tomorrow? Why are we leaving tomorrow?"

"Mom didn't pay the rent."

"Let's find her. You can find her. She can pay the rent,

and we can stay, Charly. We can stay."

"She doesn't have any money, and neither do"—I bit back the tears—"I."

"Sometimes, she has money. Sometimes. She said she would pay for me to have new pants."

"She's gone, Jacob, and she's not coming back. Not this time."

"But—"

"Even if she does come back, the apartment won't be here because they're taking it away from us. She didn't pay the rent."

"But, my pants. I wanted new pants. She promised."

"She's a druggie. She lied to you about the pants, and we have to leave."

"Where are we going?" He pulled on his fingertips. Bit his lower lip. "I don't want to go anywhere."

"We'll find a place. It's going to be okay. I know of somewhere downtown you can stay while I get a job."

"You're going to leave me?" He rocked back and forth. "You said you wouldn't leave me, but you're going to leave me. Dad left. Mom left. Charly left."

"I'm right here, and I'm not leaving you." I put my hand on his shoulder. "Open your eyes. I'll visit you every day."

"You're going to stay with Drake, and I'll never see you again. I don't like him. I don't want to stay with Drake, and I don't want to stay downtown, and I—"

"I'm not staying with Drake. I'm breaking up with him." Saying this out loud made it final, but the thought of leaving the only boyfriend I'd ever had hurt. Everything hurt. "Put your things in that corner." I stood. "We can bag them up later."

"No."

"Please? We need to be ready." My heart swelled. My eyes watered. I couldn't stand to let Jacob watch me lose control. I turned my back on him and opened my dresser drawer. "I'll put my things in the other corner. Let's see who's fastest."

"Can I bring everything?" he asked, glancing around the room. "I can't, can I? It won't fit in the corner. How much can I bring? My rubber ducks?"

"Bring your most important things."

He got off the bed and pulled a wooden box out from under it. His face was red but it was fading.

I threw my underwear into my corner. Then my shirts. Pants. Socks. Shoes.

Jacob opened the wooden box and pulled out a raccoon tail. "This is an important thing. I won. Amanda won first, but she gave me this, so I won too."

I shuddered and looked away. "Bring it, then. Put it in your corner."

"I have the notes, too." He held up some papers. "The clues. I still have the clues."

"You need to bring some clothes."

"Remember this one?" He laughed. "About a donkey named Rags? I found this one in the bushes. I found this one, and it told us to go to the boathouse. We found this box there. It was for oats. It's an antique. Remember, Charly?"

"Yes, I remember." The last thing I wanted to think about was that summer—the box and the tail, the clues and Amanda—it came back to me like a recurring nightmare. Thinking about Amanda had never stopped . . . Amanda and her perfect little life. My aunt gave her anything she wanted, but they were always too busy to help me. "Pick out your clothes, and I'll make something for dinner."

"We don't have anything left for dinner, Charly. What are

you going to make with nothing?"

"I'll come up with something, don't worry. Just fill your corner."

My makeup mirror was heavy. I didn't want to carry it around Denver in my backpack, but Jacob had given it to me, and I thought I might need it soon. I put it in my corner and went to Mom's room. Most of her clothes were too small, but I found a few things. Some low-cut tops. A half-shirt. Two leather short skirts. A garter belt. A pair of red high heels barely large enough for my feet. I scooped it all up along with some lipstick and eyeliner and carried the load into the hall.

The front door burst open. "Boo!"

I screamed and threw everything into the air.

Drake charged toward me, his hands outstretched, that playful yet evil look in his eyes. "Boo! Did I scare you?"

I slapped him across the face.

He put his hand on his cheek. "Hey."

"You asshole."

The playfulness drained from his face. He raised his fist. "Where were you? You were supposed to come to my place."

"I did." I cupped his fist and pulled it down. "Don't be mad. You weren't there."

"Where did you go this afternoon?"

"None of your business." I smiled and ran my tongue over my lips.

He glanced at the floor. At the clothes and makeup. "Where were you going with that stuff?"

"Nowhere."

He narrowed his eyes. "Tell me."

"No."

He raised his fist again.

"Please, don't."

My head rocked back when he hit me.
I ran to the kitchen and grabbed the carving knife.
Jacob and I left the next day.
We had to. We were evicted.

359

CHAPTER SIXTY-FOUR

Easy does it. A predator does not panic. A predator watches his prey from a secluded vantage point, moves from place to place, then kills.

A predator stalks.

A predator hunts.

Kennedy and Miss Highsmith run through the forest, scrambling, wasting precious energy.

Randall moves through the trees, a cheetah moving through oleander.

They change direction, and he adjusts.

This will be over soon.

Blasts from the arctic wind only heighten his senses.

The tracks lead straight ahead, cross a small clearing, and—there's breathing, and there's scuffling, and—they are in the trees to his right. They're trying to double back. He reverses direction, treads over the snow as fast as possible, and hides near a rock outcropping. The rocks jut out of the ground like crooked leopard's teeth. Snow and ice hang from the rocks' apex, creating a wall. He punches a hole, and with both hands, he points his pistol through the opening.

They'll never see it coming.

Miss Highsmith says something, but he's too far away to understand her words. She cannot be seen behind the trees. Kennedy responds to her, but again, he cannot make out the words.

The wind whistles.

He holds his gun steady.

The prey comes into view. Miss Highsmith leads the way.

He takes aim at her back, but she's moving fast. He wishes he had a rifle with a scope, but no matter. He can do this. He's a god with a gun.

And, he's wise.

Miss Highsmith is farther ahead of Kennedy. She's smaller. She's blocked by Kennedy.

He switches his aim and shoots.

A direct hit.

Kennedy goes down screaming, grasping her side.

Roll out the red carpet for the internet's hottest fashion blogger— Kennedy McCallister. This year, she's draped herself in her own design: Snow Blood.

Randall looks away. Gags. Swallows. Stands and walks around the rock outcropping, his pistol raised, his eyes watering from having seen Kennedy's blood soak into the snow.

Miss Highsmith pulls a rifle off her shoulder and points it at him before his vision clears.

"You son of a bitch," she says.

He points his gun at her. Cocks his head. Aims. "Where'd you find that?"

Ah, but he knows before the words leave his lips. It's the rifle he gave to Amanda. He left it in the trees after disarming her. Nevertheless, this is not his fault. It's fate. He couldn't have known Miss Highsmith would escape the boathouse and find the rifle. In fact, she must have had some kind of supernatural assistance. That lock was impenetrable. There's no way the imbecile could have helped her. No way.

This is fate.

Evolution wanted her to escape so he could cleanse the earth of her imperfections. Miss Highsmith—the prey known as Charly—standing there with a rifle pointed at him. What a vaginal neanderthal she is. What a moron.

"I'll shoot," she says. "I swear to God, I'll shoot you."

"Ah, but there is no God for you to swear to. God is dead." Randall lets the moment consume him. It fills his heart with joy. "What makes you think that rifle is loaded?"

Her body stiffens. She says nothing.

He bets she didn't even cock it. "I know where you found it. It's one of mine. It's a Winchester."

"So?"

"So, it holds five rounds with one in the chamber, but when I gave it to Amanda"—Miss Highsmith frowns—"that's right. Your cousin became a true hunter today."

"Shut up." Her arms tremble.

"When I gave the rifle to Amanda this morning, there were five rounds loaded, but none in the chamber. She shot it five times before killing Cam. Tell me, did you know she killed Cam?"

"You asshole."

"There, there. Listen. My point is, you have no bullets."

"I don't believe you."

The insolence. The arrogance.

Yet, she's not wrong. Amanda wasted four rounds on Cam, leaving exactly one. Like most newbies, Miss Highsmith probably didn't check to see if the rifle was loaded. She is also holding it all wrong, her hand too far up the stock. Her hips askew. There's no way she could hit him from there.

He steps toward Kennedy, keeping his pistol trained on Miss Highsmith.

"Stay right there," she says. "Kennedy, are you okay?"

"You're precious. Do you know that?"

"Stop." She tracks his movement with the rifle.

Kennedy shrieks, "I'm bleeding. Oh, God, please, help me."

"*I'm bleeding,*" Randall mocks, "*Oh, God, help me. Help me.*"

"Put your gun down, or I'll shoot."

Randall loves it. "I think not."

He swings his pistol toward Kennedy and fires, hitting her in the leg.

She cries out.

In a flash, Randall resumes his aim at Miss Highsmith.

She lowers her rifle in shock and stares at the blood flowing from Kennedy's thigh. "No. Why?"

Randall pulls the trigger, and the imbecile screams. He misses.

Miss Highsmith sidesteps behind a tree.

He approaches Kennedy. Stands over her. Winces at the bloody snow. Focuses on her face instead.

"Why?" she asks. "Why did you do this?"

"Because I'm a hunter. It's what hunters do." He kicks snow over the blood, but there's too much to cover up. Worms. Gray worms. He swears her blood is filled with diseased, gray worms.

He gags.

He looks away. Gazes at Miss Highsmith's hiding spot. She could try to shoot him from behind that tree, but she'd miss.

He raises his pistol. "Miss Highsmith? Are you still over there?"

No response.

"Miss Highsmith?"

"Come and get me, coward."

"I think not."

"Come on. I'm over here."

Snow and ice crackle behind the tree.

Is she on the run?

He aims his pistol at Kennedy's lovely emerald eyes. "It's you who should come over here. I'm not going to chase you."

He waits.

He waits for nothing. "Miss Highsmith? Don't you want to save your friend? Are you still there?"

Nothing.

"Oh, dear Kennedy. You imbecile. Your Barry will be so disappointed when I tell him you went back to Denver alone."

"No." She blocks her face with her hands. "Please."

"When you don't call him tomorrow, he'll wonder if it was something he said, but don't worry. He'll get over you. Social media slags such as yourself are a dime-a-dozen to men like him."

"Please. Don't."

"He won't miss you."

Randall looks to the sky.

There's a small break in the clouds over the horizon. The blizzard might let up soon.

Bang.

CHAPTER SIXTY-FIVE

My plan failed miserably. I tried to distract Randall by taunting him. I begged him to come after me, to chase me, but he didn't fall for it.

Bang.

He shot Kennedy.

He shot her point-blank.

He shot her in the face.

Panic took the reins.

I was too rattled to think I could hold the rifle steady and shoot him.

Rather than stay and fight, I took flight.

I ran.

The world became a white blur of snow and confusion. Dodging trees in the snowdrifts, I got turned around. I couldn't tell which way was back to the cabin. Now, I stand here freezing, watching the wind blow ice crystals against the tree trunks. The crystals stick to the bark and sparkle. They stick to my cheeks. They burn my pores.

Gripping the rifle we found near Cam's body, I fight

through a copse of evergreens.

He's coming after me. Randall. He must be.

Pine needles poke my hands. My face. My feet are heavy. With each laborious step, the snow weighs me down. I plow through the frozen expanse. He called my bluff. He knew I would miss if I tried to shoot him back there, and now . . .

Kennedy is dead.

Amanda is dead.

Cam is dead.

Cam's body was crumpled in a heap near the rifle. Randall said Amanda shot him with this rifle. I don't know whether to believe that or not, but it doesn't matter anymore because—everyone is dead.

Oh, God.

They're all dead.

I want to cry.

But I never cry.

Ever.

And I don't dare cry now.

I stop and listen. There's no sound other than the breeze blowing through the trees. Snowy ghosts spiral around me. It's nearly silent out here. Randall might not be chasing me after all. An image of Amanda's lifeless body—no longer bragging, winning, or breathing—surrounded by a sea of blood floats on the white, white snow mixed with the ghosts in my mind, and I realize my eyes are closed.

My teeth ache from the cold.

My shoulder blades shiver.

I lean against a tree, barely managing to stay upright.

I almost drop the rifle.

My heart pounds as if it's about to explode.

Whether Randall is coming or not, I must press on.

I must find Jacob.

The wind is wicked, and my pulse is loud, blood pumping through my head, an avalanche coming down. Beat and pump, and beat and pump. I trudge through the snow. Randall doesn't seem to have followed me. He must have taken a different route back to the cabin. It's hard to be sure. What *am* I sure of?

Everyone is dead. Kennedy. Amanda. Cam.

And, Tyler.

My God. Poor Tyler.

Earlier, I listened closely when Hector's voice came through Randall's radio. He'd said everything had gone as planned. No deviations. He probably hunted Tyler down like an animal and killed him.

That bastard.

Poor Tyler.

I force his gentle eyes out of my mind. His touch. He didn't deserve to die.

No one did.

I must focus, but—what if they ran across Jacob in the woods? What if they took the carving knife away from him?

What if they shot him?

No.

Stop it.

My mind is making things up now.

Jacob is alive. He's got to be.

I break through the trees into a clearing. There's the road. The driveway to the cabin meanders up the hill. Scattered trees dot the top near the makeshift firewood stand. I can see the cars and the snowmobile. The front porch and the cabin.

The cabin looms over me like an impenetrable castle.

Someone speaks, but I'm not close enough to understand

them. Crouching and walking at the same time, I move from tree to tree until Hector and Barry come into view. They're standing behind the Humvee. Barry opens the back and pulls out a briefcase.

"This ought to do it," he says.

"Thank you." Hector takes the case in hand. "It was a pleasure doing business with you. I hope it was everything you expected."

"It was." His face beams beneath his greasy dark curls. "I'm on top of the world. I won't soon forget this trip."

"Excellent. That's what we like to hear."

"Where's Mr. Thorne? I'd like to thank him."

"No need. We're done here."

"Oh." Barry closes the hatchback and steps toward the cabin.

"Stop." Hector grasps Barry's shoulder. "I have some bad news."

"What is it?"

"Randall radioed while you were taking your celebration piss in the woods. Kennedy won't be returning to Denver with you."

"What?" He looks up at the cabin.

"She left a couple of hours ago. Something about how she couldn't stand being cooped up here without the internet anymore. An associate of ours took her to town on the snowmobile."

"I don't understand." He scratches his head. "She should've been too hungover to leave. I thought she'd sleep all day."

"Nope."

"Let me just check." Barry heads for the porch.

Hector follows close behind. "There's no need to do that,

Mr. Rockwell. She's gone."

The Humvee is unlocked. It's right there, not twenty yards away. I could hide inside and go with Barry. Once we find civilization, I could tell him about Kennedy. What really happened. We could get help and come back for Jacob. It reminds me of the last time I left him. He lived in that miserable shelter for over two years. But, this is different. I'd come back for him this time because, if I didn't—if for some reason I couldn't—they'd kill him.

"Mr. Rockwell," Hector shouts. "Do not go inside. Your excursion is over. Kennedy isn't here."

Barry turns around. "Why didn't you tell me she left?"

"Mr. Thorne didn't want it to affect your hunt. Now, please, leave. We have other clients inside. You can contact your girlfriend when you get to town."

"Let me—"

"No. I can't allow you to interrupt the next excursion." He unbuttons his denim coat and thrusts the bottom back, exposing a gun tucked into his pants.

Barry shakes his head. "Fine. I'll leave."

I'm too late. I can't get to the Humvee now.

Jacob is in one of two places. He's either in the cabin or frozen to death in the woods. He was serious about finding Randall. There's no way he would have climbed back into the Humvee.

"Good. I'll follow you down the mountain."

Barry opens the driver's side door and gets inside. The engine starts. He backs up, turns, and slowly descends the hill, riding high in his enormous vehicle. Hector follows in his truck. He passes by my hiding spot, his fat face glued to the windshield, carefully keeping his tires inside Barry's tracks.

I sneak to the snowmobile. The gas tank is full, but the

key is gone. Hector lied to Barry about Kennedy receiving a ride from an associate, but he didn't lie about the snowmobile. I left it by my car miles from here when I ran out of gas. Someone must have filled it up and driven it back to the cabin. Maybe the "associate" Hector referred to is real. My thoughts are so blurry. Could Randall have had time to retrieve the snowmobile *and* take Amanda hunting?

Maybe.

I spent hours locked in the boathouse cage—half asleep, half awake.

A lot could have happened.

Randall could have retrieved the snowmobile while I was talking to Jacob. He could have been gone when Jacob left looking for him, carrying that carving knife. Swearing he was going to rescue me. He'd been so confident. So fearless.

I hope his exuberance has faded.

I hope he's hiding in the cabin right now, warm and untouched.

I hope he's not dead like everyone else.

I race to the porch as if the wind isn't trying to hold me back.

The awning failed to keep the snow off the porch, but it did protect the windows. Yet, I can't see inside because of the curtains. I creep along the wall, hoping Randall isn't waiting for me inside. If he is, I don't want him to hear me coming. All I have left is the element of surprise. At the same time, it's warm in there. My feet will fall off if I don't wrap them in a blanket soon. I take a quick, painfully frostbitten step, and something flutters in my peripheral vision.

It's a piece of paper taped to the window.

I reach for it, but the wind gets there first. The paper flies into the air, swooping this way and that. I bound off the porch and chase after it. So much for not surprising Randall. The paper comes to rest near the firewood stand, and I snatch it up.

Behind the house of boats, where one hundred years ago, a mountain man gave a donkey named Rags a box of oats, you will find the next of these notes.

Jacob.

It must be him.

He must have taped the note to the window.

I read it again.

I hold it up to my nose.

It doesn't smell old, but it doesn't smell new, either. This must be the note from our childhood. Jacob must have brought it along with the raccoon tail. He must be trying to help me find him.

He's alive.

CHAPTER SIXTY-SIX

RANDALL

This excursion ends now. There have been too many mistakes. None of which can be blamed on Randall, of course. It's all on Lance. Lance told him to go to the cabin in Colorado, and the cabin in Colorado has always been the mountain cabin. Not the new location in Pueblo. Lance didn't explicitly say Pueblo. He gave Randall the wrong location for Barry's excursion, and now those inferior animals who showed up at the mountain cabin are dead.

All except for two.

Jacob and Miss Highsmith are somewhere in the woods, and Randall will find them. He will hunt them down and kill them. He'll tie up these loose ends before his boss arrives, and everything will be okay.

He pauses along the trail leading deeper into the forest. The ache in his leg makes him feel alive. He will not lose. He expands his chest, sucks in the frigid air, and releases a frosty cloud. So refreshing. So full of life. So much control—yet, it shouldn't have gone this way.

But, adaptation is the key to survival.

He repeats this to himself because of Ronald.

Adaptation is the key to survival.

Adapting to changing circumstances kept Randall alive, which is why his brother had to die.

Rest in peace, Ronald.

Adaptation is why all the inferior animals died today, their bodies stinking up the mountainside. The Zaroff cleanup crew has their work cut out for them. That is, if Randall decides to keep using this location for future excursions. Damn his boss. None of this would have happened if Randall had been in charge. Nevertheless, he will be soon. Very soon. When Lance arrives this afternoon, they will have a heart-to-heart conversation about the future of Zaroff Excursions.

Together.

Alone.

In the woods.

Randall spies divots in the snow. Buried footprints. It's a blessing the clouds ceased their discharge earlier this afternoon. The clearing of the sky was meant to be. He glances this way and that, looking for the boulder mentioned in the note he found behind the boathouse.

A boulder named Stew . . . broke in two.

Hilarious.

One of the loose ends is trying to find the other, leaving stupid notes taped to the cabin, hidden behind the boathouse, and only Darwin would know where else. He suspects Jacob is behind the notes. Miss Highsmith is too smart to do such a thing.

Jacob is a retard.

Randall memorized the notes and left them behind for Miss Highsmith to find. It's perfect, really. He will follow the clues until he finds Jacob, and then he will kill him. Miss

Highsmith will follow the clues as well, and Randall will be waiting for her. By the time Lance arrives, the loose ends will be all tied up.

The trail leads around a hill. He's been here many times before, but rarely in the winter. Mother Nature can't confuse him by pulling her wintry disguise over the wilderness. He's a true hunter. He is prepared for anything. He was prepared when he visited this part of the woods last summer—as he does every year. Boots, rations, zip ties, his walkie-talkie, GPS—the tools of a survivor.

A conqueror.

Another twenty minutes or so, and he'll arrive at the boulder. He'll find the next clue, and perhaps it will instruct him to turn around. Head back toward the cabin. That would be good. His annual visits to the boulder are enough.

He thinks of Tyler's hiking boots again. He pictures Barry gunning Tyler down. Tyler's expensive jacket. His thin neck. That constant doubt in his eyes. He looked so much like Ronald.

Ronald had to die, just like Tyler.

Suddenly, Randall is not in the mood to trek by his brother's resting place, even if it means finding Jacob.

But, he must.

It is apropos.

Today is the day his brother's death will be justified.

Today, Randall takes over Zaroff Excursions. The sacrifice will have been worth it.

He needs to focus.

He must tie up the loose ends no matter where it takes him. The loose ends? Jacob, Miss Highsmith, and . . .

Barry?

Is Barry taken care of?

Yes.

Barry must be dead by now. Hector promised to kill him at the cabin.

That fat slug had better have done it.

Randall didn't want to have Barry killed. Referrals from clients like the wealthy Bartholomew Rockwell are incredibly important to Zaroff Excursions. Randall's *new* Zaroff Excursions. Barry was the perfect client, but with Kennedy's disappearance and Miss Highsmith still on the loose, Randall had to ask Hector to finish Barry off. He had to adapt. No one other than Hector can leave this mountain alive.

Not today.

Too much is at stake.

To be sure, he uses his walkie-talkie to radio Hector, but the slug doesn't answer. Some affirmation that Barry is dead would be nice, but he trusts Hector. He has no choice. Hector is not like his brother. Hector's motives can be trusted. Ronald's could not. Ronald wanted to expose the organization. Hector only wants to retire.

Sweat accumulates behind Randall's ear and runs down his neck. The trickle chills his back. His hips stiffen as he steps over a log. No. He does not miss his brother. No. He did what he had to do. He did to Ronald what Hector had to do to Barry. He picked off the weak from the herd. Separated the chaff from the wheat.

It's okay.

It had to be done.

Concentrate.

Tie up the loose ends, and move on.

The broken boulder lies on the other side of the trees ahead. Beyond the boulder, a few paces down the hill—that's where Ronald died. Sometimes, in the summer heat on his annual visits, Randall can smell his brother's blood clinging to the Aspen leaves. It always makes him sick.

Sometimes, he wishes it were him instead of his brother, but—no. He can't do that.

Randall is not the weak one.

Ronald was.

He shot Ronald in the back.

It was a mercy killing.

That's right. Mercy. Mercy for the sake of mankind. Ronald did not die in vain. He died for Zaroff Excursions. He died for the good of evolution.

A soft murmuring comes from the other side of the trees. It's not a sobbing sound, but it's close. He steps off the trail and circles around, heading toward the boulder, keeping his cover.

He stops, knocks snow off a drooping limb, and presses it down until he can see the trail.

Until he can see that simpleton standing there.

Jacob Highsmith.

CHAPTER SIXTY-SEVEN

Everything I own fits inside my Jansport backpack if I organize it the right way. Everything except my art, but that's okay. It's no good anyway. It's a temporary relief to paint. Take my emotions out on an unsuspecting canvas and then throw it all away.

I'll never throw away my makeup mirror. I don't care how heavy it is. I'll never leave it behind. Jacob gave me this mirror for my birthday.

I miss him.

It's been two years since we ran away from Windcrest. In a way, I've been running ever since. Before living with Lucas, I dated Mark, and I was able to take everything I owned with me when we broke up—except my paintings, of course. He had a basement apartment beneath a two-story townhome. It was nice, but not as nice as Grant's place. Grant's high-rise had a terrific view of the Rockies. I'd hoped things would last longer with Grant, but there I was, standing outside his bathroom, holding my mirror with both hands, getting ready to pack.

"I want you out here now, bitch." Grant threw my backpack over the bed. It landed on my feet. "And don't come back."

He was drunk.

I was drunker.

Things were fuzzy, but getting kicked out wasn't a surprise. "Can I stay until tomorrow?"

"No."

"But it's cold outside. And it's late."

"I don't care."

I unzipped my backpack, wrapped a shirt around my mirror, and slid it inside.

"Whore," he said.

"I'm not a whore." I shoved my other things into my pack—high heels, skirts, shirts, tampons, and papers. A toothbrush. "Are you sure I can't stay until morning? I have nowhere to go."

"Why don't you go to the Cabaret?"

"All I said was, I'm eighteen now. I'm old enough to strip, but I'm not going to do it."

"That's not what Alicia said."

"Screw her."

"No. Screw you." He pointed down the hall. "Get out."

As I left Grant's apartment for the last time, I took the last swallow of my beer and dropped the bottle on the floor. Peace out. I never loved him. I never loved anybody. I hoped that last swallow would keep me warm. At this time of night, the temperatures would be below freezing, and the streets in downtown Denver would be covered in ice. My coat would only keep me warm for a while, and if I didn't find somewhere to go, I'd turn into a Popsicle.

I stepped into the elevator and pressed "G" for ground.

Maybe Lucas would take me back, but I doubted it. To make that work, I'd have to sleep with him. He's got this nasty mole on his back, but it might be worth it. Christmas was coming. It would be an early present for him and somewhere to crash for me.

It might be worth it.

Then, I pictured his goatee.

And the mole.

No. Definitely not worth it.

Sure enough, the ice outside Grant's apartment building coated the sidewalk, and Broadway Avenue glistened beneath the streetlamps. Half drunk, I decided to walk it off. I didn't have the money to spend wandering the city in an Uber. I decided to let the brisk night air sober me up. I headed east, away from downtown, toward the side streets. Toward the ragged alleys.

Toward Five Points. The drug neighborhood.

It wasn't safe to go to Five Points at this time of night, but I was drunk, and I knew people there.

The wind tore through the urban corridors, trying to inflate my coat. Trying to kill me with its subzero torrent. I didn't completely disagree with the wind's desire. I wanted to disappear. Curl up and die. It was after midnight. Dark. Cold. Empty.

The night was dark, cold, and empty, and so was I.

And, I was drunk.

Did I want to die?

No.

That was the booze talking.

I needed somewhere to stay.

There might not be anyone at Five Points.

What about Lucas? The goatee and the mole?

I needed to suck it up and call him, but—my phone. I didn't have my phone. Rushed and confused and ten sheets to the wind, I'd left Grant's without it.

What about Mark?

I couldn't remember where Mark lived. Before him—Neil? Was that guy named Neil? I vaguely remembered living with a Malcolm, and before him . . .

Drake.

I'd never forget Drake.

Back at Windcrest. Back before Jacob and I ran away.

I could never go back to Drake. Our relationship ended badly. Very badly. He hit me. I nearly stabbed him with a knife. But, that was eons ago. Two years is eons when you're only eighteen.

The wind threatened to freeze me to the core.

I pulled my backpack straps tight to keep the frigid air off my spine. The streetlamps came and went as I ambled down the slippery sidewalks. At times like this, the past was a blur. Memories came out of nowhere like dreams—visions filling me with guilt and remorse. Life would have been different if I hadn't left Jacob at the shelter. His face haunted me. I told myself not to go there, not to think about him, but the memories always returned whenever I got drunk.

Jacob had been with me the first time I put everything I owned in this backpack and hit the streets. Then, I left him.

I left him, and I missed him, but I left him.

My teeth chattered.

I pulled my collar around my neck.

Somehow, I had wandered off the main street into an alley. Dumpsters guarded the back doors to the restaurants, bars, kitschy clothing stores . . . I stumbled in the snow and put my hand on the brick wall. Some doors had lights on above them, but most did not. Some dumpsters had room to hide behind them, but most did not. My stomach turned on itself, sending a burning sensation up my throat. Beer bubbles and acidic anguish.

I wished I wasn't alone.

I wished I hadn't left Jacob.

He had cried and pulled on his fingers. He had run to the window and screamed for me not to leave, but—I didn't have a choice. I had no money. I couldn't take care of him. No guys would have given me a place to stay, towing my neurodivergent brother around with me everywhere I went.

Talk about baggage.

I didn't have a choice.

But tonight, I did.

Tonight, I could go to a shelter. I could look for him.

Or, I could curl up and die behind a dumpster.

CHAPTER SIXTY-EIGHT

The simpleton stands there in the middle of the trail, holding a bag. He stands in the middle of the broken boulder, shaking. Nearly crying. So pathetic. So unworthy of a place on this earth. It begins to snow, and the simpleton appears to be trying to watch each flake as it falls. What a waste of space. What a moron.

What a retard.

Randall is the opposite of Jacob. Randall has stealth. He has cunning. He is the predator. The fittest. He slinks through the trees, stepping lightly, circling around, and coming up behind the fool.

"Who's there?" Jacob says.

Randall stops cold. Steps behind a tree. He's only a few feet away.

"Charly?" Jacob pulls something out of his bag.

Randall could shoot the fool in the back of the head from here. Easy peasy. He reaches into his pocket, unstraps his pistol, and pulls it out. He takes aim and licks his lips.

"I heard you." Jacob turns around. "You're here, but

you're not on the trail. You're—who are you?"

Before Randall can pull the trigger, Jacob takes off.

Randall stows his gun and chases after him.

Something shiny flashes up and down as Jacob pumps his arms.

The simpleton has a knife. He took the carving knife.

Jacob looks over his shoulder. It slows him down. Randall catches him, grabs his elbow with one hand to stabilize the knife, and wraps his arm around Jacob's neck. The knife falls to the ground, and Randall brings the boy down. They slide on the snow, coming to rest against a log. Randall presses his forearm into the back of Jacob's neck, forcing the retard's face into a pile of frozen pine needles. "So, it was you . . ."

"Wha?" Jacob asks, his voice muffled by the pine needles. Randall relieves the pressure enough so the cretin can be heard. "What was me? You're hurting me. What was me?"

"You took the carving knife from the kitchen."

"Get off. You're hurting me. Get off. Charly. Help."

"You shouldn't have done it. You shouldn't have taken it." Randall pulls his gun out and presses the muzzle against the back of Jacob's head. "Stand." He grasps Jacob by the collar. "Do you know how many problems you have caused me?"

They stand.

"You're evil," Jacob says. "You're an evil man. Evil."

"No, I'm not." He pulls Jacob onto the trail. Kicks the knife off to the side. Grips the butt of his gun tightly and punches Jacob in the face with it. "I'm diligent."

"Ah. Ow." He covers his eyes. "Why?"

"Shut up." Randall hits him again and spins him around before the blood from Jacob's nose can sully his senses. He shoves Jacob in the back. "Walk."

Ahead, the boulder collects fresh snow. The snow falls harder now. Beyond the boulder lies Ronald's resting place. It's close, but not so close as to be tarnished by killing Jacob right here. Yet, Randall fears he would see the simpleton's stupid face each time he visits Ronald. And he'd hate to scare Miss Highsmith away, assuming she found those stupid notes. "Where's your sister?"

"Charly," Jacob shouts. "She's Charly. Charly. Help."

"*Charly. She's Charly*—where is she? When did you see her last?"

"Charly."

"Stop yelling, or I'll hit you again."

"You'll break my cheekbone, and I won't be able to talk. I won't be able to tell you where I saw Charly last. I won't."

Randall grabs Jacob's shoulder, spins him around, hesitates, then grips the cretin's ear and twists it.

"Ah. Charly. Charly. Charly." He shakes his head free. "Charly."

"*Charly. Charly. Charly*—oh, shut up."

"Charly. I'm here. I'm here. Help me."

"Wait." Randall grasps Jacob's collar and pulls him close. "You're right, half-wit. Keep it up. Yell for her."

"Charly."

"That's it. Yell."

"I want to go home. I want to leave. I want Charly."

"That's a good boy. Keep it up. Let's see if she can find us."

Randall raises his pistol and gazes down the trail.

He waits.

Jacob yells.

CHAPTER SIXTY-NINE

Streetlamps glowed above a major street at the end of the alley. The alley's dumpsters slept in the shadows between the brick apartment buildings. Millennials slept in the units above, warm and comfortable.

I shivered.

I wondered where I was.

Had I gone the wrong way?

How had I gotten here?

Why was I—then I remembered the fight.

Grant.

I'd gotten drunk and left him.

I stood in a dimly lit alley, considering whether to stay and sleep behind a dumpster or find a shelter. My backpack was heavy. I'd packed all my things and left Grant for good, wandering out into the cold, searching for a place to stay. If I fell asleep here, I'd likely freeze to death. A fitting fate for someone like me.

A whore.

Grant had called me a whore.

Voices came from the street. I slunk along the wall, staying in the dumpster's shadows until I reached the end of the alley. Two men stood across the street. The taller one handed the other a baggie and patted him on the back. It wasn't a friendly pat. More of a *here-you-go-now-get-the-hell-out-of-here* pat.

I knew the taller man.

Antonne Sands.

Drug pusher extraordinaire.

I first met him in City Park not long after leaving Jacob in the shelter. I'd been sleeping under a bench when a drug dealer twice Antonne's size woke me up and insisted I buy some rock. The dealer was huge, with a wart-ridden, flabby face. A real ogre. He followed me through the park, yelling at me, calling me names I'd never heard before—slunt, dunt, cooz. Antonne came up behind him and swept his feet. He went down hard. Antonne pulled a knife and threatened to tell other drug dealers how the ogre had trespassed on their turf.

The flabby-faced creep skulked away like a child.

Unlike the ogre, Antonne never pushed drugs on me.

We never dated.

He was my savior.

For a time, Antonne Sands was my only friend.

Looking back on those early days, I should never have slept in the park like a homeless person, but my pride kept me from staying in a women's shelter. I could have. The bruise Drake had given me decorated my cheek for weeks after running away. Denver had plenty of places for battered women to go, but they weren't for me. Instead, I wanted a job, some money, and to rescue Jacob from the shelter. Then, I met . . . Neil?

Was it Neil?

My brain was so fogged.

No. It was Malcolm. Malcolm was the first guy I dated after Drake, and he let me stay with him for three months. Then it was Neil. Then it was the next one, and the next one, and—time ran away from me.

Two years.

I couldn't believe I hadn't seen Jacob in two years.

I stood on the corner, shivering, watching Antonne sell drugs, wondering if Jacob was still in the shelter. He could have found a foster home by now. He could have been rescued by someone else. He could have moved on while I was stuck wandering through life like a homeless person, going from place to place.

First one, then two snowflakes fell onto my face. Then, hundreds gathered on Antonne's black knitted skull cap. I considered asking him for a place to stay, but our relationship had never been that way, and I didn't know where he'd been. I hadn't seen him in months.

My toes began to lose feeling.

The short guy with the baggie walked away, and I stepped into the light, gingerly navigating the icy crosswalk. "Antonne."

"Charly. Shh." He waved for me to hurry, glancing up and down the street. "Not so loud." The whites of his eyes glowed in the dark. He wore a thick black jacket and dark blue jeans. Some stitches on his skull cap had come loose, and the Raiders skull logo hung sideways. I'd always liked the Broncos better, not only because we lived in Denver, but because Dad had always said we were a Broncos family.

The whites of Antonne's eyes shone brightly despite the streetlamp's attempt to turn night into day. "What are you doing out here?"

"I broke up with Grant."

"You mean Mark?"

"Sure. Whatever."

"You looking to score something? I didn't think you used."

"I don't."

And I didn't. I never had, but that night, I wanted to.

I wanted to die.

I wanted to curl up and die, and I thought, maybe this is how it starts for addicts. Maybe this is how my mom went from vodka to crank.

One cold, lonely night, looking to die . . .

CHAPTER SEVENTY

CHARLY

My bitter hands clutch the note I found taped outside the cabin window.

Behind the house of boats . . . you will find the next of these notes.

Standing knee-deep in the snow by the firewood, I turn to go, and the wind whips my face and shakes the paper. It chills my soul. Low-hanging clouds fly across the sky, darkening the property. I make my way around the cabin, staying close to the wall so no one can see me through the windows.

A snowflake lands in my eye.

I stop. I squint.

Another flake hits me in the face, and then another.

The snow becomes frantic, obliterating the landscape below. The scenery reminds me of a painting I created years ago. It was the first art I'd done after living on my own for the first time. I called it "Sugar Daddy Whiteout." It was a reminder of each guy I'd ever lived with. After painting their faces, I'd covered the canvas in white so I could forget them. So I couldn't see them.

So I could move on with my life.

It hadn't worked as well as I'd hoped.

Now, standing on this hill by the cabin, I need to find Jacob and run away all over again.

I can barely see my hand in front of my face. This is a real whiteout. I know the boathouse is down there. Randall might be in the cabin behind me, though, so I continue to stay close to the outside wall, avoiding the windows, until I have no choice but to make a break for it. I descend the hill at full speed, running through the snow. If Randall came back from the forest before me—and he most likely did—then he could be inside the cabin waiting for me. I only hope he doesn't see me. Thank God Jacob left the note. Thank God he's not in there with that madman.

The rifle bounces against my back. I grasp the shoulder strap and pull it tight. Earlier, I checked. I've got one shot left. Randall was wrong when he told me the rifle had no bullets. I hope he really thinks I'm out of ammunition so I can surprise him. And Jacob has the carving knife. Together, if Randall comes after us, we'll have a chance.

The deep snow covers everything behind the boathouse except for a large box. The kind of box that rides in the back of a truck. Jacob must have knocked the snow off when he opened it to hide the next note. I grasp the latch and swing the lid up. The metal makes a loud *clang*, but I don't care. I've found the next clue . . .

A boulder named Stew fell off the mountain and broke in two. If you follow the trail and stay to the right, you can visit Stew, and under the log on his left, you'll find your next clue.

The split boulder.

I only vaguely remember the boulder from my childhood, but I vividly remember Amanda's face when she found a clue there. So cocky, standing in the boulder's divide. She won the game that day, and now—now she is gone.

She'll never win again, and I'll never lose.

What a horrible thought.

My long-held resentment rushes through me, and I realize it was never her. It was my father. He was the one I should have blamed, not her. She didn't take his love away from me the day she won the game. He did. He's the one who left.

And now, she's gone.

There's no time to think about this now. I've got to keep moving.

I attempt to close the lid more quietly than I opened it, but it slips out of my fingers and bangs down. Why did I try? If Randall heard the first bang—if he came outside the cabin to see what it was—then he might be standing on the deck right now. If he is, he can't see me hiding behind the boathouse. But if I'm to follow the directions on the note, I'll have to venture into the open.

I listen for him.

The wind blasts through the wilderness beyond.

If he's coming, I can't hear him over the squall.

Crouching, I peer around the corner.

Snow flurries spiral off the lake, pushed by the wind. The snow lets up, revealing the woods. Jacob's footprints lead across the open space and into the trees. The falling snow obscures the cabin. I can't tell if Randall is on the deck or on his way toward me. The wind blasts again, thrusting my hair into my face. I wish I were dead. The chill is unbearable, but

I've got to find Jacob before I freeze to death. Before he freezes to death.

I rub my ankles, trying to warm them. My feet are a lost cause.

With everything I have, I sprint into the open.

"Hey," someone yells from the deck.

I keep running.

"Stop."

It's a man's voice. It's got to be Randall. He's seen me.

Just before disappearing into the woods, I glance back.

A dark figure comes down the deck stairs. Tall. Ominous.

The snow on the trail isn't as high as it was in the open. I speed up.

The man yells again, but he's too far away. I can't tell if it's Randall's voice or not, but it must be him. Hector and Barry left.

I follow in Jacob's footprints.

I'm fast.

I build a lead.

When the trail divides, I take a chance. Instead of following Jacob's footprints, I choose the path not taken and make new prints. If Randall comes behind me, he won't know which prints to follow. After a few feet, I leap off the trail into the trees, hoping to make it look like I stopped at a dead end. I trudge through the snow until I rejoin the original trail and run.

The air stings the tip of my tongue. A throbbing pulses behind my eyes as I scamper through the trees. As I scan the forest for Jacob, fear creeps in, wrapping itself around me.

It threatens to slow me down.

But I won't let it.

I have a rifle.

Jacob has a knife.

Randall has it coming.

But, if possible, I'd rather not confront him. I'd rather find Jacob, sneak back to the cabin, and steal a car. Or the snowmobile. If I could trick Randall into getting lost, we might have time to escape. I turn around and walk backward at the next juncture, sweeping my footprints away. Again, I hope he won't know which way I went.

I do this again the next time the trail splits. And, again.

I think it's working. I haven't heard anyone yell since leaving the boathouse.

I've only heard the wailing wind.

Maybe he didn't follow me.

The boulder can't be much farther.

Stew, where are you?

I press on.

Everything will be okay. I have a bullet. Jacob has a knife.

Where is that boulder?

The trail slithers up a hill into a copse of slender evergreens. Nothing is familiar. I'm not sure I went the right way, and how would I know if I had? It's been so long, and I'm so cold. My legs are fatigued. They don't want to move anymore.

"Charly," a voice calls out. "Charly. I'm here. I'm here, Charly. Help me."

"Jacob?"

CHAPTER SEVENTY-ONE

CHARLY - THEN

It was a warmth, seeing a familiar face after wandering the frigid streets of downtown Denver all night, drunk and alone. It was a warmth to see Antonne. Drug dealer extraordinaire.

Before I left the alley and crossed the street to his corner, I'd wanted to die. My head was stilled fogged from drinking. I'd wanted to curl up and die before I saw him. Before I remembered how he'd saved me in the park two years ago. Before his smile melted the frosty air between us on this cold and lonely night.

He saved me back then.

He could save me again.

I wouldn't have needed him if I hadn't left my cell phone at Grant's apartment, but here I was. Drunk, alone, and desperate.

"Where have you been?" I asked.

"Jail," he said.

"Is that where you got that?" I pointed at the black snake coiled on his neck.

He touched the tattoo. "No. I got this before I went in."

"It's nice."

"Yeah." He spoke slowly, smooth and warm. "What you doing out here, girl?"

"I'm freezing." I wrapped my arms around my chest. Snow gathered around our feet.

"You're looking fine, girl. You still got that dope nose. Cute." He put his finger on the tip of my nose and grinned, the corner of his mouth rising, exposing a canine. "How long's it been? A year?"

"Something like that. You're still working the same job, I see."

"Yeah." He glanced up and down the street. "I'm moving up in the world. The can was good for that. I met some good blood in there. What you been doing?"

"I started painting."

"Oh, yeah? That's something." He pinched his nose and sniffed. "Like houses or art shit?"

"Paintings. Art."

"I ain't never been into doing that, but I like it. You got some in there?" He reached for my backpack. "It looks loaded."

I stepped back. "It is."

"You making any money with it?"

"No. I paint for fun. It's a release."

"I know what you mean." He put his hand in his jacket pocket. "I got plenty of release."

"No doubt."

"You want some?"

"I've got my painting." I glanced back at the alley.

"Where you going tonight?"

I stared at him. The snow fell, the wind blew in my face, and the night threatened to take me, luring me back into the alley, back to a dumpster where I could lie down, fall asleep, and freeze to death. Where I could curl up and die.

"Girl, you need somewhere to crash, don't you?" He tipped his head back. Looked up at the streetlamp. "That ain't art in your backpack, is it?"

"No. I had to leave my paintings."

He pulled out a cell phone and checked the screen. "Come back to my crib. I'll put you up. We can do some art." He nodded toward his pocket. Winked. "I got plenty of art supplies."

"I don't know."

"Come on, girl. It'll be a release."

"I just need to sleep, and I don't have any money."

"It's free of charge for you, Charly." He bounced on his toes. Suddenly antsy. Cold. "Nobody pays the first time."

A lone car passed through the intersection behind me, tossing slush upon the curb. I turned to see it better and spied a homeless man across the street. He stood at the end of the alley like a guard. His gray wool trench coat hugged his body, and he wore one of those old hunting hats with ear flaps.

A red scarf hid his face.

Antonne put his hand on my shoulder. "You can't go wandering. It's too cold. Come with me." The whites of his eyes lit the night. "We can do some beautiful art together."

"Can't I just crash on your couch?"

He stepped back. Smiled. Raised his hands. "You can sleep when you're dead, and tonight—whooh—tonight we won't be dying. We'll be flying. Come on, girl. Trust me. After we paint a couple of pictures with this"—he patted his pocket once more—"sleeping will be the last thing you'll want to do."

My feet had gone numb. My knees were locked up. My back muscles strained to hold my spine straight, burdened by my backpack. I wanted to throw up.

I nodded. "Okay."

Antonne gently took my hand. "This is going to be righteous, girl. You'll see."

"Stop," called out the homeless man.

We turned toward him.

"Let go of her."

Antonne dropped my hand and charged into the street, chest out, chin up, hands in the air. "You got a problem, man?"

"No," the homeless man said.

"Antonne, wait." I followed him into the intersection. "Ignore him."

"It looks to me like you got a problem." Antonne stopped in the middle of the street a few feet from the man. "What's your problem?"

The man didn't move.

I put my hand on Antonne's shoulder. "Leave him alone. Let's go."

The homeless person's eyes focused on me, peering over his scarf. His face was completely hidden, and his hands were buried deep in his woolen trench coat pockets.

He wore leather shoes, and they shined.

"How long you been there?" Antonne asked.

"Go," the man said. "Get outta here and never talk to Charly again."

"The hell I will, asshole." Antonne puffed his chest.

"This is your last warning."

"Come on, Antonne." I pulled on his shoulder.

He pushed me away.

The man pulled out a gun and shot the streetlamp. Glass came crashing down behind us, bouncing on the sidewalk.

We ducked. Covered our heads.

"Leave her alone," the man said, "or I'll put *your* lights out with the next shot." His phantom black shadow stretched down the alley toward the dumpsters. His scarf a red mask of death. His gun raised.

"Shit. You crazy bastard." Antonne grabbed my hand. "Come on."

"No." The man tilted his head to the side. Took aim at us. "She stays."

"Fuck you." Antonne let go of my hand and bolted down the street.

I stood.

"Don't move," the man said.

"Who are you?"

"Don't move. I don't want to kill you."

CHAPTER SEVENTY-TWO

I've found Jacob.

He's calling my name.

The boulder named *Stew* must be around the corner because that's where Jacob's voice came from. The clues have led me to my brother and—

"Charly. Help me."

I sprint around the bend.

The evergreens cast prickly shadows over the trail.

Two figures stand in the snowy distance, the boulder farther on, behind them.

I rush forward.

Freezing cold sweat drips from my brow.

"I want to go home." Jacob's voice carries his pain. "I want to leave now. I want to go home. Help me, Charly."

"I'm coming," I shout. "I'm—"

Randall has a gun to my brother's head.

I stop cold.

It can't be.

Randall was behind me.

Who came out of the cabin?

I remember watching Hector and Barry leave earlier. Hector followed Barry down the driveway in his truck. They left. They would never have come back. This isn't possible. Whoever came out of the cabin couldn't have been either of them.

Who was chasing me?

"Help, Charly. Help. Get the knife." Jacob tilts his head. The butt of the carving knife sticks out of the snowbank just off the trail to his left.

I pull the rifle off my shoulder.

Randall presses his pistol against Jacob's cheekbone. "Drop it."

I take aim. "No."

"I want to go home, Charly." Jacob stands with his back straight, his eyes fixed on mine. "I want to go home. Get the knife, Charly. Stab him. Stab him like a raccoon."

"Jacob," I say. "It's going to be all right."

"I agree," Randall says. "We didn't wait long, and now that you're here, Miss Highsmith, everything *is* going to be all right."

"You found the notes." Jacob smiles.

I take a step closer. His left eye is swollen. The bastard must have hit him.

"You followed the notes, didn't you, Charly? Didn't you?"

"Yes, I did. That was good."

"*Yes, I did,*" Randall mocks, "*that was good. I'm so good . . .*"

"Shut up," I scream.

"Ah, but it was good. Very good indeed. Now, drop your rifle."

"No."

"Very well." He shakes his head. "You can't hit me from there anyway. You're holding the rifle all wrong, and oh, that's right. You're out of bullets."

"Get the knife, Charly." Jacob stares at me through the blizzard, unblinking, undeterred by millions of snowflakes. "Stab him in the back like a raccoon."

"Like a what?" Randall asks.

"Kill him and cut off his tail like a raccoon, Charly. Do it like he's a raccoon."

Visions of Cam stabbing the poor beast when we were kids ravage my mind. The animal's pitiful screaming. The blood. The tail held high in the air. Amanda winning the game. My father hugging her on the deck. The divorce.

Amanda dying.

Randall killing her.

Randall killing everyone.

I have one bullet left. He's lying. I *know* I have one bullet left.

Randall shakes Jacob by the collar. Moves the muzzle to his temple. "That's it. Time to kill off the crazy. Evolution is going to owe me for this one."

"No," I say. "Stop." I lower the rifle. Randall is right. I can't hit him from here.

"Thank you," Randall says. "But, I still have to do my duty. It's the natural order of things. You understand."

The knife is two strides away.

"I'm not afraid of you." Jacob's body stiffens. "I'm not afraid of evil. Not when Charly is here. Charly is going to win, aren't you, Charly? Cut off his tail, Charly. Cut it off."

I take another step forward.

Randall's forearm flexes. His trigger finger moves.

The blizzard takes a breath.

"Randall." A man's voice comes from behind me. "Put the gun down."

"Mr. Dawson." Randall pushes a ghastly smile onto his face. "I'm so glad you made it, but I wasn't expecting you until later. Hector said you were stuck in Texas." He tightens his grip on Jacob's collar. "I'm merely tying up some loose ends here."

"Drop your weapon, Randall. It's over."

I glance behind me.

"Dad?" Jacob asks.

The snowstorm spins out of control.

My stomach tightens.

My breath stops.

"Lance," Randall says, "you don't understand. I can't drop my weapon. These people aren't on an excursion. They showed up uninvited. They crashed the party, as it were. We've got to protect the organization."

"Drop it." The lines in my father's face are deep and long, and he's thinner than I remember, but it's him. He stands there, his pistol raised, aiming at Randall, his graying hair muted by the forest's shadows. "This is an order, Randall. Drop your weapon. Now."

My heart speeds up. It races out of control. It makes me gasp for air.

The miserable thing wants out of my chest. The pounding is unbearable.

My heart pushes its way into a part of me it hasn't been for a long, long time.

It pushes its way into a dark, dark place.

My heart—my dad smiles at me and says, "Hi, Care Bear. I've missed you."

CHAPTER SEVENTY-THREE

CHARLY - THEN

The man behind the red scarf stepped into the alley and pointed his gun at me. He hid in the shadows. I didn't get a chance to see his eyes. His hunting hat, woolen trench coat, and shiny leather shoes all but disappeared in the darkness. The breeze blew the snow sideways, carrying it toward lower downtown. I grasped my backpack straps and prepared to run.

Light glinted off broken glass in the street.

Snow gently landed on the glass, melting on impact.

It was quiet.

Antonne was long gone. Some savior he was. He'd left me standing beneath the shattered streetlamp and rounded the corner up ahead only a few moments ago. Exhausted, the first signs of a well-deserved hangover pounded in my temples.

I didn't want to run.

I wanted tonight to be over, one way or the other.

"Get over here," the man said, his East Coast accent lifting his words. "Get outta the street."

"No."

"I don't want to hurt you, but I will if I have to." Using his gun, he gestured toward the shattered streetlamp. The other lamps weren't afraid of him, still shining as if nothing was wrong. "You should know, I never miss. Come here now, or I'll take off one of your kneecaps."

I walked to the curb.

He pulled out a flashlight and switched it on. The glare blinded me. "Listen very carefully, Charly."

"How do you know my name?"

"Listen." He raised his voice. "You gotta do what I say, or I'll do worse than shoot you in the knee."

"You said you wouldn't hurt me."

"I said I didn't *want* to hurt you, but that's up to you." He motioned down the alley with his gun. "You see that green dumpster down there?" He said *dumpsta* not *dumpster*. Some of his words were from Boston, and some were from New York.

The green dumpster slept at the other end of the alley. "Yes. I see it."

"Think of this as a game. A treasure hunt, as it were. I'm gonna leave that way"—he pointed in the direction Antonne had run—"and pay your drug dealer friend a visit. You're gonna look behind that dumpster."

"Antonne didn't do anything."

"Don't worry. I won't hurt him. I'm only gonna remind him to stay away from you."

The alley narrowed at the far end. I imagined myself peering behind the dumpster only for someone to jump out and grab me. Kidnap me and sell my organs, or worse, sell me to some pervert.

At least I'd have a place to stay tonight.

"What if I don't do what you say?" I asked.

"I'll know if you don't. Like I said, I don't *want* to hurt you."

"You might as well shoot me, then. I'm not going down there." I took a step toward him. "Go ahead, shoot me. Put me out of my misery."

"You ought to think about someone besides yourself." He circled around behind me and backed onto the sidewalk. His eyes were brown. "Suicide is selfish."

"Shoot me." I raised my hands. "I don't care anymore." Years of doing whatever men had said in exchange for a place to stay caught up with me. Years of belittling myself in the name of survival. I couldn't believe I'd considered staying with Antonne earlier. I was going to do drugs with him. I was going to become my mom. If not that, I'd planned on hiding behind a dumpster, curling up and freezing to death.

Drugs or death.

I had chosen drugs.

Now, this man offered me death, and I wanted to go out in a blaze of fire. "Shoot me." I took another step toward him.

"If I shoot you, who will rescue Jacob from the shelter?"

"What?" I stopped. My heart jumped. "Jacob?"

"Go to the dumpster. Look behind it. You owe it to your brother. He's still where you left him. He needs your help."

A streetlamp flickered and went out. The wind blew snow in my face. An apartment window rattled high above. Snowflakes clung to the man's woolen trench coat. He lowered his gun. "Go on. Take a look down there. Do it for Jacob."

"Who are you?"

"You'd better hurry, Charly. Your brother's not getting any younger. No one wants him."

The man in the red scarf turned and walked away.

I examined the buildings on both sides of the alley. Some doors had lights on above them, but most did not. The red brick apartments above the doors reached for the sky. No lights glowed in the second floor units.

Or, in the third.

Or the fourth.

All was quiet.

I had nothing to lose.

CHAPTER SEVENTY-FOUR

Randall stands tall on the snowy trail. He's in control. He has full control of the situation. He's holding a gun to the retard's head, and there's nothing Miss Highsmith nor his boss, Lance, can do about it.

"Dad?" Jacob says. "Is that you?"

Randall has control, but when Jacob speaks—oh, the weakness in the simpleton's voice. Lance stands on the other side of Miss Highsmith, pointing a gun directly at Randall's face, demanding he drop his weapon, and Miss Highsmith waves her rifle around like an idiot, and the simpleton is calling Lance his dad, and—Randall has control, and he knows he shouldn't, but he mocks Jacob right in front of Lance. *"Dad? Is that you? Dad, is that you?"*

Lance creases his forehead. Glares.

Randall lets go of Jacob's collar and grasps his neck. He shoves the muzzle into Jacob's ear. Two seconds. That's all it would take. Pull the trigger, swing the barrel toward Miss Highsmith, and pull the trigger again.

Loose ends all tied up.

Then, he'd be alone in the forest with his boss.

As planned.

Ah, but the best-laid plans of mice and men often go awry. Not so for Randall. He is the only deserving man here. Lance is a mouse. Jacob is a mouse. Miss Highsmith, standing off to the side of the trail with her back turned, facing Lance, and her rifle lowered—she is less than a mouse.

She's a woman.

"Dad?" Miss Highsmith's body tenses up. It would be so easy to shoot her in the back of the head from here. "Where did you come from? You're—I thought you were dead."

"It's him," Jacob says. "It's him, Charly. Look, it's him. It's Dad."

Randall tightens his grip on Jacob's neck. "Shut up."

"It's Dad!" Jacob croaks.

"Why are you calling him that?" Randall asks.

"Drop your gun, Randall." Lance lowers his voice. "This is your last warning."

"No." Randall shakes Jacob. "I have everything under control."

Miss Highsmith turns around. The wind blows her hair back, revealing her entire face. She's white. It's like she's seen a ghost. "Let him go."

"Dad," Jacob rasps.

"*Dad. Dad. Dad.*" Randall can't help himself. Why does the simpleton think Lance is his dad?

Could it be?

The wind rips across the trail, pushing Miss Highsmith's hair back into her face, slightly knocking her off balance.

Dad . . . could it be?

Could Lance be their dad?

Yes.

Of course, he is.

The cabin. The location. It makes sense now. This location was one of the first for the organization. Lance must have owned it back then. Perhaps he still owns it. For some reason, Miss Highsmith thought he died and left it to her in a trust fund. Whatever Lance was attempting to do, it didn't work. Nevertheless, he is not to be underestimated.

"Dad," the simpleton says, "you're here. You came back."

"Quiet, Jacob." Lance keeps his gun trained on Randall. "It's going to be okay. Mr. Thorne is going to put his gun away and let you go, aren't you, Mr. Thorne?"

Randall laughs. The simpleton is the perfect shield.

"You know I can take you out with one shot, Randall," Lance says. "I don't miss."

"That's rich." Randall's chest swells. "The great Lance Dawson is going to take me out. Tell me, *Lance*, how many children have you been hiding all these years? This one?" He squeezes Jacob's neck. "That one?" Miss Highsmith steadies her rifle, foolishly aiming it at Randall. "One or two more? I bet you have a woman in every city, don't you?"

"It's over, Randall."

"Actually, it's just beginning. The new Zaroff Excursions, that is. But, I want to know something. What were you afraid of? Why'd you hide these fabulous children from the organization all these years?"

"What's he talking about?" Miss Highsmith asks.

"Put your gun down, Charly." Lance has a hitch in his throat. He's scared. He's weak. Randall knows why he kept his children a secret, but he wants to hear Lance say it. He wants to hear Lance admit he's weak. "Back away, Care Bear. You need to get out of here."

"Don't call me that." Miss Highsmith trembles. "I hate it

when you call me that. I need to think."

Lance raises his voice. "Go, Charly. Run."

"She's not going anywhere," Randall says, "unless, of course, she wants me to shoot her brother in the head."

"Where were you, Dad?" Jacob speaks fast. Randall relaxes his grip. Why not let the retard take a few final breaths? "Where were you? Charly said you were dead, but you're not dead. Where were you?"

"Let him go." Miss Highsmith's rifle shakes like an old-style alarm clock going off.

Randall's confidence grows. "No. I think not." This is working out so perfectly. The great Lance Dawson. A father. That's some significant leverage. Randall owns him now. "Answer the dullard's question, *Lance*. Tell us. Where were you?"

Lance shakes his head.

"No? You don't want to say? Okay, allow me to make a conjecture. Based on the age of these two, you had them before you helped found the organization. Before you became the leader. Somehow, you kept them a secret from us all these years. I should have known you had a weakness like this. An Achilles heel, as it were."

"Get the knife, Charly." The simpleton nods toward the hillside. "Cut his tail off. Like a raccoon. Like a raccoon."

"For the last time," Lance says, "drop your gun. That's an order, Randall. It's over."

"Oh, it's over all right."

"What's he talking about?" Miss Highsmith asks. "Is it true?" She glances back at Lance. "Did you leave us for him?"

"No. It's not like that. Not—I left to protect you. That's all. Now, go. Get away from here."

"I can't."

"Yes, you can. Trust me, Charly. Jacob will be fine."

"No. I'll never trust you." Her arms shake. She focuses her attention back on Randall. She's still holding the rifle all wrong. It's laughable. "You left us. You broke all your promises. You never came back. You made our lives a living hell. You—goddamn you."

"Not true," Lance says. "I came back."

"No, you didn't." She spins around and aims her rifle at him. "You broke all your promises. You lied. I should shoot you."

This is the best day of Randall's life. Ronald would be so proud.

"Care Bear, please, trust me. I couldn't let you know. I couldn't risk the organization finding out about you."

"Don't call me that!"

"I'm sorry."

She shakes her head. "And, the organization? This human hunting business? Are you the leader? How is that possible . . . Randall is lying, isn't he? You can't be the leader of . . . of *this*. You wouldn't."

"I wouldn't lie about that," Randall says. "Your father was quite the leader." He winks. "*Was*."

"Charly, please, listen to me." Lance's voice is so stressed. It's so wonderful. "You must go."

"So, you *are* behind all this. You're the reason Amanda is dead. Did you know he killed her? Did you know Cam is dead? Kennedy? Tyler?"

"Charly, please."

"Is this all a game to you? These, whatever they're called . . . excursions? How many people have died because of you?"

"It's not like that." Lance's lips tremble.

He looks like he's about to cry.

This is so wonderful.

"Don't listen to him, Miss Highsmith. It's exactly like that." Randall retightens his grip on Jacob's neck. "And now, it's your brother's turn to go on an excursion. Would you like to join us?"

CHAPTER SEVENTY-FIVE

I marched down the alley and approached the green dumpster like I had nothing to lose. I pretended the dark doorways didn't bother me. Behind the dumpster, I found a metal box nestled on a stack of soggy newspapers. Inside the box, there was a piece of paper.

A note.

Though the woman was stout, she didn't have it all. To save her brother from the shelter, she needed something from the mall. She left him alone years ago, acting like a wench, and now all she needed was the next clue, hidden beneath a bench.

It was a game. A treasure hunt.

It was my dad's game.

The man—or whoever left the note—knew about the game. Jacob must have told him. Jacob must have met him at the shelter and told him about the summer Johnathan invented the game.

The summer Amanda won the ultimate prize.

Undeterred by time, my hatred for her resurfaced. I pictured her holding the raccoon tail and my father hugging her.

And just like that, the game was on.

Hangover be damned, I wanted to win.

Though the woman was stout . . . she needed something from the mall.

The mall.

The 16th Street Mall.

Bordered by shops and restaurants on each side, the 16th Street outdoor mall ran across fifteen blocks in downtown Denver. Cars were never allowed on the mall—only free buses. But at this time of night, no one would be there.

Getting drunk is stupid. Fighting. Forgetting. I wished I hadn't left my phone at Grant's apartment now more than ever. But I had a clue. I had hope. I headed for 16th Street, reinvigorated. I passed 20th Street. 19th Street. 18th Street. The note said the next clue was under a bench. I passed 17th street. My shoulders ached. My frozen feet wanted to break. I stepped onto the 16th Street mall and found a bench. There was no note, but there was another bench. Again, no note, but another bench. And another. The mall went on forever. There had to have been a hundred benches lining the street.

Maybe more.

I took the note out of my pocket.

Though the woman was stout . . .

Why stout? I wasn't stout. I was tall. Very tall, on average. Not stout.

Yet, the note was clearly referring to me.

Stout.

I wasn't stout, but Stout Street was.

Three blocks up, on the corner of 16th and Stout, I found

the next note sealed inside a plastic baggie taped beneath a bench at the light rail station.

I tore it open.

The man's name is Trey, he's a valet, and he works at the Cabaret. There's not much else to say except 2708-A.

I raced back down 16th Street. The Cabaret was somewhere near the end. Since running away, I had considered becoming a stripper several times. I had applied for work at the Cabaret twice, and twice, they'd turned me down for being underage. I'd been forced to live with my boyfriend du jour because I could never afford my own place.

Grant kicked me out because he thought I was going to work at the Cabaret.

He thought I was a whore.

Cabaret.

Du jour.

French words.

I was sobering up, but I still felt funny.

I took deep breaths, walking as fast as I could.

This was no time to get delirious. And, there was no time. The club would close soon, and I needed to find a valet named Trey. Fortunately, the snow had stopped falling, but that only made it seem like it would get warmer. In reality, the air stiffened, and the darkest hour of the night brought with it the coldest hour of my life.

Confused, I went the wrong direction down Glenarm Place, reversed, and forced myself to run toward the Cabaret, racing against the clock. Men poured out of the beige, windowless club. Suits. Greasy hairdos. Cuff links and neck chains. Some headed for the parking lot. Others lined up at the valet booth.

I got in line.

"Hey, baby. Nice backpack." The man in line before me had bloodshot eyes, and he blinked when he spoke. "You on your way to school?" Scotch and cigars—he reeked.

I turned away. Said nothing.

The man drowsily sensed my disinterest and returned to bantering with his buds. One of them had a sash that read, *I'm a groom, so groom me.* They were next in line for the valet. "And I gave her a fifty, and she didn't do anything extra."

"It doesn't always work."

"Lap dances at this place suck."

Gross.

The valet took the man's ticket and ran into the lot. The group stepped aside, and another valet entered the booth. "Can I help you?" His badge read, *Trey.*

"Yes." I handed him the note.

"2708-A. Got it. I'll be right back." He went inside the club and returned a few minutes later with a box. At first glance, I thought it was the same box from the dumpster.

"Thank you," I said.

I carried the box down the street, speedily walking away from all the testosterone. Trying to go unnoticed.

It didn't work.

A man called after me. Offered me a place to stay.

For the first time in my life, I turned down a place to stay when I needed one. I ignored him and turned at the next intersection. Alone, sitting on the steps beneath the awning of a fancy hotel, I opened the box. It contained an envelope and another note.

You're almost there, Charly, and then you'll win. One sacrificial act will vanquish all your sin. Take this money, find your brother, and take care of him. You can never change the past, but you can always change. You can always adapt. You can always rearrange. Take this money, vanquish your sin—your life is waiting to begin.

I opened the envelope. Federal First Bank of Colorado. It was a bank statement with my name on it. The balance was enormous. There was enough money for me to lease my own apartment. Enough for a car. Enough for me to find Jacob and give us a place to live.

Forever.

And that's what I did.

CHAPTER SEVENTY-SIX

I have not come this far in life, suffering the guilt from leaving Jacob at that shelter, then rescuing him, only to watch him die at the hands of a psychotic hunter. I didn't do it because I had to. I did it because I love Jacob, which is more than I could ever say for my dad.

My dad.

Johnathan Highsmith.

He came back. I can't believe it, but he came back, and—

Randall has his gun rammed inside Jacob's ear.

Johnathan has his gun pointed at Randall.

Johnathan. My dad. The head of Zaroff Excursions.

He doesn't know love.

He's a murderer.

I have my gun pointed at him. Everyone is dead because of him.

The three of us are in a stalemate, and I'm caught in the middle, glancing between Randall and Johnathan.

Jacob is surprisingly calm.

This is all Johnathan's fault.

"I helped you, Care Bear," he says. "I swear. I was always there. Helping you. Put the rifle down."

I should kill him. My finger is on the trigger. If he calls me Care Bear one more time . . .

"Don't worry, Lance. She'll miss." Randall flashes a cocky smile. "She doesn't know how to use a rifle."

"His name's not Lance," Jacob says. "It's Johnathon. He's my dad. Johnathan."

"Shut up." Randall tightens his grip.

"Get the knife, Charly." Jacob speaks as if he's waiting in line at the post office. "It's over there in the snow. I dropped it. Stab him like a raccoon, Charly. Cut his tail off."

I sneak a glance at the snowbank. The carving knife handle sticks out of the snow, but I don't need it. Even if I did, even if my rifle jammed, I can't reach it from here. I need to end this now. I need a reason—one final reason—to pull the trigger and kill my dad.

Then, Randall.

"Please, Charly." Johnathan doesn't take his eyes off Randall. "You've got to believe me. I helped you your entire life."

"You're lying. You never helped me."

"I did. I gave you the money. You've got to believe me. Put the rifle down."

"The trust fund money? I don't have that yet."

"No. The money in Denver to get you and Jacob started. At the valet. I helped you save Jacob from the shelter."

"You?"

I'd always hoped it had been him, but I never allowed myself to believe it. After he was gone for so many years, it was too painful to think he could be anything other than evil. I couldn't let go of my anger toward him. It was easier to believe someone else had met Jacob in the shelter and decided to help us. A friend of some wealthy do-gooder maybe. Every day that had passed without my father's return only reinforced my thinking. Until now. "You? It was you in the red scarf?"

"Yes. That was me. I waited weeks for you to leave that boyfriend. I knew you would. You always did. I was always there, watching. Waiting. Look at me. I came back. In a way, I never left. I love you, Care Bear."

"For the last time, stop calling me that."

"*Care Bear.*" Randall's voice pitches higher. "*Care Bear. Care Bear.*"

"Sweetheart. Put the rifle down. You don't want to shoot me."

The hell I don't.

Dammit.

He's right.

I don't want to shoot anyone. Too many have died already. Time slows down. Snowflakes land on the rifle's barrel. I struggle to keep my trigger finger steady while the rest of my body trembles.

"Let's go on our own excursion," Randall says. "What do you say, Lance? Sorry. I meant Johnathan. Let's go for old time's sake. We have plenty of prey to hunt." He shakes Jacob.

I swing my gun toward Randall. "Don't you dare."

"Charly," Johnathan yells. "Drop it. You'll accidentally shoot your brother."

The gunsight wavers up and down. Side to side. I can't control it. My nerves are shorting out.

"Please," Johnathan says. "Put the gun down and go for help. I'm not going to let him hurt anyone else. You have to trust me."

"No, I don't. You're just like him. You're a murderer."

"Not anymore. I'm shutting down the organization. I faked my death and left you all my money. After assuming another identity, I'll run into you at a restaurant somewhere. Introduce myself. Make up for lost time. Please, I'm coming back, and Zaroff is over. You've got to believe me."

"Believe him, Charly." Jacob's colorless lips bend at the corners. He stands still like it's not freezing out here. "Believe Dad. There is too much of me in the way." He glances down. "I'm in the way. There's a ninety-two percent chance you'll hit me if you try to shoot him. There's ninety-two percent of me in your way, Charly."

He's right. I lower the rifle.

"Good girl," Randall says.

I step back. My heels butt up against the snowbank.

"Go for help," Johnathan repeats.

The snow has stopped falling. Behind him, the trail curves around the mountain. It leads to the cabin. To freedom. "I can't leave Jacob here."

"Then put the rifle on the ground so I can negotiate with Randall in peace."

"Negotiate?" Randall says. "Yes. Negotiate. Let's do that." He squeezes Jacob's neck. "Let's go on a hunt. You and me. We can talk while we hunt this one."

"Ow. Stop hurting me." Jacob grasps Randall's hand and pulls. "I'm not afraid of you. Not when Charly's here."

Randall pushes the muzzle harder into Jacob's ear. "Do as Daddy says, Miss Highsmith. Put the rifle down."

"Okay, okay," I say. "Okay." I lay the rifle on the ground.

"Not good enough." Randall strikes Jacob on top of the head with the butt of his pistol.

"Ah. He's hurting me." Blood trickles down Jacob's forehead. "Get the knife, Charly."

"No," Johnathan yells. "Kick the rifle over here."

I do as Johnathan says. The rifle comes to rest at his feet. The knife is on the other side of the trail, out of my reach. It's all up to him now.

"Excellent," Randall says. "Now, how do we want to do this? Should we give them each a head start, or should we hunt one at a time?"

Johnathan eyes him. "You know the rules."

"Very well. One at a time it is."

Johnathan points his gun at me.

"You—you liar," I yell. "What are you doing?"

"Quiet," Randall shouts.

My molars are going to explode. The tension in my shoulders pulls on my neck. It draws my head back. High above, a gray cloud splits in two. "You liar!"

"Get the knife," Jacob yells.

"Everyone be quiet," Randall shouts.

My chest heaves. I lower my chin. Lean forward toward Johnathan. I catch my breath and glare at him. I glare at his gun. He holds it steady with both hands and blinks.

He keeps his gun trained on me.

Then, he blinks again.

"She has a point," Randall says. "You are a liar. After your impassioned speech there, I wonder how sincere you are about this hunt. You say you faked your death and plan to end Zaroff. Is that true?"

"Only partly. I faked my death to get further away from these two. They weren't supposed to be here. They've been dragging me down for years, and now there's only one way to end this. They must die."

"Uh, huh." Randall narrows his eyes. "Why should I believe you?"

"Because everything I've ever done is for the organization. I'm doing this for the sake of the herd. I'm willing to sacrifice them for the sake of the herd. I know you understand that, Randall. You understand sacrifice."

"Yes, I do."

"I haven't forgotten about your brother."

Randall's face turns red.

"I haven't forgotten about Ronald," Johnathan says.

"Don't say his name." He swallows hard.

"Ronald would have wanted you to—"

"Stop saying his name." He closes his eyes. Scrunches his face.

Johnathan blinks. Then, he winks at me.

Stunned, I don't know what to do. I shake my head, confused.

Johnathan winks again, and I nod my head.

Randall lets go of Jacob's throat with his hand and wraps his arm around Jacob's neck. He pulls Jacob off his feet.

Jacob begins to choke. Coughs. Slips in the snow, trying to stand.

Randall points his pistol at Johnathan. "I don't believe you. I can see it in your eyes."

"Trust me," Johnathan says. "I'm with you. Zaroff Excursions is going to live on. It must. It's for the good of mankind. For evolution. For the thrill. Come on, let's go on this excursion. Let's prove we deserve to be at the top of the food chain." He glances at me. "Let's hunt her first. Then him. They mean nothing to me."

Jacob gets his footing and stands upright.

"Nothing?" Randall keeps his gun trained on Johnathan. "It means nothing? Prove it."

Johnathan aims his gun at Jacob and shoots.

Blood explodes out of my brother's thigh. Randall lets go of him and jumps back.

I lunge across the trail and dive into the snow, reaching for the carving knife.

Randall stumbles and hits the ground. He rolls, holding his pistol with both hands, aiming at me.

I fall short of the knife.

Randall stops rolling and lies on his stomach, propping himself up on his elbows. The barrel of his gun is an endless black tunnel. It hangs in the frosted air, then an orange flash fills my world.

Then, a bang.

I cover my head.

The sound ravages my ears.

I roll away, feeling for where he hit me. My legs, hips, ribs, neck, head—nothing.

He missed.

He actually missed.

I scramble to my feet.

Jacob jumps on top of Randall. Flailing, he knocks the gun out of Randall's hand.

I pick up the knife.

"Go." Johnathan coughs. "Run, Charly. Run."

I turn toward him, and gasp.

He lies on his back, his hands on his chest, blood bubbling through his fingers.

Randall's bullet must have hit him.

Jacob sits on Randall's chest, beating his face. "I hate you. I hate. I hate. I hate. I hate you. You're evil." One blow after another, he mercilessly connects with Randall's jaw.

Randall grasps Jacob's shoulder and throws him to the side.

I leap toward them and bury the knife into Randall's thigh.

My favorite spot.

He shouts. He grasps his leg and screams. He screams like a raccoon.

I back away.

Randall can't keep the blood from becoming a fountain. His face turns green.

I pick up the rifle. "Don't move."

He sits up, rests his back against the snowbank, and looks at me. Blood gushes through his fingers. "You're so weak." He swallows as if he's about to vomit. "You're like Ronald."

Jacob goes to Johnathan. Crouches next to him. Turns to me. "He's dying, Charly. He's dying. He's going to die."

"The retard is right, Miss Highsmith. I shot him in the chest." Randall lifts his gaze. He smiles. "He's going to die. I'm the head of Zaroff Excursions now." He blinks slowly. "Finally. I'm at the top of the chain."

"Not for long," Charly says.

"You won't shoot me." His eyes flare. "You're weak. You won't survive."

"Yes. I will."

He reaches for his gun.

I pull the trigger.

His head explodes.

EPILOGUE

CHARLY

"I'm sorry." My mom rests her chin on her chest and gazes at her crippled hands. She grips her coarse, assisted care center blanket. Tries to pull it to her face and fails. Her room smells like antiseptic. Like the staff is getting it ready to give to someone else. "I didn't mean for any of this to happen."

"I know, Mom. You don't have to apologize."

"But, I—"

"Where are we going after this?" Jacob asks. "I want a new phone. Can we buy a new phone?"

"You can stop fidgeting and sit down." I glance at the clock. "We're going to be here a while."

He leans his crutches against the wall and sits near the window. The lemon-yellow sun blazes outside, melting yesterday's snow. My jacket makes me hot, but I don't want to take it off. It's usually colder in here.

"I didn't know any of that," Mom says. "Zaroff Excursions? It's so strange. Johnathan never hunted after we were married."

"He traveled a lot for work, didn't he?"

"I suppose."

"And you weren't always aware of what was going on around you. Not with your problems."

"That's true."

"Why did you give me the keys to the cabin?"

"It was a mistake. Johnathan showed up out of nowhere with his will. I didn't read it all, and when I saw the word 'estate,' I thought everything belonged to you. I didn't know he'd been using the cabin. I didn't know it wasn't included."

"He was here? You said he died. You said he had a heart attack."

"I'm sorry."

"Stop apologizing. Did you lie to me on purpose?"

"He made me. I knew how much you'd missed him all these years, and he said he would come back into your life if I told you he was dead. He said it was the only way he could leave you his money." She blinks slowly. "It wasn't his fault. He didn't know I still had a key to the cabin."

So . . . it was true. What Johnathan said about faking his death. About running into me at a restaurant a few months from now. What he said about following me, spying on me, and watching over me.

And he had come back.

Too little, too late.

My mom shakes her head. "I never thought in a million years he was hunting people. It's insane. I knew others used the cabin, but I thought he rented it to them. I—hunting people? Murdering them? I'm so sorry. This is all my fault."

"Stop it."

She lifts her chin off her chest. A tear streams down her cheek. "Charly. I'm so—"

"Stop it." I take her hand. "I know you're sorry. You've

been sorry all my life."

"But what you went through. Amanda and Cam."

"It's over now."

"And Jacob."

"He's fine."

"I'm fine." He sits by the window, his injured leg outstretched. "I'm fine. The doctor says my leg will heal fast because I'm so young. It will leave a scar. I wanted a tattoo, but a scar is better. It proves we won, right, Charly? We won?"

"Right." I swallow the lump in my throat. "We won."

And more importantly, Randall Thorne lost. His buddy, Hector, gave me a scar on my cheek, but I took Randall's life. I don't regret it. It's been one week since I ended his game. Only one week, but I know, just as I will never forget my father's face the night he left the cabin—the night he left to run Zaroff Excursions—I will never forget the shock on Randall's face the day I pulled the trigger.

The day I blew his head off.

"We're going to buy me a new phone," Jacob says. "I left mine at the cabin. My phone is in the bedroom at the cabin, and we can't go back there because of the police. Because of the evil man. Because he shot me, but the slickhead told on him. The slickhead saved us."

It's true. If it hadn't been for Barry, Jacob might have eventually bled to death alongside Johnathan. The bullet didn't hit any major arteries, making me wonder if he only shot Jacob in a desperate attempt to convince Randall he was serious about ending Zaroff Enterprises. I'll never know.

After Barry led Hector down the mountain, he went to the nearest police station and reported Kennedy missing. Hector drove away. Barry gave the police our location, and we were rescued. Later, when they questioned me, I described

Hector as best I could, but they still haven't located him. Barry was released, and Hector became the sole suspect in the murder of Tyler Evans. I wasn't there, so I don't know who shot Tyler, but at a minimum, Barry was an accomplice. Jacob and I think he used his money to avoid jail somehow.

Typical slickhead.

"Charly saved me first, though." Jacob has done nothing but grin at me since we left the hospital last week. "She stopped the evil man."

As far as jail goes, I'm not concerned for myself. There will be court dates in the future. I'll attend them, but the detectives assured me this will be an open and shut case. Self-defense. With Randall Thorne and Johnathan Highsmith—a.k.a. Lance Dawson—gone, Zaroff Excursions will fold. The police and the FBI will make sure of it. The organization was much larger than I'd thought. According to the news, they ran excursions in eleven countries, employing over fifty people. They routinely hired black market contractors to clean up their messes. The police found Amanda, Cam, Kennedy, and Tyler before the cleanup crew arrived.

Last night, I slept more than two hours straight for the first time since the massacre. It's probably why I'm in a better mood today. I swore I'd never come back to this place. Mountain Crest Healthcare Center—the bridge between this world and the next. When I left Mom here three weeks ago, I left her to die.

I never imagined my world could change so much in such a short time.

Now, Johnathan is dead. For real this time. And the others are gone.

All I have left is my mom.

And Jacob.

"Charly." My mom lifts her hand and places it on top of mine. "Thank you for taking care of Jacob. I wish I'd done things differently."

"Like I said, it's over now. You don't have to be sorry. You didn't know about the cabin."

"It's not the cabin. It's—it's everything. Thank you for being his mom when I couldn't. You've always been so strong."

"I didn't have a choice."

"Yes, you did. You could have left him in that shelter. You could have taken the money Johnathan gave you and disappeared. Bought drugs." She shudders. Her shoulders shake. "It's what I would have done."

"I know."

"Oh"—she squeezes my hand—"this damn life. I tried, but I could never be who I wanted. I could never change. There's always been two of me—the addict and the woman. Does that make sense?"

"Yes."

"And the addict always won."

"I know. Please, don't apologize again."

"I won't, but I want you to forgive me. Promise me you'll forgive me."

"I already have. I've made my peace."

"You deserve peace. Peace and serenity."

"So do you, Mom. So do you."

She closes her eyes.

Her hand slides off mine.

She falls asleep.

Jacob and I walk across the parking lot. The sun blazes down upon us, but it will soon be dark. Storm clouds to the west creep over the Rocky Mountains.

I begin to cry.

But I never cry.

Ever.

A few days later, my mother dies in her sleep, leaving Jacob and me on our own.

And that's okay.

We've been here before.

ACKNOWLEDGMENTS

Thank you!

Above all else, I want to thank you, fearless reader, for journeying into the mountains with Charly and Jacob. Readers like you make the world of fiction a wonderful place for us all. Otherwise, this book would be nothing more than a tree falling in the woods, not making a sound.

I also want to thank my editors, critique volunteers, and reviewers, especially my first reader, Kim. Without her, I'd be lost in the woods, surrounded by the silently falling trees.

GET AN EXCLUSIVE BONUS STORY

Dear fearless reader, there is always a FREE short story, novella, or full-length novel available on my website at:

https://topaine.com/free

ENTER TO WIN A GIVEAWAY

Several times a year, my publisher and I sponsor giveaways as a thank you for reading. Past giveaways included Kindle Paperwhites, Amazon Gift Cards, Headphones, my novels, and novels by other authors. Check out the current giveaway at:

https://topaine.com/giveaway

DID YOU ENJOY READING THE EXCURSION?

If so, I'd love to hear from you. Please send me an email at topaine@topaine.com and let me know your thoughts. If you'd like to hear about upcoming releases from me, follow me on Amazon, BookBub, or sign up for my newsletter at:

https://topaine.com

You can also connect with me on:
- Facebook – https://facebook.com/topaineauthor
- Instagram - https://instagram.com/t.o.paine
- Twitter - https://twitter.com/topaine

A review on Amazon, Goodreads, and/or BookBub would mean the world to me. Reviews are the single most important factor in an author's success and longevity. If you enjoyed this novel, please consider leaving a review, even if it is only a line or two. I would very much appreciate it.

ALSO BY T.O. PAINE

The Resentment
"A Wickedly Sharp Suspense Thriller"

The Teaching
"A thriller based on the author's experience living in a cult."

ABOUT THE AUTHOR

T.O. Paine holds a master's degree in information systems, and when he is not writing, you can find him running or cycling through the mountains of Colorado, USA. He has run over thirty marathons, ridden over twenty 100-mile cycling events, and completed an IRONMAN.

T.O. resides with his wife, two children, and a Boston terrier who stares at himself in the mirror, questioning his existence.